DARK SISTER

Also by Graham Joyce

Dreamside

DARK SISTER

Graham Joyce

HEADLINE

First published in 1992
by HEADLINE BOOK PUBLISHING PLC

10 9 8 7 6 5 4 3 2 1

British Library Cataloguing in Publication Data

Joyce, Graham
Dark Sister
I. Title
823.914 [F]

ISBN 0-7472-0629-5

Printed and bound in Great Britain by
Clays Ltd, St Ives PLC

HEADLINE BOOK PUBLISHING PLC
Headline House
79 Great Titchfield Street
London W1P 7FN

To my Mother and Father
– who never put me through any of this

ACKNOWLEDGEMENTS

Special thanks to three wise women who in another age would probably have been burned for their extraordinary talents: my editor, Caroline Oakley, for her vision and shaping skills; my GP, Alison Rhodes, for her knowledge of the healing arts; and my wife, Suzanne, for her unravelling of the legal scrolls and much more besides. Also to Nick Cooper of the Leicester University Archaeology Department. Thanks too for the sustaining friendship and encouragement of Pete Blythe, Alan Grapes, Sandra Mahoney, Phil Marlowe, Jo Porter, Tam Tansey and Pete and Anne Williams. Finally, to the one who sits just outside my window.

PROLOGUE

Hide it! Now, before they come. You must hide it.

Because come they will, and when they do come they will burn you. They will tear down your house stone by stone, and when they find it they will set to uncovering all your treasured secrets, until they cry: Here it is! Here she is! We have found her out! This surely is a one!

Bring her to a public place! Bring wood! Bring fire! Burn her!

So listen to me when I tell you to hide it. Because I am one who knows.

And when they cannot burn you, when the flames flicker out and the ribbons of smoke die in the dry wood, then they will shout in their confusion and they will do such things to you, such torments that I cannot speak of it.

Why? Why, when you cannot harm them? When you are nothing but the wind in the trees? When you cradle your weakness in your art? And what are they that they must put you to the torch? For you are just a meek, frail thing. A soft pigeon. A little bird.

They will tear your heart.

So hide it! Find a place.

But quickly.

They are already coming.

1

When Alex had ripped out the boards, in a cracking and splintering of
wood, he called Maggie. The kids came too, along with Dot, their
Labrador-cross, who had a sniff at the results.

'I knew it!' Maggie said. 'It's beautiful!'

Alex was more doubtful. 'It might be when it's cleaned up.'

It was a standard Victorian fireplace, with a wrought-iron and tiled
surround. Maggie was already rubbing at the tiles, exposing bright, floral
patterns. The grate was intact, though choked with soot and debris.

'It's got to be swept. Kids, take all this wood out the back.' Alex liked
to have his gofors around when he was doing a job.

Maggie was already making inroads into the debris with a dustpan
and brush when she jumped back.

'Ugh!'

The children crowded closer. 'What is it?'

Maggie looked as though she wanted to be sick. 'Come away from
it.'

'What is it, Mummy?'

Alex poked at the debris in the grate. Mixed in with the soot were
what seemed like sticks and straw. 'I see it,' he said. 'It's nothing. Only
a dead bird.' He lifted it out on the dustpan. It was a large, black-
feathered bird with wings spread. Obviously it had been there for some
time. It was desiccated, though not decayed; its feathers were choked
with dust and soot, its eye had whitened over and its beak was hanging
open. Alex waved it at the kids.

'Ugh!' said Amy.

'Ugh!' said Sam, with fascinated eyes.

Even Dot seemed to wince.

3

'Take it away, Alex.'

'It must have nested in the chimney at some time. Then got trapped. Happens all the time.'

'What will you do with it, Daddy?'

'We'll have it for Sunday dinner. Blackbird in parsley sauce.'

'Take no notice, Amy, he's being silly. Get it out of the house, Alex.'

'Will we give it a proper burial, like Ulysses?' Amy wanted to know.

When Amy's goldfish Ulysses had died, they'd given it a 'proper burial' in the garden, so Alex took the bird outside, dug a hole for it and covered it over.

Amy patted the soil with the spade. 'Will it go to heaven now?'

'Yep,' said Alex. 'If you look up at the sky you'll see its white soul flying towards heaven.'

It was an afternoon in late October, and the sky was as blue as a bird's egg. Amy looked up at the sky for a long time. Then she looked back at her father. He could see that at five years old she was already beginning to distrust some of the things he said. It made him sad.

'Let's go back inside.'

It had all started the night they'd gone over to the Suzmans for dinner. First the car wouldn't start.

'What are you getting mad about?' Maggie said.

It was the kind of remark guaranteed to nettle Alex further. He tried to think why he *was* getting angry. It had started to rain, the kids were playing slap in the back of the car and Maggie was looking at him. She wore too much make-up. Whenever they went to the Suzmans, Maggie felt insecure; and whenever Maggie felt insecure she put on too much make-up.

He got out of the car, flung open the bonnet, and was impotently fiddling with the plug leads when the engine coughed into life, fan blades narrowly missing lopping off the tops of his fingers. Now he really had something to be mad about.

Maggie still had her hand on the ignition keys. 'Magic touch,' she said, smiling at him as he climbed back inside.

'Trying to amputate my fingers, were you?' Her smile disappeared. He looked at the heavy red lipstick at war with her flaming chestnut hair. Who could stay angry with someone so nervous about meeting old friends that she had to plaster her face like that? Alex couldn't. 'Forget it.'

He turned to the kids in the back. 'If you two don't stop slapping each other I'm going to bang your heads together.' He'd never banged heads, and probably never would, but Maggie turned and nodded to them as if to say *he means it*.

'This is supposed to be enjoyable,' she said.

'So why isn't it enjoyable?' said Amy, imperiously adult.

But the visit to the Suzmans had turned out to be enjoyable after all. Amy and three-year-old Sam were whisked off by the Suzman kids, giving their parents the chance to show Alex and Maggie around their monster of a new house. Bill Suzman, a commercial lawyer, had managed to get in before the house prices went crazy. Alex had missed the boat, as usual.

After Alex and Maggie admired the way the towels were folded in the bathroom and so on, Bill cracked open the wine, Anita drew attention to their new compact-disc player and located the right music, and they settled down in front of a rip-roaring log fire.

Maggie looked into the flames, firelight reflecting in her hair and in the wine glass at her lips, and Alex knew exactly what she was thinking. Marriage, proximity to another person, he supposed, cultivated a knowingness, a rough telepathy. It was something you acquired in exchange, when ardour faded. But he loved to do things to make her happy, and if she, too, wanted an open fire, she could have one.

'Nice fireplace,' Alex observed.

'Original Victorian,' Bill said, getting up to stroke the marble mantelpiece. He always stroked anything he wanted others to admire: his CD player, his mantelpiece, his wife. 'Look at those tiles. Perfect condition. Been boarded up for years. We had to rip out an old gas fire to get to it.'

'That old fire had protected it,' said Anita.

'You wouldn't believe,' Bill continued, 'the state of the thing we took out. You're an archaeologist, Alex; you'd appreciate it. One of those sixties plastic log-effect things. You plug 'em in and a rotating fan casts shadows on a very unconvincing orange light.'

'Ghastly,' Maggie agreed, and they laughed more at the word than at Bill's description.

5

'We've still got one,' said Alex.

There was a pause. 'I'd forgotten about that,' said Anita.

'What the hell,' said Bill. 'Is dinner ready?'

Dinner was indeed ready, because Anita had hired some help for the evening, a gesture beyond Maggie's comprehension and budget. Silverware gleamed, crystal glimmered, and no one seemed unduly worried when Sam seemed deliberately to tip a glass of claret on to the snow-white tablecloth.

'Why did you do that?' said Alex, exasperated.

Sam giggled and showed everyone a mouthful of half-chewed dinner.

Otherwise the meal went well. Alex and Bill cackled a lot and guzzled wine. Anita said sophisticated things about antiques, in which she had a 'hobby' business, and Bill stroked her arm a lot. Maggie paid attention to keeping the children in order. Then she won the others' interest by telling them about a psychic evening she'd attended for a joke; but she caught herself in the middle of the story. The two men were gazing at her, entranced by her enthusiasm, but Anita was looking at her strangely, so she allowed the story to tail off.

But it had been a pleasant evening, the conversation had stayed light, friendly. With the kids asleep in the back of the car, Maggie drove them home.

Alex, mellowed by the wine, said, 'Why did you stop halfway through your story about the psychic?'

'I don't think Anita liked me grabbing the limelight.'

'Why d'you say that?'

'Just a feeling.'

'It's your imagination. Anyway, to hell with Anita. That was your story, and your chance to tell it. She wouldn't stop for you.'

'No. You're right. I think Anita doesn't like me because I've got red hair.'

'Nonsense. You're drunk.'

'No I'm not. Anyway it's not my hair. Not just that anyway. It was a . . . feeling. Sometimes I look at people and I . . .'

'And you what?'

'Never mind.'

'Go on! Say it!'

'No. You'd just laugh at me. You always do.'

'Yes, I probably would.'

'Did you see that lovely open fireplace, Alex? Do you think . . .'

'Don't ask. The answer is yes.'

Which is how Alex had come to be tearing out the old gas fire from their lounge the following day, which was a Saturday. The moment he'd seen Maggie staring into the fire at the Suzmans', he'd remembered what had irritated him.

Every time they visited Bill and Anita's immaculate house, Maggie returned discontented. Consequently his precious weekends (designated for watching *Sports Report* from the comfort of the couch while lubricated by tins of beer) were spent trailing around home improvement stores the size of aircraft hangars. Death by DIY. Previous visits to the Suzmans had spurred the conversion of the cellar into a playroom for Amy and Sam, and the erection of a lopsided conservatory at the rear of the house. However longsuffering he was about it, Alex just wanted to make Maggie happy. He would look at her moist eyes and her long, curling chestnut hair, like a Pre-Raphaelite painting, and generally he would give in to whatever she wanted.

With the gas disconnected, the fire had lifted out easily enough. Alex had had more difficulty with the boarding. A strong frame had at some time been constructed out of thick lengths of wood, leaving only a small vent for the passage of the gas fumes up the chimney. But now that part of the job was done. Meanwhile someone had to stop Sam juggling with the loose soot, and Alex decided that was women's work. He put his coat on and adjourned to the Merry Fiddler.

Theirs was a large Victorian villa with a huge, overhanging gable front. It was described by estate agents, when they'd first bought it, as a character property, and character properties were Maggie's enthusiasm but not Alex's. Character properties were like character people. Their qualities, entertainments and rewards came in equal measure with their usually hidden faults. Alex had doggedly devoted much of his leisure time in the past five years to beating back elements permanently poised to invade the sanctuary he was trying to build for his family.

There was the cellar with a damp problem he'd finally conquered in order to turn the place into a playroom for the children. There was a woodworm problem he'd poisoned into submission. There was a silverfish infestation astonishing even the experts from Rentokil. The high-ceilinged rooms had demanded the installation of powerful central heating just to secure the beautiful plaster mouldings round the light fittings. And he was still embattled over a roof leak which thwarted him by shifting nine inches every time it was 'fixed'.

Embattled yes, and if occasionally he broke ranks and deserted the front line in favour of the Merry Fiddler, Maggie let him go. She said nothing as he went out, and checked the Yellow Pages for a chimney sweep.

She primed the children for the arrival of the sweep. They'd seen *Mary Poppins* on video, and she told them stories from her own childhood. When she was a kid, the chimneys had been serviced by a local man who played the ventriloquist to keep curious children amused. He pretended to have a midget assistant who spoke from up the chimney, and would send Maggie outside to check if his brush had cleared the chimney pot. Amy and Sam were fascinated. They sat by the window, waiting eagerly for the man to arrive. Maggie told them they should 'touch' the sweep for luck.

When he arrived that afternoon Maggie was enormously disappointed that he wasn't black from head to foot, and that he brought with him a suction machine instead of a set of brushes. The modern version was a bespectacled young man in a clean set of blue overalls. He had no sweep's humour for her children. When Amy and Sam ran forward to touch him almost before he got through the door, the young man looked at the spot on his overalls where the children had put their fingers. Then he looked (sourly, Maggie thought) at the children. Maggie quickly showed him where to set up his equipment.

Sam rapidly lost interest in this unpicturesque sweep and waddled away to play with Dot, but Amy remained, watching his every move. She was utterly spellbound. She inched forward, gazing over the shoulder of the man as he knelt before the fireplace, until she was almost breathing on his neck. Maggie was about to shift her out of his way, but she was checked by a second thought, almost like another voice in her head. *Why not? Why not let her look?*

The first thing the sweep did (though it didn't seem right to call him a sweep when he was only a man with a machine which sucked) was to put his arm up the flue, bringing down more debris, straw and sticks into the grate.

8

'Hello,' he said, withdrawing his arm. 'Something else here.' He was holding some dirty object in his hand. It was a book. He scraped away the soot and the dust. 'People hide things up chimneys, then forget all about them.'

He flicked the pages open, as if looking for something pressed between the leaves. Maggie was mesmerised. She felt a thrill of possessiveness, almost childish in its intensity. *My book*, she wanted to say. *My house, my chimney, my book.* She objected to his large, sooty thumbs imprinting on the cover. She wanted to snatch it from him, but instead she said, 'Do you find many things?'

'I once found five hundred quid—'

'Sweeps are lucky,' she blurted, unable to take her eyes from what lay in his blackened hands.

'You didn't let me finish. It was in forged notes.' Finding nothing between the pages, he lost interest in the book. 'Here.' He passed it to her and got on with the task of sweeping, or rather sucking, the chimney.

That evening they had a crackling log fire going in the lounge. They all sat round it staring into the flames as if it was some new form of light entertainment, except for Dot, who commanded the place in front of the fire and immediately went to sleep, as if the entire thing had been introduced for her benefit alone. The newly exposed fireplace showed off to great effect. An ornate, black, cast-iron surround was inset with beautiful ceramic tiles in rich autumnal colours. The design had an oriental feel, depicting peacocks and other exotic birds entwined in mysterious looking shrubs and trees. Maggie had polished them until they gleamed. The glaze on the tiles was perfectly preserved, not a single chip or scratch anywhere.

It was, they both agreed happily, even better than the Suzman specimen.

Alex was initially fascinated by what had been found hidden inside the chimney, and every now and then broke the hypnotic spell of the fire by reading aloud from the book.

It was a leatherbound diary. It was soiled and slightly charred, but still legible. Alex struggled to decipher the handwriting, and insisted on reading out what seemed to be mostly shopping lists. His first flush of excitement soon dulled though, as Maggie knew it would. Maggie's had not; but for some reason she felt compelled to disguise her interest in the thing.

'It belonged to someone who lived here,' said Alex. 'Actually lived here over a hundred years ago!'

Maggie pretended to stifle a yawn. 'Will you give it to your museum?'

'No, I bloody won't. It'll end up in a box on a shelf in a cupboard in a back room on a forgotten inventory.'

'Some archaeologist you are.'

'I know too much about the bloody business.'

'Did Daddy swear?' said Sam.

'He said it's time for your bed,' said Maggie.

'No he didn't,' said Amy.

Amy had a pageboy head of silky blonde hair, and a habit of looking suddenly from under her fringe. Her eyes were the impenetrable blue-grey of the mist from a lake. They disarmed. They challenged. Sometimes it was mightily disconcerting to be wrong-footed by a five-year-old.

'You never miss a trick, do you?' said her father.

'No,' said Amy, looking into the fire.

2

Amy had been home from school about an hour. She and Sam had been playing spitting games in the garden. It was three days after the discovery of the diary in the fireplace. Maggie was busy at the kitchen sink – busy in that abstract way of gazing into the soap suds as if they revealed fleeting patterns of the future – when a bespattered Amy and Sam ran into the kitchen.

'Dot dug it up! Dot dug it up!'

'And it wasn't dead and it's gone on the roof!'

'If you've been spitting . . .' Maggie started, noticing the suspicious dribble on Sam's chin, but something about the children's urgency made her stop.

'She did! Dot dug it up, so it isn't dead!'

'What isn't dead?'

'The bird we buried on Saturday. It isn't dead yet.'

'Nonsense.'

But Amy insisted Maggie should come and look for herself.

Out in the garden, Maggie could see Dot snuffling in the corner by the wall and looking vaguely guilty as she approached her. The dog was hacking, as if trying to clear its mouth of something unpleasant. Amy pointed to the spot where Alex and the children had made a shallow grave for the bird they'd removed from the fireplace. The earth had been disturbed.

'Dot dug it up and got it in her mouth and then the bird flew away. I saw it.'

'Yes it did,' said Sam.

Maggie looked into the cloudless blue of Sam's three-year-old eyes. He was going through a phase of lying habitually about almost

11

anything. But Amy was usually a more reliable witness.

'It can't fly away when it's dead, Amy. Dot must have eaten it.'

'Dot ate it,' said Sam.

'No she didn't!' Amy protested. 'I saw it fly!'

Maggie took a stick and poked at the disturbed soil. It was true, nothing remained there now.

'There it is!' Amy shouted, pointing above her mother's head.

Maggie turned. Perched on the rusting pole of her washing line, not six feet away, was a sleek blackbird, its eye fixed on her. She waved her arm, expecting it to fly off, but it didn't move. It sat there, immobile, watching her. Maggie instinctively took a step backwards.

'That's not the same one. There are hundreds of blackbirds around here.'

'It is the same one,' said Amy, 'it is.'

'Kill it,' said Sam.

Maggie felt the prickly contagion of her children's fear and excitement. It transmitted to her, like static. It paralysed her. It left her almost shell-shocked, unable to step out of the moment. She had a picture of herself, of them all, her, her children and the bird, all caught in a web.

Then she became conscious that Sam and Amy were waiting for her to do something. Ridiculous! It was ridiculous that this small, unremarkable bird should make her afraid like this! At last she picked up a bit of wood. Advancing slowly, she waved the stick before her. The bird, in its own time, hopped from the pole to the wall before flying away.

Maggie collected up the children and ushered them indoors.

3

Alex came home late that evening complaining bitterly about the dig at the castle. A policy change had been made over his head. Since the episode with the bird, Maggie had had a particularly tiresome time with the kids. Amy had stood on watch in the garden and had flatly refused to come in even when it had begun to rain; and when Maggie took her eye off Sam for three seconds while fetching Amy, he'd promptly emptied a box of breakfast cereal into the dog's dish. What's more, her period was about to start, and she frankly didn't give a shit about Alex's grubbing about in the castle ruins.

Meanwhile Alex directed at Maggie the speeches he would like to have made at work. 'Living archaeology he calls it! So now we have to build a walkway round our work so Joe Public can come and watch us in action. Can you believe it?'

'Haven't you ever stopped to watch three men digging a hole in the road?'

Alex ignored her, tearing off his work clothes and throwing them in a corner of the kitchen. 'I told him, just so long as you don't want to put us under a glass case at the end of it. Didn't know what I was talking about. Pretended not to. How would he like it? How many people have to tolerate having their work closely observed by the public?'

'Footballers. Actors. Policemen. Dentists . . .'

'Exactly. Run me a bath, would you?'

'Any particular temperature?'

Alex changed to a wheedling voice. 'Sorry; you know how I like to be pampered when I get worked up about the job. And it's not as if you have anything to do all day.'

He reached out to her in supplication but she pushed past him and

13

went hammering up the stairs. In the bathroom she slapped the plug in the hole and throttled the taps open to release ferocious jets of hot and cold water; then she thumped heavily down the stairs, shoved him aside and snatched up his discarded work clothes. Alex made to say something conciliatory, thought better of it, and turned to make his way quietly up to his bath.

While Alex soaked, Maggie shepherded the kids to bed, still nursing her indignation. She came downstairs and put a match to their new living-room fire. It was crackling nicely when Alex appeared wearing an old dressing gown she hated. He collapsed into an armchair and picked up a magazine.

She waved a glossy leaflet at him. 'This came today. Want to look at it with me?'

Alex glanced up, and looked pained. It was a prospectus for the local university.

'Do we have to go through this again? We've discussed it enough times.'

'Alex, I really want to do this course. It's important to me.'

'But it's the wrong time. You've got a young family to think about. Responsibilities.'

They had discussed it before; many times, and without resolution. The words they used had been repeated so often they'd become symbolic. Maggie used language like 'important' as a stinging missile. Alex in turn sent up big barrage-balloon words like 'family' and 'responsibilities'. The words were all there, but they'd stopped talking to each other.

Underneath it all, Alex was secretly afraid he might lose her, to someone or to something else. It was an unspecified anxiety he chose not to analyse. And the more Maggie sensed this secret fear, the more trapped she felt.

'I'll go mad if I don't do something. I mean really mad. I'm already going mad hanging around here. Weird things have started to happen.'

'What weird things?' He put down his magazine.

'Today. There was a bird. In the garden. It *looked* at me.'

'It looked at you?'

'Yes. It *looked* at me.'

Alex laughed. 'Well. I daresay it did.'

Maggie stared at him. He pretended to duck back behind his magazine.

'You,' Maggie said at length.

'Uh?'

'You.'

The magazine went down again. 'Are you premenstrual?' he said smugly. 'Do you want a cuddle?'

She outstared him. The grin vanished from his face. She had to take deep breaths between her words. 'You don't – know – what – I'm talking about! You just – sit – there and you – DON'T KNOW WHAT I'M TALKING ABOUT!'

'All right! Stop shouting and tell me what you are talking about!'

She waited until she felt more composed. 'There was a bird, in the garden, and it looked at me! Not in any ordinary way. And it frightened me. The children saw it too.'

'What kind of a bird?'

'A blackbird.'

'An ordinary blackbird?'

'It wasn't ordinary at all. It looked *into* me. Through me. I can't explain it. It was as near to me as you are now, and it wasn't at all afraid. I tried to make it go away and it wouldn't.'

'Perhaps someone had tamed it. Looked after it.'

'Not this one.'

'How do you know?'

'You weren't there.' She chewed her lip, wondering whether to tell him the rest. 'The children said it was the bird you buried in the garden.'

'What?'

'Amy said that Dot dug it up and it flapped its wings and jumped onto the roof.'

'Ridiculous.'

'I know it sounds ridiculous, but the bird was gone from where you put it and I told Amy that Dot must have eaten it or something but I didn't believe it myself.'

'Look, you're just—'

'I know! I know! I'm just neurotic! A completely neurotic house-wife with two children and a dog and a dog's dish and a husband in a dirty old dressing gown! You don't seem to see the point!'

'So what is the point?'

'The point is . . .' Maggie had to draw a deep breath so she could

15

remember the point. 'The point is that every day I'm stuck here I feel like a bird in a wire cage and I want to get out!'

Then she saw Sam standing in the doorway in his pyjamas. The shouting had woken him, and he was blinking at her with moist, frightened eyes. She gathered him up and brought him over by the fire, and told him it was all right, they were only playing a shouting game.

That night in bed, she did something which she didn't do very often. When Alex put his hand on her belly, she turned away from him. He said nothing. They lay awake in the dark, and it was some time before either of them drifted off to sleep.

4

Amy was at school and Sam was asleep on the sofa. Maggie had a precious moment to herself. She'd been woken in the middle of the night by a thump from downstairs, where she'd found Sam sleepwalking. She'd tried to pick him up to carry him back to bed but he'd woken to complain about nightmares, so she let him climb in with them. Alex had snored on and Maggie had sighed with guilt. She knew the shouting had disturbed Sam.

Sam had developed a touch of conjunctivitis, and after a bad night his eye looked sore. Maggie had a large, very old *Family Medical Dictionary*, passed on to her by her grandmother. Her family doctor told her the healthiest thing she could do with it was toss it on a bonfire; he told her books like that only scared people. But she kept it, consulting the brittle, yellowing pages every time her children suffered some complaint or other.

She read that conjunctivitis was an inflammation of the membrane that linked the eyelids and covered the white of the eye; she read that any but the slightest cases required immediate attention as blindness might result; and she read that a serious form was caused by gonorrhoea. She felt rather alarmed by all of this information. The book was returned to its shelf under the stairs, out of the doctor's sight.

Sam turned in his sleep. Maggie thought about phoning the clinic for advice; it might even produce another visit from the doctor. She liked him. He was a young, handsome Asian GP with a wonderful sense of humour, who always seemed prepared to stay longer than was strictly necessary. She picked up the telephone, looked up the number, and then something made her replace the handset.

She noticed the diary resting alongside the phone. The diary the sweep had found up the chimney. It was odd: Alex must have left it there.

She made herself a coffee and sat down to leaf through the pages. As well as what appeared to be shopping lists, the diary contained lists of herbs, what Alex had called 'folk remedies'. Her idea was to see if she might find some gentle salve to apply to Sam's eye.

Opening a page at random, she found a list written in beautiful copperplate handwriting. In places the blue ink had mellowed to purple and black with age, but the author was meticulous and neat:

Acacia	*Anise*	*Broom*	*Comfrey*	*Elder*	*Eucalyptus*
Eyebright	*Hazel*	*Lavender*	*Marjoram*	*Mastic*	*Mistletoe*
Mugwort	*Nutmeg*	*Peppermint*	*Pimpernel*	*Sandalwood*	*Spearmint*
Thyme	*Wormwood*				

That was all. There was no other entry on the page. Whether it had any relation to the date at the head of the page, 7th February 1891, Maggie had no idea. Neither did she know enough about herbs to deduce why this selection had been grouped together. The previous page contained a similar list:

Balm of Gilead   Cedar   Cinquefoil   Cypress   Fern   Honeysuckle ...

On the following page, another list of herbs, rather longer.

Maggie turned the pages more quickly. Some entries seemed to be no more than shopping lists, with no reference to herbs; occasionally there was a more intriguing entry. On one page was written simply:

Sell your coat and buy betony.

There were also practical remedies.

All headaches. Make herbal sachet of light-blue cloth, sew into equal parts bruised leaves lavender peppermint mugwort clove

*marjoram tie on blue thread and wear round neck. Sniffing is effi-
cacious.*

But beneath that entry was written:

A. hates me because of my red hair.

The diarist too was a redhead! Maggie immediately felt a strange affin-
ity with the writer, for reasons unclear to her. Why should a detail of
physical appearance – trivial in itself – excite in her a wave of sympathy and identification? Redheads weren't denied the fruits of the earth
any more than anyone else and, in her experience, never laid claim to
any sisterhood which might exclude a blonde or a brunette. Once,
before she was married, a boyfriend had teased her that redheads more
readily assumed the powers of a witch; but he was always inventing
things, and she'd laughed it off. Yet there it was, and Maggie decided
that whoever the diarist was, she liked her for it.

She leafed through the diary rapidly, alighting on whatever looked
interesting. There were several 'remedies', listing the preparation of poul-
tices, salves, ointments, oils, and some which seemed simply intended
to make smells. Many, however, were useless, since they didn't say what
complaint they claimed to remedy. The diarist might have known, but
Maggie couldn't guess. Then she found something for Sam.

*Soreness of eyes all eye complaints. w.m. juice of fern camomile
eyebright. Salve then sachet w clove garlic 1 eucalyptus 2 sage 2
saffron. Blue cloth. Can also bring f.*

It all sounded a bit messy. But, she reasoned, it couldn't be any
worse than having chemicals dropped into your eye, which was all the
family doctor – however kindly he was – would prescribe. These were
earth remedies, Maggie argued to herself, natural healing agents that
had been handed down over hundreds and hundreds of years only to be
ridiculed and dismissed by a medical industry too clever for its own good.

She put down the diary and moved to where Sam was stirring on the
sofa. She put her hand on his forehead and he opened his eyes. There
was still some inflammation in the corner of one eye.

19

'Want to come shopping with me?' she asked.
'No,' said Sam.
'No?'
'Yes.'

5

Three days later Sam was still running around with a sore eye. He also had a dirty brown stain near the bridge of his nose where Maggie applied her homemade herbal remedy. Alex had quizzed her about it.

'Ointment,' she'd said. He'd sniffed and let the matter drop.

Alex didn't seem to notice that Sam carried a sachet of herbs on a string round his neck. The herbs were sewn into a light blue cloth, and Sam carried it cheerfully, calling it his treasure.

Unfortunately it just wasn't working.

Maggie had been conscientious. She'd dragged Sam around the shops to pick up every herb mentioned in the list. There'd been no difficulty in collecting them from general health food stores, except for the one called eyebright. The assistants all looked blank at that one, and when pressed on where she might try, they shook their heads pathetically. Then another customer, overhearing, suggested she might try a shop in the Gilded Arcade.

The Gilded Arcade was an original four-storey Victorian shopping precinct. It was unfashionable and off the main drag; consequently the many tiny stores which operated from it were special interest or frankly eccentric. Rents were low and businesses had a habit of changing hands rapidly. The hollow echo of the arcade, its fitful little flights of business, and the peeling gold-leaf railings of its catwalks gave it the impression of a giant aviary. Colourfully dressed young people looked over the railings for hours, at different levels, like perched exotic birds. Maggie approved of the unorthodoxy of the place, and its air of dilapidated grandeur.

The shop she was looking for was called Omega. She passed kiosk-sized shops peddling memorabilia, second-hand period clothes, specialist books, and found Omega at last on the uppermost level. Pulling Sam by the hand, she opened the door and a tiny bell tinkled. A man sat behind the counter reading a book. He looked up from the book, but didn't speak.

The shop seemed chiefly devoted to herbs and spices and books about alternative medicine; that is to say its shelves contained rows and rows of jars with handwritten labels, and where there were no jars there were books and pamphlets.

Maggie turned her back on the man at the counter, pretending to study a selection of pestles and mortars, but she felt his eyes following her. She picked up one set made of stone but quickly replaced it on the shelf. When she turned back to him, he raised his eyebrows in a jocular fashion. Sam just stared at the man.

'Eyebright. I want a herb called eyebright. Do you know what it is?'

'Of course.' It was said in a lethargic manner. The man was in his mid-forties, with thinning shoulder-length hair and a wispy beard. His weathered face and heavy build seemed at odds with his thin, reedy voice. '*Euphrasia officinalis* if you want to get technical. Euphrosyne by any other name. Red eyebright to me and thee. What d'you want it for?'

She resented the question. 'I only need a small amount.'

'Please yourself,' he said, getting up and crossing to a shelf on the far side of the shop. He reached for a jar. 'Only trying to be helpful.'

He weighed some of the herb on a beautiful set of brass scales. 'Gender, Male. Planet, Sun. Element, Air. Ask for Euphrosyne another time, because that's what most people call it.'

'Do you know a lot about herbs?'

The man opened his eyes wide and looked at her as if the question was stupid. 'Anything else?'

She shook her head and paid for the herb. Her fingers trembled in her purse. As she was bustling Sam out of the door the man said, 'Next time come to me for the other things as well. I do it half the price you paid in those health shops.' She turned to look at him, but he already had his head back in his book.

After that she drove out of town to Osier's Wood. It wasn't necessary to drive so far to collect a few stalks of fern, but the place had pleasant associations. She and Alex used to walk there. They'd even made love there one hot summer afternoon; but only once. Alex was put off after claiming to have seen an adder weaving through the fern stalks.

She had an idea Sam had been conceived that time in the woods.

'Know what, Sam? You were made in these woods.'

'No,' said Sam.

'No? I'll give you no!' She waved a freshly cut fern at him.

'Yes!' said Sam, running away. They played a game of hide-and-seek in among the trees before going back to the car.

The following day Maggie had to return to the Gilded Arcade. When she went into the shop, the man was seated in exactly the same position, reading the same book, as if he hadn't moved a millimetre since she'd left the premises the previous day. Almost without looking up, he pointed to the selection of pestles and mortars. 'They're all over there.'

She had indeed returned to buy a pestle-and-mortar set, having decided the previous evening that, if she was going to make an ointment out of her ingredients, they'd need to be pounded first.

'Are you a mind-reader as well as a herbalist?'

The man looked up, pleased with himself. 'Where's the little boy?'

'With his childminder. I get two hours' relief a week. I'm glad to see there's something you don't know.'

'I can always spot a first-timer. They come here to ask for the more obscure stuff. Then they get it home and realise they need some way of preparing it. Then they remember seeing all these.'

'How did you know I'd been to the health food store first?'

'That was more difficult. You had a carrier bag spelling out their name in big letters.'

Maggie smiled to herself and turned to finger the implements lined up in the window. She liked the man now she realised his offhand manner was nothing other than gamesome. She picked up a brass pestle. 'What do you recommend?'

'The ceramic ones chip if you're not careful; the wooden ones splinter and don't take to anything hot; and I don't like to think of the metal ones leaving some of themselves in your mix.'

'Stone, then?'

'Every time.'

'Not cheap, are they?'

'Please yourself. Take the brass.'

'No, I'll take the stone.'

'And I wasn't being nosy yesterday. I was genuinely trying to be helpful.'

'Then you must know the eyebright is for eye infections.'

'The little chap. I noticed his eye was sore.'

'Isn't that how it got its name?'

'Eyebright? No. Applied to the eyelids it aids clairvoyance.'

'Are you serious?'

He looked at her hard, but his eyes were swimming with suppressed mirth. 'I never joke. Tell me what you're making.'

She told him. He nodded thoughtfully. 'Not my first choice. But it's an interesting one, and it won't do him any harm. Where did you get it from?'

So she told him about the diary and the lists of remedies. 'And there were the initials w.m. – does that mean anything to you?'

He shook his head. 'As for the sachet, that's a bit of indirect herbalism, if you follow me.'

'Should I ignore that part?'

'Oh no. And it'll give you something to do with your time.' There wasn't a flicker from him to indicate irony. Then he gave her some useful advice for preparing Sam's eye ointment. As she turned to leave the shop he said, 'This diary. I'd really like to have a look at it some time.'

'I might show it you,' she said, 'and then again I might not.'

And the tiny bell tinkled as she went out.

Three days later, all Sam had to show for his mother's incursion into the world of herbalism was a dirty face; that and the gay little sachet round his neck. Maggie inspected the remains of the sticky paste she'd concocted and judged it time to revert to orthodox pharmacy.

For some reason she'd hidden from Alex her new collection of herbs and her stone pestle and mortar. She wasn't sure why exactly she'd made a secret of the thing. Perhaps she was placing it beyond his ridicule, because nothing was more certain than his scepticism for anything unscientific.

Unscientific.

No, it was more than that. Much more. Alex's was like many people's scepticism: it was almost rabid, it was desperate. He used scepticism to seal himself off from whatever he was afraid lay out there. Like the yards of draughtproofing he bought for the house, or his damp-proofing, or his endless leak treatments. Worse, she knew that in his darkest heart he nursed some kind of suspicion about her. Something they'd never discussed, and never would, but which lay between them, like a sword hidden beneath the sheets.

She knew what Alex feared was her power. Powers he didn't possess. The power to be surprised, to be delighted, to exult, to be mystified by events. The power to be afraid without fear of showing it. The power to resist the stolid pull of the ground. There was something in her he recognised as a deep flirtatiousness, not necessarily with other men, but with the world itself, with the unknown, and he was afraid that one day it would carry her away from him.

Beyond all that, she wanted this to be something exclusively her own. That's why she'd hidden the herbs. She wanted the opportunity to experiment freely. Somehow that gave her a feeling of another kind of power; power not just over Alex, but over the preparations she made with her herbs.

So she hid everything in a lockable trunk in the spare room. It was full of old photographs and memorabilia neither she nor Alex could bear to dispose of but at which they never looked from one year to another. She bundled everything in a black scarf and buried it at the bottom of the trunk.

Sam came out of the garden and into the kitchen waving a stick. Maggie held his face to the light and looked doubtfully into the corner of his eye. 'It was worth a try, Sam. But we'll have to stop using that stuff; it's not doing any good.'

'No!' said Sam.

'For God's sake stop saying no every time I speak to you.'

'The lady said.'

'What?'

'The lady in the garden.'

'What lady?' Maggie felt a shiver run through her.

'In the garden. She said use it tonight. She did. She did. She told me.'

Maggie looked out of the window at the walled garden with the dwarf birch in the corner. There was no one there. She knelt on the floor beside Sam. 'Tell me about this lady.'

'You can't see her. She's gone. And she's only this big.' He stretched out his thumb and first finger. Then he changed his mind and made her a bit smaller. 'No, this big. She rides on a rat.'

'What did she say about the ointment?'

'She said you have to put it on me tonight. Yes she did.'

'That boy,' said Alex angrily. Maggie was startled. He was towering in the kitchen doorway, looking down at them. He must have been watching them for some time. He looked huge and frightening. 'We're going to have to do something about this constant lie-telling. He needs a good shaking.'

Alex stormed past them and clumped heavily upstairs. He'd had another bad day at work. Maggie collected Sam to her, and hugged him.

6

Maggie applied her herbal ointment to Sam's eye that night, and the next morning there was a distinct improvement. By the following morning, his conjunctivitis had cleared up completely. Now all they had to worry about, said Alex, was Sam's deep-rooted habit of telling lies.

'He's just a child. He makes up stories. So what? That's what children are supposed to do. He'll grow out of it.'

Alex wasn't having any of it. 'It's not stories. It's lies. Lies. Every single word that comes out of his mouth is a lie. Ask him what his name is and he says anything other than Sam. Ask him where he lives and he talks rubbish. He tells people his mother is the lady at the sweet shop. If he says yes, we all have to pretend he means no.'

'He's only three years old, for Christ's sake!'

'He's nearly four and there's something wrong!'

'It's just a phase he's going through, Alex. Your mother told me you were still wetting the bed when you were nine.'

Alex didn't like to be reminded of such things. Maggie could tell that the remark had angered him, because unlike most people, Alex spoke more quietly when he was angry, stopping occasionally for big breaths. 'It is not a phase. It is a steady condition.'

'I mean all children do it. Have pretend playmates and the like. That's what I meant to say.'

'Amy certainly never did it. Not on this scale. And neither did any of our friends' children. He needs to see a child psychiatrist.'

'At three years of age! You're the one who's crazy, Alex!'

'You think it'll help him if we wait until he's thirty? Now's the time to do it, so he can be straightened out.'

27

'Straightened out? I don't want him straightened out. I'm not putting Sam at the mercy of a shrink.'

'What's a shrink?' Amy wanted to know.

'It's a special doctor,' said Alex, 'who looks after little children.'

'No it's not,' said Sam.

It seemed easier to communicate through pointless argument than by any other means; at least that's all Maggie and Alex seemed to be doing. The matter went unresolved, they turned their backs on each other.

Meanwhile Maggie returned to the diary, flushed with the success of her first efforts. She found the page listing the remedy she had used and underneath it made an entry herself. She wrote the dates, the quantity she had used, and the words *Sam's conjunctivitis cleared up.* If only the diary had a herbal for banishing fibs and tall stories.

While flicking through the pages, settling here and there on remedies, she made a discovery. Some of the pages with ink entries contained further notes, but in pencil and so faintly written that a cursory glance could easily miss them. These entries, too, were mainly lists, written in the same perfectly formed copperplate hand, but they occasionally included additional commentaries. Maggie was astonished she'd failed to notice them before; but then the pencil marks were so weak, they were a strain to read.

Rue is a mighty powerful one, a mother of herbs. I heard her called Ruta, Bashoush and Herb of Grace and more. This is of Diana, though it is hot and indeed it is of the element of Fire.

Now rue they used for that Great Plague, but it was denied. It grows best if stolen, which I have. Gather in the fresh morning because a poison to pick later. Some say the sight. I know that to eat leaves will not talk in sleep, which is the tongue of angels and demons. The crushed leaf, when breathed back full, will clear the brain of envious thought. And rue water kills the flea.

Now I will use rue on A. she bothers me so: I know this one for she taught it me: Nine drops of the rue oil added to a bath with salt for the nine nights as follows the moon in her waning will break the spell she has on me, for she wearies me. And I know others:

Rue, vervain, St John's wort, dill
Hinder witches of their will

Maggie felt a strange thrill. She set the diary down and turned to check on Sam. He was playing happily behind her chair, swinging an old biscuit tin loaded with toy soldiers. She picked the book up again and re-read the page. What she'd taken to be simple herbalism was obviously something more. *Rue, vervain, St John's wort, dill . . .*

She leafed through the pages, searching for more pencil entries.

Listening. This I dearly love above all things. And I can with or without I make a simple. On a windy day, with the sun just up, or fast on the dusk which is my favourite to lie down in a tall leafy bower or such and listen and wait on the wind. And I wait and I wait and there he comes with such messages as are written in the wind in the leaves some time I fear my heart will break. And should I infuse a simple it is the mugwort and I make a tea and sweeten with honey. Or that if I make a pot then into the boil the bay laurel, mugwort and cinquefoil and I breathe them. But for listening I say I can without a simple or a pot.

Maggie read on:

Some words of the mugwort, also called witch herb and old uncle harry and artemesia and felon herb. Why 'uncle' I cannot tell, for mugwort is a she-plant and another of Diana whose other name is Artemis. Her planet is Venus and her element the Air.

Now she is very good for the sight; in a simple or pot or the fresh leaves rubbed on mirror or the crystal. She also wards off fatigue and I have walked long distances; and wild beasts stay away from it. Now pluck before sunrise during the wax moon: A. says, and is insistent, that it should be from a plant as leans northward. Also her powers are strongest when picked at the Full.

A few pages on Maggie stumbled across the name of the diarist.

P.B. come to me and was full of woe, I never seen so much woe, she being barren. Bella, she says to me, three years and no child! I counselled her and I had a bit of Patience Dock so I stitched her a sachet as we talked. I didn't want to give her any of my Man, he being so rare these days so I put bryony, which is good and she wasn't to know. I told her eat poppy and sunflower seed in a cake, and sent her off to find some mistletoe. Well I hope for her but I'm afraid I can't see it.

Now A. chid me for all this, for her saying is 'be silent as the sacred oak'. She says folk turn. But I say we must help, and there's the end of it.

So now she had the diarist's name. It was Bella. Red-haired Bella. And Bella was some kind of witch.

Maggie read on as if the diary contained hard news. Some of the pencilled entries she didn't entirely understand; others were merely the elaboration of uses of herbs. She was so absorbed in the diary that she jumped when Sam gave a yelp from behind the chair.

'It bit me!' he bawled. He held his hand up to her and she saw a thin stream of blood running between his finger and thumb.

Maggie saw the culprit. The corner of the biscuit tin had become twisted and a sliver of metal extruded from the edge. It was razor-sharp. 'Naughty tin!' she said. 'We'll throw you away for doing that!'

'It wasn't the tin,' said Sam. 'The tin didn't bite me.'

Maggie took Sam's little white hand and put it to her mouth, sucking the crimson beads of blood. 'Who did, then?' she said soothingly.

7

Alex came back from work to find Maggie, Amy and Sam playing a game in the yard. A large blue candle was set in a brass holder in the middle of the yard, its flame flickering in the light breeze. It was Amy's turn to jump.

> *Jack be nimble, Jack be quick*
> *Jack jump over the Candlestick*

And Amy jumped. She cleared the candle easily and shouted, 'Mummy's turn!' Maggie stepped a few paces backwards, said the rhyme and took a healthy run. She cleared the candle by several feet. 'Cheating!' shrieked Amy. 'Cheating! You have to stand still and then jump.'

'What's going on?' said Alex.

'Shut up!' Amy shouted. 'Sam's turn!'

But Sam was scared to try. 'Scaredy-pants!' Amy bawled. 'It's easy.'

'Don't want to.'

'Can I have a go?' said Alex.

Alex stood before the candle and cleared it easily from a standing position. 'No!' Amy bellowed. 'You have to say Jack! You have to say it!'

'OK.' So Alex did it again, reciting the rhyme.

'Now Sam has to do it.'

'Not if he doesn't want to.'

'He's boring.'

'No I'm not.'

'I know,' said Alex, lifting up Sam. 'I'll do it holding Sam, then we'll have done it together. All right, Sam?'

Sam nodded. Amy complained that it didn't count, but they did it anyway, reciting the rhyme together. Maggie hadn't done it properly, so she was put to the task again.

'Did you know that Jack's another name for the Devil?' said Alex. 'This game was supposed to be an old pagan cure for something or other.'

'Eczema,' said Maggie.

'Really? That's handy, because Amy's got a touch of . . .' He looked at his wife strangely.

'What does pagan mean?' Amy wanted to know.

'Sort of . . . wild,' said Alex.

'No it doesn't, Amy. It means the people before Christianity. They had lots of different gods.'

Alex considered for a moment. Then, still holding Sam, he said, 'Bet you can't do it backwards!'

'Backwards?' said Amy.

Alex stood with his back to the flaming candle and said:

> *Candlestick the over jump Jack*
> *Quick be Jack nimble be Jack*

He jumped backwards. He landed awkwardly, his leg buckling under him. Sam landed on his chest.

'Careful!' Maggie shouted.

Sam thought it was a giggle, but Alex had sprained his ankle. He picked himself up.

Amy noticed the candle had gone out. 'You said that's bad luck, Mummy. You said it's bad luck if the candle goes out.'

'It's always bad luck,' said Alex, hobbling back up the path, 'to twist your ankle.'

'Bad luck stupid shit!' cackled Sam. He picked up the candle and threw it at his father. 'Stupid shit backwards!'

Alex straightened up and looked at Maggie in astonishment.

'I don't know!' she protested. 'He must have picked it up from the kids at the childminder's.'

That evening, with the children in bed, they sat by the fire. Alex was watching a game show on the television with his foot up and a bag of ice cubes draped over his ankle; Maggie had her head in a magazine.

'You know that diary we found?'

'Hmmm?' said Maggie. She didn't look up.

'I was looking for it earlier. I couldn't find it.'

'It's around somewhere.'

'I was telling a colleague at work about it. He's interested. I said I'd let him have a look at it,'

'Hmm.' She turned a page.

'So where is it?'

'Where's what?'

'The diary.'

She looked up. 'Where have you looked?'

'I've looked all over.'

'Last time I saw it it was by the telephone.'

'By the phone?' said Alex. 'What was it doing by the phone?'

'I don't know. I certainly didn't put it there.'

'Well who did? More to the point, where is it now?'

'I don't think it's a good idea to lend it out anyway.'

'Oh, you don't?' Alex was getting annoyed. 'Can I ask why not?'

'We won't get it back.'

'Don't be ridiculous. It's only Geoff; he wants to see it.'

'It's fragile and it's valuable,' she flashed angrily, 'and it belongs to this family.'

Alex was rather taken aback by this show of defiance. 'All right. All right. Keep the bloody diary.'

He pretended to become re-engrossed in the TV game show. After a while he snapped the television off and stood up.

'What are you up to?'

'What?'

'You're up to something, Maggie. What is it?'

'What the hell are you talking about?'

'All right. Have it your own way. Meanwhile something's got to be done about Sam.'

'Something?'

'He's out of control. Completely out of control.'

Maggie took the remark as it was intended: a criticism of her capacity as a mother. She pursed her mouth. She was boiling. She said nothing.

Alex went to bed, hobbling up the stairs with his twisted ankle. Maggie followed an hour later. It was a cold bed. Two backs turned make a deep, dark valley down the middle, where sleep is hard to find.

8

Alex had Sam booked in to see a child psychiatrist within the week. He made private arrangements, an expensive move calculated to infuriate Maggie. Mr De Sang – he didn't like to be called doctor, although he possessed all the credentials – insisted on an initial meeting with the parents together, followed by individual meetings, followed at last by meetings with Sam.

Maggie had put up massive resistance, but Alex was determined. It had been their single biggest dispute in seven years of marriage. Maggie said it would only happen over her dead body, Alex declared that could be arranged. Alex said he'd drag her there kicking and screaming if necessary and Maggie claimed that would be the only way. Alex alluded to a history of mental illness in Maggie's family (a minor nervous complaint) and Maggie reminded him of disorders in his own (a single case of epilepsy).

'If you *really* want to screw him up,' bawled Maggie, 'why not just throw him into a pit of snakes.'

'Seems like you've already accomplished that much.'

'What do you mean by that?'

'Work it out for yourself.'

The truth was Alex didn't know what he meant. It was just something to be said in the momentum of fierce argument. It was a wild shot, but it silenced Maggie for a minute.

She recovered to say, 'So Sam's got to be dragged off to a qualified child abuser just because you're for some reason furious with me?'

To Alex's credit, he'd considered that possibility. He'd analysed his own motives for wanting Sam examined. He was genuinely uneasy about Sam's relentlessly disruptive behaviour. Amy was growing up as straight as a pine tree while Sam, psychologically speaking, was like something from a hall of mirrors. He'd enjoyed none of the closeness with the boy he'd adored in bringing up his daughter. Maggie had found a way of handling him, sure enough, but all he ever got from the child was a gaudy procession of lies, tantrums, breakages, blue fits and foul language. He loved Sam, but found the boy a minute by minute horror show.

To Alex's debit, he failed to understand his proposal for dealing with Sam masked a deeper unease. His self-analysis wasn't thorough enough to make him realise he was trying to get a grip on a family he sensed was nudging away from his sphere of dominance. It frightened him at too deep a level to admit this might be happening. At some level he sensed malign things incubating in the umbrageous waters of the family relationships, but the knowledge of it only ever spoke to him in his dreams. He was a rational man. He grabbed at rational, surface solutions. He thought all that was needed was a strong hand on the tiller.

De Sang wore suede boots and a drab suit, its jacket supplementing a large, buttoned cardigan. He was a tall, thin man with a fleecy white head of hair. Though he had a chair behind his desk, he didn't seem to like to sit on it; throughout his interviews with Maggie and Alex he sat on the arm of his chair, on the edge of his desk, on his windowsill, anywhere but his chair. In a day's work he covered miles of ground without leaving his office.

When agreeing to take on Sam he managed to convey the impression he was doing all concerned a favour. 'Meanwhile what Sam needs above all else,' he said, parking his bum on the warm radiator and folding his arms, 'is stability.'

'He's got stability,' said Maggie.

De Sang looked at her a long time before answering. 'Children Sam's age are moving through a precise stage of development. They have a habit of responding acutely to the emotional environment in which they're located. If Mother is pleased, they know it without anything being said by Mother. If Father is angry, they know it even before Father has outwardly shown his anger.'

Alex nodded, interested. Maggie looked away, guessing where all this was leading.

'This *empathy* of early childhood begins to thin out as kids become more verbal – as they learn to talk better. It's a survival faculty we mostly lose. But Sam here, he's still in that empathy mode, reflecting some of the emotions generated around him.'

Alex agreed. 'Makes sense. I mean—'

'You can tell all that from one meeting?' Maggie interrupted rudely.

'I can recognise a pattern when I see one,' said De Sang. 'We all like to think of ourselves and our relationships as unique – and in some ways they are. But underneath . . . If there is tension in the house, Sam will find a way to reflect it back. If there's a mood of opposition, or contradiction—'

'But what's been said about tension or opposition?' She looked at Alex.

'Mrs Sanders. You're paying me to be blunt.'

'It's all right,' said Alex, getting up to leave. 'I appreciate the directness. It's already making sense.'

He shook De Sang by the hand.

Maggie was livid.

'What the hell did you tell him about us?'

'I didn't tell him anything.'

'Bullshit. You practically did his job for him. Now he doesn't even have to earn his fee. Stability! Stability? Couldn't you even let him look at Sam first, before blaming everything on our disagreements?'

'The idea is to help the man sort it out, not to mystify him!'

'Rubbish! You had your tongue so far up his arse I couldn't even see your head waggling.'

Alex stared at her. She'd never previously directed language like this at him.

'All I said was that there are certain *tensions* in the household. That's all I said.'

'Did he ask you if we're fucking?'

'Sam is listening to every sweet word you have to say.'

'Did he ask you? Did he?'

'What's that got to do with it?'

'That means he did! Yes! I'm right! And you told him. Jesus Christ!'

Sam looked up wide-eyed at his mother. 'Baby Jesus.'

'All right! What do you suggest we do with the child? I'm sure you've got some terrific ideas. What does your book say? Rub him down with mustard and garlic? Or thrash it out of him with a hazel switch? When are you going to be a PROPER MOTHER TO OUR CHIL-DREN?'

Now it was Maggie's turn to stare at him for raising his voice. Alex stormed off to work, leaving her to take Sam home.

But before she did, she stopped by the Gilded Arcade, to look in on the man she thought of as Mr Omega. She peered through the window and thought he must have finished reading his book; at any rate he had his back turned and was weighing out measures of herbs in small plastic bags. He didn't look up when the bell tinkled. Sam pointed up at the tiny bell, waiting for it to ring again as the door closed.

'Rue, vervain,' said Maggie, 'St John's wort, dill . . .'

'Hindreth witches of their will.' He didn't look up from his task, but she could tell he was smiling. 'You've learned something.'

'Only we say hinder. We don't go in for "hindreth".'

'Brought that book in for me to see?'

'No.'

'Right. Sell her old stock, won't we, Sam?' He winked at the child. Sam buried himself in Maggie's long skirt.

'How did you know his name?'

'You told me. Last time you were in.' She suddenly remembered telling him, and she felt stupid.

'If you're going to ask me all these questions,' he said a few minutes later, 'you'd better sit down. I'll make you some coffee. Or herb tea if you prefer, but personally I can't stand the stuff.' He dragged a chair beside the counter and she sat. He gave Sam a doll on strings to play with.

'Coffee will be fine. What does it mean when certain herbs are referred to as "hot" or "cold"?'

'It refers to the energy of the plant. If its effects are stimulating and aggressive, or electric, then they're said to be hot. If they're relaxing, passive and magnetic, then cold. I prefer it as a gender classification, male and female, but then I suppose I'm an old sexist.' He sat down and swept a hand through his thinning hair.

'I suppose you are.' She looked across her coffee cup at him and their

38

eyes settled on each other a moment too long. Maggie looked away. 'What if a plant was said to be of Diana?'

'Oh, you're getting a bit fey there. All these herbs are supposed to have associated deities. The old gods. I can't be bothered with all that stuff.'

'Does it matter when a plant is picked?'

'Does it matter how long you cook a lasagne? Or a panful of carrots? Of course it matters!'

'I still don't see why.'

'She doesn't see why, Sam. Look, if you want to be scientific about it, did you know the weight of a plant increases during the waxing of a moon? Fact. Photosynthesis. So some new matter must be created. Then the weight returns to normal as the moon wanes. Fact.'

There was something invitingly humorous and ironic about the way he levitated his eyebrows each time on the word *fact*. As though he was seducing her into a conspiracy to which he only jokingly subscribed. Certainly he wasn't the most physically attractive man in the world, but he exuded a deep sense of calm and self-possession; it tempted one to want to stay and bathe in it for a while.

Maggie had a deeply intuitive nature, and great powers of empathy when they were allowed exercise. It depended on context or on precise individuals, on the combination of active agents, like sugar and yeast. Here was such an interaction. The bond was immediate. She saw through to him. She saw a level of sadness beneath all of his ironies. It excited her instincts. Questions fizzed.

'What's manzanilla?'

'Camomile.'

'What's devil's milk?'

'Celandine.'

'And old gal?'

'Old gal is elder.'

'And old man's mustard?'

'Yarrow. Where are you getting all these names from?'

'You seem to know them all. Can you sell me some laurel, mugwort and cinquefoil?'

'Going listening, are we? I really wouldn't mind getting a look at that book of yours.'

Maggie giggled. 'Got any suggestions for a love potion? Or at least I'll settle for a peace potion. Something to restore a bit of harmony to a fractious household.'

'Not getting along with the old man, eh?' He jumped out of his chair and started to reach down jars from the shelf behind him. 'Let's see what we can do.'

Maggie too got to her feet, bombarding him with questions as he shook herbs into the brass pan of his weighing scales. She leaned comfortably against the counter. Both were too preoccupied to notice the door open.

Sam, playing with his doll on the shop floor, did notice. His eyes shot up to the bell as he waited for it to tinkle; but this time it failed to ring. An old woman stood in the open doorway.

Sam looked at his mother and the shopkeeper, but they had their backs turned. He looked again at the silent bell, and then at the woman standing over him. She wore a long grey coat, black woollen stockings and heavy black shoes. A dark hat was pulled over her head, shadowing her face. Wisps of hair the colour of smoke poked out from under the brim. She stared hard at the two people engrossed at the counter, her face set in an expression of impatience. Then she noticed Sam.

The old woman bent down towards him. Her movement was slow, snake-like. She put her face close enough to his that he recoiled from her pungent breath. Sam looked over to his mother. He wanted to call her, but the space across the floor of the shop seemed to expand outwards until she was a great distance away, too far to hear him. The woman took the doll from him and put it inside her coat. She straightened her back, turned and walked out of the shop, closing the door behind her. Sam raised his eyes to the bell again. It was silent.

Maggie suddenly looked up from the counter, where they were still measuring out herbs.

'What is it?' the shopkeeper wanted to know.

'I don't know.' She looked at Sam and snatched him up from the floor.

'Something wrong?'

'Nothing. Only . . . Just a strange feeling. Forget it.'

He dispensed the herbs in little plastic sachets. 'As for your old man, blend the oil I told you about. Then rent a porn film from the video shop.'

'Should I drop the oil in his food?'

'Not unless you want to poison him. You're meant to wear it. It smells good.' Maggie paid for what she'd bought. 'Can I have my dolly back?' the shopkeeper asked Sam.

Sam buried his head in his mother's clothes. 'Come on, Sam. Where's the dolly? Give it back to Mr Omega.'

'The lady took it.'

Maggie apologised. 'He makes up porky pies I'm afraid.'

'The lady took it!' Sam almost screamed.

'Don't worry about it. It must be around here somewhere. My name's not Mr Omega by the way. It's Ash. Let me know how you get on.'

He opened the door for her, and this time Sam heard the bell tinkle over their heads, and then again as Ash closed it after them.

9

Alex came home in buoyant mood. He picked up the kids and swung them round and chattered about his work. His nostrils twitched once or twice, but whether in savour of the spicy goulash simmering on the stove or of Maggie's newly acquired and liberally applied oil, it was impossible to tell since he made no comment.

'Things are going haywire at the castle; all our ideas have been scrambled by things turning up which shouldn't really be there.'

'What sort of things?' Maggie stirred the goulash.

'The layer we've worked for the last three months is supposed to be fifteenth century; today we suddenly find our way into the twelfth century with all this stuff.'

'Stuff?'

'Yes, stuff. Stuff. Nothing important. Shards of pottery. A coin and a tin plate. Just all from the wrong period. We'll have to go back to the drawing board and retrace the foundations.'

'Were there any bones?' Amy always wanted to know if there were any bones. Alex had once brought a skull home to show them, but Maggie had refused to keep it in the house. If her own unease wasn't enough, Amy had demonstrated far too great a fascination for the object. She'd wanted it for a plaything, and the line had to be drawn when Maggie had discovered her cleaning its grinning teeth with a pink toothbrush. Out went the skull.

'No bones. No skeletons. Not even a dog bone.' His nostrils twitched again and he sniffed. He looked at Maggie. 'What's for tea?'

Maggie had prepared her perfume using an eyedropper she had originally purchased to treat Sam's conjunctivitis. Ash had sold her oils of

43

gardenia, musk, jasmine and rose geranium, and she blended them a drop at a time until the scent seemed satisfactory. Ash had told her to use her instincts in judging the strength of the smell.

It wasn't that she was prepared to compromise over the issues which had been dividing them; she was still angry about the question of Sam and his visits to De Sang's private practice. But she was exhausted by the arguments, and genuinely concerned that the tension in the household might be harming her children. Despite her antipathies towards De Sang, his words hadn't completely missed their mark.

So she made her scent, her oil perfume, and hoped for the best. She applied it behind her ears, and on her wrists; and for good measure she also anointed the pillows in the bedroom and the cushions on the sofa in the lounge.

Alex complimented her on the goulash, which was a good sign, and the first kind words in over a week. Then after dinner he switched on the TV, plumped up the cushions and stretched out on the sofa to watch a game show. By the time she had put the children to bed and washed the dishes, he was almost asleep himself, dozing in front of the set.

She sat in her chair, looking at him. She was asking herself if she still loved him. She thought she did, thought she might. Once he'd been the one with all the ideas, the initiator of adventures. Now he dozed in front of game shows and colour cartoons. The routines of work and the responsibilities of parenthood strapped him in. She felt a wave of compassion for him; he was doing all he could to protect her and the children from the storm, while she longed for nothing more than to be allowed an occasional walk in the wind and the rain.

Alex roused himself. He got to his feet, blinked at her and smiled weakly. Then he went up to bed. After a while she followed him, but he was asleep before she got there. She undressed and held her scented wrist to her face, inhaling the perfume as she looked at him. The scent produced a deep, sensuous ripple in her and she had to smile. It wasn't love and it wasn't passion and it wasn't enchantment either; but it was better than arguing.

Tomorrow she would go listening.

In the afternoon she deposited Sam with Mary the childminder and returned home to consult the diary. It recommended dawn and dusk as the best moments for the exercise, but these were times not usually available to her: the afternoon would have to do.

She boiled spring water – from the supermarket – on the kitchen stove. Then she shredded the bay laurel, the mugwort and the cinquefoil and tipped it into the pan. She covered the pan with a lid and left the mixture to simmer.

Returning to it half an hour later, she lifted the lid and sniffed the fumes. It didn't smell particularly strong, so she inhaled more deeply, twice, before replacing the lid. She felt nothing in particular. She was disappointed. There seemed nothing stimulating about the concoction; if anything it made her feel slightly drowsy.

But she was committed. She took a thermos flask and filled it with the hot brew, screwing the cap on tight. She put on her coat, picked up the flask and her car keys, went out and drove to Osier's Wood.

It was quiet but for the breeze stirring in the trees. Maggie left the car and crossed the brook into the willow-fringed woods, finding a spot near the place where she believed she and Alex had created Sam. Here she sat under an oak. She unscrewed the cap of the thermos flask and inhaled the hot fumes rising from the brew. She practised breathing in from her diaphragm, pushing out below the rib cage as she inhaled. She did this until the brew went cold; then she sat back to wait.

When Alex got back from work that evening, the telephone was ringing and no one was answering. He unlocked the front door and burst in to answer the phone just before the caller hung up. It was Mary the childminder. She didn't mind that Maggie hadn't been to collect Sam, but she wanted Alex to know she expected to be paid for the extra hours. Alex mumbled an apology and promised to collect Sam himself.

He replaced the receiver and looked uselessly around the living room. The car was missing from the driveway, and he hadn't a clue why. His only thought was that something might have happened with Amy, and that Maggie must be with her. He was ready to trudge round to the childminder's to collect Sam when the telephone rang again. This time it was Anita Suzman on the line.

Anita had gone to school to collect her own children, who finished half an hour later than Amy's younger class, only to find Amy hanging around in the playground with a teacher. She'd waited a while longer and had then decided to take Amy home with her. That had been over two hours ago, and she'd been telephoning intermittently ever since. Was anything wrong?

'Wrong?' said Alex. 'I don't know. I've just this minute got in. And there's nobody here.'

'Well, you're there now.'

Alex, his mind still on other things, was astonished at the logic of this remark. 'Yes.'

'So. Would you like to come and collect Amy?'

'Amy?'

'Yes. She's your daughter, remember?'

'I'm sorry, Anita, I'm not with it. Thanks for picking up Amy; it's good of you. I'd come at once but Maggie seems to have taken the car somewhere.'

'Would it help if I brought Amy to you?'

Anita even offered to pick up Sam on the way after Alex had explained his predicament.

The children looked none the worse when she arrived with them. She took off her coat and sat down without being invited. It wasn't even six o'clock but Anita looked as though she was dressed for a big night out.

'Going somewhere this evening?' Alex gave her a glass of wine.

'No. Why do you ask?'

'I don't know,' said Alex. He hadn't seen Anita since they'd all dined together at her house and he was reminded how attractive she was. She relaxed easily into his sofa and crossed her long legs. The nylon of her tights hissed as they meshed.

'I see you got your open fire,' she said.

'Oh that. Yes.'

'Cosy and romantic. An open fire.'

'Is it? Yes, I suppose it is.'

She put down her wine glass. 'What's going on?'

Alex took a deep breath. 'Maggie wants to go and study a course at university. I don't want her to, so she's finding all sorts of ways to punish me.'

Anita was about to answer, but suddenly Maggie was standing in the doorway.

'Maggie! We were just talking about you.'

'I heard. How are you, Anita?' She unbuttoned her coat, sat down and picked up a magazine.

'We were worried about you. Everything OK?'

'Why shouldn't it be?'

'Anita collected Amy from school,' said Alex calmly. 'She also collected Sam. Mary has been phoning all afternoon to ask what's going on.'

'Are the kids all right?'

'The kids are fine,' said Anita.

'That's all right then,' Maggie looked at Alex, 'isn't it.'

10

'This garden needs digging.'

'What?' Alex had followed Maggie outside after Anita left.

'I'm going to plant a herb garden. I want my own herbs.'

'Why the hell are you talking about herb gardens? Where have you been all afternoon?'

'And I want the money for some garden tools.'

'Did you have to be so bloody rude to Anita?'

'I don't like her.'

'You made that pretty obvious.'

'Didn't you see why she was waiting? So she could enjoy the spectacle of us having a row.'

'Anita is our friend!'

'Correction: she's your friend. Correction: she's the wife of your friend.'

'She was looking after Amy and Sam while *you* were falling down on the job of being a mother.

'It won't happen again.'

'Are you going to tell me where you were?'

She turned to look him in the eye. 'I was having a conversation. With myself. I found out some things. I found out you don't love me, for example.'

'Here we go again. Here we go.'

'You only want to own me. You can't stand the idea of me having any life of my own. I'm not allowed my own life. I'm just a . . . clip-on accessory to your own world.'

'The old song.'

'Why don't you listen to me? Just for once?'

Alex looked up in exasperation. He saw Amy and Sam watching them from a bedroom window. 'Look at that! Look at those kids! No wonder they're so twisted and fucked-up and miserable and unhappy when they've got you for a mother, disappearing and reappearing without a word! Just look at them!' Alex dived back indoors.

Maggie looked up at the children, saw them move away from the window. Twisted and fucked-up and miserable and unhappy. She knew it wasn't the children Alex was describing at all; it was themselves.

She turned and saw the bird perched on the washing-line pole. It was a blackbird, stock-still, head cocked to one side as if listening. Its eye was focused on her. She stared at it for a long time, until it flapped away.

That evening hit a new low. They didn't exchange a single word. Alex made himself a bed on the sofa.

Maggie lay awake in the feverish dark. She felt anxious, troubled by thoughts too abstract to pin down. Still light-headed from the episode in the woods, she was unable to keep her mind from what had happened there.

In one sense there was little to be said. Listening, that's all that had occurred. No more, no less than that. Yet it was as if she had listened for the first time in her life, and discovered that beneath the ordinary sounds of the world was something else.

The first change was a miraculous softening. Her brittle edginess dissolved in the peace of the woods, and so too did her visual impression of the trees, branches, ferns, grasses, and the silky feel of the leaf-mould beneath her. Everything softened. The silence of the place distilled out, and even when a wood pigeon broke cover, the whirr of wings and flicking of branches was muted and distant.

At one point she thought she must have fallen asleep, but knew she hadn't. Time had simply gone awry. She had overstayed her allotted period by two hours. And she had indeed heard a voice, whether in the leaves or in her own head. It was soothing and, in turns, excitable. It was reassuring. It knew things she had thought forgotten. It was a voice she hadn't heard for many years, a neglected, private voice.

It was her own, inner voice, demanding to be heard.

It spoke to her in a language half-formed, in bits of words, sometimes archaic in sound; it whispered in strange accents. Strange, but familiar enough to be none other than her own mind, yet fragmented and reformulated, and at last fractured into a small crowd of ghostly women at her back.

No, she hadn't fallen asleep, because as she opened her eyes and looked around her she felt intensely awake, her perception had sharpened. Squinting up through the branches, she saw that the leaves formed patterns. They structured the light between the leaves, stringing it together like beads on a necklace, or suspending the light in parabolas, like spiders' cobwebs.

The woods took on a moist-canvas effect. She too felt she helped to generate this moistness, and was happy to be a part of the rich mulch of woodland decay and fertility. She found herself blowing gently on the back of her hand, to remind herself to stay conscious; and the act chased a sensuous ripple through her body. She felt moist, inside and out.

And then as she closed her eyes again, the effortless whispering returned. Sometimes it was no more than a beat beneath the surface of life, a rhythm, an existential hum. Then it was the versifying rustle again, which she knew must be the leaves in the trees, but which was urgent in its desire to speak, to tell, to reveal. She had opened a faucet on something shut down for a very long time, and now it would not be closed off. It waited for the twilight between dozing and sleeping and then it began again, elusive, at the periphery of consciousness, but relentless as a river.

The following day, with Alex at work and Amy at school, Maggie set about cleaning up in the kitchen. The pan of dirty herb water sat on the stove. She tossed the reeking remains into the sink where they instantly formed a pattern on the stainless steel. A face suggested itself in the mash of leaves, and a shape like the omega outside Ash's shop in the Gilded Arcade; but Maggie'd had enough of clairvoyance for a while, and she rinsed the leaves away.

She did some washing, and when she came to peg it out she found something dangling from the line. It was the wooden doll on puppet strings which Ash had given Sam to play with in his shop. Maggie couldn't think how Sam had managed to bring it home with him unnoticed, but there it was. She took it down. It was an expensive toy, hand-carved and brightly painted. She decided to return it, or even to offer to pay for it, that afternoon. She also decided to show Ash the diary.

She went and fetched it from its hiding place and began leafing through the pages. It was a curious feature of the diary that she continued to discover, here and there, pages of faintly pencilled entries she'd previously dismissed as blank pages. As if the volume of contributions increased every time she closed the book. Her eyes fell on an entry on the right-hand page, dated 21st March. There was the usual list of herbs written in pen, and underneath a pencilled entry in the same fastidious hand.

First day of spring, and so I have a one should any ask me for help with a-courting. And why not, for I love the young, let them do, I being too old, well not so old but here it is, and it is the hand-fasting. Gardenia for harmony. Musk for passion. Jasmine for love. Rose geranium for protection. Yarrow for seven years' love and to stop all fear.

Maggie read it again. It was almost identical to the recipe given to her by Ash! Only the yarrow was different.

These being all essences, but for the yarrow, which wants the dried herb, a pinch mixed with these essences. Then pour off into two jars, and then each anoint the other from their own jar, by the moon, asking. And after the seventh night, the remaining poured into one jar and both jars be hidden in some secret place. And there's the handfasting.

Maggie looked at the recipe sadly. It would be fun to try, she thought, but the idea of getting Alex to agree to join in a witch's love ritual, smearing each other with oil, depressed her. She might as well try to persuade him to fly from the bedroom window after their last spat.

On the left-hand page of the diary, the previous day's entry, was another recipe:

Dwale. Now she is a harsh mistress. A. says she is my lady, as she has my name. She is from the valley of shadows, and she stalks

*those who would use her. Sleeping, madness and death. The leaves
soaked in wine vinegar and pressed against the temples brings sleep
and eases intolerable headaches and agues. Two of her beautiful
berries might kill a small child. A. told me they once used her juice
as cosmetic – well she can keep it. Deadens pain of childbirth. A.
says now I must use her against my enemies.*

   Dwale is sacred to Hecate and should be picked May eve.
It is one for the flying, as last night I found out,
God help me, for I may have come too far in this

The entry seemed to have broken off. Underneath these words, and
scrawled in another, barely literate hand was a further entry. Maggie
had to turn the diary on its side and squint hard to make it out.

   Ha for there ain't no turning back

It was curious. It had obviously been written by some person other than
Bella, the author of the diary. Maggie had always assumed that the diary
had been a very private thing; that she shared its exclusivity and sense
of dark secrets only with its author. Here also were the first signs of the
diarist's distress.

   She closed the book and told Sam to put on his coat.

Ash was fascinated by the diary. He ordered Maggie to make coffee while
he leafed through its pages. Sam was allowed to play on the floor with
the doll. 'Dwale,' he said, 'is an old witchy word for deadly nightshade.
You know, belladonna.'

   'That's why Bella says it has her name.'

   'Deadly is right. Don't be tempted to try any of this. There are easier
ways to cure a headache. But who is this mysterious A.?'

   'I don't know. She keeps cropping up, doesn't she? I can't tell if she's
a friend or an enemy.'

   'That's right. Bella seems uncertain about it herself. I get the impression Bella is always looking over her shoulder at A. There are some
interesting recipes in here. Would you mind if I copied them?'

   Maggie did mind. She prickled. 'No. Go ahead.'

   'Maybe you wouldn't mind lending it to me for a while.'

She felt, not for the first time, the thrill of possessiveness. 'No. That's not possible.'

Ash looked up from the pages and into her eyes. 'Not even for one night?'

'It's not possible.'

Something told him not to push the matter. He nodded. 'I'll make some notes. If that's all right by you.'

They chatted about the contents of the diary as Ash scribbled down some of the formulae. Much was already familiar to him, but one or two concoctions took him by surprise. 'Bella was into listening to the wind. Have you tried it?'

'I have,' said Maggie.

He looked up again. 'Tell me about it.'

Sam was happily playing on the floor with his puppet. He wasn't dextrous enough to manipulate the strings, but he cheerfully dragged the wooden doll across the floor and gave it a half-formed voice. The doll told him it was sleepy, so he laid it on the floor beside him and felt sleepy himself. He could hear his mother and Ash murmuring at the back of the shop. Their soft, lilting voices retreated slowly, grew muffled and far-off, and the distance between him and them seemed to expand. Their presence diminished and grew cloudy, and his eyelids became heavy.

His arm holding the doll lifted slowly into the air. The strings were held taut, the doll's feet lightly brushing the floor. He felt a slight tug on the strings, and then another tug, in the direction of the door. The door stood ajar. Sam looked up at the tiny, silent bell. Then he looked out of the door and saw her.

It was the old woman. The old lady who had stolen the doll from him last time they came in here. She was outside on the catwalk, squatting, her back to the painted safety railings. She was looking directly at him. She held out her hand with her index finger crooked towards him. She made a trigger movement with her finger, and the puppet strings went taut again, and tugged in her direction. Sam looked from the puppet to the old woman. She repeated the gesture, and the doll seemed to want to walk towards her. Dragging the puppet, Sam left the shop and walked over to her. The sound of shoppers' activity on the level below echoed strangely in his ears. Sounds, shouts became frozen.

Her eyes seemed washed-out, only vestigial traces of hazel colour remaining. She waited until Sam approached her; then she moved her outstretched finger to her nose and pressed it. Her tongue shot out. Sam giggled. Then she grabbed the loose flesh under her chin, tugged it, and her tongue disappeared back into her mouth.

'Can you do it again?' said Sam.

She did it again. Sam was enchanted. Then the old woman straightened her back, beckoned him to follow her, cocked her leg over the safety railings, and jumped.

They were four levels up. Sam leapt at the railings and pressed his head to them. Down at ground level he could see dozens of tiny people walking to and fro. They were the size of his toy soldiers. He could also see the old woman. She was suspended in mid-air, only a few feet below the catwalk.

She took two steps, walking on air. She looked back at him, beckoning him to follow. Sam giggled, and climbed up on the railings.

Ash took a slurp of tea. 'My wife and I are going to take a walk on Wigstone Heath on Saturday. Why don't you come? Bring the kids.'

'That would be nice,' Maggie said. 'I'll ask Alex. Though I don't expect you'll have much in common.'

'That doesn't matter. We can have a picnic if it's not too cold.'

Maggie was delighted at the thought of new friends, what's more her *own* friends. Everyone she knew was connected through Alex. Maybe she would lend Ash the diary for a night after all.

There was a fluttering at the window that made her look up. It was a bird, fanning its wings and swooping at the window, as if it was trying to get inside. Its beak and claws tapped against the window as it hovered against the glass.

'Christ!' Ash shouted. He pointed at something outside and leapt to his feet. Maggie saw he wasn't pointing at the bird, but at Sam, who had cocked a leg over the railings on the catwalk, and was preparing to swing himself over the edge.

Ash vaulted the counter and rushed out. He flung himself at the rails and collected Sam in his arms just as the boy was about to let go. Maggie, coming up behind him, ran at the rails. She could see shoppers huddled on the ground fifty feet below, pointing up at them. The drop flashed like a blade, and she wanted to vomit. She looked up and saw the bird, fluttering at the windows roofing the arcade.

It was a blackbird. It escaped through an open skylight.

11

De Sang was expecting her. His receptionist told Maggie to go right in. She pushed open the door and saw the white-haired psychologist lying face down on the carpet, blowing out his cheeks and moving across the floor with a breaststroke motion. Also blowing out his cheeks was Sam, happily swimming beside him.

'Come and join us,' said De Sang. 'We're having a race to see who can get to the other side the slowest.'

'To the island,' shouted Sam between gulps of air.

'I mean to the island.'

Sam was having a great time. Maggie might even have joined them, but she'd put on a new skirt to come and collect Sam. 'I don't want to get wet,' she said.

De Sang didn't get up, so Maggie sat down. She bit her nails. 'Are you getting some clues to his character?'

'No,' gulped De Sang. 'We're just playing.'

Maggie crossed her legs and looked around the room. On the walls hung a grey diploma, almost obscured by lots of kids' paintings in bold, primary colours. 'Is this how you win their trust?' She was trying hard to sound friendly.

De Sang mouthed at her like something inside a glass tank. 'No. Just playing.'

'No talking!' Sam shouted.

De Sang reached the wall and got to his feet. 'I win so I lose,' he told Sam. 'Time to go home.'

'NO!' screamed Sam.

'Captain Hook,' he said. Sam looked thoughtful and stared at the carpeted floor. 'Swim outside and get your coat.' Sam did as he was told, breaststroking towards the reception. De Sang was red in the face from his exertions. He perched on the edge of his desk, drying off. 'Great,' he said.

Maggie watched Sam swimming out of the room and had to laugh. Then she became serious again. 'So can you tell me why he tried to throw himself over the railings?'

'No idea. Can you?' He smiled.

'How much are we paying you?'

'Lots. Hope I'm worth it. Who is Mr Ash?'

'The shop owner. The one who grabbed him in time. Ash saved his life.' He looked at her. 'No, I'm not having an affair with Ash.'

'Good Lord. Did I suggest you were?'

'No, but you gave me a look. A *psychological* look.'

'In that case I'll have to be more careful.'

It was Maggie's turn to look at him. His face was wreathed with lines. He managed to make a virtue out of his scruffiness, and for this reason she thought she could like him after all. 'Somehow we got off on the wrong foot, didn't we, Mr De Sang? After all, we both want the same thing.'

'We're making progress already,' he smiled.

Alex declined to go walking with them on Wigstone Heath. It was a blustery day, and he preferred to curl up on the sofa in front of the TV, sipping lager from the tin. Maggie festooned the kids with hats and scarfs and took Dot along with them to meet Ash at a prearranged spot. When they got there, he was sitting in his car alone. His wife hadn't felt well enough to come. Maggie wished she'd left the children with Alex.

Wigstone Heath was a wind-blasted stretch of moorland, dotted with stunted bushes and outcrops of rock eroded into eerie shapes. A stone circle called the Dancing Ladies commanded the elevated middle of the heath; and at some distance, leaning slightly into the wind, was a large single standing stone, the Wigstone from which the heath had taken its name. It was like a solitary broken tooth. They headed for the stone circle.

The wind was sharp as a scythe. It made Maggie's ears ache. Dot, at least, seemed to enjoy herself, running ahead and sniffing the path in front of them. Maggie told Ash about De Sang.

'All he seems to do with Sam is play with him.'

'So?'

'Well, I could do that.'

'Then why don't you?'

Maggie wondered why she didn't.

The children ran round the stone circle, attempting to leap from one stone to another. Dot cocked her leg against one ancient megalith.

'What is it?' Amy wanted to know.

'It's a stone circle.'

Amy sighed as if her mother was an idiot. 'But what's it for?'

'It's a mystery,' said Ash. 'Sometimes it's more fun when we don't know the answer. Then it can be anything we want it to be.' Amy looked less than impressed with this. 'All right, I'll tell you the legend. There were these nine ladies. They were dancing naked here one midsummer night. And a wizard put a spell on them, so that if they were still dancing when the sun came up they'd be turned to stone. Well, the night was so short, it took them by surprise. But they were so beautiful the wizard couldn't take his eyes off the dancing ladies, and he got turned into stone too.' Ash pointed over at the solitary standing stone across the heath. 'There he is.'

Amy counted the stones in the circle. They seemed to confirm Ash's story. She walked over to the single stone. 'She's happier with that explanation,' Maggie said.

'But it sort of takes away from the mystery, don't you think?'

'I'm sure there's some deep meaning to it.'

'Yes,' said Ash. 'I'm sure there is.'

They all sat in Ash's car and had sandwiches and tea from a flask.

'You didn't forget to bring the diary, did you?' Maggie asked him. It had been on her mind all day.

'No, I didn't forget.' He produced it from the dashboard. 'And I've got something to show you.' He flicked open to a page which was blank but for a few herb names written on the first two lines. 'What do you see?'

Maggie took the diary and held it up to the window. She could see nothing more than what was obvious. She shrugged.

'Watch.' He took the book from her and pressed his palm down on the page. After a minute he took his hand away and half a page of pencil writing had appeared.

59

'How?'

'Some trick with the pencil graphite and chemicals I suppose. More successful at hiding it on some pages than on others.'

'That explains why I kept finding stuff on pages I'd already looked at.'

'You probably surfaced some of it just by keeping it in a warm place, and by exposing the pages. You'll find more in there than you thought.'

'Have you read all of it?'

'I haven't had it long enough. I was about to ask. Though I suppose you'll want it back for a while now I've showed you that little trick.'

'I suppose I will,' said Maggie, already engrossed in the magic writing.

'Be careful with it,' said Ash. 'Strong stuff.'

'Yes.'

Be careful.

So why am I afraid? When I take such care?

Is it A. whom I fear? Or is it this craft that seduces me? When it steals my every thought? And though I have this and that to attend to, always I think the craft the craft, and return to it, and when so many wonderful things are shewn to me that I cannot otherwise. Wonderful things, falling one upon the other.

And I may do good with it, that's best of all.

But A. torments me and says I play and am not true to the path. Why do I let her abuse me? Why listen? But she says I have not yet come to my fork in the path, as all will and must, says A. Then she flatters me and says I must come to my fork in the path early because I am this and I am that. And it is at the fork I must make the DECISION.

In her few quiet moments Maggie read and re-read the new pages of the diary as Ash had revealed them to her. Recipes for salves and ointments and healing herbs were numerous; but more mysterious were the diarist's outpourings over her misgivings, and the strange courtship with the unnamed A. Maggie did not understand the meaning of these fretful passages but felt in some way they were speaking to her. They were at times like an echo of her own doubts, and yet like the diarist she felt the irresistible seduction in the unfolding of mysteries promised behind the words.

Certain passages made her blood quicken.

There is a fork in the path in the woods, as I now see, and one is the way out, and one is bathed all in the blue light. This is the path of DECISION as I take it. But howsoever A. will have it, I say I am on the path of the blue shining, and the DECISION is made. But A. says I will never do at that.

No, I would not go naked. There's an end. I am resolved not to be put off, nor teased, nor threatened nor bullied no more by A. For now I see she wants me for her own uses, to do this or that EXTREME thing.

Though she struggled to make a coherent picture from these entries, Maggie had, at least, discovered some continuity.

In spite what I wrote a few days ago, today I went naked for the LISTENING, and there is an end to all talk of play. It was the blue lighted path, but not lighted in an ordinary sense, and even A. says yes and how yes it was the DECISION. And it is made. And it shut her mouth for a while, and I'm glad of the bit of peace, so I am.

I'd just as lief not prove her right, but it brings me such reward my heart hammers to tell of it. And dangers, there are dangers I never guessed, but such reward! My heart is like a scales, up, down, I don't know.

I am still afraid, and A. says that is proper.

What was it that had pitched the diarist into such raptures? Maggie wanted to know what great step it was that appeared to have been taken. There was the *listening* mentioned again. Maggie had already been seduced into sampling that the afternoon she'd forgotten to collect the children. Extraordinary things had happened, in their small way, and certain emotions had been excited; but there were no blue lights or shining paths or spectacular decisions to be made.

Meanwhile she found a preparation for treating Amy's eczema; and

61

an inhalant for treating her own sinus complaint, which she used with some success. She had an itch for the creativity of the thing, which made her cast around for subjects. But it wasn't ointments and herb baths she wanted, it was more. The diarist's excitement infected her.

Maggie had never had an affair since marrying Alex, though she had once come close. But, in hiding her herb collection from him, in poring over her diary in secret moments, and in plotting snatched intervals away from her family, the entire enterprise felt a little like that. She was cagey about what she'd been doing and careful not to let anything slip, but her curiosity pulled like desire.

The diary was full of mysteries waiting to be undressed. Her work with oils was deeply sensuous; streaming with exciting, public perfumes and with private, arousing musky odours. Her secret world was full of novel moods and new histories, and was charged with possibility. It was a potent, dangerous seduction; and Maggie was seducing herself.

One morning, about half an hour before dawn, Maggie woke up – as indeed she'd asked herself to before falling asleep. She slipped out of bed and dressed hurriedly. Alex snorted and turned in his sleep but didn't waken.

In the kitchen she shredded and boiled her concoction of bay laurel, mugwort and cinquefoil, inhaling the fumes before pouring the brew into her thermos flask and carefully disposing of the dregs. She got in the car and drove through the empty streets.

Grey light was peeling into dawn when she arrived at Osier's Wood. She parked the car and took her flask and a blanket. There was a heavy dew and mist, a will o' the wisp streaming from the woodland and across the distant meadow. The woods were eerily silent. Trees stood in dark ranks, prodding branches at her in strange, silent gestures. They enfolded her, tree trunks closing behind her like gates.

She found her way to the middle of the woods, dawn light creeping dimly through the fenestrations of the trees. She listened. There was nothing but the occasional drip of dew from a branch. Then the moistness of the trees and the leaves and the earth became a kind of sound to her, a dull harmony. Black and grey and green branches were twisted and drawn around her, like an exotic alphabet she hadn't yet mastered, but which she *would* learn. She put down her flask and her blanket and took off her coat. The decision had been made. She glanced around her before starting to undress.

It was cold, October-dawn cold, but she stripped and stood naked, looking up at the trees, as if she was waiting for something. Leaf mould oozed between her toes, her nipples became erect. A shaft of light lit up the dew on the bark of a tall silver birch. She moved to it, collecting dew on her fingers and putting the droplets to her mouth as if they were honey. They tasted strangely sweet. The glinting silver birch took on a lavender hue. She put her tongue to the bark. She licked, inhaling the deep smells of the bark, the smells of moist, old wood and the fungal odours.

A breeze rippled through the woods and she shivered. She threw the blanket round her shoulders and sat at the foot of an oak. Opening her flask, she inhaled the steam, and it made her feel drowsy. She ran a hand through her long hair, tossed back her head, and listened.

The wind in the tree told her many things.

It told her true things and false things.

It was a friend and a false friend. It told her secrets and lies.

It whispered what she must do to love her husband, and what she must do to kill him.

12

Maggie became aware that she was looking at a live thing. Its striped markings blended in so well with the leaf mould and the autumnal ferns that she hadn't noticed it. A tiny movement betrayed its presence, and she came to, instantly recognising the black and grey-brown chevrons marking its length: adder.

It was no more than a yard from her bare foot, and it was looking at a small bird alighted on a moss-rich, rotting log. Maggie couldn't understand why the bird didn't take flight. It was a tiny jenny wren, close enough for her to see that it was looking at the adder. Then she realised it was hypnotised. It was paralysed by the gaze of the snake.

The adder was a late hibernator. Most of its cousins would be settled in for their winter sleep, and for that reason Maggie felt it was a significant moment. It was present for her. It was a message from Nature.

Maggie narrowed her eyes and stretched her neck. She made a low hissing noise. It seemed madness, but she thought she could project her will into the snake. 'Leave it.' She wasn't sure if she spoke these words or only thought them, but they emerged like a rattling breath caught in the back of her throat. The adder's eyes flickered from the bird to her. Maggie clapped her hands and the wren flew off. The adder slipped away into the ferns.

She gazed for a while at the spot where the adder had been, before suddenly feeling bitterly cold. She had no idea how long she'd been there. She dressed and made her way back to the car.

The hedgerows were ablaze with berries and wild fruit. Maggie felt as if her eyes had been stripped of scale. Black-red elderberries jostled for her attention with poisonous ruby berries of black bryony, healthful hips, brilliant whitebeam, blue juniper, wild crab apple and the shining black pods of deadly nightshade. The season had delivered, and the bushes were an open treasure chest. She determined to come back later, to collect.

Alex, Amy and Sam were sitting quietly round the table having breakfast when Maggie got back to the house. Dot slunk away as she entered the kitchen. She was greeted by silence.

'I've been for a lovely walk,' she announced, a trifle too enthusiastically. 'You should all do the same if you know what's good for you.'

'Early start?' said Alex, buttering his toast.

'I figured it's the only time I can have to myself. If I don't want to be accused of neglecting anyone.'

'Shall we see,' said Alex, 'if we can get through an entire Sunday without having a bust-up?'

Amy looked at Maggie as if the decision was entirely up to her.

Alex went along to the Merry Fiddler for a lunchtime drink with his cronies. He always made a point of inviting Maggie, and she always made a point of declining to join him. Didn't she have the Sunday roast to think about?

The children vanished with Dot down into their converted cellar playroom while Maggie got busy. Not until pans were bubbling and steaming on the stove did she go down to check on them.

They were playing quietly on the rug. Dot was scratching herself in the corner. Alex had made a decent job of converting the cellar. He'd wood-chip-papered the walls and laid a floor of wooden tiles only six months earlier. Maggie noticed a rust-coloured stain spreading from beneath the rug.

'Who spilled something?' she asked crossly. The children looked up with wide eyes. 'Off the rug. Come on! Up! Up!'

The children got off the rug and Maggie pulled it aside to reveal a large, reddish-brown stain, four or five feet in diameter. It was dry. Someone had spilled paint, she guessed, and had tried to hide it with the rug. Only Dot looked vaguely guilty. Maggie fetched a bucket and a scrubbing brush. She scoured at the wood tiles, but the stain showed no sign of lifting. She scratched at it; it wasn't paint and she couldn't work out what it might be. So she tried a solvent, but that didn't lift it.

Amy, standing on the other side of the stain, said, 'It's a face.'

Maggie stood beside her and saw that she was right. The stain formed an identifiable face; features only half-formed in places, ugly, contorted, but nonetheless a face.

'Hmmm,' said Maggie, and she covered it up again with the rug. She returned to the kitchen to attend to the roast.

'It's the lady,' Sam told Amy after Maggie had gone.

'What lady?'

'The lady at the shop. And she's been in the garden. She has.'

Amy tried to sound like her father. 'Are you telling lies?'

'She has! She rides a rat! She's been in the garden!'

'All right. I'll lift up the rug and you spit on her face. Go on. You spit on her face.'

'No, I'll lift up the rug, and *you* spit.'

'You're scared.'

'You spit, Amy. Go on.'

So Sam lifted up the rug and Amy spat on the face. Then they put the rug back.

'Don't say anything,' said Amy.

'Great dinner!' said Alex, wiping gravy from his moustache. 'Tell Mum thank you for a great dinner, kids.'

'Thank you for a great dinner,' said Amy.

'Thank you for a great dinner,' said Sam.

This was Alex's way of trying to make peace. The lunchtime beer had made him frothy and exuberant. He got down from the table and put a match to the fire he'd prepared earlier, picking up the Sunday newspaper before flinging himself on the couch.

'Before you get too comfortable,' said Maggie, 'would you have a look at the playroom floor? I think there's damp coming up from underneath.'

Alex looked at the fire, then at his newspaper. He let the paper slide to the floor. 'Sure.'

He went down into the playroom and checked out the tiles. That was his Sunday afternoon gone. He had just enough tiles in reserve to replace those ruined by the staining. Lifting out the old ones, he found no sign of damp. It was puzzling, but he simply relaid the new tiles. It took him the best part of two hours.

'Job done,' he told Maggie, returning to his couch minus the lunchtime cheer. 'Probably something in the woodstain.'

Ten minutes later the fire was roaring and Alex was snoring.

Maggie decided to make an effort herself. She was not so self-absorbed as to suppose her relationship with her husband would mend on its own. She knew that marriage was sometimes a job of work. It needed routine maintenance with full commitment and sleeves rolled. If only she could find a way of blending that with her newfound interests.

Gardenia for harmony. Musk for passion. Jasmine for love. Rose geranium for protection. Yarrow for seven years' love and to stop all fear.

Harmony! Passion! Love! If only.

She would be prepared to settle for the first and least of these, if only it were that simple. Yes, it was easy enough to make a pretence at harmony. Be sweet, Maggie! Be pliant! Save your spices for the family casserole and don't ask for more, Maggie!

But that wasn't harmony. That was the paralysis of a weak heart. When inside she was scalding.

Passion, once there had been plenty of that. There had been a time in the beginning when they'd been afraid to get out of bed for fear the other might not be there when they returned. Now there were times when, making up her face before a mirror, she might pause to remember some of that passion, and to stretch briefly like a cat, letting go a deep, sensual sigh. Love. Protection. Protection from what? From these adulterous fevers? Or from the fear that – even at that moment – invisible hairline cracks were appearing in the myth of cosy domesticity, a myth she'd never previously had time to challenge.

Maggie didn't want to lose any of it – Alex, the children, the family hearth. But she'd become terrified by a sense of how fragile the thing was, how a moment's inattention might break it. Seven years' love and to stop all fear. Well, they'd had seven years' love, and maybe they'd worn it out. That was her biggest fear of all, that something irreplaceable was already spent.

She'd prepared her oils by the method of *enfleurage,* filling small jars with leaves or petals, immersing them in olive oil and leaving them for a day or two; then repeating the process several times, throwing away the old leaves and introducing fresh leaves into the same oil, until it became saturated with the fragrance. Finally the oil was strained through filter paper into a bottle. A few drops of benzoin tincture were added as a preservative before the bottle was tightly stoppered.

She was becoming an adept enthusiast of the art, using both instinct and olfactory good sense to decide when an oil was ready. She blended her oils with the eyedropper and added a pinch of yarrow herb.

She sniffed the result. It made her smile. It wasn't exactly what she expected, but an irrational belief sat inside her like a guiding spirit. Any residual scepticism she possessed was no more than a skin stretched over the void. Old doubts were drying, cracking, sloughing off, freeing the bright, moist creature underneath.

Then pour off into two jars, and then each anoint the other from their own jar, by the moon, asking.

She poured the blended oil into two small, opaque bottles; one for him and one for her.

That night, she waited until they were undressing by the soft light of the bedside lamp. Alex sat on the bed unbuttoning his shirt. She knelt behind him and began to massage his neck. He was tense, his muscles stiff as hawsers.

'That's nice.'

She dipped her fingers. He tried to look across his shoulders. 'Keep still,' she said softly. She ran a hand through his hair.

'Would you rub my neck, Alex? Just for a moment?' She slipped off her blouse, handing him a small jar. 'Use this.'

'Strong stuff.' He kneaded it into her shoulders and into her back. The oil glistened along her spine and on her smooth, pale skin.

'Something from the Body Shop . . . That's enough. Come here.' She took the bottle from him, held his hand, kissed it and wiped it across her own brow. Then she got up, set the two bottles on the windowsill to receive the moonlight and switched off the lamp. She parted the curtains a little, to let in the soft rays of the waxing moon, and climbed into bed beside him.

'Do you love me?' she asked.

'You know I do.'
'Swear by the moon.'
'What?'
'Swear by the moon that you love me.'
Alex snorted.
'I mean it,' said Maggie. 'I want you to.'
'It's not Sam who needs a psychiatrist.'
'Just do it. Say it.'
'All right. I swear by the moon I love you. Can I go to sleep now?'
'Yes. You can go to sleep now.'

13

Maggie decided that the children's playroom needed cheering up. She tossed out a couple of old, broken, hard-backed chairs and introduced two brightly coloured bean bags. She also placed a few potted plants around the place; a parlour palm and a geranium brought indoors after a successful summer. She was placing the geranium on a low table when she was gripped by a strange notion.

A momentary giddiness came over her and as if caught in a flash photograph she saw Alex working at the castle dig.

'How could that be?' she said aloud. Sam looked up from his toys and smiled at her.

'He won't like that, will he, Sam?'

'Yes.'

'Go and fetch your coat. We're going out.'

The dig in the hollow outside the castle was underway as usual. For work, Alex wore wellingtons and overalls and a permanently knitted brow. He was directing a couple of students to set a series of level indicators. Round the perimeter of the dig area a wooden boardwalk had been constructed, to allow visitors an uninterrupted view of live archaeology. The public, however, had not been persuaded to desert the cinemas or their leisure centres or even their armchairs in favour of live archaeology. The idea had not been a vast commercial success, and it annoyed the hell out of Alex to be on display to schoolkids and the odd courting couple. But on this day he looked up and saw Maggie marching Sam along the wooden planks towards him.

'Hullo. What's up?'

'Found anything?' asked Maggie.

'Not really.'

'You haven't dug up anything interesting today?'

'Not even a button. Why?'

'Not even a button,' Sam repeated.

Maggie stepped off the walkway and paced across the sward to the far rim of the hollow. 'Dig here.'

'What?' Alex laughed.

'Just dig here.'

'Why?'

'Because you'll find something.'

'You can't just dig anywhere you like, can you, Sam? The place would look like a rabbit warren, wouldn't it, Sam?'

'No,' said Sam.

'Please yourself,' said Maggie. 'Come on, Sam.' She swept Sam up in her arms and walked back the way she'd come. 'Say bye bye.'

'Bye bye,' said Sam.

And they were gone. Alex looked at the spot Maggie had indicated he should start burrowing. He shook his head and turned back to the job of supervising the dig.

Back at the house, Maggie began to make a more systematic study of the diary. She had begun to re-read the entries day by day, hoping to glean more information about its author, Bella. But it was problematic. She wasn't convinced that the entries had been made chronologically at all, and still some of the pages contained nothing more than lists. Other pages needed raising, which she did either by pressing them with the palm of her hand or, more effectively, by applying a warm iron to them. Occasionally the heat failed to bring up an entry in full, but Maggie was learning more all the time.

Stinging nettles burn the finger to touch it. But to boil takes out the sting. Then it will do as a remedy against the poison of hemlock, mushrooms, quicksilver and henbane, and the oil of it takes away the sting that itself makes. Gather in July and August, and will also give you good protection.

Other entries were eccentric and inconsistent.

A. says white moths are the souls of the dead. But I say this is twaddle, and that we should separate these superstitiousnesses from the true knowledge.

On the following page was an entry which Maggie was unable to read in its entirety.

Now I take back what I said about the white moth for [missing] and was angry with me and showed me and told me that I should not gainsay my dark sister. My fear did [missing] I thought I should die. Why do I let my dark sister lead me? For we put the [missing] which use of the flying ointment I now abjure. Shred and powder the dwale and hemlock and [missing] and hellebore and steep in hogsfat. But that you should [missing] and go courting death, for Hecate, and I have seen her [missing] that you should fly and I am afraid to look upon her face [missing] and a warning for all who take that path.
Why do I let my DARK SISTER lead me so?

Maggie did her best to recover the missing words, but she was unable to raise them on the page. Some oily substance had stained the paper there, and the full prescription was lost. Flying ointment she'd heard of before; but who was the dark sister, if not the mysterious A.?

Sam was enjoying himself in the cellar playroom, swimming like a slow fish. It was a good game, but better when there was someone else to play it with. When his friend the doctor was swimming, it was easier to hear the sound of the waves and the splash of the water. He liked the doctor.

Sam got up from the floor, and looked around for something else to do. He had a crate of bright-coloured plastic bricks in the corner, next to the potted geranium. He waddled over to the crate and tugged it away from the wall. Then he felt something wet splatter across his face.

It hit him sharply across the cheek. Someone had spat at him. He lifted his hand to his face and wiped at the spittle. It was slimy and cold. He looked around him, but there was no one else in the room.

He was still looking to see where the spit had come from when a second gob slapped him hard in the face. This time he knew where it was coming from. Sam wiped his face, backing slowly across the floor away from the low table bearing the potted geranium.

Maggie came down the steps to the cellar to check on Sam and found him crouched against the wall.

'Sam? What are you doing?'

'Nothing.'

'Are you all right?' She picked him up.

'Yes.'

But Maggie's nerve ends were prickling. She looked around the playroom. There was a disturbing smell in the air, a bitter tang, not strong, but pervasive. She looked at the pile of toys. She looked hard at the potted geranium. She looked at the new bean bags. Then she noticed the stain creeping from under the rug.

She had a bad feeling. Sam was strangely subdued.

Still cradling Sam, she swept the rug aside with her foot. The peculiar discoloration of the wood tiles had returned. It had come back exactly as it had before. Maggie stooped to wipe a finger across the surface, but it was dry. The marks she'd previously identified as a face had reappeared. She kicked the rug back into position, re-covering the offending stain.

'Tell me, Sam.'

Sam didn't want to speak. His fear of earning disapproval for telling lies, Maggie knew, was bringing on an unhelpful reticence. He muttered something inaudible.

'What was that? Tell me, Sam. You can tell me anything.'

'It was the lady.'

Maggie shivered. 'Come on, let's go upstairs and light a fire.'

14

After three days, and against his better judgement, Alex got a dig going on the spot indicated by his wife. Truth be told, he had more helpers than he could usefully employ, and he set three volunteers on the task to keep them from under his feet. They roped off a square and set to work.

On the second day, Alex was as surprised as anyone when things started to turn up.

At first they hit what was a Norman wall forming part of the castle's foundations. These remains pre-dated the main castle by a few hundred years, but were in no way remarkable. The medieval castle builders had simply capitalised on what was, after all, a prime defensive site. The volunteers were instructed to cut a section along the Norman wall and below it.

What was remarkable was the unearthing of artefacts *below* the wall's remains, artefacts some five hundred years more recent than the building of the wall. Of the several explanations for this, Alex favoured slippage of land. The 'Maggie dig', as he came to call it, was after all adjacent to a hollow in the grass, and successive generations of coal mining immediately below the site had caused considerable subsidence over the years. But he later dismissed this and theorised that the new finds were some kind of intrusion on the site.

Apart from shards of pottery and glass, the first artefact to show up was a rusted dagger. It was ceremonial rather than martial, with a long blade and a cumbersome, wrought handle. The knob of the handle was a grinning gargoyle head, with half-folded wings projecting back. The implement was cast in a rough bronze material and studded with three tiny red stones, something like fire-garnet. It had no place among the debris of a Norman wall.

Then its twin turned up not three feet from the first. Alex temporarily abandoned the main venture and flung himself into the Maggie dig. He personally turned up half a tin plate and a few coins which were easy to date as sixteenth-century.

Maggie crowed. 'You should have listened to me in the first place.' She glowed with pride; with deep, private satisfaction, and with secret vindication.

'A lucky guess,' Alex laughed. 'There's stuff littered all over that mound. How could you have known?'

'Instinct. Don't knock it. I just had this tremendous feeling about it.'

Instinct? Maggie didn't know what to call it. But she accepted it as a gift from her recent handfasting ritual. She didn't want to compromise the gift with too many questions. It was an important confirmation that powers were aggregating to her.

'Well, I'm going to throw a couple more people into it tomorrow. See if there's anything worthwhile.'

Alex was always easier to be with when his work was going well. And for that Maggie secretly thanked her handfasting oils (even at that moment drawing down the moon's soft rays). It was a circuitous means of recapturing affection, certainly, but she didn't mind how it worked. Alex wouldn't admit it, but he was grateful to Maggie for giving him a diversion from his otherwise unproductive dig.

He kissed her hand before getting up from the table, and she thought again of her jars of oil standing on the bedroom windowsill. Maggie felt she had learned something about the extraordinary lightness, and indirection, of magic.

'So it was a ritual knife?' Anita Suzman was fascinated. Alex and Maggie had asked the Suzmans over to dinner. Alex had been regaling them with accounts of the dig – the principal dig – and had broken off to tell them about his most recent discovery.

They all got down from the table and sat round the roaring fire. Alex shrugged. 'Certainly looks like that to me. But for what kind of ritual, who can say?'

'What made you break off from the main dig?' Bill said, stroking Anita's arm.

Alex irritated Maggie by leaning back in his chair, thrusting his hands in his pockets and looking sage. 'There were impressions in the earth around that spot. Looked like it had been interfered with at some time, but not enough to be obvious.'

'Was it what you people call a hunch?' said Anita. Maggie noticed how she couldn't take her eyes off Alex.

Alex looked sheepish.

'More wine for anyone?' said Maggie.

'Actually, I'll have to come clean. It was Maggie who told us where to dig.'

Now Anita and Bill's attentions turned to Maggie. 'I can't explain it,' she told them.

'Maggie's gone a bit . . . weird lately. A bit fey.'

'Fey?' Bill looked puzzled.

'Oooh,' said Anita, a teasing note. 'Perhaps she is a witch after all.' Maggie wondered just exactly what she meant by 'after all'. She glanced over at Alex.

The wine had made Bill's cheeks red and his eyelids sag. 'Eye of toad,' he said stupidly, 'wing of bat.'

Maggie challenged him. 'What is eye of toad?'

'Eh?'

'I thought so. Just advertising your ignorance, Bill? All those things like eye of toad are just code names for different plants and herbs. Eye of toad is camomile. Bloody fingers are foxgloves. Beggar's buttons are just burdock. That's all. No big mystery.'

'Consider yourself told,' said Anita.

'I do,' said Bill.

'Our kitchen is like a herbalist's grotto these days,' Alex said glumly. No one said anything. 'An alchemist's chamber.'

Maggie got up. 'I'll go and wash the dishes.'

Anita followed her into the kitchen. She insisted on helping while the men swilled the rest of the wine and chortled like schoolboys.

'I'd like to learn something about herbs,' she said.

'Oh,' Maggie shrugged, 'I don't know that much about it myself.'

Anita looked disappointed.

* * *

After the Suzmans had gone home, Maggie went upstairs and waited for Alex. It was after midnight of the seventh evening of the blending of the handfasting oils. The moon outside the window was strong and bright. She held one of the jars up to her eye, and the moonlight became a starburst in the opaque glass. Silver light ran from the bottle like drops of mercury.

Yes, she breathed. *It might.*

She poured the oil from this jar into the second jar. Then she took the empty one and hid it in her secret chest. She undressed in the moon's soft light, and anointed herself with some of the newly blended oil. Then she sniffed at the perfume still glistening on her skin; a deep, sensual draught. It thrummed her nerves; her muscles were treated to an involuntary spasm.

It affected her. She felt strong.

'What are you doing in the dark?' Alex said as he came into the bedroom.

'Don't put the light on.'

He was slightly tipsy. The wine had made him perspire, and he smelled good. It was an attractive manly odour she'd thought she'd ceased to appreciate through familiarity. He stood against the bed, fumbling with the buttons on his shirt.

Maggie flung herself on him.

Alex gasped for breath as he bounced back against the mattress with Maggie astride him. She tore the shirt off his back, buttons bulleting across the room. Alex strangled a protest as she rained bites and kisses on him, pinning him by his arms. A strange noise was coming from her throat. It made him want to laugh. Giggling, he tried to throw her off, but she was amazingly strong. She was gulping loudly between biting and kissing and sucking at his neck and shoulders. Pinning his chest with one hand she tore at his trousers with the other, scratching him with her sharp fingernails.

Then he was completely naked and she was stretched over him. It was as if someone had thrown open the door to a giant, white-hot furnace. There was a roaring in his ears. Maggie was drenched in perspiration and some incredibly strong scent. Her arched back glittered in the moonlight. Still a strange rasping came from her throat as she licked and kissed the length of his body from his scalp to his toes, her tongue rough like a cat's. It seemed to him she had momentarily lost awareness of who and where they were.

He was massively aroused by the fury and ardour of her attack. He tried to turn her over, to turn her on her knees so he could penetrate her from behind; but he couldn't find the strength to shift her.

'Maggie,' he said. 'Maggie!'

She took his cock inside her mouth and sucked until it hurt, drawing her sharp nails from his shoulders down to his feet. Energy crackled from her like a discharge of electricity. She settled herself with a shimmy, and he felt the furnace heat of her as she lowered herself onto him, flinging her head back as his full length went inside her. She convulsed at the penetration, her breasts shivering in the liquid light, nipples erect to the moon. There was an overpowering odour of sex and sweat and scent, and a moment when Alex thought he was going to pass out. She pressed her hands on him, cooling him with her fingers. She stretched herself across him and the contact of her nipples and her skin made him hallucinate briefly, seeing and feeling her as eels of warm light.

'What are you doing to me!'

She went on until he was exhausted, exhausted and sore. No one had ever performed on him like that. He lay back on the bed, panting, with Maggie still sitting astride him, herself panting, finished, the sweat gleaming on her back and on her breasts, drops of perspiration pearling the moonlight. Her face was in shadow, but her teeth were white and sharp. The whites of her eyes glittered with lunar light, flashing in the dark. She looked frightening, like a goddess, or a demon.

'Now,' she said when she'd recovered. 'How long have you been fucking Anita?'

15

Alex denied it. He told Maggie she was insane. What could she say? That the trees told her? That the wind in the bushes had whispered in her ear one day when she was naked in the woods? That she knew the trees sometimes lied in order to help, but that this time she believed them? She had no evidence to confront him with, nothing at all to go on other than her instincts.

But she was determined to find out.

'You be careful,' said Ash. 'You just be careful.' He dropped the catch on the shop door to make sure Sam didn't find his way out onto the catwalk. He could live without a repetition of recent events.

'I've spent all my life being careful. That's the trouble.'

'But you're getting into a dangerous game here. This isn't like making a herb pillow.'

'That's why I'm asking you to help me.'

Ash looked hard at her. She looked pale. Her copper hair was drawn back fiercely into a Scandinavian plait; her blue eyes were moist. 'This is not an under-the-counter sale you're talking about. I don't even stock these things. They're poisons.'

'Listen to this.' She read from the diary. '*All questions will be answered and all matters settled. Take care to gather only on the moons as I have said and make the banishments which A. assures will keep us from the harm of demons. Honour Hecate, she says, and she will love you for her own; abuse her and she will imperil your soul. And all this can I testify. All questions will be answered and all matters settled, but that you fly.*' She put down the diary. Sam was hanging from her arm, looking into Ash's eyes. 'But you see it, don't you? This *flying ointment*. It's an aid to clair-voyance, isn't it? That's what they mean by flying! That's all it ever meant!'

'I know all that, Maggie, but what I'm telling you is the ingredients are all highly toxic, deadly even. I mean that's what all that stuff about Hecate is saying: watch out, she'll kill you!'

'Not to those who treat her with respect.' Maggie was urgent. Ash had never seen her so animated. 'And anyway. You've done it yourself. Once or twice.'

He was shocked. 'How do you know that?'

She half-closed her eyes and squinted at him; a strange, seductive gesture. 'The trees told me.'

He looked away, feeling his cheeks burning. Her intuition was strong, and it was correct. He had experimented with the flying ointment, and had singed his wings. But what made him blush was something else. If her intuition about him was so strong, then she would also have guessed his feelings towards her.

'Fly with me, Ash.' He started straightening shelves. He couldn't look her in the eye. 'You could show me how.'

Alex went back to his dig and tried to shut the events of the previous night out of his mind. The discovery of the ritual daggers had been reported locally, producing a trickle of extra visitors to the site. The presence of these spectators only irritated him more. He marched along the specially erected boardwalks in his heavy wellingtons bellowing 'Excuse me', all but bundling people out of his way.

He was conscious of the scratches and the bruises and the bites Maggie had imprinted on his body. She'd acted like a wildcat; he'd never before seen her like that. She'd been possessed by uncanny strength. Plus there was her insistence about Anita. He'd denied it a dozen times, but she was implacable. For the first time in their marriage she'd done something that made him slightly afraid of her.

No, that was untrue. There had always been something in her to make him a little afraid. A reckless streak. A promiscuous gap in her integrity that he felt would one day be used to take her away from him. It was a demon-worm that had always gnawed at him over the years, despite his best efforts to deny its existence.

Some of the things she'd done to him last night made him wonder. It occurred to him she might have been taking lessons from someone else.

* * *

'No,' said Ash, 'I can't help you.'

'Then I'll do it myself.' Maggie tapped on the diary. 'I've got all the information I need.'

'It's dangerous. Leave it alone.'

'That's why I asked you to help me.'

'I'm not going to. Don't ask me again.'

'Come on, Sam.' Maggie slipped the diary into her bag and got up to go. She tried to open the door, but couldn't manage to release the catch. Ash had to open it for her.

'Wait. If you're serious about it, let me make a suggestion.' He rushed back to the counter and took out his address book, copying something onto a scrap of paper. 'Do you know the village of Church Haddon? There's someone there you might go and see. Old Liz. She's a strange soul but don't let her frighten you. At least she won't let you come to any harm. Just see what she's got to say, first. Please.'

Maggie shrugged and put the address in her coat pocket. Ash watched her dragging Sam along the catwalk to the stairs, and felt sad.

16

Alex had been charged with collecting Sam from De Sang's clinic the following afternoon. De Sang maintained an open-door policy, so that parents need not feel excluded from some esoteric process going on behind lock and key. The receptionist smiled at Alex as he passed her desk and walked into De Sang's room.

De Sang was seated in a hard-backed chair in the middle of the room. His hands were tied in front of him, his face was painted an assortment of vivid colours, and his trousers were round his ankles. Sam, face also painted, was running round his chair whooping and waving a paperknife he'd found on De Sang's desk.

'Come in! Come in!' De Sang shouted. 'Pull up another chair!'

Sam had already found another chair and, shrieking with delight, was drawing it alongside De Sang. Astonished, Alex dropped into the chair. 'Hands, Daddy! Hands!' shouted Sam. Alex looked at the psychologist.

'HANDS!' Sam screamed angrily. He'd found more string.

'Better do as he says,' said De Sang. 'Looks like he's got us.'

Sam looked furious with his father. Alex held out his hands and Sam wound the string round them so many times he didn't need to tie a knot. 'You don't mess with Peter Pan,' said De Sang in a stage whisper. His face was a garish patchwork.

'Peter Pan!' yelled Sam. 'Peter Pan! TROUSERS!'

'Sam made a discovery while he was here today. He went to the toilet and was so eager to get back in here he forgot to pull up his trousers. Result: he fell over. We made it a learning experience: man with trousers round his ankles can't go anywhere.'

'TROUSERS!' bellowed Peter Pan.

'He's Peter Pan. I'm Smee.'

85

'Who am I?' said Alex.

'Oh. Just one of the nasties.'

Peter Pan picked up the paperknife and waved it menacingly.

'Better do as he says,' De Sang said again.

'How can I put my trousers down with my hands tied?' Alex was serious.

Sam looked disgusted. He put the knife down. 'Come here, Daddy. And no tricks. NO TRICKS!'

'He knows all the tricks by now,' said Smee, 'so there's no use trying anything.'

Sam unwound the string from his father's hands. Alex lowered his trousers, sat down and allowed his hands to be bound again. Armed with greasepaint pencils, Sam set to work on Alex's face.

Alex wasn't too comfortable about it all. 'Made any progress today?' he tried to sound casual.

'Not really. We've been playing most of the time,' De Sang said chattily. 'Although we did have a little sleep earlier on, didn't we, Sam?'

'Sleep?' said Alex.

'KEEP STILL!' Peter Pan bellowed.

Then he noticed, amid the children's paintings on the wall, a framed diploma qualifying De Sang as a hypnotherapist. 'Oh,' he said, realising. 'Look-into-my-eyes sleep.'

'Pardon?'

'Hypnosis.'

'Good Lord, no. I mean sleep sleep. I was a bit tired and so was Sam, so we lay down on the floor over there and had a ten-minute nap.'

Alex felt stupid. 'I mean, were you looking for dreams or . . . something.'

'No, we just wanted a nap.' Alex could see De Sang's grin behind the swirling clouds of smudged colour. 'You don't hypnotise or dream-analyse a three-year-old. It's all there on the surface. It only gets buried as we get older.'

Alex wanted to ask *what* was there on the surface. He'd suddenly remembered how much he was paying De Sang for all of this. They were interrupted by the receptionist entering the room. If she was at all surprised by the sight of two men sitting with their trousers down, she made a good show of disguising it.

'Your next clients are here. You might want to wash your face.'

'Thanks Sheila!' chimed De Sang. 'Time to go home!'

'No!' shouted Peter Pan.

'Sam,' said De Sang. *'Captain Hook.'*

On hearing the magic words, Sam cheerfully resigned himself, and unbound De Sang's hands, grudgingly doing the same for his father. Without being asked, he trotted off to find his coat.

Alex and the psychologist pulled up their trousers.

'Are we making any progress?' said Alex.

'Early days.' De Sang looked hard at him, smiling.

Under the pressure of this smiling gaze, Alex felt obliged to say something, anything. 'He's been a bit better at home.'

'Really? That's excellent.' Alex wished he would stop smiling from behind all that greasepaint. Then De Sang touched Alex's elbow and stopped smiling. 'Your wife, Maggie. She's a very clever, very intuitive lady. I think she's understimulated and I think she feels undervalued.'

Alex suddenly felt something immense turning on a delicate fulcrum; an entire burden of blame shifting towards him. 'So it's my fault, is it?'

'Stop. Stop there. Both you and Maggie, like most people, have this incredible ability both to apportion blame and to feel blame being apportioned to you. This is not about blame. This is about life. I'm telling you this as a friend might tell you.'

'I thought this was going to be about Sam,' Alex protested.

'Of course it's about Sam. Now: shall we go and wash this stuff off our faces?'

The next day Maggie had the freedom afforded by being able to leave Sam at the childminder's. She decided to pay a visit to Old Liz.

It was a fifteen-mile drive to Church Haddon. Maggie found the place easily enough, parking in the street and walking the hundred yards or so to a grey, tile-roofed cottage at the bottom of a cinder pathway. An old collie came to bark at her from behind a half-closed gate, and she hesitated.

A few yards away, the door to the cottage stood partially open. Maggie waited for the commotion to summon the householder from the shadowy interior, but no one came. The dog barked furiously, blocking her way.

Maggie looked the collie in the eye. 'Don't be silly,' she said and the dog stopped barking instantly, coming from behind the gate to lick at her heels. She scratched it behind the ears, and it followed her down the path.

In front of the house was a vegetable patch. The cottage door showed its original wood, greying beneath a coat of flaking green paint. A rusting horseshoe was nailed over the lintel. Maggie hovered nervously on the threshold. She had to fight an impulse to retreat down the path, get in her car and drive home. She glanced over her shoulder before knocking softly on the door.

There was no answer. She tried to peer inside but was unable to see past the gloom of the immediate shadows. Smells hovered in the doorway; kitchen smells of bottled jams, vinegar and yeasty odours. She knocked again, a little harder.

The door nudged open a further inch under the pressure of her knock. The shadows within seemed to deepen. Maggie waited. She set a foot on the stone threshold and took a decision to push open the door.

'You wants to be careful.'

The voice from behind made Maggie spin round. An old woman stood square on the path not three yards away. She was leaning heavily on a stick, evidently having been watching Maggie for some moments.

'You wants to be careful, going places you've no rights to go.'

Old Liz was a skinny woman, bespectacled, iron-grey hair tied back and folds of loose skin hanging from her face and neck, making her look like a turkey in need of fattening. She was chewing or sucking at something in her mouth. 'Goin' in people's houses.'

'I'm sorry. I wasn't going in, I was just . . .'

'I know what you was doing.'

'I thought no one was in. I was just about to go.'

The old woman said nothing. She leaned on her stick, chewing vigorously, eyeing Maggie. Her eyes were dull, black beads behind the thick glass of her spectacles.

'Ash suggested that . . .'

'I knew you was a-coming.'

'Oh? Did Ash tell you then?'

'Ash? You knows Ash, do you? No, Ash told me nothing.'

'Oh?' Maggie said again. *So how did you know?* was the question she for some reason felt unable to put.

When Maggie took a step towards her, Old Liz reached down smartly and pulled up a bit of grass or herb from alongside the path, crushing it and rubbing it between thumb and forefinger. The gesture stopped Maggie in her tracks. She felt bewildered. The old woman didn't take her eyes from her for a second. A taste of bile rose in her mouth. For some reason this awful old woman frightened her. What was Ash thinking of in sending her there? She wanted to go home.

Suddenly Old Liz seemed to relax. Then she was pointing her stick at Maggie. 'I sees it. It's all there, it is. But you don't even know when-the-day! You don't! Heh heh!'

'Pardon?'

Old Liz fastened the garden gate and then pushed past Maggie to go inside. 'Yes, we knew you was a-coming all right. But it's been a time, hasn't it!'

Maggie didn't know whether she was expected to follow, until Liz snapped at her. 'Come in and shut the door behind you. You'll be lettin' all th'eat out th'ouse.'

Liz slumped into an armchair underneath a grandmother clock. Maggie couldn't sense any heat to let out; in fact it was marginally colder inside than it was outdoors. There was no fire to see, and Liz wore what must have been at least five layers of woollens.

Maggie closed the door and turned to explain. 'Ash from the Omega bookshop in town, he told me—'

'Never mind all that,' Liz said irritably, 'get that kettle a-going.' She waved her stick fractionally towards the stove. Maggie did as she was told.

The old woman had made the kitchen her living quarters. A door gave way on to another room behind, but it was firmly closed. Some kind of larder was curtained off near the sink where Maggie splashed water into an aluminium kettle. The kitchen had a musty smell, like bacon curing, plus another scent which Maggie quickly identified. She looked up and tied to the rafters were bunches and posies of herbs hanging to dry. There was a huge range oven in the corner of the kitchen, but it obviously wasn't operational. Maggie put the kettle on a gas stove.

'My grandmother had one of these ranges in her kitchen.' Maggie tried to make conversation. 'They're lovely. They really are.'

'She did, did she?' said Liz, tapping her stick on a floor made up of offcuts and irregular lengths of different carpets. 'Well, listen to this.'

And she sang a verse of song in a cracked, tuneless voice, tapping her thigh occasionally with her free hand.

> *I'm a-going on me way, a-going on me way,*
> *I sees this I sees that, I sees what I see,*
> *I knows as I'll not tell a soul,*
> *For it's nowt to do wi' me.*

When she'd finished, Liz sat back. Maggie smiled, but Liz looked as if she didn't want her to smile. They sat in embarrassed silence for a while. Maggie wished Ash had been there to make a proper introduction.

'Ash, that is the man at the shop, in town—'

'Never mind all that,' said Liz. 'Two beans, a bean and half a bean, and half a bean again. How many?' Then she spat something from her mouth on to the rug in front of her. Maggie saw that it was a bean.

'I'm sure I don't know.'

'Not clever then, are you?'

'I'm afraid I'm not.'

'Then there's those clever ones who pretend as they're not clever. You could be one o' they?'

Maggie tried to force a smile. Then the old woman leaned forward out of her chair.

'Two. You've two little ones. Now then, how do I know that?'

'I'm sure I've no idea. How did you know?'

'That kettle's a-boil,' said Liz.

Maggie made the tea. The old woman got up and stood over her, supervising with silent but intense vigilance. For a second time Maggie thought she wanted to go home.

'Ash thought you might help me.'

'He's no good. He comes here, then as soon as he comes he goes away again. What's the use o' that? Eh?'

Maggie could think of nothing to say.

'How much will you give me?' said Liz suddenly. Maggie was taken aback by this directness. Liz chuckled. 'I'm just kiddin' on. I always say that to Ash. Heh heh. How much will you give me, I always say. And he says, as much as you want. Heh heh, that's a good 'un ain't it? As much as you want. You can say it. Say: as much as you want.'

'As much as you want.'

'Heh heh heh!' Liz thought this was hilarious. Then she turned serious, and said sharply, 'Listen here, missie; I've never had anything as I haven't earned. So you be careful.'

Maggie didn't know what she was being accused of. 'I am careful.'

'Yes, you're a one, I can see that. Liz can see that, but it's clear you ain't all released. You don't know when-the-day.'

'Sorry?'

'You ain't expressed at all. Not released. Though I sees you are a one.'

'A one what?'

'Don't try and kid on at Liz, because you're just a girl. A slip.'

Maggie relaxed for the first time since entering the cottage. 'Do you mean—'

'Hoi!' Liz silenced her with a wave of her stick. 'None o' that.'

Liz's eccentricity made Maggie smile. She shook her head, as if trying to flick away the very charm of the old woman's strangeness. 'All right. What do you mean by saying I'm not released?'

Liz dropped her stick and slowly put her arms round her own shoulders, hugging herself. She lifted up her knees and hugged them into herself as far as she could, old limbs parodying the younger woman opposite. Liz was grinning and blinking at Maggie from behind her spectacles.

'I'm doing my best!'

Liz unfolded herself. 'Your best might not be enough for what's at call.'

'And what is at call?'

'You tell me.'

'Ash thought you might help me with the flying ointment.'

'Pssshhttttt!' Liz dismissed her with a wave of the hand and looked away.

'Will you?' Maggie said after a while.

91

'Listen to this:

> *'I'm a-going on me way, a-going on me way,*
> *I sees this I sees that, I sees what I see,*
> *I knows that I'll not tell a soul,*
> *For it's nowt to do wi' me.'*

Liz sat back in her chair and closed her eyes. Within seconds she was asleep and snoring gently.

Maggie sipped her tea. The grandmother clock ticked on over Liz's head, the heavy pendulum swinging from side to side. Maggie felt extraordinarily drowsy herself. She had to resist a temptation to close her eyes. She studied the old lady sleeping in the chair, still grasping her walking stick. She was tempted just to get up and leave, but she thought it too ill-mannered. She sat, and waited silently.

Presently Liz opened one eye and looked at her. She roused herself in her chair. 'If you draw that curtain back,' she said indicating the larder, 'you can pour us a glass of elderberry wine.'

'I can't.' Maggie looked at the clock. 'I've got to pick up my little boy in half an hour or there'll be hell to pay.'

'Eh? Got to go? What's the point of comin' 'ere at all if you've got to go?'

'Sorry. Can't be helped.' She stood up.

'You comin' again tomorrow?'

'Can't.'

'Go on then. Bugger off,' said Liz.

Maggie turned at the door. 'Can I come back again next week?'

'You just bugger off,' said Liz, looking hard at the wall.

Maggie let herself out. She stopped at the gate to take a breath before walking back to her car. She didn't know whether to feel amused or irritated by the old woman. Certainly the meeting hadn't produced the help and guidance she was looking for.

She wasn't looking for an explanation necessarily, but for a context, a framework for understanding. The inspirational message about where to dig in the castle grounds had left her feeling a little too pleased with herself. She hadn't felt the need to question it. But the sexual frenzy of the other evening had astonished even her. It was not as if something had taken her over; she was not possessed. On the contrary, she'd remained ultimately in control of what was happening. But the ferocity of the power which had suddenly been made available to her had genuinely shocked her.

Liz had not been able to offer her anything. Old people want to talk, Maggie thought as she drove home, but they don't want to listen, or to respond, or to give. Liz wasn't so much different from many very elderly people she'd met, half senile, cantankerous, demanding.

She resolved not to bother the old woman again.

17

'I was talking to Mr De Sang,' said Alex.

'Oh yes?'

'He's got some interesting views.'

'Yes?' said Maggie. The children were in bed. The fire was dying in the grate and Dot commanded her usual position stretched before it, twitching occasionally in her dog dreams.

'He was talking about something he called *projection*. Do you know what that is?'

'You're about to tell me.'

'When Sam feels upset by his mum and dad arguing, he naturally projects a threat to his security and happiness. He then deals with this projection by contradicting everything, or by bad behaviour, in order to get the attention and security he really needs.'

'It's a neat enough theory.'

'Similarly,' said Alex, 'when Maggie feels unhappy, she contemplates separation or even infidelity. But she can't admit this to herself, so she *projects* this on her husband.'

'De Sang told you that?'

'No. I'm just trying to work things out.'

'I see. The name of the game is Alex has found a new word.'

'Don't be angry. I'm trying to help.'

'This is not a good way of doing it.'

'Got a better idea?'

'Yes. Come for a walk with me. Now.'

'It's after eleven!'

'All the more reason to go. When did we last take a midnight stroll? There's a beautiful new moon out. Can't you see how important it is to do new things? Walk under a new moon? Strip the scale off our eyes?'

'Why?'

'Because I want to show you things! You always used to be the one to show me things, and now I want to show you things. We need it. We need to share things. When did we stop sharing things? When did we stop caring about what's happening inside each other's head? When did we stop watching for each other's reactions?'

'We don't need to go outside to do that.'

'Oh, come on, Alex! The world is a different place at midnight. There's a power to it.'

'It's impossible! What about the kids?'

'Wake them up! We'll take 'em with us.'

'What's the matter with you? Amy's got school in the morning.'

'They'll both learn more this way. Life doesn't have to be lived by timetable!'

'For Christ's sake. I'm going to bed.'

He left Maggie pleading to an empty room and went upstairs. Moments later he heard the front door click shut. He looked out of the window and saw her get into the car, accompanied by a sleepy but happy-looking Dot.

Maggie parked the car and a brilliant new moon lit her path through the woods, Dot snuffling at the damp, leaf-moulded way ahead. She had a list of plants and herbs to gather from the hedgerows at the perimeter of the woods, but first she wanted to collect something more mercurial: a sense of the trees at night, a sense of dark places.

The new moon glimpsed through the trees was white, virginal, maiden. Her crescent was turned upwards, like a pair of horns; her light traced delicate patterns, moist on the leaves of the trees, running between shadows. The wood was a world of silver and black, a newly minted world. The cool of night fanned Maggie's face. Her skin was silver, the dog was silver, the east-facing boughs of the trees were illuminated, all half-plated with bright silver, all generating a soft lustre. Maggie went deeper into the woods.

There was no sound. The earth swallowed their footfalls, even Dot trotted on in an envelope of shining silence. The absence of sound conferred visual intensity; trees stood in ranks making outlandish gestures, like spectators arrayed along the path; huge fungi festooned along fallen trunks were pumped full of intoxicant night air; bracken heads coiled like snakes. The night was spinning something of itself on an unseen wheel, something fine, elusive. Maggie stopped and listened. Dot stopped.

There was a presence in the woods.

It was like a low breathing, of trees exhaling. Far off, a dog-fox barked, three times. Dot's hackles rose, and Maggie felt her own flesh ripple, the hair stir on her neck. It was like a signal, and her body was answering. A call, indicating they were in the presence of something magnificent, something holy, something terrifying.

Maggie realised she'd been holding her breath. Her throat was constricted. She released a sigh, hardly daring to disturb the stillness. The trees rustled in answer; they encroached, embracing her, and the rustle of leaves on the uppermost branches was like the swirl of a cape as the breathing came closer. Dot lay down on her belly and put her head between her legs. Maggie wanted to do the same: fling herself on the ground and hide her head. The hair on the nape of her neck bristled. Her skin crawled.

But she knew she must stand tall and win the respect of whatever was out there. A voice came into her head.

Just to look at you.

Then a perfume, streaming from the earth. Not just the moist wood smells, the decay of leaf, of fungus and bark, not just that which was always there. Something else. A spice, some bright herb, a mother-earth smell; a signal-scent, property of the presence arrayed in the woods before her, behind her, all about. A hot wave flushed over her, followed by a chill shiver.

Maggie was paralysed. The moonlight in the woods had become a ring of silver fire all around her. A drop of dew – one brilliant, tiny, concentrated sphere of moonlight – dropped from a leaf and splashed her forehead. She was anointed. She tipped back her head and opened her mouth, and a second drop, like a silver coin, was placed on her tongue.

A name came to her, and she knew now in whose presence she stood. It was a name she had come across in the diary. It rippled free from some place deep inside her and presented itself on her tongue.

It was a name which had meant little to her when she'd first stumbled across it, but which now magically described the moment in all its full-ness. To state the name was to state the nature. The tree branches swirling like a dark cape confirmed her presence. The moon's horned coronet. The earth-spiced perfume and the holy ring of silver flame. The anointing, the gift. She had been granted speech.

'Goddess,' she breathed. 'Hecate.'

Alex sat up in bed pretending to read a novel. He was only pretending to himself. It was well after one o'clock and Maggie hadn't returned. He was both annoyed with her behaviour and concerned for her safety. Scrambling from his bed, he tugged back the curtain. Outside, a sickly white moonlight poured down from a cloudless sky. New moon, Maggie had said. He thought the moon had a diseased look.

He pulled on his dressing gown. There was something he wanted to check out while Maggie was gone.

The spare room . . . He was convinced Maggie had been storing something in there, hiding something from him. Perhaps it was the excessive interest she'd shown in wanting to restore the room to some sort of order; or maybe it was the way in which the door had only lately been kept clicked shut that had tipped him off. He'd intended to confront her about it directly. So why hadn't he?

The spare room, being no more than a tiny shoebox shape, was useful only as storage space. It had become a dump for old clothes, worn-out appliances, broken toys, boxes of books and papers – anything they couldn't bear to throw away. He went rummaging, unsure what he was looking for exactly, but certain there was something to be found.

He cleared a lot of old shoes from the foot of the wardrobe to get to a large cardboard box underneath. He had an allergy to the dust he was disturbing. It brought on a sudden perspiration and a fit of sneezing. His temperature shot up, making him angry with the box he was endeavouring to wrestle out of the wardrobe. It was wedged against the wooden uprights, and he tore at it to release it. When he finally ripped open a corner to reveal a length of white, flouncy lace, he realised it was only the container for Maggie's wedding dress. He stuffed the box back in the wardrobe, hurling shoes on top of it.

A kind of madness swept over him as he prowled the room, tossing clothes aside and tearing open sealed boxes of old archaeology journals and papers. Then he noticed the trunk. It was partly concealed by a pile of paperbacks stacked on top of its closed lid. He pawed the books to the floor and rattled the lid. It was locked. The key was normally left in the lock. He thumped the lid angrily.

He went downstairs and came back with a file, easily snapping the lock. The trunk was overspilling with photograph albums and wallets of snapshots. He lifted all of them out before convincing himself they were hiding nothing. He slammed the lid back down on the trunk.

He was restacking the books on the trunk when another idea chased him back to the wardrobe. He lifted out the shoes and felt the weight of the wedding-dress box. He shook it. It rattled. He lifted it and something slid inside. He had to stand the box on end before it would come out of the wardrobe.

The long, white silk and lace dress was folded in half and wrapped in delicate tissue paper. Alex lifted it from the box as if it might disintegrate in his hands. Underneath was what he was looking for.

The diary, plus a collection of other objects. There was the jar of hand-fasting oil – he failed to recognise it as the one from which Maggie had massaged him over a week ago. He took off the top, sniffed it and stood it on the trunk. There were other items: a stone pestle and mortar; a wooden-handled knife; a brass incense pot; a wooden stick stripped of its bark; an enamel pot; a bottle of olive oil; a collection of coloured candles (some partially burned); an eyedropper; needles and cloth; and assorted candle holders.

'What the hell . . .'

In addition to all of this, and laid out in neat, alphabetical order, were dozens of clear plastic sachets containing various herbs, all neatly labelled. There were also a number of miniature ceramic pots, which inspection revealed to contain scented oils.

Alex sighed. He picked up the knife and the stripped branch of wood. Then a tiny hand tapped him on the shoulder.

Alex leapt backwards in terror, scattering books and the jar of hand-fasting oil from the trunk. It tumbled to the floor, spilling its contents on the carpet. Amy stood in her pyjamas biting her thumb.

'How long have you been standing there?' Alex had to put a hand on his drumming heart.

'I was having a bad dream,' said Amy. She looked about to cry.

He sighed again, but this time with relief. He held out his arms to her. 'Were you, my darling? Come here, let me cuddle you. Is that better? Shall I carry you back to your bed? Here we go. Or do you want to come to our bed?'

'Your bed.'

'Anything you want, my darling. Anything you want.'

Alex carried Amy back to his room and tucked her into bed. He stroked her hair and promised to return to her in a few minutes. Then he went back to the spare room, replacing everything as he'd found it. He located the jar he'd knocked to the floor and cleaned up the mess. He even tried to disguise the accident by refilling the jar with some of the olive oil. The box was restored to the foot of the wardrobe and layered over with shoes. He switched off the light, returned to his own room and climbed into bed beside Amy.

Maggie arrived half an hour later, by which time Amy was asleep. Alex also pretended to be asleep. She slipped into bed beside him, and he felt a wave of cold pass from her. A draught of woods and earth smells came from her hair.

18

The Maggie dig turned up a third knife identical to the first two, and another half tin plate. Alex was having to keep an eye on both archaeological efforts simultaneously. He didn't entirely trust his mainly volunteer crew to do a decent job. He needed to be in both places at once. He was afraid they might miss some vital but unspectacular piece of scientific information in their eagerness to turn up museum-quality artefacts.

'Just slow down, for God's sake!' he was always telling them. 'It's the fine details that count.' He'd started bawling people out, and never heard himself until it was too late.

When the third dagger and the second half-plate appeared, he marshalled the crew into working around the objects with a fine brush until he – and only he – could lift them out. The half-plate was a perfect match to the first, cleanly sliced down the middle. It was found at a distance of eighteen inches from its other half. The first two daggers had been set at approximately two feet apart; the third was two feet from the second dagger and four feet from the first.

Alex marked the points of each find and connected the markers with a line of tape. It produced an isosceles triangle, its equal sides each inter-secting the position in which the half-plates had been found. Alex instructed the three student volunteers he'd assigned to the job to dig round the apex of the triangle.

'WHAT'S THAT?' he screamed at one of the students, a youth with his hair tied back in a pony tail.

'This?' said the student, holding up a delicate trowel.

'Yes! That, that, that stone-breaking implement! What is it?'

The boy looked at the object in his hand as if someone else had put it there. At length he said, 'It's a trowel.'

'This is not a fucking quarry! This is surgery! Use SOMETHING ELSE!'

Alex stormed back to his main dig, leaving the students to exchange looks.

In the playroom Maggie was prising up wooden tiles. Every evening Amy took a great delight in checking on the worsening stain under the rug and reporting back that it was taking on the semblance of a face more and more with each passing day. Maggie made a great show of scoffing at the idea to Amy, but admitted to herself that it was indeed easy to recognise a face in the pattern of the staining.

She'd moved the rug aside herself from time to time and saw what was unmistakably a pair of eyes (though rather far apart), a nose (though set at something of an angle) and a mouth turned back in an expression of sadness and suffering.

Alex had already established that there was no damp rising through the floor. There was nothing spilled or running between the tiles. Now Maggie had decided to leave the stained area untiled. Beneath the tiles was the bare concrete which Alex had put down over the original cellar floor. She simply laid the rug across the exposed concrete and tossed the stained tiles in the bin.

While his mother was upstairs discarding the tiles, Sam charged around the playroom brandishing his plastic sword. He hacked and slashed at an opposing army, single-handedly putting them to flight, ran his sword through a few small enemies and stabbed a bean bag for good measure. Then he slumped on the bean bag, recovering his breath while deciding what to do next.

Something moist struck him sharply on his cheek.

Something had spat at him.

He heard a hiss. He stood up from the bean bag and turned unsteadily. Slap. It struck him again, stinging and wet on the cheek. It burned like a slap to the face.

He knew where it was coming from. He turned to face the potted geranium.

Inside the plant was a living, full-sized face. An old woman's face. Sam recognised her. She leered at him, and grinned, blinking her eyes.

Her face was made of leaves, her skin green, wrinkled and veined like the leaves of the geranium, her teeth yellow.

It was the old woman who had stolen his doll. Who had beckoned him along the catwalk at the Gilded Arcade. She hissed at him. She produced hands out of the branches of the plant, brown hands with cracked yellow fingernails. She hissed again and opened her mouth. Her long black venomous tongue unfolded from between her cracked lips, a foot long, like a snake, inching towards him.

Sam's screams brought Maggie running down the cellar steps. She found Sam stamping his feet, screaming in an hysterical high-pitched wail, sucking in air in huge gulps between screams, his eyes streaming. He was hacking violently at a plant on a low table with his plastic sword. Maggie scooped him up in her arms but he did not stop screaming or swinging his plastic sword.

'What is it, Sam?'

He only shrieked more hysterically.

Maggie carried him out of the playroom and up the stairs. The leaves and broken branches of the geranium lay in an untidy scattering at the foot of the low table.

19

'Never put a geranium where there's a child.' This was Old Liz's advice.

Maggie had changed her mind about not visiting her again. It bothered her that there was simply no one to whom she could turn for support; at least no one who could remotely understand what she had to say, let alone help her to say it. Alex wouldn't begin to listen. Ash at the shop was sympathetic, but somehow always on guard. However senile or even lunatic the old woman had originally appeared, Maggie decided she was the nearest to a kindred spirit available.

If there was a conclusion to be drawn from that, Maggie had steered away from it and had returned to Old Liz's house to recount the episode with Sam and the plant. Ash had told her Liz had a liking for sherry, so Maggie had brought her a bottle. The old woman had accepted the bottle without a word, setting it down and withdrawing from her pantry a bottle of homemade elderberry wine. 'As for geraniums, no child will thrive with one. I know that. And you should know that.'

'Why should I know that?'

Liz took a sip of blueblood elderberry wine. 'Why, she says?' tapping her stick on the rug. 'Why? Because you're a one as knows, or says you are.'

'I've never said anything!' Maggie protested.

Liz grinned and made the same slow gesture she'd made on Maggie's first visit, hugging herself like some deeply repressed thing. 'But,' she said, dropping the pose, 'I see you're opening. Like a flower.'

Liz pulled such faces when she spoke that Maggie wanted to laugh. 'Is that what you see?'

Liz became serious again. 'A one's got to be open to the world if a one's goin' to find her way. That's why you've got a money box. Open to the world.' Maggie smiled. She hadn't heard it called a money box since she was a girl. Liz uncrooked a finger and jabbed it at her, backwards and forwards. 'Stick it in, stick it in, stick it in. That's all those fellas can do. Stick it in. Good for nowt else. That's why they don't know anything. They can't.'

'Don't you get men who . . .' Maggie picked up Liz's circumspect language. 'Who are ones. Can't men be ones?'

'Oh, you do get 'em. Oh you do. You do.' The old woman leaned forward. 'Some.'

'Is Ash one?'

'Pssshhttt!!!' Liz waved her stick. 'What you want to talk another for? Eh? You don't talk another! Eh?' She seemed quite angry.

The rebuke made Maggie feel like a little girl. She couldn't understand why Liz tolerated her when her presence so easily inflamed her. And then her acid manner would dissolve instantly, with equal unpredictability. She began to suspect the old woman might be teasing, playing with her.

'I'm sorry—'

'Do you like it? I said do you like it?'

Maggie realised she was referring to the elderberry wine. 'It's lovely. Do you make it every year?'

'Take one o' them bottles for that husband o' yorn.'

'That's very . . .' Maggie tailed off. She'd suddenly spotted a way in. 'Would you show me how to make it as good as this?'

'How much will you give me?' Liz said, quick as a flash.

'Whatever you want.'

Liz rocked with laughter. She pulled a grubby handkerchief from her sleeve to wipe the tears from her eyes. 'There's a good 'un! That's a good 'un, ain't it?' She laughed again, a high laugh. 'That's what Ash says.' She recovered. 'I might show you. I might. There's a lot to know about the owd gal.'

Old girl. That was a term Bella used for elder in the diary. Maggie took the diary from her handbag and tried to show it to Liz, but the old woman seemed to grow annoyed. She waved it away. 'Books! You don't want books! Books'll do you no good at all, and no one any good. Them as write 'em is the worst, and them as read 'em; there's no good in any of 'em. Books!'

It seemed important to put up some kind of argument. 'There must be *some* good books! What about the Bible?'

'Bible? Eh? That only gives the worst ones an excuse to argue. Did it mean this, did it mean the other? No. We don't want these books.'

Maggie slipped the diary back inside her handbag. 'When do you pick the elder? For the wine, I mean.'

'Owd gal, well now . . .'

The old woman was a fund of both lore and practical information regarding the virtues and vices of the magnificent elder. Not only concerning the making of wine, but also of jam, and a lot more besides. It was a plant, she observed more than once, 'as runs both ways'. Maggie took this to mean it could have both beneficial and malign properties, something Liz had also said of the geranium. She wouldn't have elder wood in her house, and said a child's cradle should never be made of elder. Maggie wondered if Mothercare knew about these things. The leaves kept flies away from a house, Liz maintained, and were useful for toothache and depression. Pinned on a stable door it would stop any horse from being hag-ridden, and before Maggie could ask about that, Liz told her an elder cure for warts and a conciliatory rhyme used by woodcutters:

> *Owd gal give me some o' thy wood*
> *And I'll give thee some o' mine*
> *When I grow into a tree.*

Maggie's head was spinning with information when the old woman surprised her by suggesting they go out and pick some from the hedgerows.

'Can you get about on your stick?'

Liz chuckled and pulled herself to her feet. 'We'll see. Pull that door to behind. Let's look to the owd gal. Come on, what're you waiting for?'

Alex was fast losing patience with the volunteers at the dig. He claimed they were drifting from the precise spot where he'd instructed them to work. If he didn't supervise them on the original dig they disturbed and confused his sophisticated system of depth markings; if he didn't oversee them on the Maggie dig they started hacking at the earth like navvies.

'You do understand plain English?' he'd shouted.

'Yes,' said the boy with the pony tail, 'I've got an A level in the subject.'

Alex glowered. He could see the other students turn away to hide their smirks. He was livid, clenching his fists at his sides until his knuckles turned white. Someone came up behind him and said he was wanted on the telephone.

'What?'

'Said it was urgent.' The man from the ticket office pointed across the site. 'You'll have to take it in my pay box.'

Alex had to walk fifty yards to the ticket office. He snatched up the phone. It was their childminder.

When they returned from the field, Maggie looked at the clock and let out a groan. 'Oh no! I'm going to be late for Amy and Sam!' She laid her bag of elderberries on the table. 'I'm going to have to fly!'

'Eh? But you've only just got here!' Liz protested. 'What's the use o' coming if you're going to go before you've arrived?'

'Can't be helped!' Maggie swept out of the door.

'Bugger off then,' the old woman shouted.

She went to the gate and watched Maggie scurry down the cinder path, climb into her car and speed away. 'Aye,' she said to herself. 'You might or you might not do.'

When Maggie arrived home, Alex and the children were at the kitchen table, eating sandwiches.

'Sorry,' said Maggie. Alex remained tight-lipped. She brushed Amy's hair from her eyes. 'You all right?' she said. Amy nodded, holding a crescent of a sandwich to her mouth. Sam, too, was all right. Everyone was all right. Except Alex.

Maggie put a hand on his shoulder. 'Alex, it's just that I met this wonderful old lady and she wanted me to go for a walk with her . . . I know I've let you down again.'

Alex spoke so calmly, and in such measured sentences, it was obvious he was boiling inside. 'I was summoned today, *summoned*, from my place of work, by no other than my son's childminder. I had to leave off the responsible task of supervising several incompetent and insolent layabouts, risking the project and thus my professional reputation, in order to mollify the said angry childminder . . .'

'Alex . . .'

He held a finger in the air. '. . . in order to carry out one of the few simple tasks allotted to my wife in any working day. In the general ratio of distribution of tasks and workload in a relationship between two people, I must declare – no, protest – that this is a *tad* unfair.'

'Alex, I'm sorry. Look. I brought you a peace offering.' Maggie handed him the bottle of elderberry wine.

Alex looked at the bottle, stood up and took it outside. There was the sound of it smashing in the yard. Alex disappeared past the kitchen window, looking intent on a visit to the Merry Fiddler. Maggie held her head in her hands.

'Daddy's angry,' said Amy.

Sam smiled, because he thought it was all a kind of game.

20

Alex called his team together the following morning. He wanted to give them a pep talk. The dig was working out badly, discipline was awry and morale was plummeting. He felt responsible.

His normal style of managing a dig was through the device of what he called 'pretend panics'. If he felt things slipping, he would gather everyone together, tell them there was a threat of bogus authorities closing the dig, call for greater commitment to prove everyone else wrong, and then hand round the cigarettes. It usually did the trick.

But this was different. He felt depressed about the work, and about his relationship with his team. To the volunteer diggers and students alike he seemed as approachable as a pit of snakes. He got wind of the fact that they referred to him, in whispers, as Vlad the Impaler. He decided to do something he'd never done with subordinates before. He decided to take them into his confidence and be open and honest with them.

The team stood around in a loose half-circle at the site of the dig looking bored and barely awake, waiting for him to say his piece and get it over with.

'Let's sit down a minute, shall we?' said Alex. He squatted on his haunches. They exchanged a few looks before following his example.

'I wanted to have a few words with you before we started work today. Things haven't been going well and I wanted to make an apology to you all.' Faces that had been looking away suddenly looked at him. They'd been expecting a collective bollocking, an exhortation to work harder and laugh less often. 'That's right, an apology. I've been behaving like an arsehole lately and I haven't been the help to you I should've been. At first I blamed them upstairs, because of some of the pressures on this dig to succeed. But that was only because I wasn't honest

111

enough to admit to myself that I've got problems at home, and that's why I've been taking it out on you. So I apologise and it won't happen again, OK?'

A few people looked nervously at each other. Mostly they stared at the ground.

Alex smiled. 'Just to show I mean it, I'm buying the beers at lunchtime for anyone who'll join me and Vlad the Impaler at the pub. That's all. Let's get on with it. Anyone want a ciggie before we start?'

Well, it worked, up to a point. The team rolled up their sleeves and went to work in a relaxed sort of way. One or two students came up to him with suggestions. Richard, the boy with the pony tail working on the Maggie dig, suggested they strike back from the marked triangle of daggers instead of away from the apex. Alex approved and offered advice.

He was good to his word and bought everyone foaming beers at the Malt Shovel. He laughed along with his crew in all the right places, and spread a bit of gossip about some of the local museum staff. By pretending to be relaxed, he could almost become relaxed. He enjoyed it; he was sitting next to a very pretty student called Tania, and the beer was going down well. When everyone started to shuffle and look at their watches, he extended the lunch break by calling in another round.

'Crush the leaf and the berry together. Then make an oil out o' that. Seven days.'

'How much?'

'Much as you like.'

'And the dwale?'

'Four or five berries crushed up, fresh, on the day.'

She'd brought Sam with her to see Liz. The boy crawled on the floor as Maggie's questioning took on a new note of seriousness. There was an urgency in her voice discomforting to Old Liz. Maggie was impatient. She wanted it all too quickly.

Maggie had all the information she needed from the diary, but what disturbed her, and why she sought some kind of sanction from Liz, was the ambivalence of the reports. Accounts of wonders were scrambled with dire warnings. *Abuse Hecate and she will imperil your soul.*

Maggie had hoped for approval, encouragement, advice from Old Liz. She wasn't getting it. Liz answered her questions directly, but with a pursed mouth and a firm neutrality which did nothing to ameliorate Maggie's fears. She stuck to the bare facts, the cold ingredients. She steered away from all discussion of effect, and refused to be drawn into talking about the diary's promise of revelations and terrors in equal measure. This was a speculation in which Maggie was on her own, with only the diarist's obscure accounts to excite her hopes and inflame her fears.

But it raise me up. Oh the wonder! And to have all questions answered. It raise me up and it break my heart. How terrible her wrath! Sleep, coma and death walk behind. Now there are toad-stools in the woods, but A. cautioned me against, for they en-feeble the will for flying whereas I need all strength. I stuck to A.'s direction and stayed within her compass and I have A. to thank for saving me from ruin and demons. We must help one another, and I see a good side to her. I have A. to thank for the banishments, and here they are.

The diary contained an exact formula for the flying ointment, the proportions of deadly nightshade described as dwale, the wolfsbane, cinquefoil and soot, mixed in a carefully described oil base. Hogsfat was mentioned. There were precise specifications of when to collect the herbs. Finally there was a string of words and phrases described as 'banishments'.

Beneath all of this was written: *Never abuse her. Never never never.*

A light passed from Liz's eyes. They reset like hard, black beads, fixed on the younger woman. Maggie felt probed. If ever she'd been under-estimating Old Liz, it stopped there.

'I see as you's set on it, girl.'

There was a moment of heavy silence. Maggie picked up where she'd left off. 'So, the wolfsbane as you've said. What's this about hogsfat?'

'That's just for keeping warm, that's all that is.' Liz suddenly stiff-ened and looked over at Sam. 'Here! Call 'im out o' there! That's no place for little boys!'

Lifting her stick she jabbed it in Sam's direction. He'd managed to crawl over to the curtain closing off Liz's pantry. He was on his hands and knees, with his head behind the curtain when Maggie lifted him out by his belt. Liz darted a hand down the side of her chair and pulled a humbug out of a grubby paper bag.

'Here,' she said to him, 'bit o' suck.' Sam trotted over to her to collect the sweet, but Liz grabbed his outstretched hand. She put her face close to his. 'Keep your nose out o' them lady's petticoats. You hear me? No place for a little boy to be lookin'. Them's lady's petticoats. You hear me?' She let him go. Sam was terrified. He retreated to the safety of his mother's side.

'Well, you shouldn't go nosing in other people's things,' Maggie said.

'Rooting, he was. Does a little boy good to be frit anyhow, and it'll keep him down when he's older. Wouldn't hurt you to be frit, either.'

'What do you mean?'

'I've looked at you, girl. You want it too quick. You wants it all now. Well, you can't have it now. Now, I've thought maybe I'll give you a bit of this and that. We all need a little sister. There's not many more years left in me, I know that. And maybe I shoulda done more in this, but it's the little sister as comes to you, that's the way it was with me, that's the way it is. And I need a little sister to give this and that before I moves on. But I look at you, girl, and, well, I just don't know.

'No, I just don't know.' Liz shook her head. 'You've got summat settled on your shoulder. And I wants to say, here! Knock it off! But it won't be knocked off easily. It's of your own making, and it might suck you dry afore you're through with it. So maybe you are the little sister, come as you 'ave to me, but I don't know.'

Maggie was unable to answer any of this. Instead she offered Liz a determined look. 'So this hogsfat, it's not necessary?'

Liz shook her head again, perhaps in exasperation. 'You wants something as'll keep you warm if you're in your birthday suit.'

'But what if you're indoors?'

'How you going to fly if you're indoors?' Liz chuckled. 'How you going to do that?'

'But you don't really fly,' said Maggie. 'Not really. I know that much.'

'Psssshhhhttt!!' said Liz.

Despite a late start, the afternoon went well. Nothing new was unearthed but the mood of the dig had lightened. Alex was much happier now he was able to share a joke or two with his team. He winked at Tania, and he made free with the smokes.

'Watch out for your fingers. Have a bowl of water to wash your hands clean. When you fly you get a tingling in your fingers, and they go into the mouth, and then you're in a mess. You take care and have that water by you.'

'I'll remember,' said Maggie.

'Rub it all over.'

'Sky clad.'

'Psshhtt! I never calls it that. Daft talk. Rub it all over.' Liz made a massaging motion at her temples and on her throat and wrists. 'Here. And in the money box.'

'How much time?'

'Oh. You want a full night.'

'As much as that?'

'And a day to get over it. Oh yes.'

'Oh,' said Maggie. That was the kind of time she didn't have.

21

Find it! Find it! She had to find it!

She went back to the wedding-dress box and broke two fingernails trying to heave it clear of the bottom of the wardrobe. It wouldn't come free. She grabbed at the old shoes littering the foot of the wardrobe and flung them angrily across her shoulder. Crack! They hit the far wall.

She stopped to take a breath, sucking at a broken fingernail. Then she reached inside the wardrobe and tore frantically at the cardboard until the lid ripped in half. She stripped out the soft tissue lining paper, flinging it aside before dragging out the wedding dress. She balled the dress and hurled it across the room, where it landed, draped like a weeping bride across the closed trunk. Then she tore the rest of the empty cardboard box to shreds.

She waited for a moment, listening, breathing heavily.

Scrambling across to the trunk, she flung open the lid, scattering books, toys and the dress before proceeding to empty it of its contents. Files, photographs and documents were scooped onto the floor.

Maggie wanted to cry with frustration, but she was in too much of a rage for tears. And she couldn't find the diary.

She thumped heavily down the stairs and marched into the lounge. 'What the hell have you done with it?'

Amy looked up. Sam looked up. Even Dot, sprawled before the fire, looked up. Alex, to whom Maggie's fury was addressed, did not look up. He didn't even let his newspaper dip.

'I said what have you done with it?'

'Done with what?'

Maggie lashed the newspaper out of his hands. 'You know perfectly well what I'm talking about. I want to know where you've put it!'

Alex had actually been waiting for Maggie to make the discovery. It had only been a matter of time. He'd gone into the spare room, removed the box from the bottom of the wardrobe and emptied its contents. He'd replaced only the wedding dress, so that a cursory glance might not betray the deed.

He reassembled his newspaper, smoothing out the creases before answering. 'I don't want it in the house.'

'I don't care what you want or don't want, I asked you what you'd done with it.' Maggie stood over him. The children watched.

'And I've told you I don't want it in the house. It's not healthy for the kids. I've destroyed it. Don't bring anything else into the house, or I'll destroy that too.

'The diary? What about my diary?'

'I've told you. I burned the whole bloody lot. That's an end to the matter. Now stop shouting and give us all a break.'

'Give you a break? After what you've done I wouldn't piss on you if you were on fire!'

Maggie stormed upstairs. Moments later she clattered down the stairs and went out. Alex heard the car drive off. He saw his children staring at him, and he hid his burning cheeks behind his newspaper.

Maggie drove blindly. It was a misty night, and she drove with her lights full up, ignoring the flashing headlamps of oncoming traffic. What was this compulsion? Her own rage at finding the diary removed had taken her by surprise. She'd panicked, actually panicked on discovering it had gone; then she'd lost control of herself when Alex said he'd destroyed it.

At times she'd thought her compulsion was motivated by a rebellion against Alex's heavy-handed control. But now she knew it was much more than that. She'd felt invaded, violated by the idea of Alex laying his hands on her secret store. The diary was hers, and hers alone. She wanted it back, wanted to feel its leather covers in her hand.

She drove with a growing sense of direction. And as she drove, she had to face something about herself for the very first time. This business with the diary. These experiments. Up until that moment she'd considered the enterprise to be a kind of flirtatiousness. Something to be dropped whenever a more interesting attraction came along.

She'd been fooling herself, she now appreciated, for some time. It was real. It was serious.

She didn't want to take her rage to the woods. It would pollute the place, she felt; it would rob it of its hitherto good associations. Instead she drove north, twenty-five miles, to Wigstone Heath where she'd walked with Ash and the children.

The fire in her head was still raging when she parked the car and got out. The moon was pale, obscured by fine mist hanging before her like delicate webbing. There was barely enough light to make out the path in front of her, but she had to walk. She passed the dark, hunched shapes of stunted bushes and the smooth-shouldered outcrops of rock, threading a route towards the Dancing Ladies.

She wandered from the path, then found it again. Her feet became sodden with the moisture from the grass, and as she put distance between herself and the car, so her anger began to blend with remorse. What Alex had done was unforgivable; but her words to him, for their children to hear, were possibly even worse. She could imagine Sam repeating them to De Sang, or Amy using them at school. Words like sharp knives, given to small children to play with unsupervised. The words whispered back at her, razors inside her head, and what hurt her even more deeply was that at the moment she'd said it to Alex, she'd meant every syllable.

She reached the Ladies, the dark stones leaning at angles, cold, damp, impassive as gravestones. Maggie leaned her back against one of the stones and wept.

Alex, tight-lipped, a choking stone in his throat, put the children to bed. They knew that this evening was not a night to argue. They undressed and got into bed without fuss.

'Can we have a story?' Amy asked, so diffidently and so tentatively that Alex thought his heart would break. He read them a tale from an anthology of fairy stories, but mechanically, and without his usual fun and playfulness with the characters' voices. It was unsatisfactory, but he completed the story. He closed the book and looked at his two children. Far from being asleep, they were staring at him wide-eyed.

They looked somehow distant from him, like someone else's children, or, worse, like offspring of another species, a life form very similar to humans but not the same. Alex suddenly felt a terror for them and for the long lives stretching before them. 'Go to sleep now,' he said, switching off the light.

'Can we have the light on?' said Amy.

Alex conceded, switched the light back on and closed the bedroom door behind him. He went downstairs and poured himself a large whisky. All he wanted was to protect his family. He worked hard for them; he wanted to love his wife and children and to be loved by them in turn. This was hardly, he was certain, a complicated set of aims.

He knew he'd provoked Maggie beyond measure, but he'd been astonished by her vehemence. She'd been angry with him before, sure enough, but Maggie's recent behaviour had been surprising in many ways. He wondered who exactly had been teaching her these new tricks.

Tricks like choice phrases. Like a taste for midnight strolls from which she returned with clothes dishevelled and grass in her hair. Like afternoons spent in mysterious places which made her forget her responsibilities towards her children. And suddenly discovered passion and tricks in bed. Most of all the tricks in bed.

Alex poured himself another hefty Scotch, and stared into the fire.

Maggie sat at the foot of one of the standing stones. Her head felt clearer. Sometimes weeping worked like a release of sexual tension, giving vent to energies which might otherwise go spiralling destructively inside. Or sex, looked at in a certain way, could seem like crying. And it seemed to her that the stones had wept in sympathy – not with tears, of course, but with the formations of moisture deposited on them by the mist. The clouds had parted slightly to give the moon a keener light, sparkling on the droplets collected on the stones. Nine ladies weeping.

A preternatural circle. Stones hominoid in shape. Certainly feminine. Dancing ladies. What were the names of the nine muses? She knew she could hang her unhappiness on them, or any other feeling for which she needed to find resolution. They would take it, dance with it, convert it, give it back. Was that their true purpose? To make a pool? A well you added to, or took something from?

But this feeling! Moonbathing, that's what she was doing. She wanted to be moonburned as she stalked round the circle. The moonbright droplets glittered on the east-facing shoulders of the stones.

Maggie retraced her steps to the car and returned with a plastic film

120

canister she'd found in the glove compartment. She went from stone to stone, collecting tiny droplets of moisture from each one in the plastic container. The act was entirely whimsical, inspired by the moment. It did no more than cover the bottom of the canister, but it was nonetheless precious. Moon-blessed. Holy water.

She left the circle and paced out the distance to the solitary standing stone. Already she'd resolved to replace the collection of herbs and plants and oils destroyed by Alex. Everything could be restored. The diary was a great loss; that much was irreplaceable. But now she had Liz to help her, to see her through.

Everything was going to be all right, Maggie decided, as she approached the solitary standing stone, the eponymous Wigstone. Ash had explained to her the origin of the name. 'Wikke' was the Anglo-Saxon word for the craft of the wise: witchcraft. It derived from the word for the willow tree, wikker, still in use to describe basket and other woodcraft. The subtlety and pliability of the wicker branch paralleled the mental prowess and agility of the true witch: the ability to manipulate not by strength but by the subtle stroking and weaving of existing force. And here was the stone, the Witch's Stone.

It was almost twice the height of the nine Ladies, mysteriously connected, but distant, withdrawn and watchful. Maggie collected moisture from the rough-hewn block, squeezing the beads of water into her canister. She was intimidated by a sense in which she was intruding, pillaging; but somehow felt it was all sanctioned. As if this theft was permitted.

Sanctioned? Permitted? By whom?

No sooner was the question considered than she began to feel the presence. *The presence.* It was unmistakable, a richness of moment, exactly like the time in Osier's Wood.

But stronger.

The voice inside the silence. The slender, teasing fingernail extending out of the darkness to touch her spine below her neck. The prickling of the skin which was her due. Maggie gasped in awe. She slipped and reached to steady herself on the stone, accidentally scything her finger on a sharp flake of granite. The blood trickled into her canister.

There was a new stirring.

No accident.

Once again, words. Where did they come from? Was it her heart speaking?

As she turned away from the stone, the mist on the ground flapped like the hem of a long skirt, then settled again. It formed in a circle round the Dancing Ladies. It rolled, slowly, like a living thing. A breeze picked up and brought in a smell of spice, of incense.

Yes, stronger than the encounter in the woods. Maggie knew she had raised it with her rage, with her tears, and finally with her resolution. It was terrifying to be able so to do. It was chilling. It was momentous.

'You are everywhere,' said Maggie.

Again words came back. *Just to look at you.*

Words. Speaking to her in the back of her brain. Words soft and indistinct like the mist, but nonetheless present, and insinuating. Maggie froze. Her flesh crawled. It was stronger than ever and she wasn't ready. Something was going to happen, and it was too soon. She was unprepared for this. Not ready, she thought. I'm not ready to see your face. Not yet.

The encircling mist wavered. Maggie moved away from the stone and ran across the brooding heath as fast as she could manage. She raced along the unlit path, careering into stunted shrubs, bouncing off boulders along the way. Her hair streamed out behind her. The muscles in her thighs seemed to lock, heavy as tree roots. She struggled to lift her legs. She ran in the direction of her car through the mist, panting with exhaustion and delirium.

She ran in terror, an involuntary strangled murmur emitting from her vocal chords. But through it all was a strange delight. When she reached the car she was almost giggling hysterically, the way a small child might if pursued by an adult in a game.

The living-room light was still on when she got back to the house. She sat in the car for a moment, composing herself.

She let herself in and went through to the lounge. Alex was seated with his back to her. He was gazing into the dying red embers of the fire and nursing a tumbler of whisky. An empty bottle stood on the mantelpiece.

Alex got up slowly, clutching his glass. He turned round and took a step towards her, swaying slightly. He put his head on one side and smiled. 'Been with your lover?'

'Don't be silly, Alex.'

'You look a bit flushed. Whyzat?' His head fell forward.

'Alex, I—'

'You've got a nerve. Accusing me.' He drained his tumbler and let it fall on the floor. It bounced harmlessly on the deep-pile carpet.

'Stupid thing to do.'

'Stupid,' Alex mimicked heavily. A high, mincing voice.

'Alex, I want to tell . . .'

But she wasn't allowed to finish. Alex drew back his fist and his first blow broke Maggie's nose. She reeled back into the wall. Next he crashed his fist into her eye and Maggie saw stars, not like in the cartoons, but white-hot needles of light at the back of her vision. He had to pick her off the floor to strike her a third blow, and by the time he split her lip, her eye had already swollen shut.

Alex left her sprawled on the floor snuffling snot and blood, and went upstairs to bed.

22

'I wish you'd come to me first. If you'd been here the morning after he hit you I'd have had an injunction slapped on him that day, to keep away from both you and the house.'

Alison Montague didn't look like Maggie's idea of a solicitor. She was pretty, under thirty, and she dressed in a suit so sharp you could have sliced your finger on it. She wore power earrings and she worked for Sedge and Sedge. Her room didn't look like Maggie's idea of a solicitor's office either. It had floral curtains and a play area in the corner complete with toys, to amuse clients' children.

'As it is,' Ms Montague arched her eyebrows, 'you walked out on them, and that sets you at a disadvantage.'

'I wasn't thinking about the consequences. I just wanted to get away.'

Maggie's broken nose didn't look too bad, though the bruises round her eyes had changed hue from lavender to a dirty yellow. It was a matter of some relief that her loosened canines hadn't shown any sign of falling out, and the swelling had gone from her lips.

'I understand that. No woman should have to put up with violence. How's this bedsit working out?'

Maggie shrugged. 'It's not the house I want. It's the children.'

'And you say he's asked you to go back?'

'Practically on his knees.'

The morning following the violence, Maggie had slipped out of the house before Alex got up. She'd had no intention of facing him. She knew exactly what she was going to do.

After all, Alex had hit her. Hit her! The man who had never previously so much as raised his fist in anger. It had shocked her to the root.

125

She thought she knew the man she'd been living with for seven years. Where had he suddenly found this depth of violence? It was as if something had possessed him, some demon.

She was not so naive about the world as to be surprised by the notion of marital violence. A kick, a slap and a punch was as common a feature of the average British marriage as the Sunday roast. But not theirs. That wasn't how they lived their lives. But now he'd placed the argument beyond her. When Alex had struck her, he'd punched a hole in the fabric of her idea of who she was in the world.

He'd hit her, but she knew how to punish him. Even if it meant suffering herself. She had to make a stand. Not for her new way of life – that was suddenly all secondary, mere detail at the periphery of the violent event – but for her integrity. For her sense of wholeness.

She would suffer over the children. But, she resolved, Alex wouldn't hit her again.

She had spent the morning in the casualty ward at the hospital, before returning to study postcard adverts in the post office and local newsagents' windows. Alex had indeed broken her nose, but the small fracture on the upper septum didn't require her nose to be reset. In any event, keeping her good looks was the last thing on her mind. She'd looked and felt terrible, shivering and wiping her painful nose with the back of her hand and squinting through a closing eye. But by afternoon she'd found a bedsit in the New Markets area of town, two miles from home. It wasn't particularly cheap, the room smelled damp, and the heating was coin-regulated by a ferociously hungry gas meter. The kitchen and toilet were shared with two other bedsits on the same floor, and the shared bathroom came complete with a toadstool growing in the corner.

But it was better than getting smashed in the face.

After telephoning to check no one was home, Maggie went back to collect a few essential belongings and installed herself in her bedsit. She spent two nights there before calling Alex.

He begged her to come home. She refused. For one thing her face still looked like a halloween pumpkin, and she didn't want the children to see her that way. Of course she could lie, but she had an idea they'd know. It wasn't possible they could have slept through the crashing violence. She also refused to tell him where she was living.

She spent a long time on the phone talking to Amy and Sam, and promised to phone again the following evening.

Alex had woken from one nightmare into another. That morning he didn't open his eyes to some slow realisation of what he'd done; he woke up to an instant consciousness of guilt and self-loathing, and a taste like wet sand in his mouth. He crept downstairs to find Maggie, searching the house in vain.

He desperately wanted to cry, but he couldn't.

The implications of her absence hit him as soon as the children got out of bed. He got Amy ready for school and dropped her off outside the gates. Then he returned to the house with Sam, stupidly hoping Maggie might have appeared. He was already late for work when he decided to take Sam with him. It would be a nuisance, but he could keep Sam close by while supervising the dig.

So he believed. Initially Sam thought it wonderful to be at Daddy's place of work. Alex carried him on his shoulders, and Sam thought this a wonderful game. For five minutes. Then he wanted to get down. Some of the diggers made a fuss of him for a while, incurring Alex's pleasure; then, realising what a brat Sam could be, their interest cooled and they got on with their work. Sam demanded total attention from his father; the more complex and sophisticated Alex's instructions to or discussions with individuals on his team needed to be, the more desperately Sam wanted to disrupt them; the closer the supervision Alex needed to offer, the more Sam screamed to be included.

He yelled. He kicked. He cried. He spat.

After a fraught half-hour, Sam started pulling up carefully laid depth markers, and wailed when they were snatched from his hands. Later, while Alex was showing someone how to shore up a wall, Sam tumbled into a ditch containing a foot of clay-coloured water.

Alex felt his anger swelling, that Maggie could leave him with these problems. Then he remembered what he'd done and he checked himself. Sam, wet and howling, now had to be taken home for a drying out. Tania offered to help, and Alex was pathetically grateful.

On the fourth night Maggie agreed to have dinner with Alex. He wanted to book a table at the Grey Gables but Maggie didn't want sweet wine and cut-glass. She stipulated the Pizza Palace and opted for mineral water.

He was late because his babysitter was late. Maggie had covered her bruises with make-up, to spare his feelings.

'Come back. I'm sorry.'

'No. I'm not ready.'

'Please, Maggie.'

'I said no and I meant it. If you ask me again I'll get up and walk out.'

'But what do you want?'

'I just want to see the children.'

'Who's stopping you? See them any time!'

'I mean without you. When you're not there.'

'Anything. I'll make it easy for you.'

A girl in a baseball cap came to take their order, pencil poised. 'Sharing or separate?'

'Separate,' said Maggie.

Alex muddled through the first few days. He was able to make arrangements here and there. Anita Suzman helped out, and Tania took an afternoon off from the site to look after Sam at home. One session with Sam, however, proved more than enough for most, and Alex had to revise his arrangements with the childminder.

'How long is it going to go on for?' Tania asked him at the site.

'No idea. We're like a weatherhouse couple. She comes to the house in the evening and I have to go out to the pub. She's very civil and all that; but as soon as I get back, she has to leave.'

'Seems like she's having it all her way at the moment.' Alex looked at her. 'Well, she doesn't have to take any responsibility for the kids, but she hasn't lost the emotional contact.'

'I hadn't thought of it like that. Maybe I should start making some conditions.'

'No,' said Tania. 'That'd just be using the children for barter.'

'Hey! Alex!' It was Richard calling him. He'd been working solidly on the Maggie dig. 'Come over here!'

Alex had let it run for a few nights before putting his foot down. He told Maggie that the present arrangement was causing too much distress. He told her the only way he would allow her to see the children was if she'd move back in with them.

Maggie went away furious. She felt tricked. She was supposed to be the one laying down the conditions, not Alex. Now he'd seen how desperately she wanted to be with Sam and Amy, he'd called her bluff.

She wasn't frightened for her children, she knew they were in no danger, Alex's outburst notwithstanding; but the idea of not seeing them drove her to distraction. She found herself running through the events of the past weeks, wondering if she was asking too much, wanting to capitulate, talking herself out of it, then changing her mind over and over again in gymnastic flips.

She cried a lot. She felt she was disintegrating. But she refused to return on Alex's terms, and sought legal advice, looking for custody of the children.

'What I'll aim for,' said Ms Montague, eyes bright and earrings a-dangle, 'and I'm not saying we'll get it automatically, is an injunction to get him out of the house and a residence order so that you have custody of the children.' She had a habit of inclining her head to one side as she spoke.

'It suddenly seems a bit unfair to Alex,' said Maggie.

'Unfair?'

'I mean, I'm the one who started messing him around. I can see how it might have looked to him, me slipping off at night . . . I feel like I'm the one who started the trouble, and he'll end up without the house and without the kids.'

'Sod that! He shouldn't be so ready with his fists!'

Maggie was startled. Ms Montague's earrings were waggling a mite enthusiastically. 'He's never done it before, you know.'

'I'm more concerned he doesn't do it again. If you want me to make an application for custody with a residence order, be ready to go to court some time in the next two weeks. Meanwhile I'll prepare an affidavit as to his behaviour, which you'll have to swear is true.'

'What happens to that?'

'You sign it and I have it filed at court.'

Affidavits. Injunctions. Sworn truths filed at court. It all seemed so ritualistic and incantatory; so grave and so monumental. Maggie nodded agreement.

She walked home from the offices of Sedge and Sedge to her depressing bedsit in New Markets. It was the last day in November, it was cold and damp, and it was already dark at five in the afternoon.

The house she'd found was three storeys high and her room was on the middle floor. Someone kept a motorbike, leaking oil from its crankcase, in the downstairs hallway. Someone else on the ground floor played solid thrash at volume from 2 p.m., presumably when they got out of bed, to 2 a.m., presumably when they went to bed. It was playing when Maggie turned the key to the front door.

In her room she switched on the gas fire and pushed coins into her meter. It was like having a pet, it needed feeding often. Unable to visit Amy and Sam, she faced another empty evening.

Making coffee in the shared kitchen facility was Kate, who occupied the next room. Kate looked like a figure from an Aubrey Beardsley drawing and wore the kind of make-up other people would only use for a pageant. She described herself as 'late gothic' but she was really a friendly, chatty Cleopatra in black denim, and though there were ten years between them, Maggie felt as if Kate was the elder of the two.

'Is he always like this?' asked Maggie, meaning the noise from downstairs.

'Never stops. I'm gonna firebomb his room one of these days.'

'Don't. I'm directly above it.'

'Perhaps I won't. Doing anything this evening?'

'No one to do anything with.' Maggie smiled at her.

'Me neither,' said Kate. 'Fancy going somewhere?'

23

Richard had discovered a fourth dagger at the Maggie dig, ceremonial, bronze, identical to the others but snapped at the hilt. It was rather obvious from its position where a fifth might appear.

'It's not a triangle at all,' said Tania. 'Another dagger over there would make a circle. They've been placed in a ring.'

Alex called in another couple of volunteers. They all worked through their lunch break and within a couple of hours the fifth blade came to light. They marked out the exact location of the blades with wooden stakes.

'Could there be more?' someone asked.

'I doubt it,' said Alex. Everyone stood round the circle, hands on hips, staring down at the wooden stakes.

'Why not?' Tania wanted to know.

Alex rubbed his chin. 'I dunno. I just doubt it.'

'What if,' said Richard, stepping over the stakes and removing the original triangle of white marker tape, 'what if it isn't a circle at all?'

He took a new length of marker tape, wound it round one of the stakes and carried it across the diameter of the circle to a second stake. Thence across the circle again to the stake adjacent to his starting point, making two sides of a larger triangle. Instead of closing the triangle, he crossed the circle again to the fourth point, then to the fifth, and back to his starting point.

He'd marked out a five-pointed star.

It was a good game. 'What if you're both right?' said Alex, taking the tape from Richard's hands. He inserted a short stake between each of the dagger positions before unwinding the tape to complete a circle round the five-pointed star. Now they were all staring down at a classic pentagram.

'I think we'd better keep this quiet for the time being,' said Alex. 'We don't want people to get stupid ideas.'

Everyone nodded sagely. None of them wanted people to get stupid ideas.

But Alex found he had a problem keeping those self-same stupid ideas out of his head. He was thinking about Maggie, and about how she might have known where he should dig. He was still convinced you could pick almost anywhere on this site and unearth something, but the extraordinary nature of the discovery complicated things. He could deny it no longer.

He was trying to relate this discovery to other things about Maggie's recent behaviour. He'd read enough of the diary to form a rough understanding of its contents. He could stop guessing about the other items he'd found alongside the diary, and about the sphere of her new interests. And if she didn't have a lover (and he'd concluded after all that he'd been wrong, and she probably didn't) then what was it she'd been up to at ungodly hours of the night?

For the first time, he felt a nagging fear about the safety of his children. For the first time a question was raised in his mind about the stability of their mother. Because the stupid ideas just wouldn't go away.

Maggie was having a good time. She was having to shout to make herself heard above the band, and was throwing back a dirty concoction of lager and blackcurrant juice, a drink to which Kate had introduced her. It was standing room only at the Seven Stars. Gutbucket blues at maximum decibels and a fug of sweating bodies, writhing cigarette smoke and beery, frothblowing chatter. They were being corralled by two youths in black leather.

'What's he say?' Maggie shouted in Kate's ear.

'He says do we want a drink.'

'I don't know. What do you think?'

Both youths held a pint glass in one hand and a crash helmet in the other. Kate beckoned to one and shouted in his ear. 'Two lager and black, but you won't get a shag out of it.'

Maggie's lager went up her nose. The youth grinned stupidly and went to the bar. Maggie felt some of Kate's carefree youth rubbing off on her. Kate had lent Maggie a leather jacket after telling her she looked too prim for where they were going. She was learning a lot from Kate. Like the fact that if you take the piss out of men they come back for more.

'Thanks. Now get back on your Lambretta,' she said to the youth when he handed her a red lager.

'I ain't gorra Lambretta. I've gorra Norton.'

'That makes all the difference. That makes you a person with a Norton.'

'A Norton?' said Maggie. 'Isn't that a two-stroke?'

''Ere Derek. She thinks a Norton is a two-stroke.'

'This is great, boys. I could talk about motorbikes all night.'

''Ere! Are you trying to take the piss?'

'Get back on your Lambretta.'

Several red lagers later Maggie and Kate were on the back of the two motorbikes speeding through the freezing November night. They were heading towards Wigstone Heath at Maggie's insistence. Maggie was on the pillion of the lead bike. They'd taken a cross-country lane, and she was hugging her motorcyclist out of fear and exhilaration rather than any desire for intimacy.

It was cold on the bike, cold. But wrapped in her borrowed leathers she exulted in it! It was loud, deafening even; she loved the deep, throaty roar of the Norton as it climbed through the gears, and the lash of the wind in her face. Her arms were clenched round the waist of the stranger controlling the machine and her thighs gripped the vibrating saddle. She wanted a bike!

The rider turned his head and shouted, 'Where now?' She heard his muffled words through the crash helmet.

'Keep going! Keep going!'

She turned to see the second bike and caught a wave from Kate. Maggie was aroused even though she knew she was just using these boys for their engines, their machines. She could fold herself across them and they would take her where she wanted to go. The bike hit top gear as they found a flat stretch of road. Maggie sensed a change of gear inside herself as they sped towards Wigstone Heath.

She felt a growing awareness as they approached the heath. There were things in the passing shadows which began to take on a faint luminosity. A boulder. A road sign. A twisted shrub. She was sure she saw a hare crouched in the hedgerow. She looked over her shoulder, and these things seemed to hold the light from the headlamps long after the bikes had passed. She felt strange. There was a growing disquiet as they got nearer to the heath. The initial giddy excitement of the ride was deserting her.

This began to seem less than a good idea. What were they going to do when they got there? It was wrong. She was using the boys, using their engines between her thighs. Playing with them. It was not for her to take them there. It was an abuse of privilege.

It gave her a bad feeling.

But she didn't know how to stop it. The bikes were cruising towards the heath, locked into a kind of trajectory, moving forward in a steady drone. Then at a bend the motorcyclist dropped down through his gears and slowed to take a sharp corner, leaning the bike into the road. Maggie saw a huge black shadow step out of the hedgerow in front of them, and the next thing she knew she was sailing through the air.

Then Kate was picking her out of the hedgerow. 'Maggie! Maggie!'

She was winded and scratched, but she was all right. Dazed, she got to her feet. The injured Norton lay on its side in the hedge, engine still squealing, back wheel spinning. Its rider staggered over to her. His leathers had been sliced open and there was a bloody gash down his arm. His friend Derek silenced the squealing bike.

'There was something in the road! There was something there!'

'I saw it,' said Maggie. But she was more interested in what she had grasped in her clenched fist. It was a branch of belladonna, deadly nightshade, black berries clustered and gleaming with a dull light. She looked up at the stars in the clear, cold sky. They were brilliant. 'It's incredible! Dwale! Deadly nightshade! She's everywhere!'

'What?' said Kate.

'She's amazing!'

'That girl's concussed,' said Derek.

'Don't talk rot,' said Maggie sharply.

He held up two fingers in front of her eyes. ''Ow many fingers do you see?'

'Get away, you stupid sod. I'm as clear as a bell.'

The evening finished there. After that, no one was in the mood for completing the journey. The forks were twisted on the Norton. It was barely roadworthy. They returned at a steadier pace, and the boys said goodnight and dropped them off back at the house.

Music thumped from the ground-floor room. Maggie made coffee and they sat in her room. 'That cut on his arm,' she said fretfully. 'If I had my stuff here I could have helped him. Really I could.'

'What stuff?'

'Oh, herbs and stuff. Never mind. I'll sort it out. It was just a warning, you know. She didn't want me to take those lads up there.'

Kate looked at her strangely, as if she might be concussed after all. 'You know what you are, Maggie? Witchy.'

'Yes,' said Maggie. 'And I'm sick of that fucking music.'

The branch of deadly nightshade was still in her pocket. She took it out and handed the leather jacket back to Kate. Then she found a length of cotton and a pin.

'What are you doing?' said Kate.

'She gave me a warning tonight. I have a feeling, a feeling she might balance it with a gift.'

'What are you on about? Where are you going?'

Maggie didn't answer. Kate followed her downstairs to the door vibrating from the thrash music. Maggie pinned the cotton to the cross-frame over the door so that the branch of deadly nightshade hung at roughly eye level. Then she hammered on the door, and without waiting for an answer, returned upstairs to her own room.

'What are you doing?' hissed Kate.

'I don't know, Kate. Sometimes I just feel *guided*.'

'Guided by what?'

'I don't know. I honestly don't know. Listen.'

They listened. After a few moments the music was silenced.

'It's stopped!' said Kate.

'Exactly.'

24

Morton Briggs, dispensing law for Moore, Bray and Toot, looked exactly like a solicitor ought to look. A tangy, residual nicotine roosted in the weft and warp of his old suit. This initial, benumbed impression was perfectly complemented by a minutely knotted, egg-stained tie. A pair of tortoiseshell spectacles rested halfway along a large, puce-coloured nose. The overall effect was of confidence and complacency imparted in equal measure. Alex felt somewhat reassured.

Briggs' office was lined with books so heavy they were obviously not designed for lifting from the bookcase. The last book on the shelf, *Law Reports 1966–67*, had a cover faded on a diagonal line up to the point where the sun daily reached its finger. The gas fire of the unreconstructed Victorian office generated a warm fug, and so did the bulky presence of Briggs himself.

'No, I think we'll leave that for the time being,' Briggs said, twisting a pencil in his huge pink hands. 'We should save that for later. It might be our trump card.'

'So you don't think she'll win custody at the hearing?' Alex found Briggs' easy confidence infectious.

'Not at the initial hearing, I don't. She left you, don't forget. We'll oppose the injunction on the grounds of the children's interests. The judge will have little option but to preserve the status quo while he asks for reports to be prepared by the Court Welfare Officer. Then the real battle starts.'

The real battle. If Briggs imparted confidence, it didn't make Alex feel any less depressed. He'd been appalled by this latest development. To his utter astonishment, an apologetic stranger in a black raincoat had turned up at his door, and had pushed a summons into his hands.

Alex had never before received a court summons. 'Do I have to accept this?' he'd spluttered, looking at the envelope in his hand as if it was coated with cyanide.

'I'm afraid you already have,' said the process server over his shoulder, the hem of his raincoat flapping as he retreated down the path.

He'd immediately picked up the phone to tell Maggie what he thought of it. He regarded it as an almost irreversible step on a downward spiral. When they could only communicate with each other by employing professionals, they had nothing left.

He'd pleaded with her to no avail, and he went on pleading. He'd apologised for striking her until he was sick of hearing the wheedling sound of his own voice. He'd even heard himself offer, preposterously, to accompany her on midnight walks under a moon of her choice; though he'd qualified his pleading by insisting that she come home, live with them, and behave like what he called a 'proper' mother.

She had adopted a siege mentality, he'd decided, and the only way to deal with her was to starve her out. Starve her, that is, of family affection by proscribing all physical contact with the children. Then the solicitor's letter had landed on the mat, and stakes had been raised in a way he'd neither anticipated nor wanted.

'How long will that take?' Alex asked Briggs dolefully.

'For reports? Three months at least.'

Alex looked at Briggs and Briggs looked back across the top of his spectacles. Then the solicitor laid down his pencil and pushed himself back in his chair an eighth of an inch. Alex realised it was a signal: audience over.

Briggs escorted him to the door. 'I'll be in touch,' he said.

'Hello, stranger!' said Ash, when the bell above his shop doorway tinkled.

Maggie closed the door and as she turned the light fell on her face.

'You look like you've been in a fight!' Ash laughed, seeing her fading bruises. Maggie just stared at him. Ash stopped laughing. 'Oh no. You have been in a fight.'

Maggie sat down while he put the kettle on. She had to wait while he dealt with a brief flurry of custom before she could tell him. Ash took her hand, put it to his mouth and kissed it.

'Bastard.'

'Perhaps I deserved it, Ash.'

'Don't say that. Victim's mentality. All you did was go for a walk.'

'He still thinks I've got a lover.'

'And you still think *he* has.'

'What makes you say that?'

The bell tinkled and another customer came in. It was a young man who wanted to buy a set of Tibetan temple bells. Ash explained that he was a herbalist.

'I get a lot of that,' he said. Maggie was still waiting for an answer. 'Liz. She's a clever old bird.'

'You've been talking to Liz? But I never said anything to Liz about it.'

'That's what I mean by clever. She picks up a lot about what's not said by listening to what is said.'

'And what does she say?'

'She says you've got it.'

'It? You mean the *it* we're not supposed to talk about?'

'That's the one. Tell me about this grotty bedsit you're living in.'

'It's not so bad. I'm enjoying the freedom. I can do what I want for the first time in my life. I can please myself. That reminds me, I have to make a new collection, herbs, plants, oils, everything. From scratch. From the beginning. I've got loads to learn and lots of time. I want you to help me.'

Ash did help her. He went walking with her. They collected what they could from the hedgerows, and he told her what she could expect in the spring. As for the more exotic herbs, he donated a quantity from his own stock and refused to accept payment. Maggie felt she was abusing his good nature, and in the end she forced him to accept a nominal sum.

He also helped her in the selection of her tools and implements. She'd lost everything when Alex had thrown out her equipment along with her herbs, so she needed a new knife, mortar and pestle and other practical equipment. Ash suggested she do things properly. He pointed out that the equipment was represented by the Tarot suits: knife for swords, mortar and pestle for cups, wand for batons and a pentacle drawn on an altar cloth. Why not consecrate the full set at the same time?

Christmas was approaching. The city had been decorated with lights.

A grand tree stood in the marketplace. Ash shut up Omega one afternoon so they could spend a couple of hours together shopping.

The event made her miss her children. Every previous Christmas shopping expedition she'd cursed them for getting under her feet, yet now she wanted them to be with her. But she also liked being with Ash. He was so unlike Alex, this tall man with the ready humour. Christmas shopping had always made Alex irritable and stressed; Ash turned it into a game, always ready with a quiverful of words for the people serving them. They might come across someone griping and complaining in the marketplace press of Christmas shoppers, and he could turn their mood with the right words. Not clever words, not smart words, but just the right words. Stroking words which would dispel provocation and restore perspective.

The approach of Christmas also meant the approach of winter solstice, Ash explained.

'The twenty-first of December. Shortest day. It's the same festival when you think about it. Just older.'

Maggie remembered Alex telling her that religion had its own archaeology, layers of different ages built on the same site.

'That's when we should consecrate all this stuff,' said Alex, meaning the knife, mortar and pestle and other equipment.

'The twenty-first. That's the day of the custody hearing.'

The custody hearing took place in the depressing precincts of the County Court. Maggie was talking to her solicitor when she saw Alex come in with his.

'Is he any good?' said Maggie.

'Bumbling and inefficient,' said Ms Montague, fiddling with an earring, 'but quite nice.'

Alex saw Maggie whispering to a woman in a dark suit in the waiting area. He stopped Briggs as they came through the door.

'Is that her solicitor?'

'Montague? Yes.'

'What's she like?'

'Arrogant and incompetent,' said Briggs, pushing his spectacles back onto the bridge of his nose. 'But otherwise a decent sort.'

Despite this composite of incompetence and inefficiency, the court managed to deal with the issue in under six minutes. The judge would not uphold an injunction over the property but issued a restraining order 'protecting' Maggie from further assault. He ruled for the status quo pending reports to be submitted by the Court Welfare Officer. A date would be fixed for another hearing. Maggie, declining the opportunity to return to the house, was granted access to the children on two days a week.

'What I told you,' said Briggs to Alex, gathering his papers.

'What we expected,' said Montague to Maggie, clipping her briefcase shut.

Leaving Maggie and Alex to wonder why they'd even bothered to go along. Maggie expected Alex to wait behind afterwards. She thought he'd at least want to talk. He didn't.

The six-minute experience tipped Maggie into a deep trough of depression.

Ash did his best to take her mind off it.

'Why the winter solstice?' Maggie asked as they drove. She stared bleakly through the passenger window into the pitch dark outside. Spots of rain dotted the windscreen.

'Because now the days will get lighter. It represents progression towards the light. A good time to consecrate these things.'

'Can't you do it for me?'

'You make your own dedications.'

'Who shall I dedicate them to?'

'Don't ask me things for which you already have the answer.'

It was approaching midnight. They got out of the car and began walking across the shadowy heath. Low cloud obscured the moon. The wind screeched around the stunted bushes and buffeted the rocks. It flapped the hems of their coats.

'It's fucking freezing,' said Maggie, stumbling along the path.

'You chose this place.'

'I suppose I owe her one here. Doesn't your wife mind you running around the heath at this time of night?'

Ash treated the question as rhetorical. They reached the standing stones and it started to rain. Maggie laid out her equipment: altar cloth, knife, mortar and pestle and the hazel wand she had cut and stripped from the hedgerow a few days earlier. Ash stood looking at his watch. He wouldn't let her start until midnight. 'If we're going to do this at all, let's do it properly. I'm just glad there's no one here to see us.'

At midnight Ash lit the paraffin-soaked brand he'd brought with him. It looked dramatic. It sent shadows running for cover behind the standing stones. Spots of rain hissed on the flame.

'What shall I say?' cried Maggie, her wet hair plastered to her head.

'Make it up,' said Ash. 'It really doesn't matter.'

'Have I really got to say it aloud?'

'Oh yes.'

Maggie squatted. She re-ran the events of the day, and for the first time allowed her depressive feelings to roll over and through her, like a storm cloud passing over acres of fertile fields. Tears pricked her eyes, but somewhere in that moment she found words. Words of power. The rain battened on her tears as she offered up each piece of equipment in turn, each to the four points of the compass. She dedicated them and asked that they be imbued with power in return. Ash stood in the circle patiently but self-consciously holding the flaming brand aloft until she'd completed the cycle.

She was drenched. The cold and the rain took hold of her. They penetrated her clothes and eased their way into her. They possessed her bones. It was like being entered by a spirit, but it was elemental cold and rain. She had a momentary sensation of damp heat at her lips, breasts and vagina. She shivered. It was a deep, earth-charged spasm.

'Finished?'

She nodded. Ash put out the flame. Maggie collected up her equipment, wrapping them in the soaked altar cloth, then came over to stand beside Ash.

They stood in the silence, the rain still falling. Then it fell harder, very hard, bouncing high off the stones.

'Well,' said Ash.

'What do we do now?'

'We go home, of course.'

During the drive back, Maggie sat in silence.

'What is it?'

'Oh, I don't know. I'm disappointed,' she said. 'I expected something to happen. To feel something more. To see something. Anything. But she just wasn't there tonight.'

'Oh no, she was there all right.'

'Well, I didn't feel her.'

'No. She takes her gifts very modestly. But she was there all the time. You'll see.'

'How will I see?'

'Oh, I dunno. She'll give you something back in return.'

Two days later, Alex agreed to let her have the children for an extra afternoon. He was taking them to his parents' house in Harrogate, where they would spend Christmas. She wanted to give them their presents before he spirited them away. She took them to a burger bar – which previously she'd always strictly refused to do – and bought them everything they asked for.

The time came for Alex to collect them. He piled the kids in the car and turned to her before leaving, pulling a gift from his coat pocket. Whatever it was, it was beautifully wrapped in expensive red and green paper and trimmed with gold thread and a golden bow. It had a label: To Maggie, love from Alex xxx.

'Can I open it now?' said Maggie. She was battling not to let him see how upset she was about the children.

'I wish you would.'

She tore open the wrapping paper. It was Bella's diary.

'I thought you'd burned it!'

'How could I – me, an archaeologist – burn something like that?'

'Thank you for giving it back to me. Happy Christmas.'

'Happy Christmas, Maggie.'

She cried after he drove away.

25

Christmas Day was bleak. Maggie woke with a hangover and a palate like a carpet soaked in sticky liqueurs. She'd been out with Kate to a pub on Christmas Eve. A drunk with Jesus Christ hair and the smell of vomit in his beard had spent the night trying to kiss her. She'd turned down two offers of bed and one of salvation when the Church Army had arrived with collecting tins just before midnight.

Now all she had was the vengeance of the morning after in her dismal bedsit. Kate had gone home to her parents' house. Even the thrash music (which hadn't started up again since she'd left her calling card) would have been almost welcome. The house was as quiet as a tomb.

She was beginning to wish she'd taken up the offer to spend Christmas Day with Kate's family. She switched on her gas fire and went to wash in the bathroom. The fungus in the corner exuded malintent. When she returned to her room, the gas had died. She emptied her purse onto the table, finding not a single coin for the meter. She flicked on her portable TV set. Every channel seemed to be showing cartoons. She got back into bed.

And there she stayed until midday when there came a hammering on the front door. Maggie got out of bed, tied her dressing gown round her and padded downstairs and along the cold corridor.

'Ash!' He was standing holding a gift-wrapped present. She hugged him, almost bowling him from the step in her enthusiasm. 'Oh Ash!'

'Didn't like to think of you here alone. Thought you might need cheering up.'

She took him inside and made him wait in the kitchen while she dressed.

'Cold in here,' he observed when he was allowed inside.

'This is the worst Christmas Day of my life. You've no idea what it's like to be on your own for Christmas Day.'

Ash looked at her strangely. 'Put your coat on,' he said. 'Time you met the wife.'

'I couldn't intrude, Ash. It's not fair.'

'Do as you're told. You're not staying here all day.'

So she let him bully her into spending Christmas Day at his place. She carried her still-wrapped gift to the car and climbed in beside him. It was a half-hour drive along roads that were almost empty.

Ash lived in a large, slightly gloomy detached house with rampant ivy trailing the facing wall. The lounge had a coal fire burning behind a brass fireguard. Ash moved it aside and she took advantage of the warmth. Maggie looked around her as Ash poured them both a sherry. It was a most conventional room, disappointingly so with its Dralon suite and velvet curtains and its brass ornaments grouped around the fire. She'd expected something more . . . bohemian, more eccentric.

'Cheers,' said Ash, tipping back his sherry.

'Isn't your wife going to join us?'

'The wife. Right. Time for you to meet the wife. Come through to the study.'

Ash pulled her by the wrist and led her down the hall to a room at the rear of the house. He opened the door and propelled her into the room ahead of him. 'Maggie, meet the wife.'

Maggie looked back at him in puzzlement. There was no one. But every eccentric or bohemian detail she'd expected to be exhibited in Ash's house had been crammed into this room. It was a study. There was a green leather-inlay desk the size of a sports field standing against the far wall. A winking word processor suggested he'd spent some of his Christmas morning at work. The walls were covered with large maps studded with pins and coloured ribbon connecting geographical positions. Otherwise framed prints covered all available wall space.

The room was heavy with the pungent smell of incense. And on shelves or on freestanding display tables was an extraordinary collection of figurines, statuary, carvings and fragments of bas-relief. The room was a museum, but with the aura of a shrine.

'They're all . . .'

'That's right,' said Ash. 'The goddess, in all her different incarnations. I collect them. Actually I study them. It's my hobby when I'm not in the shop.'

'And the maps?'

'I'm tracing her movements, across history. See? She started out here, in Africa, and her influence spread to Asia and Europe. Then with the migration of the peoples . . . Only her name gets changed, she doesn't change.'

'It's incredible!' She lifted a figurine from a table.

'That's the Ephesian Artemis. And it's original, in case you were wondering. From somewhere in Asia Minor about 1000 BC. You went straight to it. Clever lady; I'm impressed. Most of the things you see here are reproductions. Some I had specially made.'

Maggie weighed it in her hand. The lifelike representation had a dozen mammary glands. 'It must be worth a fortune!'

'Yep.'

'But why do you . . .'

'Refer to it all as "the wife"? Because it's here. It's a good excuse, if ever I want to get away from someone. And because I spend so much time with her . . . Come on. Let's go back to the other room.'

Maggie carefully replaced the figurine on the table. He closed the door softly on the goddess, and poured another glass of sherry.

'So you're not married after all. You don't have a wife.'

'I did have. She died in a car accident three years ago.' Ash looked into the fire. This was the sadness Maggie had sensed in him from the beginning. 'Actually there's another reason why I call all that "the wife". Janie – my real wife – started all that research. She was writing a book. I'm trying to finish it for her. I don't have her brilliance. It's taking a long time.'

He was trying to make light of it, and he wasn't doing it very well. She could see he'd never let it out to anyone; intuition told her he'd choked it all back. 'Do you know,' he was saying, 'people say time will help you get over it. Well, they're wrong. When you lose someone, the world becomes a changed place. And it's changed for ever.'

She wanted to hold him, but it wasn't possible.

'I'm being morbid!' he said brightly, suddenly.

'No you're not.'

'Yes I am. Drink up! Open your present! There's a turkey cooking. Can you smell it?'

Oh yes. Maggie could smell the bird cooking.

They pulled crackers and wore paper hats and drained two bottles of claret and had a jolly dinner. It was slightly self-conscious jollity, but it was genuine. They were relaxed in each other's company, and they were both desperately relieved not to have to spend the day alone.

After dinner they sat through part of a television church service, before Ash switched it off and put some music on instead.

'Don't you believe in the miracle of the Virgin birth?' Maggie asked, ironic.

'No more than I believe Santa Claus comes down that chimney.'

'You don't like the Christian Church, do you? I could see while you were watching that.'

'No, I don't. I despise it. Don't misunderstand me: Christ was the greatest teacher ever. A healer, in more ways than one. But if he was here today he'd have nothing to do with the Christian Church.'

She'd got him on his subject. 'Take the Virgin Mary,' he continued. 'Our most recent incarnation of the goddess. But what did they do, these old patriarchs? They took her sexuality away. The virgin mother. And that's how they took her *power* away. Who do you think is that second woman you always see standing at the crucifixion?'

'What? You mean Mary Magdalene?'

'That's right. The prostitute, so called. The demoniac cured by Christ. She's the same person, the same Mary. But they split off the two halves of the goddess. The magdalene is the sexy half. The virgin's dark sister if you like.'

Dark sister. The phrase rang bells. 'Why did you say that? *Dark sister*?'

'Isn't that what she is? A shadow, always in the background, but always there. Come to think of it, Jesus was probably married to Mary Magdalene.'

'Where do you get these outrageous notions?'

Ash smiled and nodded towards the study. 'From the wife. But what really makes my blood boil about the Christian Church is the slaughter. All of those women in medieval times, literally millions across Europe, who were tortured and slaughtered and burned. Wise women. Healers. Simple herbalists, some of them, like me. Some of them just lonely old anti-social women. Victims of prejudice and fear. All put to the torch. Actually, they used to hang witches in this country, not burn them. But no one in the Christian Church, even to this day, seems prepared to show the slightest remorse for what they did. And they're still trying to do it! Do you know they had a campaign against my shop, because of some of the books I sell?'

'I'd heard about that, yes.'

Ash waved a hand through the air, as if he wanted to swat a barmy world.

In the evening they played a round of Scrabble and drank more claret and a few glasses of brandy. Then just to prove how committed to Christmas he was, in a deep-down sort of way, Ash produced a packet of dates, and they were in such good spirits they ate them all.

It seemed perfectly natural they should snuggle on the couch to watch a late film on the television.

'Would you like to stay here?' Ash asked her sleepily. She nodded. 'You can have my bed,' he said. 'I'll make a bed up on the couch.'

'That's not necessary. I want you to sleep with me.'

He kissed her lightly, but then looked at her hard. 'I'll stay on the couch.'

'Why?'

Ash vented a deep sigh. 'One of the greatest, most wonderful pleasures for a man in this world is the secret pleasure of an erection. After my wife died, the goddess took that pleasure away from me. I'm waiting for her to give it back.'

Maggie felt an overwhelming surge of love for Ash. Or was it a tide of compassion? Whatever, she felt the need to hold him, to cradle him, to impart love.

'It's all right,' she said. 'I want you to sleep with me anyway. Just to be with you.'

Maggie knew Ash had some crying to do.

26

Boxing Day blues.

Ash left to fulfil a promise to visit his dead wife's parents. He went around midday, and though he suggested Maggie should avail herself of the house, she found herself wandering back to her bedsit. The place was still empty apart from her; then in the afternoon the thrash music started up again from the ground floor.

Maggie telephoned Alex. Alex's mother answered stiffly before putting him on. He was amenable.

'What have they said? Have they taken your side?'

'What do you expect?' said Alex. 'Let's not get into it, eh?'

'Have the kids been behaving?'

'Amy is queening it over everything and they're spoiling her to death; Sam has been a little swine since the moment he got here. He's crying for you all the time and he's smashing anything that's put in front of him. Mum and Dad bought him an indestructible truck and he threw it on the fire.'

'Let me speak to them.'

Maggie asked Amy to share her toys with Sam, and she asked Sam to be a good boy.

'How's your Christmas?' Alex said when he came back on the line.

'Quiet.'

Maggie broke a long pause by asking. 'When are you coming back?'

'Couple more days. Will you be home when we get back?'

'No . . . Maybe. I'm thinking about it.'

'Yes. Think about it.' Alex put the phone down.

Maggie was thinking about it. She wanted her home back. She wanted her children back. About Alex she wasn't so sure. There was one

151

particular question about Alex to which she wished she had the answer . . . She'd confronted him with her suspicions, but it wasn't enough. She wanted to *know*.

Maggie returned to her room and fed coins into her gas meter. She wanted the place to be warm for what she was about to do.

First she set up her table with the altar cloth and the implements she'd consecrated on Wigstone Heath. She unboxed her Christmas gift from Ash, three ornate brass incense burners which she set out in a triangle around the room, and set cones of incense smouldering.

Then she proceeded to mix her flying ointment.

She operated partly on information from the diary, partly on the basis of warnings and tips delivered by Old Liz. Getting information out of Liz was never easy, in that it came either in fragments or sudden outpourings. Checking or recapitulating anything was out of the question. It was like trying to catch rainfall: you collected only what went straight into the vessel.

It scared her deeply. Yet she wanted to do it, had to do it. She needed more than ever to prove to herself she was not some feeble spirit to be fisted around the house. The recollection of Alex's stinging blow to the mouth came to her. It gave her the strength to proceed.

Using a base of almond oil she mixed her quantities with the precision and care only fear could marshal. Her hands trembled; her throat was dry even as she used her mortar and pestle to grind the ingredients. She invoked the name of a protective spirit given to her by Ash.

Once, when she was a girl of twelve, she'd ascended the ladders to the top diving board at her local swimming pool. She'd never faced the top board before. Up there she found a short queue of dithering boys her own age, all failing to pluck up the courage either to jump or make the dive. Two boys walked to the extremity of the board and came back. They couldn't do it.

The boys had turned and, shamefacedly, had parted for her. Followed by their eyes, she'd stepped to the edge of the board. The cries and the splashes in the pool below had become remarkably hollow, had seemed to come from another world. Aware of the shivering boys behind her she'd dropped off the board, slipped through the air, and plunged, seemingly for ever, towards the water.

Emboldened by her example, the dithering boys were now all leaping from the top board. On reaching the side of the pool, she'd felt a strange trickle inside herself. She climbed out of the pool and went immediately to the changing rooms. Her first menstrual period had started.

She mixed belladonna, juice of wolfsbane, poplar leaves, wild celery and cinquefoil. To this she added a tiny ball of black resin which Liz had given her, and followed Liz's advice that she compound a kind of cold cream rather than an oil. Liz had told her that she should blacken the cream by adding soot, though she hadn't explained why. Maggie did as instructed.

These were different waters, darker waters, and they scared her far more than that leap from the top board. Far more, even, than had the red, mercurial trickle heralding a new phase of life. But now, as then, she was busy disguising her fears from herself.

Even though she'd had her oils awaiting *enfleurage*, the operation took her two hours. She placed a bowl of water and a towel beside her. Then she was ready.

She locked the door.

She undressed and sat naked on the floor, inside the triangle of incense burners. She sat with her eyes closed for ten minutes, trying to address her mind to the matter. Music thumped from the room below, but despite this distraction she found she could easily come back to her question. When she was satisfied, she opened her eyes and reached for the prepared ointment.

It wasn't easy, because she was afraid. Her stomach squeezed. Her hand shook. Her mouth was dry. *Why am I doing this?* she thought. *Why? Why?* She looked at the black paste she had spent so long mixing. The incense in the room hung heavy. She felt nauseous. The black pool beckoned. *Because you must*, came the answer from inside her head. It was a voice she'd heard before, in the woods, on the heath; female, intimate, insinuating. *Because you are what you are.*

She smeared the paste across her forehead, into her temples, on her throat and round her wrists. She massaged it thoroughly into her skin, but only at these precise points. Then, as Liz had insisted, she took a quantity of the paste on her fingers and pushed it up inside her vagina. It seemed a perverse act, but Maggie knew of other intra-vaginal treatments, so maybe it wasn't so strange. She wiped her hands on her thighs, smearing them in the process with sooty streaks, before washing

153

her hands in the bowl of water. Then she sat back to concentrate again on her question.

She was perspiring heavily; even though she was fully committed now, the fear had not diminished. Someone had once taught her to meditate; so she tried to slow her racing heart by closing her eyes and silently repeating a mantra to herself, without losing sight of her question.

The meditation technique relaxed her a little. She vented a huge sigh, a release of anxiety, and started to feel strangely languid. It was a pleasing sensation, almost a numbness, a distancing from her body. It lasted for ten or fifteen minutes, though she was already losing her sense of time.

Then suddenly her heart rate went up. It started knocking heavily inside her, and she was engulfed by a terrible, blinding headache. She opened her eyes and was astonished to see great blisters of sweat oozing from her body, the perspiration glittering like light on frost. Her vagina was burning inside and her throat was parched. She instinctively reached for the bowl of water, then remembered having used it to wash her hands. She tried to get up, but the movement made her vomit. She was sick into the bowl of water, twice, three times, until she was retching, unable to produce anything and at the same time unable to draw breath.

Then the retching stopped, and a profound numbness swamped her body. The pain in her head receded, as did the burning in her throat and vagina. She was breathing heavily, feeling only overwhelming relief that the pain had gone. She drew herself upright, her legs folded under her, her eyes screwed shut. Although she was still panting heavily, the frightening heart rate was beginning to slow. Instinctively, as if to give her lungs more room in which to work, she thrust forward her chest and pushed her arms back behind her. Then she tried to open her eyes.

Light hit her like a slap in the face. The instant she tried to open her eyes, she felt as if she had been grabbed by two giant claws, one round her neck, one squeezing her buttocks, and flung up, up, up into blackness, hurtling against a cinnamon hot wind. It was like being shot out of a cannon. White-hot sparks exploded and buffeted her as she travelled through the blackness, detonating behind her closed eyes. Her blood was roaring in her ears.

Then she suddenly came to a stop. She was suspended in mid-air. All pain had gone, all sense of heat and odour, all sound. This time she could open her eyes. She was in a grey corridor, unable to discern whether indoors or outside. All was muffled as she moved slowly along the corridor. Grey or black shapes, ambiguous things, fracturing shadows, drifted by her with languid movements like fish in an aquarium. Sometimes the shapes stopped, disappeared, reappeared, moved on. They could be geometric in form, or irregular. Maggie felt confused, lost.

She reached out at one of the shapes, and as her hand passed into it, the shape folded, quit. It changed into a face, mouthing words at her, words she couldn't hear.

The face was very old, androgynous, perhaps female, Maggie couldn't be sure. It hovered close, mouthing silent words, chilling but not threatening. Maggie moved away, but the face followed at her shoulder. Trying to speak was useless. It took her an age simply to turn and look into the eyes of the hovering face; then a long stand-off as she looked back without result, without consequence. Again Maggie moved away, and again she was followed. The face mouthed its words again, and again, until slowly it penetrated. *What do you want? What do you want?* the face was asking her. It wanted to help her.

Maggie tried to remember her question. It seemed a long way from here. She'd forgotten it. She would have to go back to her room to remember her question, and it was too far . . . too far away.

Then she recalled the question. She deliberately brought it to mind. The face disappeared immediately, and in its place, like a parting in the fabric of the grey corridor, was a scene. Maggie drew closer.

An elegant pair of hands, jewelled hands, a woman's hands, were carefully wrapping a Christmas gift. All Maggie could see were the hands, the gift and the wrapping paper. The paper was expensive, pretty green and red material shining and winking in the strange light. The gift was Bella's diary. The hands finished wrapping the gift, and now Maggie could see to whom they belonged. Anita Suzman. She was talking to someone behind her. Anita was naked, spread across a bed, lying on her stomach. She waved the gift in the air looking across her shoulder as she spoke. A man's bare arms slid under her stomach, lifting her from beneath her belly, raising her onto her knees. It was Alex. He parted her legs and Maggie could see his erection as he moved closer to Anita, slowly penetrating her as he leaned across her arched back. Anita's eyes closed and her head dropped forward in pleasure.

Anita slipped out her languorous tongue and licked the pretty bow decorating Alex's Christmas gift to Maggie as he took her from behind.

The sound of someone hammering on the door brought Maggie round. She came to on the floor, flat out on her back. She had her hand in a bowl of water and vomit. The gas fire had gone out and she felt cold.

'Maggie! Maggie! Are you in there?' The hammering got louder.

'Who is it?' Maggie croaked, unable to get off her back.

'It's Kate. What're you doing?'

Maggie dragged herself to her feet. She felt weak. She slipped on her dressing gown, sat on the bed and put her head between her knees.

'Maggie!'

'I'm all right!'

'Then open the door.'

Maggie staggered over to the door and opened it a few inches.

'God! Look at you!' said Kate. Maggie suddenly remembered the sooty flying ointment.

'Run me a bath if you want to do something for me.'

Kate did as ordered and stood back as Maggie came by with the bowl to tip down the toilet.

'Must have been one hell of a party,' Kate said nervously.

Maggie only looked back at her through a stray curl, but with a baleful eye.

27

Alex softened a little in the New Year. He let Maggie have the children for an extra day a week. It was always Saturdays he wanted her to have them, which was convenient for him, but she was grateful for any contact. Sam's conjunctivitis had returned, so she made a repeat preparation of the eye lotion that had cured him before.

Maggie's savings were dwindling. She was going to have to do something about money. Meanwhile Ash paid her to run Omega two days a week. He said he was glad of the days off, but she didn't see how he could afford it. Business was less than brisk. Maggie persuaded him to broaden his stock. They started selling sets of Tarot cards and handcrafted jewellery; she got him to take a wider range of books. He grumbled something about turning his herbal kiosk into an occult emporium, but let her have her head. Trade improved, and she felt she had at least done something to earn his generosity.

Entertaining the children every Saturday proved to be a drain on her scant resources. Previously it had been something she hadn't had to think about. So she started taking them to see Liz, which cost nothing.

'I know'd you was coming,' Liz said, eyeing Amy, whom she'd not met before. Amy stared in fascination.

Liz scrabbled an arthritic hand down the side of her chair and proffered a humbug.

'Take it,' said Maggie.

'Thank you,' said Amy stepping forward. Liz clasped her hand in arthritic fingers, but lightly, drawing her close and planting a kiss on her cheek. Amy showed none of the fear of Liz evinced by Sam.

'She's an angel,' said Liz. 'A little dove, a little pigeon. Pretty, eh?'
Amy blushed.

'Me!' shouted Sam.

'Yes, here's a suck for you. I'm not leaving you out.'

'Say thank you!' said Maggie. He wouldn't. Maggie put the kettle
on to boil; she didn't have to ask. Liz had got her stove burning. Maggie
was relieved; it was cold outside.

Liz saw her looking. 'I told you, I know'd you was a-coming. So I
got a good fire going.'

'How did you know?' said Amy.

Liz leaned forward and tapped her nose. Amy turned and smiled at
her mother. She sat on a hard-backed chair and gazed at Liz. Sam
crawled under the table.

Maggie wanted to tell Liz about her flying experiments, but in words
the children wouldn't understand.

'A little too much belladonna, I think, Liz.'

Liz's stick tapped involuntarily. 'Oh? Oh? When was this then? Now
I sees it.'

'Boxing Day.'

'Boxing Day? Boxing Day? Where was the mistress on Boxing
Day?'

Maggie hadn't thought about the moon at all. 'I didn't—'

'You've got to look out for the mistress. She's to be waxing when
you're mixing, and in one of the air or earth signs. Where did you do
it?'

'In my room.'

'Pssssshhhhttt!!!! That's not proper. You'll come to grief, you will.'

'Yes, well, it was a bit messy. Still, I got what I wanted.'

'You be grateful then.'

'Liz, there was a face. It seemed like someone helping me.'

'Oh yes. How do you think we'd go on if we didn't have someone
helping us? Help and be helped. That's it. We're here to help one
another, mark that, Amy?' Amy nodded. The old woman seemed to drift
off into some reverie sparked by her own words.

'Did you give her anything?' Old Liz said at length.

Maggie was confused. 'Give what?'

'Oh, she'll not be pleased with you if you didn't give anything for her help. Her might not come to you again. You've got to give something to your dark sister if her's to help you.' Liz fumbled in her sweet packet and held out a humbug to Amy.

Amy took the humbug. Liz tossed another to Sam, who was playing happily under the table.

'So that's my dark sister? But what do you give? And how do you give it?'

'Any way you like. Give an offering. Flowers, they like flowers. Or give her the next pleasure you gets off a man!' Liz hooted with laughter and her stick slapped at the floor. 'She'll like that even better! He-he!'

Maggie waited until Liz's laughing fit had subsided. 'Speaking of that, have you got anything that can put the lead in a man's pencil?'

'Yes,' Liz said quick as a flash, 'and I knows who you wants it for!'

Poor Ash, thought Maggie, to be spoken about like this. But she believed she could help, and Liz did have this uncanny intuition . . .

The talk of gifts reminded Maggie she'd brought a bottle of sherry for Liz. She'd left it in the car so she sent Amy off to fetch it, while she herself went to use the toilet, a cold, cobwebby brick outhouse at the bottom of the garden.

Sam crawled unnoticed behind the curtain into Liz's pantry. The dusty fabric of the curtain closed behind him, with a silent jingling of the brass rings suspending it from the rail. Liz had told him to keep out, he knew. But he wanted to take a look.

It was cool in the pantry. Cool and quiet. He sat on the stone floor and looked up from floor to ceiling. Layer after layer of shelves, groaning to capacity. Bottles and jars everywhere, innumerable, those nearest the ceiling gathering dust, those resting on the cold stone floor collecting cobwebs. There were glass jars and stone vessels; green bottles and brown; giant Kilner jars; enamel jugs and crock tubs; pots and demijohns; flasks and vases and open-topped cans, jostling for position on the shelves.

Some were unlabelled, some hand-labelled, some with their original brand labels fading, peeling, sticky from spillage. Those glass jars whose contents he could see were stuffed with black and yellow beans, or jams or fruit preserves or exotic-coloured powders and leaf branches.

Sam touched the stopper on a bottle resting on the floor. The stopper fell off and went rolling between his feet and along a phalanx of bottles standing at the back of the pantry. He moved to fetch it, but was distracted by a sharp odour issuing from the unstopped bottle. He put his nose to the bottle: it was like cherry pop, sweet, sugary, but it stung his nose like the smell of disinfectant. He took a tiny swig but it tasted sour. It made his eyes water. He could see the scent streaming from the bottle: a brown ribbon coiling in the air, passing under his nose and moving slowly across the pantry.

And now the pantry was full of smells. There were familiar smells and smells he didn't know; rich, pungent odours and sharp, spicy confections. Garlic and toffee. Vinegar and vanilla. Lemon and malt. Hundreds of smells, leaking from their glass jars and bottles. The air was full of dim-coloured thin ribbons of scent, like party streamers travelling slowly through the air, looping, tangling, drifting . . .

Suddenly a movement, seen out of the corner of his eye. A scuffling in the back of the pantry. Sam turned to look. Peering from behind a stone bottle was a large grey rat.

It looked at him with shining black eyes. Deep black pools. It lifted its fat head into the air, vibrating its whiskers and baring cracked, yellow teeth for Sam to see. Sam got a whiff of the animal, a hot, dirty stink of rodent. He tried to turn his head away, but he was caught, mesmerised.

The rat moved forward from behind the stone bottle, and Sam recognised, riding on its back and brandishing a match of wood, a tiny lady he'd seen before. The one he'd seen in his garden riding the rat. The lady who'd stolen his doll. The lady who had called him over the balcony in the shopping arcade.

She had him. Sam wanted to call out, but he was too afraid to move. Where was his mother? Where had Amy gone? He was paralysed. As soon as the lady appeared, there was a roaring in his ears, and a disturbance in the airstream. The ribbons of scent, still visible, quivered and creased. The jars and the bottles on the shelves vibrated, thrumming with energy, inching precariously towards the edge. The entire bottled contents set up a din in his ears, until he looked up and saw shelf after shelf of trembling jars and jugs and flasks and bottles threatening to topple.

And the contents of the jars had been changed. The huge jar of black and yellow beans had become wedged full of live, angry, buzzing wasps. The jar of leaf branches had become a tangle of black centipedes waving their legs at him. A jar of fruit preserve had changed into a human face, a boy's face, squashed into the jar, its nose and lips rammed up against the glass like leeches, its eyes blinking slowly at him. They were all going to fall.

And fall they did. First a glass jar containing a white-hot star fell from the shelf and smashed on the stone floor, sizzling caustically before it died. Bottles toppled, spilling pools of bubbling, steaming blood. Then a jar smashed to the left of him, spreading little boys' penises near his feet. The whole pantry was coming down around his ears. The curtain behind him lashed open as the din got louder.

'Now then! Now then!'

It was Old Liz, standing over him. She sank her arthritic claws into Sam's shoulders. He looked up to see her above him, her tongue thrust forward at astonishing length. Instantly she retracted her tongue and spat something, a bean, with great velocity across the pantry. The bean struck the rat. Its rider vanished instantly and the rat scuttled away. The jars stopped vibrating, the coloured ribbons of scent disappeared.

Sam was white with fear. His face was contorted in a scream he was too afraid to release. Liz pulled him to her and he hugged her, burying his head in the folds of her old skirts, setting up a wail and crying hysterically now.

'Hush then. Hush then. Now you knows. Now you knows what's in Liz's pantry.' She brushed his hair gently. 'And now *we* knows, don't we. We knows this little one is *overlooked,* don't we? But we won't say anything, will we? 'Cos she's got enough to be reckoning, your mother, now ain't she? Hush up now.'

Sam pointed at the smashed jars of jam and fruit on the stone floor. 'I didn't do it,' he blubbered, 'I didn't.'

'We knows. We knows who did it. Hush up afore your mammy comes in.'

Liz looked behind her and saw Amy staring at them. She was holding the bottle of sherry she'd fetched from the car.

'You saw?' said Liz.

Amy nodded.

'Well, you saw it done. Now you keep it hid, little miss. Keep it here,'

Liz tapped the side of her nose, 'and not here,' she said, tapping her lips.

Amy nodded again.

'And when the time comes, you just remember Old Liz, see?'

Maggie returned to find them standing over the mess in the pantry. 'What's been going on here?'

'Nothing to worry on. We've had a little accident.'

'Oh, Sam! Let me clear it up, Liz. For God's sake, Sam.'

'Don't blame the lad. There's a rat in there as scared him.' She turned Maggie back with her hand. Maggie made to insist, but the astonishing strength of Liz's grip prevented her. 'Any clearing up and I'll do it. You leave that alone.'

Liz sat back in her chair under the clock, and Maggie was surprised to see how Sam was clinging to her. Within moments he'd fallen asleep in her arms and Amy was settled at her feet. Maggie had the feeling something beyond the breaking of a few jars had happened, but she couldn't tell what.

'Where were we? I knows. We were talking about Ash,' Liz said in a low voice. 'And about the lead in his pencil.'

'Yes,' said Maggie.

28

Alex collected Sam from De Sang's clinic one afternoon, to be presented with an envelope which, De Sang assured him, contained his final report on the boy. Sam was sitting in the consulting room, drawing with wax crayons.

'Final?' said Alex.

'Sam doesn't need to spend any more time here. You'd only be wasting your money.'

'But I thought his behaviour had been improving lately . . .'

De Sang looked sceptical. 'Read the report. At this stage, a good child-minder will work out a lot cheaper.'

'But what are we supposed to do?'

'It's all in the report.'

Alex made to tear open the brown envelope.

'I prefer you to discuss it with your wife,' De Sang told him. 'Then if nothing's clear, come back to me and I'll go through it with you. But you won't need to.'

Alex was taken aback by the abruptness of it all. He didn't know what to say. De Sang called Sam over. 'Captain Hook!' he said, and Sam happily waddled off to get his coat. 'Of course,' De Sang went on, 'if you're keen to spend your money, we'll happily keep Sam – at the usual rates.'

'No, no,' said Alex, and within a few minutes he was walking away from the clinic with Sam trotting happily at his side, wondering whether De Sang had just abused him or done him a favour.

When he got home, he opened the envelope and pulled out the typed report. It said:

* * *

Report on Samuel Sanders prepared by Dr James De Sang

Playing games

After observing Sam on a number of occasions I have arrived at the following understanding of his behaviour.

Sam is a healthy little boy, who like all children enjoys playing games. Games are very important. For children they are the means by which they come to understand social behaviour. Sam has reached the stage of development at which these social games come into being.

In this sense Sam is learning the rules that govern life. These rules and morality are actually the same thing. It's all about behaviour which is acceptable, and behaviour which is not. Morality is a game. It's distinct from play, but it's still a game.

Up until about the age of three children do not adhere to the rules. After this time, they might imitate rules without understanding them, and will often change them to suit their own interpretation of the game. By the time the child is seven, it will usually begin rigidly to adhere to the rules in a genuine social manner.

Sad, isn't it? Sad, I mean, that we lose this capacity simultaneously to interpret whatever's going on in a number of different ways.

But that's life. Sam, however, shows no sign of imitating the rules (the second stage I mentioned above). This is what his parents tell me.

Now, I find that when Sam is in my clinic, he is very happy to imitate the rules. Not only that, I find him a very bright, creative little boy willing to invent rules to be shared. These perfectly healthy signs lead me to conclude that his environment may not be providing him with the best model for behaviour. Here in the clinic we PLAY THE GAME. We try to say what we mean and mean what we say to Sam. We find he responds well.

His unwillingness at home to imitate the rules and instead to display defiance, aggression, violence and hysteria (again as his parents tell me) indicates to me that his model at home is of someone NOT PLAYING THE GAME.

Since it is important for Sam at least to imitate the rules, I suggest
that his behaviour at home would be improved if all were to
PLAY THE GAME.

Hard, isn't it? But again, that's life.

I'm being as direct as I can here, because I know I'm addressing intelligent people. To do otherwise would, after all, be playing
quite a different game.

De Sang had signed his name at the foot of the report. Also enclosed
was an invoice.

Alex dropped the report on the table and ran a hand through his hair.
He picked up the telephone and dialled. A strange voice came on the
line, and he asked it to fetch Maggie from her room. 'Can you get over
here?' he asked her.

Maggie read the report for a second time before folding it and handing
it back to Alex. He snatched it from her and slung it across the room.
'The man's a fucking lunatic! He's the one who should be certified!
Running around with his trousers down for three months to come up
with that! And do you see what he wants to charge? We're not paying,
that's for sure.'

'No,' said Maggie, 'we must pay.'

'You're joking! He won't get a brass ring out of me. Who does the
charlatan think he's trying to kid? He can whistle for it!'

'It's as clear as a bell. And of course we have to pay him.'

'Clear? What's clear? What do you mean clear?'

'The report is precise. De Sang knows what he's talking about.'

'I don't believe I'm hearing this. The man is just taking the piss!'

Maggie looked into the fire. 'The man is speaking clearly and accu-
rately from the heart,' she said calmly. 'He's telling us there's nothing
wrong with Sam. He's saying you and I are the ones who have to grow
up.'

'Where are you going?'

'To the pub,' said Maggie.

29

'I don't know what's wrong,' said Alex. He buried his head in his pillow. Things weren't going well for him. He was under pressure.

Firstly there was the constant stress of having to get Amy ready for school and Sam to his full-time childminder, plus keeping them fed, clean, clothed and living in a house fit for human habitation. The expense of paying childminders to look after Sam and to collect Amy from school was starting to make work look like a waste of effort. And work itself wasn't without its share of problems.

The archaeological dig at the castle had resumed in January. Alex needed to produce results from his original dig if he wanted the project to be extended. Funds were tight, as always, and he had to fight for resources merely to erect a rain cover over the diversionary Maggie dig. That small site had filled up with water over the Christmas period, and had to be drained before work continued.

Maggie herself was still refusing to come home. The court hearing would be upon them in a few weeks, and that would incur heavy legal fees. His financial worries alone were enough to drive him to distraction. He was beginning to wonder if he were the one who needed a psychiatrist.

Except that psychiatrists had already demonstrated their dubious abilities in the form of James De Sang. Alex was still fuming over that report, and the accompanying bill. He was going to have to find a way to pay it. He wondered if he could arrange some paid overtime at work.

But that raised the problem of looking after Amy and Sam. And as for extra time, he could hardly claim it when here he was taking extended lunch breaks for the occasional secret rendezvous between the sheets.

Anita gave up stroking Alex's flaccid cock. For her, too, it had been a disappointing session. She felt she was losing him somewhere. Lately he seemed less inclined to make the effort to see her.

'Don't worry about it. Being anxious about it will only make it worse.'

'Telling someone not to be anxious is guaranteed to make them anxious.'

Anita was nettled. 'Sorry, I'm sure.'

Alex softened. 'I didn't mean to take it out on you.'

'Do you think she knows about us?'

'Who? Maggie?'

'Yes, Maggie.'

'No, I don't think she knows about us.'

Why did he lie to Anita? Was he afraid she might want to stop seeing him? Or was he just trying to keep his two worlds apart, so he could be a more accomplished liar should he have to face Maggie's accusations again?

Alex thought hard about it. He'd been careful not to do anything to arouse Maggie's suspicions, yet she'd confronted him forcefully, directly, on the night she'd ravished him. Ravished him? She'd *fucked* him, before demanding to know what he was up to. He was still slightly dazed. Never had he been so completely overwhelmed by a woman's ardour. He couldn't have stopped it if he'd wanted to, no more than he could resist a hurricane. The force of it had utterly subdued him. It was like being staked out and flayed.

He didn't know that night whether something primal had been given to him or taken away from him. Perhaps, he reasoned, that's why the affair with Anita had begun, because Maggie had in some mysterious way unmanned him. There was, he admitted to himself, a disgraceful immaturity in the notion that he'd done all this to re-assert himself.

Rationalising, he thought; it's all rationalising after the event! Just like Maggie's suspicions, powered by jealousy or maybe by intuition, it was all unfathomable, emotionally based, unknowable. She didn't *know*, she couldn't *know*. That's why he'd denied it, and went on denying it. And now here he was rationalising away his adulterous relationship with Anita, when the thing had happened simply because she was *there*.

She'd always been there. He'd always been deeply aware of her. He smelled her whenever she came into a room. It's simple: you observe the contract to pretend it doesn't exist and then *bang!* one day you're forced to admit it. It was a universal contract, in operation every day between women and men, a Devil's Contract, damned if you break it, damned if you don't. For there she was, coming round to his house smelling like a lynx, and always at the times when Maggie seemed most distant. Anita, shaking her platinum-and-golden hair; Anita, crossing and re-crossing her long legs so that her nylons hissed, until his head was full of thoughts of her wearing nothing but her animal perfume.

And always between them this astonishing, fragile tension when they were alone for a few moments: the drying of the mouth, the involuntary stiffening of muscles. Like a spring coiling and tightening. So strong, this feeling, and so dangerous to the two of them that it had to remain unspoken. Until finally it had to give. Only one act could break it.

When, one lunch break, he'd almost collided with her in the street, it seemed natural that they should decide to go to eat together. Anita was magnificent, he decided. She was one of those women who wear little or nothing in the way of rings, necklaces and accessories, yet who light up like a jeweller's window. Alex had long nursed an archaeologist's fantasy of gently uncovering fascinating layers of her perfumed clothing, ultimately to reveal the golden trove, which he would kiss. That day she was wearing a black, tight-fitting dress, black nylons and black heels. The sheen of her natural complexion and the precious-metal highlights of her hair contrasted provocatively with her carefully constructed lipstick pout. He wanted to eat her.

So when a decent table couldn't be found anywhere, at any price, it also seemed natural to go back to Anita's house for coffee and a sandwich. And when Anita's back was turned in brewing the coffee, Alex noticed her hands were trembling as much as his; so to stop his own hands from shaking he took a deep breath and put his arms around her from behind, letting his hands rest on her belly. Anita set down the jug she was holding and went very still. Neither of them spoke. Then she let her head tilt back on to his shoulder, and when he saw that her eyes had closed, he let his fingers splay across her thighs. He reached his hands under her dress. She moved to stop him, but ritually and without conviction. His cock was straining through his clothes, stabbing at her bottom. He felt her underarms perspiring heavily. She reached behind and pinched him savagely and he returned by probing inside her panties with his fingers, sliding a finger into her up to the second knuckle. Inside she was scalding. Then she grabbed his hand away and lifted it to her mouth, sucking the finger that had been inside her. She turned round, clasping her arms around his shoulders, locking her mouth against his and somehow *climbed* onto his hips, fastening her thighs around him.

She kissed him ferociously. He struggled to carry her that way – still kissing – through to the lounge, where he tipped her into an armchair and ripped away her shoes, her tights and her panties. There was no archaeologist's fantasy of hidden treasure, it was too urgent, too hot. He pulled her dress up around her waist to reveal her soft, tanned belly, and when she loosed his trousers for him his cock sprang out angry and engorged, swollen like a bee-stung thing.

He put his tongue inside her cunt until he was dizzy with the smell of her. She grabbed a fistful of his hair, drawing his head back, locking mouths with him again, wanting to taste herself on his mouth.

She spoke through the kiss. 'Come into me.'

That was the first time. It had all happened the day before Maggie had made her accusation. After that he'd met Anita for long, searching lunchtime sessions almost every second or third day. God, the potency of those afternoons, thought Alex wistfully.

Where had it gone?

He stroked Anita's hair. 'No,' he lied again. 'Maggie hasn't got it in her to suspect.'

'I'm not so sure about that.'

Alex looked at her.

'Bill's got the same . . . problem you have.'

'What problem? Can't get it up, you mean?' He snorted. 'What's that got to do with anything?'

'I wonder if it's Maggie's doing.'

'*What?*'

'Something she's doing to me, I mean. Something she's working. She knows about us. She hates me.'

Alex jumped out of bed and buttoned on his shirt. 'Hocus. I've seen what she does. Herb tea and a couple of joss sticks.' He thought about Maggie's 'dig here' prediction. He kissed her. 'I've got to go back to work.'

* * *

That afternoon Maggie was at Omega, unpacking new merchandise she'd ordered for the shop. Here she had a collection of talisman jewellery – metal discs on thin chains, the discs engraved with obscure glyphs and symbols. The silver bell rang behind her, and she was surprised to see Anita, dressed, as usual, as if she was looking for an opera to attend.

'Heard I'd find you here,' she said brightly.

'Anita!'

'Haven't seen you in ages. Thought you might like some company.'

Maggie flashed back to her flying vision, saw Anita's pink rump thrust in the air. 'You've taken me by surprise.' She found herself offering Anita a chair and a cup of tea, much against her instincts.

'I've been worried about you, Maggie.'

'Why should you be worried?' Maggie went back to unpacking her boxes.

'Not just you. Both of you. I saw Alex the other day and he doesn't look well. You don't look well either.'

'Really? I feel great.'

'I know he wants you back. And he's been seeing rather a lot of that student from his dig, the one who—'

'Tania. Nice girl. Looks after the kids sometimes.'

'You should go back to Alex. You two were made for each other.'

'To be honest, I'm enjoying the space. I'm not sure I want to go back.'

'But you miss the children terribly.'

Maggie bit her lip and opened another box of talismans. Anita, at least, knew when to change the subject. 'They look interesting. What are they?'

'Talismans.'

'Protective powers?'

'No, you're thinking of an amulet. Here, this is an amulet. But these are talismans. They're like batteries. You wear a talisman to increase your powers; an amulet to ward off powers.'

'You're really into this, aren't you. What's this one mean?'

'It doesn't "mean" anything. It's a love talisman. It's made of copper because that's the metal of Venus. This is the symbol of the planet, and this one is of its guardian spirit.'

'Charming. Can I buy one?'

Maggie hadn't yet priced the stock. She'd thought of selling them at around ten pounds. 'Handmade. Thirty pounds, seeing as I know you.'

Anita took out her cheque book. 'Not cheap, are they?'

Over the site of the Maggie dig, Alex had finally managed to erect a rickety shelter to keep off the rain, and to arrange for a drainage ditch to be dug, to lead the water from the new hole. Tania had been put in charge of the Maggie dig. He didn't actually say it was a reward for occasionally babysitting his children.

Meanwhile he had enough worries over the original project. An unearthed wall had collapsed; vandals had appeared one night and moved the markers on an entire section; and the dearth of positive results of the project was clouding its future. Alex was scratching his head, his mind not on the job, when Tania came up behind him. She was about to say something when he asked her if she could babysit that evening.

'I can't do it every night, Alex.'

'Sure. I know. I mean, think about it, will you?'

'I'll think about it. Anyway, we've found something. You'd better come and look.'

They'd excavated a length of narrow-bore lead pipe inside the dagger circle. It was disintegrating, but so far it was still in one piece. About three inches in length had been uncovered.

'Is it old?'

Alex looked closely at the white layer of oxidation on the surface of the pipe. 'Oh yes,' he said. 'Oh yes. Let's have it out.'

'Can you give me a lift if I come round tonight?' said Tania.

'I'm still keen to learn a few things,' Anita said after Maggie had seen out a customer. She didn't seem to want to leave, and Maggie couldn't think how to get rid of her.

'What things?'

Anita gestured at the rows of shelves. 'These things. Herbalism. Talismans.'

'What do you want to know?'

'Lots of things. How to attract someone. How to repel someone. How to know what another person is thinking.'

Maggie looked at her. Anita had something she desperately wanted to ask, but couldn't. She gave the impression she was waiting for Maggie to open the subject. Well, she could wait. 'Not easy, those things.'

'But you do have some knowledge.'

'Very little.'

'Don't bullshit me, Maggie Sanders. I'm not completely without insight myself you know.' Anita's eyes fizzed. 'I know what you do.'

Maggie's laugh was like the silver bell above the door. 'I don't know what you're talking about.'

'Alex is one thing. Bill is another. You'd better lay off.'

Maggie dropped what she was doing and turned round. 'Anita, hadn't you better explain what you're talking about? Because I'm getting confused.'

But Anita, if she was about to explain, didn't get the opportunity, because Ash came in at that moment. 'Afternoon, ladies!' he said, in his vaguely ironic and proprietary voice. Maggie introduced them.

'I thought there would be someone,' Anita said, getting up to leave.

'Pardon?' said Ash.

'On the scene.' Ash looked at Maggie, and then back at Anita, who said, 'Do you make magic together? Silly me. Of course you do. I have to go.' Anita turned and left the shop.

Ash stared after her.

'Alex's lover,' said Maggie.

'Oh,' said Ash, as if that explained everything. 'Sexy lady.'

'Some people think so,' said Maggie.

She held up her new talismans for him to see.

30

Maggie didn't give up trying to persuade Ash to fly with her, but he resisted stubbornly. She also tried to get him to talk about his own experience of flying, but all he would say was that it differed for different people, and that it was an experience he was most reluctant to repeat.

She could understand that. Her own recent efforts had succeeded in poisoning her. Despite exercising great care, it had taken her two full days to recover properly from the effects of flying. The nausea, headaches, night sweats and bowel disorders had been a grim toll to have to pay. But she was convinced that the preparation had been fundamentally correct. What had failed, she suspected, was something in her mental preparation, some inability to *transform* the poisonous properties of the flying ointment. She thought it was something Ash might know about.

Maggie stayed at his house occasionally, though not often. She'd made the mistake one night of giving over her best efforts to cure Ash of his impotence. The undertaking failed. She sucked him and squeezed him and teased him with her sharp fingernails and licked him from head to toe with her darting tongue, all to no avail. Though he pretended otherwise, she knew he was mortified. All she succeeded in doing was augmenting his anguish.

The craft she kept in reserve. Liz had given her strict instructions on that, and Maggie was too afraid to see the craft fail to do otherwise. But she continued to press Liz on the use of the flying ointment. She was whipped on by overwhelming curiosity, yet too afraid to go it alone again.

While Ash held out against her, she turned to the diary, where she found another of Bella's entries on the subject of flying. It was not helpful, and it only redoubled her store of anxieties.

Last eve I did fly again and survived, but by the skin of my teeth, thanks be to Hecate, and ere I got what I wanted I was out of it. A. forced me into it though I'd not a mind for it. Why do I let her bully me? I'll have done with A. if there's a way for it. I'll kill her off, my dark sister, so I will. And though I don't feel poorly, the banishments being correct, my hands are all a-tremble at what I did see.

Now at least I have some knowledge on A. for I seen HER dark sister and HER dark sister and so on, all in a line like tied with May blossom or something of the sort which I couldn't make out. But I'm done, and I'll not fly again, no.

Maggie decided that Bella was a witch of little resolve, for there was another entry a few days later.

I did fly again last eve though I'd said I'd not and I did intend but that I had A. tormenting tormenting tormenting me that I'd not SHIFT and I'd not used the flying ointment three times in the same moon, so since she was on her back but carrying water, the moon that is, I went along and did. A. left me alone a bit then, as she knows how I am towards her of late.

A. says I'm not discreet enough and she says I'll pay. But things are not as they were.

None of it was much help, except that the references to banishments were intriguing. There had been at least one earlier reference to banishments and something about 'preservation from demons'. Maggie understood these demons to represent the physical discomforts she'd endured, and put the question to Ash.

'Don't ask me. She's probably referring to the banishing rituals.'

'What are the banishing rituals?'

'I'm not telling you. It only encourages you to go away and do something dangerous.'

'Isn't it more dangerous if I don't know?'

'There are all kinds of banishing rituals. The idea is that the ritual keeps away any undesirable forces and influences. Some of them are complicated procedures where you have to wave a sword at the points of a star and so on; others are just about the time of day it's safe to work – dawn, midday, dusk.'

'Can you make up your own?'

'You shouldn't underestimate these rituals. It's something about keeping your intentions pure, and your mind unclouded.'

'I'm going to fly again. If you won't join me, will you at least watch over me?'

Ash groaned.

More artefacts were turning up at the archaeological dig, but they raised more questions than answers. Tania and her colleagues had found a metal handle with a back plate and screw holes. Then they unearthed another piece of metal, square-shaped, again a plate with screw holes, but with a circular hole in its middle.

'These things were probably screwed to something wooden which has rotted,' Alex told them. 'See if you can find the screws. Also, take a section of earth and see if you can find anything in the soil which might suggest an imprint left behind by a wooden casket or something. Take it slowly.'

They found a second metal handle. It almost certainly belonged to a large box of some kind. The function of the other fragment, the metal plate with a hole in the middle, was more difficult to guess. Then Alex saw Tania trowelling at the earth, her hair scraped back and tied in a pony tail, bending over in her tight jeans. He had a lewd thought. He packed her off to fetch the five-foot length of lead pipe they'd already unearthed. When she came back, the lead pipe fitted snugly inside the diameter of the metal plate.

Alex was supposed to have a lunchtime rendezvous with Anita that day. Instead he invited Tania to join him for a drink at the Malt Shovel. She accepted, and if she was surprised that he didn't invite the others, she said nothing.

He bought her lunch and a glass of white wine. 'Can you come round tonight?'

'I don't want to babysit for you again, Alex.'

'Not babysitting. I thought you might like dinner at my place. We could open a bottle of wine and *speculate* about what these objects might be.' He narrowed his eyes on the word.

Tania had wide-open brown eyes, and they didn't blink. 'That would be nice,' she said.

Alex planned to have the kids in bed by eight o'clock and Tania in bed by eleven. He hoped she could do for him what Anita, lately, couldn't. He wondered, with vague feelings of guilt and suspicion, what Maggie would be doing that evening.

Ash had agreed, under protest, to supervise Maggie's flying experiment that evening. He made his study available, knowing how uncomfortable her bedsit could be. He also told her what he knew about 'banishments' and fashioned a ritual for her, half from memory, half invented, but in any case a precise order of events which they rehearsed twice in order to get clear.

They'd agreed to begin the process at dusk. The flying ointment was prepared. Incense was ignited in Ash's study, already smouldering in brass bowls as the sky began to darken outside. Maggie began to feel the itching, the claw squeezing at her bowels as the hour approached. Why am I doing this? she asked herself again. What's driving me? A bitter taste lined her palate, as if the memory of her first flying experience was a metallic dust secreted in her saliva. Deposits of anxiety. Ash felt her jitters.

'You don't have to, you know. No one's making you.'

'I don't know why; but I must.'

'I'll make you some herb tea. Settle your stomach.'

Maggie saw her chance. 'Good idea. You sit down. I'll do it.'

She made the herb tea, but not one Ash had ever drunk before. This was one of Liz's. She sweetened it with honey.

'Mmmmm. Good. What is it?'

'My secret,' said Maggie. 'I'm going to take my bath.'

'Don't be long. It's almost dusk.'

Maggie took a perfumed bath. She knew enough about aromatherapy by now to scent the gardens of paradise. She'd made her own bathing mixture from sea salt, rosemary, frankincense and cypress. After drying, she anointed herself with the protective oils of hyssop and basil.

Liz had also passed on a love scent. The old woman had made it up for her and had given it to her with a wicked smile and instructions to use it sparingly. Maggie had to beg her to reveal the formula. It contained jasmine, red rose, a minute quantity of lavender, a bit of musk and ylang-ylang oils.

She came from the bathroom wearing her dressing gown. Ash was in the study wearing a loose-fitting jogging suit, lighting tall red and white candles. The incense was a specific compound of sandalwood and rosemary, pungent and sweet, streaming from the brass bowls and coiling in the air like serpents. He saw she was wearing one of her engraved copper talismanic charms.

On the rug Ash had made a large circle out of a length of clean, white rope. The circle was broken at the two ends of the rope. Outside the circle stood a bottle of mineral water to answer the ravaging dryness of Maggie's first experiment. Inside the circle was a bowl of water for washing and the jar of flying ointment. Maggie gave Ash a nervous smile, slipped off her dressing gown and stepped into the circle. She sat cross-legged on the rug, naked but for her talisman. Ash closed the circle behind her by overlapping the two ends of the rope.

Maggie composed herself. She dipped her finger in the water and touched her forehead. Repeating the words Ash had taught her, she made her dedications to Hecate and asked for protection: *I have purified myself and my heart is filled with joy. I bring gifts of incense and perfume. I anoint myself with unguents to make myself strong.*

Outside the circle, Ash watched, fascinated. The perfume from the censers hung heavy in the room. Her hair was like burnished copper in the flickering candle light and her skin was flushed rose-pink from her scented bath. Her eyes were half-closed as she repeated the ritual dedications, a slight bloom of perspiration on her brow. She reached for the jar of flying ointment and began to massage it into her wrists. She rubbed it into her temples, her ankles, round her throat and finally put her fingers inside her vagina.

'Wait!' said Ash. He slipped off his tracksuit, opened the rope, entered the circle and closed it behind him. He crouched down beside her, dipping his hand in the water and touching it to his brow, exactly as she had done.

'Ash! What are you doing?'

'Wherever it is you're going, I'm coming with you.'

He repeated the words, massaging the flying ointment into his ankles, wrists and throat: *grant me the secret longings of my heart.*

179

'No cheating,' said Maggie. She put her fingers in the jar of ointment and smeared it on his cock, then reached behind him and pushed her forefinger up his anus. Ash gasped. Then she kissed him full on the lips and smiled grimly. 'Now wait.'

They sat in complete silence for ten or fifteen minutes before she began to feel the faint dizziness and the perspiration on her brow. There was a taste somewhere in the back of her sinuses reminding her of her first experience. Again a burning, in her bowels and throat and inside her vagina, the dry heat which made her want to retch. But this time she saw the heat as a silver light climbing up the column of her spine. She visualised the heat as a silver sword, tip of the blade extending, as if she could control it, *transform* it, neutralise its poisonous properties, make it useful. The shimmering blade of light climbed up her spine and inserted itself into the tenderest parts of her brain. Suddenly there was a wild knocking inside her – from her heart, it must be the heart – and then a strontium flash inside her brain, shock waves producing a profound numbness throughout her body.

Suddenly her head swelled, balloon-like, racing outwards at speed until it jerked to a stop, two inches from the ceiling and the walls of the room. She touched the ceiling and her fingers stuck to it like suction pads. She realised she was on the ceiling, not hanging from it, but on it, inflated massively. Her head and hands were so large, she could see nothing of the room. Ash? Where was Ash? She blinked and saw Ash, also on the ceiling with her. He was looking back at her with huge, round eyes. Their bodies were gargantuan, obstructing all view of the study. She put a hand on Ash's arm and instantly there was an explosion as he shot away, a distance of a million miles in a fraction of a second, leaving a laser trail of light like a spaceship from a science-fiction movie.

Then another explosion as he was back with her again. She looked into his eyes. They were stormy black holes, clouds racing across them chased by high winds. She went into them, passed through them, and he was already inside there, waiting for her. They held hands and went hurtling through lilac skies, buffeted by hot spice winds, until they came to an abrupt stop.

They were together in that grey corridor she had visited before. She tried to speak to Ash but couldn't. Grey and black shapes drifted past her vision, dissolving, re-forming. Then the familiar face was beside her, the face that had helped her before, questioning without words. Maggie told her she had a gift to offer.

The face disappeared and in its place was a familiar scene within a parting in the grey corridor. It was Alex, raising Anita to her knees. Maggie didn't want to witness the event a second time. She waved it away and it changed. Alex was still there. This time he was at home. He was lying on his back, in bed. Tania was with him. Nothing was happening.

Tania was also lying on her back, sheets drawn up to her waist, her doe-eyes gazing at the ceiling.

'Perhaps you're trying too hard,' she said.

Alex turned over and bit the pillow. Tania's sympathy was even more provoking than Anita's.

Hitherto, the evening had gone well. Tania had turned the kids on to something called 'Cowboy's Glory', which was nothing more than the beans on toast Alex could never get them to eat. The children, by now accustomed to Tania's presence, had gone to bed without too much fuss. Alex's party-piece lasagne had turned out well, and the first bottle of claret had given way to a second. Then Amy had come downstairs at the wrong moment to find her daddy removing Tania's blouse and sucking Tania's brown nipple.

'What are you doing?' Amy had wanted to know.

After Amy had been settled again, Tania and Alex removed to the master bedroom. But there, despite a lot of spirited wrestling and imaginative foreplay, the point had somewhere been lost. And though his body couldn't give him an erection, his mind was still ablaze with lust. Alex didn't want Tania's sympathetic clichés or her banalities, he wanted a night of deep sex. The kind of sex that went on until the early hours, and then even further, the kind of sex that left you sore. He wanted Tania to help him prove that Anita had a problem and he didn't; that Anita was being passed over by the angels of lust and he wasn't; that where Anita exuded something dispiriting and deflatory, he was still clean.

At first he felt this was some kind of punishment cooked up for him by Anita. Then he changed his mind and thought it was all Maggie's doing. Then he wanted to blame Tania. He felt angry at her, lying there staring up at the ceiling, but he couldn't think why. So he settled for a compound resentment of all three, lying in the dark in a sullen, curdled silence; but of the three, mostly he cursed his wife.

Maggie came to on the floor, lying on her side inside the circle. The censers had burned out but the scent was still heavy in the air. The candles had burned down. Ash was lying next to her, one arm round her. Her throat was dry. There was a slight tingling throughout her body. She reached outside the circle for the bottle of mineral water and gulped it back. Then she noticed something about Ash.

'Ash! Ash!' She put the bottle to his lips and trickled mineral water into his mouth. He coughed and came round, blinking at her. He groaned.

'You OK?' he asked.

'I feel fine. Weird but fine. Really. What about you?'

'A bit shaky. Otherwise fine.'

'Was it like your last time?' said Maggie.

'Nothing like it.'

'Ash, haven't you noticed anything?' Ash looked puzzled as he drew himself up. Maggie nodded at his lap. Ash had a monster erection. His cock was pointing straight up at the ceiling, engorged, the swollen purple head bobbing slightly as he looked down at it.

'Goddess! You've come back to me!'

He sat on the floor, looking delirious with happiness. Maggie got up and placed a hand on each of his shoulders. She hoisted herself over him. 'I owe this one,' she said, gently lowering herself down the length of his aching shaft, 'as a gift.'

'Goddess!' he said.

31

Sam's nightmares wouldn't go away. There was a fat rat scuffling in his dreams. And when he woke up from these nightmares he would see the old lady in his room. The rat-rider. And when he awoke it was as if he came back from these bad dreams clutching a black fragment, a ragged swatch of the dream itself, and that torn piece of dream was the old woman. She could appear anywhere in the shadows of the unlit room. As the coat draped over the back of a chair. As the lampstand in the corner. Among his box of toys. Under the bed. Oh, she would fade shortly after he'd woken up, too soon for him to wake anyone else, but not before she'd let him know she was there.

Amy had returned from one of her mother's visits to Liz with a vague sense that she must protect her brother. Liz had hinted and tapped her nose in a frightening way, leaving her with a feeling of responsibility. *Remember me*, Liz had whispered, *remember me*. When Sam became hysterical at the thought of sleeping another night alone, Amy had surprised her father by offering to let Sam into her room. Jealous of her space, like so many growing girls, Amy had up until now always refused Sam the opportunity of even *looking* in her room.

Alex had moved Sam's bed into Amy's room. Then one night Amy was awakened by the sound of Sam crying and pleading in his sleep. She saw him sit up in bed and gaze across the room, eyes wide. Amy looked over and saw an old woman in black clothes, firmly embedded in the wall. Only her head, hands and feet were visible, protruding from the wall. The rest of her torso was elsewhere, seemingly sunk behind the wallpaper and plaster as if it was made of styrofoam. She was eyeing Sam with a vicious smile.

'Sam,' Amy whispered.

The smile on the old woman's face turned into a sneer. She rotated her head slowly, until she was looking at Amy. Then she faded.

Amy got out of bed and put the light on. Sam was whimpering. She climbed into bed beside him and cuddled him until he fell asleep, just as her mother and father had done with her when she was smaller.

In the daytime, Sam would never set foot in the cellar playroom alone. If he did go down there, he would cling to his sister, and if she tired of him, he would cling to Dot's collar.

One day, in the excitement of a game with Amy, he almost forgot his troubles in the playroom. As he raced across the room the rug slipped from under his feet and he cracked his head. The rug had shifted to reveal the face, more prominent than before, and more malevolent. The rust-coloured stain bubbled moisture, glistening on the bare concrete as they looked on.

Amy touched the stained floor, and the rust colour transferred to her finger. 'It's wet,' she said quietly.

She looked at Sam. He seemed very small.

'Wait here.'

'No,' said Sam.

'Dot's here. You'll be all right.'

Sam put his hand under Dot's collar and slithered behind her. Amy ran up the stairs and into the kitchen. Sam heard her drawing a stool across the floor. Then he heard a cupboard opening, a rustling, and Amy climbing down from the stool. In a few moments she was back in the playroom.

She had something in her mouth. Sam and Dot watched as Amy stood before the face in the floor. She stood over it in silence, as if she was thinking. Her arms hung lifeless at her sides, her head was bowed slightly, drawn into her shoulders. She stayed like that for a long time.

Then she pushed her tongue out of her mouth. Sam got a brief glimpse of something sitting on her tongue, before she drew her head back and spat it violently at the face on the floor. It landed in the middle of the face.

Nothing happened. Dot sneezed, but Amy stood her ground. Then the face began to blister and bubble in tiny spots. It peeled back, like old paint, and within five seconds the stain had disappeared. In the middle of the floor was a dried bean.

'What did you do?' said Sam, still hanging onto Dot's collar.

Amy picked up the bean and settled the rug back into place.

Alex appeared in the doorway. 'You kids are too quiet for my liking. Everything all right, Amy?'

'Yes,' she said, pushing past him.

Sam followed her out, and so did Dot.

32

'Listen to this,' said Maggie. She and Ash were lying in bed, candles flickering, empty wine bottles gathering in number, sound of wind and rain lashing at the window. She was reading to him from Bella's diary, pieces she'd read herself many times.

A. drives me, she drives me and drives me, my wicked dark sister. Always having me do the next thing and the next thing until I know I shall lose my wits. I'm out of patience with her but she's too strong for me, and knows it, and she does so keep on at me until she has her way. I am weak, for I know that without me she can do nothing, so why do I let her drive me?

Last night it was on the heath, and I performed the shifting, and it has done nothing but left my wits in shreds and I can hardly hold this pen for trembling. No, I'll not talk of it, not even in this secret journal.

Only my dark sister knows.

Oh, the blackbird.

And A. says I'm too careless with my coming and going, but I say to her that she is the one who drives me hither and thither. A. says I'll pay for indiscretion, but I've told her if I pay, then she'll pay too, and she knows it.

All this because I give a herb scrying and a love simple to one who lives near and came asking for it. What can we do, when they ask us?

Maggie closed the diary. 'Why was she so paranoid, do you think?'
'Old Liz will tell you enough stories to answer that. There was a wise

woman near her who was thought to have dried up a spring. When she died the villagers pulled her cottage down brick by brick. This wasn't the middle ages, this was forty years ago. She probably had reason to be paranoid.'

'Who?' said Maggie. 'Bella? Or the mysterious A.? You said you thought of them as the same person.'

'I do. A. is Bella's alter-ego, I assume. She gives her the excuse to go and do the things she really wants to do. The dark stuff, the things she can't face in herself.'

'You mean Bella was a schizophrenic?'

'I suppose so. Something like that. Maybe not barking mad, but certainly hiding behind this A. character she's always complaining about. See how she always blames what she does on A.?'

'I don't see it like that. I think A., whoever it was, was another witch. A separate person altogether. Leading Bella on.'

'The way that diary leads you on?'

Maggie wasn't happy about that remark. 'What are you getting at?'

'Never mind.'

'No, say what you were thinking.'

'It was what we were saying about paranoia. You're steeping yourself in a lot of heavy craft these days. If there's one thing I do know, it's that the craft has also got a dark sister, and her name is paranoia.'

'I'm old enough to know the difference.'

'Really? I know you've been working something against Anita and Alex.'

Maggie was surprised. 'How did you know?'

Ash produced a strip of leather with five knots tied in it. Each of the knots was singed with a crude alphabetical representation. 'These five letters wouldn't add up to the name of anyone we know?'

'Ash!' said Maggie, not at all annoyed. 'You've been rooting through my handbag!'

'I'm getting very fond of you, Maggie, but ligatures? Just be careful. It's a wrong path.'

Maggie looked away. The rain and the wind beat against the bedroom window.

* * *

Whatever Ash's objections, he swallowed them and indulged Maggie. She practically took over the business at Omega for him, and business flourished in her hands. What could he say? If he lost some of his old customers, he gained three times as many new ones. Maggie also had a shrewd idea of how far Ash's integrity could be stretched. There was a lot of junk she could have stocked – bogus products carrying extravagant claims, miracle cures, lucky silver pixies – which she didn't. She respected his 'what you see is what you get' philosophy on merchandising, and never tried to breach it.

He indulged her for what she'd done for him. And Maggie found in him a companion and lover who was excited by spontaneity. If they wanted to wake up at a ridiculous hour and go walking by a lake or in the woods, they did so. One time they drove in a thick night fog to a flight of canal locks, just to hear what the place *sounded* like when you couldn't see it. Dawn, midnight and dusk. These were the goddess hours, the moments imbued with magic capability. Sometimes, however, even Ash balked.

'No, Maggie, no! I'm not going out on the heath on a night like this. Listen to that wind!'

'But that's what Liz meant about flying indoors. It's why we felt like we were crashing into the ceiling. Next time we have to fly outside.'

'Not in the middle of winter, we don't. Go back to sleep.'

But Maggie lay in the dark unable to sleep. The wind outside, far from deterring her from a visit to the heath, only stirred something in her breast. She looked tenderly at Ash sleeping beside her, but she heard voices in the wind. Something was calling softly from the heath, and from the hills beyond the heath.

She did not know what was calling her, nor if the voices were all inside her head. But it was beautiful, eerie, a low chorus of women's voices. *One of us*, they sang, *you have always been one of us*. It pulled her like the moon pulling on the tides. She was approaching her period; she felt the mysterious blood connection. How could she tell Ash? He was a man. How could she ever tell him about voices he couldn't possibly hear and was never meant to hear?

There was a rumble of thunder. She knew it was a night for her to go. She slipped out of bed and went to look out of the window. Ash woke up, blinking sleepily at her. She kissed his lips. 'I won't be long. Don't worry.'

'Not flying, are you?'

'No. It's a Macbeth night. I just want to feel it a little.'

Ash groped for his shirt. 'I'll come.' She wanted to tell him it was a girls' only night, but she was touched by his sleepwalker's loyalty.

Ash drove steadily towards the heath through the rain. There was the first spear of lightning. The rains lit up against the headlights, swirling silver sparks.

'What is it?' said Maggie.

They were about halfway to the heath. Ash blinked into his rear-view mirror. 'For a minute I thought somebody had been following us. But it's nothing.'

'And you said *I* was paranoid.'

They reached the heath and parked the car. The trail was pitch-black, but by now they knew their way in the darkness. The rain had stopped. The storm had passed overhead, but there was still the distant rumble of thunder and the occasional fork of lightning. The afterbreath vapours of the fission and the smell of ozone touched everything. The earth was fingered with mist. Maggie breathed deep. She felt her powers magnified, quadrupled. She danced along the path ahead of Ash.

'The goddess! Hecate! All around us! She passed by this way! Smell her!'

The grass was heavy with rain. The standing stones were wet, glistening with water droplets, exuding their own smells. Maggie walked round the circumference of the circle, inside, brushing her hands against the nine stones. Then she stepped quickly out of her clothes. She pressed her naked back and her thighs to the wet, erect granite, luxuriating in the suck of heat from skin to rough stone and the transmission of cold from stone to bone.

'Come on, Ash! Feel the rain between your toes!'

'It's freezing!' he countered. But she was on him, pulling his sweater over his head. Giggling, the pair fell to the ground, rolling in the wet grass. Maggie got up and danced away. There was another feeble flash of lightning, seeming to come from behind one of the stones. Ash stood up and stared into the darkness.

'Did you see something, Ash?' Maggie was breathless. She put her hand on his arm.

Ash continued to gaze into the blackness. 'I don't think that last flash was lightning.'

'What do you mean?'

'I don't know.'

33

It was the day of the custody hearing. Both parties had made their visits to the Court Welfare Officer, and both parties concluded that the Court Welfare Officer was biased against them. A report was duly compiled and a date set for the hearing in chambers. To attend, Alex dusted off the only suit he possessed, and tied his tie in a strangling, tiny knot. Maggie put on too much make-up and wore high heels.

Briggs for Alex and Montague for Maggie. Morton Briggs exuded an easy confidence which Alex didn't share. Alice Montague did her best to put Maggie at ease. 'Judge Bennett,' she said. 'That's very good for us.' Each side was introduced to and interviewed by their respective barristers and the case was up and running by 10 a.m.

While the Welfare Officer's inconclusive report was being read out to the court, Alice Montague, sitting next to Maggie, whispered in her ear, 'Apparently your husband's not calling anyone as a witness. Any idea why?'

Maggie shrugged. She had no idea whether it was significant or otherwise. She herself was calling her childminder who, despite recent difficulties, had guaranteed to testify to Maggie's qualities as a fit parent. Maggie's worst fears were that Alex would drag in Anita Suzman, programmed to say hateful things about her ability as a mother; but it looked as though Alex was happy to proceed without witnesses.

However he may have looked, Alex was not happy about much at all. He was beginning to squirm at what he'd done since first receiving the summons, and he was even more nervous about the possible consequences of his actions. But Maggie had started this! She'd elected for the legal path! He'd pleaded, appealed, and begged; but she was not to be diverted.

So be it. Alex had actually uttered those archaic words aloud one day, an oath resonating with biblical weight. *So be it.*

It was, he'd decided, time to regain control. Things had got out of hand and now he was reining in. Emotional appeal had failed, familial affection had lost its way. He had a terrible feeling that Maggie's powers (and only now was he beginning to see them as powers, female, dissipatory, undisciplined) were on the ascendant, and their single tendency was disruptive. He knew he must meet her head on with cold, hard logic. He saw how the brittle, masculine lines of the law could serve him and not her.

Maggie, after all, had taken the decisive step on a road where he could match her yard for yard. He would fight to keep household and children by all means available. No, he wasn't happy about this. He wasn't *happy* about any of it. But he had switched off the emotional response and had abandoned himself to a close study of the rules of play. And the rules of play had a habit of taking over from the original reasons for the engagement.

Maggie soon realised why Alex wasn't troubling to call witnesses, and so did Alice Montague. Alex's barrister presented a large cardboard box containing a collection of small jars, bottles and packets of herbs.

'Your honour,' said the barrister, 'what we have here is a collection of herbs, hedgerow plants, oils, incenses – all of dubious medicinal value – which Mrs Sanders gathered together when she became obsessed with notions of healing, witchcraft and other practices which I can only describe as occult.'

Maggie felt Alice Montague stiffen beside her. Alex had lied when he'd said he'd burned all of her herbs. She tried to look at him, but he was staring straight ahead.

The judge, who had not spoken a word and seemed not to be listening, took his spectacles off, as if the gesture would help him understand more clearly. 'Occult?' he said.

'Yes, your honour, occult. It seems Mrs Sanders discovered an old diary composed by some eccentric former occupant of the family home. She became obsessed with the bizarre remedies and treatments suggested by the diary, so much so that she began a campaign of experiments on her own children.'

The judge put his spectacles on again and looked hard at Maggie.

Then he began poking around in the cardboard box, sniffing at some of the containers almost theatrically. 'You are married, aren't you, Mr Boyers?' he said to Alex's barrister.

'As your honour knows.'

'And doesn't your wife keep a spice rack in her kitchen?'

'Indeed she does, your honour, but—'

'And does that make her an inferior mother to your children, would you say?'

'Indeed not, your honour, though I must say—'

'And haven't you ever rubbed a dock leaf on a nettle sting, Mr Boyers?'

'Most certainly I have, though . . .'

'Though what, Mr Boyers?'

Maggie was astonished. The judge seemed to be teasing the barrister, giving him the run-around. She looked at her solicitor, and Alice Montague winked.

'Though what I would say, your honour, is that—'

'And did you not find the application of said dock leaf to said nettle sting an effective remedy?'

'Yes, your honour.'

'And if your wife told your children to use this method of relief, would that make her a bad mother? No, Mr Boyers, it won't do.' The judge turned his nose up at the contents of the box and waved it away. 'Can we have this removed?'

Alex's barrister lifted something else from his bench and handed it to one of the court ushers. 'If your honour would care to study this then I assure your honour that he might look at the contents of the box in a somewhat different light.'

The case practically closed itself from that moment. What the barrister had given the judge was a photograph, taken at night, showing Maggie romping naked on the heath inside a stone circle. She appeared to be dancing, and the expression on her face suggested some delirium. In the background, smiling demoniacally (it might be assumed), was a bearded man, Ash, also partially naked.

The custody hearing which would normally be expected to last a full day was over by lunchtime. Alex was awarded custody, with no variation of the current access arrangements.

* * *

'The bastard's been having me followed!' cried Maggie outside the court-room.

'That's right,' said Alice Montague. She was trying to comfort her.

'But isn't that illegal in itself? Following people?' Maggie's make-up had run. Her face was like a cracked painting. 'Surely it's illegal to follow people.'

Ms Montague shook her head. 'He must have commissioned a private investigator. That photograph—'

'It wasn't how it looked! We were only—'

'You don't have to explain anything to me, Maggie. At least try to comfort yourself with the fact that the judge awarded you good access to the children.'

'Isn't there anything I can do?'

'See your children as often as you can. Things might change. Maybe in the future you'll be able to work out some kind of agreement.'

'Agreement? After the way he's behaved today? I couldn't care if he stops breathing! You're married to someone all this time and you think you know the best and the worst of them. But you don't! You're living with a stranger. How could he have done this to me, whatever the arguments? It's unforgivable! I don't want an agreement! I want him dead for doing this!'

'Try not to be bitter, Maggie.'

Bitterness. Bitterness was not something to be buttoned on and off like a coat. It was a cancerous spot, like a lump in the chest or a stone in the throat. It deposited a taste in the mouth which wouldn't wash away. Maggie shook hands with Alice Montague and left the building, her high heels clicking angrily down the stone steps to the busy street.

'Maggie.' It was Alex, waiting outside for her.

She paused briefly and flashed him a look before marching away, her coat flapping in the wind. Alex was frightened by what he'd seen in her eyes.

'Try not to be bitter, Maggie.' This time it was Ash, offering the same ineffective advice. Maggie had gone back to Omega, and he'd shut up shop to spare time to try and console her.

'Everyone tells me not to be bitter. But it's easy for you to say that.'

Maggie sat looking oddly composed. But she didn't deceive herself.

She knew if she didn't project a composure of sorts she would break something. She had to shut down her feelings, but even so she felt them working, agitating, trembling at hideous depth, like molten lava. Some rage inside her was loose and shifting, dissociating from herself.

'Yes, it's easy for me to say that,' said Ash. 'But it's also easy for you to give in to the kind of thoughts you're having right now.'

'We can't all be so noble.'

Ash let that one go. He handed her a cup and saucer. She hadn't looked him in the eye since she'd come into the shop. He was a little afraid of her. The appearance of her anger was too cold. 'Look, you've lost a legal fight, but you've got access to the children. Think positive. There are other ways you can make this work for you.'

'That's right.' She suddenly turned to face him. 'There are other ways.'

'No,' said Ash, realising. 'That's not what I meant. I was talking about using your access time creatively. Getting the most out of it. I know what you're thinking, and you'd better put away those ideas right now.'

'A lot of other ways.'

'I tell you, Maggie, it's a wrong path. A wrong path. It'll come back on you. Are you listening to me, Maggie? Maggie?'

34

Liz was kneeling over her doorstep, whetting a wooden-handled knife on the stone threshold. It was a knife so old it had lost half its blade width on a lifetime's sharpening. A low, throaty singing came from her as she worked. Her voice wobbled with the vibrato of age, but Liz could still hold to a melody.

> She become a rose
> A rose all in the wood
> And he become a bumblebee
> And kissed her where she stood
>
> She become a hare
> The hare run down the lane
> And he become a greyhound dog
> And fetched her home again.

A shadow fell over her threshold and she looked up. 'Here she is.'
'Here I am.'
'Know'd you was coming.' Liz went on whetting her knife on the step. 'Where's that little gel? Ain't you brung her to see me?'
Maggie stepped over her and went inside to make a brew. 'I've lost her. I've lost both the children.'
Liz stopped what she was doing. 'Lost? What's all this talk of lost?'
Maggie bit her lip and explained the consequences of the court decision.
'Why,' said Liz, 'that's not lost. You proper turned me over when

you said as they was lost. I thought they was dead. Nothing's lost until they're dead.'

'I want them back, Liz!'

'And so you shall have them back. But not by bleating about it, you won't.'

'Will you help me?'

'I'll not.'

'But you could, Liz. You could help me get my children back.'

'And I've told you I'll not. I knows what you've got a mind to do, and it's nowt to do wi' me, but I'll tell you this: stay off of it.'

'You don't know what I've got in mind. Why do you say you do?'

Liz straightened her bent back and waved the knife at Maggie. 'I know more than you think. You mark it. More than you think. I knows what you put on that husband o' yours, and on his fancy woman. That's surprised you, hasn't it? And you think yourself clever; but never mind, because that was no more than justice. Justice. But this other, it's wrong path. Now I've telled you and I'll say no more. But you mark it.'

Maggie looked away. In one sense she was surprised by what Liz had known about what she'd done; but in another way she'd always recognised that Liz had a sight beyond her own.

'Did you mark it?' Liz demanded.

'Yes,' said Maggie, like a sulky schoolgirl.

'Good. Now fetch my coat and we'll go for a blow in the fields. For I don't like you coming in my house with all this on you.'

They walked along the edge of a sparse copse and across a field. Liz's old collie trotted ahead of them.

'Spring not far off,' said Liz. 'Smell it?'

'Yes. It's in the air.'

'Not in the air. In the ground. In the growing. That's what you smell. Feel better for a blow?'

'Yes, I do feel better.'

'Blow away some o' that what's a-settled on your shoulder.' She pointed her stick at a plant with a yellow flower not unlike a dandelion head. 'Coltsfoot. Earliest I ever seen coltsfoot. Weather's a-changing. Get me some o' that. Good for the lungs. Coughs. Very good.'

Maggie stooped and picked the plant by the root. 'What do you know about *shapeshifting*?'

'Psssshhhhtttt!' went Liz. She still hated anything mentioned openly.

Maggie ignored her. 'That diary of mine, the one I told you about. It mentions it. It says that, well, it's the way to true power. Is that so?'

Liz walked on, tight-lipped.

'I mean, have you ever done it?'

Liz stopped. 'Wouldn't tell you if I had. And there's an end to your questions, ain't it?'

'But why not?'

'I don't know who you might tell. You might be a blabbermouth for all I know.'

'Look here, Liz. All the time I've been coming to you I haven't said a word about anything to anyone. And if you know half what you claim to know, you'd know *that*.'

Liz chuckled to herself, and flicked her stick in the direction of a wooden stile. 'Let's head up there. You can collect me some firewood as we go.'

Maggie was accustomed, and never objected, to being used as a packmule on these walks. She collected a few logs and stacked them under her arm.

'No no no,' said Liz. 'You still don't know your wood. That 'un won't burn. A one should know her wood. Here:

> Oak shall warm you well
> That's old and dry
> Logs of pine do sweetly smell
> But sparks will fly
> Birch will burn too fast
> Chestnut scarce at all
> Hawthorn logs be good to last
> Cut them when leaves fall
> Holly log it burns like wax
> You may burn 'em green
> Elm logs like to smouldering flax
> No flame to be seen—

Are you listening?'

'Yes, Liz.'

'No you ain't. You're letting things play. And you ain't a-listening.'

Liz leaned and Maggie hoisted herself on the stile, and they were quiet for a few minutes. Then Liz said something Maggie didn't understand.

'I was thinking how I might tell it you all. I was even thinking how I might give you the line when my time comes. And that can't be long. But I don't know, gel; there's a hardness in you of late. Today you're as tight as a drum, and I don't know.' Liz looked off into the trees.

Maggie said, 'But I only wanted to ask you if it was possible. This *shapeshifting*. To ask you if you'd ever . . .'

She tailed off because this time it was Liz who wasn't listening. She was gazing at a blackbird perched on an elm branch not six feet away. Perfectly still, its feathers were sleek and black, its beak a brilliant orange. Its head was cocked, its eye fixed on Liz's eye; or maybe Liz's brilliant gaze had skewered the bright eye of the bird. Nothing needed to be said. Maggie had her answer. The old woman had *shifted in her time*. She knew the way, and she had the wisdom of transcendant experience. She had tasted the flame many, many times.

The blackbird flew away.

'Put this thing out of your mind,' said Liz, 'and concentrate on them children o' yours. I'm worried you're bringing a shadow over them. Who knows, maybe it's better if you don't see 'em for a while. But if you really want them back, then go and talk to him. Talk. That's the proper way. Folk must talk.'

Liz moved off without looking back to see if Maggie was following. Maggie trailed at a short distance. They climbed the gentle incline of a hill, and Liz seemed lost in deep thought.

'Come to me on Saturday morning,' she said at last, 'and I'll give you what you need for the *shifting*.'

'Shall I bring the children?'

'Leave 'em where they are.'

'I thought you wanted to see Amy?'

'And I said not.'

Maggie didn't argue.

35

Fifteen miles. It was fifteen miles from Church Haddon to town, and then fifteen miles back again. That, she considered, was a tidy step, and with her arthritis it might even finish her off. But it had to be done.

Old Liz had already covered the first three miles and was stroking her stick through the hedgerow. 'Come out, felon. Come out, old uncle harry.' The mugwort was common, but not being in flower for some months yet, it was difficult to locate. She was in sore need of it, if she was going to survive this hike. 'Come out, felon.'

Three times already Liz had detected the plant, but in each case after finding it, she'd rejected it. 'There, there, uncle.'

Liz had woken that morning, dawn's light breaking in through the uncurtained window, with a certainty Maggie's children were in danger. 'Amy and Sam,' she'd muttered, hauling herself out of bed. 'We must look to Amy and Sam. Yes.'

At times like these, she'd thought ruefully, she could have done with a lift in Ash's car, or someone's car. That engine, she would have been the first to admit, was better than any amount of craft. Certainly she could have telephoned Ash; she had his number on a scrap of paper somewhere. But if she were to involve Ash, then he would tell Maggie, and all would know and all would be known and she might just as well stay at home.

No.

She would have to walk.

That fifteen miles and back would have been nothing to her in her younger days. She would have taken that at a clip. But this arthritis and this bad hip, well, it held her up. And she didn't have a lot of time.

Old Liz didn't even consider the matter of breaking her appointment

203

with Maggie. These other things were too important. Maggie could make her own way. Anyway, it wasn't for Maggie she was doing this, it was for those children. Liz had woken up bothered by what she'd seen in those children.

Liz had known Maggie would bring trouble from that very first afternoon she'd come to the house. What power she'd seen in her that day as Maggie had hovered on the threshold, unaware that Liz was watching from behind, what potential! For a moment Liz had been afraid, surprised and afraid. She'd had to stoop down and find a bit of something that day, to keep Maggie back until she'd got her full measure. Then she saw how Maggie had no idea of her own capacity; it was all corked, but like a cork leaking under pressure of fizzing elements. For a moment Liz's heart had leaped, thinking Nature had sent her a little sister; but then she'd had to quiet herself with the realisation it was impossible.

Maggie hadn't got a clue! And that made her a danger. One voice inside Liz told her to have nothing to do with the girl Ash had sent her; but another part of her had spoken up, and yes, she'd seen the fine qualities in Maggie; and didn't she herself have a need of at least someone?

A little sister, to make the pass? No, Maggie wouldn't do for that. But for Liz, there were no others of potential in sight. Not a one. And there was no greater crime, no uglier sin than to go to the grave without having passed on *the know*. This was sacred when all things were profane, and as Liz knew in her aching limbs and in the groaning of her joints, every day the Old Enemy came ever nearer. No, Maggie could not be the one to take the pass, but there were other possibilities. The next best thing was to give her a bit of instruction. It wasn't enough, it wouldn't satisfy, but what else was there?

Liz was eighty-three years old. She didn't want to guess how many more years might be hers. But it had gnawed at her for a long time now that she might die never having found a little sister. Was it a punishment, she wondered, for the misdemeanours of her early years? She would rather have faced the torments of any Christian hell than allow that to happen.

So when Maggie had first appeared, Liz saw a rightness in it, a compromise, and also a sign that she herself was not much longer for this world, and she resigned herself to the idea. But then the shadow had crept over Maggie, and Liz had begun to have her doubts. *The know* was for those who struggle with purity of heart. Wasn't that how she'd been taught? The craft was not to be sullied by sourness of motive. Even with right intention, the path was fraught and dangerous.

But thankfully she was able to see past Maggie. Past and beyond. There was hope, like a crystal glimmering in the shadows, and Liz could see it.

'Come out, felon herb!'

Liz found a young plant under the hedgerow. It was leaning north-wards, and this had her nodding with satisfaction. She drew a penknife from her pocket and unearthed the mugwort by the root. Then she sat down on the grass.

It was still early. The grey clouds were streaked with bands of white light, and the day could go either way. Liz stripped the fibrous roots from the plant with her knife and cleaned the stem with her spittle. Then she took a small vial of oil from her pocket. She poured the yellow oil on to the stem, massaging it into the stem with her fingers. The stem turned brown and the sap bubbled to the surface. Liz looked about her to make certain no one was watching, and kicked off her shoes.

She cut a chunk of the stem with a knife and put it in her mouth, chewing vigorously while removing her thick socks. Still chewing, she stripped the leaves and rubbed them into the soles of her feet. When this was done she stuffed the crushed leaves into her shoes, saving a few which she rammed into her pocket. Then she put her shoes and socks back on again, stood up and set off again.

Maggie arrived at Liz's cottage at around ten o'clock. She pushed at the door handle, expecting it to swing open, but was surprised to find the door locked. Liz's collie was already barking at her from behind the door, but she knocked anyway. There was no answer.

Odd that Liz should have locked her door; Liz *never* locked her door. Even when she went out on one of her walks across the fields, she tended to leave it ajar. She had no fear of burglars or intruders, and, as she said herself, she had 'nothing worth pinching'. Maggie knocked again. Getting no response, she stepped over to the window to take a peek inside.

It had been inconvenient for her to visit Liz this morning. The old woman had insisted that she shouldn't bring the children with her, and this had necessitated a telephone conversation with Alex to change the standing arrangement. Since the custody hearing, Maggie had been stiff and formal with Alex, collecting and returning the children exactly as agreed, even though Alex claimed to want to be generous and flexible with the arrangement.

Alex, of course, now wanted them to be friends. He wanted everything to be civilised. Whenever she called at the house, Maggie accepted his invitations to have a coffee, but thwarted his efforts at conversation with the frozen hostility of perfect good manners. She answered his questions with the briefest of replies and deliberately failed to pose any of her own. She would look at her watch intermittently, and made transparent excuses in order to leave. She played the part of the stranger who disguises boredom with studied politesse.

Today she'd had to break the formality by asking Alex if he would agree to changing her day with the children. Even though he'd arranged to see Anita, Alex was perfectly amenable. He was happy, he said, for Maggie to see the children any time she wanted.

Now Liz wasn't there. Maggie squinted through the windows at the gloomy interior of the cottage. Her first thought was that Liz was ill, but Maggie could see her empty bed in the room adjacent to the kitchen, its crocheted blankets folded neatly. Liz never used the upper floor of the cottage; she slept in a bed downstairs to save her arthritic legs.

The dog continued to bark. No, Liz was out. Maggie went back to her car. She would sit and wait. Liz had no transport, she couldn't have gone far.

When Anita Suzman drove past the Sanders' home that morning she was disappointed to see Amy, Sam and Dot playing in the driveway. Saturday was Maggie's time with the children; Anita had arranged to spend an uncluttered hour or two with Alex. But she was also puzzled to see an old woman, apparently watching the children from the gateway. As she drove past, she felt an irrational thrill of concern for the children. Something seemed amiss.

Anita was discreet enough always to park her conspicuous bright red Cabriolet two streets away. She locked her car and walked back to the house. As she approached, she could see the old woman still in the gateway. Anita hung back to watch.

The grizzled old woman was beckoning to Sam. He didn't seem to want to go at first, then he stepped over to her. Amy and Dot had disappeared. The old woman stooped over Sam. She had her hands on his shoulders, and was whispering in his ear. Then she produced something from the folds of her black skirts and hung it round Sam's neck. Sam tried to lift it off, but she pressed it back on him, hiding it inside his T-shirt.

Anita didn't like the look of what was happening. She walked towards the gate, quickening her pace. When the old woman saw her approaching, she stiffened and walked away smartly in the opposite direction. Anita watched her turn a corner out of sight.

'Sam, come here.'

Sam was playing with the string round his neck. Anita pulled it from inside his T-shirt. Dangling from the grey string was a neat little cloth sachet. Anita stretched out a hand, wanting to take a closer look, but Sam pulled away from her. 'Amy!' he shouted, running back up the path in search of his sister. 'Amy!'

Anita followed him round to the back of the house, and stepped in through the back door. She found Alex up to his elbows in washing-up suds. She brushed her lips against his cheek.

'Who was that old woman outside?'

'What woman?' said Alex, drying his hands.

'Outside the gate. Talking to Sam.' She went through to the lounge and made herself at home.

'I've no idea. Shall I go and look?'

'She's gone. I think I chased her away.'

'What was she doing?'

Anita never answered because the telephone rang. It was Maggie. She'd discovered she wasn't as busy as she'd expected, and wanted to know if she could have the kids after all.

'Sure,' said Alex. 'No problem at all. When do you want to pick them up? About an hour? Fine. See you then.' He put the phone down. 'That bitch is playing games with me.'

'Why do you say that?' The old woman was forgotten.

'First she arranges to have the children today, which is why I said I could see you. Then she phones this morning, desperately sorry, can't have them. Now she wants them again. She's testing my patience.'

'I'm sure she's not, Alex.'

'Yes, she is. Every time she comes here she does it. Very polite. Nothing to say. No emotion. No talk. Nothing.'

'What do you expect? She's still furious with you, and I don't blame her.'

Alex looked at her. No matter what time of day it was, Anita always looked as if she was about to hit town. She wore a tight-fitting black dress, black tights and heels. Her lips were glossed and her eyes painted. She was utterly desirable. He put a hand into her honey-blonde hair and kissed her.

'You can hide upstairs when she comes,' he said.

'No, I'm not staying. That's what I've come to talk to you about.'

'What are you saying?'

'It's over. It has to be.'

Alex looked away.

'Bill suspects something,' Anita went on, 'and I think we should quit while we're ahead. Anyway, you know it was running out of steam, don't say it wasn't.'

Alex wasn't saying anything.

'It was good while it lasted, Alex. It was good, wasn't it? Wasn't it, Alex?'

36

Sunday morning Maggie was back at her bedsit. She was lying awake in bed, staring at the ceiling and thinking about Ash. The previous day, after failing to find Liz, she'd spent a few hours with the children before returning to Ash's house. There she'd made a big mistake.

'Ash, I intend to get my children back by any means.'

'Please! Not again, Maggie.'

'By any means.'

Ash was making her a casserole. He stopped chopping vegetables. 'I can't argue with you while I'm cooking. All that confusion, it goes straight into the cooking. And then you eat it. Did you know that?'

Maggie knew that. 'You said to me you'd be a friend whatever happened, Ash. I believed you when you said that.'

'And I meant it. And I always will. But to be a friend to you now is to tell you to drop this stupid idea. These methods will not bring your children back to you. They will only poison your own mind. If you want them back, you have to go and talk to Alex and work at it.'

'I can't believe I'm hearing this!'

'Maggie, if you try to work something against Alex you might even succeed in hurting him. But you've forgotten the first principles of this business. It's *wrong path*. It will return on you threefold. I believe that. It's the scariest thing about it.'

'I don't intend any direct harm.'

'I know exactly what you intend! You want to try this shapeshifting because you think it will bring you access to the children and some kind of special influence over them. I've been to the places your mind is going, Maggie! I know what I'm talking about!' Ash collected up the chopped vegetables and threw them all away. The dinner was ruined before it had even started cooking.

'It can't hurt anyone, Ash. I'm going to ask you one more time to help me.'

'Are you deaf?'

'I need your help. Please don't let me down when I need you most.'

'I said count me out!'

'Ash, if you're not with me, you're against me.'

Ash looked stung. He stopped clearing things away and grabbed her arm. 'Don't try to lay that on me, Maggie. Don't you ever!'

It was their first dispute, and it was deeply acrimonious. She felt betrayed.

The door swung open and Kate entered the room. She was holding a copy of the *Sunday World*, a tabloid with a nasty reputation and a high circulation. 'Have you seen this?' Kate hissed.

Maggie sat up in bed as Kate laid the pages before her. It was a double-page spread, with a banner headline trumpeting COVENS OF ENGLAND. There was a large photograph of a smiling, pleasant but dotty-looking elderly woman in a Queen of the Nile headdress. She claimed to be – or the newspaper proclaimed her to be – Empress of the Witches of England. There were other photographs. One of them clearly depicted Maggie and Ash frolicking naked within a stone circle. Maggie was named, Ash was named, and Ash's shop in the Gilded Arcade was named.

'But where did they get the pictures?' Kate wanted to know.

Maggie groaned.

37

Spring solstice, 21 March, a Monday morning. Alex was trying to get the children ready for school and childminder, chivvying, coaxing, bullying, rummaging for clean clothes which weren't there because he hadn't washed them, dishing up a dog's breakfast because he hadn't shopped for a week, trying to let the real dog out and bring the milk in, to iron a blouse for Amy, pour a mug of tea for himself, find the minder's overdue cash, locate Amy's schoolbook which she couldn't go without . . .

Alex wasn't coping.

Anita had had enough of him. Tania, tired of playing the surrogate mother, had refused to help him all weekend. And the children's real mother had deserted him.

Maggie! Where are you, Maggie? For God's sake, Maggie!

Sam was being a brat, refusing to get out of his pyjamas, shouting and standing on a stool pressing the timer pads on the microwave oven. Alex could have cheerfully shut him inside it and switched to hi-power. Instead he dragged him off the stool and gave him a vicious slap across the leg. Sam started howling.

'Shut that before I really give you something to cry about,' Alex growled. Sam obviously thought he'd already got something to cry about, because he didn't let up. Alex grabbed a pullover and took off Sam's pyjamas.

'What's this?' he demanded, seeing for the first time the new, blue sachet hanging on a grey string round Sam's neck. 'Did your mother put this dirty thing on you?'

'Noooooo hoooo hooo,' howled Sam.

Alex showed him the back of his hand. 'What have I told you

about telling me lies? What have I told you?'

'Noooooohooo, she didn't.'

'What? I said did your mother?'

'She didn't,' said Amy.

'You shut up,' said Alex sharply, and Amy shut up.

'Noooo,' wailed Sam, and then, seeing no way of avoiding another slap, wailed, 'yes, noooooo, yes.'

Alex pulled the string over Sam's head and tossed the sachet into the rubbish bin. Amy went to retrieve it until Alex shoved her roughly out of the kitchen. 'Leave the filthy thing where it is. Go and get dressed before you get the next slap.'

So Amy started crying too, and Dot came back in barking furiously at Alex, until Alex kicked her and she went whimpering into the garden. Alex looked around him at the detritus. The breakfast room was like a disaster area. He surveyed the failed breakfast and the piles of dirty laundry and his wailing children looking back at him through tears, and he felt like crying himself.

'Maggie,' he said softly, 'Maggie.'

Spring solstice, and Maggie was preparing. She was careful to combine all the elements of magic she'd learned with some she didn't understand. She was confused about the significance of planetary alignment (something Liz dismissed with a gesture), but with Venus exalted in Taurus, she blindly hoped this would offset her malefic intention.

For she admitted malefic intention. She wanted possession of her children, by any means. She wanted unhappiness and disgrace to fall on her husband. She believed that the rite of *shapeshifting* would confer on her the power to achieve these things.

After reading about herself in the newspaper, she'd returned to Liz's cottage. The old woman was again sharpening knives on the doorstep. Liz had been evasive about where she'd been the day before, saying only that she'd had an 'errand' to run, something that couldn't be neglected. She had also seemed unwilling to let Maggie cross the threshold. She didn't want her in the house. It wasn't that she was in any way unfriendly; she just whistled up her collie and insisted that they go for a 'blow' across the fields.

'Are you going to tell me what's to be done, or am I going to have to go it alone?' Maggie asked her, fearing further evasion.

'Oh, I'll tell you,' Liz said, hobbling along the grass pathway with her stick. She said her feet were bad from having walked a 'step'. 'Because it's in you, and it wants out, so we must have it. And it might be the only way.'

'What do you mean, the only way?'

But Liz only pointed with her stick to a bush in the hedgerow. 'Mistletoe, in flower. Cut a piece; you'll need some.'

Maggie got that and other more complicated instructions, plus a new *oleum magicale*, different to the flying ointment.

On the way back from visiting Liz, she called on Ash to show him the newspaper. He held his head in his hands.

'I'm sorry, Ash; I've brought this on you.'

'No, you haven't,' he said. 'No, you haven't.'

She returned to her bedsit, going to bed without eating. Liz had told her that the rite of *shapeshifting* required lengthy preparation and that she should fast for twenty-four hours.

Alex eventually dropped Amy at school and Sam at the childminder's. He arrived late at the site to find everyone in a state of excitement. There had been a spectacular find under the pentagram.

Tania and her crew had cleared the area of the staked circle. Initially the area close to the circumference of the circle had yielded nothing. But towards the centre, by working more boldly across the diameter of the circle, they found what for some days now everyone had expected. It fulfilled certain fantasies of the type Alex had tried to suppress. They'd discovered human remains. First to come to light was a rib cage.

Everyone stopped working on the main dig and either joined the effort or stood around watching.

The archaeologists worked sideways, sweeping across from the rib cage, to mark the parameters of the find. Most of the skeleton was still firmly embedded in the earth. They dusted off extruding shoulder and knee bones. It was small enough to seem obvious what they were dealing with.

It was a child. The words swept around the group. *A child.*

Alex made them slow down the operation. There was too much

excitement about the find, and he was afraid clumsy strokes might break up the skeletal pieces. He got everyone working with fine brushes. Those involved looked more like they were painting the bones than excavating them. Soon the watchers grew bored at the slow rate the thing was surfacing, and went back to their own jobs.

The bones got nicknamed Minnie.

Alex supervised, fussily. By lunchtime they had exposed the entire flank of the rib cage, and Alex began to have his doubts. The rib cage was too large to have been a child's, and he said so. There was something unnatural about the position in which other bones were coming to light. They were compressed into an extreme foetal position. The thigh bone was drawn up, and the skull, which they had just begun to touch, seemed slumped forward.

'I want an exact record of the position in which the skeleton is found. There's something odd about it. Go extra careful, please, this is not a sprint to the finish.'

They proceeded now to work across the top of the remains, so as not to disturb the earth on which the bones rested.

Spring solstice and Ash, as usual, took the lift to the fourth floor of the Gilded Arcade. On stepping out of the lift he realised some sort of commotion was going on outside Omega. There was a picket.

About nine ladies of pensionable age and a sad, solitary-looking gentleman in a dark suit crowded the doorway of his shop. Some held placards. One proclaimed NOT IN OUR CITY. Their chatter generated a hubbub of excitement.

'Morning, ladies! Morning, sir!' Ash called cheerfully, gently shouldering his way through the white-haired scrum. The hubbub stopped. They moved aside for him and stood in a silent half-circle, watching as he took out his keys. No one said anything. Their eyes raked him from head to toe, looking for the mark of the beast. At last Ash had the door open. He turned before going inside. 'Bit of rain in the air,' he said.

A tall woman with white cropped hair stepped forward. She had the spark of the mad evangelist in her eye. She carried a placard which read LEST YE FORGET. Ash, at least, couldn't remember the reference. 'Satanist!' she said.

Ash smiled pleasantly. 'Please. If you're going to call me names, can't you find some accurate ones?' He stepped inside and closed the door behind him.

Maggie spent the day preparing. She fasted, meditated, repeated her mantras, sipped water, brought her purpose to mind. She had decided that, when the time came, she would go out to Osier's Wood. She would have preferred to conduct the business within the safety of Ash's house, or even at her own bedsit, but she knew it wasn't possible. The woods had been the place where she'd had her first real scent of the possibilities within her; her first encounter with the spirit of the goddess. Her room constrained her; it had neither power nor resonance.

Hecate was choosy. Hecate was careful. Hecate preferred the seclusion and deep mystery of the woods.

At noon Maggie lit candles and incense and repeated the banishing ritual she had employed when flying with Ash. It had protected her then. She would repeat it again at dusk, when the moment was right.

She practised mental projection of the things she expected to happen, exactly as Liz had told her.

At one o'clock she practised relaxation and breathing exercises.

At two o'clock she drank a little saline water and gathered together everything she would need. Before leaving, she concocted her 'listening' brew, and filled a thermos flask. She climbed into her car and drove out to the woods.

It was a dry, sunny day, warm for the time of year. She parked her car at a distance of half a mile from the woods and walked the rest of the way.

Deep in the woods, she found her spot, the hidden place she had discovered before, the tree-ringed tiny glade where Hecate had made her presence felt. She still had three hours before dusk. She settled down and spent half an hour practising her visualisation exercises. Then she opened her flask and inhaled the listening brew. She felt relaxed, and sat back to listen to the sound of the wind in the trees.

Alex had ordered a U-shaped trench to be dug round the skeleton so that it could be worked on from three sides. Now the bones stood out on a promontory of earth, a bed attended by a team working in hushed concentration. Something other than a dig now, the enterprise had become an operation of delicate flensing of the earth around and between the bones.

It had become clear that Minnie was not an infant or a child after all. It was an adult of small stature, whose awkward burial posture was due to having been squeezed into an unnaturally small space.

'Stop!' said Alex.

They all stopped.

'What is it?' asked Tania.

'What's up?' said Richard.

Alex stroked an imaginary beard and looked hard at the earth on one side of the remains. Then he walked round the other side, crouched, touched the soil and then straightened up. 'Carry on,' he said.

The delicate flensing resumed. Alex had an irritating habit of letting ideas boil inside his head. He distracted everyone by jogging from side to side, getting in close, stopping individuals with a gesture and then retiring without a word.

'Shit!' he said. 'Stop! Everybody stop!'

Everyone let their brushes and implements hang at their sides. Alex got in close, eyeballing the earth near the still-covered skull.

Tania exploded on everyone's behalf. 'For Christ's sake, Alex!'

Alex rubbed sweat from his eyes. 'It's not your fault, it's my fault.'

'WHAT isn't our fault?'

'Just nobody touch anything for a moment.' He folded his arms and stared at the trench. Tania turned away and mouthed silent words at the sky. He saw her. 'Come here. What's this?'

He pointed at the earth below the back of the skull. Tania got in close, everyone else huddled behind her. 'I don't see anything.'

'Exactly.'

'What do you mean, "exactly"?'

'I mean you can't see anything, but I can. I should have seen it before. See this ragged pattern in the soil? The dark stain? It's the imprint left by rough-grained wood. Packed hard against the earth, see? Where wood has rotted and compacted into the soil. Everywhere else it's been broken up by worms and the like. But not here. Or here. And we've been so eager to get at the old bones we've ruined any traces of whatever it was buried in.'

'Is that a tragedy?' said Tania.

Alex looked at her as though she were a child. 'Minnie here was a full-grown adult squeezed into a small box. Some information about the box would have helped.'

'We haven't disturbed the area behind the skull,' Richard put in. 'Or underneath. That might turn up some information.'

'Let's hope so,' Alex said glumly. It was true. He should have known better.

By late afternoon, another discovery was made. The set of bones was missing its left hand. Attention turned to the other side to reveal the right hand was also missing. The two feet had also been amputated before burial. They'd each been lopped off with blade strokes that cleanly severed bone.

At Omega, Ash was vainly trying to maintain an attitude of business as usual. It was difficult. The evangelists took it in turn to press their noses up against the window to see what he was doing. He was writing in a ledger, and this was clearly causing speculation outside. He deliberately affected a demonic grin, and made a great show of dipping his pen in the veins of his forearm; but he was actually preparing no more than his accounts.

Lunchtime had come and gone and not a single customer had passed through the picket. Then in the afternoon a young man braved the storm. He was so enthusiastically received by Ash that he went out and came in again.

Ash didn't know whether to close up and go home or grit his teeth and stay on. He thought that closing would be giving in to them; on the other hand, by staying open he was only playing their game. By late afternoon he'd decided to close early, but to confuse them by leaving the window blinds up and the sign declaring the shop open.

He came out jangling his keys and the picket parted.

'Excuse me! Excuse me!' It was a rather elderly lady addressing him, a woman with a heavy overcoat and a sweet, round face. 'Would you be good enough to tell us if you're closing now, because we don't want to wait here unnecessarily.'

Ash was astonished. Then he laughed out loud.

'Well, we can be civilised about it, can't we?' she said.

Ash was about to reply when he noticed a silver brooch lying at her feet. He picked it up. 'Is this yours?'

The old woman was taken aback. Then she smiled at him and gently rested a hand on his arm. 'Do you know, my husband gave me that before he died. I must have dropped it and I'd have been heartbroken if I'd lost it. Heartbroken.' She was beaming at him.

Ash pinned it back on her coat. Well, at least one of them didn't hate him.

The tall woman, 'Lest Ye Forget', stepped forward. 'You want to throw that brooch away, Mary, now he's touched it. It's tainted. You want nothing to do with it.'

Ash saw the sweet smile die on the other lady's face. He saw her look from him to the interlocutor, and to the brooch. He saw a tear begin to form in her eye and he was outraged. He stepped towards the tall woman. 'You,' he said. 'You'd have been there, wouldn't you? Cheering them on at the hangings and the burnings. It's how people like you enjoy yourself. You'd have been at the front of the queue!'

Ash marched off along the catwalk, watched all the way by the silent picket.

Maggie had cleared an area to make a small, smoky fire, as she'd been instructed. Liz had told her to study the smoke from the fire before beginning the ritual. She followed this with a relaxation exercise, before commencing her serious preparation.

She unzipped and emptied her bag. First she laid out her circle with the long length of white rope, leaving the ends open so that she could enter when the time was right.

She lit incense and repeated her banishing ritual.

Outside the circle she marked the four points of the compass. At north, at the station of Earth, she deposited a handful of soil she'd brought from the site of the Dancing Ladies, and she spoke the name of Uriel. South of the circle, at the station of Fire, she set a beeswax candle in a ceramic wind-protector. She lit the candle and invoked the name of Michael.

At the station of Water, at the eastern point, she set a jar of rain-water, earlier consecrated with salt. Here she spoke the name of Gabriel. The last point, on the western side of the circle, was the station of Air.

Here she placed a sprig of mistletoe in flower. Liz had told her that the seasonal fruit of the mistletoe was preferred, but that if Maggie insisted on this particular time, then the mistletoe in flower would have to suffice. It was dedicated to Raphael.

She still had an hour or so before dusk. She sipped a little wine in which mistletoe had been steeped, and waited.

It was approaching five o'clock at the site of the Maggie dig, and every-one wanted to stay on. After discovering the absence of hands and feet on the skeleton, they'd pressed on to reveal that some kind of device was attached to the skull. Alex held up that part of the operation so that he might record the exact position in which it lay. Having done so, he was ready to give permission for them to uncover the device.

He was as eager as everyone else to stay on and work in the dark if necessary. But he had a problem.

'No, I won't,' said Tania. 'I'm not missing this. What do you take me for anyway?' She thought Alex was just using her.

'No, I can't,' said his childminder when he telephoned. She thought it was high time Alex faced up to his responsibilities.

'No, I'm sorry,' said Anita, when she too received his telephone call. She thought it was Alex's way of trying to rekindle things.

'Not even for old times' sake?' he pleaded.

'Especially not for old times' sake. Have to go; Bill's due back.'

Amy had already been picked up from school by the childminder and was waiting to be collected along with Sam. That was the arrangement. Alex was running out of options. In desperation he tried to ring Maggie. First he rang the telephone in the hall of her bedsit. Someone answered but told him Maggie was out. Then he looked up the number for Omega in the Gilded Arcade. There was no reply.

He went back to Tania.

'No, Alex. Absolutely not.'

He drew her away from the others. 'Please, Tania. I'm going to make a big media buzz out of this and I promise I'll tell them it was your dig. You'll get a job somewhere on the back of this. It'll look good for you. Think about it. Please help me out.'

'I don't need this pressure, Alex.'

'Please. I'll never ask you again.' He held out the keys to his car. Tania looked back at the dig, and then at Alex. Her cheeks were burning. She snatched the keys from him.

'This is absolutely the last time.' She was already marching away across the grass.

'You're a life-saver!'

'Fuck off, Alex,' she shouted over her shoulder.

He turned back to his skull, rubbing his hands together in satisfaction.

Tania collected Amy and Sam from the childminder and drove them back to the house. At least she knew they'd become fond of her, and were better behaved for her than ever they were for Alex.

'Can we have Cowboy's Glory?' Amy said, climbing out of the car.

'Yes, you can have Cowboy's Glory.' Tania was too goodnatured to dump her anger on the kids. So she opened cans and knocked out rounds of beans on toast. When they'd finished eating, she sent them off to play so she could get on with some clearing up. The house was a shambles. Sam reluctantly followed Amy down into the playroom.

Liz stood on the doorstep of her cottage. She was chewing something. Chewing, and staring out across the fields into the gathering dusk. The cottage door was flung wide open. Behind her, the old collie sat whimpering. Liz turned slowly, and silenced the dog with a look.

She was afraid for them. She'd worn herself out walking that great distance to the Sanders' house on Saturday, and then back again. It was too much at her age. She'd done her best to help Sam. But she'd been disturbed by the arrival of Alex's lover. That had been unfortunate. She just hoped that she'd done enough.

Liz turned her attention back to the grey horizon, across the fields, and to the graded advance of dusk.

Dusk came into the woods with stealth, insinuating itself into the smoke of her small fire. Maggie tied back her hair, slipped off her clothes and stepped inside the rope, closing the circle behind her. It was cold, as she'd anticipated. In preference to the hogsfat mentioned in Bella's diary, she rubbed herself with an embrocation fluid, which numbed as well as warmed her. Liz had sanctioned this variation.

She performed her banishing ritual for the third and final time.

She unstoppered her new *oleum magicale*. It was filmier than the flying ointment, more opaque, highly scented with sandalwood and wisteria. She applied it to her body as before, to her temples, wrists, ankles, glandular points, intra-vaginally; but also a smear under her eyes, and a single drop on her tongue. Already the oil on her face stung her eyes. On contact with her skin it released strong vapours. She was forced to close her watering eyes as a bitter, acrid taste spread over her tongue, numbing her mouth and depositing a pellet of bile in her throat.

She struggled to open her eyes against the vapours. She needed to stay alert to what was happening in the physical world around her. Liz had told her that she must respond to the first thing to appear.

'What if nothing comes?' she'd asked.

'It will,' Liz had said. 'It will.'

It could be an adder. It could be a bird. She would know when it approached the circle. But it would not enter the circle until she invited it in. She forced her eyes open against stinging tears. She waited, gazing at the smoke from her small fire as Liz had instructed her, visualising forms rising from the smoke, weaving smoke and dusk into a single grey tapestry.

The most hideous feature of the discovery was not the amputation of limbs, but what was strapped to the skull's head.

Alex had decided to get the generator going and fix up a floodlight before allowing any more progress on the excavation. When everything was set up, they had returned to exposing the back of the skull and discovered the brank – a metal cap, fitting like a cage across the skull and face, with a cruel spike protruding from the brank into the open mouth. A V-shaped lip extruded a few inches from the brank at the other end of the spike.

With the skull itself half-bedded in the earth, Alex crouched down to take a close look. He'd seen a brank before, but not one quite so vicious as this. The floodlight scored stiff shadows on the white skull behind the bars of the brank.

'What's it for?' someone asked him.

'For keeping the victim quiet, I should think.'

Turquoise light. Everywhere, turquoise light, shot through with deep blue veins. Maggie's heart hammered. A numbness coursed through her body, leaving only the sensation of a thrumming heart. Her body was anaesthetised but her senses were alert. She had to keep her head still; any swift movement brought hot knives of pain to the frontal lobes. Despite the ethereal light she could see every leaf, every branch, each blade of grass with absolute clarity. The details took on an artificial, plastic quality, an imprint of a design, as if placed there by some unseen hand; but her eyes had been sharpened to the uniqueness of each leaf, each fern and log.

Waves. The woods were subjected to a gentle swell and fall like waves, a swell and fall she took to be the rhythm of her own breathing. The waves rippled in sympathy with her, as if part of her; she could no longer feel the extremities of her physical form. Her sensations extended as far as the range of her vision. She was what she could see. If an upper branch swayed in the wind, she felt the movement deep in her bowels. If a fern moved in a breeze, she felt a string drawn through her heart. The rotting of a log she felt as an infinitely slow burn somewhere inside her.

The upper fronds of the closest ferns waved, and she felt a slow, sinuous progress along the earth towards her. A cold underbelly pressed to the leaf mould, moving closer. A sinuous rippling through the dead leaves. Would this be it? The first thing, Liz had said, the very first thing. The slippery, gliding sensation continued through the ferns, moving closer to the rope circle. Then it stopped, suddenly.

It had been beaten. Something else had alighted outside the circle ahead of it.

It was a bird. A blackbird, but seeming brilliant blue in the turquoise light. Sleek feathers, still moist from the day the world was first made. It had stopped at the edge of the circle, head cocked, looking at her, eye to eye. Maggie knew this creature. She'd known it for a long time.

'Come in,' she said.

The bird hopped inside the circle.

222

Maggie felt an unexpected wave of sadness inside her, and a hot, salt tear squeezed from her left eye, nestling on her cheek. She could see the moisture there, lensing turquoise light. The bird flew at her, hovering near, wings vibrating the air and fanning a wind at her face; beak dangerously close to her eye, it dipped and sucked the teardrop into its beak. Then it was gone.

Maggie stood up and looked around her, around the circle. The objects she had placed outside the circle remained in place, but there was no bird. It had gone, and with it, she thought, her chance. She felt unsteady on her feet, so she crouched down again, her knees drawn up to her ears.

She felt a scorching pain inside her and had to spit a string of black bile from her mouth. Then a pain, of the type she'd not experienced since the birth of her son. She found she could relieve the pain by puffing her rib cage up and out and forcing her arms behind her back. Her body trembled violently. Sweat broke out on her brow and she couldn't stop the shivering. She puffed her chest out again and hawked another string of blue-black bile from her throat.

Then vomit. She was panting uncontrollably. Her chin retracted into her neck and she lost its shape. Her breathing was being constricted. She hawked again, trying to loosen the sensation of choking. She felt her feet scrabbling claw-like in the soft earth, trying to keep a foothold as her body convulsed. Suddenly she couldn't breathe.

She panicked. She tried to shake her head out, shake it free of what was happening, but she was paralysed. She was retching. Spit; if only she could spit she might loosen what was choking her air passage. But in the effort of spitting, her mouth puckered and extended outwards, her nose curving into a sharp point.

It was too ugly. She shook in terror. Then she felt a series of clicks in her joints, a sound like the cracking and resetting of bones. Please stop! She wanted it to stop! She tried in vain to reverse what was happening to her by dint of mental power. She felt her heart sink inside her into a tight ball, threatening to burst. Blood sang in her ears. Her skin flushed from scalp to toe, gooseflesh standing high, rippling across her body in a wave. Blue-black feathers erupted from her white skin as she scrabbled in the earth to keep her balance. She was turning in circles now, struggling against the metamorphosis, gagging for air. Stop! Oh stop!

Her wish was granted. The process was arrested halfway. She sobbed in relief, breathing heavily now. She'd managed to stop it. Then she tried to straighten her back, but was unable. She strained, but the effort only produced a cracking of bones and sickening pain. She waited. Tried again. She was unable to move.

Panic took her again. Liz! Ash! She wanted to cry out but there was only a terrible gagging, and no one to answer. It wouldn't move forward, and she couldn't reverse it. She was stuck.

No air. A gagging in her throat. Her lungs compressed. Choking. Panic. She couldn't scream, she was unable to make any kind of noise.

Her eyes began to bleed. A jelly-like substance drew across them. She was choking. She was paralysed. She was going to die. Then she tried to relax. Think through what had happened. Think the process through from the beginning. She gave a final push, trying to heave herself into another world.

Only the brank was holding the skull in one piece. Alex identified a clasp at the side of the contraption, and attempted to clear the loose dirt from it with a fine hairbrush. The jaw of the skull gaped in a lopsided rictus. Alex put the brush aside, pursed his lips and blew delicately on the dust around the clasp. The metal cage of the brank fell apart. The lower jaw slipped from its bed of earth and bounced at the bottom of the trench, followed by half of the disintegrating brank.

Free. She was free. Free to fly in the turquoise light. Up, up, beyond the branches, above the trees. Into the ethereal light. There were two directions in which she could fly. The direction of space, of distance. And the direction of memory. She flew in the direction of memory.

Flying down the line. Down the ethereal light, turquoise yolk, unfolding, veined with brilliant blue. She flew into Far memory. Pain. Bella. Pain. A. Pain. Dark Sister. Understanding. The long line, understanding.

Far memory. Far memory. Far memory.

And returned. Flying now in the direction of distance. Ordinary blue

space. Trees. Road. Cottages. Swoop on cottage – no, not there. Trees.
Road. City. Castle – no, not there. Trees. Road. City. House. Find.
  Far flying. Far flying. Far flying.

38

Amy sat at her desk in the cellar, colouring by numbers; Sam was placing his soldiers and toy motors in a long procession, yard-long plastic trucks lining up behind a tailback of matchbox-sized models, with no sign of impatience. He played in his own world, happily naked but for a soiled white vest. The cellar playroom had one high window, looking out at ground level. Something brushed against it and Amy looked up.

Dusk was yielding to darkness outside, a preternatural light, colour-sucking. Amy turned to look at Sam, still intent on his serpentine procession of toys and tiny figures. An old woman stood over him.

Amy had never seen her before but felt she knew the old woman. She was very old. She was dressed in black. Long skirts. Strange garments. Amy froze. She felt a cold wave peel her flesh open like a fruit. The old woman became aware of Amy's eyes on her. She turned her head slowly and mouthed silent words at Amy: *stay back*. Her eyes were like the grey smoke Amy had seen coiling from a garden bonfire. They had fire in them, and imminent flame. The old woman turned back to Sam.

Amy slipped her hand into her pocket.

Sam looked up from his snaking procession of toys and saw his mother standing over him. He smiled at her. She smiled back.

'Sam,' said Maggie, 'listen to me. Tell Amy to go away. Tell her, Sam.'

Sam looked over at his sister. She was staring at them. There was something wrong with her. She was shrunk back against the desk. Her skin was white, all colour drained from her cheeks. She looked sickly. She held her fist clenched tightly in her pocket.

'Tell her,' Maggie said softly, smiling at him. 'Tell her to go away.'

Sam went back to extending his carnival procession. 'Amy, you have to go upstairs,' he said without interest.

'No,' Amy said, so sharply that Sam looked up at her again.

'Listen to me, Sam,' Maggie whispered, but with more urgency. 'Sam. Sam. Tell your sister to get out of this room. Tell her to get out.'

'I told her.'

'Well, tell her again!' Sam looked at his mother. She wasn't smiling any more. Her faced seemed cracked, like a cheap mask. Then she smiled at him again and everything seemed all right. 'Sam. Tell her again!'

Amy darted up behind Sam and hung something round his neck. It was the herbal sachet Liz had made and given him and his father had torn from him; Amy had retrieved it from the bin.

The old woman rounded on Amy. She mouthed words, but seemed to have difficulty speaking. But her intention was clear. 'Take it away from him!'

Amy cowered behind her brother. 'No.'

Sam was confused. He couldn't understand why Amy seemed so afraid or why his mother was screaming at her. He looked back at Maggie again. She smiled at him. 'Sam, you don't want that dirty thing round your neck. Take it off.'

Sam fingered the string.

'No,' Amy shouted.

'Yes, take if off, Sam. And then you can come with me.'

'Where?'

'Anywhere you want, Sam. But take it off.'

Sam took the string with the sachet from round his neck and offered it to his mother. She stepped back. 'Just throw it aside. That's all you have to do.' He let it fall to the floor. Maggie held out her hands to him.

Amy saw the old woman with her arms outstretched. She could see that Sam was going to her. She picked up the discarded sachet.

The old woman turned her head again, slowly, towards Amy. Her eyes were bitter grey smoke, full of loathing. She shook her head from side to side. Amy flung the sachet in her face, and the old woman disappeared.

'Where did Mummy go?' said Sam.

The playroom was silent. There was nothing. They looked at the desk where Amy had been sitting, her colouring-by-numbers exercise uncompleted. They looked at Sam's procession winding across the floor.

A snake was in its place. A fat, bloated, glistening serpent, with adder markings, its tongue flickering lazily. They backed away.

'Over here!' said a voice. The children wheeled round and crashed into the old woman, who had been standing immediately behind them.

This time Sam saw her exactly as Amy did. As he'd seen her before. Rider of rats. Stealer of dolls. Walker on air. The old woman in black, only now she held a tiny blade, a silver knife angled towards his genitals. Her eyes were smoke.

'All I want,' she said, struggling to speak against a hoarse, cracked voice, 'is my magic penny-purse. My moly-sack. My cursing pouch.'

Sam's hand went instinctively down to protect his wrinkled, little-boy scrotum. The old woman nodded slowly.

Then she leapt, grabbing and twisting his vest, easily lifting him in the air with one hand and slamming him against the wall. Sam screamed and kicked his feet, thrashing against the wall as she angled the wicked blade towards his genitals.

Amy, too, screamed, and inside her scream she heard Liz saying, Remember me, Amy, remember me.

The herb sachet lay discarded on the floor. Amy grabbed it and tore it open, flinging a shower of leaves in the air above the old woman's head. She exhaled a foul jet of air at Amy and dropped Sam to the floor. Then she turned to face Amy, bringing her blade round in a sweeping, slashing arc.

Remember me. Amy threw her head backwards, narrowly avoiding the blade. Then it happened.

Sam saw Amy grow to full adult height. Her body expanded and reset. Her face changed, and where Sam had seen his sister, now he saw Liz. The head Amy had flung back to escape the knife was now bearing down towards the old woman, tongue thrust forward, releasing a torrent of foul, watery substance at her. It was a jet stream of undigested beans, hard, white pellets travelling at bullet velocity, striking the old woman full in the face. The room trembled violently. There was a loud, painful ringing in Sam's ears. He put his hands over them and closed his eyes.

When he opened them again, Tania was picking him off the floor.

'What's all the screaming about?' she said. 'What's going on?'

Sam looked around him. Amy was standing close by, unhurt, looking at him strangely. She looked white-faced, but normal again. There was no sign of the old woman, or of Liz. Where they'd both seen a snake, now there were only toys again.

'Oh, for God's sake!' said Tania. She was looking at a pool of vomit on the floor. 'Come on then, which one of you's been sick?'

Sam looked at his sister. 'Amy,' he said.

39

The following morning at the site, Alex was confidently holding a press conference. The local media were out in force, along with a few representatives of the national press. A small battery of photographers and cameramen grouped themselves round the site of the Maggie dig.

Tania was still at his house looking after Sam and Amy, listening to Alex pontificate live on local radio. She'd stayed overnight when Alex had returned late, praising his acuity over the conduct of the dig, consoling him over the mishap with the skull. She was a capable ego-masseuse.

It was a school holiday, and Alex had promised Tania that Maggie would collect the children at nine thirty, and that she'd be able to join him at the site. It was now eleven thirty, and no sign of Maggie.

'Obviously the burial was ritual in nature,' Alex was saying on air, 'we just don't know what kind of ritual was involved.' He'd rounded off some of his vowels for radio and his voice indicated he was really rather pleased with himself. 'We can deduce that the victim was a woman by the nature of the skeletal remains.'

'And what is there to suggest the victim was alive at the time of burial?' the radio journalist wanted to know.

'The brank was a medieval device for keeping people quiet, silencing them. There was also a length of pipe that fitted into a breather hole attached to the burial casket. I think the victim was squeezed into a tiny box and cruelly kept alive by the breather pipe. Water could be trickled into the victim's throat by means of the pipe and this curious attachment to the brank, prolonging her agony. It's some kind of oubliette, designed to keep the victim alive, at least for a while.'

The journalist observed that this was a grisly find. Alex agreed that indeed it was. Tania, fidgeting in her chair, repeated the word oubliette

231

like a black curse. The news report moved on to a feature about school dinners in the county.

She snapped off the radio. 'Thanks for not mentioning me,' she spat. 'Get your coats on, kids. We're going up to the castle.'

At the site, Alex was answering another journalist's questions. The reporter filled two and a half pages of his notepad and moved on. Tania arrived with Amy and Sam. Alex remembered he hadn't mentioned Tania in any of the publicity, as he'd promised.

'Hi!' he beamed. 'How are we doing?'

'You're a lying bastard,' said Tania.

'Don't start! Here, you can still get in on the act.'

Another man came up beside Alex and put his hand on his arm. It was a tall, bearded man with thinning hair.

'Can I have a word, Mr Sanders?'

'By all means. This is Tania. She's in charge of the dig. Which paper are you with?'

'I'm not with any paper. My name's Ash. Your wife's in hospital.'

Maggie had been found in the early hours of the morning, wandering naked along the fringes of Osier's Wood. She'd been reported by a passing motorist and picked up by the police, who'd taken her to the Royal Infirmary. Somehow they'd managed to get Ash's name and address out of her.

Ash drove Alex and the children to the hospital. He sat outside with Amy and Sam while Alex went in to see Maggie. Everyone was subdued.

Alex choked when he saw Maggie lying in bed. She had a bloodless pallor and a bruised look. She was heavily sedated. He laid his head on her breast and cried, and she ran her hand through his hair saying, 'It's all right. I'm all right. It's all right.'

'How did we let it get to this, Maggie. How did we? When we love each other.'

'It's all right. It's all right.'

Alex came out accompanied by a junior doctor fingering a paging device. Ash looked at the doctor, the children looked at Alex.

'She's dopey,' the doctor was explaining, 'because she's been injected with one hundred milligrams of Largactyl. It's a stiff dose. She may say a few strange things but she'll be passive.'

'Don't you want to keep her here? I mean for observation?'

'We'll arrange for your GP to make a domiciliary visit.' Alex didn't respond. 'Frankly,' said the medic, 'we need the beds.'

Ash stood up. 'Alex, it's time for you to take Maggie home with you.'

Alex was in a daze.

'And I don't mean just for today. I mean home for good.'

'Yes.'

'I'm very fond of Maggie. She's helped me. But I know what she needs. She wants her family back. She wants her home and her children. She's going to need help. A lot of space and a lot of love.'

'Yes.'

The nurses got Maggie ready, and Ash drove them all home. He pulled up outside the house and kept the engine running. 'You'll need to collect Maggie's things from the bedsit,' he said to Alex when they climbed out of his car.

Maggie turned. 'Ash . . .'

He wound his window down but the wink he gave was a mite too rapid. 'You'll be all right. Drop by the shop when you're feeling a bit better.'

Ash drove off.

40

Maggie did not get better easily. The family GP made his visit, concluded she was out of danger and left Alex with a further prescription for Largactyl tablets to be used if her behaviour became disturbed. She remained bedbound for several days, and even though there seemed little – at least outwardly – that ailed her, she showed no sign of wanting to come downstairs. Mostly she sat with a pillow propping up her head, her long, red hair combed in waves against the white slip either side of her, and stared at the wall.

Alex fussed, cupped her hands, talked to her softly, asked her if she wanted anything. She answered, faintly, always briefly, always offering up a weak smile, but she never wanted anything. She ate little. 'It's all right,' she said. 'It's all right.'

Alex took days off work, washed, cooked, kept the children in order, saw they were well turned out. Supervision of the dig had to be placed in the hands of a subordinate; care of Maggie was Alex's immediate priority. Anita and Bill Suzman visited and brought a ridiculously lavish bouquet of flowers and fruit. Kate from the bedsit came with a gift of an outrageous pair of dangling earrings to cheer her. Ash dropped by, and spent an hour holding her hand. But she had very little to say to any of them.

Worst of all was the lack of recognition she showed her children. There was no warmth, no affection, no interest, nothing. Alex tried to make them spend time in their mother's company, but it was pointless, even counterproductive. He stopped trying and simply made sure they kissed her goodnight each evening before going to bed, but even that was a mechanical act. Once she looked at Amy and recoiled slightly, but otherwise they were like strangers. Alex despaired.

The GP arranged a visit by a psychologist. He stayed for forty minutes, gave Alex some banner words like 'traumatic neurasthenia' to think about and prescribed a course of anti-depressants which came in pink and white capsules.

One evening when Alex was talking to her, she turned to him and said, 'Why do you call me Maggie? My name is Bella.' Alex was so astonished he simply stared at her, saying nothing. Her voice was changed, it was softer, wheedling. Bella. Bella. He suddenly remembered it was the name of the diarist.

'Where's your diary?' he asked.

'Hidden.'

He kissed her gently and closed the door behind him. He knew the diary wasn't hidden at all. It was among the things he'd recovered from her bedsit. He found it immediately, and sat down to read it before the open fire.

The pages were filled with entries he hadn't seen before. He thought they must be Maggie's work, though they were written in the same copperplate hand as the original entries. He leafed through, towards the end of the diary.

Now they are whispering about me. A. said it would come to this. All of them, even those I have helped. There's P.B. and R.S. and all I've to reckon with. This is how I am to be repaid.

Oh why did I not heed my dark sister?

It meant nothing to Alex. He turned over a page.

P.B. has lost her infant and puts it about that she must be over-looked and I'm the one. If this is gratitude. And all I did was to help this one and this other one. A. laughs in my face at that and tells me they will come for me. And yesterday a pantry window broken by lads hurling stones, and that no accident. A. says I must shift if I am to get a purchase on them, though that above all things makes me afraid down to my bowels that I lose my wits. What shall I therefore do?

I know I must hide this journal. Hide it, for it has all I know. For if they were to come and take this, then it would give them all they want, and there would be an end to it. I know a place where none will look, and I'll have a board made to keep it. Let them come and take me, they won't have this, for as long as this survives, I do too.

And then again:

Gerard come and he makes my board for me for the hearth, for he is a kind soul and I done this and that for him and all the children of his and he says he fears for me. He warns me they are after doing something, he has heard all the talk and they turn on any as try to speak up for me now. And he tells me it were better if I should go but where can I? At my age, and with what little I have, there is no place for me to go.

I have only this house and what little else besides.

Gerard tried to comfort me, but there's no comfort. I should have hearkened to A. who predicted all this, and never been a help to no one if this is how I am to be repaid. Where does all this hating one another come from?

And in the night I hear a scuffling and I come down to find a blaze in my hall. They have soaked a rag and pushed it through the letterflap and it catch at the curtains at the door and who knows what if I hadn't put it out. And what next?

Will they torch everything they don't understand? And is it because I know this and that one among them? That I know all their affairs and their transgressions and wrongdoings when they come here and tell me? Help me get with child by him, help me lose that child with that one. Is it because I know them all? When all I ever did was to be a soft bird among them with a brave heart, a blackbird, to help them along here and there. A. spat and call me a fool, and she tell me there is only one way out.

Tonight I'll go with A. and I'll shift, whatever the consequences.

There was one final entry in the journal. The fine copperplate writing was distended. There was a lack of the usual continuity. It suggested a note of hysteria in the diarist.

I have taste the flame
I have taste the flame and it burn my breath
It scorch away my words I have none No words
I have taste the flame

This was Bella's final entry in the journal. Only blank pages followed. There was no more information about her fate. Alex closed the diary and put it aside. He looked at the dull red fire shifting in the grate below the chimney where they'd first found the diary. It seemed to him a long time ago.

One day Maggie got out of her bed and came downstairs. Without saying a word she flung herself into housework, cleaning floors, washing clothes, wiping paintwork.

'You don't have to do that,' said Alex.

'I know, Alex. But I've got to do something to snap out of it. If I lie in bed any longer, I'll lose my mind.'

He nodded. At least it was a glimpse of the old Maggie; but she looked so frail and ill he just wanted her to rest.

'You've got work to do at the castle. Go back to your job, if you still have one. You've got a family to support.'

She made a show of eating again, though it was only a show; and Alex allowed himself to be persuaded to return to work. Maggie was still distant from her children, particularly Amy. Alex would catch her staring hard at them while they played or were occupied in some activity. He would distract her and she would come to with a start. But the children detected an unexpressed hostility in her, and kept their own distance.

'Nimble be Jack quick be Jack,' she murmured one time.

'Sorry?' said Alex.

'What?'

'Did you say something?'

'I don't think so.'

Maggie gazed into the fire. The children were in bed and Alex was beside her on the sofa.

Alex had been meaning to bring up an old question. There was something lying around the house which still bothered him. 'All those old herbs and things, Maggie. Maybe we should throw them out.'

Maggie jerked her head towards him. Her lip twisted and her face contorted into a sneer. She barked at him like a dog. 'SHE HASN'T GOT IT IN HER TO SUSPECT!' It was something he'd once said to Anita, but how could Maggie know? And then, barking still, 'GOOD, WASN'T IT, ALEX? WASN'T IT? WASN'T IT?' Her eyes blazed with fire and her face had distorted into something else, an old face. The voice was nothing like her own.

Alex looked at her in astonishment. Then her hand went to her mouth, and she was Maggie again.

'Maggie?'

She was trembling. 'Alex, I'm sorry, I don't know where these things come from. I swear it.'

But it wasn't like the first time, when Maggie had thought she was Bella, and had spoken in that gentle, wheedling voice. This was coarse and violent.

'Maggie, it's happened before.'

'I remember. It takes me over. Then I remember. Hold me, Alex.'

'You're not going to bark at me again?'

'Just hold me.'

But it happened at other times. In a rare moment Maggie was chatting playfully to Sam when suddenly she barked at him. 'SAM! MAMMY WHORE DADDY WHORE WHO'S FUCKING WHO?' The boy was terrorstruck. Amy, seeing it, took his hand and Maggie instantly snapped out of it. She wept to see him so frightened of her. She gathered him up in her arms. 'I'm sorry, Sam! Mummy's sorry! Mummy's not well! Do you understand? Not well!' But Sam didn't understand, and her anguish and her tears only frightened and confused him further. Amy, watching it all, was also frightened and confused.

That night as they lay in bed, Maggie told Alex about the episode. He held her and tried to comfort her, but she was afraid she would one day lose control and do something harmful to the children. She felt a hovering presence; she described it as being like a lift rising inside her, its doors threatening to open on reaching the top to reveal . . . It was always there, always waiting. He couldn't understand, and there was nothing he could do but hold her and try to reassure her. He kissed her tears away.

But in truth Alex was hanging on to her by his fingernails. He was terrified. He was burdened by pieces of a jigsaw he was too afraid to push together. Indeed, he felt his survival, the survival of all of them, depended on keeping the things apart in his own mind. The Maggie dig, the experiments of which he knew, the diary, her shocking outbursts: they stood like a hooded figure on the horizon beckoning him towards some overwhelming conclusion. But it was as if the hooded figure couldn't really exist unless it established clear eye contact, unless it *knew* that he *knew*. It skirted at the periphery of his vision, making signs, bidding for attention, wanting him to *look up*.

But he would not look up. He would resist. This was not the Maggie he knew, but he hoped if only he could pretend for long enough that things were creeping back to normal, then the hooded figure on the horizon might dissolve. All he had to do was avoid looking up.

He hadn't dared to touch Maggie since her illness, but one night he brushed her lips with his and let his tongue probe inside her mouth. She stiffened, and then bit hard into his tongue. Alex jumped back, spitting blood. The bite had sunk deep. Maggie's face was contorted and ugly. 'HOW DO YOU LIKE FEEL OF BRANK THE BRANK THE BRANK?'

Just as suddenly she realised what she'd done, and was sobbing hysterically and reaching out for him. Alex was out of his depth and drowning.

Later, lying awake in the dark, Maggie said, 'I want De Sang. He can help me.'

'What? That charlatan? What can he do for us?'

'I've told you. He can help me.'

'We'll get proper psychiatric help.'

'No. I want De Sang.'

'He won't help us, Maggie.' Alex despaired at the idea. 'I didn't even pay his bill.'

Maggie made an appointment to call on De Sang the following afternoon. She took Sam. He ran into De Sang's consulting rooms and flung himself at the man. 'Well, well, well! And how are you, young man?' De Sang stooped down beside Sam and spoke quietly to him, as though confiding the biggest secret in the world. 'I want to have a talk with

240

your mummy. Do you think you can keep Captain Hook tied up in that hallway for a while?'

Sam waddled out of the room.

'My receptionist will keep an eye on him,' De Sang said, offering her a chair.

'I've just paid her,' said Maggie. De Sang glanced away.

'So,' he said after she'd outlined her story. 'There's Maggie, and there's Bella, and there's . . .'

'A.'

'And you don't know her name?'

'No. But I think Bella does.'

'And why do you think I can get Bella to tell us?'

Maggie pointed to the hypnotherapy diploma peeping from behind children's paintings on the wall. 'I want you to conduct a regression. Isn't that the word?'

De Sang shook his head. 'That isn't an everyday use of hypnotherapy.'

'No. But then you're not an everyday kind of psychologist.'

He smiled at her. Then he moved over to his couch, kicked off his shoes and lay down, as if he were the patient. 'Let's you and me have a talk, Maggie.' He settled his head against the pillow. 'Just us witches.'

41

De Sang agreed to try something. He argued that the sessions should be conducted at Maggie's home. Her psychological difficulties had been generated in the home, he pointed out, and should be resolved there. Alex made a point of being out.

De Sang arrived, and asked Maggie to make herself comfortable in the living room. He took off his jacket. 'I want you to be very relaxed. The fact that I know you trust me is going to make this a lot easier,' he said. She nodded.

'Maggie, have you been thinking about that word I gave you? I'm going to speak that word now. I'm going to say the word, and you'll remember it just how I showed you the other day. All right?' Again Maggie nodded. 'And the word is, the word is, Maggie, what I told you . . . Wait. Before I tell you the word again, Maggie, I want you to get comfortable. Come on, let's shift these cushions around, that's better. Now take a deep breath, because I'm going to say the word, deep breath, good, that's good, and another, and the word is . . .'

De Sang had lowered his voice. He was almost murmuring. There was a cadence to his speech, a compelling rhythm, and even though he was saying very little, it was like a spool unwinding.

'Maggie, I'm ready now to say the word, it's just a question of saying the word. Maggie would say the word herself but you can't, Maggie. You can try but it's too difficult, isn't that right, Maggie? You buried the word so deep you can't bring yourself to say it now, can you? Isn't that right?' Maggie nodded drowsily. De Sang gently took one of her hands in his. 'But it won't matter because I'm going to say the word for you. That's why I'm here, to say the word. I'm going to whisper the word to you, Maggie, and the word is *delphi*.'

Whereupon De Sang jerked Maggie's hand violently towards him in a short, snapping movement. Maggie's head lolled to the side, her eyes closed.

De Sang nodded in satisfaction.

'Such feelings of relaxation; you'd like to keep your eyes closed and remain relaxed, exactly as you are, why not, trusting me implicitly, knowing you're safe, quite safe, and I'm going to count to three and repeat our secret word and you are going to go deeper, all the while remaining aware of the sound of my voice, knowing you're completely safe, one, two . . .'

This time there was no sudden movement, but the sound of Maggie's deep breathing became louder, until it became almost like the purring of a cat. De Sang repeated this process, and then again a third time. Noiselessly, he got up and prowled softly around the room. Maggie sat with her head back, a slight rasping issuing from her throat in time with the rise and fall of her breathing.

At last De Sang stopped, leaned over her and said, quietly, 'You can come to any time you want. Any time you want.'

Maggie stirred. She lifted her head, rotated her neck as if to ease stiff muscles, and then opened her eyes. She looked directly at De Sang.

As easy as that, De Sang thought. 'Hello, Bella.'

Maggie held his gaze. 'I don't know you.'

'Yes you do, Bella. You know me. I'm De Sang. I want you to trust me.'

She looked suspicious. 'Have you come to take me away?'

'No, Bella. I'm here to help you.'

She started to weep. 'They took me away. They put me in that place. I didn't do anything. They took me away.'

'Don't cry, Bella, please don't cry.' De Sang took her hand again and sat on the arm of the chair. 'I promise you I'll help you.'

'They hurt me.'

'What did they do, Bella? What did they do?'

'They came for me. They said I was wicked. They put me in an asylum. I only tried to help them. But they didn't find my secrets. I hid them. They're coming for you! Hide them, said A. Hide! Hide! Hide! I hid them.' She became subdued and weepy again. 'They hurt me.'

'You lived here, didn't you, Bella? This was your house?' She nodded, yes.

Go straight for the split, thought De Sang. 'Do you know whose house this is now?'

She looked around her wildly. 'This is my house.'

'Yes, Bella. But can you tell me who lives here now?'

'I live here!'

'You did live here, Bella. But that was in the past. Someone else lives here now. Do you know her name?'

She flung herself forward in the chair, eyes wild, barking at him like a dog. 'DON'T HURT DARK SISTER!'

De Sang stepped back a pace. *Too fast. Fool.*

'It's all right, Bella, it's all right. Relax, just relax. I want to help you. I promise they'll never take you back to that place. I promise you.' She relaxed back into her chair. 'Your secrets, Bella. You hid them. You were right to hide them.'

'Yes, hide.'

'You hid them up the chimney, didn't you?'

She stiffened. 'Yes.'

'They're safe. We found them. No one can hurt you now. Bella? Are you the dark sister?'

She looked confused again. The mention of the words seemed to disorient her. 'Dark sister? No . . .' She started to tremble.

'It's all right. I'm helping you. Like A. helps you. A. helps you, doesn't she, Bella?'

'No!'

'Is she your dark sister? This A.? Is A. your dark sister?'

'No . . .' She was trembling, shaking her head weakly from side to side.

'Bella. Who is A.? Tell us who she is.'

She leapt up again, hissing in De Sang's face, 'DON'T! DON'T HURT DARK SISTER! DON'T DARK SISTER! DON'T DARK SISTER! DON'T! HURT! DARK! SISTER!'

She was shaking uncontrollably, thrashing her arms and screaming at De Sang. Blood appeared at the corner of her mouth.

She's having a fit! 'Bella,' De Sang shouted above her screams, 'I'm going to touch your head and you are going to go to sleep!'

He touched her brow and instantly she fell back onto the cushions. De Sang examined her. She'd bitten her tongue. She'd also wet herself: *petit mal*.

He brought her out of her hypnotic state.

Maggie was distressed and embarrassed on realising what had happened. She was concerned that nothing should be said to Alex about her minor fit. He would have chased De Sang out of the house.

'Do you remember anything?'

'Turquoise light,' said Maggie. 'That's all.'

'I met Bella.'

'And A.?'

'Briefly, I think. But that's something much more volatile.'

'What did I tell you?'

'Nothing you couldn't have told me from reading the diary. But that's not the point. Bella's only a screen. To stop me, or you, from getting to A.'

'I'm not deliberately screening her.'

'I know that. At least not consciously. Maggie, I'm afraid I pushed it too far too soon. Let me see your tongue.'

He examined the self-inflicted bite.

'It's the mark of the brank,' said Maggie.

'What?'

'Never mind. Sometimes I say things and I don't know what they mean. Promise me you'll try again, whatever happens.'

De Sang did try again.

He adopted the same routine, relaxing Maggie, evoking his keyword, applying the powers of suggestion, surfacing the persona they referred to as Bella. Only Bella was proving less communicative.

'Aren't you speaking to me today, Bella?' She shook her head, no. 'Don't you trust me any more, Bella? Has someone told you not to talk to me?'

She looked away.

'Is it her? Has she told you not to talk to me? That's it, isn't it? Your dark sister. She's told you to have nothing to do with me, hasn't she?'

'No.' She pushed out her bottom lip in a pout, looking like a child, except that her face was wreathed in lines of pain and suffering.

'Why would that be? Why would your dark sister not want you to have anything to do with me? She's not afraid of me is she?'

'She's not afraid of YOU.'

'Can I speak to her?'

'She'll tell you to get to hell.'

'I'd like to talk to her. Has she said anything to you about me?' No answer. She was refusing even to look at him. 'Is she a healer, too? A healer like you, Bella?'

'She *was*.'

'I want you to give her a message, Bella. Next time she speaks to you. Tell her my name is De Sang. Tell her I'm also a healer.'

'She'll spit in your eye.'

'Tell her. Tell her I can help her.'

Suddenly she turned and looked at him for the first time that day. Her face had transformed. It was no longer the pouting baby. It was the sneering face again, more animated, more energised than the deadpan of Bella, a cold sparkle in the eyes. It was a new personality. She threw her head back and said, 'HA!'

De Sang stared at her for a long time. 'Thank you for coming,' he said at last.

42

Alex was cultivating serious doubts about the value of De Sang's treatment. He'd tried to stay back as far as possible, but since the psychologist insisted on conducting these sessions at the family home it was impossible to keep things at arm's length. He was jealous of Maggie's implicit faith in the man. He was also irritated by the way De Sang let Sam climb all over him. Beyond all that he believed these sessions were making Maggie, if anything, more withdrawn from her family. He managed to smother all these misgivings with a stiff civility. He offered De Sang a glass of vodka.

'Who is this other . . . personality you're trying to get through to?' Alex wanted to know.

'It's the A. of the diary. That's all I can tell you. Bella haunts Maggie, and A. haunts Bella. A. manipulates Maggie through Bella, and uses her as a shield to stop me getting near her.'

'But are they – were they – real people?'

'Maggie's the only real person.'

Alex looked exasperated. 'I'm out of my depth.'

'No, you're not. Just think of it as archaeology.' De Sang drained his glass and declined a refill. 'If only I had something on A. I could get to her. Provoke her. If I had her name, for example.'

'When is Mummy going to play with me again?' said Sam.

'When she gets better.'

'Is she tired?'

'She's very tired,' said De Sang.

Amy walked by, carrying a doll. 'It's because of Annis.' She was heading for the cellar playroom.

De Sang watched her go down the steps. He put down his empty vodka glass and followed her.

'What did you say, Amy?'

'Annis. It's because of Annis.'

'Why did you say that?'

Amy shrugged. She thought for a moment, then shook her head.

'It's important. Who told you?'

'Mummy must have told me.'

'When?'

'While I was asleep.'

It was true, the sessions did sometimes make Maggie increasingly withdrawn and uncommunicative. She had her good moments and her bad spells. De Sang was afraid to push Bella too far about her dark sister; the hysterical reaction she'd demonstrated, the *petit mal*, made him anxious about the frail condition of Maggie's psyche. He was genuinely afraid her presiding personality might become completely swamped. In psychological terms, there was the danger of triggering a true psychosis.

But she was still seriously unwell. Physically her condition was so alarming he felt it necessary to prescribe a course of steroids. De Sang decided to make his move.

'Hello, Bella,' he said. Maggie was responding more easily to the suggestion with each session. 'I've come to talk to you again. Have you gone quiet on me?'

There was no answer. She blinked and looked away.

'I'm worried about Maggie.'

As he'd expected, the name produced a look of confusion, a disorientation. He pressed on. 'We might have to have her taken away.'

Bella's bottom lip protruded. Her chin tucked into her neck and her eyes filled with water.

'You wouldn't like that, would you, Bella? You wouldn't wish that on anyone. Not again.'

'They hurt me.' Little girl's voice.

'No one's going to hurt you any more. And no one's going to hurt Maggie. If you help me. Will you help me?'

'How?'

'Don't pretend you don't know, Bella. There's someone I have to talk to. Only, you've got to let her in.'

Bella shook her head violently.

'If you won't help me, then Maggie will be taken away. And you'll see it. Because you are Maggie, aren't you, Bella?' She was still shaking her head violently. De Sang was afraid of another fit. But he knew he had to force the split. 'Shall I call you Maggie, Bella? Or shall I call you Bella? Or shall I call you by your other name. Annis?'

Her head stopped shaking and she flung herself back into the chair, arms out wide. She'd blanked out.

De Sang realised he was sweating profusely. He wiped his face with a handkerchief before proceeding. 'Bella. Bella, I know you can hear me. I want you to listen to me, listen to my voice. You know I'm here to help. Bella, I'm going to count to five, and on the count of five I'm going to touch you and you'll become relaxed. One, two, three, four, five.'

He touched her brow and she vented a deep, deep sigh, her eyes remaining closed. 'That's good, Bella, that's very good. Now stay with my voice. I'm going to take you even deeper. Deeper. Because I want you to remember. I think it's before your time, Bella, long before your time. Remember before your time. How it was. And when I bring you back it will not be as Bella, and not as Maggie. You will remember.'

'Yes.'

The sudden response took De Sang by surprise. The voice was barely more than a whisper. Her eyes remained closed, but her head shifted slightly on the cushion. Her tongue licked at her lips and she swallowed hard.

'Annis?'

She didn't answer; continued to lick her lips and swallow uncomfortably, as if with difficulty. Then, 'Yes.'

'Annis. You've led us a dance.'

'Dance?' Still a whisper.

'Who are you?'

'I am Annis. I am only a small bird.'

'You've been frightening people. Little Sam.'

She continued swallowing with difficulty.

'You hurt people, Annis.'

She opened her eyes and looked at him. Some splinter of light in them made him afraid. 'They are the ones who hurt. They hurt me.' She gasped.

'Are you thirsty, Annis?'

She nodded, and he gave her a glass of water. She crooked her fingers round the glass and sipped the water painfully.

'Who are you, Annis?'

'Healer. Harm none. The priests. They came for me.'

'Like Bella.'

'Bella is weak.' Her eyes closed again. He took the glass from her.

'Annis? Annis? Listen to me, Annis.'

But she didn't respond. Her breast rose and fell with her heavy breathing, a soft rattle issuing from her throat.

Then she said, 'You are a priest.'

'No,' said De Sang. 'I'm a healer. Like you.'

'No; you are a priest. New words. New gods.'

'I don't think you can know me, Annis.'

'Yes. I know you. You were there. You were the priest.'

And Annis was gone, and Maggie was awake, shivering, shivering intensely.

43

Ash had been brooding. His visits to Maggie, grudgingly allowed by Alex, had not convinced him she was getting any better. On that issue, he and Alex saw eye to eye. He paid a visit to Liz, because he had no one else to talk to. He poured it out to her in a state of such agitation his fingers trembled round his teacup.

'It's a do,' Liz said when he'd finished. She sat under her grandmother clock, the pendulum swinging from side to side, its loud ticking beating back the silence. She chewed at her inner cheek and stroked her dog. 'Yes, it's a do. You're missing her bad, ain't you?' she said. 'Why did you give her up so easy?'

'It wasn't easy, Liz. But it was her kids. It was destroying her to be apart from them. And deep down she loves Alex, I know she does. And though she didn't see it like that, I was standing in the way.'

'You're too good, Ash. Some people are just too good for their own selves.'

'She's ill. Very ill.'

'What about this one that's seeing her? What do you say to him?'

'The psychologist? I don't know. She trusts him. But it may not be enough.'

'She trusts him, eh?' Liz looked thoughtful at that.

'What do you know, Liz?'

'What'll you give me for it?' Liz laughed. Ash chuckled, but she saw there was no mirth in it. She got up stiffly and took his teacup from him. 'I'm still aching from a step out I took.' Then she lifted a bottle from her pantry and poured them both a glass of elderberry wine. 'I knows,' she said, 'of this one as is grabbing hold of her and won't let go. I've seen 'er.'

253

'Seen her? What do you mean "seen her"?'

'She been hooking on to them children. She were in my pantry one day. I seen her all right.'

'Do you mean the one they're calling Annis?'

'We don't say no names, do we? You should know that if you know anything. We don't say no names, but yes, that's the one. I been looking out for them children, so I been . . . agin her . . . as you might say.'

Ash stroked his beard. 'Is it – she – like a spirit trying to get possession of Maggie?'

Liz waved a hand through the air. 'Soft. You'm soft, Ash. You know nothing. She ain't a spirit as is trying to get in. She's a spirit as is trying to get out. How you ever going to understand anything when you're so soft?'

'What about the one called Bella?'

'Same.'

Ash shook his head. 'Maggie told me it all started with a bird. A black-bird.'

'Aye, and she told me that story. And she were like you, soft, couldn't understand this, didn't know that. Talk it on for ever, she would. I says to her, no, the bird wasn't trying to get in you, it were trying to get out of you, but she couldn't see it.'

'The familiar?'

'Whatever you wants to call it. The bird, then this one she's got trapped on her shoulder now, then the other one . . .'

'Annis and Bella.'

'And more, as much power as you've got. All in you. And will come out, if you're a one. All for you to use. But if you'm careless and choose wrong path, why, they'll want to use you, won't they?'

'But why does Annis attack the children?'

'Who else is taking Mammy's time and her wherewithal? It's all her vital, draining off to the children. So she don't want that, this one doesn't. She wants 'em out of the way so she can draw more vital for herself. Particularly the lad. He's taking a lot of her. So she goes for the lad. And there's something about that lovely gal she's afeared of.'

'Amy?' Ash's head was swimming.

'That story with the blackbird. When it all started. Maggie breathed its spirit back to life. Now I never done nor seen that. But I believe it. Because, mark my words, there were more than just Maggie's power in the air that day.'

'You're losing me, Liz.'

Liz took a swig of elderberry wine and smacked her lips. 'That's because you're soft. You want it all laid out in a line for you. And then it's not the thing it is.'

'Go on.'

'No. I'm proper talked out now.' She stared down at the rug under her feet.

After a while, with nothing more said between them, Liz closed her eyes. Ash could tell from her breathing she'd drifted off to sleep. The clock ticked loudly. Once or twice she smacked her lips in her sleep; at one point she snored, in a sawing kind of way.

Ash gazed at the floor, and then at Liz's collie lying at her feet. Its ears pricked up and it looked back at him with sympathetic but help-less eyes. He thought he should get up and leave Liz to her snooze; she wasn't going to come up with anything for them. Then a sharp spasm went through him, and Liz opened her eyes.

Her stick had fallen to the floor. She leaned over and picked it up. 'Yes, you'd best be on your way,' she said, getting to her feet to see him out. Ash was a little surprised. Normally he had to endure Liz's abuse whenever he wanted to leave.

'She lost something, Ash. When she was shifting. When she went a-flying. She lost some of herself and her's got to find it again.'

'Where to look?'

'What did your mammy tell you whenever you lost something? Look where you lost it.'

Liz came as far as the gate with him. 'Tell that one,' she said, 'to ask her about the Singing Chain.'

'The Singing Chain?'

'That's it. And the Death Lullaby. Ask that.'

'What are they?'

Liz looked cross with him. She raised her stick. 'It's nowt to do wi' you. And you shouldn't even know. Now get off and ask him.'

'Just one more thing, Liz. All this talk of a dark sister. Is Annis the dark sister? Or Bella? Or these spirits she sees when she's flying? Or is it the Hecate she talks about?' Or even you, he thought. 'I mean, I'm lost.'

'Is it because you're a man you'm so soft?' said Liz. 'These are all her dark sister. Coming out in different clothes. But there's only one dark sister,' and she tapped the side of her head, 'and she lives in *here.*'

Ash shook his head and walked to his car. He got in, turned the key in the ignition and looked through the rearview mirror. Liz stood at her gate gazing after him, her collie at her side. She was pointing her stick at him.

Ash reported all of this to De Sang at his clinic. He got a frankly sceptical response.

'So far, all the information we've been working on has been internal to the workings of Maggie's mind. Bella is a character from a journal Maggie knows practically by heart. Annis is a similar story. Alex says she's just using bits of information emerging from his archaeological dig at the castle.'

'And what do you think?'

'What difference does it make? Her behaviour and her health are what counts.'

'But you told me you got Annis's name from Amy. That's external to Maggie's mind. Where did that come from?'

'I'm assuming Maggie found a way of telling Amy, so Amy would tell us. That's an indication of the mind's natural subconscious will to heal itself.'

Ash shook his head. 'There's more to it. I know you think she's just weaving a story around herself. But don't you think this spirit of Annis might somehow have a life of its own?'

De Sang looked hard at him. 'I'm a psychologist,' he said, 'not a fucking mystic.'

De Sang was running out of ideas. His sessions were hitting the same impassable bedrock. His aim in surfacing the persona of Annis through hypnosis was to achieve integration of Maggie, Bella, Annis all. And he was willing to try anything. He tried a long session, hoping tiredness might offer some subtle change in the subject's response.

'Annis,' said De Sang. 'I want to talk to you again. I want to ask you some questions.'

'Always questions.'

It was after midnight, and De Sang was struggling to keep the weariness and hint of desperation from his voice. He'd been working with Maggie since early afternoon, unable to get beyond or away from Annis.

'You've told me, Annis, that you mean no harm. But I don't believe you. You frighten Bella. You've terrified Sam. Now you're threatening Maggie's life. Healers don't do this. Why, Annis?'

'The brank of time.'

'So you've told me. But what does that mean?'

She sighed deeply and looked at De Sang from under heavy, drooping eyelids.

'Then tell me why you want to hurt Sam. Tell me that.'

'Because of his mother's love. It drains us. Makes us weak. Her love makes us all weak. She put balm on his eyes; he saw me and I was in.'

'In where?'

'Your world.'

'She put balm on his eyes? Meaning Sam's mother?' No answer. No recognition. 'What of Amy? You didn't attack Amy.'

'The girl? She is . . . is a one. She has the know.'

De Sang prowled the room, parking his bottom in turn on the windowsill, the table and against the mantelpiece. Finally he dropped to his haunches in front of her before playing his wild card. 'Annis, what is the Singing Chain?'

Her eyes flared open. She looked astonished. De Sang himself couldn't hide his own surprise at her reaction, and when she registered that, she relaxed again. 'If you know of that, then you must know what it is.'

'I also know of the Death Lullaby.'

She shook her head complacently. '*That* you can *never* know.'

'Then tell me about the Singing Chain.'

'Let me sleep.'

'If you tell me.'

She snorted. 'The Chain. It is the passing on of power from a one to another one. That's all. When we are dying, we find a one and give them our power, our hopes. The Singing Chain. My Chain is very long. As long as life itself.'

'But how is the Chain passed on?'

'By the singing. Of the Death Lullaby. The most powerful of our many songs of power.'

'Sing it to me.'

Again she snorted with contempt. 'No *man* was ever given this song. It is the property and chain of the wise women. Healers. And besides, to sing the Death Lullaby is to invite death. It is Hecate's song.'

'If you sang it to me, I would die?'

'Fool. You are not a one. I would die. I. It is for the passing on, to a one. Now I want to sleep. I am weary of this.'

'But tell me, Annis. Why didn't you pass on the Singing Chain? Why didn't you die?'

'My time was taken from me.' A fat tear welled in her eye. 'They broke a Chain of two thousand years. My little sisters of two thousand years!' Then she snarled, suddenly nasty again. 'Let me sleep, you priest!'

'But you want to die, Annis! You said you wanted to hand over the Singing Chain! You told me that. Why not give the chain to Maggie! Then you could die and leave her alone, and the Chain would survive. Why not, Annis? Why not?'

Her eyes closed. 'Here,' she beckoned feebly. 'Closer.' She was whispering. De Sang put his ear close to her mouth. 'Closer. I will spit out the brank. Come closer.'

He was ready for her to tell him. She grasped his lapel. Then without warning she sat upright, launching an agonising high-pitched scream into the passage of his ear. De Sang shrank back in pain, but she grasped him firmly. He couldn't get away and the scream became louder. Her mouth was distended to ugly, shocking dimension. The membrane-splitting shriek paralysed him with a pain like red-hot needles drawn through the most tender, fleshy parts of his inner ear. The scream burned. It was a scream of hurt and fear and agony and hatred, an occult screech calling across the centuries. The scream set up an excruciating, dangerous vibration on the sensitive tympanic membrane inside his ear. He thought his eardrum must burst.

Alex rushed into the room and the scream stopped. De Sang flung himself away, falling to his knees against the wall. He put his hand to his ear, and there was blood on his fingers. He looked at her, sitting on the chair, and she was grinning at him.

Grinning at both of them, with evil satisfaction.

44

'I have to fly,' said Maggie.

'What?' hissed Ash. 'Are you mad? Don't you think that would just be enough to tip you over the edge?'

Ash had a kind of contract with Alex to visit Maggie one afternoon a week while Alex was at work.

'You told me yourself what Liz said. If you've lost something, you have to go back and look for it where you lost it.'

'It's madness!'

'De Sang can't help me any further. I need you to fly with me, Ash.'

'But how is flying going to help you?' Ash protested. 'You lost yourself in the *shifting*, not in the *flying*.'

'Flying is to knowledge as shifting is to power. Knowledge and power. That's the difference between the two. You have to trust me over this, Ash. I have to see, to know. There are some things I need to find out. That's my only way back.'

'I don't see the logic.'

'Now you're beginning to sound like Alex.'

'And anyway, Alex would never stand for it. He wouldn't allow it for a second.'

Maggie clouded over. 'Alex will have to accept it. That's exactly what this whole thing was about in the first place.'

Ash recognised the determination in her eyes. He'd seen that look before. How Maggie had changed over the time he'd known her. And yes, it was true, that was exactly what this whole thing was about in the beginning. He could see how she would tell Alex, and how Alex wouldn't be able to stop her.

'Remember the time we flew together, Ash? It was wonderful. Our love protected us. You can be there for me, protect me again. I gave you something that day, Ash. Something no one else could have given you. You owe me.'

How could he argue? 'It'll never work, Maggie. Alex would never forgive me. Haven't I encouraged you enough? Made you ill with it?'

'You can persuade Alex for me.'

'Me? He's not going to listen to me!'

'You owe me.'

Alex, as predicted, hit the roof. Maggie had persuaded Ash to wait with her until he returned from work. She sat her husband down and told him.

'Is this your fucking idea?' he snarled at Ash.

'No, it's mine. Ash was firmly against it. But he's agreed to help me if I'm determined to go ahead. Which I am.'

'It's not going to happen.'

'You can't stop it.'

'I'll stop it. Whatever it is you do, I'll be there. I'll stop it. It's lunacy! Sheer lunacy!'

'Then we'll simply go somewhere else to do it.'

'Does De Sang know about this?'

'What do you care about De Sang? You don't value his opinion.'

'He won't allow it! He simply won't tolerate it!'

Maggie took hold of Alex's hand and spoke to him very calmly and very seriously. 'Alex, the days when you have the last word are over. You have to understand that, or all of this will have been for nothing. I've come back to you because I love you and I love the children. But the way we were before is over. It has to be. There will be times when I have to decide what's best for me, and you'll have to accept that. We're moving forward or not at all.'

Ash had been sitting quietly listening to this exchange. 'Can I say something?'

Alex looked at him. 'No you fucking can't! You've done your piece to get Maggie in this state! Maggie is my wife, not yours, and while we're talking you'll just keep your fucking mouth shut.'

'Can you leave us, Maggie?' said Ash.

Maggie let go of Alex's hand and went out. Alex stood up.

'WHERE ARE YOU GOING? GET BACK HERE!' The door clicked softly behind her. Alex was left looking red-faced and impotent.

'Are you going to sit down?' said Ash.

'No, I'm not.'

'Fine. Then I'm going to stand up.' Ash did so, and took two steps towards Alex. He had a height advantage of at least four inches. Alex tensed.

'She's decided she must do this thing,' said Ash.

'I don't have to listen to any of this.'

'You're going to listen to it all. And if you don't, I'm going to walk in there after Maggie and I'm going to take her away from you.'

'Don't flatter yourself.'

Ash took a step closer. 'Want to put it to the test?'

Alex looked away.

'I could go in there and she would come with me. And nothing would make me happier than to have an excuse to take her away from you. A lot of this is down to you. Now you have a choice. You let her do what she's going to do anyway, or you lose her for ever. Simple. Now, are you going to make that choice?' Ash could see he already had. 'And don't think about bleating to De Sang about this. He doesn't need to know.'

Ash called Maggie back into the room. 'I've managed to persuade Alex to accept this course of action. He won't stand in your way.'

Alex had tears in his eyes. 'What if you die, Maggie? What if you die?'

'*I'm* not going to die.'

45

The final ritual was to be conducted at Ash's house, in his study. This was not merely to spare Alex's feelings. There it was that they'd conducted the early, successful flying experiments; the room had positive associations for them. Maggie persuaded Ash that flying would be enough. Flying was to knowledge, she said again, as shifting was to power. In any event, Maggie couldn't face the depredations of the shifting again, and Ash would have nothing to do with it; the flying was itself terrifying enough, and Maggie knew it would take them where they wanted to go.

They were fastidious in their preparations, trying to re-create exactly the conditions which had made their early experience a positive one. The process was begun at dusk: incense was set to smoulder in brass bowls, red and white candles were lit. Separately they took a purifying, aromatic bath. The only thing absent was the aphrodisiac tea and the love scent. Maggie certainly didn't want to complicate what was already a confusion. As before, she wore an engraved copper talisman round her neck. Ash also wore one.

Ash was a knot of tension, but in Maggie he found a focus of resolution. Even so, she was sensitive to his anxiety. 'You don't have to join me, Ash.'

'It's all right.'

'You could simply watch over me.'

'It'll be all right.'

The hour came. They slipped off their dressing gowns and stepped into the rope circle. Maggie closed it behind her. They were naked but for their talismans. They dipped their fingers in the bowl of water and made the banishments: *I have purified myself and my heart is filled with joy. I bring gifts of incense and perfume. I anoint myself with unguents to make myself strong . . .* They watched each other apply the flying ointment. Ash had an erection which wasn't there the first time round. Maggie had the bloom of perspiration on her; Ash was sweating heavily. She leaned across to him and kissed him full on the lips. *Grant me the secret longings of my heart.*

Ash sat cross-legged, his erection bobbing angrily, stimulated by the tingling heat of the flying ointment. They'd pretended to each other, tacitly, that it wasn't going to happen; but in a moment she was lowering herself onto him. The moment had taken them over. Both could feel the heat of the flying ointment inside and out. Ash made love to her as though it might be his last time on earth, and she writhed in his arms like a bitten serpent. Orgasm catapulted them into a state of hallucination. Ash saw their bodies replicate, locked in an endless procession of loving and birthing, a girdle of light spinning from their glowing, corporeal and coupled form, spreading round the planet; Maggie saw it as an unbroken scallop of light, an eternal caravan of reincarnation fanning from the circle and sourcing from their act of love. His hot seed was inside her, and each seed ran like the mercurial thought, each seed a ball of energy she could ride to take them anywhere she wanted to go.

Maggie passed out of consciousness and came to in that familiar, timeless grey corridor. Ash was there. Grey and black geometric shapes drifted by, fracturing, re-forming. The helping face appeared. Maggie promised a gift, and the face changed to become the parting in the grey corridor. This time the parting revealed nothing but an ethereal light. She moved towards the light and Ash wanted to follow her. She made him understand he couldn't come with her; that he must stay behind, stay and safeguard a way back for her. They were beyond speech. She was unable to explain. She waved him back, turned and stepped . . .

Into the turquoise light! Swimming, flying in the turquoise light!
    The light of far memory. Far memory.
    And she sits in a chair, in the middle of a room she should know. She is waiting. They are coming for her, but she no longer has any fear,. She has placed herself beyond terror, with her secrets, which are also safe. Only she knows where they are, hidden behind a fireplace boarded with wood, where they will never look. She sits, waiting patiently,

knowing of their approach, sensing that they are close. It is summer and the smell is high. A smell of decomposition and sadness, from within the house. Her dog and two cats lie decomposing in the kitchen. Flies are thick in number. She herself is starving, but she cannot eat. She has placed herself beyond hunger.

There comes the hammering on the door. Again. Then a splintering of wood as they force their way in. Oh, Bella. The splintering sound becomes a ripping sound, like a tearing not of cloth but of the ethereal light as she is flung again – into the turquoise light!

And she is no longer Bella, and they have her at the gibbet and the rope sore round her neck. The gibbet, and the gibbering crowd. Faces. She recognises faces in the crowd. The light goes out as the hood falls over her head, her legs kicked away and she swings, oh swings, and the small crowd gasps and is silenced, for her neck has not snapped, only burned on the hemp rope, and she swings, choking, and there is a rumour and consternation from the crowd, and they cut her down.

The Scottish way, they say, they will the Scottish way, and they parade her bare-breasted and carrying the brands of the irons on her breasts, as they taunt and spit. She is carried to the place in the square where she sees them, bundling faggots high in the place of burning. And again faces she should know. The women bundling the faggots high, she knows them! Two redheaded women, and another old woman with loose skin at her throat like a turkey's wattles.

The old woman spits at her as she draws near, curses her, pushes her towards the pile of faggots. Confusion. Betrayal. The men leave off her and let the woman take up the cry, spitting, cursing, and this old woman is among the most vicious, though drawing close and taking her roughly, and under cover of this action presses something into her hand. Here, little sister, she says in a whisper, an underbreath that betrays her own fear, here, little sister. And it is a pressing of the herb dwale, belladonna, which will be her only relief from the flame. She is comforted in her torment, knowing her sisters have not abandoned her; she bends double in disguise of swallowing the dwale and the old woman pretends to cuff her and heap curses upon her head.

Yes, she is beyond all help, and her only fear now is for the Chain. How shall she pass the Chain when they will not let her little sisters draw near? How shall she chant the song of dying to a one? Two thou-

sand years and the Chain broken? And how shall she, Annis, truly die if not by the Death Lullaby? Oh, little sisters! Oh, little sisters! My heart is a little bird! Tear it from my breast!

And they are surely other sisters heaping high the faggots of wood to burn her! And there are others she should know. Here the white-haired priest whose name she should know, damning her, book and bell; and here another man whose bed she should know full well, bearing the torch to ignite the wood. Who are these men?

The dwale takes effect, clouds sense, closes her eye, glory to the little sisters who did not forget her in her hour. And though the fire licks lazily at the wood under her, trailing thick grey plumes of smoke, she sees the sisters watching, watching in stillness while others bray, names she should know, names which confuse her, Liz the elder, Bella the redhead, and this other flame-haired one turning her face is Maggie.

Confusion! The dwale has befuddled her senses. How can this be if she is Maggie? I am Maggie; no, I am Annis. The dwale. And there comes the pungent smell of burning chestnut in her nostrils. Chestnut! The sisters! They know!

The flame gutters out. She comes to, still alive, unburned. Rumour and fear in the crowd. They light the faggots of chestnut brush again. A second time it smokes and will not catch. The sisters! Oh, the sisters!

Three times they light the wood. It smoulders, thick, acrid coiling serpents of smoke, but it will not catch. Three times. The sisters know, piling the wood high with sweet chestnut of the season and it will not burn! Chestnut scarce at all: who has the knowledge of the wood? Sisters, you have saved me from the noose! You have saved me from the flame! Come to me now and take the Chain! The dwale has made me weary of this world and it is for you and no other I am ready. Come, those of you who are maiden, and let me print on your lips the lullaby of death and departing! In the midst of smoke and death I am in song!

Annis! Maggie!

But they cannot draw near lest they betray their natures, those sisters. And worse is to come.

She passes from consciousness and they take her down, many even afraid now to manhandle her. For what work is this? What trickery? What truck with demons?

The white-haired priest. He approaches, bell and book. His voice quavers. So be it. If she shall so defy death, then grant her a living death. They say she can curse. Then sever her hand and foot that she may not point her curse at any man! They say she speaks magic words to her like. Then brank her that she be denied all faculty of speech. They say she can fly. Then bury her, so that if she sprout wings they be no help for her! And keep her alive that she endure her living death. Do this in God's name!

And they sever her hands and her feet, and cauterise the bloody limbs with burning brands. And they brank her head, and the spike bleeds her tongue. And they squeeze her into a tiny casket and bury her, leaving a breather pipe with which to water her and make hers the torment of many days and nights.

And in the night the brave sisters come, whispering words to her though she cannot answer them, and trickling potions to her lips to assuage her agonies. And they bury moon plates and knives and ask for the intervention of Hecate, to keep her heart from hatred. But the potions and her agonies derange and confuse her, and one night there comes a one, a sister. The sister whispers to her, whispering strange words in the blackest hour, rare words in the darkest night of her suffering.

I have come to you, *says the voice.* I am Maggie, and I will take away the brank of time.

Maggie woke inside the rope circle, cradled by Ash. She was shivering and weeping. Ash had draped one of his white shirts round her shoulders.

'I was there, Ash,' she wept. 'I saw it all.'

'You're back; you're safe. It's all right.'

Ash had come to some time before Maggie. On recovering he realised Maggie was still out cold, but weeping. Maybe she was dreaming, but in her unconscious state she was racked by a deep, distressing sobbing. He'd tried to make her come to. Then he'd broken the circle to find something to drape over her shoulders, returning to hold her in his arms until she recovered consciousness. He got her to sip a little water.

'I was watching. I saw everything. Yet I was Annis at the same time. I was both Maggie and Annis.'

'Drink this.'

'She was one of the innocents, Ash. They twisted her. I know what she wants. They hurt her; oh, how they hurt her.' Maggie sobbed in his arms. It was tearing her heart. 'Did you see it? Did you see it?'

But Ash hadn't seen it. He'd been left waiting in that grey place, that mysterious corridor between seeing and understanding, the memory of which was already fading for him. Whatever she'd seen was not for his eyes. Now there was nothing he could do but believe what Maggie told him.

'I understood, Ash. All of us. We're all branked by what life does to us. You. Me. Alex. Amy and little Sam. All of us, Ash. We're all waiting to take the brank away. And it hurts. It hurts.'

Ash held her, until her sobbing had exhausted itself.

46

Maggie told everyone what she wanted and whom she wanted. De Sang was recalled and Ash was dispatched on an errand. Maggie asked Alex to stay close by. She wanted him to be there, to know.

Maggie's feverish sense of authority betrayed to De Sang that something had happened, but in performing what was required he kept his suspicions to himself. He was sceptical about what else he could offer; he was also deeply apprehensive after the experience of Annis's occult scream.

'On the count of three I will touch you lightly and you will come to us as before, calm, and rested. One, two, three. There. Hello, Annis. You've been away.'

The session was conducted in the lounge, as before. She blinked and looked at De Sang. Then she looked at her hands.

'How do you feel, Annis?'

A sneer came across her face. 'Priest.'

'No, I'm not the priest. Not any more, Annis. I'm a friend of Maggie. You know who Maggie is, don't you?'

She looked blank.

'You don't have to play with us, Annis. Maggie is the one who will help you.'

She licked her lips, and spoke with difficulty. 'Water.' De Sang handed her a glass and she drank painfully.

'Maggie wants you to tell me the Death Lullaby. The song of death and departing. She wants you to tell me.'

Silence.

'You know you want to, Annis. Then you can be free.'

Silence.

It was broken by a ringing on the doorbell. Alex went to answer it. De Sang heard muffled voices in the hallway. He resumed the interrogation.

'Let me ask you something else. Who taught you the Death Lullaby?'

'A one.'

'And you have to give it to another one? But it can't be a man? What happens if a man sings the Death Lullaby?'

'No man can know it.'

'But if he did?'

'No power. Only women can know. Deeper in the cycle of life. Spring from womb, grow a womb, spring from womb.'

'I understand. So I don't want you to tell it to me. I want you to tell it to Maggie.'

Silence again. Then: 'No need. I have it for her.'

'But if you don't, then two thousand years of craft will be broken, Annis. A hundred generations of witches, and the Singing Chain broken. For ever. Give it to Maggie. Let her take it.'

'No need. We are one.'

'No, no, Annis. You are separate. You must separate. She doesn't have the Chain. You have it.'

No answer.

De Sang was already at the end of his rope. He didn't believe in the existence of the Singing Chain, whatever it might be, and therefore wasn't surprised when he was unable to find it. He belonged to a school trading only in the cantrips of logic. But Maggie had given him a key she claimed would unlock the secret. He sighed. 'I have a message for you from Maggie. She wanted you to have this special message.'

'Tell.'

'She asked me to say to you the following words. Are you listening, Annis? She asked me to say: *I am Maggie. I will take away the brank of time.*'

Her eyes flared open. She rotated her head slowly to look at De Sang. There was lambent fire in her eyes, but for the first time there was also loss, confusion, doubt, hurt. She started to tremble. It was the onset of a fit, the profitless finale of many of these sessions.

'Don't run away, Annis! Don't run away!' He was terrified she would simply hide from the conflict he'd set up for her, hide behind her fit. Already her breathing was deepening and she was closing her eyes. 'Keep your eyes open, Annis. Look at me. If you won't tell us, we're going to have to kill Maggie.'

She came to again. 'You won't.' Her demeanour had changed. She'd become protective.

'You said it, Annis! I'm the priest. I'll have her taken!'

'DON'T TOUCH HER!'

'I'll burn her. I'll have her buried alive, Annis!'

'DON'T YOU TOUCH HER!'

'It's why you're still here! If we kill her, we can kill you!'

'DON'T BRANK SISTER! DON'T BRANK SISTER!'

'Then tell Maggie! For heaven's sake tell Maggie the Death Lullaby! Tell her!'

'I can't! Don't you see I can't!' She was screaming. Crying and screaming.

'You can, Annis! You want to! She can take away the brank!'

'She can't! She can't!'

'Why can't she? Why?'

'Because MAGGIE IS NOT MAIDEN!'

De Sang was astonished. Maggie had persuaded him Annis was ready to pass on the secret. She'd been certain. Plausible even. He'd believed it really might happen, if only because of her own conviction. Suddenly he felt crushed, defeated. Not maiden. He realised for the first time it was not that Annis didn't want to pass on the Chain to Maggie; she was unable. In Annis's mind, the Death Lullaby could only be passed on to a virgin. The play had been made, and it had failed. De Sang didn't even know if there was such a thing as a Death Lullaby, or a Singing Chain. The convolutions of Maggie's unhinged mind had simply turned another flip, rendering the solution inaccessible. She had placed herself beyond reach. He had failed.

Behind him the door opened silently. De Sang turned and saw, advancing into the room, an old woman. He thought she must have been eighty years old. Her face was wreathed with care lines and her hair was iron-grey; loose flesh, like wattles, hung from her chin. She walked with a stick, yet she moved forward with a light, fluid step. He guessed her name.

It was Liz. Before her was Amy, blinking shyly. Liz had one claw-like hand clasped on her shoulder. Ignoring De Sang, she propelled Amy towards the chair. The two women locked eyes. The sky outside was beginning to darken.

'I'll give you a one,' said Liz.

'No,' said Alex, hovering uncertainly by the door.

'And all things will be well,' said Liz.

There was silence.

Liz leaned across the chair, and spoke gently. 'This is the gift. She will take away the brank. Come on, old gel. You in your turn. Me in mine. And her in hers.'

Maggie shuddered at Liz's words. Then she looked at Amy, her eyes blue glass. 'The brank of time,' she murmured. She beckoned Amy with a tiny gesture. 'Come here.'

Amy looked at Liz. She was afraid.

'Go to her,' said Liz. 'Remember what I've told you.' She gave Amy a gentle push, and backed off. 'Well?' she said, turning to Alex and De Sang. 'Get you out! This is not for you.'

Neither Alex nor De Sang showed any inclination to move. Ash was also hovering in the hallway, having delivered Liz to the house at Maggie's request. Alex started to protest.

'OUT!' shouted Liz, rushing at them. 'OUT!'

Startled, they went, and she slammed the door after them. She took up position against it, like a sentry.

'Now,' she said, 'you have your gift. And the way is clear.'

Amy looked at her mother. She was still afraid of her. She didn't seem like her mother. Behind those features she saw an older face, the face of an enemy. But it had softened. Amy saw pain and sadness and suffering in that face, and a hunger for revenge that had only tormented herself. Amy understood nothing of this, she only felt it. She looked into her mother's eyes, and saw that blue glass, and behind that rivers of ice, running, congealing, thawing, refreezing, running free again. The rivers of ice were hundreds and hundreds of years old.

Her mother took her left hand, and gripped her third finger tightly. She was silent for a while before she intoned in a kind of chant:

'My dark sister was Stella. And hers was Celinda. Hers Isabel. Hers Lizabeth. Hers Jean. Margaret. Ciss. Annie. Hers Peg. MyraRuthRowena. HazelBessElla. Melusine and Mag. GretaClaraAlwyn. CorrinnaFredaMalekinUlrica. JeannieAmeliaMicolMaugElfledaElfreda

MinaEricaIsolda. EilianMurielGwynethMorganRhonwenEnaBridged
SheelaRinganMoiraCatti. Una. Hers Tryam. MolleeGlastieBood
KirreeCaithBrythMaeveSheena. Ethna. EtainRoanneeLhiannon
CarridwenFuamach and Arian. Fionn. Nuala. Sadbh and Lorreeak. And
Alethea from across the great sea.

'That is the line. Now it is yours, and you must remember. Many
names. But you will remember them all. Because this is the Singing
Chain. This is the far memory.'

Amy felt her mother's hand tighten round her finger. The ice rivers
were running free.

'Now give her the song,' urged Liz. 'The Death Lullaby. And you
will be free.'

Amy saw her mother sigh and run her tongue along her lips. She
beckoned Amy forward and kissed her hard on the mouth. She fell back
and stared at the ceiling. Then she began singing, so softly Amy had
to strain to hear words which meant nothing, but which she would never
forget.

Baby born is born to die
Even Mother's tears will dry
By 'n' by

All is none and none all
Baby die 'fore baby crawl
By 'n' by

Dead men lie still
But truth they will
By 'n' by

When baby live
Then all's to give
By 'n' by

When baby live again
No more a witch's pain
By 'n' by

* * *

Her mother closed her eyes and went to sleep. Amy stared at the rhythmic rise of her breast and knew that Annis had gone for ever, and that her mother would soon be well. Liz came up slowly behind her. She put her gnarled old hand on Maggie's brow and nodded with satisfaction. Then she ran her hand gently through Amy's hair.

'No telling. Ever.' Amy nodded. She knew. 'When I'm finished, when my time comes, I shall call you, and you shall have my line too. Two lines joined in one. And what a one you shall be!'

Amy looked up at Liz. And her eyes were pure and clear.

47

Maggie was mending. She was well enough two weeks later to make an expedition to see Liz, along with Alex and the children. When they got there Ash was nursing a glass of elderberry wine. He kissed Maggie and told her how much better she looked; and he was relieved not to have to pretend it was true. A rose flush was back in her cheeks and she'd regained her lost weight.

Liz pronounced that spring was painting the hedgerows, and that they should all go out for a 'blow', but Ash wanted to leave. He made his excuses. Alex tried to persuade him to come along, but he couldn't be tempted.

'That's right,' said Liz. 'You bugger off.'

Ash kissed Maggie again, shook hands with Alex and got into his car.

'And don't come back till the next time!' Liz growled after him. She opened the gate and they went walking across the field. Her collie stared after Ash as if it couldn't understand why he wouldn't come with them.

Liz was no stranger to Alex any more. After the evening at his house, Liz had left Maggie to sleep and had taken charge, mobilising people, giving instructions, heaping abuse where necessary. She'd emerged from the room with Amy to tell them Maggie was 'mending' and needed putting to bed. When De Sang said he wanted to give Maggie a sedative after the punishment she'd been through, Liz gave him a tongue-lashing. De Sang looked round nervously for someone to grin at, and concluded he had no option but to accept this colourful new authority in the household. Liz snapped at him that he should make himself useful by getting the kettle going, and no one seemed more amazed than himself when he jumped to it.

Hadn't Alex got work? she demanded before scolding him for getting under everyone's feet. She busied herself with cooking up a weak broth, which she stipulated was for Maggie and no one else. Meanwhile Ash, seeing that Maggie was in the safest hands possible, slipped off quietly without telling anyone.

He hadn't the heart to stick around.

Amy had stolen the show by sitting regally in a chair with her hands folded in her lap. Occasionally she would approach Liz and whisper something in her ear, some question or other, to which the old woman would nod and answer simply yes or no; a little conspiracy which vexed De Sang and dismayed Alex. Most of the time Amy sat apart from the others, with her head slightly cocked, as if listening to some internal music; or as if she was counting. Or reciting in time to a rhythm only she could hear.

Sam just seemed baffled by it all. Liz, with whom he never felt entirely secure, had turned the premises upside down. Her presence was like a wind blowing through the house. Amy, after receiving permission from Liz, told him he had nothing more to worry about from 'the lady', that he wouldn't be troubled again. He sensed that something had happened to Amy, but was no more party to it than were either his father or his erstwhile psychologist. They were all three adrift in the same boat of ignorance, and he sat staring stupidly at his sister.

For the next few days Alex was subdued. A renegotiation of rights had taken place at a mysterious level beyond words. He was coming to terms with it. He knew he'd have to yield up his taste for control if things were going to work, and when that actually started to happen, he began to relax; and soon he learned that he'd lost nothing but an angry pride.

He was feted over his archaeological discovery in the castle grounds. His reports on the excavations appeared in academic and popular journals, and in all his writings he freely acknowledged the mysterious assistance of his wife in the 'dig here' episode. He offered the information up to his readers exactly as it had happened, and without senseless speculation.

Meanwhile Sam at least wasn't at all unhappy about the idea of going for a walk across the fields. Inside Liz's cottage, he gave the pantry a wide berth.

It was indeed a beautiful spring day. They climbed a stile and walked beside hedgerows cloudy with May blossom. Lapwings had returned to the field in number. Amy had her arm linked with Liz's. Occasionally the old woman would stop and point her stick at something in the hedge or growing in the grass. 'Shepherd's purse. Can stop a bleeding wi' that one. You mark it,' she said. Or, 'Groundsel. Lady's friend. Tell you when you're older about that one.'

Sam noticed how closely his mother and father, walking behind Liz and Amy, were marking this blossoming relationship. Because Amy seemed to glow in the attention. The sun lit up her golden hair and there seemed something changed about her. Tagging along behind, he could only gaze in awe and admiration at his sister.

His shining, dark sister.

TACKLING UNEMPLOYMENT

Tackling Unemployment

Richard Layard

Director
Centre for Economic Performance
London School of Economics and Political Science

First published in Great Britain 1999 by
MACMILLAN PRESS LTD
Houndmills, Basingstoke, Hampshire RG21 6XS and London
Companies and representatives throughout the world

A catalogue record for this book is available from the British Library.

ISBN 0–333–72232–9

First published in the United States of America 1999 by
ST. MARTIN'S PRESS, INC.,
Scholarly and Reference Division,
175 Fifth Avenue, New York, N.Y. 10010

ISBN 0–312–21577–0

Library of Congress Cataloging-in-Publication Data
Layard, P. R. G. (P. Richard G.)
Tackling unemployment / Richard Layard.
p.   cm.
Includes bibliographical references and index.
ISBN 0–312–21577–0 (cloth)
1. Unemployment—Great Britain.   I. Title.
HD5765.A6L38   1998
331.13'7941—DC21   98–16548
                                                     CIP

This book is printed on paper suitable for recycling and made from fully managed and sustained forest sources.

10   9   8   7   6   5   4   3   2   1
08   07   06   05   04   03   02   01   00   99

Printed and bound in Great Britain by
Antony Rowe Ltd, Chippenham, Wiltshire

To Gordon Brown

Contents

PART II   REMEDIES FOR UNEMPLOYMENT

Preface

This is one of two books, *Tackling Unemployment* and *Tackling Inequality*, which reproduce my main articles on these issues. A complete list of publications appears at the end.

I am grateful to Tim Farmiloe of Macmillan for proposing the idea of publication. He also suggested I write a personal credo which appears at the beginning of the volume.

RICHARD LAYARD

Acknowledgements

The author and publishers acknowledge with thanks permission from the following to reproduce copyright material:

Chapter 3: Elsevier Science (NL, Sara Burgerhartstraat 25, 1055 KV Amsterdam, The Netherlands) for D. Grubb, R. Jackman and R. Layard, 'Wage Rigidity and Unemployment in OECD Countries', *European Economic Review*, Vol. 21 (1983).

Chapter 5: Blackwell Publishers for R. Jackman, R. Layard and C. Pissarides, 'On Vacancies', *Oxford Bulletin of Economics and Statistics*, Vol. 51 (1989).

Chapters 6, 16, 18: *Economica* for R. Jackman and R. Layard, 'Does Long-term Unemployment Reduce a Person's Chance of a Job' (1991); for R. Jackman and R. Layard, 'The Efficiency Case for Long-run Labour Market Policies' (1980); for R. Layard, 'Is Incomes Policy the Answer to Unemployment?' (1982).

Chapters 7 and 14: Cambridge University Press for R. Jackman, R. Layard and S. Savouri, 'Mismatch: A Framework for Thought', in F. Padoa Schioppa (ed.), *Mismatch and Labour Mobility* (1990); for R. Layard, 'Preventing Long-term Unemployment: An Economic Analysis', in D. Snower and G. de la Dehesa (eds), *Unemployment Policy: Government Options for the Labour Market* (1997).

Chapter 8: Centre for Economic Performance, LSE, for R. Jackman, R. Layard, M. Manacorda and B. Petrongolo, 'Europe vs. US unemployment: Different Responses to Increased Demand for Skill?' (1997).

Chapters 9 and 19: *Scandinavian Journal of Economics* for R. Layard, C. Bean, 'Why Does Unemployment Persist?' (1989); from R. Jackman and R. Layard, 'The Real Effects of Tax-based Incomes Policies' (1990).

Chapter 10: OECD for R. Jackman, R. Layard and S. Nickell, 'Combatting Unemployment: Is Flexibility Enough?' in *OECD Proceedings: Macroeconomics Policies and Structural Reform*, copyright OECD (1996).

Chapter 11: London School of Economics for M. Blaug, R. Layard and M. Woodhall, 'The Causes of Graduate Unemployment in India', in R. Layard, M. Blaug and M. Woodhall, *The Causes of Graduate Unemployment in India* (1969).

Chapter 12: European Centre for Work and Society, Maastricht, for R. Layard, 'Unemployment in Britain: Causes and Cures' (1981).

Chapter 15: Employment Policy Institute for R. Layard, 'Preventing Long-term Unemployment: Strategy and Costings, in *Economic Report*, 11(4) (1997).

Chapter 17: *Economic Journal* for R. Layard and S. Nickell, 'The Case for Subsidising Extra Jobs' (1980).

Chapter 20: Employment Institute for R. Layard, 'How to End Pay Leapfrogging', in *Economic Report*, 5(5) (1990).

Chapter 21: *Quarterly Journal of Economics* for R. Layard and S. Nickell, 'Is Unemployment Lower if Unions Bargain over Employment?' (1990). © 1990 by the President and Fellows of Harvard College and the Massachusetts Institute of Technology.

Chapter 22: Centre for European Policy Studies for G. Basevi, O. Blanchard, W. Buiter, R. Dornbusch and R. Layard, 'Europe in 1984: The Case for Unsustainable Growth', *CEPS Paper*, 8/9 (1984).

The author is extremely grateful to Richard Barwell, Marion O'Brien, Sunder Katwala and Keith Povey for skilful and devoted help in preparing this volume for publication.

1 Why I am an Economist*

I turned to economics because I wanted a framework for thinking about the problems of society. I was already in my early 30s, so it was quite a decision. But I was not disappointed.

As an undergraduate I had read history and then begun a part-time masters' degree in sociology while teaching in a comprehensive school. I remember well at that stage thinking that I understood how society and the economy worked. In fact I even began to write a sixth-form textbook on the subject.

But then I was asked to become the research officer for the Robbins Committee on Higher Education, which was to launch the great university expansion of the 1960s. In the first few weeks of our work, a memorandum came from the Treasury asking 'Should extra public money be spent on higher education or on renovating the decaying cities of the North?' I realised I had no framework at all for thinking about such a question.

So, when the Committee's work was done, I set about learning economics – not easy at any age and certainly not at 31. I was comforted to be told that James Meade had not understood the subject for the first five years, until he suddenly realised what it was all about. Fortunately I was well motivated and I already had questions I wanted answering.

It was a real culture shock. Though I had always believed in the mixed economy, I had never much liked the profit motive. To be among people who thought it wonderful was at first quite uncomfortable, but I soon took it on board. The majority of the British intelligentsia did not do so until quite recently. What they perceived as a new philosophy of 'market economics' was in fact the stock-in-trade of mainstream economists throughout my working life.

But what I really liked about economics was the breadth of the issues it could handle – from taxation and transport to education, health and crime. Since many people question this universalism of economics, let me try to explain what I think economics can and cannot do. I shall do it in the form of seven propositions, beginning with positive economics and moving on to policy.

---

* Prepared for this volume.

1

WHAT I BELIEVE

Economics is about rational choice and about systems

Economics is about two things – rational choice and systems. Positive economics begins with rational choice which tells us how individuals and companies will change their behaviour if faced with different alternatives. These responses can be predicted because to a degree individuals and companies are maximising some objective function subject to constraints. When altered circumstances change the constraints, behaviour changes in predictable ways. In common parlance, people compare the benefits and costs of different actions and adjust until there is no scope for increasing the excess of benefit over cost.

From this approach to the different agents in the economy, we then model the working of the system when all the agents interact. When they come together in a 'market', this determines the terms ('prices') which constitute the opportunities for the individual agents. Thus the 'market' determines the prices and also the allocation of resources – of which the most important is the use of human time. There can be no coherent economic analysis of any problem without an equilibrium model of how agents interact to determine a set of prices and quantities.

Too much of empirical economics is conducted without a theory of how the system is working. People run wage equations which show that house prices affect wages without reference to what causes house prices. And so on. There has to be theory, but the theory must be driven by facts.

Positive economics should start from facts

When we set up the Centre for Labour Economics in 1980, we discussed what were the big issues we should investigate. One distinguished theorist said we should investigate 'why unemployment was too high'. But most of us jumped on him, saying we should investigate first why unemployment was what it was. Only if we understood that could we fruitfully discuss whether it was too high.

This means that we must start from facts. Of course some facts are more interesting than others – and generally the things we want to explain will be things which have a big impact on human welfare or on people's ability to make money. But that is a matter of motivation. The research strategy must be driven only by facts – many facts. And the aim of the research is to find an explanation which is as consistent as possible with all of them.

Thus economics which starts with one fact and looks for a theoretical explanation of it is unlikely to be fruitful. I once taught a labour economics course jointly with a distinguished theorist, who claimed to have revolutionised contract theory by insisting that workers must in fact be indifferent to being laid off. I asked him why he believed this. He replied that it must be so, and offered an anecdote about a case where an involuntary separation became voluntary through the offer of increased redundancy pay.

Economics cannot be based on the odd anecdote. It should start from a serious body of facts and try to find a theory which encompasses them. Theory is vital in economics and too few applied economists work on it. But the reverse is equally true. Unfortunately in our profession too little prestige is derived from knowledge of facts. But facts should be as important for theory as they are for empirical work.

The best kind of theory is theory which leads to estimable equations, so that we can find out whether the theory is true. It took me years to learn this, and without the shining example of Stephen Nickell I might never have learned it.

But how scientific can economics ever be?

Positive economics should aspire to be a science

We have to be realistic. At present we have few controlled experiments. So most of our evidence comes from non-experimental data where too many variables are changing across the different observations for us to get very precise estimates of causal effects. In practice we proceed in a Bayesian fashion, basing our views on many pieces of evidence, and modifying them as further evidence accumulates. We rarely base our views on one test or estimation. Thus when we report standard errors on coefficients the reason is not usually to test whether the coefficients are different from zero, but to help us form some estimate of what the effect is – taking into account other estimates we know of and their standard errors.

One of the striking differences between economists and many other social scientists is that they are not usually testing whether a relationship exists but what it is. The aim is to build a coherent explanation. Economists generally focus on the coefficients in their equations (how much y changes as a result of a given change in x), while many other social scientists find it enough to ask whether an association exists. In addition, economists realise that most relationships are multi-variate and get frustrated by the bivariate correlations still produced by so many other social scientists. It is one of the glories of economics that econometrics has set a standard which is now being followed more widely in the social sciences.

Even so the controlled experiment and the natural experiment generally provide clearer evidence than non-experimental data. I greatly admire economists like Orley Ashenfelter and David Card who have tried so hard to find good quasi-experimental evidence and to make sense of it. Unfortunately there is so far only limited evidence of this type. As time passes, we shall get more of it and the information revolution will also yield much larger numbers of observations on non-experimental data. So the future for economics as a science is bright.

But for the moment we are still in the Middle Ages. Economists are better placed than others to make sense of economic reality and, if we do not do it, others even more ignorant will take over. So it is right that economists should go beyond pure science and offer the most coherent explanation they can of what is happening – even when the evidence is contradictory and a judgement has to be made. It is perfectly proper that the judgement should be based not only on systematic research but also on personal experience of life. Certainly this is the spirit in which Stephen Nickell, Richard Jackman and I have approached the explanation of European unemployment.

The key requirement is that the explanation be consistent with the main facts. Not only must it explain the thing of greatest interest (for example, aggregate unemployment or inflation) but it must be consistent with more detailed facts (such as the structure of unemployment or price movements). Many theories fall at this first hurdle. For example, Paul Krugman has hypothesised that 'US inequality and European unemployment are two sides of the same coin'. The idea is that the demand for labour has shifted towards skilled labour. In response to this, relative wages of the unskilled fell in the USA, while in Europe they did not, so that unemployment rose. But the corollary of this mismatch explanation is that for skilled workers in Europe the unemployment rate should have fallen. But in fact it rose by at least the same multiple as did unskilled unemployment. So Krugman's theory of why European unemployment rose falls at the first hurdle. Without checking on the intermediate predictions the theory would have appeared consistent with the facts.

The separation between theory and empirical work in the profession is unfavourable to the spirit of checking against the facts. For a theory article to be published it is often sufficient that it be clever and internally consistent. There is no soupçon of requirement to provide evidence. Even worse, I discover from the chairman of one editorial board that it is generally dangerous to include evidence when submitting a theory article because the evidence might not be of equivalent standard to the theory. If this is true, it cannot be good for the development of economic understanding.

In my opinion there is another criterion for a plausible explanation of events.

A plausible explanation describes the behaviour of people and companies in ways they themselves would recognise

There are two polar styles in economics, with a spectrum in between. At one pole are those who are content with explanations that appeal to economists but not to anyone else. An example is the theory that unemployment fluctuates due to intertemporal substitution in labour supply. This was never remotely plausible to any unemployed person, but wasted the time of millions of economics students. Our profession is so sheltered that it is quite possible for it to play its own games without worrying when there are literally no spectators from outside the profession.

But in the end the theories which prevail are those where the economist has checked his model with practitioners. He has said to an economic actor, 'Here is my model of why you do what you do', and the actor has said, 'Yes, that makes sense'. Surely every economist should perform such checks.

It is nice to be an economist because on the whole it has been the most successful social science – in predictive ability and therefore in public prestige. Yet in many ways this is surprising because the theory of rational choice explains such a small part of human behaviour.

Human wellbeing depends on more than individual opportunities

Economics explains the behaviour of individuals with given tastes as their opportunities change. It does not explain their tastes. Thus economics is much better at explaining *changes* in behaviour than the *levels* of, say, consumption or time use. Culture is a key factor here, though as the world becomes more homogeneous there will be fewer such differences to explain.

A second major weakness of standard economics is that it ignores many key variables that affect utility and therefore affect behaviour. For example, if you get a pay rise and I do not, I become unhappy. This may affect my work effort. The simplest form of efficiency wage theory is one where effort depends on the individual's wage relative to some concept of the fair wage. In that case, work effort will not be correctly predicted by a utility function that ignores these externalities.

This is extremely unfortunate from the point of view of positive economics. It is even more serious from the point of view of normative or 'public' economics. For example, if I work harder and earn more and this hurts other people, then this provides an extra argument in favour of income taxes.

It is most unfortunate that the thousands of economists who think about how to maximise a social welfare function $W(u_1, \ldots, u_u)$ should have devoted so little attention to what actually generates utility. It is one reason why politicians often disregard the advice of economists – because they know better what affects utility than the economists who think that income and prices say it all. Obviously psychologists and social psychologists have to come to the rescue here, but they will not provide the insights that we need unless we work with them. Among the few honourable examples of economists who do this are Richard Thaler and Andrew Oswald. One of Oswald's most important findings is that being unemployed reduces a person's happiness by much more than the cost of the income loss. This means that social welfare depends not only on output but also negatively on unemployment. The usual welfare triangle will give quite the wrong idea, especially if we treat leisure as a normal good.

Thus any sensible policy analysis is bound to use an eclectic approach. Most of the economists I most respect do just this, rather than using one simple model as a guide. They also recognise that any policy choice must allow for issues of fairness as well as efficiency.

Public choices must always involve issues of income distribution

When I took up economics in the 1960s the common view was that 'economic policy' was about how to achieve efficiency – maximising the size of the cake. It was then the task of 'social policy' to decide how the cake should be distributed and used. This distinction between economic and social policy was a disaster, since every policy decision affects both the size of the cake and its distribution. The focus on efficiency had been rationalised by the Kaldor criterion, which said that a change was good if the gainers gained enough to be able (hypothetically) to compensate the losers, by lump-sum transfers. The criterion was philosophically absurd since a change could be morally justified along these lines only if the compensation were actually paid. It is also practically unhelpful since in the practical world lump-sum transfers (with no incentive effects) are impossible to orchestrate and any policy generates losers as well as gainers.

Yet in the early postwar period much of the thinking of economists about the problems of distribution was conducted as if lump-sum transfers were possible. Thus arose the postwar welfare state which considered that poverty was best dealt with through cash redistribution, rather than by enabling people (where possible) to be productive and earn a decent living.

Thinking improved greatly through the work of James Meade, Britain's greatest postwar economist and founder of the subject of 'public economics', and his great successors Jim Mirrlees, Tony Atkinson, Joe Stiglitz and Amartya Sen who was a great influence for good at LSE during the 1970s. They all started from the point that lump-sum transfers were impossible and we are in the world of second-best. It followed that if the objective was to maximise a social welfare function $W(u_1, ..., u_n)$ subject to behavioural constraints, we should always find that the marginal social value of a pound was different in the hands of different people. Normally the value would be higher in the hands of the poor than of the rich. So income distribution must be taken into account in evaluating every policy.

I stressed this in my first textbook, on *Cost-Benefit Analysis* (1972), and I felt it so strongly that, when I later wrote a microeconomics textbook with Alan Walters (1978), we put welfare economics at the front of the book. The result was that Amartya Sen called it the most left-wing micro text available. But a second result was that it never captured the market. However, I still think that no policy remarks should be included in micro textbooks until the issues of welfare economics have been properly discussed.

Thus policy choices depend on a well specified social welfare function involving ethical judgements, and on sound knowledge of behavioural relationships. The policy problem will suggest which behavioural relationships most need understanding. For example, income tax policy obviously requires knowledge of labour supply responses. But the spirit in which the behavioural relationships are studied should be totally detached. And indeed it is a very good thing that many economists have no interest in advocating policies or in making a fortune – they just want to explain what happens.

If the economics I learned in the 1960s was a little confused on issues of income distribution, in most other ways it was remarkably sound. Some people say that economists have totally changed their tune since the 1960s. This is simply untrue.

Little has happened to make economists change their political philosophy

There was in fact little wrong with the mainstream approach of the majority of British economists in the 1960s. They accepted the profit motive and favoured private production of most goods and services (at least three-quarters of GDP). They were unenthusiastic about trade unions and believed that redistribution was a key role for the state. They also believed that, where individuals are ignorant or exposed (as in education and health), state provision is necessary for efficiency and fairness. Most of them thought competition was important in the private economy and were suspicious of 'industrial policy'. Almost all believed in free trade, except for some development economists. As regards macroeconomics, they considered the key instruments of short-run policy were fiscal policy and interest rates.

So what has changed? For most of the economists I respect, only two things of importance. First, in 1970–2 we switched from the Phillips curve to the expectations-augmented Phillips curve – an important change technically, leading to a de-emphasising of demand as opposed to supply-side issues. But it was hardly a change of political philosophy. Second, we became more aware of government failure as well as market failure, and in the 1980s were converted to the privatisation of telecoms and the debureaucratising of many state functions through the establishment of public agencies.

But the idea that the economics profession in Britain has changed its basic tune is quite simply untrue. The profession has surely been at fault in not explaining clearly enough what it believed – leaving this too often to people at either extreme. Hence people have the impression that economists always disagree with each other – an impression largely overstated by the media because anything else makes the analysis too tame.

At least I can honestly say that my own position has changed little except in the ways I have said. As early as 1980 I was writing that the welfare state had taken the wrong tack in its approach to unemployment, and needed instead a Welfare-to-Work approach.

I also have the impression that most of those who hold more right-wing opinions than myself now also held similar positions in the 1960s. The main change has been a reduced number of left-wingers; most have moved to the centre while a few have unhelpfully proclaimed that economics has died, rather than noting that it was always a complicated business.

Compared with people from some other disciplines, most British economists are now polite and helpful to each other. When they disagree with each other, they usually understand why – rather than simply failing to make contact. This comradeliness makes it a pleasant profession to work in, and is perhaps at its best in Britain's leading economics department at the London School of Economics (LSE), where I have had the pleasure to work throughout my professional life.

THE BOOKS

The sequence of my interests has been heavily influenced by problems of concern in the external world, and perhaps I should describe the sequence briefly as an explanation of the papers gathered together in *Tackling Inequality* and *Tackling Unemployment*.

Education and income distribution

I became an economist in the 1960s. This was a time of strong educational expansion caused by the rapidly rising demand for educated people, coming partly from the space race. This raised the stock of educated people, which in time depressed graduate earnings. So in the 1970s educational expansion largely stopped. In consequence, there was eventually a shortage of educated people, and the rewards to educated people again rose. This produced a second great expansion from the late 1980s, and at the time of writing education is the top priority of all three British political parties.

I have always believed that most people can reach a good educational level if the motivation and opportunities are there. The motivation is largely affected by the pay of people with different types of skill, which is in turn determined by the interaction of demand and supply. But it is also affected by the degree of subsidisation provided by the state.

A key issue in educational policy is therefore the degree of subsidisation at different levels. This can be resolved only by taking into account considerations of equity as well as efficiency. In the 1960s the discussion of education and income distribution focused on the impact of education on annual earnings. This was the great contribution of Becker and Mincer. They showed how the variance of education helped to explain the inequality of annual earnings. But the policy implications went largely unanalysed. On the one side more educated people earned more. But on the other side students were poor. What followed?

It was clear that one could think about the distributional issues only by looking at the incomes of different people over their whole lifetimes. Philosophically, the same applied to issues like health, child support and pensions where one function of the state is to redistribute between different points of life, but another is to redistribute between lifetimes. I therefore developed a cost-benefit framework for analysing the efficiency and equity impact of policies, where equity is evaluated in terms of lifetime income.

When Lyndon Johnson launched the War on Poverty, he believed that education was the key to a more equal society. But then Jencks pointed out that education explains only a small fraction of the variance of annual earnings, making it appear a weak tool of equalisation. But if, as I argued, annual earnings was the wrong concept and it was lifetime earnings that mattered, then a key role for education was re-established.

I tried to show this using relevant empirical material – and comparing the effects of different educational policies with cash redistribution. Since people live in families the analysis has to be done using family income per head rather than individual income. It requires also a knowledge of supply responses.

This led me into the study of family labour supply, since the scope for redistribution is limited by the size of the labour supply response. On the other side, however, I was struck by the consideration that, in trying to keep up with the Joneses, people might be induced to work excessively.

I had the good fortune at this time to meet Orley Ashenfelter who played an important role in bringing the rigour of American labour economics to Britain. I was also asked by the Royal Commission on the Distribution of Income and Wealth to write a report on the causes of poverty, which enabled me to set many of these issues in perspective. At the same time I wrote the microeconomics textbook with Alan Walters to make sure I understood the subject.

In the area of education my other interest was in education as an industry and its incentives (or lack of them) to be efficient. The dominant technology in the education industry has changed little since the invention of book and blackboard, while the technology of communication has been totally revolutionised by post, radio, television, cassette player and computer where there are huge economies of scale. I argued that to be cost-effective the industry had to change. But the problem was, and remains, the incentives facing teachers. Now at last there is some sign that things are changing.

By the late 1970s I was thinking of writing a book about economics and human nature – in other words about what makes people happy and what this implies for policy. But, instead, the second oil shock sent unemployment rocketing up and I thought it would be more useful to work on unemployment.

Unemployment

Though I knew little about the subject, in 1980 I signed a contract to write a book called *Unemployment*. The book was published in 1991 with three authors – Richard Jackman, Stephen Nickell and myself. Working with them has been the most satisfying experience of my working life. Throughout the 1980s we were developing our ideas in a series of articles, but I always felt (and continue to feel) that the idea of a book is always the best incentive for getting a real perspective on an issue. Partly for that reason, but also in order to stimulate debate, I wrote a smaller popular book in 1986 called *How to Beat Unemployment*, reflecting where we had got to at that point.

Looking back, I think our main contributions on unemployment were these.

1   We focused attention on the average level of unemployment over the cycle (the NAIRU) and tried to explain this. We insisted that both positive and normative analysis of unemployment should start from a *general equilibrium* framework, in which the artificial distinction between macro and micro had no place. All the various factors at work should fit into a single model, which could handle the reality of individuals flowing through unemployment as well as the other forces at work. The most fruitful model turned out to involve a function for wages (or more strictly labour cost), a price function and a hiring function.

2   We argued that a key clue to higher European unemployment was the outward shift of unemployment at given *vacancies*. This suggested that something was making the unemployed less effective as fillers of vacancies.

3   One possible explanation for this was increased *mismatch* by skill, region or industry. But we rigorously derived an appropriate measure of mismatch, between the pattern of jobs and the characteristics of job seekers – and this suggested that mismatch had not increased.

4   A more plausible explanation was the huge increase in the proportion of the unemployed who were *long-term* unemployed. We were able to show how for a given unemployment level, vacancies and wage pressure were higher the higher was the proportion of long-term unemployed within the total. This has now become the conventional wisdom, and there is growing support for the corollary – that the welfare state should be re-designed to prevent people entering long-term unemployment.

5   The key issue to focus upon was the wage curve – i.e. the level of real wage cost associated with any given level of unemployment. The main factors influencing unemployment could all be analysed through their influence on the wage curve. Important factors included are *wage bargaining*, where we developed a plausible model of decentralised bargaining (perhaps the first) which explained why (despite the turnover of workers) firms tended not to

contract but to adjust their employment in response to the size of the labour force.

6 For all the main *policies* we tried to develop relevant models. For active labour market policy we developed models to analyse the degree of substitution and displacement (much exaggerated in public discussion), and we showed in a plausible way how a tax-based incomes policy would work. George Johnson was a great stimulus to all our policy analysis.

Meantime I was fortunate enough in 1982 to be appointed to the Macroeconomic Policy Group set up by the European Commission, and including Rudi Dornbusch (as its first chairman) and Olivier Blanchard. Both have been wonderful colleagues. They focused my mind on the absolute necessity of a blending of macro and micro. They also forced me to think about problems on a wider international canvas, and in my time in the group we produced four reports urging a more proactive employment strategy in Europe.

Economic reform

In 1989 Dornbusch and I formed a new group including also Olivier Blanchard, Larry Summers, Paul Krugman and Andrei Shleifer. This was the time of economic transition, and our group produced three books on reform, including one on its impact on migration.

In 1991 I was invited to become an economic adviser to the Russian government and spent much of 1992 there. Thereafter my monthly visits became shorter and shorter, but we still had a strong team in Moscow producing *Russian Economic Trends* and contributing to the Russian policy debate within the government and the media. We had a monthly press conference. The work I did on Russia was largely macroeconomic, including writing a macroeconomic textbook about the Russian economy. But I also studied the labour market and analysed the remarkable labour market flexibility there which helped to keep unemployment in check.

Progress in Russia was always going to be difficult, given Russia's unique legacy of 75 years of Communism. Up to the end of 1996 I was fairly optimistic and progress was indeed being made. John Parker and I recorded our views in a co-authored book which we titled *Russia Reborn?* but the publisher insisted on calling it *The Coming Russian Boom*. From December 1996 onwards I became more pessimistic, as reflected in the monthly updates of *Russian Economic Trends*. The problem was not, as is often said, that Russia was having inappropriate market solutions foisted on it, but that local and national governments were interfering in every aspect of the economy and preventing new firms from developing. From autumn 1997 my anxieties increased, as it became obvious that Russia was next in line for a speculative attack after the

Far East. Early and resolute action by the West could have preserved financial order, but it was not taken.

In the meantime the British policy world has become a lot more attractive to someone like myself. The Labour Party has adopted on a large scale the kinds of policy in which I believe – preventing long-term unemployment and ensuring a minimum level of skill for all. We now have a real opportunity to put our ideas to the test.

I cannot end without a tribute to the LSE which has been my working home. It provides a wonderfully stimulating environment, in which there is always someone who knows the answer to your questions and someone who will help. The hand of management is light, so that if you have an idea you can implement it.

I came to LSE in 1964 to set up with Claus Moser the Higher Education Research Unit. In 1974 it became the Centre for Labour Economics and in 1990 the Centre for Economic Performance.[1] Since 1980 it has had a block grant from the ESRC, whose support has been constant and unswerving. And it has attracted the best in-house research group of economists in Europe and two fine deputy directors Charles Bean and David Metcalf. I am deeply grateful for their help. But equally important has been the wonderful administrative support over the years of Pam Mounsey, Bettie Jory, Phyllis Gamble, Joanne Putterford, Philomena McNicholas and, above all, Marion O'Brien and Nigel Rogers. I have been truly lucky.

Note

1.　Strictly, from 1964–7 it was called the Unit for Economic and Statistical Studies on Higher Education, and from 1974–7 it was the Centre for the Economics of Education. But the key break points were 1964, 1974 and 1990.

References

Layard, R. (ed.) (1972) *Cost-Benefit Analysis* (Penguin Modern Economics Readings); Second Edition (edited with S. Glaister) 1994 (Cambridge University Press).

Layard, R. (1986) *How to Beat Unemployment* (Oxford: Oxford University Press).

Layard, R. (from 1992) *Russian Economic Trends*, 4 quarterly issues (London: Whurr).

Layard, R., S. Nickell and R. Jackman (1991) *Unemployment: Macroeconomic Performance and the Labour Market* (Oxford: Oxford University Press).

Layard, R. and J. Parker (1996) *The Coming Russian Boom* (New York: The Free Press).

Layard, R. and A. Walters (1978) *Microeconomic Theory* (New York: McGraw-Hill) reissued as McGraw-Hill International Edition, 1987.

Part I
Explaining Unemployment

2 Introduction to Part I

World unemployment rose sharply in the mid-1970s following the first oil shock, and again in the early 1980s following the second. But in the USA unemployment then fell back to earlier levels; in Europe it did not. This experience provides a real challenge to economists – as a phenomenon requiring explanation, and as a problem calling for a policy response.

At first it was not clear how long the higher unemployment would last, and it was natural to explain it as a temporary response to shocks. In the 1970s there were two big real shocks to OECD countries – the rise in the real cost of imports (especially oil) and the fall in productivity growth. These shocks then set up inflationary pressures which led to increased inflation or increased unemployment or both. In other words the Philips curve trade-off between unemployment and changes in inflation shifted towards higher unemployment. And the shift was bigger the greater the 'real wage rigidity' in the coefficients of the wage equation. As Chapter 3 shows, such an approach explained quite well the growth of unemployment in the 1970s, and the differential growth across different countries.[1]

But one would expect that eventually an economy would absorb real shocks. Yet, as the 1980s progressed, unemployment in Europe failed to fall, and further explanations had to be sought. Various facts struck one in the face. First, much of the extra unemployment in Europe was long-term unemployment. Second, European countries tended to provide unemployment benefits for very long periods – often indefinitely. Third, long-term unemployed people have much lower exit rates from unemployment than people who became unemployed more recently. And, fourth, vacancies in many European countries were as high in the mid-1980s as they had been in the early 1970s.

LONG-TERM UNEMPLOYMENT

The following explanation took shape. There had been an initial shock. This had increased long-term unemployment, but because of long-duration benefits there was limited pressure for long-term unemployment to fall. The extra long-term unemployed people exerted very little downward pressure on wages because employers did not want to hire them. In consequence vacancies remained unfilled even though there were more unemployed people around: they were not the right kind of unemployed people.

Nickell and I set about investigating these ideas (see Chapter 4). It did indeed appear that the number of long-term unemployed exerted a much smaller downward effect on wages than the number of short-term unemployed. And vacancies fell less when long-term unemployment rose than when short-term unemployment rose.[2]

HYSTERESIS

This approach also explained why wage pressure depended not only on the level of unemployment but also on its rate of change – the so-called 'hysteresis issue' whereby wage pressure depends not only on the current state of the labour market but also on past history. Our explanation was simple. If unemployment is falling, short-term unemployment is low relative to long-term unemployment. Thus for a given level of unemployment, wage pressure will be more when unemployment is falling. Our estimated relationships bore this out.

If long-term unemployment is the key, the policy consequences (see below) are clear. But there was another quite different explanation of hysteresis put forward by Blanchard and Summers (1986).[3] This explanation was based not on the nature of the 'outsiders' but on the number of the 'insiders'. Insiders set wages in their own interest only – without regard to the number of outsiders. Thus if actual employment is low in one period, the equilibrium level of employment next period will also be low. If demand expands, employment will indeed rise but this will be inflationary.

This explanation of hysteresis was difficult to reconcile with a number of basic facts. Even in recession most firms are hiring workers: why do the remaining workers 'permit' this? Moreover, when the labour force grows, employment generally rises: why? And, even more problematic, vacancies in many countries were as high in the later 1980s as in the early 1970s: why?

Empirically, the debate between the two approaches could be resolved only by using firm level data to find out whether the number of insiders in a firm is more important, or the number and types of unemployed in the local labour market. Later on Nickell and Wadhwani (1990) did such a study and confirmed that what mattered most was the number and types of unemployed.

LAYARD–NICKELL MODEL

The time was ripe to look simultaneously at all the possible factors affecting unemployment within a unified framework. Stephen Nickell and I did this in what has become known as the Layard–Nickell model. This appears in Chapter 4.

The model has two main equations – for labour cost and prices. In equilibrium, wage and price surprises are ruled out, and the real labour cost set by wage setters must equal the real labour cost set by price setters. Unemployment is the variable that brings them into line.

We had already made two earlier attempts at the model[4] in which we also incorporated aggregate demand – in a rather complicated way. But we eventually concluded that the *IS* relationship is the best way to handle the short-run determination of unemployment, with inflation then moving up or down according to our model, so long as unemployment differs from its equilibrium level.

There is one further wrinkle. If relative import prices rise, this tends in the medium term to increase wage pressure. So the equilibrium level of unemployment in the medium term can clearly be reduced by a real appreciation of the currency – but only at the expense of the trade balance.

In the model all the main factors affecting equilibrium unemployment do so through their effects on wage pressure. These factors include the treatment of the unemployed; wage bargaining; labour market mismatch; employment protection; and taxation. Each of these are treated in the chapters which follow.

THE EFFECTIVENESS OF THE UNEMPLOYED

A key clue to the causes of higher unemployment is the fact that vacancies have not fallen while unemployment has risen. To investigate this Richard Jackman and I joined forces with Christopher Pissarides, a pioneer in the theory of labour market flows (see Chapter 5). We estimated the first 'hiring function', from which it was clear that in Britain the effectiveness of the unemployed as fillers of vacancies had fallen steadily.[5]

Why was this? One obvious hypothesis was that long-term unemployment was not just a symptom of high unemployment but a mechanism which reduced the effectiveness of an unemployed person – he became demoralised or stigmatised by employers. And this was one reason why in micro data the exit rates from unemployment are much lower for long-term than for short-term unemployed people.

However there is an alternative explanation for this phenomenon – that the best people get jobs quickly so that the long-term unemployed are worse people (and were so when they started unemployment). This issue is difficult to disentangle from micro data, but it is clearly important for policy purposes. Chapter 6 provides a test of the 'selectivity' explanation based on aggregate data, and finds strong support for the notion that long-term unemployment does in the context of the British benefit system have a markedly detrimental effect.

Thus long-duration benefits of the kind common in Europe have an extra strong effect on the level of unemployment. They make it possible for people to remain unemployed; and, as the people continue in unemployment, they then become less and less likely to find work. In other words they get 'excluded'. This effect of long-duration benefit is strongly confirmed in the cross-country cross-section reported in Chapter 10.

MISMATCH

There was however another obvious reason why vacancies might have risen at given unemployment rates: the pattern of skills among the unemployed could be increasingly out of line with the pattern of skills demanded. Or the pattern of geographical location of the workforce might be increasingly inappropriate.

How was this issue of mismatch to be investigated? Some people said that mismatch should be measured by the variance of sectoral unemployment rates; others said it should be the coefficient of variation; and so on. To resolve this issue requires a proper model in which for each type of labour there is a wage function and a demand function. In the wage function the log sectoral wage appears to be a linear function of log sectoral unemployment. As Chapter 7 shows, it follows that the equilibrium level of total unemployment rises when there is an increase in the spread of unemployment rates across groups even if the mean remains constant. This is because the fall in unemployment for a low-unemployment group increases wage pressure more than the rise in unemployment for a high-unemployment group reduces wage pressure.

We therefore computed the movement of relative unemployment rates for most OECD countries since the early 1970s. In general, there was no increase in the relative dispersion. We can therefore rule out increased dispersion as a cause of increased unemployment. This does not mean that the *level* of dispersion does not matter and should not be reduced. Indeed we show that, in Britain, unemployment is at least 50 per cent higher than it would be in the absence of mismatch.

In the preceding analysis, worked out in the 1980s, no effort is made to explain the evolution of unemployment for each of the different groups. Perhaps for this reason, our argument about mismatch was not everywhere accepted. Chapter 8 therefore explains separately the movement of unemployment for each separate group.[6] Its main point is that if extra mismatch explained increased European unemployment, the unemployment rate of the unskilled should have risen, but in addition the unemployment rate of the skilled should have *fallen*. Since in fact it rose, the extra unemployment must have come from the some other source than mismatch: there must have been an increase in *aggregate* wage pressure arising, for example, from the working of the benefit system.

WAGE BARGAINING

This brings us to the question of wage bargaining. Bruno and Sachs (1985) had already suggested that coordinated bargaining at a national level might produce lower wage pressure (and thus lower unemployment) than would result from decentralised bargaining. But it took us some time to find a plausible model of decentralised bargaining. Most of the standard models implied that in the presence of turnover the union would prefer that employment fell steadily. Eventually Stephen Nickell and I found a framework in which existing workers face a stochastic demand curve. Their chances of continuing in their present job depends on the wage set in the bargain, and they care about their expected wage. This leads to a sensible framework set out in Chapter 9 in which the individual wage bargain is indeed affected by the number of insiders but more so by the effectiveness of the outsiders (the unemployed).

Thus far the conclusion was that high European unemployment (relative to the USA) was due mainly to the European welfare state and to some unduly high minimum wages (linked to high employers' social security contributions). However many others argued that the main problem in Europe was labour market rigidity due to laws on employment protection. When the *OECD Jobs Study* (1994) talked about labour market rigidity as *the* problem, *they* meant by 'rigidity' more than just employment protection but many people focused on this as the central issue. Were they right?

EMPLOYMENT PROTECTION

The role of employment protection can be investigated at many levels – disaggregated and aggregated. At the aggregate level it is clear that employment protection discourages hiring and thus increases long-term unemployment. It also discourages firing and thus reduces short-term unemployment. There is no *a priori* way to know the net effect. Empirically, one way to resolve this is to include employment protection in a cross-country regression in which one tries to explain country level unemployment by all the main factors that might be affecting it.

This is done in Chapter 10. The effects on long-term and short-term unemployment is as predicted, and the net overall effect is negligible.

OTHER CAUSES

Other causes that have been adduced for unemployment include social security taxes on employers, excessive hours of work and excessive work by old people. These too are investigated in Chapter 10 and receive no support.

GRADUATE UNEMPLOYMENT IN INDIA

I end Part I with my earliest work on unemployment – on graduate unemployment in India. Chapter 11 was written in 1967 with Mark Blaug.

Our explanation was in terms of 'wait unemployment'. Graduate wages are rigid, and people flood into the colleges until the expected income of graduates equals that of non-graduates. This explanation is very similar to the explanation of urban unemployment being developed at the same time by Harris and Todaro (1970).

Notes

1. For an earlier approach also Jackman and Layard (1982). In both these papers our model had no long-run solution for the level of real wages. In all our subsequent work we rectified this, though some writers still believe that in the USA there is no long-run solution (Blanchard and Katz, 1997).
2. See Budd, Levine and Smith (1988).
3. See also Lindbeck and Snower (1989).
4. Layard and Nickell (1985, 1986).
5. The article was originally written in 1983 and also included a complete theory of the determination of vacancies. Since it was (I think) one of the more interesting pieces I have written, it was especially difficult to get it accepted. The theory of the determination of vacancies was published in Layard, Nickell and Jackman (1991), pp. 272–5.
6. It also proposes a sounder index of mismatch than was used in Chapter 7.

References

Blanchard, O. and L. Katz (1997) 'What We Know and Do Not Know about the Natural Rate of Unemployment', *Journal of Economic Perspectives*, 11(1) (Winter), 51–72.

Blanchard, O. and L. Summers (1986) 'Hysteresis and the European Unemployment Problem', in S. Fischer (ed.), *NBER Macroeconomics Annual 1986* (Cambridge, MA: NBER).

Bruno, M. and G. Sachs (1985) *Economics of Worldwide Stagflation* (Oxford: Basil Blackwell).

Budd, A., P. Levine and P. Smith (1988) 'Unemployment, Vacancies and the Long-term Unemployed', *Economic Journal*, 98, 1071–91.

Harris, J. and M. Todaro (1970) 'Migration, Unemployment and Development. A 2-sector analysis', *American Economic Review*, 55: 126–142.

Jackman, R. and R. Layard, (1982) 'An Inflation Tax', *Fiscal Studies* (March).

Layard, R., S. Nickell, and R. Jackman, (1991) *Unemployment: Macroeconomic Performance and the Labour Market* (Oxford: Oxford University Press).

Layard, R. and S. Nickell, (1985) 'The Causes of British Unemployment', *National Institute Economic Review* (February).

Layard, R. and S. Nickell, (1986) 'An Incomes Policy to Help the Unemployed', Employment Institute; reprinted in J. Shields (ed.), *Making the Economy Work* (London: Macmillan).

Lindbeck, A. and D. Snower (1989) *The Insider–Outsider Theory of Employment and Unemployment* (Cambridge, MA: MIT Press).

Nickell, S. and S. Wadhwani, (1990) 'Insider Forces and Wage Determination', *Economic Journal*, 100, 496–509

OECD (1994) *Jobs Study* (Paris: OECD).

3 Wage Rigidity and Unemployment in OECD Countries (1983)*

with D. Grubb and R. Jackman

1 INTRODUCTION AND SUMMARY

Real wage rigidity is often blamed for causing unemployment in the wake of adverse real shocks, like changes in productivity or the terms of trade. Likewise nominal wage rigidity is blamed for causing unemployment in the wake of adverse nominal shocks, like falls in nominal demand.[1] However, there has been relatively little systematic discussion of how these concepts should be defined. Some authors (e.g. Sachs, 1979) have defined real wage rigidity as the opposite of nominal wage rigidity, with the US nominally rigid and Europe really rigid.[2] The rigidity of European real wages has then been used to explain why Europe has experienced a greater increase in unemployment since 1973 than the US. But in this discussion real wage rigidity has not been measured in a way which would in fact predict how much unemployment would result from a given real shock. The discussion has focused on the degree of nominal inertia in the system. But the unemployment cost of real shocks does not depend primarily on the degree of nominal inertia but rather on the effect of unemployment in the Phillips curve.

In Section 2 of the paper we therefore offer our own definitions of real and nominal wage rigidity, based on the unemployment consequences of the corresponding (real or nominal) shocks. Real wage rigidity is the inverse of the long-run coefficient on unemployment in the wage equation. Nominal wage rigidity is real wage rigidity multiplied by the sum of the average lags in the wage and price equations. It follows that nominal and real wage rigidity can

* *European Economic Review*, 21 (1983), pp. 11–39. © 1983 North-Holland Publishing Company. The authors are extremely grateful to T. Casas-Bedos for computing assistance, to C. Bismut, W. Buiter, G. Fethke, R.J. Gordon, S. Nickell and J.B. Taylor for helpful advice and comments, and to the Social Science Research Council for financial support.

well coexist, and in fact across nineteen OECD countries the estimated correlation between them turns out to be positive (though insignificant).

In section 3 we estimate wage and price equations for nineteen countries, from which we derive our measures of rigidity. We then examine the role of these rigidities in 'accounting for' the different unemployment experiences of the different countries. First we show how the 2 per cent higher OECD unemployment in the 1973–80 period (compared with 1960–72) can be accounted for mainly by the slower rate of growth of feasible real wages of given employment. This slower growth has arisen in about equal measure from the more rapid increase in relative import prices (which were previously falling) and from the fall in the rate of productivity growth.

If one then examines the position in the different countries, one can ask: Do the different unemployment experiences (in so far as we can explain them) correspond mainly to differences in shocks or to differences in real wage rigidity? The answer is that in our estimates it is the degree of rigidity which matters most. The estimated correlation between real wage rigidity and increased unemployment is −0.5. (Countries also differ importantly in the trend growth of unemployment.) Countries with notably low real wage rigidity include Switzerland, Japan, New Zealand, Sweden and Austria – all countries with notably low increases in unemployment. The US has notably high nominal wage rigidity, due to its long lags, but does not appear to have low real wage rigidity.

In section 4 we try to explain why countries differ in the wage response to unemployment and to current prices. On the basis of a simple model, we hypothesise that the response to unemployment will be higher the higher the variance of nominal and real shocks experienced. In addition the response to current prices will be higher the higher the ratio of nominal to real disturbances (the Fischer–Gray result) and the higher the degree of policy accommodation to inflationary shocks. Our empirical investigations provide little support for these hypotheses, however.

Finally we note that our estimates of rigidity are based on a model in which the constant term in the wage equation does not alter over the relevant period in response to changes in real wage growth actually experienced. In fact there must be some adaptation. With the limited historical evidence available, it is not easy to estimate such a model for any one country. But for the OECD as a whole we have estimated an adaptive model, which tends to confirm that our earlier approach to the wage determination process in 1973–80 may have been quite realistic.

2 CONCEPTS

Economists are interested in wage rigidity because it causes unemployment to increase in the face of adverse shocks. So the natural measure of wage rigidity is the extra unemployment which occurs in the face of a deflationary shock.

Suppose we begin with the simplest possible wage adjustment function,

$$\dot{w} = \dot{p}^e - \beta(U - U_0) + \dot{q}^e \tag{1}$$

together with a labour demand function written in the form of a price equation,

$$\dot{p} = \dot{w} - \dot{q} - \gamma\dot{U} \tag{2}$$

Here small letters denote logarithms and w, p, and U are money wages, prices and the unemployment rate, respectively; $\dot{w} = w - w_{-1}$ and similarly for other variables; $\dot{q}$ is the feasible growth rate of real wages at constant unemployment (reflecting capital accumulation, labour force growth, technical progress and relative import prices); $\dot{q}^e$ is the target rate of real wage growth when U equals U_0.

Adding (1) and (2) gives[3]

$$\dot{p} - \dot{p}^e = -\beta(U - U_0) + (\dot{q}^e - \dot{q}) - \gamma\dot{U} \tag{3}$$

A real shock in this framework is represented by a fall in $\dot{q}$ relative to $\dot{q}^e$. It is apparent from (3) that a real shock may be associated in the short-run with higher unemployment or faster than anticipated inflation. However, the total unemployment caused by the shock is independent of the short-run response. To see this, suppose that for one year $\dot{q}$ falls by $(-\Delta\dot{q}_0)$. We can then accumulate the differences on both sides of the equation – differences being taken from the no-shock case. This gives

$$\sum_t \Delta(\dot{p}_t - \dot{p}_t^e) = -\beta \sum_t \Delta U_t - \Delta\dot{q}_0 - \gamma \sum_t \Delta\dot{U}_t$$

Since the economy will return to the original level of unemployment, $\sum \Delta\dot{U}_{t=0}$. It is also reasonable to suppose that the cumulated errors in the inflation forecast were zero both before and after the shock, so that the left-hand side is zero. It follows that, if ΔU_t is the unemployment change caused at time t by the initial shock,

$$\sum_t \Delta U_t = (1/\beta)(-\Delta\dot{q}_0)$$

These are the point years of unemployment caused by the shock. So the proper measure of real wage rigidity (RWR) is $1/\beta$,

$$RWR = 1/\beta$$

Equivalently the proper measure of real wage flexibility is the reciprocal (β). This measure is independent of the government's policy response to the shock – it depends only on the assumption of zero long-run errors in inflation forecasts.

We could also of course ask what would be the effect of a permanent fall in $\dot{q}$ (of $-\Delta\dot{q}$), rather than a one-period shock. If $\dot{q}^e$ did not adjust, we can see from (3) that, so long as price expectations are satisfied,

$$\Delta U = (1/\beta)(-\Delta\dot{q})$$

Once again the measure of real wage rigidity is $1/\beta$. As we shall show, over the medium term this approach seems to explain a good deal of the stagflation of recent years.

2.1 A model with nominal inertia

All this is fairly obvious. But how does real wage rigidity relate to nominal wage rigidity? Nominal wage rigidity can only arise if there is some nominal inertia in the system. This might arise from overlapping wage contracts, or from adaptive expectations of price inflation. Let us assume that price expectations are correct apart from a white noise error, and that inertia comes from the role of lagged wage inflation.[4] This gives a wage equation (omitting the error term) of

$$\dot{w} = \alpha\dot{p} + (1 - \alpha)\dot{w}_{-1} - \alpha\beta(U - U_0) + \alpha\dot{q}^e \tag{1'}$$

In this equation we have, reasonably enough, imposed linear homogeneity on the nominal variables. We have also modified the coefficient on unemployment, so that β continues to measure the long-run effect of unemployment on real wages; and we have modified the constant term, so that $\dot{q}^e$ continues to measure the long-run rate of growth of real wages at $U = U_0$.

In this system, how does the rate of inflation vary? Focusing on wage inflation, (1') and (2) give

$$\ddot{w} = (\alpha/(1 - \alpha))(-\beta(U - U_0) + (\dot{q}^e - \dot{q}) - \gamma\dot{U}) \tag{3'}$$

This is the basic equation of this paper.

Let us first confirm our earlier analysis of the question of real wage rigidity. A one-period fall in $\dot{q}$ will increase inflation. So long as the government is unwilling to allow a permanent increase in inflation, $\dot{w}$ will ultimately have to return to its original level, so unemployment will have to increase to produce an equal and opposite long-run effect. Since $\sum\ddot{w}_t = 0$ and $\sum\dot{U}_t = 0$, we find as before

$$\sum\Delta U_t = (1/\beta)(-\Delta\dot{q})$$

The degree of real wage rigidity equals the inverse of the long-run coefficient on unemployment in the wage equation.[5]

This definition of real wage rigidity assumes of course that inflation has to return to its original level. If inflation were allowed to rise permanently, then the economy could adapt to a real shock with less unemployment.[6] So how arbitrary or uninteresting is the assumption that inflation returns to its previous level? It is noteworthy that since about 1972 most countries have been unwilling to tolerate a permanent increase in the inflation rate. So we would argue that our definition of real wage rigidity is of considerable practical relevance.

What is the natural definition of nominal wage flexibility? Consider a nominal shock. Suppose the government reduces the rate of growth of nominal income by $(-\Delta \dot{w})$ points and then holds it constant. Ultimately the rate of wage inflation will fall by $(-\Delta \dot{w})$ points. But if $\sum \ddot{w}_t = -\Delta \dot{w}$, it follows that

$$\sum \Delta U_t = [(1 - \alpha)/\alpha](1/\beta)(-\Delta \dot{w})$$

So the natural measure of nominal wage rigidity (NWR) is[7]

$$NWR = [(1 - \alpha)/\alpha](1/\beta)$$

This expression is very interesting. For $(1-\alpha)/\alpha$ is the average lag of wages on prices. The longer the lag of wages on prices, the less the rate of change of inflation per year for a point year of unemployment. Hence, to achieve a given total fall in inflation, more point years of unemployment are needed. By contrast if there is a zero lag, there is no nominal wage rigidity. Even a little unemployment will set off an infinitely fast decline in inflation, as falling prices chase falling wages and vice versa.

So nominal wage rigidity is real wage rigidity times the average lag (AL),

$$NWR = RWR \cdot AL$$

Across countries, unless there is a strong negative covariance of real wage rigidity and the average lag, one would expect that countries with high real wage rigidity would also have high nominal wage rigidity and vice versa.

So how did the opposite idea arise? Suppose we rewrite (1') as

$$\dot{w} = \alpha \dot{p} + (1 - \alpha)\dot{w}_{-1} - \beta^*(U - U_0) + \alpha \dot{q}^e \quad \text{where} \quad \beta^* = \alpha \beta$$

Then

$$RWR = \alpha/\beta^* \quad \text{and} \quad NWR = (1 - \alpha)/\beta^*$$

Hence for a given coefficient on unemployment in the Phillips curve, the more rapid the pass-through of prices into wages the greater the real wage rigidity, but the greater the nominal flexibility. By contrast if the pass-through is slow, real wages can be easily altered by a price shock, whereas underlying inflation will respond only sluggishly. This is the line which is stressed by Sachs and others.[8] But our estimates suggest that countries differ as much as β^* as in α.

At this point it may be worthwhile showing how the preceding analysis can be generalised in a model with unrestricted lags in the wage and price equation. Consider the homogeneous model

$$\dot{w} = \alpha(L)\dot{p} + \theta(L)\dot{w} - \beta^*(L)(U - U_0) + \alpha(1)\dot{q}^e \qquad (1'')$$

$$\dot{p} = \gamma(L)\dot{w} - \dot{q} - \gamma\dot{U} \qquad (2')$$

where $\alpha(L)$ is a polynomial $(\sum \alpha_i L^i)$ in the lag operator (L) and hence $\alpha(1) = \sum \alpha_i$.[9] We can no longer get a simple expression, like $(3')$, linking contemporaneous $\dot{w}$ to contemporaneous U, $\dot{q}$ and $\dot{U}$. But if U and $\dot{q}$ are held constant, the system will converge on a steady rate of change of wage inflation given by[10]

$$\ddot{w} = (1/(AL_1 + AL_2))[(-\beta^*(1)/\alpha(1))(U - U_0) + (\dot{q}^e + \dot{q})] \qquad (3'')$$

where AL_1 is the lag of wages on prices in the Phillips curve equation, AL_2 is the lag of prices on wages in the price equation, and $\beta^*(1)/\alpha(1)$ is the long-run effect of unemployment on real wages.

The expression in $(3'')$ also tells us the cumulative change in $\dot{w}$ that will occur as a result of a temporary increase in U (measured in point years) or in $(\dot{q}^e - \dot{q})$, again measured in point years. Thus it enables us to answer all our earlier questions about the unemployment consequences of real shocks or of inflation reduction. The general expressions for wage rigidity thus become

$$RWR = \alpha(1)/\beta^*(1) \quad \text{and} \quad NWR = (AL_1 + AL_2)(\alpha(1)/\beta^*(1))$$

Our whole analysis depends of course on the assumption that the equation for wage inflation is linearly homogeneous in nominal variables. This seems eminently reasonable. If it were not so, the permanent rate of inflation would vary with the level of unemployment, and most evidence contradicts this. Of course if the coefficients on the right-hand variables summed to less than one, a real shock such as a one-period fall in $\dot{q}$ could produce effects on inflation that were eliminated without any increase in unemployment.[11]

The discussion so far has been based on the total cumulated unemployment in response to a real shock, regardless of its time path. However, one might feel that rigidity should be defined in terms of impact effects rather than total effects. This leads to the same general conclusions as before. To investigate this question we need to introduce a policy feedback rule, such as

$$\dot{U} = \phi\ddot{p} \qquad (4)$$

Taking this together with $(1')$ and (2) and starting with a steady inflation rate gives us an impact effect of

$$-dU/d\dot{q} = 1/((1 - \alpha)/\phi + \beta^* + \gamma)$$

As before, the unemployment effect is lower, the lower the pass-through of prices into wages (α). It is also lower the higher β^*. Unlike the total effect, the impact effect will also vary with the degree of non-accommodation, ϕ (positively), and with the elasticity of demand for labour, $1/\gamma$ (positively). For the lower the elasticity of demand for labour the less real wages have to fall, since a small increase in unemployment is consistent with a greater excess of real wages over q. Hence less unemployment has to emerge when q falls.

2.2 An adaptive wage equation

The discussion so far has assumed that the only force which affects the target rate of growth of real wages is unemployment. The constant term in the wage equation ($\alpha \dot{q}^e$) has been taken as invariant. Thus we have relied entirely on unemployment to change the intended growth of real wages. However the target level of real wage growth can also be affected by the experience of past real wage growth. Indeed it must be affected by this if the NAIRU is not to vary with the permanent level of actual real wage growth. One might therefore wish to broaden the concept of real wage flexibility to include the speed with which real wage targets adjust to actual experience.

The most general approach might be as follows. One might assume that wage payments are designed to achieve a target real wage (ω^*) except insofar as this is modified by the effect of unemployment. Thus, assuming price expectations are fulfilled, the actual real wage is given by

$$\omega = \omega^* - \beta(U - U_0)$$

In one version of this model $\omega^* = \dot{q}^e t$. This is the assumption of the Cambridge Economic Policy Group and modified versions have also been estimated by Sargan (1964) and Branson and Rotemberg (1980).[12] Clearly in this model unemployment must continue rising for ever if the feasible real wage growth ($\dot{q}$) is less than $\dot{q}^e$. This is even less plausible than the conclusion of our earlier model that the level of unemployment will be permanently higher if ($\dot{q} - \dot{q}^e$) is reduced.

We clearly need a better approach. A general model would specify ω^* as a distributed lag on past ω:

$$\omega^* = \sum_{i=1}^{T} a_i \omega_{-i}$$

The form of lag must be such that in the long run the gap between ω and ω^*, which determines the level of unemployment, is invariant with respect to the long-run rate of growth of real wages. It will, however, vary with changes in the growth rate of real wages, so that[13]

$$\omega^* = \omega - \ddot{\omega} \sum_{i=1}^{T} c_i \ddot{\omega}_{-i}$$

Since a fall in real wage growth ($\ddot{\omega}_i < 0$) will tend to make subsequent real wage targets too high, one would expect that all the c_i coefficients would be positive.

If real wage targets are too high, unemployment will have to rise (or price expectations be falsified). If $p = p^e$ and real wage growth fell by $(-\Delta \dot{q})$ i periods ago, unemployment will now be given by

$$U - U_0 = (\omega^* - \omega)/\beta = (c_i/\beta)(-\Delta \dot{q})$$

The cumulative effect on unemployment of a permanent fall in $\dot{q}$ will be

$$\sum \Delta U_t = [(1 + \sum c_i)/\beta](-\Delta \dot{q})$$

Thus

$$RWR = (1 + \sum c_i)/\beta$$

is the most natural measure of real wage rigidity we have to offer.[14] $1/\beta$ appears as usual but is now multiplied by $(1 + \sum c_i)$.

However, the c_is are not easy to estimate, as the time series do not embody enough change in the rate of growth and estimation is complex due to small sample bias. In this paper we do not attempt to estimate the c_i coefficients, though we have done so elsewhere for the OECD as a whole.[15] For the average OECD country, the estimated number of point years of unemployment caused by a permanent 1 percentage point fall in real wage growth was 8.2. This compares with infinity in our non-adjusting framework. However, the profile of extra unemployment in the first seven years was remarkably flat. The increase in unemployment (assuming price expectations satisfied) was, for selected years:

t	0	1	2	3	4	5	7	10	15	20
$U(\%)$	0.57	0.70	0.71	0.69	0.64	0.58	0.46	0.32	0.17	0.09

Turning to our earlier model (($1'$)), for the average OECD country, the long-run coefficient on unemployment is just over one. This implies unemployment costs in each year (for a one per cent fall in $\dot{q}$) of rather under one, which corresponds quite well with the numbers above for the earlier years. Our earlier framework may thus be reasonably adequate for analyzing the medium-term causes of the current stagflation. In the empirical work in this paper we confine ourselves to the earlier framework.

2.3 Accommodation and the time path of unemployment

The discussion so far has been based on the total cumulated unemployment in response to a real shock, irrespective of its time path. The reason for this is that the time path will depend on the policy response: the unemployment increase can be indefinitely postponed so long as higher inflation is tolerated. It is therefore a virtue to have a simple measure that does not depend on the policy response.

However, it is also interesting to consider what might determine a country's policy response, and how this in turn could affect the path of unemployment. One might imagine that the amount of unemployment a country chooses will be a function of its level of inflation, $U = f(\dot{p})$. If inflation is high people will be willing to tolerate more unemployment than the NAIRU in order to reduce inflation; and if inflation is low they will be willing to risk higher inflation for the sake of less unemployment. Thus, if there is a NAIRU $(\overline{U})$ given by the wage and price equations, there must be an equivalent 'natural' level of inflation $(\bar{\dot{p}})$ given by $\overline{U} = f(\bar{\dot{p}})$

The following simple model (in continuous time) generates this behaviour. Both unemployment and inflation are disliked, so that the political welfare function is given by

$$S = - \int_{0}^{\infty} (U^2 + \phi^2\dot{p}^2)e^{-rt}dt$$

where r is the discount rate. Suppose for simplicity that the wage and price equations combine to give[16]

$$\ddot{p} = -\beta(U - U_0) + \dot{q}^e - \dot{q}$$

There is now a temporary shock to productivity growth which raises inflation to (let us say) $\dot{p}_0$. The optimal path of unemployment and prices is now given by[17]

$$U_t - \overline{U} = (z/\beta)(\dot{p}_0 - \bar{\dot{p}})e^{-zt} \quad \text{and} \quad \dot{p}_t - \bar{\dot{p}} = (\dot{p}_0 - \bar{\dot{p}})e^{-zt}$$

$$z = (\sqrt{r^2 + 4\beta^2\phi^2} - r)/2 \quad \text{and} \quad \bar{\dot{p}} = r\overline{U}/\phi^2\beta \text{[18]}$$

As we would expect, the natural level of inflation (to which the system converges) is higher the higher the discounting of the future inflation gains from higher employment. It is lower the more inflation is disliked and the stronger the effect of unemployment on inflation.[19] In any one period the feedback rule makes excess unemployment proportional to 'excess' inflation,[20]

$$U_t = \overline{U} + (z/\beta)(\dot{p}_t - \bar{\dot{p}}) = \text{(for small } r)\, \overline{U} + \phi(\dot{p}_t - \bar{\dot{p}}) \tag{4'}$$

Returning to the effect of a shock, the cumulated unemployment caused is best looked at assuming the initial level of inflation to be the natural level. Initially inflation rises by $(-\Delta\dot{q})$ so that $\dot{p}_0 - \bar{\dot{p}} = -\Delta\dot{q}$. The undiscounted sum of the extra unemployment that follows is

$$\int_0^\infty (U_t - \overline{U})\mathrm{d}t = \int_0^\infty (z/\beta)(\dot{p}_0 - \dot{p})e^{-zt}\mathrm{d}t = (1/\beta)(-\Delta\dot{q})$$

This is the formula we have been using all along. The discounted sum of the extra unemployment is

$$\int_0^\infty (U_t - \overline{U})e^{-rt}\mathrm{d}t = (1/\beta)(z/(z+r))(-\Delta\dot{q})$$

This is no longer proportional to $1/\beta$, though for reasonably small r it will remain approximately so.[21]

3   EMPIRICAL ANALYSIS OF EFFECTS OF WAGE RIGIDITY

To investigate the role of real and nominal wage rigidity we first estimate wage and price equations for each of nineteen OECD countries. From them we construct our measures of real and nominal wage rigidity, and then use them to 'account for' the different unemployment experiences of the different countries in recent years.

The wage equation is estimated in the following form

$$\dot{w} = \alpha\dot{p} + (1-\alpha)\dot{w}_{-1} - \alpha\beta U + \delta t + \text{constant} \tag{5}$$

where t is time (allowing for changes in U_0 and $\dot{q}^e$). To obtain the price equation we need an expression for $\dot{q}$ (the feasible rate of growth of real wages), and assume this is equal to $x - \frac{1}{2}s(\dot{m} + \dot{m}_{-1})$ where x is trend productivity growth, s the share of imports in GDP in 1975, and m is import prices relative to domestic prices (all variables are defined in appendix C).[22] Hence

$$\dot{p} + (\dot{x} - \tfrac{1}{2}s(\dot{m} + \dot{m}_{-1})) = \theta\dot{w} + (1-\theta)\dot{w}_{-1} - \gamma\dot{U} + \text{constant} \tag{6}$$

Both equations are estimated by 2SLS,[23] the price equation being estimated in level form with an autoregressive error. The data are annual data for 1957–80.

Having estimated our coefficients of real wage rigidity, $1/\beta$, the nominal wage rigidity, $(1 - \alpha\theta)/\alpha\beta$, we can use them to 'account for' the movement of unemployment by combining (5) and (6) to give

$$U = (1/\beta)(-\dot{x} + \tfrac{1}{2}s(\dot{m} + \dot{m}_{-1}))((1 - \alpha\theta)/\alpha\beta)(-\ddot{w})$$
$$+ (y/\beta)(-\dot{U}) + (\delta/\alpha\beta)t + \text{constant} \tag{7}$$

This says that unemployment will rise *ceteris paribus* if feasible real wage growth falls or if wage inflation falls. We shall examine how far inter-country differences in unemployment experience are 'due to' differences in real shocks or in the degree of disinflation, and how much to differences in rigidities.

3.1 Results

Tables 3.1 and 3.2 show the results for the wage and price equations.[24] In all countries unemployment tends to reduce wage inflation and in most countries the coefficient is significant. We also tested for the effect of $\dot{x}$ in the wage equation and it was generally insignificant – average t-statistic = 0.9.

In Table 3.3 we derive the measures of real and nominal wage rigidity. The average level of real wage rigidity is about unity, so that a one percentage point shock to feasible real wage growth requires an extra point-year of unemployment to purge the resulting inflation.

There is a substantial spread of real wage rigidity coefficients. We tested whether in (5) there was a significant difference in the $\alpha\beta$s across countries. A χ^2 statistic for the hypothesis that all the $\alpha\beta$ coefficients were equal was $\chi^2(19) = 49.6$, clearly rejecting the hypothesis.[25] Among the coefficients that are relatively well determined, the most striking feature is the low level of rigidity in Switzerland, Japan, New Zealand, Sweden and Austria.[26]

Turning to nominal wage rigidity, we note first that the average lag in the average OECD country is about 0.8 of a year, and the average nominal wage rigidity is thus less than the average real wage rigidity. The average lag is strikingly long in the USA, making this the most nominally rigid country in the OECD.[27] Switzerland, Japan and Austria are (with Finland) the most flexible countries. In Figure 3.1, we plot the two measures of rigidity against each other – the correlation is 0.27.

We can now put our coefficients to use in accounting for the growth of unemployment in recent years. The sharpest change has been the much higher level of unemployment in the years since 1973 (here 1973–80 inclusive) as

Table 3.1 Wage equation ((5))[a]

Country	Const./100	$\dot{p}$	U	t/100	SE 100	R^2	DW
Australia	4.00	0.89	−0.89	−0.19	2.07	0.75	2.09
	(3.4)	(6.2)	(2.3)	(2.1)			
Austria	8.31	0.87	−2.19	−0.17	2.42	0.52	2.15
	(2.8)	(4.2)	(1.7)	(1.7)			
Belgium	8.39	0.85	−1.25	0.28	1.80	0.65	2.55
	(5.8)	(5.1)	(4.7)	(3.7)			
Canada	5.00	0.39	−0.64	0.06	1.01	0.66	1.65
	(4.3)	(3.9)	(3.4)	(1.7)			
Denmark	4.50	0.77	−0.52	−0.04	2.18	0.53	2.24
	(3.8)	(4.2)	(1.9)	(0.6)			
Finland	6.10	0.83	−1.19	0.21	2.14	0.56	1.31
	(4.0)	(4.5)	(3.0)	(2.4)			
France	8.18	0.87	−1.69	0.45	1.20	0.75	1.95
	(5.3)	(5.7)	(3.9)	(4.3)			
Germany	6.38	1.19	−0.77	−0.17	2.30	0.56	1.73
	(4.4)	(4.8)	(1.8)	(1.9)			
Ireland	9.64	1.20	−0.77	0.22	2.45	0.77	1.98
	(4.0)	(7.4)	(2.4)	(2.2)			
Italy	10.23	1.03	−0.88	0.09	3.33	0.67	2.07
	(3.2)	(5.8)	(1.8)	(0.9)			
Japan	18.77	1.09	−8.09	0.07	2.69	0.66	1.27
	(5.8)	(6.2)	(4.9)	(0.8)			
Netherlands	8.53	0.95	−1.95	0.14	2.55	0.64	1.55
	(4.4)	(5.2)	(3.1)	(1.1)			
New Zealand	1.42	0.41	−1.31	0.05	2.54	0.31	2.00
	(1.7)	(2.0)	(1.2)	(0.5)			
Norway	3.11	0.70	−0.49	0.06	2.50	0.49	1.56
	(0.8)	(4.3)	(0.2)	(0.7)			
Spain	7.85	0.89	−0.62	0.21	5.25	0.38	2.19
	(2.6)	(3.4)	(1.0)	(0.8)			
Sweden	7.38	0.94	−2.45	−0.15	3.42	0.50	2.33
	(1.8)	(4.0)	(1.2)	(1.4)			
Switzerland	3.26	0.90	−7.14	0.02	1.17	0.73	1.34
	(6.4)	(5.5)	(4.2)	(0.5)			
UK	4.00	1.01	−0.42	0.04	2.63	0.69	2.04
	(1.9)	(5.7)	(0.6)	(0.2)			
US	1.73	0.26	−0.24	0.03	0.94	0.31	2.68
	(1.8)	(1.6)	(1.3)	(0.8)			
EEC	7.48	0.98	−1.03	0.13	2.31	0.66	2.01
average	(4.1)	(5.5)	(2.5)	(1.2)			
OECD	6.51	0.84	−1.76	0.08	2.35	0.59	1.93
average	(3.6)	(4.7)	(2.3)	(0.9)			

Note:

[a] The *t*-statistics are in parentheses (absolute values). Average *t*-statistics are algebraic averages, taken net of sign. The coefficient on $\dot{w}_{-1}$ is 1 minus the coefficient on $\dot{p}$. The equation was estimated in the form $\dot{w} - \dot{w}_{-1} = \alpha(\dot{p} - \dot{w}_{-1}) - \beta^* U + \delta t + \text{constant}$. Hence R^2 measures the proportion of $\text{var}(\dot{w} - \dot{w}_{-1})$ explained.

Table 3.2 Price equation ((6))[a]

Country	w	U	t/100	p	SE 100	DW
Australia	0.57	−4.29	1.56	0.04	1.41	1.80
	(7.0)	(15.6)	(18.0)			
Austria	0.64	−5.78	−0.77	0.59	2.46	1.51
	(2.9)	(2.4)	(4.0)			
Belgium	−0.47	−4.76	0.22	−0.15	1.47	1.96
	(3.9)	(16.9)	(2.3)			
Canada	1.30	−1.79	−1.08	0.21	2.02	1.73
	(4.8)	(3.9)	(8.0)			
Denmark	0.88	−2.55	−1.20	0.24	1.73	1.78
	(5.3)	(8.5)	(13.2)			
Finland	1.02	1.08	−0.13	0.99	2.40	1.36
	(4.5)	(1.6)	(0.2)			
France	0.58	2.67	0.12	0.96	2.01	1.53
	(2.1)	(1.8)	(2.2)			
Germany	0.61	1.06	−0.11	0.49	1.56	1.56
	(4.0)	(2.2)	(1.2)			
Ireland	0.71	−1.01	0.56	0.78	2.14	1.65
	(5.8)	(1.9)	(2.2)			
Italy	0.45	−4.93	0.17	0.86	4.07	1.42
	(2.1)	(2.8)	(0.3)			
Japan	−0.43	−36.79	1.51	0.28	4.50	1.82
	(1.2)	(7.1)	(7.1)			
Netherlands	0.70	0.07	−0.22	0.57	2.95	1.44
	(2.8)	(0.5)	(0.8)			
New Zealand	0.87	−0.95	−0.35	0.99	2.93	1.38
	(2.6)	(0.5)	(0.5)			
Norway	0.71	0.35	0.31	0.91	2.58	1.01
	(3.6)	(0.2)	(0.8)			
Spain	0.58	2.11	−1.41	0.69	4.12	1.50
	(3.0)	(2.2)	(2.7)			
Sweden	0.48	−1.97	−0.92	0.76	2.32	1.53
	(3.3)	(1.0)	(4.4)			
Switzerland	0.39	−1.94	0.44	0.70	1.27	1.70
	(1.5)	(0.4)	(3.7)			
UK	0.67	−0.92	−0.13	0.46	1.51	1.67
	(5.9)	(1.7)	(0.8)			
US	1.02	0.26	0.09	0.91	1.22	1.06
	(2.5)	(0.9)	(0.4)			
EEC	0.52	−1.30	−0.07	0.53	2.18	1.63
average	(3.0)	(3.4)	(1.1)			
OECD	0.59	−3.16	−0.07	0.59	2.35	1.55
average	(3.5)	(2.8)	(0.1)			

Note:
[a] The *t*-statistics are in parentheses (absolute values). Constant term not shown. The coefficient on w_{-1} is 1 minus the coefficient on *w*. The estimated equation was $p + (x - \frac{1}{2}s(m + m_{-1})) = \theta w + (1 - \theta)w_{-1} - \gamma U + \mu + \varepsilon/(1 - pL)$. R^2 is always 0.994 or more.

Table 3.3 Real and nominal wage rigidity

Country	RWR (SE)	NWR (SE)	$AL_1 + AL_2$
Australia	1.00 (0.50)	0.55 (0.27)	0.55
Austria	0.40 (0.22)	0.20 (0.17)	0.51
Belgium	0.68 (0.16)	1.12 (0.26)	1.64
Canada	0.60 (0.26)	0.77 (0.36)	1.28
Denmark	1.48 (0.86)	0.61 (0.56)	0.41
Finland	0.70 (0.23)	0.12 (0.24)	0.17
France	0.51 (0.13)	0.29 (0.17)	0.57
Germany	1.54 (0.87)	0.36 (0.40)	0.23
Ireland	1.55 (0.68)	0.19 (0.27)	0.12
Italy	1.17 (0.67)	0.61 (0.46)	0.52
Japan	0.13 (0.03)	0.18 (0.06)	1.35
Netherlands	0.49 (0.16)	0.17 (0.15)	0.35
New Zealand	0.31 (0.28)	0.49 (0.46)	1.59
Norway	1.43 (5.80)	1.03 (4.47)	0.72
Spain	1.45 (1.50)	0.78 (0.97)	0.54
Sweden	0.39 (0.35)	0.22 (0.21)	0.57
Switzerland	0.13 (0.04)	0.09 (0.04)	0.71
UK	2.39 (4.22)	0.78 (1.55)	0.32
US	1.09 (1.14)	3.14 (2.57)	2.88
EEC average	1.23	0.52	0.52
OECD average	0.92	0.62	0.79

compared with the years before (1960–72). This should be accounted for by (7), with $\overline{U}_{73-80} - \overline{U}_{60-72}$ equalling (apart from errors) the equivalent terms on the right-hand side.

For OECD countries as a whole the average changes (1973–80 average values – 1960–72 average values) were

U	$(-\dot{x})$	$\frac{1}{2}s(\dot{m} + \dot{m}_{-1})$	$(-\ddot{w})$	$(-\dot{U})$	t
2.0%	1.8%	0.9%	0.6%	−0.3%	10.5

Explaining Unemployment

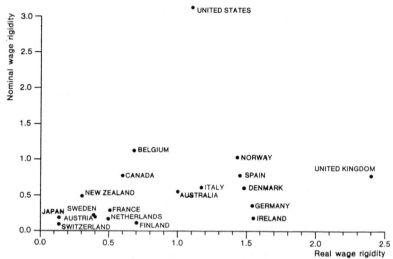

Figure 3.1 Real wage rigidity and nominal wage rigidity

The average values of the corresponding coefficients are

0.92   0.62   1.3   0.0008
(*RWR*)   (*NWR*)

However, one cannot multiply average values of variables by average coefficients. The appropriate exercise is performed in Table 3.4. This shows for each country each of the terms in (7), as well as the total explained increase in unemployment, and the actual increase. For the average OECD country the amount of extra unemployment explained was

		%
Due to	$-\Delta \dot{x}$	1.3
	$\Delta \dot{m}$	0.9
	$-\Delta \ddot{w}$	0.2
	$-\Delta \dot{U}$	-0.4
	Δt	0.8
Total explained		2.8
Actual total		2.0

Thus the analysis somewhat overpredicts the increase in unemployment which happened – perhaps because it does not allow for any adaptation in the constant term in the wage equation.[28] Interestingly the results suggest that the slowdown in productivity growth may account for more of our present day

Table 3.4 Accounting for the growth in unemployment (Δ = 1973–80 average minus 1960–72 average), percentage points

Country	$\frac{1}{\beta}(-\Delta\dot{x})$	$\frac{\frac{1}{2}s\Delta(\dot{m}+\dot{m}_{-1})}{\beta}$	$\frac{1-x\theta}{x\beta}(-\Delta\dot{w})$	$\frac{\gamma}{\beta}(-\Delta\dot{U})$	$\frac{\delta}{\alpha\beta}At$	ΔU Explained	Actual
Australia	0.9	0.6	0.1	–2.0	2.2	1.8	2.7
Austria	0.9	0.1	0.2	–0.5	–0.8	–0.1	–0.1
Belgium	0.9	0.5	1.6	–2.7	2.4	2.7	3.1
Canada	0.9	0.4	–	–0.2	0.9	2.1	1.8
Denmark	3.0	1.8	0.3	–2.9	–0.8	1.3	2.9
Finland	1.2	0.5	0.1	0.2	1.9	3.9	2.3
France	0.9	0.2	–	–0.5	2.8	3.5	2.8
Germany	2.5	0.9	0.2	0.6	–2.3	2.0	2.4
Ireland	2.6	3.4	–	–0.8	3.0	8.3	3.9
Italy	4.4	1.1	–0.4	–1.4	1.0	4.8	1.5
Japan	0.7	0.1	0.3	–0.7	0.1	0.5	0.6
Netherlands	0.8	1.0	0.3	–	0.7	2.8	2.8
New Zealand	0.3	0.4	0.4	–0.1	0.4	1.4	0.8
Norway	1.2	2.4	–0.1	–	–1.3	2.2	–
Spain	–1.2	0.3	0.5	3.1	3.5	6.3	4.8
Sweden	1.0	0.4	0.3	0.1	–0.7	1.2	0.2
Switzerland	0.3	–	0.1	–	–	0.4	0.3
UK	2.6	1.6	–0.4	–0.6	1.0	4.1	2.6
US	1.4	0.5	0.1	0.1	1.2	3.3	1.7
EEC average	2.2	1.3	0.2	–1.0	1.0	3.7	2.7
OECD average	1.3	0.9	0.2	–0.4	0.8	2.8	2.0

problems than the growth of relative import prices or the trend growth in the NAIRU.

Thus, at the level of the OECD as a whole, our wage and price equations simulate the behaviour of the data reasonably well when 1973–80 is compared with 1960–72. How well do they do on a country basis? One would expect some variability due to the higher sampling error. The data are plotted in Figure 3.2. The regression of ΔU on $\Delta\hat{U}$ gives the following:

$$\Delta U = \underset{(1.7)}{0.0064} + \underset{(4.2)}{0.48\,\Delta\hat{U}}, \quad R^2 = 0.52, \quad SE = 0.0099$$

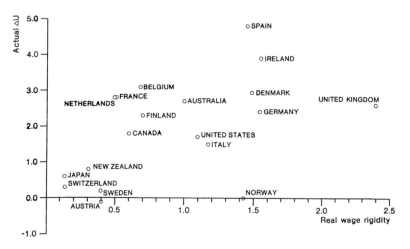

Figure 3.2   Real wage rigidity and increase in unemployment (1973–80 minus 1960–72 ($R = 0.50$)

It may also be interesting to find out which components account for most of the variability between countries. For this purpose we regress ΔU on the five components (as shown in Table 3.3). Denoting the first term $T(-\Delta \dot{x})$ and so on, we obtain

$$\Delta U = -0.004 + 0.46\,T(-\Delta\dot{x}) + 0.38\,T(\Delta\dot{m}) + 1.36\,T(-\Delta\ddot{w})$$
$$\quad\ \ (0.8)\quad\ (1.5)\qquad\qquad (1.2)\qquad\qquad (2.0)$$

$$+ 0.36\,T(-\Delta\dot{U}) + 0.61\,T(\Delta t), \quad R^2 = 0.65, \quad SE = 0.0096$$
$$\ \ (1.5)\qquad\qquad (4.1)$$

The coefficients here should ideally be unity. It appears from the t-statistics that the trend growth of NAIRU 'explains' more than any other component, but all components are reasonably important.

However, from our present point of view the really interesting issue is whether unemployment differences mainly reflect different external shocks or different responses to the shocks, due to different degrees of rigidity. To investigate this we regress ΔU on the shocks *and* the coefficients,[29]

$$\Delta U = -0.004 + 0.016\,(1/\beta) + \ 6.5\,(\delta/\alpha\beta) + 0.075\,(-\Delta\dot{x})$$
$$\quad\ \ (0.6)\quad\ (3.7)\qquad\qquad (5.1)\qquad\qquad (0.4)$$

$$+ 0.009\tfrac{1}{2}s(\Delta\dot{m} + \Delta\dot{m}_{-1}) + 0.84\,(-\Delta\ddot{w}), \quad R^2 = 0.79, \quad SE = 0.0074$$
$$\ \ (0.03)\qquad\qquad\qquad\quad (2.5)$$

Table 3.5 Shocks (Δ = 1973–80 average minus 1960–72 average), percentage points

Country	$(-\Delta\dot{x})$	$\frac{1}{2}s\Delta(\dot{m}+\dot{m}_{-1})$	$(-\Delta\ddot{w})$	ΔU
Australia	0.90	0.59	0.19	2.87
Austria	2.23	0.20	1.20	−0.11
Belgium	1.31	0.74	1.45	3.13
Canada	1.53	0.62	0.04	1.77
Denmark	2.00	1.20	0.50	2.90
Finland	1.79	0.71	0.77	2.26
France	1.79	0.36	−0.02	2.79
Germany	1.61	0.60	0.69	2.40
Ireland	1.68	2.20	0.06	3.92
Italy	3.77	0.98	−0.62	1.47
Japan	5.26	0.87	1.57	0.58
Netherlands	1.64	1.95	2.04	2.81
New Zealand	0.97	1.27	0.73	0.82
Norway	0.83	1.70	−0.11	3.38
Spain	−0.80	0.21	0.61	4.77
Sweden	2.64	1.10	1.43	0.15
Switzerland	2.00	0.00	1.18	0.28
UK	1.09	0.66	−0.57	2.56
US	1.28	0.44	0.44	1.66
EEC average	1.86	1.09	0.44	2.75
OECD average	1.77	0.86	0.59	1.95

This shows that the actual differences in real shocks (shown in Table 3.5) account for virtually none of the inter-country variation. It may not be surprising that differences in relative import prices account for little, since one would suppose that changes in raw material prices, if properly measured, should affect the feasible real wage in most OECD countries (except materials producers) by much the same amount. The striking feature of the equation is the powerful effect of real wage rigidity $(1/\beta)$ in 'explaining' the differences. The crude correlation between real wage rigidity and the change in unemployment is shown in Figure 3.2. The correlation is (-0.5).

We should stress at this point that the inter-country comparisons we have just undertaken in no sense provide further evidence in support of our model. The model is to be judged only by the performance and plausibility of the individual price and wage equations. The inter-country comparisons merely illustrate the implications of the model.[30]

4   EXPLANATION OF WAGE RIGIDITY

We now come to the most speculative part of this paper. It is interesting to consider what influences might determine our key parameters. The first of these is α, the degree of indexation of wages to prices. Gray (1976) has suggested that this should optimally vary positively with the ratio of the variances of nominal to real shocks.

The other parameter is β, the degree of real wage flexibility. Lucas (1973) offers the proposition that β should vary positively with the ratio of the variances of aggregate to relative demand shocks. However, in the Lucas model inflation and employment are related by the aggregate labour supply function, whereas we see them as related by a wage-adjustment function.[31] Even so, one might expect that our β would also vary positively with aggregate demand shocks, and in addition with aggregate supply shocks. One might also suppose that if agents wished to minimise the variance of output, they would index wages more the greater the degree of monetary accommodation.

These conjectures are consistent with the following simple model. Measure all endogenous variables by their deviations from the values that would hold in the absence of shocks. If y is log output and l log employment, the production function is

$$y = ((\eta - 1)/\eta)l + u, \quad \eta > 1 \tag{8}$$

giving a demand for labour function

$$l = -\eta(w - p - u) \tag{9}$$

The demand for output is determined by the degree of monetary accommodation (λ) according to

$$y = (\lambda - 1)p + v, \quad \lambda < 1 \tag{10}$$

here u represents an unobservable supply shock and v an unobservable demand shock.

As in the Fischer–Gray model the short-run supply of labour does not appear. The expected value of employment can be thought of as corresponding to its long-run equilibrium value or some value determined by collective bargaining and union power.

The aim is to select w so as to hit this level of employment. Since the level of employment cannot be precisely determined, the aim is to minimise the variance of l. If only prices and employment can be observed, this requires a wage rate based on current prices and employment. We assume that employment is only observed with error, observed employment being $l - e$. The wage rate is then

$$w = \alpha p + \beta(l - e) \tag{11}$$

where α and β remain to be chosen optimally. The solution is[32]

$$\alpha = (\sigma_v^2/\sigma_u^2 + \lambda\eta)/(\sigma_v^2/\sigma_u^2 + \eta) \tag{12}$$

Since $\lambda < 1$, the degree of indexation is higher, the higher the ratio of demand to supply shocks (as in the Gray result). The higher the degree of monetary accommodation, the greater the degree of wage indexation. As regards the effect of employment on inflation,

$$\beta = 1/(\sigma_e^2[1/\sigma_v^2 + 1/\eta\sigma_u^2]) \tag{13}$$

Thus the effect of employment on inflation is higher, the greater the variance of both demand and supply shocks. Interestingly, once endogenous indexation is allowed for, the coefficient β is not affected by the degree of accommodation in this model.[33]

4.1 Empirical analysis

To investigate whether there is any support for (12) and (13), we need first to construct measures of the variance of demand and supply shocks (σ_v^2 and σ_u^2). For this purpose we ran second-order autoregressions of nominal income ($p + y$) and of the underlying feasible real wage (q) for the years 1957–72, since one would expect behavioural responses (especially in the pre-1972 years) to be moulded by these experiences.[34] σ_v^2 and σ_u^2 are the residual variances of the equations. The results are shown in Table 3.6 (first two columns).

We also need to estimate the feedback equation (i.e. to find an empirical counterpart for (10)). The variables in this equation were expressed in terms of innovations. However since we do not know what information lag is appropriate, we have for present purposes estimated a feedback equation in terms of untransformed variables.

In this context we rely on (4') which we derived earlier. This assumes that governments have a reaction to the rate of inflation (rather than to the level of prices net of trend). Given the lag between the government reaction and changes in employment it seems natural to express this relation as

$$U = \phi \dot{p}_{-1} + at + \text{constant}$$

The results, estimated with an autoregressive error, are shown in Table 3.6. Though these results are not altogether satisfactory, they have some interesting

Table 3.6 Variance of shocks and estimated accommodation equation[a]

Country	Variance of shocks σ_v^2 (nominal) $\times 10^4$	σ_u^2 (real) $\times 10^4$	$\dfrac{\sigma_v^2}{\sigma_u^2}$	Accommodation equation Coefficients on $\dot{p}_{-1}(\phi)$	$t/100$	$Const./100$	p	SE 100	DW
Australia	3.5	0.12	109	−0.01 (0.2)	−0.02 (0.5)	1.72 (4.1)	0.35	0.46	1.64
Austria	3.7	0.25	31	0.00 (0.0)	−0.12 (3.7)	1.41 (3.5)	0.61	0.28	1.22
Belgium	2.4	0.06	9	−0.03 (0.4)	−0.04 (0.8)	2.18 (4.4)	0.60	0.53	1.19
Canada	2.3	0.06	35	0.23 (0.7)	−0.01 (0.1)	4.78 (4.2)	0.66	0.88	1.94
Denmark	3.0	0.07	45	0.13 (1.5)	−0.30 (3.9)	0.04 (0.0)	0.81	0.47	1.44
Finland	3.6	0.33	11	0.04 (0.6)	0.06 (1.0)	2.21 (4.4)	0.41	0.69	1.58
France	2.9	0.11	27	0.03 (1.6)	0.13 (6.6)	2.15 (11.9)	0.64	0.17	2.01
Germany	4.7	0.14	34	0.22 (1.9)	−0.16 (2.4)	−0.17 (0.2)	0.76	0.45	1.39
Ireland	5.5	0.33	17	0.04 (0.6)	−0.04 (0.6)	5.47 (6.9)	0.86	0.41	1.60
Italy	1.9	0.20	9	0.04 (0.3)	−0.24 (1.5)	5.46 (3.3)	0.88	0.86	0.78
Japan	10.8	0.03	323	−0.04 (1.4)	−0.03 (1.5)	1.47 (6.3)	0.67	0.17	1.39
Netherlands	5.7	0.29	19	0.12 (1.9)	−0.01 (0.1)	0.76 (1.5)	0.61	0.45	1.16
New Zealand	3.8	0.29	13	0.05 (2.3)	0.01 (0.8)	0.05 (0.3)	0.35	0.12	1.46
Norway	2.2	0.28	8	0.04 (0.6)	−0.70 (2.6)	1.34 (3.7)	0.12	0.39	1.71
Spain	11.6	0.19	61	0.01 (0.4)	0.08 (3.8)	1.91 (8.6)	0.22	0.32	1.30
Sweden	1.5	0.16	9	0.10 (1.6)	0.02 (0.0)	1.56 (4.0)	0.39	0.42	1.85
Switzerland	1.9	0.29	6	0.01 (1.2)	−0.07 (3.2)	−0.03 (1.0)	0.58	0.02	1.67
UK	1.3	0.18	7	0.09 (1.3)	0.08 (2.2)	1.90 (4.1)	0.45	0.37	1.52
US	2.8	0.01	232	0.60 (2.0)	−0.11 (1.1)	2.65 (2.1)	0.60	0.82	1.90
EEC average	3.4	0.20	21	0.08 (1.1)	−0.07 (0.1)	2.22 (4.0)	0.70	0.46	1.39
OECD average	3.9	0.18	53	0.09 (0.9)	−0.08 (0.4)	1.94 (3.8)	0.56	0.44	1.51

Note:
[a] The *t*-values are in parentheses.

features. The least accommodating countries (with highest ϕ) are, in order, the US, Denmark, Germany, Ireland, the UK, Canada and the Netherlands.

We can now attempt to estimate the indexation function (12) in linear form,[35]

$$\alpha = a_0 + a_1[\sigma_v^2/\sigma_u^2] + a_2\phi$$

We expect to find a_1 positive and a_2 negative – indexation should be less when a country is non-accommodating. To the extent that $\lambda\eta$ and η are large we shall not be surprised if (σ_v^2/σ_u^2) does not show up as having much effect. The estimated equation is

$$\alpha = 0.92 + 0.0001\,(\sigma_v^2/\sigma_u^2) - 0.99\,\phi$$
$$\quad\quad\quad (0.15) \quad\quad\quad\quad (2.6)$$

The result is satisfactory in relation to ϕ. However we should point out that this is entirely due to the observation for the US which is both long-lagged and non-accommodating. The ratio of variances seems to have little effect.

Turning to the equation for β this is estimated in linear form as

$$\beta = 0.86 + 2327\sigma_v^2 - 1025\sigma_u^2, \quad R^2 = 0.09, \quad SE = 2.17$$
$$\quad\quad\quad (1.28) \quad\quad (0.02)$$

This again is not particularly satisfactory, and the positive result for σ_v^2 is entirely due to the high value of both variables in Japan.

On the basis of these results one might be tempted to conclude that economic theory could say little about the reasons for the spread of coefficients among OECD countries other than outliers like Japan and the US. However this would be premature. There is scope for producing better theories and better tests. But we do suspect that there will always remain a role for institutional differences, going back into history.

Appendix A:
The Role of Lags

Define $\psi(L)$, $\beta(L)$, and $\gamma(L)$ to be polynomial functions of the lag operator (L). Using these functions the wage and price equations can initially be written

$$\dot{w} = \psi(L)\dot{p} - \beta(L)U + \text{constant} \tag{A1}$$

$$\dot{p} = \gamma(L)\dot{w} - \dot{q} \tag{A2}$$

We have suppressed the term in $\dot{U}$ in the price equation since we are going to assume U is constant. We have also for the moment suppressed the lagged $\dot{w}$ term in the wage equation.

Substituting (A2) into (A1) gives

$$(1 - \psi(L)\gamma(L))\dot{w} = -\beta(L)U - \psi(L)\dot{q} + \text{constant} \tag{A3}$$

Suppose we define $\phi(L)$ by

$$1 - \psi(L)\gamma(L) = \phi(L)(1 - L) \tag{A4}$$

Then

$$\phi(L)\ddot{w} = -\beta(L)U - \psi(L)\dot{q} + \text{constant}.$$

If $\dot{q}$ and U are constant, $\ddot{w}$ will be given by

$$\ddot{w} = (1/\phi(1))[-\beta(1)U - \psi(1)\dot{q} + \text{constant}]$$

What is $\phi(1)$? Differentiating (A4) by L gives

$$-\psi'(L)\gamma(L) - \gamma'(L)\psi(L) = -\phi(L) + (1 - L)\phi'(L)$$

Setting $L = 1$ we find

$$\phi(1) = \psi'(1)/\psi(1) + \gamma'(1)/\gamma(1)$$

since by homogeneity

$$\gamma(1) = \psi(1) = 1$$

But $\psi'(1)/\psi(1)$ is the average lag in the wage equation (AL_1) and $\gamma'(1)/\gamma(1)$ is the average lag in the price equation (AL_2).[36] Hence in the long run,

$$\ddot{w} = (1/AL_1 + AL_2))[-\beta(1)U - \dot{q} + \text{constant}] \tag{A5}$$

44

If we now introduce lagged wages into the right-hand side of the wage equation, we have a new wage equation

$$\dot{w} = \alpha(L)\dot{p} + \theta(L)\dot{w} - \beta^*(L)U + \text{constant}, \quad \alpha(1) + \theta(1) = 1$$

or

$$\dot{w} = (\alpha(L)/(1 - \theta(L)))\dot{p} - (\beta^*(L)/(1 - \theta(L)))U + \text{constant} \tag{A6}$$

This is equivalent to (A1) with

$$\alpha(L)/(1 - \theta(L)) = \psi(L) \quad \text{and} \quad \beta^*(L)/(1 - \theta(L)) = \beta(L)$$

Since (A1) gave rise to (A5), (A6) gives rise to

$$\ddot{w} = (1/AL_1 + AL_2))[-(\beta^*(1)/\alpha(1))U - \dot{q} + \text{constant}]$$

This is (3″) in the text (once the constant is separated into U_0 and $\dot{q}^e$-terms).

We have estimated that if U and q are constant, (3″) will eventually hold in each year. But we also have to establish that a given number of point-years of U will produce a cumulated change in $\dot{w}$ given by the same formula. In general, ignoring $\dot{q}^e - \dot{q}$, we can write

$$\ddot{w} = \sum_{i=0}^{\infty} g_i[U_{-i} - U_0]$$

If U_i diverges from U_0 in any one year the cumulative change in $\dot{w}$ will be $\sum_{i=0}^{\infty} g_i$ times the divergence. But this is exactly the same as the effect on the permanent level of $\ddot{w}$ of a permanent divergence in U from U_0.

Appendix B: Derivation of Results in Section 4

The model is (8)–(11). Substituting to eliminate y, p and w yields

$$\left(1 + \eta\beta + (\eta - 1)\frac{1-\alpha}{1-\lambda}\right)l = \eta\frac{1-\alpha}{1-\lambda}v + \eta\beta\varepsilon + \eta\left(1 - \frac{1-\alpha}{1-\lambda}\right)u \tag{B1}$$

It is apparent that the parameters α and λ enter only in the combination $(1-\alpha)(1-\gamma)$ Writing $\psi = (1-\alpha)/(1-\lambda)$ and rearranging gives

$$l = \frac{\eta\psi v + \eta\beta\varepsilon + \eta(1-\psi)u}{1 + \eta\beta + (\eta-1)\psi} \tag{B2}$$

In the wage contract, α and β are set such as to minimise the variance of l. For any given value of λ, choice of α implies choice of ψ. Thus we set β and ψ to minimise

$$\mathrm{var}\,(l) = \frac{\eta^2\psi^2\sigma_v^2 + \eta^2\beta^2\sigma_\varepsilon^2 + \eta^2(1-\psi)^2\sigma_u^2}{(1 + \eta\beta + (\eta-1)\psi)^2} \tag{B3}$$

First-order conditions for β and ψ are given by

$$\beta = \eta\frac{\psi^2\sigma_v^2 + (1-\psi)^2\sigma_u^2}{(1 + (\eta-1)\psi)\sigma_\varepsilon^2} \tag{B4}$$

and

$$\psi = \frac{(\eta-1)\beta^2\sigma_\varepsilon^2 + \eta(1+\beta)\sigma_u^2}{(1+\eta\beta)\sigma_v^2 + \eta(1+\beta)\sigma_u^2} \tag{B5}$$

If one were to assume a given value of α, as well as λ, so that ψ is determined exogenously, then (B4) gives the optimal value of β. Substituting $\psi = (1-\alpha)/(1-\lambda)$ gives the expression in n. 33.

A simultaneous solution for β and ψ can be derived by substituting for σ_ε^2 from (B4) and (B5). The resulting expression, after rearrangement, can be written in the form

$$(1 + \beta\eta + (\eta-1)\psi)(\psi\sigma_v^2 - \eta(1-\psi)\sigma_u^2) = 0 \tag{B6}$$

The first term in (B6) cannot be zero since $\eta > 0$, and, from (B4), β must then take the same sign as $1 + (\eta-1)\psi$. Hence

$$\psi\sigma_v^2 - \eta(1-\psi)\sigma_u^2 = 0$$

(12) follows from this, and (13) follows from (12) and (B4).

46

Appendix C: Data

The data sources are as follows:
OECD *Main Economic Indicators* (*MEI*)
OECD *National Accounts* (*OECD NA*)
OECD *Labour Force Statistics* (*OECD LFS*)

(1) *Wage Inflation*
Definition: Average hourly earnings in manufacturing (most countries).
Source: Most countries: *MEI* various. France, Italy and Netherlands: *ILO Yearbooks* chained. UK: *British Labour Statistics Historical Abstract, Economic Trends Annual Supplement* and *ILO Yearbooks*.

(2) *Price Inflation*
Definition: Ratio of consumer expenditure to constant price consumer expenditure (1975 prices).
Source: *OECD NA.*

(3) *Employment rate*
Definition: Unemployed as percentage of employed and unemployed (unemployed is based on country definitions, and employed includes self-employed).
Source: *OECD LFS* (most countries).

(4) *Trend productivity growth*
Definition: See text.
Source: Employment: *OECD LFS* (most countries). GDP: *OECD NA.*

(5) *Import prices relative to consumption deflator, multiplied by share of imports in GDP*
Definition: Import price is value of imports divided by volume of imports at 1975 prices.
Source: *OECD NA.*

(6) *Unit value of world manufacturing exports* ($)
Source: *UN Yearbook of International Trade Statistics* (various issues) – tables for world exports of market economies by commodity classes.

(7) *Sterling/dollar exchange rate*
Source: *IMF International Financial Statistics.*

Notes

1. By a 'real shock' we mean one that (in the final equilibrium) leads to a change in the real wage, and by a 'nominal shock' we mean one that does not.
2. Branson and Rotemberg (1980) adopt a more complex approach, based on the specification of the adjustment mechanism.
3. This makes it clear that U_0 is the long-run level of U when $\dot{p} = \dot{p}^e$ and $\dot{q} = \dot{q}^e$.
4. In the equation $\dot{w} = \alpha_1 \dot{p} + \alpha_2 \dot{p}_{-1} + (1 - \alpha_1 - \alpha_2)\dot{w}_{-1} - \beta U +$ constant, OECD average coefficients (with t-statistics) were 0.78 (3.0) on $\dot{p}$ and 0.11 (0.4) on $\dot{p}_{-1}$.
5. As we shall see below it is independent of the average lag in the wage equation.
6. For example consider the simple model $\dot{w} = \dot{p}_{-1} - \beta(U - U_0) + \dot{q}^e$ and $\dot{p} = \dot{w} - \dot{q} - \gamma \dot{U}$. Suppose $\dot{q}$ falls by one unit in period 1, and then returns to its previous level. If U remains constant $\dot{p}$ will be one unit higher in period 1 and thereafter, while $\dot{w}$ will be one unit higher in period 2 and thereafter. Hence $\dot{w} - \dot{p}$ falls permanently by one unit in period 1. U has never changed.
7. This is Gordon and King's (1982) 'sacrifice ratio'.
8. As regard the importance of α, our analysis is exactly the same as Sachs'. Branson and Rotemberg (1980), however, do not impose linear homogeneity. They estimate a function

$$\dot{w} = (\gamma_1 + \gamma_2)\dot{p}^e + \gamma_1(\dot{q}^e t - (w - p)_{-1}) - \beta U + \text{constant}.$$

   If this is homogeneous ($\gamma_1 + \gamma_2 = 1$), this is said to indicate real wage stickiness. If $\gamma_2 = 0$, this is said to indicate nominal wage stickiness. These definitions are based on whether the adjustment mechanism (to a given real wage target) is better described in real or in nominal terms. We comment later on term $\dot{q}^e t - (w - p)_{-1}$.
9. This is the appropriate coefficient on $\dot{q}^e$ since by the homogeneity assumption $\alpha(1) = 1 - \theta(1)$, which is the long-run coefficient on $\dot{w} - \dot{p}$.
10. See appendix A.
11. This is so in Bruno's (1980) reduced form equations. Suppose $\dot{w} + \alpha\dot{p}_{-1} - \beta U +$ constant ($\alpha < 1$). Then if the government chose to keep unemployment constant (by appropriate demand management), the level of inflation t periods after a one-period fall of one point in productivity growth would be α^t points above its initial level.
12. Some modification is needed to explain why in equations regressing $(\omega - \omega_{-1})$ on ω_{-1} and t, the coefficient on ω_{-1} is generally much less than unity. This can be explained by a partial adjustment scheme such as

$$\omega^* = \lambda(\dot{q}^e t - \beta U) + (1 - \lambda)(\omega_{-1} + \dot{q}^e).$$

   However, so long as $\lambda \neq 0$ the implication is that unemployment will rise for ever so long as $\dot{q} < \dot{q}^e$.
13. See Grubb, Jackman and Layard (1982, Annex 2).
14. In this formulation a fall in $\dot{q}$ followed by a return to normal $\dot{q}$ has no long-run cost, whereas it does in our earlier case, which was non-adaptive.
15. Grubb, Jackman and Layard (1982). The estimating equation was

$$\dot{w} = [(a + bL)/(1 - dL)]\ddot{w}_{-1} - \beta U - \beta'\dot{U} + \text{constant}.$$

   This was estimated using Monte Carlo methods.

16. The equations could take from the form $\dot{w} = \dot{p}_{-1} - \beta(U - U_0) + \dot{q}^e$ and $\dot{p} = \dot{w} - \dot{q}$

17. Proof available on request.

18. If we use a more general welfare function

$$S = -\int\limits_0^\infty [(U - U')^2 + \phi^2(p - p')^2]e^{-rt}\,dt$$

inflation converges on

$$\bar{p} = p' + r(\overline{U} - U')/\phi^2\beta$$

19. When inflation is at its natural rate, the marginal benefit from a further unit reduction of inflation (which is $\phi^2\dot{p}/U$, measured in terms of U) equals the amortised marginal cost r/β. For a more general discussion of optimal inflation policy, see Phelps (1972, 1978).

20. This gives us the rule for monetary accommodation. With constant velocity $\dot{U} = -\xi(\dot{m} - \dot{p})$ and we require $\dot{U} = (z/\beta)\ddot{p}$. Hence we set $\dot{m} = \dot{p} - (z/\xi\beta)\ddot{p}$.

21. Half of the extra unemployment will be eliminated in $0.7/z$ years, which would be about 4 if $r = 0.04$, $\beta = 1$ and $\phi^2 = 0.04$ (values which would make $\bar{p} = \overline{U}$). The excess welfare loss is a more complex expression since

$$\int(U_t^2 - \overline{U}^2)dt + \int(\dot{p}_t^2 - \bar{p}_t^2)\,dt \neq \int(U_t - \overline{U})^2 dt + \int(\dot{p}_t - \bar{p}_t)^2\,dt$$

22. The static version of this equation should hold exactly if the production function is of the form $Y = f[aF(L, K), M]$ where F is Cobb–Douglas and L, K, M are labour, capital and materials. Trend productivity is treated as a function of time consisting of linear segments (one per business cycle). It is found by estimating on annual data 1951–80 the function

$$l = \beta l_{-1} + (1 - \beta)y - f(t)$$

where l is log employment, y is log GDP and $f(t)$ is the log productivity term. In Grubb, Jackman and Layard (1982) we discuss at some length how far trend productivity growth change can be considered exogenous and conclude that it can to a considerable degree.

23. Instruments were $w_{-1}, w_{-2}, p_{-1}, p_{-2}, t, U_{-1}, y_{-1}, (p + m)_{-1}, x$ and current import prices (\$) divided by the world price of manufacturing exports (\$).

24. In Grubb, Jackman and Layard (1982) we estimated similar equations and checked their stability using the Chow test for the period up to and after 1973. In the majority of cases this was satisfied at the 5 per cent level.

25. This test is based on the fact that if all coefficients are equal to the same value $\bar{c}$, t-statistics testing the hypothesis that $\hat{c}_i = \bar{c}$ are asymptotically normally distributed.

26. If the wage equation is estimated with $\dot{p}$ replaced by $\dot{p}_{-1}$, the pattern of real wage rigidity is similar. The t-statistics for the US and UK are now above 2. The UK is averagely rigid in real and nominal terms. The US is averagely rigid in real terms but well above average in nominal terms. In the $\dot{p}_{-1}$ equations the average lag is

constrained to be at least a year. The OECD average *NWR* becomes higher (0.90), the average *RWR* lower (0.45) and the average lag higher (1.77).

27. The α coefficients in the wage equation were significantly different across countries; $\chi^2(19) = 59.1$.

28. Another likely reason is that, due to measurement error in U, $\alpha\beta$ is biased down and hence $1/\beta$ is biased up.

29. We do not include *NWR* since the coefficient on it should be approximately proportional to $(-\Delta\ddot{w})$ which is close to zero.

30. There is a problem if U is not measured in a standard way in all countries. Suppose for example that $U = aU^*$, where U^* was an internationally standard measure. Then, if the true Phillips curve is $\ddot{w} = -\beta U^*$ and we estimate $\ddot{w} = -\hat{\beta}U$, $\mathrm{E}(\hat{\beta}) = \beta/a$. Equally $\Delta U = a\Delta U^*$. Hence there is an element of spurious positive correlation across countries between $1/\hat{\beta}$ and ΔU. However we doubt whether the correlation observed in Figure 3.2 would disappear if unemployment were everywhere measured on, say, US definitions.

There is a further problem if the true Phillips curve does not depend on labour market tightness but on, say, the output gap. This would again cause spurious correction of $1/\hat{\beta}$ if the Okun coefficients differed between countries. However, we were not able to estimate as good Phillips curves for the output gap and theory would not lead one to expect it.

A somewhat different problem arises if the model is fundamentally false. For example, consider the following simplified model: $\ddot{w} = -\beta U$, and suppose that in each country there are two observations so that β is estimated as $-\Delta\ddot{w}/\Delta U$. If across countries $\Delta\ddot{w}$ and ΔU are independent, then ΔU will be positively correlated with $1/\hat{\beta}$. This finding will only be meaningful in so far as the original estimate of the $\hat{\beta}$'s reflected a true causal process.

31. We do not find it helpful to think of the tightness of the labour market as constant over the cycle, when vacancies in the UK fluctuate between 100,000 and 300,000 and similarly in many European countries.

32. See Appendix B.

33. (i) Taylor (1980) conjectured that it would be, but his model did not allow for differential indexation. If α and λ are fixed,

$$\beta = (\eta((1 - \alpha)^2\sigma_v^2 + (\alpha - \lambda)^2\sigma_u^2))/((1 - \lambda)(\eta(1 - \alpha) + \alpha - \lambda)\sigma_e^2)$$

If all shocks are nominal, greater accommodation leads to higher β, but nothing definite can be said in the presence of real shocks.

(ii) In our model the response of inflation to employment would become infinite, if employment could be observed without error. A possible alternative explanation of sluggish wage adjustment in the face of unemployment might be if there was aversion to variation in real wages as well as employment. In this case the objective function of wage setters could be $E(l^2 + \xi(w - p)^2)$. The solution is now complete indexation ($\alpha = 1$), and wages adjust to unemployment according to $\beta = \eta/\xi$.

34. If we use data to 1980, the results are similar.

35. As a crude approximation, if $y = (\lambda - 1)p$ and $U = \phi p = -\frac{1}{3}y$, then $\lambda = 1 - 3\phi$

36. If $\alpha(L) = \alpha_0 + \alpha_1 L + \alpha_2 L^2 + \cdots = \sum \alpha_i L^i$, the average lag is $\sum i\alpha_i / \sum \alpha_i$. But $\alpha'(L) = \sum i\alpha_i L^{i-1}$, so that $\alpha'(1) = \sum i\alpha_i$, $\alpha(1) = \sum \alpha_i$

References

Branson, W.H. and J.J. Rotemberg (1980) 'International Adjustment with Wage Rigidity', *European Economic Review*, 13, 309–32.

Bruno, M. (1980) 'Import Prices and Stagflation in the Industrial Countries: A Cross-Section Analysis', *Economic Journal*, 90, 479–92.

Gordon, R.J. and S.R. King (1982) 'The Output Cost of Disinflation in Traditional and Vector-Autoregressive Models', *Brookings Papers on Economic Activity*, 1, 205–42.

Gray, J.A. (1976) 'Wage Indexation: A Macroeconomic Approach', *Journal of Monetary Economics*, 2, 221–35.

Grubb, D., R. Jackman and R. Layard (1982) 'Causes of the Current Stagflation', *Review of Economic Studies*, 49, 707–30.

Lucas, R.E. (1973) 'Some International Evidence on Output-Inflation Trade-offs', *American Economic Review*, 63, 326–34.

Phelps, E.S. (1972) *Inflation Policy and Unemployment Theory* (New York: Norton).

Phelps, E.S. (1978) 'Inflation Planning Reconsidered', *Economica*, 45, 109–24.

Sachs, J. (1979) 'Wages, Profits and Macroeconomic Adjustment: A Comparative Study', *Brookings Papers on Economic Activity*, 2, 269–333.

Sargan, J.D. (1964) 'Wages and Prices in the UK', in P.E. Hart, G. Mills and J.K. Whittaker (eds), *Econometric Analysis for National Economic Planning* (New York: Macmillan).

Taylor, J.B. (1980) 'Output and Price Stability: An International Comparison', *Journal of Economic Dynamics and Control*, 2, 109–32.

4 The Labour Market (1987)*

with S. Nickell

1 INTRODUCTION

> The biggest single cause of our high unemployment is the failure of our jobs market, the weak link in our economy.
>
> (White Paper, March 1985, *Employment, The Challenge for the Nation*, pp. 12–13)

Most people are dissatisfied with Britain's economic performance over the last 15 years, and many blame the institutions of the labour market. It is a natural argument, since our most obvious economic failure is the rise of unemployment.

But can one argue that unemployment has nearly trebled since 1979 because our labour market institutions have got so much worse? Clearly not. Up to 1979 our institutional arrangements did become a bit more rigid, but since then they have become a bit less so. So the rigidity argument cannot be of the form, 'Unemployment has risen because rigidity has risen'. It must be of the form, 'Unemployment has risen because the system has been subjected to deflationary shocks, and a rigid labour market has been unable to absorb them'. This will be the central theme of this chapter. We shall not discuss the deflationary shocks, which are the subject of other chapters in this book. Rather, we shall focus on the reaction in the labour market.

First (in Sections 2 and 3), we shall look at the labour market as an aggregate, and try to explain why unemployment has ratcheted upwards in the way shown in Figure 4.1 (p. 54). The central mystery is why, at present levels of unemployment, wage inflation is not falling. One approach is to focus on the

---

* Chapter 5 in R. Dornbusch and R. Layard (eds), *The Performance of the British Economy* (Oxford: Clarendon Press, 1987), pp. 131–79.

The authors are extremely grateful to Andy Murfin and Paul Kong for help with this paper. Jonathan Haskel kindly did the flows analysis of Tables 4.1 and 4.2. We are also grateful to David Stanton, Patrick Minford and Graham Reid for helpful comments, and to the Economic and Social Research Council and the Esmée Fairbairn Charitable Trust for financial assistance. Data sources are available on request, and are as in Layard and Nickell (1986a) and Nickell (1986). A longer version of this paper is available on request (Layard and Nickell), 1986b); this contains further evidence on the matters discussed in Section 4 and also a full discussion of hours of work.

impact of long-term unemployment on attachment to the labour force. According to this account, a sharp deflationary shock increases the number of long-term unemployed, many of whom effectively withdraw from the labour market. A rival, although related, interpretation focuses on the role of the unions. If unions are concerned mainly with 'insiders' and there is a contraction of employment, the unions become concerned with a smaller proportion of the labour force.

To discriminate between these two approaches, we shall deploy one of the basic facts about the labour market: that unemployment has risen hugely while vacancies are now as high as they were in 1977–8. The fact that vacancies exist in that (limited) abundance argues in favour of the explanation in terms of workers' incentives to take work and firms' incentives to fill vacancies, as against explanations that focus solely on the role of unions in holding down the number of jobs, once this number has fallen.

A quite different explanation of unemployment focuses on structural issues and the rigidities in the structure of relative wages (rather than of the general wage level). In Section 4 we show how inflexible relative wages are in this country – whether by industry, region, age, or sex. This makes unemployment higher than it would otherwise be. But there is no evidence that these problems have worsened in a way that could explain the *rise* in unemployment.

Thus far, we have been concerned with employment (an input) rather than with output. But the test of the labour market is not only whether it can use the labour available, but whether it can use it to produce something. In Section 5 we therefore look at productivity. Sections 3–5 each end with a summary.

2 AGGREGATE UNEMPLOYMENT

Some basic facts

We shall begin with some basic facts. Unemployment has quadrupled since 1970 (see Figure 4.1). The most relevant series we have is for male unemployment, since measured female unemployment depends so much on women's varying entitlements to benefits. Male unemployment (on the official pre-1982 definition)[1] has increased from 4 to 17 per cent – mainly through two huge steps, one in 1974–6 and the second in 1979–82. On the OECD's standardized definitions, male unemployment is now nearly twice as high in Britain as in France, Germany, Italy, or the United States.[2] And male employment is now lower than it was in 1911.

The increase in unemployment has come about almost entirely through an increase in the duration of unemployment. As can be seen from Figure 4.2, the inflow into unemployment in recent years has been rather less than it was in the late 1960s, though about a fifth above its level in the late 1970s. There has been

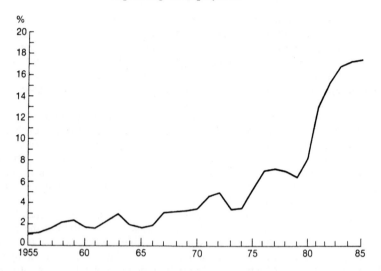

Figure 4.1 Male unemployment rate, 1955–85 (pre-1982 definition of unemployment)

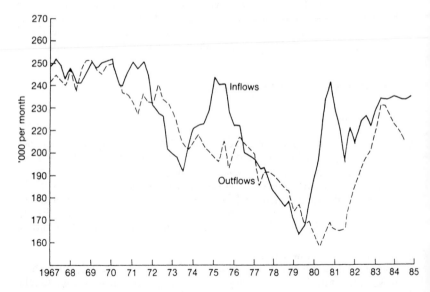

Figure 4.2 Male unemployment inflows and outflows, 1967–85 (pre-1982 definition of unemployment)

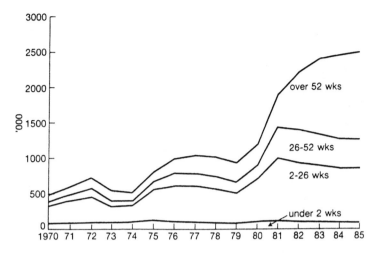

Figure 4.3 Male unemployment by duration, 1970–85 (pre-1982 definition of unemployment)

a huge build-up of long-term unemployed – that is, of those unemployed for over a year (see Figure 4.3). In fact, since 1981 short-term unemployment has actually fallen a bit, while long-term unemployment has soared.

Unemployment of this kind must be both inefficient and inequitable. It must be inefficient since it cannot reflect any necessary search or redeployment of labour and in fact causes huge depreciation of the stock of human capital. It must be inequitable since it reflects the concentration of the total man-weeks of unemployment in a very small proportion of the population. The number of men who become unemployed is roughly $2\frac{1}{2}$ million a year – only 16 per cent of the male workforce. But the stock of unemployed men is nearly $2\frac{1}{2}$ million. So those who do become unemployed can expect on average to remain so for roughly a year.

The rise in unemployment has not been matched by a commensurate fall in vacancies. Vacancies are indeed low (about two-thirds of their average level in the 1960s), but they are at about the same level as in the economic troughs of 1958, 1963, and 1971–2 and above their level in 1976 (see Figure 4.4). The outward shift of the u/v curve is thus a basic puzzle which we have to explain.

While unemployment has risen, the labour force has not stood still. Indeed, it has risen continuously since 1971 (except in 1983), though much more slowly than in the United States and Japan. The increase is entirely due to the rising number of women in the labour force. This reflects partly the size of the adult

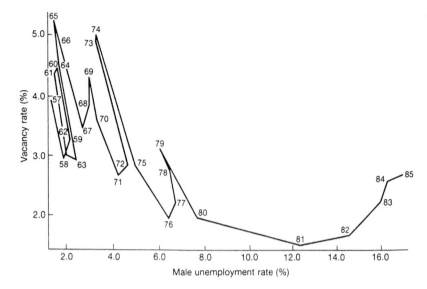

Figure 4.4 Vacancies and male unemployment, 1957–85

population, but also the increasing participation rate of women. By contrast, the participation rate of men has fallen, mainly owing to earlier retirement.

The mechanism by which labour supply affects employment is through its effects on wages. At some level of unemployment, wage inflation will be stable – increasing at lower unemployment and falling at higher unemployment. Figure 4.5 therefore shows the history of wage inflation, while Figure 4.6 shows changes in wage inflation against the level of vacancies. There is clearly some relationship.

A labour market model

To explain the movement of unemployment, we shall present a simple model. This draws on earlier work (Layard and Nickell, 1986a), but simplifies it and extends it to focus on the apparent ratchet effect in the level of unemployment.

In the long run, unemployment is determined so that there is equality between

1. the 'feasible' real wage, implied by the pricing behaviour of firms, and
2. the 'target' real wage, implied by the wage setting behaviour of wage bargainers.

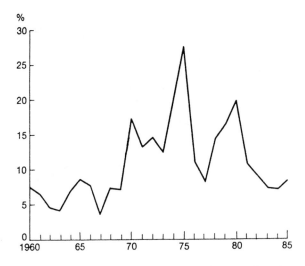

Figure 4.5 Rate of growth of hourly earnings of male manual workers, 1960–85

Figure 4.6 The change in rate of growth of hourly earnings (male manual) and the vacancy rate (×5), 1963–85

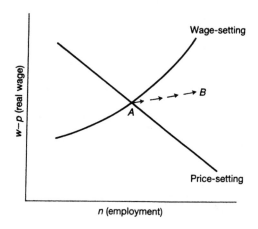

Figure 4.7   The consequences of a positive demand shock

This is illustrated at point *A* in Figure 4.7.

Let us go behind the curves, starting with the price-setting relationship determining the 'feasible' real wage. We shall define prices (*p*) as the price of value added; i.e. at the level of the firm, final prices adjusted for changes in materials' prices, and at the level of the whole economy, for changes in the price of imports. Firms set their value added prices as a mark-up on hourly labour cost (*w*). But this mark-up will tend to rise if output is higher. Since output is related to employment via the production function, it follows that the real wage falls as employment rises, as in Figure 4.7. The mark-up falls if inflation is greater than expected ($p > p^e$), both because prices will not be adjusted enough upwards for the higher wages, and because firms will underestimate competitors' prices and keep their prices low to retain business.[3]

Wages in turn are set as a mark-up on expected prices. The mark-up increases as employment rises and is also affected by a whole host of wage pressure variables (*z*), to which we return later. If inflation is greater than expected the mark-up will fall, since, when prices turn out to be higher than expected, the real wage achieved will be lower than the real wage bargained for.

In the longer run, the growth of the capital stock will lead to productivity improvements, which, on the one hand, will lead firms to reduce their mark-up of prices on wages and, on the other hand, will lead firms and workers to bargain for a higher mark-up of wages and prices.[4] Thus, in static, log-linear form we have the following model:[5]

Price setting:

$$p - w = \alpha_0 + \alpha_1(p - p^e) + \alpha_2(n - l) + \alpha_3(k - l)$$
$$(\alpha_1 < 0, \alpha_2 \geq 0, \alpha_3 < 0) \tag{4.1}$$

Wage setting:

$$w - p = \beta_0 + \beta_1(p - p^e) + \beta_2(n - l) + \beta_3(k - l) + z$$
$$(\beta_1 < 0, \beta_2 > 0, \beta_3 > 0) \tag{4.2}$$

where w = hourly labour cost (including employers' labour taxes)
$\quad\ p$ = value added price
$\quad\ k$ = capital stock
$\quad\ l$ = labour force
$\quad\ n$ = employment (note the unemployment rate $u = l - n$)
$\quad\ z$ = 'wage pressure' (the influence of mismatch, employment protection, replacement ratio, union power, incomes policy, relative import prices, and employers' labour taxes).

There are many points worth noting abut this framework. First, it is very general. For example, if $\alpha_1 = 0$ and $\alpha_2 = -\alpha_3$, then (4.1) becomes the standard labour demand equation for a competitive industry. Similarly, a restricted version of (4.2) yields a competitive labour supply equation. On the other hand, if $\alpha_2 = 0$ we have the pure mark-up or normal cost pricing model, where prices are unaffected by demand in the short run. Second, to complete a model of a closed economy, we may add the following equations:
Production function:

$$y - k = f(n - k) \tag{4.3}$$

Aggregate demand:

$$y = y^d(x) \tag{4.4}$$

where y = value added output
$\quad\ x$ = exogenous determinants of real demand.

So, given the resources of the economy as specified by k and l, the model will, in the short run, yield w, p, n, y for any given level of demand (x), price expectations (p^e) and wage pressure (z). In the longer term, when price surprises are ruled out ($p = p^e$), the model reveals, for given z, the level of y, n, $w - p$, and y^d consistent with no surprises. If no surprises is synonymous with stable inflation, these levels correspond to the NAIRU (non-accelerating inflation rate of unemployment).

The great advantage of writing the model as we have done is that (4.1) and (4.2) alone will yield the no-surprise (or NAIRU) values of employment and the real wage, and are thus eminently suitable for analyzing long-term unemployment trends.[6]

In order to see how the model operates, we consider, first, the consequences of an aggregate demand shock starting from a position of equilibrium $(p = p^e)$. This is illustrated in Figure 4.7. An increase in real demand raises employment, and this tends to raise prices relative to wages in the price equation, and wages relative to prices in the wage equation. The only way in which these tendencies can be made consistent is via the positive price surprise brought about by a rise in inflation. This tends to offset the consequences of the rise in the level of activity on both sides of the market, leading us to a point such as B, which is below the wage line and above the price line. (Note that the effect of a positive price surprise is to raise the price-determined real wage.) So we have the standard result that a positive demand shock will raise employment, raise inflation, but have an indeterminate impact on the real wage. However, we can be more precise on this latter point in certain special cases. If the product market is competitive, then $\alpha_1 = 0$ and $\alpha_2 = -\alpha_3$ in (4.1), as we have already noted. Thus B must lie on the price line, which slopes downwards. The real wage must, therefore, fall. On the other hand, under strict normal cost pricing, $\alpha_2 = 0$ and the price line is horizontal. Under these circumstances the real wage must rise, since B must be above the horizontal price line.

Turning to the consequences of a supply shock, in Figure 4.8 we illustrate the outcome of a rise in wage pressure, z (a negative supply shock). If real demand remains fixed, then we move to a point such as B, with a fall in employment and positive price surprises generated by rising inflation. The real wage has risen, and we have the combination of inflation and 'classical' unemployment typical

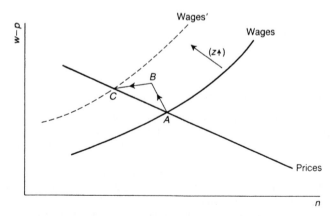

Figure 4.8   The consequences of a rise in wage pressure

of such a shock. If the rise in wage pressure is permanent, real demand must fall if inflation is to be stabilized. This may happen either autonomously (via real balance effects, for example) or as a result of a conscious policy shift. In consequence, we move to a new equilibrium at C, with lower 'equilibrium' employment and a real wage that will be higher to the extent that prices are influenced by demand. In the extreme case of normal cost pricing, the price line is horizontal and the real wage will revert back to its original level. The additional unemployment will then apparently be entirely 'Keynesian', although it has, in fact, been brought about by the rise in wage pressure.

It is clear from this analysis that the wage pressure variables are the key to the long-run analysis of unemployment. It is also clear that focusing on the real-wage outcome will not be very useful in trying to understand what is happening. The real wage that finally emerges has as much to do with the pricing policy of firms as with labour market activity.

Our next step is to attach some numbers to the fundamental model. Our equations are based on Nickell (1987). The dynamic versions of each equation are (annual data 1956–83):[7]

Prices:

$$p - w = \alpha_0 - 0.61\Delta^2 w - 0.51\Delta^2 w_{-1} - 0.253u +$$
$$0.075\Delta u - 0.338\Delta^2 u - 1.07(k - l) \qquad (4.1')$$

Wages:

$$w - p = \beta_0 - 036\Delta^2 p - 0.104\log u + 0.532u$$
$$-1.174\Delta u - 0.356\Delta^2 u + 1.07(k - l) + z \qquad (4.2')$$

A number of points are worth noting. The price surprise terms are represented by $\Delta^2 w$ in the price equation and $\Delta^2 p$ in the wage equation. One of the key properties of the wage equation is the dependence of wages on $\log u$ as well as u. This has profound implications and we shall return to this point at a later stage. At the moment it suffices to say that a 1 percentage point rise in unemployment has a lesser impact on wages, the higher is its initial level. A final point concerns the role of the productivity variable $(k - l)$. The model imposes the restriction that increases in the stock of capital have no impact on unemployment *in the long run*. This is perfectly consistent with the data and implies that the long-run coefficient on $k - l$ is the same (in absolute value) in both price and wage equations. Were this not the case, the implication would be that firms and workers would be trying to extract, on a permanent basis, more or less than 100 per cent of the growth in trend productivity. Since this would imply either *permanently* rising or *permanently* falling unemployment at stable inflation, we decided to rule out this possibility – it seems inconsistent with the apparent consequences of two centuries of economic growth.

To understand the long-run determinants of unemployment, we can write (4.1′) and (4.2′) in their long-run form, expanding the wage equation around an unemployment rate of $\bar{u}$. This gives

Prices : $p - w = \alpha_0 - 0.253u - 1.07(k - l)$ $\qquad\qquad$ (4.1″)

Wages : $w - p = \beta_0' - \left(\dfrac{0.104}{\bar{u}} - 0.532\right)u + 1.07(k - l) + z$ $\qquad$ (4.2″)

The long-run level of unemployment is given by adding these equations to obtain

$$u = \left(0.253 + \frac{0.104}{\bar{u}} - 0.532\right)^{-1} (z + \alpha_o + \beta_0') \qquad (4.5)$$

Thus, wage pressure (z) is crucial to our explanation of unemployment.[8] The next step, therefore, is to look at the movement of the wage pressure index – see Figure 4.9. (We shall discuss its constituent parts later.) As can be seen, it

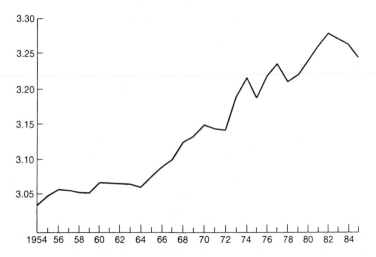

Figure 4.9   Wage pressure index, 1954–85
Note: This is based on
$z = 0.068$ mismatch $+ 0.28$ replacement ratio $+ 0.49v \log (Pm/\bar{P}) + 0.29 \Delta$
$(v \log (Pm/\bar{P})) + 0.030$ union power $+ 0.66t_1$
$Pm/\bar{P}$ is the real price of imports, and t_1 is employers' labour tax rate. The mismatch variable has been smoothed to remove its cyclical component. v is the share of imports in GDP.

moves broadly in line with unemployment up to 1980, and any divergences are identified with increasing or decreasing inflation, as appropriate. However, since 1980 the index has risen little, with the years 1980–5 having wage pressure only 4 points higher than the 1974–80 average. The long-run NAIRU (for male unemployment) is now around 12 per cent; yet actual unemployment is much higher than this, with the 1981–5 average being nearly 10 points above the level for 1974–80. Thus, the index does not seem to explain how the high unemployment of the 1980s could be accompanied by such relatively small reductions in wage inflation.

The answer to the apparent paradox lies in the fact that the short-term NAIRU is not the same as the long-term NAIRU. This arises from the dynamics of the system and especially of the wage equation (4.2′). As the wage pressure equation makes clear, wage pressure is less not only when unemployment is higher but also when unemployment is rising. By the same token, wage pressure at a given level of unemployment is higher when unemployment is falling. Thus, suppose the wage equation is, for simplicity,

$$w - p = \beta_0 - \beta_2 \log u - \beta_3(u - u_{-1}) \tag{4.6}$$

as compared with the long-run wage relationship

$$w - p = \beta_0 - \beta_2 \log u$$

In Figure 4.10 we show the long-run NAIRU at point A as usual. But suppose last year's employment was at n_{-1}. The short-run wage pressure equation (4.6) is given by the dotted line and the short-run NAIRU is at B. This is the essence

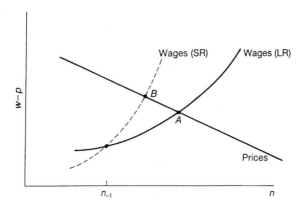

Figure 4.10 Short-run NAIRU (at B) and long-run NAIRU (at A)

of our present difficulties. We have got to a very high level of unemployment, and reducing unemployment is always liable to produce increasing inflation.

What accounts for the long-lasting effect of past unemployment in the wage equation? The evidence suggests that it results from the effect of high unemployment on the numbers of the long-term unemployed. But in order to give all theories a run for their money, we need first to consider from basic principles how the unemployment situation might be expected to influence the degree of wage pressure.

Unemployment and wage pressure

Two parties are involved in wage determination: firms and unions. Their relative importance differs in different parts of the economy.[9] Let us begin with firms. Firms, if they were free to choose wages, would set them at a level that would enable them to recruit, retain, and motivate workers. For recruitment purposes, they would choose lower wages, the more plentiful the supply of workers that they faced. Similar factors would affect the ability of firms to restrain quitting and to motivate workers, for workers are easier to retain and motivate, the more job market competition they would face if they themselves became unemployed.[10]

Thus, a key variable is the number of acceptable unemployed workers who are out there 'beating at the gates'. Since few unemployed workers (30 per cent) get re-employed in the industry of their previous job, we would expect that it was general (rather than industry-specific) unemployment that affected wage behaviour in each country. And this turns out to be the case (see p. 85 below).

But the level of unemployment on its own does not adequately measure the number of acceptable workers beating at the gates. The composition of unemployment also matters. If a high proportion of the unemployed have been out of work for a long time, the employers may consider them undesirable as workers; equally, the workers themselves may be discouraged, and may have largely given up searching. Thus, long-term unemployment represents a less effective labour supply than short-term unemployment. So employers will be influenced both by the level of unemployment and by the proportion of the unemployed who are long-term unemployed (R). As we have seen this proportion has doubled since 1979, and we shall find that this is a major factor explaining the current degree of wage pressure.

But what about the union response to unemployment? Unions too will care about the numbers of workers 'beating at the gates'. For if wages are pushed too high, some union members will lose their jobs and end up in competition with other unemployed job-seekers.[11] So if general unemployment is high, and predominantly short-term, individual unions will be less inclined to push on wages and so risk unemployment for their members.

But unions will be concerned not only with the bleakness of the world outside, but also with the likelihood that their members will be ejected into it. So another key variable will be 'fear' – the fear of job loss. The extent of job loss will of course depend on the wages that each union selects. But this will in turn depend on how unfavourable a demand curve the union faces. The union may evaluate its demand curve largely in terms of, say, last year's job loss.[12] This could be proxied by last year's rate of inflow into unemployment (I) or by the change in unemployment.

One extreme view is in fact that wage behaviour depends *only* on the change in unemployment, and not at all on the level (Blanchard and Summers, 1986).[13] This has been offered as an explanation of why wage inflation fell so much between 1980–1 and 1982–3, and so little since. The chief line of reasoning is that the unions care only about their members and set the wage so as to maintain the chances of their continued employment (see also Lindbeck and Snower, 1984). If unemployment has been low and stable for some time, wage claims will be no higher than if unemployment has been high and stable for sometime. For the unions are concerned only with ensuring the continued employment of those employed in the previous period, and this does not require a lower wage when unemployment is high. But when employment is falling, unions do moderate their behaviour in order to try to prevent employment falling further.

There are many obvious problems with this 'insider–outsider' line of argument. First, it provides no explanation of the fact that, over longish periods, the size of the labour force has a clear effect on the level of employment. This must involve some responsiveness of wages to the labour force, as well as to employment.[14] Second, given the huge level of annual turnover in enterprises, it is hard to understand why employment has not been steadily falling if wage-setting only takes account of surviving workers. Third, the theory fails to explain why it is general unemployment rather than industry-specific unemployment (or employment) that most clearly affects the wages in an industry (see p. 85 below).

But even so, it is important to investigate systematically the effect of flow variables like unemployment flows and the change in employment, as compared with the level of unemployment and the composition of unemployment by duration. This is done in Nickell (1986), and we shall summarize the results. The most successful equation is one that includes only the log of unemployment and the proportion of the unemployed out of work for over a year (R):[15]

$$w - p = \beta_0'' - 0.36\Delta^2 p - 0.104 \log u + 0.212 R + 1.07(k - l) + z \qquad (4.7)$$
$$ (7.8) (3.7)$$

IV estimates 1956–83, se $= 0.0114$

When this equation was expanded to include the inflow of unemployment, we obtained a *t*-statistic of only 1.3 and the significance of the duration term increased. When the equation was expanded to include lagged employment terms, the coefficients were

η_{-1} :   0.46 (2.2)

η_{-2} : -0.52 (2.1)

and the *t*-statistics on log u and R remained 5.7 and 4.1, respectively. However, this version of the equation fits very badly over the 1980s. So our conclusion is that the story based on the effects of long-duration unemployment is the most persuasive.

Before pursuing the implications of this, we should refer to one other issue: the impact of region-specific unemployment rates. It is often suggested that, since wage bargaining is undertaken nationally in so many sectors (e.g. the public sector) and companies (e.g. ICI and the four main motor car manufacturers), wages may be most strongly influenced by the tightness of the labour market in the most buoyant region – that is, the South-East. So we added to our standard equation a variable measuring the South-East's unemployment rate relative to the national average, expecting it to reduce wage pressure. It did so – but its *t*-statistic was only 0.7. This is not surprising, given that this variable has recently had a high value, and yet there has been little apparent reduction of wage pressure.

We are therefore ready to investigate how the duration of unemployment affect the dynamics of wage behaviour. The first step is to see how the proportion of unemployed out of work for over a year (R) is affected by the history of unemployment. The relevant equation is

$$R = 0.054 + 0.61 R_{-1} - 2.41 u + 5.58 u_{-1} - 2.18 u_{-2} \qquad (4.7')$$
$$\quad (2.1) \quad\;\; (3.7) \quad\quad (5.6) \quad\;\; (6.5) \quad\quad (2.4)$$

OLS estimation 1956–83, se $= 0.023, \overline{R}^2 = 0.84$

This equation makes very good sense. As unemployment rises, the long-term unemployed proportion falls initially, since historically increases in unemployment come about because the inflow rises. In the long run, however, the long-term proportion tends to rise with unemployment. If we now solve out for R and substitute into (4.7), we obtain, after some manipulation, (4.2′), which is how we obtained that equation in the first place (see Nickell, 1986, (26)).

Interestingly, (4.2′) is similar to what is obtained from the following directly estimated dynamic wage equation:

$$w - p = \beta_0 - 0.113 \log u + 0.425 u - 0.803 \Delta u + 1.07(k - l) + z \qquad (4.2''')$$
$$\qquad\qquad\quad (5.2) \qquad\quad (1.03) \quad\; (1.9)$$

IV estimation 1956–83, se $= 0.0125, DW = 1.81$

This was our most successful dynamic wage equation (except for one that depended heavily on unemployment lagged three years). But the important point is that (4.2‴) gives no behavioural insight into how the dynamics arise, whereas our two equations involving long-term unemployment, (4.7) and (4.7′), do just that.

We can now see how our model helps us to understand the movement of inflation. From (4.2′) we can see that in the long run, if unemployment gets high enough (above 19 per cent), further unemployment fails to reduce wage pressure, because the proportion of long-term unemployed becomes so high (see Figure 4.11).

But what happens to the rate of change of nominal wages? As equations (4.1′) and (4.2′) make clear, the rate of change of inflation is directly related to the difference between the target real wage and the feasible real wage (each measured in the absence of nominal inertia, i.e., with $\Delta^2 w = \Delta^2 p = 0$). To see this, we add (4.1′) to (4.2′) after first expanding (4.2′) around $\bar{\mu}$, setting $\Delta^2 w = \Delta^2 w_{-1} = \Delta^2 p$, and omitting $\Delta^2 u$. This gives us

$$\Delta^2 w = -0.68 \left\{ \left(\frac{0.104}{\bar{u}} - 0.279 \right) u + 1.10 \Delta u - z - \alpha_0 - \beta_0' \right\}$$

where the term in brackets is the gap between feasible and target wage. Using (4.5), this can be rewritten

$$\Delta^2 w = -0.68 \left\{ \left(\frac{0.104}{\bar{u}} - 0.279 \right) (u - u^*) + 1.10 \Delta u \right\} \tag{4.8}$$

Thus, as unemployment grows, the effect of higher unemployment on cutting inflation is reduced. This is exactly what we should expect by looking at Figure 4.11 and bearing in mind that the change in inflation is proportional to the distance between the two lines. This distance reaches its minimum when unemployment is 37 per cent, and if unemployment goes higher than this it starts to lose its power to reduce inflation. For beyond that point higher unemployment raises the target real wage more than it raises the feasible real wage. This observation is highly speculative since it lies way beyond the sample range, but it does raise the spectre that, if wage pressure became fierce enough, there might be no unemployment rate that could stabilize inflation.

More relevant to our present range of experience, the diagram shows clearly how the benefits of additional unemployment vary with the existing level of unemployment. If unemployment is low, more unemployment will have a marked effect on the change in inflation. But if unemployment is already high, the counterinflation gains from further unemployment are very limited. Thus the following table shows the (negative) effect on the change of inflation of 1 extra point of unemployment, starting from different levels of unemployment.

$\bar{u}$	Effect of 1 extra percentage point of unemployment on $(-\Delta^2 w)$
0.07	0.82%
0.12	0.39%
0.17	0.22%

(The values correspond to 0.68 $(0.104/\bar{u} - 0.279)$. This indicates, for example, that a 1 point rise in unemployment from a base line of 7 per cent (i.e. 1979 male unemployment) will cause inflation to slow down at four times the speed of the slow-down induced by a similar rise in unemployment from a base-line of 17 per cent (i.e. 1985 male unemployment). However, this is a

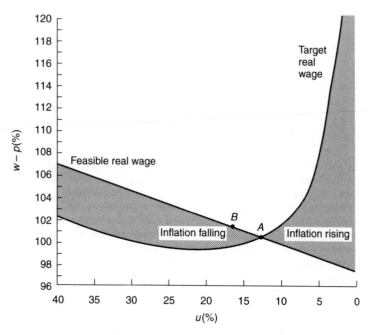

Figure 4.11 How unemployment changes the rate of inflation (using long-run wage and price equations)
Note: This diagram is drawn to scale and corresponds to 1985. *A* is the long-run NAIRU: *B* is the short-run NAIRU when $u_{-1} = 17$ per cent; and $\Delta^2 w = 0.68$ (target real wage − feasible real wage).

long-run effect. The Δu term in (4.8) reveals, for example, that, if we start from the current base-line of 17 per cent male unemployment and assume that this is 5 points above the long-run natural rate (our estimate is around 12 per cent), then any attempt to reduce unemployment down to this level at a rate of more than 2 percentage points per year will actually generate increasing inflation from the start. Even if unemployment is reduced at 1 percentage point per year, inflation will start to rise well before the natural rate is attained. This arises because of the way in which the duration structure of unemployment changes when unemployment declines. Falls in unemployment lead initially to a sharp reduction in the short-term unemployed. This withdrawal of a considerable proportion of the most active and desirable workers from the unemployed pool generates an increase in wage pressure which eases off only when the duration structure returns to normal and the major reduction in unemployment has come from the long-term end of the spectrum.

To summarize, therefore, once we take account of the fact that the long-term unemployed have only a minor impact on wages, we find that, in the long run, the inflation-reducing effects of extra unemployment decline rapidly as unemployment rises. For the same reason, the impact of changes in wage pressure on unemployment increases as the general level of unemployment goes up.

3 INFLUENCES ON WAGE PRESSURE

Having established the overall framework, we now need to look at the various wage pressure factors (z), which determine the long-run NAIRU. How far does each help us to explain the long rise in unemployment, and how does the duration of unemployment (as a more endogenous influence) fit into the story?

The wage pressure factors we shall investigate are (in order): the duration of unemployment, employment protection, mismatch, benefits, unions, incomes policy, taxes, and import prices.

The duration of unemployment and the u/v curve

To think about the first four of these influences, we need to go behind the simplified model we have been using so far, and look at the flow of people through unemployment. This gives us a relationship between the unemployment rate (u), the vacancy rate (v), and a number of shift variables (x): $f(u, v, x) = 0$. We can also conceive of the structural wage equation lying behind (4.2) as including vacancies (as well as unemployment) as a determinant of wages. The wage equation (4.2) we have used so far is therefore a semi-reduced form in which vacancies have been substituted out, using $f(u, v, x) = 0$. It therefore includes all the variables (x) that affect the relationship of vacancies and unemployment. However, to check on our interpretation of the role of these variables in (4.2), we must look directly at the structural u/v relationship. Where does it come from, and what factors affect it?

The u/v curve reflects the process by which unemployed workers are matched to vacancies to generate a flow of hirings (or job-matches). One would expect that the number of hirings would depend positively on the number of vacancies that firms are willing to fill per period, and also on the number of unemployed people looking for work per period. It will be reduced by any mismatch (*mm*) between unemployment and vacancies. The intensity with which firms want to fill vacancies will vary according to how they view the quality of the unemployed and on such things as employment protection legislation and the like. So the vacancies that are relevant per period are some proportion (*g*) that firms wish to fill. Similarly, workers may vary in their intensity of search, depending on their past experience and on the level of unemployment benefits and the like. So the unemployed that are relevant per period are some proportion (*c*). This gives us our matching equation:

$$A = f(gV, cU, mm) \qquad (4.9)$$
$$ + \quad + \quad -$$

where A is the numbers leaving unemployment per period and U and V are the numbers of vacancies and unemployed.

We can now see clearly how the proportion of long-term unemployed (R) has its effect. For both g and c will decrease as the proportion R rises. Hence (for given flows) the u/v curve shifts out as the proportion of long-term unemployed goes up. This is exactly what Budd, Levine and Smith (1988) have found.[16] The fact that long-term unemployment shows up in the structural u/v relationship adds greatly to our confidence that its effect in the semi-reduced form wage equation (4.7) is also valid.

To obtain the long-run u/v curve, we note that in a steady state the outflow from unemployment equals the inflow. This has been roughly true for the last few years, and was also true in the late 1970s. In this case $A = S$, where S is the inflow to unemployment. This gives us

$$\frac{U}{N} = \frac{S/N}{A/U} \qquad (4.10)$$

where S/N is the inflow into unemployment as a proportion of the employed, and A/U is the proportion of the unemployed who leave unemployment. The unemployment rate (relative to employment) is simply the ratio of these two proportions.

Which of these two proportions accounts for the huge rise in unemployment? A glance at Figure 4.2 shows that the increased inflow rate into unemployment (S/N) would have increased unemployment by only a fifth. The main 'cause' of increased unemployment has been the halving in the outflow rate (A/U).

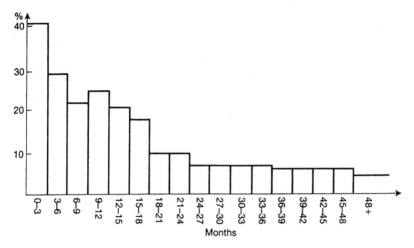

Figure 4.12 Proportion of unemployed in January 1984 leaving unemployment in the next three months

It is easy to see how the pile-up of long-term unemployment could help to explain this fall in the outflow rate (A/U). For the outflow rate is always very much lower for those who have been unemployed longer. As Figure 4.12 shows, for people who have been unemployed over four years it is now 4 per cent per quarter, compared with 41 per cent per quarter for those who have recently lost their jobs. Thus, when long-term unemployment piles up, the overall outflow rate falls, even if the duration-specific outflow rates remain constant. We can therefore examine the effect of the duration structure upon the outflow rate by constructing an index of the outflow rate as it would have been over time with the duration-specific outflow rates unchanging but with the duration structure of unemployment changing as it has. This is shown in Figure 4.13. The (fixed) duration-specific outflow rates are those for January 1984 (as shown in Figure 4.12).

As the index shows, the change in the duration structure of unemployment accounts for all of the fall in the overall outflow rate since early 1981. This is the period during which the proportion of long-term unemployed has continuously risen while (as Table 4.1 shows) the duration-specific outflow rates have changed little. Before 1981 there was no increase in the proportion of long-term unemployed, and the fall in the outflow rate was due entirely to the sharp fall in the duration-specific outflow rates (Table 4.2).

So what happened in the 1980s was this. The proportions of people leaving unemployment at each duration fell, but they fell by nothing like one-half (see

Table 4.2). This, however, led to an increase in the proportion of the unemployed who were long-term unemployed. Because the outflow rates are lower for the long-term unemployed than for those with shorter durations, an equiproportionate fall in all outflow rates leads to a more than proportionate fall in the average outflow rate.[17] If there were now a major economic recovery, the inflow into unemployment would fall sharply and so would short-term unemployment. But it is most unlikely that long-term unemployment would fall at all rapidly, unless specific measures were taken to encourage employers to hire the long-term unemployed.

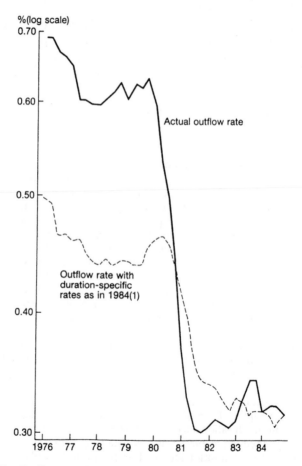

Figure 4.13 Outflow rate from unemployment (per 3 months), males, 1976–84

Table 4.1 Outflow from unemployment, 1981–85

Year	% of unemployed in Jan. leaving in next 3 months, by duration (months) in Jan.									
	0–3	3–6	6–9	9–12	12–15	15–18	18–24	24–36	36–48	48+
1981	36.7	29.4	26.1	19.3	17.4	–	–	–	–	–
1982	40.4	31.4	23.9	21.8	18.7	24.4	18.9	–	–	–
1983	39.2	28.1	21.5	20.2	17.9	23.8	10.8	8.7	–	–
1984	41.1	29.7	22.2	25.3	21.4	18.7	10.4	7.8	6.0	4.3
1985	41.8	28.6	22.7	23.7	21.1	–	–	8.1	6.4	5.1

Reverting to the u/v curve (4.9), Pissarides (1986) has shown that it exhibits constant returns to scale. We can therefore divide both sides by unemployment to get.

$$\frac{A}{U} = f\left(g\frac{V}{U}, c, mm\right)$$

which can be substituted into (4.10) to get the long-run u/v curve. Clearly, a complete model would need an equation to explain the inflow rate (S/N). This

Table 4.2 Outflow from unemployment, 1976–85

Year	% of unemployed in Jan. leaving in the next 3 months, by duration (months) in January			
	0–3	3–6	6–9	9+
1976	56.2	38.9	31.8	18.1
1977	56.0	41.4	35.1	20.1
1978	54.9	41.8	37.5	21.5
1979	56.6	41.0	35.0	16.6
1980	52.0	36.7	30.0	17.3
1981	36.7	29.4	26.1	13.9
1982	40.4	31.4	23.9	15.3
1983	39.2	28.1	21.5	13.8
1984	41.1	29.7	22.2	13.6
1985	41.8	28.6	22.7	12.1

was attempted in Nickell (1982) but is not reported here. An important factor affecting flows both into and out of unemployment is employment protection: our next factor affecting the u/v relationship.

Employment protection

If the cost of firing workers increases, employers will become more leery about hiring. Thus the proportion (g) of vacancies they are willing to fill per period will fall. Of course, at the same time the number of firings will fall also. Since in equilibrium firings equal hirings (a), in equilibrium a also falls. What happens to the u/v curve (and thus to equilibrium unemployment) depends on which of these effects dominates.

Let us begin with the facts about employment protection laws and then give evidence on their net effect. There have been three main changes. The Redundancy Payments Act 1965 introduced statutory payments when a worker is made redundant, a part of which is a direct cost to the employer. The Industrial Relations Act 1971 established legal rights against unfair dismissal (now covering all workers employed for over two years by the same employer). The Employment Protection Act 1975 extended the periods of notice required before termination.

Employment protection has been studied in some detail in Nickell (1979, 1982), with mixed results. The net impact on unemployment is unclear. As we have said, if it becomes more difficult or expensive for firms to reduce employment, this will reduce flows into unemployment. So employment protection must be a cause of the downward trend in inflow during the 1970s. But, by making employers more choosy in hiring, it will also reduce the outflow from unemployment. Both these effects were detected in Nickell (1982), but the net impact was in the direction of a reduction in unemployment. This result is, however, very tentative, since the variable used to capture the legislation (numbers of Industrial Tribunal cases) is clearly rather weak. Survey evidence is also ambiguous (see Jackman, Layard and Pissarides 1984). The most recent survey by the CBI asked employers how (1) abolition or reduction of redundancy entitlements and (2) abolition or reduction of unfair dismissal rights would affect the number of their employees. The replies were

	Definitely increase employment	Possibly increase employment
Redundancy entitlements	5%	14%
Unfair dismissal rights	3%	7%

Thus, reverting to the u/v curve, it seems quite likely that employment protection has had little effect, reducing equilibrium a and g by roughly offsetting magnitudes.

Mismatch

Another variable affecting the location of the u/v curve is the mismatch (mm) between unemployment and vacancies. Other things equal, unemployment will tend to rise if the unemployed became less well matched to the vacancies available. We can therefore ask, Are structural factors an important part of the explanation for the rise in unemployment? This is a tough question. The first issue is, Which structural dimension matters most? Probably the most serious is the regional dimension. Hardly any of the unemployed find work in a different region from the one they worked in before. By contrast, two-thirds of men who became unemployed in autumn 1978 and found work within four months found it in a different industry (24 categories) or occupation (18 categories) from their previous job.

The next issue is how to measure mismatch. The most obvious concept of a good match is one where the ratio of unemployment to vacancies is the same in each region.[18] The incidence of structural unemployment could then be measured by the proportion of the unemployed who would have to be in a different region if perfect matching were secured. This is given by

$$mm = \tfrac{1}{2}\sum |u_i - v_i|$$

where u_i is the proportion of the unemployed in region i and v_i is the proportion of vacancies. This index is charted in Figure 4.14.[19] It shows that the degree of regional mismatch has been reduced.

This may seem surprising, for many people feel that the amount of structural unemployment has risen. However, both statements are true. When we measure regional mismatch we are trying to find an index that could have *caused* an increase in unemployment. When we measure the amount of structural unemployment, we measure the *number* of unemployed people who would have to shift regions in order to restore proportionality between unemployment and vacancies. This is given by

$$SU = mm(uL)$$

In recent years structural unemployment has risen because of the increase in unemployment, but not because of an increase in mismatch. Mismatch has fallen, because the proportional rise in unemployment rates has been less in the high-unemployment regions. Structural unemployment has risen, because the *absolute* rise in unemployment rates has been greater in the high-unemployment regions.[20] But to see that regional imbalance is not a *cause* of the shift of the aggregate *u/v* curve, we have only to note that the proportional increase in unemployment at given vacancies is on average higher *within* each region than it is for the national aggregate.[21]

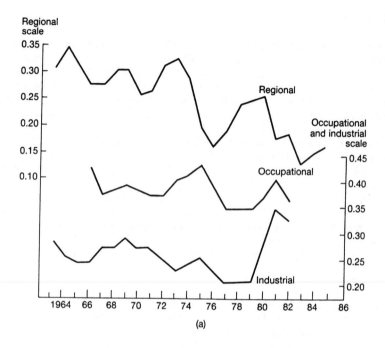

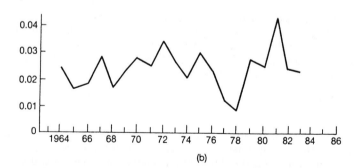

Figure 4.14 (a) Mismatch indices, 1964–85. (b) Index of change in the industrial composition of employment, 1964–83

Turning to other dimensions of mismatch, we find in Figure 4.14 no obvious trend in occupational mismatch (similarly calculated). As regards industrial mismatch, however, this was high in 1981 and 1982. This measure depends on classifying the unemployed by the industry of their last job, and unfortunately this analysis of the unemployed has now been discontinued, so we cannot tell how mismatch has been progressing recently in that dimension.

But it is important to form some view. Presumably, mismatch is increased by larger changes in the industrial structure of employment. Industrial structure did change quite sharply in 1981 and 1982, but this turbulence has now declined. To indicate this we show, in Figure 4.14, one half of the sum of the absolute changes in employment shares in each of 24 sectors.[22] There has been no major upward trend in this measure of turbulence since the early 1970s. In the econometric work reported earlier we used a simplified version of this index – namely, the absolute change in the share of unemployment falling within the 'production industries'. This suggested that since the 1960s increases in mismatch have raised wage pressure by 1 percentage point, implying a rise in unemployment of a little over 1 point.[23]

Our general conclusion is that increases in mismatch are not an important reason for the outward shift of the u/v curve. We also doubt whether employment protection is that important. So what could account for that part of the outward shift not explained by long-term unemployment?

Benefits

The obvious explanation is some aspect of the benefit system. Let us examine first the level of benefits. If, when productivity rises, benefits rise as much as wages, we should probably expect unemployment to remain unchanged. But if the replacement ratio (of benefits to net income in work) changed, we should expect unemployment to change. But the replacement ratio has changed little since the mid-1960s, though it has fluctuated considerably, rising by about 30 per cent between the late 1950s and the late 1960s.[24] So the replacement ratio cannot explain much of the increase in unemployment since 1970.

A more important factor may be the administration of benefits, and the application of the work test. There is good evidence that this was applied less strictly from the later 1960s onwards, even before the economic troubles of the 1970s (Layard, 1986). Then during the 1970s the job centres became physically separated from the benefit offices, making it even more difficult to ensure that claimants were encouraged to seek work. Since 1982 claimants have not even been required to register at job centres. Casual impression also suggests that there have been profound changes in social attitudes to living on the dole – the most obvious of these being the attitudes of students. Thus, by a process of elimination, and on grounds of inherent plausibility, there is good reason to suppose that an important reason for the shift of the u/v curve has been changes in the intensity with which the unemployed seek work at given vacancies.

Jackman and Williams (1985) have used individual cross-section data to study the intensity of job search, as measured by the number of job applications; for men who became unemployed in autumn 1978 and were still unemployed four months later, the median number of applications was one per month. (The figure in the United States seems to be four times as high.) Application rates are lower for those made redundant than for those who quit. Since the unemployed now include a lower than usual proportion who quit, this might help to explain the outward shift of the u/v curve.

Jackman and Williams also find that application rates are affected by benefits. The effect of benefits on application rates is directly in line with the findings of Narendranathan, Nickell and Stern (1985), who estimate the effect of benefits on job-finding using the same sample. The respective elasticities with respect to benefits were -0.25 and -0.40.[25] These elasticities are not high. They reflect the amount by which benefits displace the wage line in Figure 4.2 to the left. The total effect on unemployment should be slightly less than this. However, when we include the replacement ratio in our time-series wage equation, we estimate the total elasticity of unemployment with respect to benefits to be around 0.7 at the sample mean. Even this is not high. It implies that the 30 per cent rise in the replacement ratio between the late 1950s and the late 1960s increased unemployment by only about 20 per cent – or half a percentage point.

Finally, while we are considering the role of benefits, we must refer to a more indirect mechanism through which they may exert their influence. If benefits are available without time limit and without an effective work test, it is not surprising that, when employment is reduced by a major adverse shock, long-term unemployment develops with all the bad implications we have already discussed. A sensible solution seems to be the one advocated by Beveridge, that, after some time limit, public support for those without regular jobs should be provided through payment for work done (or training received) on a public programme.

Unions

We come now to a radically different way of viewing the labour market, in which unions play a crucial role. As we have already said, we do not believe that specifically union-oriented analysis throws much light on the rise in unemployment since 1979, since it cannot also explain the shift in the u/v curve (which is evidently closely related to the rise in unemployment).[26] However, the unions are an important feature of the scene, and we must attempt to clarify their impact.

We can begin with union membership. Almost half of all employees in employment are members (roughly 60 per cent of manual workers and

40 per cent of white-collar). The rates vary widely between sectors, as the following figures for 1979 show (Bain, 1983, p. 11):

Manufacturing	(%)
Manual	80
White collar	44
All	70
Construction	37
Private services	17
Public sector	82

About one-fifth of all workers are in closed shops, meaning that to hold the job they have to join the union.

But more important are the proportion of workers whose wages are determined by collective bargaining, whether or not they themselves are union members. Of full-time workers in 1978, the proportions 'covered' by collective agreements were 71 per cent of men and 68 per cent of women (New Earnings Survey for 1978). Most of the collective bargaining that matters is now with single employers, and the majority of that is at the plant level. Thus, if we confine ourselves to private sector employees, and ask what is the most important level of pay bargaining affecting their wages, the answers from the 1980 Workplace Industrial Relations Survey were as follows (Bain, 1983, p. 144):

Single-employer bargains	(%)
Plant level	30
Firm level	18
Multi-employer arrangements	
National or regional bargains	21
Wages councils	5
management decisions	26

For non-manual workers, management decision is more common, and national or regional bargains less common. Likewise, for smaller establishments, managerial decision is more common and firm-level bargaining less so. The general conclusion is that, although 80 per cent of the unionists are now in the largest 22 unions, the pattern of bargaining is highly decentralized.

What are its effects? First, unions appear to raise the wages of manual male trade unionists by about 11 per cent above those of other similar workers. This estimate comes from Stewart (1983) and is based on individual data from the National Training Survey. According to Stewart (1985), trade unions have affected wages mainly where there is a closed shop, especially where a pre-entry closed shop (now outlawed) existed.

To get some feeling for how the union mark-up has changed over time, we have to use a different procedure, based on a cross-section of industries rather

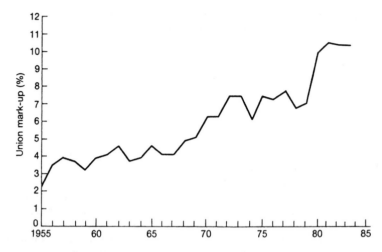

Figure 4.15   Estimated mark-up of union over non-union wages, 1955–85

than individuals (Layard, Metcalf and Nickell, 1978). The results of this, updated and scaled for consistency with Stewart, are shown in Figure 4.15. This shows that the mark-up has tended to rise over time. During the 1970s the rise was accompanied by a rise in trade union membership and, at least up to 1973, can be taken as associated with autonomous wage-push (the end of deference and all that). Since 1980 union membership has fallen somewhat, even among employees. One might therefore be inclined to explain the high mark-up in the 1980s by the disinflation of 1981–3, since deflation typically causes a rise in the union mark-up (Lewis, 1963). On the other hand, Batstone (1984) reports that shop steward organization and activity has not declined significantly since 1980, and today's high mark-up may therefore in part reflect continued militancy.

If this is the effect of unions on wages, What is their effect on employment?[27] The effect is indirect. For unions do not normally bargain over the level of employment in their enterprises (Oswald and Turnbull, 1985; Oswald, 1984). Bargaining does take place when redundancies are proposed, but experience of the last five years shows that unions' ability to affect the scale of redundancy is limited. (They do of course frequently ensure that there is maximum use of voluntary redundancy, and that compulsory redundancy follows the principle of 'last in–first out'.) Bargaining also takes place over manning levels, but this affects the ratio of employment to capital rather than the total level of employment. (Investment is not generally bargained over.) So bargains basically concern wages, and then employers determine employment subject to the wages that have been determined.

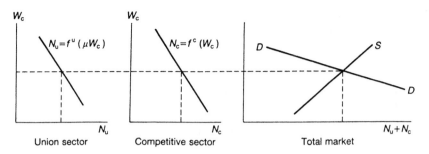

Figure 4.16 A market-clearing model of the labour market

The outcome is unlikely to clear the market in the union sector. But what about the non-union sector? Will not this be market-clearing? Suppose it is. Then all unemployment will be voluntary. Jobs are always available in the non-union sector, and workers choose not to take them, either because they want a holiday, permanent or temporary (Minford, 1985), or because it is more efficient to search for a union job while unemployed than while working in the non-union sector (Hall, 1975).[28]

This model may be depicted as in Figure 4.16 (ignoring issues to do with search). A few points should be noted. First, the supply curve is rising as a function of the real wage in the competitive sector, given the level of real benefit. It is essential to recognize the diversity of human nature in this way, and misleading to say that wages in the competitive sector are determined at the level of benefit (plus or minus a fixed mark-up) – as though all workers were equally hard-working. According to our earlier estimate from Narendranathan *et al.* (1985), the elasticity of this supply curve is in fact only 0.1 (when unemployment is 10 per cent). The next point to note is that the demand for union labour depends on μW_c where μ is 1 plus the mark-up of the union over the non-union wage. Clearly, if μ rises, the aggregate labour demand curve *DD* moves to the left; competitive wages fall, and employment falls because fewer people are willing to work. This, in essence, is Minford's account of how unions destroy employment.

There is, however, one reason that makes it impossible to accept the model as a satisfactory stylization of the system. All the evidence suggests that even unskilled markets may fail to clear, and, even more important, that the degree to which they do clear varies sharply from period to period. This evidence comes from the answers of Confederation of British Industry employers to the question 'Is your output likely to be limited in the next four months by shortages of (a) skilled labour, (b) other labour?' The answers are graphed in Figure 4.17. They show how unhelpful is the assumption of continuous market-

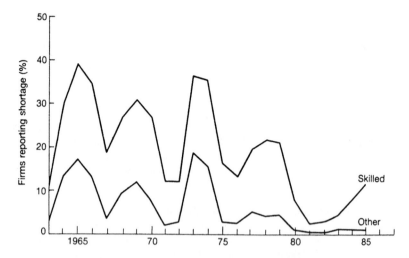

Figure 4.17   Shortage of skilled and other labour, 1963–85

clearing. They also show that the less skilled occupations (which in Confederation of British Industry firms tend to be less unionized) have a particular excess supply of labour.[29]

If the market-clearing framework helps little, how can one conceive of the effect of union power upon employment? We adopt a simple synthetic approach. In some cases wages are set by firms, and *their* efficiency wages may not be market-clearing. In other cases unions play a role in bargaining, and again their pushfulness will raise the degree of wage pressure. The final outcome (e.g. in Figure 4.7) is one where at prevailing wages more people are wanting work than there is work available. Most of them eventually get into work through the process of matching the unemployed to vacancies. Benefits slow down the speed of this matching and thus create wage pressure and reduce employment. Union power also creates wage pressure and reduces employment. In our estimates, the increase in the trade union mark-up since the 1960s has raised wage pressure by 3–4 percentage points and unemployment by 2–3 points.

Incomes policy

A standard way to reduce wage pressure is through incomes policy. A glance at Figure 4.5 shows the powerful effect of the 1975–7 incomes policy on the rate of wage inflation. (In 1975–6 the £6 a week limit equalled 10 per cent of average pay, and in 1976–7 the limit was 5 per cent.) Wadhwani (1985) has traced these dynamic effects in a quarterly model. Our annual model has been less successful at picking them up.

Of course, after 1977 the policy began to break down,[30] making some rise in unemployment after 1979 quite likely. A major problem arose from the inability of unions to control their shop stewards. This made the TUC unwilling to endorse the policy formally after the first two years (even though it did not oppose it). Bruno and Sachs (1985) have suggested that countries responded best to the oil shock of 1973 if they had rather centralized wage bargaining, making possible 'corporatist' solutions (as in Austria and Sweden). In more recent work with Bean (Bean *et al.*, 1986), we have further explored this and shown that, among 17 OECD countries, the *more* centralized countries have 'target' real consumption wages that respond *more* strongly to unemployment and to falls in the 'feasible' real consumption wage. In the scale of corporativeness Britain ranks twelfth – near the bottom. This means that it is peculiarly vulnerable to supply shocks.

Taxes and import prices

A supply shock is anything that reduces the feasible real consumption wage at given employment. If we write w^* as the log of the wage (so that $w = w^* + t_1$ where t_1 is employers' labour taxes), then the log real consumption wage is

$$w^* - t_2 - (\bar{p} + t_3) + \text{constant}$$

where t_2 is the personal tax rate, t_3 is the indirect tax rate and, $\bar{p}$ is the log final output price. The relation of the latter to the price of value added (p) is given by

$$\bar{p} = p + v(p_m - p)$$

where p_m is the log price of imports and v the share of imports in GDP. Thus the log real consumption wage is

$$w - p - t_1 - t_2 - t_3 - v(p_m - p) + \text{constant}$$

If $w - p$ remains constant, then the real consumption wage falls whenever there is a rise in taxes or in relative import prices. Thus, if taxes or relative import prices rise, and workers try to maintain their real consumption wage, they will push up $w - p$ and unemployment will have to rise to restore equilibrium. It is only if rises in taxes or relative import prices are voluntarily absorbed by workers that they do not generate wage pressure.

We estimate that all taxes except t_1 are voluntarily absorbed in the long run, but that employers' labour taxes and rises in relative import prices do increase unemployment. Since the 1960s, we tentatively estimate that labour taxes raised wage pressure by $1\frac{1}{2}$ points, and unemployment by between 1 and 2 points. The rise in relative import prices in the early 1970s raised wage pressure by $3\frac{1}{2}$ points and unemployment by 2 points, but developments in the 1980s have been more favourable, and we await their further course with bated breath.

It has often been suggested that the falls in productivity growth in the 1970s caused problems because they were resisted in wage demands. But we found no evidence that falls in productivity growth generated wage pressure.

Conclusion

Thus, to understand unemployment we have to understand the wage pressure generated at a given level of unemployment. This is now very high owing to the high proportion of long-term unemployed. Looking back over the last 15 years, wage pressure has increased partly because of union militancy, partly because of taxes, and partly because of easier social security. Mismatch has contributed little to the increase in unemployment. Even so, it is a serious problem, and we would be much better off if we had a better match between the structure of labour demand and supply. We turn now to this subject.

4   RELATIVE WAGE RIGIDITY AND THE STRUCTURE OF EMPLOYMENT

In Section 3 we focused on the aggregate labour market, analyzing its problems in terms of the inflexibility of the general level of real wages. In this section we look at the flexibility or otherwise of the relative wages of different groups, and ask how far this accounts for mismatch or other problems.

There are at least five dimensions of matching that are important: industry, region, skill, age, and sex.

Industry

We shall begin with industrial structure; for, even though many workers are not closely attached to industries, it is changes in industrial structure that primarily effect the fortunes of the different regions. The basic change in industrial structure has been the huge decline in manufacturing employment (Figure 4.18). This has certainly led to a migration of workers out of manufacturing, but to little change in relative wages.

These processes have been studied in detail by Pissarides (1978) and Pissarides and McMaster (1984a). Movement of workers between industries was found to respond to sector-specific vacancies and to relative wages, with both playing a roughly equal role in the redeployment of labour. But the role of

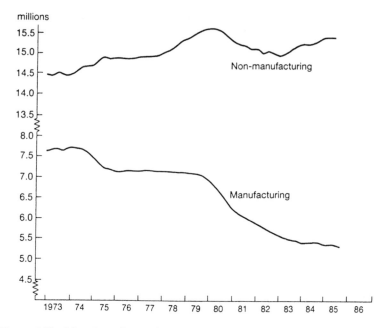

Figure 4.18 Manufacturing and non-manufacturing employees in employment, 1973–86

wages is not particularly functional, since wages do not respond to sector-specific vacancies as much as to aggregate vacancies in the economy as a whole.[31]

Region

Turning to the more serious problem of regional imbalance, workers do tend to leave the high-unemployment regions (in net terms). But the movement is much less than it would be if we had a more flexible housing market (see for example Hughes and McCormick, 1981). Moreover, the wage structure plays a small role in the adjustment process. It is remarkable how similar wages are in the different regions despite the huge differences in unemployment. This reflects the fact that relative wages react very weakly to unemployment differences (Pissarides and McMaster, 1984b). In the upshot, if a region starts with 1 point of unemployment above the national average, it will experience 12 man-years of unemployment before all excess unemployment has been eliminated. Thus, to evaluate regional policy, one could compute the present value of a policy to create a lower productivity job in the region or permit the outmigration to occur towards higher-productivity regions.

Skill

One of the most basic facts about unemployment is that it is concentrated on manual workers, and nearly half of it on semi- and unskilled manual workers. In 1983 male unemployment rates were

	(%)
Non-manual	5
Skilled manual	12
Semi- and unskilled manual	23

Why is this?

There is no doubt that relative wages affect the relative demand for labour at different skill levels. Nissim (1984), working on certain engineering industries, estimated the Allen elasticity of substitution between skilled and semi-skilled workers at around $2\frac{1}{2}$ (s.e. $= 0.3$). This is crudely illustrated in Figure 4.19 (crudely because the Allen elasticity is not the same as a 'direct' elasticity).

Given the effect of wages on demand, low-wage differentials seem an obvious explanation of the unemployment of the less-skilled. Such differentials might be due to union preferences for equality,[32] or to employers' concepts of

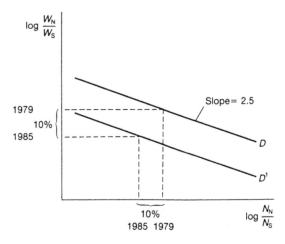

Figure 4.19   The relative demand for non-skilled workers, 1979 and 1985

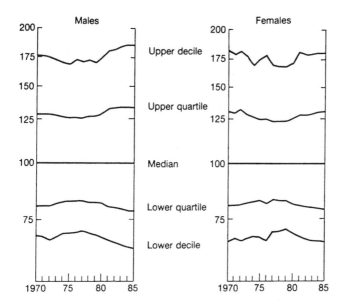

Figure 4.20 Gross hourly earnings as a percentage of median (log scale), 1970–85

efficiency wages – or even of fair wages. Wages councils do not appear to be a major explanation, since only about $1\frac{1}{2}$ million workers are covered by them alone and not also by collective bargaining.

One cannot estimate how flexible skill differentials are with respect to relative unemployment rates, since there is no adequate time-series of unemployment rates by skill. However, the evidence of the Family Expenditure Survey suggests that unemployment rates for the less skilled have risen roughly in proportion to unemployment rates for the skilled (Micklewright, 1983; see also General Household Survey). In other words, the proportional fall in employment has been twice as great for the less-skilled as for the skilled manual workers. At the same time, differentials have widened for men to an extraordinary degree (see Figure 4.20). Thus relative unskilled wages (say at the bottom decile) have fallen since 1979 by roughly 10 per cent relative to the mean. This is illustrated in Figure 4.19.

If both relative employment and relative wages have fallen, relative demand must have fallen substantially. With an elasticity of substitution of 2.5, relative demand must have fallen by around a third. This is a huge change. It must reflect partly increasing mechanization and partly the reduction of relative over-manning. But it brings into sharp focus the problems now facing the less skilled.

In such a situation there are two possible solutions. One is to improve the relative employment of the less skilled by subsidies to employers of less skilled labour (Layard, 1985). This can reduce the NAIRU by matching demand more closely to supply. The other is to train the less skilled and thus reduce the NAIRU by matching supply more closely to demand. In any normal optimization exercise, a bit of both would be indicated.

This brings us to the subject of training. If unemployment is due partly to rigid relative wages, the social returns to training are huge and greatly exceed the private returns (Johnson and Layard, 1986). For suppose that at the NAIRU skilled labour was fully employed and unskilled was not. The social return to training an unskilled person to be skilled would be the marginal product of skilled labour (rather more if skilled labour and less-skilled are complementary so that more skilled labour raises the demand for the less-skilled). But what are the private returns to training – to the firm and the worker combined? They are the skilled wage minus the unskilled wage (after adjusting both for the probability of employment). When there is involuntary unemployment of the less skilled, there is thus a huge externality in the returns to training.

This provides a strong argument for state subsidization. Other arguments stem from imperfect capital markets (higher cost of capital for workers than firms), biased information, and so on. For these reasons, the Industrial Training Act 1964 set up a levy-grant system whereby firms paid a small percentage of payroll into a fund but were rebated if they spent an equivalent amount on training. As time went by, the system lost its marginal effect as the percentage of payroll was so low relative to the amount that firms were paying anyway. Yet despite this, firms were paying remarkably little. In consequence, the general view is that British workmen are less well trained than those in other European countries (Prais, 1981). The government now organizes a two-year Youth Training Scheme which is open to all children who leave school at 16. But the second year of this has been introduced only this year, and it remains to be seen how effective it will be. Under present arrangements it will still be perfectly possible (which it is not in Germany) for someone to go straight into employment at 16 and to receive no training at all.[33] And even if the Youth Training Scheme does well, there will remain major shortcomings at the level of technician training and school education.[34]

Age

There are two dimensions of supply which the individual is powerless to affect: age and sex. Over time, youth unemployment has risen hugely relative to adult unemployment. This is due partly to relative wages, partly to relative population movements, and partly to general economic conditions. For the period 1959–85, the following regression explained relative male youth unemployment quite well:[35]

$$\log\frac{u_Y}{u_A} = 2.31 + 3.4\log\frac{W_Y}{W_A} + 0.42\log\frac{POP_Y}{POP_A} - 0.20\log v$$
$$(7.0) \qquad (0.9) \qquad (2.1)$$

$$se = 0.14, \ DW = 1.37 \ (t\text{-statistics in brackets})$$

where W_Y/W_A is relative hourly earnings, POP_Y/POP_A is 15–19-year-olds relative to 15–60-year-olds, and v is the vacancy rate.

Up to the mid-1970s, relative wages were a potent force in explaining the rise. No one fully understands why relative wages rose so much, but the best explanation seems to be the desire of collective bargainers to pay adult rates at ever earlier ages (Layard, 1982). Since the late 1970s relative youth wages have if anything fallen, presumably in response to relative unemployment. But at the same time the economic situation has worsened and relative population movements have been adverse to youth (up to now, but with an improvement hereafter). All in all, however, the performance of the British labour market in providing jobs for young people in recent years has been nothing but dismal.

Sex

When we come to sex differences in the workforce, we have to start with the huge increase in female participation. This is one of the most profound social changes of our time. After a small hiccough in the early 1980s, it seems to be proceeding unabated. The increase is entirely on the part of currently married women, the participation rate of other women having been more or less constant for the last 30 years. Most of the increase has been of part-time work.

What has caused the rush of women to the labour market? The natural first step is to look at wage levels. Women's hourly wages were very stable relative to men's up to the early 1970s (at nearly 65 per cent). The Equal Pay Act outlawed separate pay scales for men and women, and as a result women's earnings rose to around 75 per cent of men's, where they have stayed ever since. How much of this difference reflects continuing discrimination is a difficult issue. Zabalza and Arrufat (1983) argue that at least two-thirds of it reflects differences in work experience and other measurable variables; Stewart and Greenhalgh (1984) seem to indicate something more like a half.

But how far do wage movements explain the rise in women's labour supply? Up to the mid-1970s the real wages of men and women rose at roughly the same rate. Rises in men's wages tend to decrease women's labour supply (through negative income and substitution effects); rises in women's wages tend to increase it (through a large positive substitution effect, offset by a small income effect). The key issue is the relative size of these two effects. As Joshi *et al.* (1985, p. S149) show, elasticities estimated from cross-section data suggest that general wage changes cannot explain by any means all of the increase in women's participation in the early 1970s. They are however quite successful at explaining the rise in women's participation *since* the early 1970s. It is, however, remarkable that these changes have persisted so strongly in the face of the adverse economic situation.

This brings us to the question of women's employment. One would suppose on the demand side that the externally imposed rise in relative wages would have reduced relative employment. The reverse has happened. Even if we confine ourselves to the private sector, the ratio of female person-hours to male has risen since the early 1970s (see Joshi *et al.*, 1985).

Two factors must account for this. The first is the shift in labour demand towards more female-intensive industries (especially services). This indeed accounts for a part of the increase. But a fixed weight demand index[36] accounts for only half of the rise in relative female employment since 1970.

What can account for the rest? Relative wage movements would have suggested a fall. Against this, the Sex Discrimination Act which also became operative in 1976 outlawed discrimination in employment on grounds of sex. This might have been interpreted to mean that employers should not reduce relative employment when relative wages were raised by the Equal Pay Act. But one would not have expected a rise in relative employment.

One explanation may be employment protection. This might lead firms to prefer part-time workers; but in fact, only those working less than 16 hours a week are exempt and two-thirds of part-time women work more than this. (Until 1975, all workers under 21 hours were exempt – or about two-thirds of part-time women workers.)

Given the buoyant employment position of women, one naturally asks whether there might not have been a growing mismatch in terms of sex between the pattern of jobs on offer and the pattern of labour supplied. To answer this, we first need evidence on the relative unemployment rates of men and women. Using survey-based estimates, we find that in the early 1970s female unemployment was about 50 per cent higher than male, becoming similar in the late 1970s and about 20 per cent lower than male in the 1980s (see Table 4.3). This suggests that mismatch may have been lower in the late 1970s. However, to obtain a more exact measure, we need to estimate the share of vacancies that was 'female-oriented'. To do this, we take the vacancies in each two-digit industry and divide them between men and women in proportion to employment in that industry. We then construct the index $U_f/U - V_f/V$ and find some evidence that this was positive in the 1970s and negative in the 1980s (see Table 4.3). However, the mismatch now in favour of women is not much greater than the mismatch in favour of men earlier.

Conclusion

In sum, the behaviour of relative wages does not do much to even out the relative imbalances in the labour market generated by shocks to demand (as

Table 4.3 Mismatch in job opportunities by sex

| | Unemployment rates | | | Index |
Year	Male (1)	Female (2)	Female–male (3)	$\frac{U_f}{U} - \frac{V_f}{V}$ (4)
1971	3.4	5.1	1.7	−1.0
1972	4.6	7.9	3.3	6.2
1973	3.4	5.5	2.1	9.7
1974	4.0	4.9	0.9	2.7
1975	4.9	5.0	0.1	−3.4
1976	6.5	8.5	2.0	6.9
1977	6.4	8.5	2.1	8.0
1978	6.8	8.6	1.8	−6.4
1979	6.9	7.4	0.5	1.7
1980	6.6	6.9	0.3	−1.4
1981	10.8	10.1	−0.7	−6.1
1982	12.7	10.0	−2.7	−7.4
1983	12.2	9.4	−2.8	−9.8
1984	12.8	11.4	−1.4	−6.4

between industries, regions, or skills) or to supply (as with changes in the number of young people). There is however *some* flexibility in relative wages by skill, but this is not enough to prevent a large relative oversupply of the less-skilled.

5 PRODUCTIVITY

Having considered the extent to which potential labour resources are utilized, we now turn to the productivity of those resources that are actually used. In Figure 4.21 we see the path of output per head in both the whole economy and the manufacturing sector. The main features of both these series are summarized in Table 4.4. Until 1973 there is a period of relatively rapid growth, but this is followed by a dramatic slowdown. During the recession from 1979–81 this slowdown is even more marked, but from 1981 onwards there is a sharp improvement. These features are common to both series, but we shall now focus on manufacturing, since it is only here that we have enough information to enable us to analyze these changes.

Table 4.4   Productivity growth rates (% per year)

	1960–73	1973–9	1979–80	1980–4
Output per head				
Whole economy	2.5	0.9	–2.6	2.8
Manufacturing	3.5	0.9	–3.9	5.4
Output per person-hour				
Manufacturing	3.9	1.1	–1.2	5.0

The first point to note is that these shifts in productivity growth are not due to fluctuations in measured hours worked. As we can see from the third row of Table 4.4, the movements in the growth rate of output per person-hour are much the same, so we must clearly look elsewhere for an explanation. Let us first focus on the slowdown after the first oil shock. Much has been written about this phenomenon, which was common to almost all OECD countries (see, for example, Matthews, 1982; Lindbeck, 1983; Giersch and Wolter, 1983; Denison, 1983). As we can see from Figure 4.22, there was a significant reduction in the growth of the recorded gross capital stock, both for the whole economy and in manufacturing. This is clearly a contributing factor, but equally clearly it is not the whole story,[37] since the growth rate of total factor productivity (TFP) also falls sharply after 1973. In Table 4.5 we present the capital stock and TFP growth rates for manufacturing, which have a similar structure aside from 1979–80.[38] The latter series is taken from Mendis and Muelbauer (1984), which is the most careful analysis of British manufacturing productivity in the postwar period currently available. This study is based on an estimated production function which not only takes account of factor utilization but also corrects for various biases in the recorded output measure,[39] although these do not include quality changes. So the changes in total factor productivity growth can be put down to some combinations of

Table 4.5   Growth rates of capital stock and total factor productivity in UK: manufacturing (percentages)

	1960–73	1973–9	1979–80	1980–3
Capital stock	4.0	2.3	2.0	1.0
Total factor productivity	2.5	0.8	–2.3	2.5

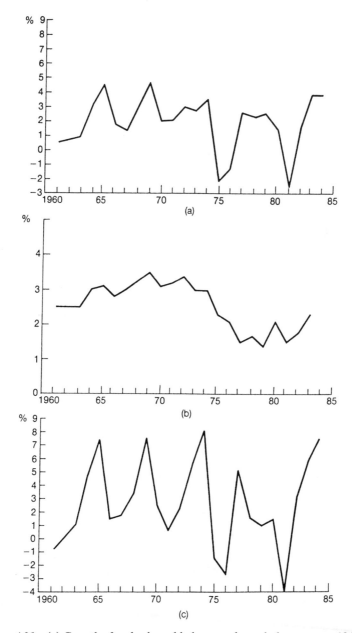

Figure 4.21 (a) Growth of real value added per worker: whole economy, 1961–84. (b) Growth of total factor productivity: whole economy, 1961–83. (c) Growth of real value added per worker: manufacturing, 1961–84
Note: (b) is centred 5-year average.

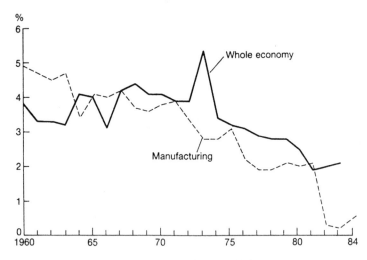

Figure 4.22   Growth rates of gross capital stock, 1960–84

'technical progress' (e.g. changes in technology or working practices), trending measurement error in the quality or quantity of output, or the inputs and changes in holiday time. The latter can be disposed of quite rapidly; for, although there has been a considerable increase in paid holidays over the relevant period, this would account for a growth slowdown of only 0.1 percentage points, according to Mendis and Muellbauer.

In their view, the key to the slow-down in measured TFP lies in the measurement of the growth capital stock. Two points are worth noting here. The strong correlation between capital stock growth and TFP growth which is clear from Table 4.5 (see also Layard and Nickell, 1986a, Figure 5) suggests that technical progress is embodied in new capital goods, and therefore that the slow-down in capital accumulation has a larger effect than might appear from a standard production function estimate.[40] The second and perhaps more important point is that the measured gross capital stock is based on the assumption of fixed service lives for different types of capital assets. In fact, however, scrapping of capital goods is hardly likely to be independent of economic circumstances. In particular, when demand is severely depressed, or when fuel and raw materials prices rise strongly in relative terms (as in 1973), then scrapping is likely to accelerate. In consequence, the measured capital stock series would overestimate the true series. There is some evidence in favour of this view. For example, Kilpatrick and Naisbitt (1986) present some

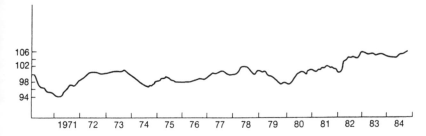

Figure 4.23 Percentage utilization of labour (PUL), 1970–84

evidence to the effect that energy-intensive industries experienced a greater than average slow-down in measured TFP after 1973. More direct evidence is provided by Wadhwani and Wall (1986), who have corrected the CSO manufacturing capital stock series using firm data on a large sample of quoted companies in the manufacturing sector. Over the period of 1972–4 they calculate that the CSO underestimated capital stock growth by 1.63 per cent over the two years and during 1974–80 overestimated capital stock growth by a cumulated 2.86 per cent. So the slow-down in capital stock growth after the first oil shock is indeed significantly more marked than would be implied by the published data.

Turning now to the more recent past, there was a dramatic fall in the rate of growth of output per person-hour in 1979–80, but since 1981 it has been rising rapidly, as Table 4.4 indicates. The initial decline is partly a cyclical phenomenon, but it does correspond to a similar decline in measured TFP, which is corrected for factor utilization. The key factor here is probably the extensive unrecorded scrapping of capital equipment which took place during this period. Thus, Wadhwani and Wall (1986) estimate that between 1979 and 1982 the manufacturing capital stock fell by 1.76 per cent, whereas the published data show a rise of 2.14 per cent over the same period.

Since 1981, output per person-hour has been rising at 5 per cent per annum. TFP growth appears to be back at its pre-1973 level of 2.5 per cent per annum according to Mendis and Muellbauer, and this is clearly part of the story. However, given that the capital stock growth remains below its pre-1973 level, there must be other factors involved, particularly with regard to the utilization of labour. Information on this is provided by the Percentage Utilization of Labour (PUL) series collected by Smith-Gavine and Bennett (1985). This series is based on a representative panel of some 131,500 operatives in manufacturing and directly measures their hourly work effort using standard work-study techniques. The series is pictured in Figure 4.23 and indicates that there has been a considerable rise in work effort over the period from the end of 1980. Indeed, hourly work effort is now around 5 per cent higher than its average in the period 1973–9 and around 7 per cent higher than its trough in the winter of 1980–1. The other relevant factor here is the fact that the capital equipment that was scrapped at the beginning of the 1980s would have been the least efficient, and this would have produced a significant one-off boost to productivity growth.

Conclusion

In summary, therefore, the recent high level of productivity growth reflects three factors: first, the reversion of total factor productivity growth to its pre-1973 level; second, a considerable growth of hourly work effort; and third, an initial boost owing to the extensive scraping of outdated equipment. The sustainability of these factors is problematic. The continuing low growth of the measured capital stock is a danger for the first of them, and the recent flattening of the work effort (PUL) series indicates problems for the second. The third cannot be sustained by definition.

Notes

1. Non-employed job-seekers registered at employment exchanges.
2. OECD, *Employment Outlook* (September 1985). The figures are standardized OECD figures for unemployed as proportion of labour force (including self-employed), and read UK 13.1, France 7.7, Germany 7.6, Italy 6.6, and USA 7.2. They relate to 1984.
3. Any tendency to use elements of historic capital cost in the price setting process will, of course, tend to exacerbate the squeeze on profit.
4. We have found that total factor productivity has no effect in our equations. This is quite explainable (Layard and Nickell, 1986a).
5. It is worth pointing out that the model (4.1), (4.2) is not (econometrically) identified as it stands, although it could be in dynamic form. However, one would not estimate it in this form but would clearly estimate the structural price equation containing the level of output market activity, along with some form of dynamic labour demand function (see Layard and Nickell, 1986a). Identification would then be less problematic.
6. One of the elements of wage pressure – real import prices – is not strictly exogenous since it depends on the real exchange rate. So the NAIRU described here is conditional on this variable. In the very long run we might expect the real exchange rate to adjust to maintain trade balance, and a very long-run NAIRU would allow for this. In practice, this would not make a very huge difference (Layard and Nickell, 1986a).
7. The price equation (4.1′) is a re-estimated version of that in Layard and Nickell (1986a), and is derived by eliminating the demand variable σ from the employment equation of the form in their Table 4 and the first price equation in their Table 5. Small terms in $\Delta^3 u$, Δl, and Δk are omitted. All the relevant

details may be found in Nickell (1987). (4.1′) corresponds to (24) in that paper. The wage equation is equation (4.7) below, with (4.7′) being used to substitute for R. Small terms in $\Delta^3 u$ and its lags have been omitted. (4.1′) and (4.7′) were estimated jointly. The data are annual (1956–83) aggregates for Britain.

8. It is worth noting that, in order to generate stable inflation in the face of a reduction in wage pressure, real demand must rise. If the rise in demand is brought about, at least in part, by tax cuts, it is easy enough to achieve a zero fall in consumption wages. This point comes over clearly in the simulation in the Treasury Paper on Wages and Employment (1985).

9. For a formal treatment of the models of wage determination being discussed here see Johnson and Layard (1986) and Nickell and Andrews (1983).

10. A simple model that captures these points is as follows. Suppose each worker in the ith firm yields net output $e\{W_i/W(1-u)\}$ where $W(1-u)$ is his expected earnings outside. The firm will choose the wage so that

$$e'\left\{\frac{W_i}{W(1-u)}\right\}\frac{1}{W(1-u)}-1=0$$

with $e''<0$. The equilibrium wage is got by setting $W_i=W$

11. In an extreme situation they could actually lose their jobs and be replaced by unemployed workers – as in Rupert Murdoch's fortress at Wapping.

12. The kind of model implied here is captured by the notion that the ith union chooses W_i to maximize expected rents $N_i\{u(W_i)-u(W)(1-U)\}$ subject to a perceived demand curve $N_i=f(W_i,I_{i-1})$ where I_{i-1} is last year's inflow into unemployment from the firm. Taking the first-order condition and *then* setting $W_i=W$ and $I_{i-1}=I_{-1}$ gives a national wage equation $W=g(U,I_{-1})$

13. If so, there would still be a long-run natural rate of unemployment. For even if the wage equation was flat, the price equation has a slope. But the implied natural rate would be very sensitive to wage pressure (z).

14. Our wage equation confirms that the labour force (L) affects employment through its effect on wage behaviour. We find that the log of the unemployment rate $(1-N/L)$ is the best explanatory variable. If $\log N$ is entered in addition, it is insignificant. To see whether the labour force was generally significant in wage equations, David Grubb has estimated the following equations for 19 OECD countries on annual data 1952–82 (the coefficients and t-statistics are unweighted averages):

$$\dot{w}-\dot{w}_{-1}=1.7+0.69\,(\dot{p}-\dot{w})_{-1}-0.33\,(w-p)_{-1}-1.91\,l+2.00\,n$$
$$\quad\;\;(3.0)\qquad\qquad(1.5)\qquad\quad(1.6)\quad\;(2.3)$$

$$-0.17h+0.26T$$
$$(0.2)\quad\;\;(0.3)$$

where h is log hours per worker and T is time.

15. This is based on (3) of Table 1 in Nickell (1987). In estimating that equation (which is based on annual data), it is impossible to detect an effect of the $\Delta^2 p$ term. However, from the quarterly wage equation in Layard and Nickell (1986a), we know that such an effect exists (albeit rather a small one, compared with that in the price equation), and we have used the estimate from that equation to obtain the coefficient on an equivalent annualized variable. The coefficients in

the Nickell (1987) equation are consistently estimated despite the presence of an omitted variable $(p - p^e)$ since the latter is orthogonal to the instruments used in the estimation.

16. They found that the doubling in the proportion of long-term unemployed since 1979 would predict about a 20 per cent rise in the level of unemployment at given vacancies. We shall show below that in fact changes in duration explain rather more than this. There are two reasons why the proportions fall with duration. One is the way in which duration affects workers' morale and employer's perceptions (i.e. the duration-dependence of the chances of outflow for a given individual). The other is a selectivity effect – that the more motivated and desirable workers find jobs quicker, so that the proportion finding jobs is lower at long durations. To the extent that we are using the duration structure to explain the falling average outflow probability, we are assuming a constant level of true state-dependence and a constant distribution of characteristics among those becoming unemployed.

17. If the proportions p_t leaving unemployment after duration t fall by a common multiple (λ) at all durations, the overall proportions leaving unemployment fall by more than λ. This applies in the steady state, and follows from the shift in the duration structure towards long durations. It can be illustrated easily in the case where the proportion leaving is λp up to duration T and $\lambda p'$ ($< \lambda p$) thereafter. Suppose an inflow of unity. The stock of unemployed is then

$$\frac{1}{\lambda p}(1 - e^{-\lambda pT}) + \frac{e^{-\lambda pT}}{\lambda p'} = \frac{1}{\lambda}\left\{\frac{1}{p} + e^{-\lambda pT}\left(\frac{1}{p'} - \frac{1}{p}\right)\right\} \quad \left(\text{with } \frac{1}{p'} > \frac{1}{p}\right)$$

when λ falls, this rises by a multiple exceeding $1/\lambda$. It follows that the average proportion leaving has fallen more than in proportion to λ. Figure 4.13 shows how the fall in the average proportion leaving can be decomposed into (1) the direct effect of changes in the ps and (2) the effect of changes in the duration structure (largely owing in turn to changes in the ps). Comparing the beginning and end-year, we can write the change in the average proportion leaving as

$$p_1f_1 - p_0f_0 = p_1(f_1 - f_0) + f_0(p_1 - p_0)$$

where p is the vector of ps and f the vector of proportion (f_t) with duration t. Looking at the right-hand side, the fall in the dotted line measures $p_1(f_1 - f_0)$, which is approximately half the total change.

18. This requires U_i/V_i to be the same everywhere. Two alternatives are less relevant:
     (a) the ratio U_i/N_i, but this does not take into account that the unemployed get employed by finding vacancies;
     (b) the ratio of $(U_i + N_i)/V_i$, but this does not take into account the fact that almost half of all vacancies are filled by the unemployed. Thus the fraction of unemployed who are looking for work exceeds the fraction of the employed looking for work by roughly the ratio N_i/U_i. If one knew exactly what fraction of employed workers were looking (λ_i), a good index might be $(U_i + \lambda_i N_i)/V_i$

19. This is taken from Jackman and Roper (1987). For an alternative index see Nickell (1979).

20. The remarks are approximate and are based on the following line of thought. Suppose two regions, with region 1 the high-unemployment region: then, first,

$$mm = \frac{U_1}{U} - \frac{V_1}{V}$$

If U_1/U falls, mm falls unless there are offsetting falls in V_1/V, which is unlikely. Second,

$$SU = U_1 - \frac{V_1}{V}U$$

So

$$\frac{dSU}{dU} = \frac{dU_1}{dU} - \frac{V_1}{V}$$

assuming V_1/V unaltered. This is positive if

$$\frac{dU_1}{L_1} > \frac{dU}{L}\frac{V_1/L_1}{V/L}$$

Since $V_1/L_1 < V/L$ (since 1 is the high-unemployment region), $dU_1/dL_1 > dU/L$ is sufficient for $dSU/dU > 0$

21. If one wished to argue that regional imbalance had worsened, one would need to argue that the share of *involuntary* unemployment in the North had risen. If we assume that voluntary unemployment is the same in all regions, this would require a huge growth in voluntary unemployment. An example is given in the table, where the total columns are actual and the other columns are hypothetical. Alternatively, we could assume more voluntary unemployment in the North (and smaller growth in voluntary unemployment in each region). But this seems implausible.

	South-East			North		
	Voluntary	Involuntary	Total	Voluntary	Involuntary	Total
1979	1	2	3	1	6	7
1985	7	3	10	7	11	18

22. That is, $\frac{1}{2}\sum|\Delta e_i|$ where e_i is the employment share. This shows the extent to which unemployment is moving from one sector to another.

23. See Layard and Nickell (1986a, Table 11), which also provides the source for similar remarks below about other z variables.

24. For a discussion of the benefit system see Layard (1986). See also Atkinson and Micklewright (1985).

25. The elasticities with respect to incomes in work were 0.96 and 0.87, respectively. This implies that, as incomes rise at a given replacement ratio, job-finding increases and thus unemployment falls. In time-series this proportion seems implausible.

26. For a fuller discussion of the shift in the u/v curve see Pissarides (1986).

27. Note that there are other effects on output through effects on productivity. Average effects on output via strikes cannot be large since in an average year only 1/4 per cent of man-days are lost that way.

28. The holiday argument is as follows. A worker will choose to be unemployed if, in the week in question, $u^i(W_c, H) < u^i(B_i, 0)$. The search argument adds in to the right-hand side an extra term reflecting the present value of the expected gain in future utility from searching rather than accepting a job at W_c.

29. Even in 1978, the duration of vacancies was as follows: skilled manual 6.2 weeks, semi-skilled and personal service 2.6 weeks, unskilled 1.5 weeks (Jackman *et al.*, 1984). Vacancy rates were similar in all occupations.

30. The limits were 1977–8, 10 per cent; and 1978–9, 5 per cent.

31. Pissarides and McMaster (1984a). In 18 sectors real wages were regressed on log national vacancies and on log sector-specific vacancies, with six and five signs wrong respectively and the sum of the two effects always positive. But real wages were significantly affected by national vacancies in eight sectors and by sector-specific vacancies in three sectors only.

32. If wages are log normal, the mean exceeds the median and the median voters will gain from equalization (Ashenfelter and Layard 1983).

33. In January 1985, 28 per cent of the 16-year-olds were in the Youth Training Scheme and 13 per cent in employment.

34. School education is dealt with in the fuller version of this paper (Layard and Nickell, 1986b).

35. For a fuller discussion (up to 1979) see Layard (1982). See also Wells (1983) and Joshi *et al.* (1985).

36. The index is

$$I_t = \sum_i \left(\frac{F_i}{M_i}\right)_{70} \frac{M_{it}}{M_t}$$

where F is female person-hours, and M is male person-hours.

37. Indeed, Mendis and Muellbauer (1984) calculate that the direct effect of the slowdown in capital accumulation explains less than one-quarter of the decline in productivity growth.

38. There is considerable evidence that the official statistics for capital stock growth in 1979–80 are highly misleading in the sense of being subject to a strong upward bias. This is discussed later.

39. The biases corrected for include the following. (a) Gross output bias, which arises because the Central Statistical Office approximates changes in value added by using gross output changes with value added weights. So if raw materials become more expensive, value added tends to increase faster than

gross output because of substitution away from raw materials, inducing a downward bias in published data. (b) Domestic price index bias: about two-thirds of manufactured output is based on current price data deflated by wholesale price indices for *home* sales. So if the ratio of foreign to domestic wholesale prices rises, the measured price increase based on home sales is too low and thus the measured volume increase is too high. (c) List price bias: although the price indices used are supposed to measure transaction prices, they are, at least in part, based on list prices. A reduction in competitive pressure is likely to reduce discounts (on the list price), and so the measured price rise understates the true price increase leading to an overstatement of the volume increase. (d) Finally, there are price controls. These tend to be widely evaded by spurious quality improvements or relabelling, and thus official price indices tend to rise more slowly than true indices when price controls are in operation with the opposite effect on output. This bias, of course, moves into reverse when controls are removed, and Darby (1984) makes much of this argument in his analysis of the US productivity slowdown.

40. Attempts at estimating putty-clay production functions do not, however, provide any evidence either way on this issue (see Malcolmson and Prior, 1979; Mizon and Nickell, 1983).

References

Ashenfelter, O. and R. Layard (1983) 'Incomes Policy and Wage Differentials', *Economica*, 50, 127–45.

Atkinson, A.B. and J. Micklewright (1985) *Unemployment Benefits and Unemployment Duration*, Suntory-Toyota International Centre for Economics and Related Disciplines, LSE.

Bain, G.S. (ed.) (1983) *Industrial Relations in Britain* (Oxford: Basil Blackwell).

Batstone, E. (1984) *'Working Order'* (Oxford: Basil Blackwell).

Bean, C., R. Layard and S. Nickell (1986) 'The Rise in Unemployment: A Multi-Country Study', *Economica Special Supplement on Unemployment*, 53, S1–S23.

Bennett, A.J. and S.A.N. Smith-Gavine (1985) 'The Index of Percentage Utilisation of Labour: Bulletin to Co-operating Firms', no. 40 (Leicester: Leicester Polytechnic, School of Economics and Accounting).

Blanchard, O. and L.H. Summers (1986) 'Hysteresis and the European Unemployment Problem' (Massachusetts Institute of Technology, mimeo).

Bruno, M. and J. Sachs (1985) *Economics of Worldwide Stagflation* (Cambridge, MA: Harvard University Press).

Budd, A., R. Levine and P. Smith (1988) 'Unemployment, Vacancies and the Long-Term Unemployed', *Economic Journal*, 98: 1071–91.

Darby, M. (1984) 'The US Productivity Slowdown: A Case of Statistical Myopia', *American Economic Review*, 73, 301–22.

Denison, E.F. (1983) 'The Interruption of Productivity Growth in the United States', *Economic Journal*, 93, 56–77.

Giersch, H. and F. Wolter (1983) 'Towards an Explanation of the Productivity Slowdown: An Acceleration-Deceleration Hypothesis', *Economic Journal*, 93, 35–55.

Hall, R.E. (1975) 'The Rigidity of Wages and Persistence of Unemployment', *Brookings Papers on Economic Activity*, 2, 301–50.

Hughes, G. and B. McCormick (1981) 'Do Council Housing Policies Reduce Migration Between Regions?' *Economic Journal*, 91, 919–37.

Jackman, R., R. Layard, and C. Pissarides (1984) 'On Vacancies', Centre for Labour Economics, LSE, *Oxford Bulletin of Economics and Statistics Discussion Paper*, 165 (Revised), see chapter 5 in this volume.

Jackman, R. and S. Roper (1987) 'Structural Unemployment', special issue on Wage Determination and Labour Market Flexibility, *Oxford Bulletin of Economics and Statistics*, February 1987.

Jackman, R. and C. Williams (1985) 'Job Applications by Unemployed Men', Centre for Labour Economics, LSE, *Working Paper*, 792.

Johnson, G. and R. Layard (1986) 'The Natural Rate of Unemployment: Explanation and Policy', in O. Ashenfelter and R. Layard (eds), *Handbook of Labor Economics* (Amsterdam: North-Holland).

Joshi, H.E., R. Layard and S.J. Owen (1985) 'Why are More Women Working in Britain?' *Journal of Labor Economics*, 3(1), S147–S176, chapter 12 in R. Layard, *Education and Inequality* (London: Macmillan, 1999).

Kilpatrick, A. and B. Naisbitt (1986) 'Energy Intensity, Industrial Structure and the Productivity Slowdown' (National Economic Development Office, mimeo).

Layard, R. (1982) 'Youth Unemployment in Britain and the US Compared', in R. Freeman and D. Wise (eds), *The Youth Labor Market Problem* (Chicago: University of Chicago Press).

Layard, R. (1985) 'How to Reduce Unemployment by Changing National Insurance and Providing a Job-Guarantee', Centre for Labour Economics, LSE, *Discussion Paper*, 218.

Layard, R. (1986) *How to Beat Unemployment* (Oxford: Oxford University Press).

Layard, R., D. Metcalf and S. Nickell (1978) 'The Effect of Collective Bargaining on Relative and Absolute Wages', *British Journal of Industrial Relations*, 16, 287–302.

Layard, R. and S. Nickell (1986a) 'Unemployment in Britain', *Economica special supplement on unemployment*, 53.

Layard, R. (1986b) 'The Performance of the British Labour Market', Centre for Labour Economics, LSE, *Discussion Paper*, 249.

Lewis, H.G. (1963) *Unionism and Relative Wages in the US* (Chicago: University of Chicago Press).

Lindbeck, A. (1983) 'The Recent Slowdown of Productivity Growth', *Economic Journal*, 93, 14–34.

Lindbeck, A. and D. Snower (1984) 'Involuntary Unemployment as an Insider–Outsider dilemma', (Institute for International Economic Studies, University of Stockholm) *Seminar Paper*, 282.

Malcolmson, J. and M. Prior (1979) 'The Estimation of a Vintage Model of Production for UK Manufacturing', *Review of Economic Studies*, 46, 719–36.

Matthews, R.C.O. (ed.) (1982) *Slower Growth in the Western World* (London: Heinemann).

Mendis, L. and J. Muellbauer (1984) 'British Manufacturing Productivity 1955–1983: Measurement Problems, Oil Shocks, and Thatcher Effects' (Oxford, Nuffield College, mimeo).

Micklewright, J. (1983) 'Male Unemployment and the Family Expenditure Survey 1972–1980', *Oxford bulletin of Economics and Statistics*, 46(1), 31–53.

Minford, P. (1985) *Unemployment: Cause and Cure* (2nd edn) (Oxford: Basil Blackwell).

Mizon, G. and S. Nickell (1983) 'Vintage Production Models of UK Manufacturing Industry', *Scandinavian Journal of Economics*, 85, 295–310.

Narendranathan, W., S. Nickell and J. Stern (1985) 'Unemployment Benefits Revisited', *Economic Journal*, 95, 307–29.

Newell, A. (1984) 'Annual Indices of the Changes in the Structure of Employment by Industry and Region', Centre for Labour Economics, LSE, *Working Paper*, 617.

Nickell, S.J. (1979) 'Unemployment and the Structure of Labour Costs', *Journal of Monetary Economics*, Supplement: Carnegie–Rochester Public Policy Conference, 11.

Nickell, S.J. (1982) 'The Determinants of Equilibrium Unemployment in Britain', *Economic Journal*, 92, 555–75.

Nickell, S.J. (1987) 'Why is Wage Inflation in Britain so High?' *Oxford Bulletin of Economics and Statistics*, 49(1), 103–29.

Nickell, S.J. and M. Andrews (1983) 'Trade Unions, Real Wages, and Employment in Britain 1951–79', *Oxford Economic Papers*, 35, Supplement.

Nissim, J. (1984) 'The Price Responsiveness of the Demand for Labour by Skill: British Mechanical Engineering: 1963–78', *Economic Journal*, 94.

Oswald, A. (1984) 'Efficient Contracts are on the Labour Demand Curve: Theory and Facts' (Industrial Relations Section, Princeton University) *Working Paper*, 178 (July).

Oswald, A. and P. Turnbull (1985) 'Pay and Employment Determination in Britain: What are Labour Contracts Really Like?' *Oxford Review of Economic Policy*, 1, 80–97.

Pissarides, C. (1978) 'The Role of Relative Wages and Excess Demand in the Sectoral Flow of Labour', *Review of Economic Studies*, 45, 453–67.

Pissarides, C. (1986) 'Unemployment Flows in Britain: Facts, Theory, and Policy', *Economic Policy*, 1(3), 499–540.

Pissarides, C. and I. McMaster (1984a) 'Sector-specific and Economy-wide Influences on Industrial Wages in Britain', Centre for Labour Economics, LSE, *Working Paper* 571 (2nd revision).

Pissarides (1984b) 'Regional Migration, Wages, and Unemployment: Empirical Evidence and Implication for Policy', Centre for Labour Economics, LSE, *Discussion Paper*, 204.

Prais, S.J. (1981) 'Vocational Qualification of the Labour Force in Britain and Germany', *National Institute of Economic Review*, 98.

Smith-Gavine, S.A.N. and A.J. Bennett (1985) 'Index of Percentage Utilisation of Labour', *Bulletin to Co-operating Firms*, 49.

Stewart, M.B. (1983) 'Relative Earnings and Individual Union Membership in the UK', *Economica*, 50, 111–25.

Stewart, M.B. (1985) 'Collective Bargaining Arrangements, Closed Shop and Relative Pay' (University of Warwick, mimeo).

Stewart, M.B. and C.A. Greenhalgh (1984) 'Work History Patterns and the Occupational Attainment of Women', *Economic Journal*, 94, 493–519.

Wadhwani, S. (1985) 'Wage Inflation in the UK', *Economica*, 52, 195–208.

Wadhwani, S. and M. Wall (1986) 'The UK Capital Stock: New Estimates of Premature Scrapping', *Oxford Review of Economic Policy*, 2(3), 44–55.

Wells, W. (1983) 'The Relative Pay and Employment of Young People', Department of Employment, *Research Paper*, 42.

Zabalza, A. and J. Arrufat (1983) 'Wage Differentials Between Married Men and Women in Great Britain: The Depreciation Effect of Non-Participation', Centre for Labour Economics, LSE, *Discussion Paper*, 151.

5 On Vacancies (1989)*

with R. Jackman and C. Pissarides

INTRODUCTION

Since 1963 British unemployment has risen by a multiple of over four. Yet the vacancy rates in the 1987 'recovery', the 1979 'boom' and the 1963 'slump' were the same (see Figure 5.1). There has thus been a striking shift in unemployment at given vacancies. Similar findings have been reported in nearly all advanced countries.[1] Thus the question which this paper addresses is how do we think about shifts in the u/v curve?

Our conclusion is that shifts in the u/v curve reflect the efficiency with which the labour market matches unemployed workers to job vacancies, and the outward shift in the UK seems mainly attributable to a fall in the effectiveness of the unemployed as job-seekers (both in terms of their own job search and their attractiveness to employers).

It is also noteworthy that the vacancy rate was on average much lower during the early 1980s than during the 1960s or 1970s. Some possible reasons for this decline are explored in an earlier draft of this paper (available from the authors on request) but are omitted from this version for reasons of space.

1 THE RELATIONSHIP BETWEEN UNEMPLOYMENT AND VACANCIES

It is helpful to begin by defining a benchmark concept of a vacancy. A commonsense definition is that used by the UK's National Survey of Engagements and Vacancies (1977), i.e. a job which is 'currently vacant, available immediately and for which the firm has taken some specific recruiting action during the past four weeks'. So what generates these vacancies? Even if there is unemployment, a firm paying the prevailing wage cannot hire as many

* *Oxford Bulletin of Economics and Statistics*, 51(4) (1989), pp. 377–94. The authors wish to record our thanks to the Economic and Social Research Council and to the Esmée Fairbairn Foundation for financial support, to Savvas Savouri for invaluable assistance in updating the data and econometric work and to Suzie Vivian and Joanne Putterford for expert typing of successive drafts of this paper.

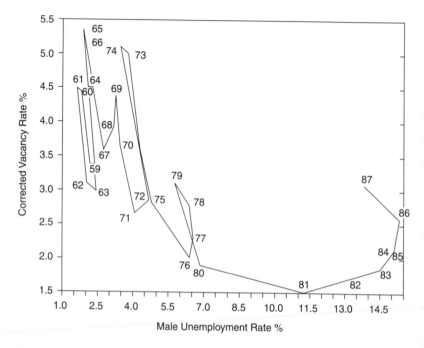

Figure 5.1 Unemployment and 'corrected' vacancies
Sources: Table 5.1 (p. 110); vacancies corrected as described in text (p. 112).

workers as it wants instantaneously. Instead firms indicate that they need labour by announcing vacancies.[2] They can of course fill these vacancies faster by offering higher wages, but at the obvious cost of a higher wage bill. They could also in principle attract more labour by advertising more vacancies, but we will assume that vacancies must be genuine. If a firm advertises x vacancies, it must be ready to employ x properly qualified people if they turn up. If it refused to do this, its future advertisements would carry little conviction.

The hiring function

At the same time as firms are looking for workers, unemployed workers are looking for jobs. Only a proportion (p) of the vacancies get filled per period, and this proportion is higher the higher the ratio of job-seekers to vacancies.[3] Not all the unemployed apply for a job in every period; the proportion who do so and are acceptable to employers is c. There are thus cu effective job-seekers.

Hence the number of engagements (e) in a period is

$$e = pv = p\left(\frac{cu}{v}\right)v \qquad (p' > 0, p'' < 0) \tag{5.1}$$

where u are the unemployed and v the number of vacancies. This can be rewritten as

$$e = f(cu, v) \qquad (f_1, f_2 > 0) \tag{5.2}$$

where f is constant returns, and both partial derivatives are positive (and so the elasticity of p with respect to u/v is less than unity).[4] There will be more engagements if there are more unemployed, they search more effectively or if there are more vacancies available for matching. With constant returns to scale, we can rewrite (2) as

$$1 = f\left(\frac{cu}{e}, \frac{v}{e}\right) \qquad (f_1, f_2 > 0)$$

or

$$c\frac{u}{e} = h\left(\frac{v}{e}\right) \qquad h' < 0 \tag{5.3}$$

In a steady state this is a relation between the duration of unemployment (which is u/e in a steady state) and the duration of vacancies (v/e). Out of a steady state u/e and v/e are not exact measures of duration, but for convenience we shall use quotation marks and refer to (3) as a relation between the 'duration of unemployment' and 'duration of vacancies'. If this relation has shifted out, it suggests a decline in the effectiveness of the unemployed as job seekers (c).

In the analysis so far we have assumed that only unemployed people are looking for jobs. We can allow for employed job-seekers by replacing (5.3) by

$$c'\frac{u'}{e'} = j\left(\frac{v}{e'}\right) \tag{5.4}$$

where u' represents *all* job-seekers, c' their average effectiveness, and e' *all* hirings. v represents all vacancies, whether filled by employed or unemployed people. It is helpful to note that $e'/c'u'$ is the rate at which a 'fully effective' job-seeker (with $c = 1$) finds a job. This rate must be the same for *all* fully-effective job-seekers whatever their status (employed or unemployed). Hence, since e/cu is the rate at which fully-effective unemployed job-seekers find work,

$$\frac{e}{cu} = \frac{e'}{c'u'} = \frac{1}{j(v/e')}$$

Thus there is a simple relationship between the duration of *all* vacancies (v/e'), *however* filled, and the duration of unemployment (u/e). Only shifts in the effectiveness of *unemployed* job-seekers (c) shift this relationship.

Clearly c is affected by the intensity of job-search which in turn may be affected by the tightness of the labour market, as reflected in the duration of vacancies.[5] Thus the empirically observed relationship will be

$$\frac{u}{e} = \frac{1}{\hat{c}} g\left(\frac{v}{e'}\right) \tag{4}$$

where changes in $\hat{c}$ reflect changes in effectiveness exogenous to the tightness of the labour market.

The u/v Curve

The discussion so far has focused on labour market flows. However, it is worth seeing what can be said about the relationship between the stocks of unemployment and vacancies, for which longer data series are available. To enable us to interpret the standard u/v diagram, we can rewrite (5.2) as

$$sn + \dot{n} = f(cu, v) \qquad (f_1, f_2 > 0) \tag{5.5}$$

where n is employment and s the separation rate, since the change in employment ($\dot{n}$) is simply engagements minus separations (sn). The u/v curve is defined as the locus of points where the employment and unemployment rates are constant, ie $\dot{l}/l - \dot{n}/n = \dot{u} = 0$, where l is the exogenous labour force. Then, dividing (5.5) by n we find

$$\frac{\dot{n}}{n} = f\left(\frac{cu}{n}, \frac{v}{n}\right) - s \qquad (f_1, f_2 > 0) \tag{5.6}$$

Let us suppose that s and $\dot{l}/l$ are constant. It follows that, for given vacancies, if unemployment is to the left of the u/v curve, unemployment must be rising.[6] If unemployment does not jump, the pattern of unemployment and vacancies will thus consist of anti-clockwise loops in a diagram where u is on the horizontal axis (see Figure 5.2). In addition the loops are vertical where they cross the long-run u/v curve.[7]

Mismatch

The preceding analysis relates to a single market. But clearly labour is not homogeneous; it differs in respect of (inter alia) region, industry and occupation. Suppose that within each sub-market there is the same relationship given by equation (5.4). Then if all markets always have the same ratio of unemployment and vacancies, the economy-wide curve will look exactly like

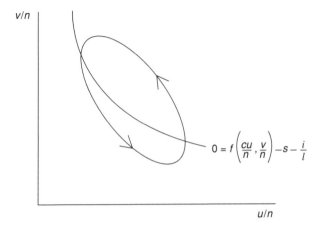

Figure 5.2 The u/v curve

the curve for each sector. But if the ratios differ between sectors, the economy-wide observations (of u and v) will lie to the right of the curve for the individual sectors, due to the convexity of the curve. A suitable index of mismatch is

$$\frac{1}{2}\sum_i \left| \frac{u_i}{u} - \frac{v_i}{v} \right|$$

where i is the individual submarket.[8] This index shows what proportion of the unemployed would have to shift sectors in order to make the u_i/v_i ratio the same in each sector.

2   THE SHIFT OF THE u/v CURVE

We are now ready to turn to the British data. As regards unemployment, we concentrate on male unemployment (excluding school-leavers), not because that is what we are interested in, but because we think it varies more closely with true unemployment than does the aggregate unemployment rate.[9] There is therefore nothing odd about relating male unemployment to total vacancies. The unemployment flows, stocks and 'durations' are shown in Table 5.1, which also shows the corresponding figures for vacancies registered at public employment offices.

Table 5.1 Unemployment and vacancies: stocks and flows (Great Britain)

Male unemployment (000s)				Registered vacancies (000s)			
Inflow (monthly) (1)	Outflow (monthly) (2)	Stock (monthly average) (3)	Duration (months) (4)	Inflow (monthly) (5)	Outflow (monthly) (6)	Stock (monthly average) (7)	Duration (months) (8)
254.4	248.7	377.8	1.52	170.0	171.0	174.0	1.02
251.0	250.3	425.8	1.70	186.0	184.0	188.0	1.02
257.7	255.7	430.8	1.68	178.0	179.0	200.0	1.12
253.4	251.1	460.1	1.83	183.0	186.0	186.0	1.00
258.1	241.7	550.0	2.28	157.0	161.0	129.9	0.80
234.6	246.3	637.7	2.59	176.0	170.0	145.0	0.85
221.6	231.6	450.2	1.94	229.0	216.0	304.0	1.41
247.5	237.9	433.3	1.82	205.0	211.0	294.0	1.39
279.5	251.1	648.3	2.58	156.0	164.0	151.0	0.92
247.5	244.9	878.5	3.59	169.0	167.0	120.0	0.72
243.1	241.5	901.7	3.73	192.0	191.0	153.0	0.80
192.3	199.5	867.4	4.35	222.0	216.0	209.0	0.97
183.0	186.7	781.0	4.18	228.0	229.0	240.0	1.05
225.7	175.3	935.6	5.34	183.0	193.0	142.0	0.74

Table 5.1 Continued

1981	223.2	189.2	1,558.2	8.24	149.0	149.0	96.0	0.64
1982	226.5	211.4	1,831.8	8.66	163.0	163.0	111.0	0.68
1983	220.7	217.2	1,977.6	9.10	179.9	177.7	135.9	0.76
1984	218.2	212.1	2,018.5	9.52	192.0	191.8	148.0	0.78
1985	226.9	224.4	2,079.1	9.27	199.6	198.5	160.5	0.81
1986	236.2	239.4	2,105.6	8.80	210.3	206.2	186.9	0.91
1987	223.6	253.4	1,951.1	7.70	224.0	219.9	232.6	1.06

Sources:

Column (1) GB Standardized inflow excluding school leavers, Department of Employment.

Column (3) Unemployment 1971–87 Department of Employment standardized series excluding school leavers; 1967–70 consistent unemployment series. Two series spliced using 1971:1.

Column (2) constructed from columns (3) and (1) using flow and level identity.

Column (4); columns (2) and (3).

Column (5) and (6), *Department of Employment Gazette*, 1967–70 (September 1973, p. 842); 1971–3 (September 1978, p. 806); 1974–9 (June 1980) p. 633); 1980–2 (February 1984, p. 541); 1983–7 *Department of Employment Gazette* (August 1988, Table 3.1) deflate UK by 1 per cent to approximate GB figure.

Column (7) *British Labour Statistics, Historical Abstract*, 1957–9; *Department of Employment Gazette*; 1960–5, (December 1966, p. 861); 1966–73 (July 1974, p. 663) *Annual Abstract* 1982 1974–80, p. 165; *Annual Abstract* 1984 1981–82, p. 119, 1983–87 *Department of Employment Gazette* (August 1988) Table 3.1 deflate UK by 1 percent to approximate GB.

Column (8); columns (6) and (7).

Notes:

1. 'Duration' is computed as stock/outflow.

2. All stocks and flows exclude school leavers and Careers Service and also Community Programme vacancies.

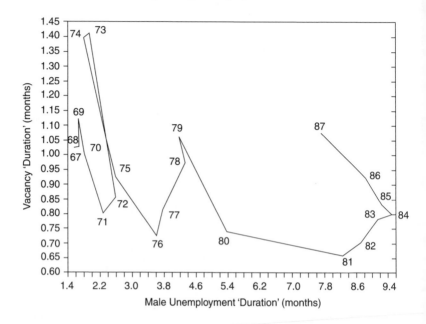

Figure 5.3 Vacancy 'duration' and unemployment 'duration' 1967–87
Source: Table 5.1 (p. 110).

These two sets of statistics give us the 'duration' relationship depicted in Figure 5.3. This has clearly shifted out, suggesting a decline in the $\hat{c}$ component of search intensity.

However, it is also interesting to look at relationships over the longer period before 1967, for which flow data are not available, and we therefore look at the *stocks* of unemployment and vacancies. The problem here is that the share of the employment exchanges in total vacancies has risen over time, especially since the Job Centre programme began in 1974. This is shown by a comparison of the flow of registered vacancies with the total turnover in the economy. The economy-wide turnover is shown in Table 5.2, together with the proportion of engagements corresponding to a registered vacancy filled (column (4)), and the proportion of separations leading to a new registered vacancy (column (5)).[10]

As Table 5.2 shows, the share of the employment service in labour market flows has expanded. To produce a corrected vacancy series we shall assume that the employment service's share in the stock of vacancies equals its share in the flow.[11] To be specific the correction factor is the inverse of the average of columns (4) and (5) in the Table 5.2. Before 1967 we assume the share of the

Table 5.2　Engagements and separations, Great Britain, 1968–84

Year (1)	Engagements (monthly) (000s) (2)	Separations (monthly) (000s) (3)	Employees in employment (December) (month) (4)	Vacancies outflow as % of engagements (5)	Vacancies inflow as % of separations (6)
1968	850	858	22.2	21.6	21.7
1969	867	875	22.1	20.6	20.3
1970	800	825	21.8	23.2	22.1
1971	716	73.3	21.6	22.5	21.4
1972	767	742	21.9	22.2	23.7
1973	833	808	22.2	25.9	28.3
1974	817	800	22.4	25.8	25.6
1975	667	683	22.2	24.6	22.8
1976	625	633	22.1	26.7	26.7
1977	641	633	22.2	29.8	30.3
1978	675	650	22.5	32.0	34.1
1979	683	675	22.6	33.5	33.8
1980	550	617	21.8	35.1	29.7
1981	467	542	20.9	31.9	27.5
1982	500	558	20.2	32.6	29.2
1983	542	492	20.8	32.8	36.6
1984	567	550	21.0	33.8	34.9

Sources: 1968–82
　Column (1): Manpower Services Commission (column (2) plus change in
　column (3) divided by 12).
　Column (2): Manpower Services Commission (based on P45, omitting deaths of
　occupational pensioners).
　Column (3): Manpower Services Commission.,
　Column (4): column (1) and Table 5.1 column (6).
　Column (5): column (2) and Table 5.1 column (5).

1983–4
We use national engagements for 1983/84 of 6.5 million and for 1984/85 of
6.8 million. *Source*: Manpower Services Commission Column (3):
Department of Employment from *Department of Employment Gazette*.

employment service to be constant. The resulting level of vacancies is plotted
against unemployment in Figure 5.1. (The *u/v* curve for uncorrected vacancies,
set out in Figure 5.4, is, of course, still more favourable to the hypothesis that
the *u/v* curve has shifted out.)

　　There is another, quite independent, source of information on the tightness
of the labour market which comes from the Confederation of British Industries
(CBI) Industrial Trends Enquiry on manufacturing, which quarterly asks
employers, 'What factors are likely to limit your output over the next four
months?'. Possible factors listed include shortages of (a) skilled labour and

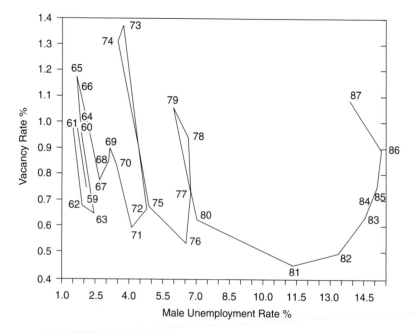

Figure 5.4 Unemployment and (uncorrected) vacancies, 1961–87
Source: Table 5.1.

(b) unskilled labour. The employment exchange data on vacancies and the CBI skilled labour index are highly correlated till 1974 since when the employment exchange data have drifted upwards relative to the CBI series.[12]

Figures 5.1 and 5.4, and both CBI series (not shown here), show that the cycles 1967–71, 1971–76 and 1976–80 lie on different u/v curves. For remember that at each point where $\dot{u} = 0$ the observation should lie on the long run curve. By contrast, as Figure 5.1 shows, the earlier cycles lie closer together.

Estimation

We now proceed rather quickly to estimation, since the basic points stand out from the figures. We estimate the relationship between the duration of unemployment and the duration of vacancies:

$$\ln\left(\frac{u}{e}\right) = a_0 + a_1 \ln\left(\frac{v}{e'}\right) + a_2 t$$

where t is time. The equation is estimated on annual data over the period 1968–87, using instrumental variables,[13] and the results are reported in Table 5.3. The simple form of the equation set out above failed the Sargan specification test, and the Gallant–Jorgensen test suggests first order autocorrelation of the residuals. We therefore re-estimated the equations including the lagged dependent variable, and the resulting equation (column (2) of Table 5.3) passes the Sargan specification test and the Gallant–Jorgensen test. We test for the structural stability by allowing for a possible parameter break in 1983. The Gallant–Jorgensen test for joint parameter stability shows the equation to be stable over the period.

The estimates in the column (2) equation, including the lagged dependent variable imply that the duration of unemployment at given vacancy durations increased from 1968 to 1987 by a multiple of about 4.94.[14] This can also be seen by inspection of Figure 5.3.

Table 5.3 Duration regressions, 1968–87
Dependent variable: $\ln(u/e)$

	(1)	(2)
Constant	0.24	0.20
	(3.82)	(6.01)
$\ln\left(\dfrac{v}{e'}\right)$	–1.04	–0.78
	(5.05)	(7.54)
$\ln\left(\dfrac{u}{e}\right)_{-1}$	–	0.514
		(6.20)
t	0.091	0.038
	(16.18)	(4.15)
Sargan specification test*	9.04	1.65
Gallant–Jorgensen test for first order autocorrelation**	2.46	0.727
Gallant–Jorgensen test for parameter stability***	–	0.79

Notes: Asymptotic t-statistics in parentheses.
* Test for structural misspecification. Under null of no misspecification the statistics are distributed asymptotically $\chi^{(2)}(3).\chi^2_{0.05}(3) = 7.81$
** Test for first order autocorrelation in disturbances. Under null the statistic are distributed asymptotically $\chi^2(1).\chi^2_{0.10}(1) = 2.71$
*** Test for a parameter break in 1983 amongst entire parameter set. Under null of parameter stability the statistics are distributed asymptotically $\chi^2(4).\chi^2_{0.05}(4) = 9.49$

Explaining Unemployment

Table 5.4 Estimates of the u/v curve, 1968–87
Dependent variable: $\ln(u/l)$

	(1)	(2)	(3)	(4)	(5)	(6)
C	−1.25	−1.40	−0.25	−3.05	−5.12	−8.07
	(1.03)	(0.12)	(0.11)	(0.88)	(9.67)	(20.67)
$\ln(v/n)$	−0.51	−0.53	−0.55	−0.60	−0.48	−0.83
	(7.68)	(5.36)	(5.23)	(3.26)	(8.24)	(10.56)
$\ln(u/l)$	0.62	0.67	0.64	0.44	0.49	
	(2.46)	(3.68)	(5.26)	(1.29)	(5.69)	
$\ln(s/n)$	0.65	0.74	0.99	0.49		
	(2.46)	(1.53)	(1.58)	(1.37)		
RR		−0.71			1.85	
		(0.34)			(2.47)	
MM			0.98			
			(0.81)			
R				0.97		3.37
				(0.53)		(7.80)
t	0.033	0.028	0.037	0.035	0.045	0.040
	(3.55)	(1.55)	(2.69)	(3.56)	(5.28)	(5.30)
Sargan specification test statistics*	0.68	0.51	0.29	0.53	4.44	0.47
Gallant–Jorgensen specification test statistics**	1.89	1.87	1.86	3.67	0.09	0.33

Notes: Asymptotic ts in parentheses.
* Sargan specification statistic which under null of no structural misspecification is asymptotically $\chi^2(3).\chi^2_{0.05}(3) = 7.81$
** Gallant–Jorgensen specification statistics which under null of white noise residuals is asymptotically $\chi^2(1).\chi^2_{0.05}(1) = 3.84 \chi^2_{0.10}(1) = 2.71$

Turning to the relationship between the stocks of unemployment and vacancies we approximated (6) by

$$\ln\left(\frac{u}{l}\right) = a_0 + a_1 \ln\left(\frac{u}{l}\right)_{-1} + a_2 \ln\left(\frac{v}{n}\right) + a_3\left(\frac{s}{n}\right) + a_4 t$$

The equation was again estimated by instrumental variables, and the results are given in Table 5.4. The results of estimating this equation, in the first column, show all the variables correctly signed and significant, and that the equation is satisfactory in terms of specification and stability tests. The equation indicates that between 1968 and 1987 the long-run level of unemployment at given vacancies rose by a multiple of around 5.68[15] (Figure 5.4), which is of similar magnitude to the outward shift in unemployment duration.

Interpreting the Time Trend in the u/v Curve

One obvious variable which might affect search intensity is the benefit/income ratio (RR).[16] Another, as noted earlier, is mismatch (MM). A third possibility as argued by Budd, Levine and Smith (1988) is the proportion of long-term unemployed (R). In columns (2), (3) and (4) of Table 5.4 we report the results of including each of these variables separately. None of the three variables entered separately was significant. However, the inclusion of these additional variables in each case also rendered the separation rate insignificant and, in the case of long-term unemployment, the lagged dependent variable also. We therefore experimented with a number of different specifications.

With regard to the replacement ratio, the results of estimating the u/v curve including the replacement ratio but excluding the separation rate are shown in column (5). The replacement ratio is clearly significant and has an appreciable significant impact (an elasticity of just under one, calculated at a replacement rate of 0.5). This estimate is consistent with the results of cross-section studies.[17] While this result is of some interest, it must be said that neither theory nor the data offers any good justification for dropping the separation rate and on the basis of the data we have used we should conclude that the effects of benefits are insignificant (column (2)). It may also be noted that the time trend in the u/v curve in the column (5) equation is as high as that in column (1), suggesting that the replacement ratio, even if significant, does not form part of the explanation of the outward shift of the curve.

With regard to mismatch, calculations of the extent of mismatch using the index described above (p. 109) are reported in Jackman and Roper (1987), and these calculations show no general increase in mismatch over the data period. Thus increased mismatch could not explain the outward shift in the u/v curve in Britain. In the regression in Table 5.4, we have used only a measure of regional mismatch as this is the only dimension for which consistent data are available over the whole period.[18] In no specification was mismatch significant and in most it took the wrong sign.

More interestingly, the proportion of long-term unemployed[19] becomes significant when either the separation rate or the lagged dependent variable is dropped, and becomes highly significant when both these other variables are dropped ($t = 7.8$). The results are set out in column (6) of Table 5.4. While the column (6) equation provides a very impressive fit of the data, its interpretation is complicated by the endogeneity of long-term unemployment. The time trend in the column (6) equation is about half that of the column (1) equations.

Finally, we re-estimated our equation for the u/v curve using our estimated 'corrected' vacancies series (see p. 112), rather than the series for officially registered vacancies. The results were very similar, except that in each equation the time trend was reduced by about half, reflecting the fact that, due to the increasing role of the government employment service over the period, the estimated number of corrected vacancies fell relative to registered vacancies.

Turning lastly to less easily quantifiable variables one possibility is that the introduction of redundancy payments and employment protection have affected the behaviour of employers.[20] First, it would discourage firms from getting rid of workers and thus reduce the flow of separations (s). As we have seen, there has indeed been a secular decline in turnover, but this factor is already incorporated in our regressions for the u/v curve. The second effect of employment protection would be to increase the choosiness of employers faced with a given number of applicants for a given vacancy, as reflected in c. This would lead to a downward shift in the hiring function, or in other words, to an outward shift in both the u/v curve and the duration relationship.

We clearly have to use judgement to determine the relative importance of increased choosiness of workers, as opposed to firms. Unfortunately the available research makes it impossible to be more precise about this. Time-series analysis is ambiguous about the effect of the legislation on total employment (though, as expected, both separations and hirings were reduced, Nickell, 1979, 1982). Surveys of employers yield contradictory results, with some reporting little effect on employment practices (Daniel and Stilgoe, 1978; Confederation of British Industries, 1984), and some reporting major disincentives to investment (Wilson, 1980).

We therefore conclude that there has been a major change in search effectiveness. There may have been many reasons for this. We have already discussed the possible role of the level of social security benefits, and the growth of long-term unemployment. But possibly a more important factor over much of the period has been the more permissive manner of social security administration (Layard, 1982, p. 43). The public attitude towards claiming benefit has also changed. During the early 1980s, for example, it became routine for students to claim benefits as a result, in part, of a National Union of Students campaign to encourage this. In addition there may have been more general changes in the work ethic.

Some people believe that higher unemployment has itself reduced the work ethic – if your neighbours have been unemployed for the last 5 years, you may not feel so bad about it. We are attracted to this idea, but our econometric work has lent it no support. Additional lags on unemployment duration or on unemployment in the equations of Tables 5.3 and 5.4 were found insignificant. So we must remain agnostic as to the causes of the change. We do however believe that our results confirm the popular belief that change there has been.

3 CONCLUSION

Our main conclusions are these.

1. If the u/v relationship results from a process of matching workers to jobs, its fundamental structure involves a relationship between the duration of unemployment and the duration of vacancies. The relationship between durations can shift only if the search effectiveness of the unemployment changes. In Figure 5.3 we plotted the duration of unemployment against the duration of vacancies for Britain. There has been a massive increase in unemployment duration at given duration of vacancies. During the 1970s, unemployment duration at given vacancy duration rose by 150 per cent. We therefore conclude that there has been a massive decrease in the search effectiveness of the unemployed.

2. In Figure 5.1 we plotted the rate of unemployment against the rate of vacancies. During the 1970s unemployment at given vacancies rose by two-thirds. In addition there was, especially in the 1980s, a massive fall in vacancies. Shifts in the u/v relation could, in principle, be caused by an increase in the mismatch between the patterns of vacancies and unemployment – across occupations, regions or industries. However calculations of mismatch suggest that, if anything, mismatch has fallen rather than risen over this period (Jackman and Roper, 1987). We therefore infer, by a process of elimination, that the u/v relation also supports the view that there has been a major fall in the effectiveness of search (at given durations of unemployment and vacancies). Either workers become more choosy about taking jobs or firms become more choosy about hiring workers. This shift may of course be due to past labour market conditions. High unemployment in the past may have undermined work habits, but we have not been able to capture any such effect by econometric methods.

The study of vacancies is in its infancy. But we are convinced that the use of these data is essential to understanding the medium-term workings of the labour market. Our main aim here has been to help explain the massive secular increase in unemployment, which is one of the major economic puzzles in Britain and other European countries.

Notes

1. Johnson and Layard (1986), Table 16.13.
2. (i) Of unemployed workers in 1979 the percentages using the following methods of job search were:

Newspapers	83	–
Job Centres	77	(15)
Asked friend	50	⎫
Asked people at place of work		⎬ (31)
Previous	42	
Other	29	⎭
Approached employers	28	(15)

Department of Employment Gazette (August 1982), p. 336. The figures in brackets indicate the percentage of the cohort of unemployed workers who had found jobs within 4 months who had heard of their job by the method shown (15 per cent was 'other'). The figures suggest that workers mainly search over vacancies rather than over firms, which may or may not have announced vacancies.

(ii) Not all posts advertised are vacancies in the sense defined, since if workers who quit give notice in advance, jobs could be advertised before they were available to be filled. But not all these slots would be filled before the quitters left.

3. This follows for example if workers and jobs are identical, and workers search randomly over vacancies. If each worker makes one job application per period the probability that a given worker applies for a given vacancy is $1/v$, and the probability that there are no applicants for a given vacancy is $(1 - 1/v)''$ $\exp(-u/v)$. Thus p $1 - \exp(-u/v)$ (see Hall, 1977, p. 356; Pissarides, 1979).

4. This follows for example from the function in the previous footnote. Earlier writers have often assumed increasing returns of the form $e = cuv$ (Lipsey, 1960, 1974; Holt and David, 1966; Holt, 1971). For an empirical test of (2), confirming constant returns and elasticity of p less than unity, see Pissarides (1986).

5. Jackman and Williams (1985).

6. In our data s is not constant. However, we still find this relationship. The reason is that in general when e changes s changes in the same direction but by less (see Table 2). Hence $\dot{n}$ and s are positively correlated, and the level of $\dot{n}$ tells us, in general, on which side of the long run u/v curve a particular observation lies.

7. See Pissarides (1985) for a formal derivation. The u/v curve can also be derived from the notion of fixed relative wages in different sectors, with sectors in different degrees of disequilibrium (Hansen, 1970). This overlooks the simultaneous existence of u and v even within any readily definable sector.

8. Jackman and Roper (1987). For a further discussion and a related index see Jackman, Layard and Savouri (1987).

9. The official registered female unemployment rate is much affected by changes in benefit entitlements.

10. A vacancy is filled either when the employment service effects a placement (shown separately in column (6)) or when the vacancy is cancelled by the employer for some other reason (namely because it has been filled elsewhere).

11. This was approximately the case in April–July 1977 when the National Survey of Engagements and Vacancies (NSEV) was undertaken. The survey findings were (*Department of Employment Gazette*, November 1978):

Monthly engagements as % of employed	2.8% (roughly as in Table 5.2)
Vacancy rate (May)	2.1%
Duration of vacancies	0.75 months
Data on registered vacancies were:	
Monthly outflow as percentage of employed	0.84%
Vacancy rate (May)	0.73%
Duration of vacancies	0.85 months

The MSC record that the vacancies they fill have an average duration of around a week (*Department of Employment Gazette*, July 1978, Table 2, p. 792). This would imply that the national vacancies (from the NSEV) filled elsewhere have a duration of roughly 1 1/2 months, and registered vacancies on the books but not filled via the Job Centres have a duration of 2 months.

12. This may be due to the decline of manufacturing as well as to the increased role of employment exchanges.

13. The instruments were $(v/e')_{-1}$, ln GDP_{-1}, world trade and corrected fiscal deficit (in *National Institute Economic Review* (February 1984, p. 80), up to 1983 and thereafter calculated from OECD, *Economic Outlook*).

14. Calculated as
$$\exp\left(\frac{20 \times 0.038}{1 - 0.514}\right) = 4.94$$

15. Calculated as
$$\exp\left(\frac{20 \times 0.033}{1 - 0.62}\right) = 5.68$$

16. The replacement ratio is a weighted average of different family types using the following proportions: single householder 0.35, married couple with no children 0.26, with one child 0.11, with two children 0.16 and with three children 0.12. The components of this weighted average are calculated from Table 6.4a of the Department of Health and Social Security, 'Abstract of Statistics for Index of Retail Prices, Average Earnings, Social Security Benefits and Contributions' (1983). This gives for each family type, data on supplementary benefits, plus rent addition *and* on net income for a one-earner family on average earnings. We compute annual income on benefit and relate it to mid-year earnings. The numbers for 1955 to 1987 are 37.5, 37.7, 36.2, 40.1, 40.6, 42.0, 42.0, 42.4, 43.9, 43.0, 47.5, 48.2, 52.6, 51.7, 50.8, 51.2, 50.6, 47.0, 46.6, 47.2, 49.2, 50.0, 51.3, 49.8, 46.0, 45.8, 50.3, 53.5, 54.4, 52.3, 51.2, 51.7, 50.2. (The rise is mainly due to the rise in rents relative to earnings.)

17. Narendranathan, Nickell and Stern (1985).

18. Data available from the authors on request.

19. For further discussion, see Budd, Levine and Smith (1988) and Jackman and Layard (1988).

20. There have been three main changes. The Redundancy Payments Act 1965 introduced statutory payments when a worker is made redundant, a part of which is a direct cost to the employer. The Industrial Relations Act 1971 established legal rights against unfair dismissal. The Employment Protection Act 1975 extended the periods of notice required before a termination.

References

Budd, A., P. Levine and P. Smith (1988) 'Unemployment, Vacancies and the Long-Term Unemployed', *Economic Journal*, 98.

Confederation of British Industries (1984) 'Attitudes Towards Employment', CBI Social Affairs Directorate (November).

Daniel, W. and E. Stilgoe (1978) *The Impact of Employment Protection Laws* (London: Policy Studies Institute)

Hall, R. (1977) 'An Aspect of the Economic Role of Unemployment', in G. Harcourt, *Microeconomic Foundations of Macroeconomies*: Proceedings of a Conference held by the International Economic Association at S'Agaro, Spain (London: Macmillan)

Hansen, B. (1970) 'Excess Demand, Unemployment, Vacancies and Wages'. *Quarterly Journal of Economics*, Vol. 84, 1–23.

Holt, C. (1971) 'How can the Phillips Curve be Moved to Reduce both Inflation and Unemployment?', in E. S. Phelps (ed.), *Microeconomic Foundations of Employment and Inflation Theory* (London: Macmillan).

Holt, C. and M. David (1966) 'The Concept of Job Vacancies in a Dynamic Theory of the Demand for Labour', in Universities–NBER, *The Measurement of Interpretation of Job Vacancies*.

Jackman, R. and R. Layard (1988) 'Does Long-Term Unemployment Reduce a Person's Chance of a Job?: A Time-Series Test', Centre for Labour Economics, LSE, *Discussion Paper*, 309. *Economica* version chapter 6 in this volume.

Jackman, R., R. Layard, and S. Savouri (1987) 'Labour Market Mismatch and the "Equilibrium" Level of Unemployment', London School of Economics, Centre for Labour Economics, LSE, *Working Paper*, 1009.

Jackman, R. and S. Roper (1987) 'Structural Unemployment', *BULLETIN*, 49(1) (February), 9–36.

Jackman, R. and C. Williams (1985) 'Job Applications by Unemployed Men', Centre for Labour Economics, LSE, *Working Paper*, 792.

Johnson, G. and R. Layard (1986) 'The Natural Rate of Unemployment: Explanation and Policy', in O. Ashenfelter and R. Layard (eds), *Handbook of Labor Economics* (Amsterdam: North Holland).

Layard, R. (1982) *More Jobs Less Inflation* (London: Grant McIntyre).

Lipsey, R. (1960) 'The Relation Between Unemployment and the Rate of Change of Money Wage Rates in the United Kingdom 1862–1957: A Further Analysis', *Economica*, 27, 1–31.

Lipsey, R. (1974) 'The Micro Theory of the Phillips Curve Reconsidered: A Reply to Holmes and Smyth', *Economica*, 41, 62–70.

Narendranathan, W., S. Nickell, and J. Stern (1985) 'Unemployment Benefits Revisited', *Economic Journal*, 95, 308–29.

Nickell, S. (1979) 'Unemployment and the Structure of Labour Costs', *Journal of Monetary Economics*, Supplement: Carnegie–Rochester Public Policy Conference, 11.

Nickell, S. (1982) 'The Determinants of Equilibrium Unemployment in Britain', *Economic Journal* (September).

Pissarides, C. (1979) 'Job Matchings with State Employment Agencies and Random Search', *Economic Journal* (December).

Pissarides, C. (1985) 'Short-Run Equilibrium Dynamics of Unemployment, Vacancies and Real Wages', *American Economic Review*, 75, 676–90.

Pissarides, C. (1986) 'Unemployment and Vacancies in Britain', *Economic Policy*, 3, 499–559.

Wilson, Lord (1980) Committee to Review the Functioning of Financial Institutions, Cmnd. 7937, Research Reports, 1 (para. 434) and 3 (p. 41).

6 Does Long-term Unemployment Reduce a Person's Chance of a Job?

(1991)*

with R. Jackman

The proportion of unemployed people who leave unemployment within a given time period is much lower for those who have been unemployed for long durations. For example, in Britain in early 1984 the proportion was 4 per cent per quarter for men who had been unemployed for over four years, compared with 40 per cent for men unemployed under three months (see Figure 6.1). Two possible explanations have been offered. (1) People may differ in their chances of employment, so that low-probability people are disproportionately represented among the long-term unemployed. (2) Long duration may actually reduce a *given* individual's probability of leaving unemployment.

There are thus two possible explanations: (1) heterogeneity, or (2) state-dependence (or, of course, some of both).

The matter is of considerable practical importance. For if long-term unemployment has a bad effect on people, it is more important that people be deflected from entering into it. In addition, if long-term unemployment can destroy human capital, it is more likely that work experience can rebuild it.

Hitherto most research on the heterogeneity versus state-dependence issue has used cross-section data (e.g. Flinn and Heckman, 1983; Heckman and Borjas, 1980; Narendranathan *et al.*, 1985). Such estimates are subject to the problem of unobservable differences between individuals. Although serious efforts have been made to model this, there is no general agreement concerning the outcome of this body of research.

In this paper we suggest a complementary approach, based on the behaviour of aggregate time series. We propose a simple test based on comparing

* *Economica*, 58 (229) (1991), pp. 93–106
We are extremely grateful to Hartmut Lehmann for all the empirical work in this paper, and to Jonathan Haskel and Peter Lanjouw for help with previous drafts. We also thank the ESRC for financial support.

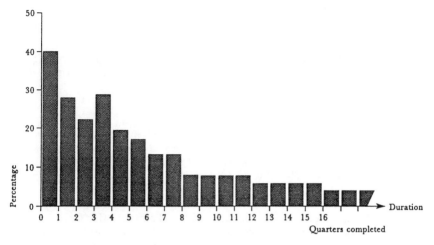

Figure 6.1   Proportion of unemployed in January 1984 leaving unemployment in next quarter: by duration (males)

changes in the overall exit rate from unemployment with changes in the exit rate for new entrants. We argue that, in a comparison of steady states, with heterogeneity of the unemployed but in the absence of state-dependence, the two would move in proportion. But in Britain over the last twenty years the aggregate exit rate has fallen by very much more than the fall in the exit rate of new entrants. This appears inconsistent with an explanation based on pure heterogeneity and suggests that state-dependence must be present.

1 THE ARGUMENT

The argument is based on a comparison of steady states. We assume that the number of people who leave unemployment (A) is determined by the number of vacancies (V) and the number of 'effective job-seekers'. Some job-seekers are more effective than others – owing to their looking harder, being less choosy about jobs or being more desirable to employers. We shall use c_i to denote the effectiveness of each type of unemployed job-seekers. It follows that the number who leave unemployment per period is given by[1]

$$A = g(V, \bar{c}U)$$

where $\bar{c}$ is the average of c_i averaged over all the unemployed. We assume that this function exhibits constant returns to scale.[2] Hence the overall exit rate from unemployment is

$$\frac{A}{U} = \bar{c}g\left(\frac{V}{\bar{c}U}, 1\right)$$

In consequence, as Pissarides and Haskel (1987) point out, the probability per period than an *individual* with effectiveness c_i will leave unemployment is

$$P_i = c_ig\left(\frac{V}{\bar{c}U}, 1\right) \tag{6.1}$$

Search effectiveness can be influenced by the pre-existing characteristics θ_i that the individual has when he or she becomes unemployed. It can also be influenced by the individual's experience of unemployment, in particular by his or her uncompleted duration, d_i. Thus, in general,

$$c_i = h(\theta_i, d_i)$$

We wish to test for state-dependence, i.e. for whether d_i affects c_i.

The inflow rate into unemployment is reasonably stable aside from cyclical fluctuations, which are not relevant to our argument which is based on a comparison of steady states (Pissarides, 1986). We shall therefore assume that the distribution of characteristics θ_i across those who enter unemployment is given by a stable density function $f(\theta_i)$. From this it follows that among new entrants to unemployment the average value of c_i is constant from period to period.

The key to our argument is that, under pure heterogeneity, the same is true of the average quality of the *total stock* of unemployment. This is because in a steady state the average duration of unemployment experienced by each type of labour is $1/c_ig$, i.e. the reciprocal of the outflow rate. If g falls, in the new equilibrium all durations lengthen by the same proportion. Hence the number of unemployed people of each type rises by the same proportion, and the average quality of the unemployed is constant.[3]

From this it follows that under pure heterogeneity the *aggregate* outflow rate would, in a comparison of steady states, move in proportion to the outflow rate of new entrants. We shall shortly see whether it does.

But first we set out our key argument more rigorously. The exit rate for new entrants is, from (6.1),

$$\left(\frac{A}{U}\right)_N = \bar{c}_Ng\left(\frac{V}{cU}, 1\right) \tag{6.2}$$

Here $\bar{c}_N$ is the average effectiveness of new entrants (and not the same as $\bar{c}$). Since the quality of new entrants is assumed not to vary over time, $\bar{c}_N$ is constant from period to period.

Under pure heterogeneity, the same is true of the quality of the total stock of the unemployed. For under pure heterogeneity each individual has an effectivenes c_i which is independent of duration. Hence the average duration of individuals of type i is $1/c_i g$ and their number is this times their inflow, i.e. $A f_i/c_i g$, where f_i is the proportion of type i individuals in the inflow and, in the steady state, the aggregate inflow is equal to the aggregate outflow, A. Hence the average quality of the unemployed stock is

$$\bar{c} = \frac{E\left(\frac{A}{c_i g} c_i\right)}{E\left(\frac{A}{c_i g}\right)} = \frac{1}{E\left(\frac{1}{c_i}\right)}$$

where E is taken using the density function $f(\ )$. Hence $\bar{c}$ is constant and independent of g. The overall exit rate is therefore

$$\frac{A}{U} = \left[E\left(\frac{1}{c_i}\right)\right]^{-1} g\left(\frac{V}{\bar{c}U}, 1\right) \tag{6.3}$$

But from (6.2) the corresponding exit rate for newly unemployed people is

$$\left(\frac{A}{U}\right)_N = E(c_i) g\left(\frac{V}{\bar{c}U}, 1\right) \tag{6.2'}$$

So the ratio of the two exit rates is

$$\frac{A/U}{(A/U)_N} = \frac{\left[E\left(\frac{1}{c_i}\right)\right]^{-1}}{E(c_i)} \tag{6.4}$$

This ratio is less than unity since the harmonic mean is less than the arithmetic mean. And, more important for our purposes, it is independent of economic circumstances (as reflected in g).

2   THE DIRECT EVIDENCE FROM EXIT RATES

We can now turn to the data to see whether in Britain pure heterogeneity holds, i.e. whether the ratio of A/U to $(A/U)_N$ has been constant. Table 6.1 shows (in index number form) the overall exit rate, as well as the exit rate of people unemployed for under three months.[4] As can be seen, between 1979 and 1985 (two points of roughly steady state) the overall exit rate fell by more than half; the exit rate of new entrants fell by one-third.

A similar difference can be seen if we compare 1969 and 1979 (again, two roughly steady states). The overall exit rate fell by 60 per cent; the exit rate of new entrants by just over one-third.

Table 6.1   Overall exit rate and exit rate of new entrants, 1969–88 quarterly rates, men, Britain (1984 = 100)

	Overall exit rate A/U (1)	Exit rate of new entrants $(A/U)_N$ (2)	$(A/U)/(A/U)_N$ (3)	$\bar{c}/c_N$ (4)
1969	597	255	234	282
1970	544	245	222	266
1971	428	216	198	237
1972	375	222	169	201
1973	505	249	203	241
1974	532	242	220	266
1975	381	199	191	226
1976	269	184	146	173
1977	259	183	141	166
1978	222	157	141	151
1979	231	167	138	154
1980	186	129	145	159
1981	118	94	126	127
1982	109	104	105	112
1983	106	102	104	104
1984	100	100	100	100
1985	103	107	96	98
1986	108	112	96	97
1987	125	125	100	99
1988	139	128	109	104

Note: Annual averages of quarterly rates.
Sources: See Appendix.

Taking the whole period from 1969 to 1985, the overall exit rate fell to 17 per cent of its original level, while the exit rate of new entrants fell to 42 per cent of its former value. So the ratio of the two exit rates fell by 60 per cent.

These findings are inconsistent with pure heterogeneity. Suppose instead that there is *some* state-dependence, with $c_i = h(\theta_i, d_i)$, and that duration reduces effectiveness ($h_2 < 0$). The effectiveness of new entrants is still invariant over time, since $\bar{c}_N = E(h(\theta_i, 0))$. But the average quality of the total unemployed stock depends on the duration structure of unemployment. If the distribution of durations has shifted towards the longer durations, then $\bar{c}$ will have fallen. Thus the hypothesis of state dependence can explain the fall in the overall exit rate relative to the exit rate of new entrants.

3 ANOTHER IMPLICATION

That, in essence, completes our test. However, it is interesting to pursue another implication of pure heterogeneity (no state-dependence) plus (6.1). This is the implication that when g falls the quality of the long-duration unemployed rises. This is because the proportion of type i entrants who 'survive' to duration d is given by

$$S_d = (1 - c_i g)^d$$

If g falls by one unit, the survival rate of those with high c_i rises most; i.e.

$$\frac{1}{S_d} \frac{\partial S_d}{\partial g} = -\frac{c_i d}{1 - c_i g}$$

which is increasing in c_1. Thus, when g falls the quality of survivors increases, and it increases most at long durations. *Hence, when exit rates fall, they should fall proportionately less the longer the duration.* A glance at Figures 6.2 and 6.3 show that this is not what happened.

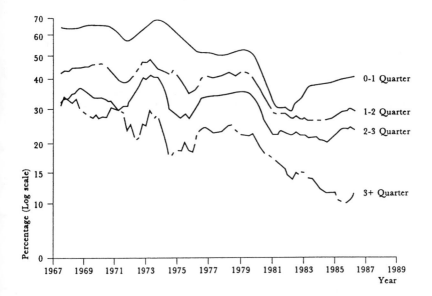

Figure 6.2 Percentage of unemployed people with given duration leaving unemployment within the next quarter (males, Britain) (4-quarter moving average)

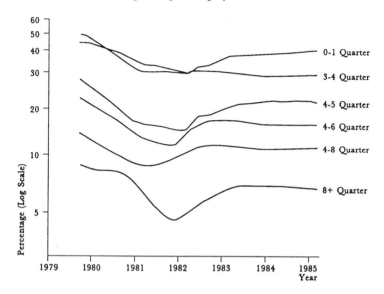

Figure 6.3 Percentage of unemployed people with given duration leaving unemployment within the next quarter (males, Britain) (4-quarter moving average)

Roughly speaking, the exit rates fell by equal proportions. This was in one sense the 'arithmetical' *reason* why A/U fell so much relative to $(A/U)_N$. Since the relative effect of duration upon exit rates was not reduced, A/U *did* fall relative to $(A/U)_N$.

4 A FURTHER ISSUE

Thus, if (6.1) is correct, the facts appear inconsistent with pure heterogeneity. It may be, however, that the specific functional form assumed for (6.1) is too restrictive. Suppose for example that, for the ith type of individual,

$$P_i = c_i g^{\alpha_i} \frac{1}{\alpha_i}, \quad \alpha_i = \alpha(c_i); a' < 0 \tag{6.5}$$

and in addition that α_i is higher the lower is c_i.[5] Thus in a downturn the exit rates of the weaker brethren would fall proportionately more than those of the stronger brethren. This effect would operate independently of duration for the individual but would lead to a sharper impact of recession on the overall outflow rate from long-term unemployment. Hence, even under pure heterogeneity, this would lead to a growth in the duration of unemployment greater in proportion than the fall in g.

To see why this is so, we note that the weaker brethren form a higher proportion of the unemployed stock than they do of new entrants. If the 'effectiveness' of the stock is to fall more than the 'effectiveness' of the new entrants, the weaker brethren must be affected by the downturn in greater proportion than the stronger brethren.

One can readily check whether the time-series data are consistent with (6.5), using the time series for exit rates at each duration. For if there is heterogeneity, the long-duration unemployed are of lower quality and hence, if (6.5) is right, should be more affected by changes in the ratio of V/U (that determines g).

Figures 6.2 and 6.3 show exit rates for unemployed people at different durations. As can be seen from Figure 6.2, the exit rates all fell between the late 1960s and the late 1970s and again between the late 1970s and the mid-1980s. Figure 6.3 shows a more disaggregated picture of exit rates since 1979. Leaving aside the '3+' category in Figure 6.2, where there have been enormous changes in the average duration of unemployment of those within the category, when one compares the proportionate falls at different durations it is rather striking how similar they are. But to make matters more precise, we proceed to regression analysis of the determinants of the outflow rates.

In the regression analysis we need to control for another implication of heterogeneity. This is that a fall in g raises the average quality of the unemployed at each duration. We have already explained why this is so under pure heterogeneity if $p_i = \theta_i g$, and it is also the case under pure heterogeneity if [6] $p_i = \theta_i g^{\alpha_i}(1/\alpha_i)$. It is also the case with some heterogeneity and some state-dependence, on reasonable assumptions. [7] Thus, when the proportions of entrants who survive to a given duration is higher, the quality of the survivors is also higher. In explaining duration-specific exit rates, we therefore have to control for changes in the quality of the survivors, as indicated by changes in the rate of survival to that duration.

We therefore estimate for each duration category (d) the following time-series equation:

$$\ln\left(\frac{A}{U}\right)_{d,t} = a_{0d} + a_{1d} \ln\left(\frac{V}{U}\right)_t + a_{2d} \ln S_{dt}$$
$$+ a_{3d}t + \text{seasonals}, \qquad d = 1, \ldots, D$$

where S_d is the ratio of numbers unemployed at that duration to numbers unemployed for 0–3 months the relevant number of periods earlier. [8] A is the outflow during the quarter, and V and U are measured at the beginning of the quarter, thus avoiding problems of simultaneity.

To explain by *pure* heterogeneity the historical falls in A/U relative to $(A/U)_N$ on the basis of (6.5), we should require that *the coefficient a_1 rise steadily* as we move from the equations for lower to those for higher durations. And on any hypothesis that included *some* heterogeneity we should expect to find a *positive coefficient a_2 on the log survival rate*.[9] If a_2 did not turn out significant, we should consider this as evidence against the importance of heterogeneity.

5   EVIDENCE FROM REGRESSIONS

What do we find? There is no tendency for the effect of the V/U ratio to be higher for the long-duration (and lower-quality unemployed. And the survival rate has an unreliable effect. Hence there is certainly no support for pure heterogeneity.

These findings are in Table 6.2. The equation is estimated on quarterly data ending in 1988(IV). The first block of regressions begins in 1968(IV), the second in 1976(II) and the third in 1979(III), since when a finer division of long-term unemployment is possible. Each block of regressions is estimated by SURE and is free of first-order serial correlation (see Table 6.2(b)).[10]

The long-run elasticity of exit rates with respect to the V/U ratio is shown in the right-hand column of the table. The results are similar whichever period we look at, and indeed the Chow test suggests no structural instability in the equation over time. In each period the elasticity of exit rates to the V/U ratio is rather below average at the long durations, the opposite of the effect required if (6.5) is to explain why A/U has fallen relative to $(A/U)_N$. The same pattern is found if the equations are re-estimated without a time trend. But, apart from this, there is no clear pattern in the results. It is true that the Wald test for identity of the long-run coefficients is satisfied only for the whole period and not for the two more recent sub-periods (Table 6.2(b)). There is thus some support for the common-sense multiplicative effect in (6.1). To the extent that there are systematic differences in the coefficients $\partial \ln p / \partial \ln (V/U)$, it is clear that they do not have the pattern that could explain the fall of $(A/U)/(A/U)_N$ if there were no state-dependence.

Thus, however, we view the time-series evidence, it supports the existence of some state-dependence. Moreover, turning to the effects of the survival rate (S), these are unreliable, and almost always insignificant, at both short and long durations.

We do not, therefore, find any evidence in support of (6.5), nor do the results on the survival rate support the existence of heterogeneity of any sort. We know there is *some* heterogeneity, but as a first approximation we suggest the following explanation of the fall in $(A/U)/(A/U)_N$.

Table 6.2(a) Regressions to explain exit rates, 1968(IV)–1988(III) dependent variable: $\ln (A/U)_d - \ln (A/U)_{d-1}$

Period	Duration	ln (V/U)	ln S_d	ln $(A/U)_{d,-1}$	$t/100$	se	LR coefficient on ln (V/U)
1968(IV) - 1988(IV)*	0–1	0.06 (2.1)	−0.16 (1.3)	−0.48 (5.0)	0.002 (0.02)	0.088	0.125
	1–2	0.09 (2.8)	−0.005 (0.03)	−0.73 (7.9)	−0.21 (2.2)	0.115	0.123
	2–3	0.15 (3.8)	0.16 (1.5)	−0.72 (9.7)	−0.09 (0.8)	0.147	0.208
	3+	(0.08) (1.7)	−0.15 (0.9)	−1.09 (10.1)	−0.34 (0.9)	0.245	0.073
1976(II) - 1988(IV)	0–1	0.07 (1.8)	−0.18 (0.6)	−0.49 (3.5)	0.10 (0.6)	0.102	0.143
	1–2	0.15 (3.6)	−0.25 (1.6)	−0.95 (7.7)	−0.48 (3.2)	0.103	0.158
	2–3	0.24 (5.3)	0.08 (0.7)	−0.87 (8.4)	−0.22 (1.5)	0.109	0.276
	3+	0.12 (2.2)	−0.24 (1.5)	−0.88 (6.5)	−0.08 (0.2)	0.162	0.136
1979(III) - 1988(III)	0–1	0.04 (0.9)	−0.67 (2.3)	−0.78 (5.8)	0.54 (2.6)	0.097	0.051
	1–2	0.14 (3.3)	−0.22 (1.4)	−1.07 (8.8)	−0.41 (2.2)	0.099	0.130
	2–3	0.24 (5.6)	0.26 (2.8)	−0.83 (8.7)	−0.15 (0.8)	0.102	0.289
	3–4	0.14 (4.3)	0.12 (1.4)	−0.64 (5.8)	−0.87 (4.7)	0.078	0.218
	4–8	0.24 (3.8)	0.08 (1.1)	−0.76 (7.4)	0.64 (2.1)	0.145	0.315
	8+	0.13 (3.3)	0.12 (1.7)	−0.52 (5.0)	−0.14 (0.4)	0.094	0.250

Notes:
Each block is estimated by SURE. The results are similar to those of OLS. *t*-statistics in brackets.
* Statistics for split after 1976(I) for these four equations are: 0.85, 1.05, 1.29, 1.37; $F_{0.05}$ (51, 81) = 1.55. (Calculations prepared on OLS estimates.)

Table 6.2(b) Tests on regressions, 1968(IV)–1988(III)

Period	LM test for serial correlations	Wald test for identical coefficients
1968(IV)–1988(IV)	0.68; $\chi^0_{0.05}$ (4) = 9.5	6.02; $\chi^2_{0.05}$ (3) = 7.8
1976(II)–1988(IV)	5.11; $\chi^2_{0.05}$ (4) = 9.5	8.04; $\chi^2_{0.05}$ (3) = 7.8
1979(III)–1988(III)	1.26; $\chi^2_{0.05}$ (6) = 12.6	28.05; $\chi^2_{0.05}$ (5) = 11.7

6 INTERPRETING THE TIME SERIES

We begin by noting the stability in the relative exit rates at different durations (see Figures 6.2 and 6.3). This suggests that, as a first approximation to understanding the time series, we can ignore heterogeneity and write the exit rate for each duration d as:

$$\left(\frac{A}{U}\right)_{d,t} = c_d g_t \tag{6.6}$$

It follows that the aggregate exit rate in period t is

$$\left(\frac{A}{U}\right)_t = \sum f_{d,t} c_d g_t = \bar{c}_t g_t \tag{6.7}$$

Since the exit rate for new entrants is

$$\left(\frac{A}{U}\right)_{Nt} = c_N g_t$$

the ratio $(A/U)/(A/U)_N$ is given by

$$\frac{(A/U)_t}{(A/U)_{Nt}} = \frac{\bar{c}_t}{c_N}$$

After an economic downturn in which g falls, the proportion of long-term unemployed rises and $\bar{c}$ falls. But c_N remains unchanged. So the overall exit rate falls relative to the exit rate of new entrants.

To see how well this account stands up, we need to construct an index of $\bar{c}_t/c_N$. (6.6) implies that the ratio of the individual c_d is the same in every year, and if this were true it would not matter which year we select to provide the weights for our index. We have actually used 1984, so that we compute $\bar{c}_t/c_N$ as

$$\frac{\bar{c}_t}{c_N} = \frac{\bar{c}_t g_{84}}{c_N g_{84}} = \frac{\sum f_{d,t} c_d g_{84}}{c_N g_{84}} = \frac{\sum f_{d,t} (A/U)_{d,84}}{(A/U)_{N,84}}$$

Thus, we use as fixed weights the duration specific exit rates for 1984 but allow the proportion of the unemployed in each duration to vary from period to period.[11]

The result is shown in column (4) of Table 6.1. As can be seen, the index is by definition equal to the observed ratio of $(A/U)/(A/U)_N$ in 1984. In any other year it could take any value. But in fact, it tracks the movement of the relative exit rates very well. The altered duration structure is clearly the main factor explaining the change in relative exit rates. Thus, even though we accept that there is *some* heterogeneity, we can understand the broad time-series movement of exit rates without worrying about it.

Finally, we can use the model of (6.7), where $g_t = g(V/\bar{c}U, 1)_t$, to explain the fall in the overall exit rate from unemployment. Taking a log-linear approximation, the overall exit rate (A/U) is explained by

$$\ln\left(\frac{A}{U}\right) = b_1 \ln\left(\frac{V}{U}\right) + (1 - b_1)\ln\bar{c} + b_2 t + \text{seasonals}$$

Estimating this with the lagged dependent variable on quarterly observations over the whole period (1968(IV)–1988(IV)), and without restricting the coefficient on $\bar{c}$, we find[12]

$$\ln\left(\frac{A}{U}\right) = \underset{(6.6)}{0.19}\ln\left(\frac{V}{U}\right) + \underset{(1.8)}{0.33}\ln\bar{c} + \underset{(2.7)}{0.33}\ln\left(\frac{A}{U}\right)_{-1} \tag{6.8}$$

$$- \underset{(3.7)}{0.65}\frac{t}{100} + \text{seasonals}$$

$$\text{se} = 0.083; \qquad LM = 0.08(F_{0.05}(1.70) = 4.0)$$

This gives a long-run relationship

$$\ln\left(\frac{A}{U}\right) = 0.28\ln\left(\frac{V}{U}\right) + 0.49\ln\bar{c} - 0.97\frac{t}{100} + \text{seasonals}$$

The Wald test that $(0.28 + 0.49 - 1)$ is zero gives 1.37 $(\chi^2_{0.05}(1) = 3.84)$, consistent with the assumption of constant returns to scale. The elasticity with respect to the V/U ratio is of the same order as that of 0.3 estimated by Pissarides (1986). But we now have an important additional explanation of the fall in A/U coming from the growth of long-term unemployment. Again, re-estimating the equation without the time trend yields essentially similar results, although now the coefficient on $\bar{c}$ is larger (0.89) and statistically significant

($t = 3.3$); but the equation now rejects the Wald test for the sum of coefficients being equal to one (constant returns to scale).

The preceding analysis counts in the outflow from unemployment in a quarter all those who leave, whether they were unemployed or not at the beginning of the quarter. In the Appendix we exclude those who enter and leave during the quarter (A_T). The restricted exit rate ($A - A_T$)/U can be even better explained by the method we have been following, and the restriction on the coefficient of $\ln \bar{c}$ is again easily satisfied.

7   CONCLUSION

To conclude, we have tested whether the time series are consistent with pure heterogeneity. On reasonable assumptions, pure heterogeneity would imply that, if the exit rate of new entrants fell by a given multiple, the overall exit rate for unemployment should fall by the same multiple. In fact, over the last twenty years the overall exit rate has fallen by 60 per cent more than the exit rate of new entrants. A test based on different assumptions also fails to support pure heterogeneity. Hence we explain the overall fall in UK exit rates from unemployment by the combined effect of (1) a fall in the ratio of vacancies to unemployed, and (2) a higher proportion of the unemployed being long-term unemployed, and hence demoralized and stigmatized in the eyes of employers.[13]

Appendix

Those who leave unemployment in a quarter A consist of

A_T those who enter and leave unemployment during the quarter (T is for transients);
A_d those already unemployed at the beginning of the quarter for d complete quarters, who then leave during the quarter ($d = 0, 1, \ldots$).

It follows that

$$A = A_T + \sum_d A_d$$

The best evidence we have on the outflow rate of new entrants comes from comparing A_T with the total number of people from which it is drawn – namely the total inflow (I) into unemployment during the quarter. Clearly, A_T/I is not a simple exit rate but is a variable that moves with the exit rate. As it happens, A_T/I has moved over the period in close proportion to A_0/U_0, where A_0 are those unemployed for under three months at the beginning of the quarter and who leave unemployment in the following three months.[14] Thus, in index number form we proxy $(A/U)_N$ by A_T/I.

Turning to the construction of the duration-index, we know that

$$\frac{A}{U} \equiv \frac{A_T}{U} + \sum \left(\frac{A_d}{U_d}\right)\left(\frac{U_d}{U}\right)$$

The index $\bar{c}_t/c_N$ is constructed as follows. First we note that

$$\left(\frac{A}{U}\right)_{84} \equiv \left(\frac{A_T}{I}\right)_{84}\left(\frac{I}{U}\right)_{84} + \sum \left(\frac{A_d}{U_d}\right)_{84}\left(\frac{U_d}{U}\right)_{84}$$

Then we construct the index $\bar{c}_t$ as

$$\bar{c}_t = \left(\frac{A_T}{I}\right)_{84}\left(\frac{I}{U}\right)_t + \sum \left(\frac{A_d}{U_d}\right)_{84}\left(\frac{U_d}{U}\right)_t$$

while

$$C_N = \left(\frac{A_N}{U_N}\right)_{84}$$

The duration categories for which exit rates are available are as follows (quarters completed):

1969(I)–1979(I): 0, 1, 2, 3+ (i.e. 4 categories),
1979(II)–1983(I): 0, 1, 2, 3, 4, 5, 6–7, 8+ (i.e. 8 categories),
1983(II)–1985(IV): 0, 1, 2, 3, 4, 5, 6–7, 8–11, 12–15, 16+ (i.e. 10 categories).

Explaining Unemployment

We then construct the following indices:

$\bar{c}_4$ (using 4 categories) for the period 1969(I) onwards,
$\bar{c}_8$ (using 8 categories) for the period 1979(II) onwards,
$\bar{c}_{10}$ (using 10 categories) for the period 1983(II) onwards

The final index ($\bar{c}$) equals

for 1983(II)–1985(IV): $\bar{c}_{10}$

for 1979(II)–1983(II): $\bar{c}_8 \frac{\bar{c}_{10}(1983\mathrm{II})}{\bar{c}_8(1983\mathrm{II})}$

for 1969(I)–1979(I): $\bar{c}_4 \frac{\bar{c}_8(1979\mathrm{II})}{\bar{c}_4(1979\mathrm{II})} \frac{\bar{c}_{10}(1983\mathrm{II})}{\bar{c}_8(1983\mathrm{II})}$

Clearly, we do not have all the information that we should like in order to analyse duration-specific flows. Ideally, we should know the weekly exit rates at each duration – and in particular for very new entrants. Instead, the data on for example A_0/U_0 tell us the 13-week exit rate of those who at the beginning of the 13 weeks had been unemployed for under 13 weeks and therefore left unemployment after anywhere between 0 and 26 weeks. This is why we have taken the exit rate of new entrants as proportional to A_T/I, these leavers being closer to the point of entry to unemployment. But A_T/I is strictly proportional to the relevant weekly exit rate only if the weekly exit rates are small. However, one cannot compute the weekly exit rate of any new entrants unless one assumes that the weekly exit rate is constant (or has some specific form) over the first 13 weeks. Any assumption here would be arbitrary. If we do assume the weekly exit rate to be constant over the first 13 weeks, we still find that $(A/U)(A/U)_N$ has fallen substantially over the period (by one-third).

Sources
I_t Inflow of males excluding school-leavers, using 1988 definition of unemployment (Department of Employment)
U_t Stock of males aged 18 and over (Department of Employment)
U_{dt} Department of Employment data disaggregated by duration according to the procedure described in Haskel (1987)
A_t $I_t - (U_{t+1} - U_t)$
A_{Tt} $I_t - U_{0,t+1}$ where U_0 is those unemployed for less than 1 quarter
A_{dt} $U_{dt} - U_{d+1,t+1}$
V_t *Department of Employment Gazette*, adjusted as in Jackman *et al.* (1989)

Notes

1. For confirmatory evidence see e.g. (6.8). Note that our formulation allows for the possibility that, when V/U changes, this affects the search intensity of each individual in equal proportion. In this case, c_i is the exogenous component of search intensity.

2. We investigate the assumption of constant returns to scale below. For further confirmatory evidence see Pissarides (1986), Jackman *et al.* (1987).

3. The average search effectiveness of those unemployed at a given duration rises, but the proportion of the stock who are at longer durations also rises, and the search effectiveness of those at the longer durations is always lower than at the shorter durations.

4. For details see Appendix (p. 137).

5. This could be the case e.g. if matching depended only on vacancies and effective job-seekers, but the intensity of job search responded more to (V/U) for those with lower c_i.

6. In the case where g has a non-proportional effect, it is convenient to rescale c_i so that, at $g = \bar{g}$, $p_i = c_i/\alpha_i$. Thus,

$$1 - p_i = 1 - \frac{c_i}{\alpha_i}\left(\frac{g}{\bar{g}}\right)^{\alpha_i}$$

and

$$-\frac{d\log(1 - p_t)}{dg} = \frac{1}{1 - p_i}\frac{c_i}{g}$$

which is increasing in c_i.

7. For example, the assumption that the duration-effect is the same multiple for each type of labour, e.g.

$$c_i = \theta_i\lambda(d_i)$$

8. If the category d is wider than one quarter, we aggregate those unemployed for 0–1 quarters in the relevant number of different earlier periods. For those currently unemployed 0–1 quarters, we measure S_d as the ratio of their number to the inflow during the previous quarter.

9. There is no obvious reason why the effects should be greater or smaller at different durations. A fall in g changes the quality of the long-term unemployed more than it changes that of the short-term unemployed, but it is not clear that the change in quality per unit change in survivor rate is greater or less at high durations.

10. The test is for first-order serial correlation between current and lagged errors *within* each equation. Note that SURE allows for correlation of current errors between equations.

11. For detailed construction of the index, see Appendix.

12. Estimates of a similar function for nine regions confirms the robustness of this equation (Jackman *et al.*, 1987).

13. For earlier discussions of these time-series issues see Budd *et al.* (1988), Pissarides (1986), Layard and Nickell (1987) and Haskel and Jackman (1988).

14.   For example, we have

	1969	1979	1984
A_T/I	241	152	100
A_0/U_0	176	138	100

References

Budd, A., P. Levine and P. Smith (1988) 'Unemployment, Vacancies and the Long-term Unemployed', *Economic Journal*, 98, 1071–91.

Flinn, C. and J. Heckman (1983) 'Are Unemployment and Out of the Labor Force Behaviorally Distinct Labor Force States?', *Journal of Labor Economics*, 1, 28–42.

Haskel, J.E. (1987) 'Notes on a Consistent Series for Unemployment', Centre for Labour Economics, LSE, *Working Paper*, 977.

Haskel, J.E. and R. Jackman (1988) 'Long-term Unemployment and the Effects of the Community Programme', *Oxford Bulletin of Economics and Statistics*, 50, 379–408.

Heckman, J. and G.J. Borjas (1980) 'Does Unemployment Cause Future Unemployment? Definitions, Questions and Answers for a Continuous-time Model of Heterogeneity and State Dependence', *Economica*, 47, 247–83.

Jackman, R., R. Layard and C. Pissarides (1989) 'On Vacancies', *Oxford Bulletin of Economics and Statistics*, 51, 377–94, Chapter 5 in this volume.

Jackman, R., R. Layard and S. Savouri (1987) 'Labour Market Mismatch and the "Equilibrium" level of Unemployment', *Working Paper*, 1009 (October).

Layard, R. and S. Nickell (1987) 'The Labour Market', in R. Dornbusch and R. Layard (eds), *The Performance of the British Economy* (Oxford: Oxford University Press), Chapter 4 in this volume.

Narendranathan, W., S. Nickell and J. Stern (1985) 'Unemployment Benefits Revisited', *Economic Journal*, 95, 307–29.

Pissarides, C. (1986) 'Unemployment and Vacancies in Britain', *Economic Policy*, 3, 499–559.

Pissarides, C. and J. Haskel (1987) 'Long-term Unemployment', *Working Paper*, LSE, 983 (October).

7 Mismatch: A Framework for Thought (1990)*

with R. Jackman and S. Savouri

As everybody knows, unemployment rates differ widely between occupations and between regions, as well as across age, race and (sometimes) sex groups. The striking thing is how stable these differences are. In all countries unskilled people have much higher unemployment rates than skilled people. Similarly, youths have higher rates than adults. In addition in most countries (though not the United States) regional differences are highly persistent – with unemployment always above average, for example, in the North of England and the South of Italy.

The first task is to document these differences (in section 1) and then to explain them (in section 2). An obvious question is why occupational and geographical mobility does not eliminate the differences between unemployment rates in different occupations and different regions. We attempt to answer this question. Our main focus is thus on the *persistent* imbalance between the supply and demand for labour across skill groups, regions and age groups. But there are additional imbalances which are *temporary*. Suppose, for example, that there are two occupations which have the same average unemployment rate over time but in one year demand shifts from one occupation to the other; this will produce a temporary imbalance until corrected.[1] Such 'one-off' structural shocks have aroused great interest in relation to the issue of real business cycles (see Lilien, 1982). They are also clearly of interest to the unemployed themselves. But they account for a fairly small fraction of the inequality among unemployment rates observed in the average year. In any event our framework encompasses both kinds of phenomena (since both reflect imbalances between the demand and supply of labour) and we shall refer to both by the generic title 'mismatch'.

---

* Chapter 2 in F. Padoa Schioppa (ed.), *Mismatch and Labour Mobility* (Cambridge: Cambridge University Press for the CEPR, 1990), pp. 44–101.

The authors are grateful to George Johnson for comments and discussions and for goading us to collect data; we are grateful to J. Hassan, B. Kan, U. Lee, R. Moghadam, M. Sadler and J. Schmitt for helping collect them. We also thank O. Blanchard, P. Diamond, S. Nickell and K. Roberts for helpful discussions and Joanne Putterford for wonderful typing.

The next question is how the *structure* of unemployment rates is related to the *average* level of unemployment. Many people in Europe attribute the rise in unemployment to increased imbalances between the pattern of labour demand and supply – in other words, to greater mismatch. The question is: have exogenous forces raised average unemployment by changing the structure of unemployment rates? To answer this question we need to develop a relevant measure of mismatch, consistent with our overall framework of explanation. We develop the theory in section 3, while in section 4 we offer empirical evidence in support of our framework. The general conclusion is that, while mismatch is a serious problem, it has not in most countries increased over time.

Since the structure of unemployment is related to the average level of unemployment, what (if anything) should be done to alter the structure? The standard recipes are to shift demand towards the sectors with high unemployment rates, and to shift supply away from them. As we show in section 5, this must be right when supply is effectively exogenous. However, the more elastic supply becomes, the less strong is the case for intervention – except where standard externality arguments apply. These externality arguments may indeed be important, so that jobs should be shifted towards less-congested regions and people should be shifted into high-skilled occupations.

Thus far the discussion of mismatch has been entirely in terms of differences in employment rates – i.e. in the ratio between total labour demand and total labour supply. But it is also instructive to look at intergroup difference in the ratio of vacancies to unemployment – i.e. in the ratio of *excess* labour demand to *excess* labour supply. We explore this in section 6 and ask how a mismatch of this kind affects the location of the aggregate u/v curve.

We ought at this point to issue a health warning. Despite its obvious importance, the topic of mismatch has so far been subject to remarkably little rigorous analysis.[2] The propositions of this study are therefore particularly exploratory.

1 THE STRUCTURE OF UNEMPLOYMENT: SOME FACTS

1.1 Occupational differences

The most striking difference in unemployment rates is between skill groups. In Britain and the United States the unemployment rate of semi-skilled and unskilled workers is over four times that of professional and managerial workers (see Tables 7.1 and 7.2). A simple measure of the dispersion of the unemployment rates is the coefficient of variation (using relative labour forces as weights). For reasons given in section 3 we use as our fundamental measure of mismatch the square of this – in other words the *variance of relative*

Table 7.1 Unemployment by occupation: Britain, 1985

	Rates (%)			% of unemployed		
	Men	Women	All	Men	Women	All
Professional and managerial	2.9	4.8	3.3	7	6	7
Other non-manual	5.9	6.8	6.7	10	48	23
Skilled manual	11.3	8.0	10.9	41	8	29
Semi-skilled manual (incl. personal services)	19.1	11.5	15.0	28	36	31
Unskilled manual	28.5	3.2	17.0	14	2	10
All	11.2	8.8	10.2	100	100	100
var $\left(\dfrac{u_i}{u}\right)$	44%	10%	22%			

Notes:
1. Unemployment is classified by occupation in last job.
2. The unemployment rate in an occupation is the number unemployed who were previously in an occupation relative to the numbers employed plus unemployed. Since many of the unemployed have never worked or do not record previous occupation, the national unemployment rate ('all') exceeds the mean of the occupational unemployment rates.
3. In calculating var(u_i/u), u is the mean of the occupation-specific unemployment rates.

Source: *General Household Survey.*

unemployment rates (var u_i/u). In Britain the variance across occupations was 22 per cent in 1985, much the same as in the United States.

In Table 7.3 we provide data for other countries (but with no skill breakdown of manual workers). Focusing on the ratio between manual and non-manual employment rates, the striking thing is how long this is in Germany (a result of their training system?).

Over time the pattern of occupational unemployment rates is remarkably stable, as revealed by the correlation between the rates in the mid-1970s and mid-1980s (see Table 7.4). But has the *spread* altered? The answer is that in no country except Sweden is there any evidence of increased mismatch since the late 1970s, though in the United States there is some evidence of increased occupational imbalance since the early 1970s.

Table 7.2   Unemployment by occupation: United States, 1987

	Rates (%)			% of unemployment		
	Men	Women	All	Men	Women	All
Professional and managerial	2.2	2.4	2.3	10	11	10
Other non-manual	3.7	4.7	4.3	13	40	25
Skilled manual	6.0	6.4	6.1	22	3	14
Personal services	7.5	7.8	7.7	13	28	19
Semi- and unskilled manual	9.3	9.9	9.4	43	19	32
All	6.2	6.2	6.2	100	100	100
$var(u_i/u)$	24%	19%	21%			

Notes: See Table 7.1.
Source: *Employment and Earnings* (January 1988), p. 170.

The next question is: where do the occupational differences in unemployment rates come from? Are they due to differences in duration or in inflow rates? As a broad generalization, mismatch stems more from differences in inflow rates than in duration. This is certainly true of occupational differences (see Table 7.5). Unemployment is highest in those occupations which have high general turnover.

Closely related to difference in occupational unemployment rates are differences in educational unemployment rates. Since education (unlike occupation) is a characteristic of a person, these rates are in many ways more meaningful. However, except in the United States and Britain, it is difficult to find time series data on these rates, so we confine ourselves here to the snapshot of Table 7.6. This confirms the much greater problems experienced in most countries by people without good academic or vocational qualifications.

1.2   Region

Unemployment rates also differ greatly between and within regions. But the regional differences are much less than the occupational differences (see Table 7.7 and 7.8). For example in Britain the variance of relative unemployment rate across 10 regions is only about 6 per cent, compared with a

Table 7.3 Unemployment rate by occupation: various countries, 1987

	United States	Australia[a]	Austria	Canada	Finland	Germany[b]	Ireland	New Zealand	Norway	Spain	Sweden
Professional and technical[c]	2.2	2.0	2.7	4.7	1.8	6.5	3.2	1.7	0.7	6.1	1.2
Administrative and managerial	2.6	2.1	0.9	4.5	–	4.3	3.7	1.0	0.2	2.9	–
Clerical and related	4.2	3.3	3.8	7.4	2.5	–	6.0	2.8	1.2	8.2	1.0
Sales	4.9	5.0	4.5	6.7	4.0	8.6	8.6	3.6	1.3	7.5	1.8
Service	7.7	6.1	8.4	11.6	4.1	6.6	9.7	3.9	1.6	13.0	3.2
Agriculture	7.1	3.8	1.7	10.0	2.7	3.2	2.54	5.0	0.7	13.2	2.8
Other manual	8.0	6.2	6.2	10.9	7.1	10.2	18.2	5.3	2.3	13.7	2.1
Average of above	5.4	4.5	4.8	8.2	4.0	7.4	9.3	3.7	1.4	11.4	1.7
All	6.2	8.0	4.7	8.9	5.0	7.5	17.7	4.1	1.5	20.5	1.9
Ratio of manual to non-manual unemployment rate	2.27	1.94	1.82	1.88	2.29	1.49	2.26	2.01	2.19	1.88	2.03
var(u_i/u) (%)	18.5	15.0	19.9	11.2	28.1	11.4	45.1	14.9	25.3	7.2	16.7

Notes:
[a] Australia (1986).
[b] Germany (1985).
[c] Occupational classifications according to International Standard Occupational Classification. The first 4 categories are treated as non-manual.
See notes to Table 7.1.
Source: ILO, *Year Book* (1988).

Table 7.4 Dispersion of occupational unemployment rates, 1973–87 var(u_i/u) (%)

Year	United Kingdom (5)[a]	United States (7)	Australia (7)	Canada (7)	Germany (6)	Spain (7)	Sweden (8)
1973		13.1					9.0
1974	23.3	15.1					9.6
1975	14.0	20.2		12.3			7.6
1976	20.5	14.0		9.2	8.8	15.2	12.1
1977	21.0	12.3	13.8	10.7		15.7	12.5
1978	16.2	12.4	18.4	9.5	9.1	16.4	12.4
1979	24.4	15.2	14.3	10.9		19.7	12.8
1980	20.4	22.7	15.1	12.4	9.1	20.6	12.4
1981	21.2	21.1	17.2	13.3		20.0	15.9
1982	21.4	*25.1*	17.4	15.1	16.9	21.4	17.4
1983	22.8	21.5	25.7	13.6		21.1	15.9
1984	20.5	19.9	22.2	11.2	14.1	16.7	*1.2.1*
1985	22.3	20.6	*19.7*	11.3	11.4	12.9	*13.3*
1986		20.6	15.0	10.8		*11.1*	*16.6*
1987		18.5		11.2		7.2	16.7
Correlation between first and last years	0.87	–	0.92	0.95	0.86	1.00	0.83

Ratio of manual to non-manual unemployment rates

Year	United Kingdom (5)[a]	United States (7)	Australia (7)	Canada (7)	Germany (6)	Spain (7)	Sweden (8)
1973		1.80					1.74
1974	1.76	1.93					1.78
1975	1.74	2.18		1.89			1.65
1976	2.13	1.94		1.71	1.04	2.08	1.91
1977	2.12	1.85	1.68	1.78		2.14	1.93
1978	1.78	1.85	2.16	1.70	1.18	1.95	2.04
1979	2.27	2.04	1.97	1.80		1.99	2.02
1980	2.34	2.46	1.97	1.92	1.27	2.04	1.96

Table 7.4 Continued

Year	United Kingdom $(5)^a$	United States (7)	Australia (7)	Canada (7)	Germany (6)	Spain (7)	Sweden (8)
1981	2.41	2.39	1.86	1.97		1.98	2.25
1982	2.53	2.58	2.14	2.04	1.69	1.86	2.34
1983	2.57	2.46	2.36	1.97		1.75	2.22
1984	2.20	2.38	2.46	1.86	1.60	1.99	1.95
1985	2.45	2.42	2.14	1.87	1.49	1.91	1.85
1986		2.41	1.93	1.86		2.00	1.98
1987		2.27		1.88		1.88	2.02

Notes:
^{a} Numbers in brackets are numbers of categories (See Table 7.1).
Sources:
United Kingdom: *General Household Survey* (breakdown as in Table 7.1).
Others: ILO, *Year Book* (1988) (breakdown as in Table 7.3, which amalgamates skilled and non-skilled manual workers).
United States: *Employment and Earnings* uses even more different classifications before and after 1983, but the trend in each subperiod is as shown above.

variance of 21 per cent across 5 occupations. Only when one gets down to travel-to-work areas do major geographical differences emerge. Across Britain's 322 travel-to-work areas the variance of relative unemployment rates is 24 per cent. But in the United States, even when we go to the 51 'states', the variance is still only about 8 per cent.

Turning to the variance in other countries, we provide comparable data in Table 7.9. These show the high persistence of regional differences in some countries (Italy, the United Kingdom, Japan, Germany) and the total absence of persistence in the United States and Australia. Thus, while the correlation coefficient of the mid-1970s and the mid-1980s, unemployment rates across British region is 0.92, across the US states it is −0.33.

How has dispersion altered? In no country is there any important increase since the mid-1970s, and in Britain it is now markedly lower than in the early 1970s. As regards the cyclical pattern of mismatch, we have investigated this only for Britain. The figures are plotted in Figure 7.1a and show a clear tendency for regional mismatch to fall in downturns and rise in upturns. In

Table 7.5 Unemployment by occupation: inflow and duration, 1984 and 1987

	Britain (1984)			United States (1987)		
	Inflow rate (% per month) (S/N)	Average duration (months) (U/S)	Unemployment rate (%) (U/L)	Inflow rate (% per month) (S/N)	Average duration (months) (U/S)	Unemployment rate (%) (U/L)
Professional and managerial	0.50	11.2	5.3	0.74	3.0	2.3
Clerical	0.88	10.1	8.0	1.58	2.6	4.3
Other non-manual	1.14	11.8	12.2	1.97	2.9	6.1
Skilled manual	1.02	14.2	12.6	2.96	2.4	7.7
Personal services						
Other manual	1.32	14.1	15.5	2.84	3.0	9.4
All	0.94	12.8	10.8	2.23	2.6	6.2

Note: The sources listed below provide data on *L, N, U* and *S* (inflow). These are then used to produce 'steady-state' estimates of duration. However the estimate of monthly inflow is an underestimate, comprising all those unemployed at a point in time who became unemployed in the previous month (it thus excludes those who enter and leave within a month). In Britain the numbers in the category on the *Labour Force Survey* (LFS) definition of unemployment are only 70% of those in their first month of benefit receipt. The *General Household Survey* is broadly consistent with the LFS.

Sources:

Britain: *Labour Force Survey* tapes. This records only previous occupation and industry for those unemployed under 3 years. The unemployment rate in each occupation is computed by taking the numbers unemployed less than 3 years who were previously employed in the stated occupation and raising it by the ratio of total unemployed to numbers of unemployed reporting their previous occupation. A similar procedure is done for those unemployed for under one month.

United States: *Employment and Earnings* (January 1988), p. 185.

Table 7.6 Unemployment rate by highest educational level, 1988, per cent

	Australia M	Australia F	Austria M	Austria F	Belgium M	Belgium F	Canada M	Canada F	Finland M	Finland F	Germany M	Germany F	Greece M	Greece F
Degree	2.6	5.5	0.8	2.4	3.2	7.7	3.4	5.5	1.2	0.7	3.0	6.9	4.2	12.7
Sub-degree	4.2	6.8	–	–	–	–	6.3	7.2	–	–	3.0	8.8	8.1	14.1
Vocational	4.7	–	3.1	3.1	–	–	–	–	–	–	5.9	8.2	–	–
Upper secondary	6.4	7.7	3.4	2.9	4.6	15.9	8.5	9.8	4.0	3.2	5.5	8.1	7.3	18.7
Other	9.5	7.8	5.5	4.9	9.0	22.4	11.2	12.7	9.2	5.6	14.4	12.9	3.9	6.2
All	6.3	7.3	3.5	3.7	6.9	17.4	7.9	9.0	7.4	4.6	6.9	9.4	4.8	9.9

	Italy M	Italy F	Netherlands M	Netherlands F	Norway M	Norway F	Spain M	Spain F	Sweden M	Sweden F	United Kingdom M	United Kingdom F	United States M	United States F
Degree	3.3	9.3	4.4	11.4	0.4	1.1	9.9	27.4	0.8	0.8	3.7	4.7	1.8	2.1
Sub-degree	–	–	4.3	10.7	–	–	11.3	21.8	1.4	0.8	–	–	4.3	3.6
Vocational	–	–	–	–	–	–	–	–	2.2	2.1	8.1	10.1	–	–
Upper secondary	9.2	20.0	4.8	10.3	1.1	2.4	18.8	33.7	1.4	1.5	7.7	7.0	6.7	5.4
Other	6.2	15.3	10.9	16.5	2.2	2.2	14.7	17.9	2.1	2.2	14.8	11.3	10.7	9.6
All	6.7	16.3	7.5	13.2	1.5	2.1	15.5	24.4	1.8	1.8	10.4	9.7	5.6	4.8

Note: 'Sub-degree' is some post-secondary education but not a degree (identified only in some countries). 'Vocational' includes any vocational qualification below a degree (identified only in some countries).
Source: OECD, Employment outlook (July 1989), pp. 85–6.

Table 7.7 Unemployment by region: Britain, summer 1988

	Inflow rate (% per month) (Inflow/N)	Average duration (months) (U/Outflow)	Unemployment rate (%) (U/L)
South East	0.80	5.7	5.3
East Anglia	0.83	4.7	4.9
South West	1.03	5.0	6.2
West Midlands	0.97	7.6	9.0
East Midlands	0.97	6.4	7.5
Yorkshire and Humberside	1.20	6.8	9.7
North West	1.30	7.2	10.9
North	1.47	7.0	12.2
Wales	1.40	6.2	10.6
Scotland	1.50	6.9	11.7
Total	1.07	6.4	8.0
var(X_i/X)	5.7%	2.0%	10.6%

Source: *Department of Employment Gazette* (October 1988), Table 2.23. The data do not relate to a steady state; the data relate to benefit recipients.

other words in a downturn unemployment rises proportionately more in the low-unemployment regions. Even so *employment* falls more *slowly* in the low-unemployment regions, bringing about substantial changes in the pattern of employment. To look at the degree of 'turbulence' in the pattern of regional employment we can compute $\frac{1}{2}\Sigma|\Delta(N_i/N)|$ indicating what fraction of all jobs in the economy have 'changed region'. This is plotted in Figure 7.1c, and shows a marked redistribution of employment during the 1979–81 downturn.

One naturally asks whether the problems of the 1980s can be attributed in general to a greater pace of change in the pattern of employment between regions. To answer this, we compute the regional turbulence index, $\frac{1}{2}\Sigma|\Delta(N_i/N)|$, for a number of countries. Table 7.10 gives averages of this for different decades. Only in Britain and the United States is the degree of turbulence any higher in the recent past then in the 1960s, and in Britain this turbulence was concentrated in the early 1980s.

Table 7.8   Unemployment by region: United States, 1988

	Unemployment rate (%)
New England (1)[a]	3.1
New York and New Jersey (2)	4.1
Middle Atlantic (3)	4.9
South East (4)	5.6
Central: North East (5)	6.0
Central: South West (6)	7.8
Central: North West (7)	4.9
Mountain (8)	5.8
Pacific (9)	5.3
North West (10)	6.2
Total	5.4
var(u_i/u)	4.1%

Note:
[a] Numbers in brackets are standard numbers for each region.
Source: *Employment and Earnings* (May 1989), Table 3.

1.3   Industrial differences

We can turn now to differences in industrial unemployment rates. These are a less well defined concept, for when industrial rates are computed, unemployed people are attributed to the industry in which they were last employed, and many eventually find employment elsewhere. As Table 7.11 shows, unemployment is well above average in construction, and in bad times manufacturing, too, gets hit. But durations are remarkably similar in all industries, with unemployment differences being due to different turnover rates.

The pattern of industrial unemployment rates is remarkably constant, as is shown in the correlations in Table 7.12. And there is no sign, except perhaps in Australia, that the dispersions have increased over time.

This does not mean that the process of industrial restructuring is not an important source of unemployment. As Table 7.13 shows, about 1 per cent of jobs 'change industry' each year. But, contrary to popular belief, there is no evidence that this process has been accelerating. People seem constantly to forget the massive restructurings of the past, such as the huge exodus from

Table 7.9 Dispersion of regional unemployment rates, 1974–87 var(u_i/u), per cent

Year	Australia (8)[a]	Canada (10)	France (22)	Germany (11)	Finland (12)	Italy (20)	Japan (20)	Sweden (24)	Britain (10)	United States (51)
1974	3.5	–	7.1	–	39.0	–	7.6	–	14.3	–
1975	3.1	7.1	3.9	–	26.4	–	4.1	–	7.2	–
1976	2.1	7.9	3.8	–	15.8	–	4.3	17.1	4.5	5.3
1977	1.5	8.5	3.5	3.6	16.6	14.3	7.2	14.6	4.9	4.4
1978	1.4	8.3	3.9	5.0	13.8	12.4	7.4	15.5	6.7	3.7
1979	2.0	9.3	4.0	6.6	13.1	12.5	7.1	11.7	8.8	3.9
1980	1.4	8.7	3.7	6.3	19.2	18.1	6.9	15.6	9.2	5.0
1981	2.9	10.4	3.2	4.9	22.4	13.1	5.9	16.4	6.6	5.6
1982	1.6	4.9	3.0	4.3	20.0	11.5	5.0	13.7	5.6	5.5
1983	0.8	3.2	3.1	4.2	16.9	9.3	5.9	10.4	5.4	5.2
1984	2.0	5.1	3.2	5.9	22.1	7.9	6.4	11.0	5.1	6.0
1985	2.6	7.1	2.8	7.3	23.5	9.7	6.6	11.6	5.0	5.1
1986	1.8	8.2	2.8	8.3	20.5	13.6	5.8	14.8	5.1	6.6
1987	2.8	9.5	2.8	–	18.8	19.6	5.4	14.5	6.3	7.8
Correlation between first and last years	–0.11	0.67	0.50	0.83	0.91	0.84	0.91	0.69	0.92	–0.33

Note: [a] Numbers in brackets are number of regions in the country.
Source: OECD, Regional Database on unemployment and labour force except for United Kingdom, which is based on Savouri (1989). UK data for 1967–73 are 12.8, 13.3, 14.9, 13.7, 14.3, 15.2, 17.5.

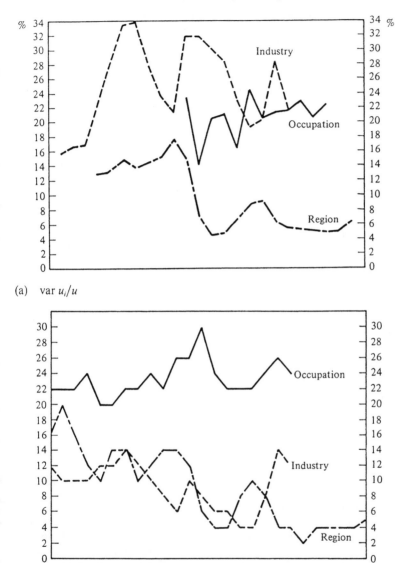

(a) var u_i/u

(b) u/v mismatch (see section 6)

Figure 7.1 (see p. 154)

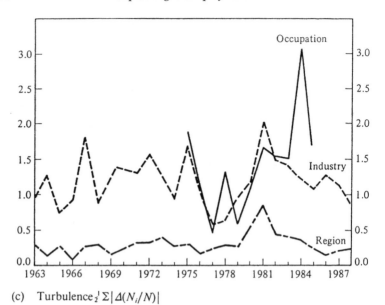

(c)   Turbulence $\frac{1}{2} \Sigma |\Delta(N_i/N)|$

Figure 7.1 Fluctuations in mismatch and turbulence: Britain, 1963–87 (shaded area = downturn)

Sources:
(a) Industry – ILO *Yearbook of Labour Statistics* (various issues).
    Regional – CSO, *Regional Trends and Regional Statistics* (various issues).
    Occupation – *General Household Survey* tapes.
(b) Jackman and Roper (1987), Table 2 updated using Department of
    Employment *Gazette*.
(c) Industry – See Figure 7.2.
    Regional – See Table 7.10 (p. 000).
    Occupation – *General Household Survey* tapes.

European agriculture in the 1950s and 1960s, which was accompanied by so little unemployment.

   In fact in most countries except the United States the rate of structural shift has been slowing down. And in Britain there is no difference between the level now and the mid-1960s, as Figure 7.1 shows. Both turbulence and industrial mismatch increase in downturns,[3] but in the late 1930s were at normal levels. Where there is a remarkable difference in both Britain and the United States is between the 1930s and the postwar period. As Figure 7.2 shows, there is every reason to think of 1930s unemployment as being due significantly to the 'problems of the declining industries'.

Table 7.10 Regional turbulence indices (averages of annual values)
$$\tfrac{1}{2}\Sigma|\Delta(N_i/N)|$$

		1960s	1970s	1980s
(E)EC	France (22)[a]	–	0.93	0.99
	Germany (11)	0.52	0.45	0.38
	Italy (20)	0.73	0.46	0.71
	United Kingdom (10)	0.23	0.28	0.37
	Australia (8)	0.49	0.48	0.51
	Canada (10)	0.51	0.46	0.53
	United States (10)	0.40	0.61	0.54
EFTA	Finland (12)	–	0.66	0.51
	Sweden (24)	–	0.35	0.50

Note: [a] Numbers in brackets are numbers of regions in the country.
Sources:
OECD, Regional Database on Labour Force and Unemployment except for the United States and United Kingdom.
United States: 1952–75: *Employment and Training Report to the President* (1982) Table D-1.
United Kingdom: 1975–88: US Bureau of Labour Statistics, *Employment and Earnings* (various issues).
  1951–68: Department of Employment and Productivity, *British Labour Statistics, Historical Abstract, 1886–1968* (London: HMSO, 1971), Table 131.
  1969–70: Central Statistical Office, *Regional Statistics*, 12 (London: HMSO, 1976), Table 8.1.
  1971–89: *Department of Employment Gazette, Historical Supplement No. 2*, 97 (11) (November 1989) Table 1.5.
Annual data available on request.

1.4 Age, race and sex

Unemployment is, of course, almost everywhere more common among young people than among adults (see Table 7.11). As so often, the difference results from higher inflow rates – and certainly not from unusual duration. The youth unemployment problem was accentuated in the 1980s by a big rise in the relative number of youths, reflecting the baby boom of the late 1950s and 1960s. In consequence, much more attention has been devoted to youth unemployment than to any other aspect (see, for example, successive issues of the OECD *Employment Outlook*). For this reason we shall concentrate mainly

Table 7.11 Unemployment by industry, age, race and sex, 1984 and 1987

	Britain (1984)			United States (1987)		
	Inflow rate (% per month) (S/N)	Average duration (months) (U/S)	Unemployment rate (%) (U/L)	Inflow rate (% per month) (S/N)	Average duration (months) (U/S)	Unemployment rate (%) (U/L)
Industry						
Agriculture	0.82	10.6	8.0	4.88	2.4	10.5
Manufacturing	0.88	16.6	12.7	2.06	3.1	6.0
Construction	1.57	12.7	16.6	4.52	2.9	11.6
Energy	0.76	10.1	7.1			
Services	0.90	11.6	9.4			
Transportation and public utilities				1.57	3.0	4.5
Distribution				2.96	2.5	6.9
Finance and service industries				2.08	2.5	4.9
Age						
16–19	3.33	8.5	22.1	10.15	2.0	16.9
20–24	1.33	15.3	16.9	4.46	2.4	9.7
25–54	0.74	13.1	8.8	1.76	3.0	5.0
55–64	0.47	19.2	8.3	0.97	3.7	3.5
Race						
White	0.92	12.6	10.4	2.15	2.6	5.3
Other	1.43	17.6	20.1	5.14	2.9	13.0
Sex						
Male	0.78	16.1	11.2	2.28	2.9	6.2
Female	1.17	9.7	10.2	2.87	2.3	6.2
All	0.94	12.8	10.8	2.54	2.6	6.2

Note: See Table 7.5 (p. 000).
Sources:
Britain: *Labour Force Survey* tapes, see Table 7.5.
United States: *Employment and Earnings* (January 1988) pp. 160, 166, 169, 170, 174, 175.

Table 7.12 Dispersion of industrial unemployment rates, 1973–87
var(u_i/u) (per cent)

	United Kingdom (9)[a]	United States (9)	Australia (7)	Canada (9)	Germany (9)	Spain (9)	Sweden (7)
1973	21.2	7.3					
1974	31.8	9.3	4.1				8.7
1975	31.8	15.3	5.7		17.6		5.1
1976	29.9	8.1	8.1	7.6	13.0	59.0	7.6
1977	28.3	6.1	8.9	9.8	12.0	60.3	2.7
1978	22.9	5.8	*11.9*	10.6	11.1	54.5	7.5
1979	19.1	5.8	8.3	8.9	11.3	57.2	3.7
1980	20.1	10.6	8.6	10.6	10.0	53.6	3.2
1981	28.2	9.4	9.6	8.3	9.5	48.6	6.2
1982	21.8	13.9	11.1	12.5	11.7	41.2	5.7
1983		11.0	24.3	12.7	10.4	37.2	4.7
1984		8.7	10.4	10.9	11.1	34.7	3.8
1985	8.8	*5.9*	9.2	12.3	26.5	*3.6*	
1986		9.9	9.1	8.3	11.7	*19.9*	5.2
1987		9.0	9.9	7.1	10.0	11.9	4.0
Correlation between first and last years	0.86	0.89	–	0.95	0.80	0.96	0.81

Note:
[a] Numbers of industrial sectors in brackets. Bars indicate breaks in the series.
Correlations are not calculated cross brackets.
Source: ILO, *Year Book* (1988).

on other dimensions of mismatch. We shall also say little about race differences (which are acute and reflect mainly inflow differences), nor about sex differences (which in most, but not all, countries are fairly small).

2 HOW THE STRUCTURE OF UNEMPLOYMENT IS DETERMINED

Why do unemployment rates differ across groups? In thinking about this, it is essential to distinguish between situations according to whether the labour

Explaining Unemployment

Table 7.13 Industrial turbulence indices (averages of annual values)
$$\tfrac{1}{2}\Sigma|\Delta(N_i/N)|$$

		1950s	1960s	1970s	1980s
(E)EC	Belgium (8)[a]	0.94	0.94	0.96	0.89
	France (8)	1.04	0.96	0.68	0.65
	Germany (8)	1.35	1.15	0.92	0.64
	Italy (8)	2.18	1.43	1.11	1.29
	Netherlands (8)	0.74	0.89	0.96	1.14
	Spain (8)	1.55	1.19	1.53	1.36
	United Kingdom (24/25)	0.91	1.12	1.17	1.27
	Australia (8)	–	1.76	1.21	1.40
	Canada (8)	–	–	0.83	0.90
	USA (8)	0.93	0.67	0.89	0.96
EFTA	Austria (8)	–	–	1.10	1.08
	Sweden (8)	–	1.45	1.52	0.67
	Switzerland (8)	–	0.90	0.99	0.50

Note: [a] Numbers of industrial sectors in brackets.
Source: OECD, *Labour Force Statistics* (various years) except for the United States and the United Kingdom. See also sources to Figure 7.2.

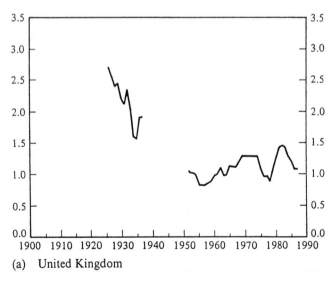

(a) United Kingdom

Figure 7.2 (see p. 159)

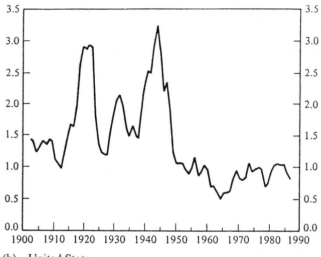

(b)   United States

Figure 7.2   Industrial turbulence index, 5-year moving average, 1900–90 $\frac{1}{2}\Sigma\,|\,\Delta(N_i/N)\,|$
Sources:

UK Industrial Employment Statistics
1924–39   Department of Employment and Productivity, *British Labour Statistics, Historical Abstract, 1886–1968* (London: HMSO, 1971), Table 114.
1948–68   Department of Employment and Productivity, *British Labour Statistics, Historical Abstract, 1886–1968* (London: HMSO, 1971), Table 132.
1969–70   Department of Employment and Productivity, *British Labour Statistics, Yearbook, 1972* (London: HMSO, 1972), Table 63.
1971–89   Department of Employment, *Gazette, Historical Supplement No. 2,* 97 (11) (November 1989) Table 1.2.
Note: For the years 1948–70, the data represents 24 industry orders, the 1948–59 data for 1948 SIC, and the 1959–70 data for 1958 SIC. The data for 1971–89 are for 25 industry orders from 1980 SIC. For the lists of the respective industries, see the above sources.

US Industrial Employment Statistics
1901–55   *Historical Statistics of the United States: Colonial Times to 1970: Part I.* D. 127–41.
1955–88   US Department of Labor, Bureau of Labor Statistics, *Employment and Earnings* (May 1989), Table B1.
Note: Index is for 8 divisions: Mining; Construction; Manufacturing; Transportation and Public Utilities; Wholesale and Retail Trade; Finance, Insurance, and Real Estate; Services; Government.

force structure is exogenous or endogenous. In the short run the labour force is already allocated between groups; but in the long run migration is possible between skill groups and regions, though not normally between sexes and races. There *is* migration between age groups, but it is unfortunately exogenous. We shall begin with the case where the labour force is taken as given, and then turn to the case where migration occurs and a long-run equilibrium has been established.

2.1   Labour force given (e.g. by age)

In the short run, the disposition of the labour force (between L_is) is given. Employment is determined by the pattern of labour demand and the process of wage formation. For simplicity we can suppose that output (Y) is produced by a CES production function that is homogeneous of degree one in the different types of labour (N_i):

$$Y^\rho = \varphi \sum \alpha_i N_i^\rho \quad (\rho \le 1, \sum \alpha_i = 1)$$

where $\rho - 1 = -1/\sigma$, σ being the elasticity of substitution.[4]

Ignoring imperfect competition, the *labour demand* for the ith type of labour is then given by

$$W_i = \alpha_i \varphi \left(\frac{N_i}{Y}\right)^{-(1/\sigma)} = -\alpha_i \left(\frac{N_i}{L_i} \frac{L_i}{L}\right)^{-(1/\sigma)} X \quad (i = 1, \ldots, n) \tag{7.1}$$

where W_i is the real wage, L_i the labour force in the ith sector, and X the productivity factor $\varphi(Y/L)^{1/\sigma}$. The coefficient α_i is an indicator of productivity of labour of type i.

Wages in each sector are determined by the *wage function*, which we shall write as

$$W_i = \beta_i f\left(\frac{N_i}{L_i}\right) X \quad (f' > 0)\ (i = 1, \ldots, n) \tag{7.2}$$

where the coefficient β_i is an indicator of 'wage push'.

The evidence for this formulation will be discussed later. Its theoretical basis is a mixture of bargaining outcomes, efficiency wages and pure labour supply (Jackman *et al.*, 1991).[5]

Both the demand function and the wage function are drawn in Figure 7.3. Taken together, they determine the unemployment rate of each group as an increasing function of its wage push relative to productivity (β_i/α_i) and also its relative size (L_i/L):[6]

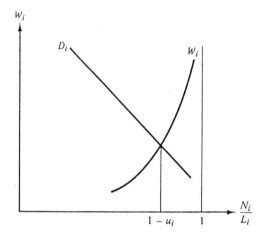

Figure 7.3 Employment and wages in a single sector: labour force given

$$u_i = g^1 \left(\frac{\beta_i L_i}{\alpha_i L} \right)$$
$$+ \ +$$

$$W_i = g^2 \left(\alpha_i, \beta_i, \frac{L_i}{L}, X \right)$$
$$+ \ + \ - \ +$$

Thus, if an age group increases in relative size, its unemployment rate will go up and its wage down. (The demand curve as drawn shifts left, since a given N_i corresponds to a lower N_i/L_i.) This is exactly what happened to youths in the United States as a result of the baby boom (see Freeman and Bloom, 1986).

Equally, the unemployment rate of a group will be affected by its turnover rate. Wage push develops if it is easy for unemployed people to find work. At a given unemployment rate, the chances of finding work are proportional to the rate at which jobs are being left; thus the wage push variable (β_i) is higher the higher is turnover. This helps to explain why unemployment is higher for young people.

2.2 Labour force endogenous (i.e. by occupation or region)

The same analysis cannot be applied to occupational/educational unemployment rates nor to differences in unemployment across regions, except in the very short run, for in the longer run the number of people in each occupation or region itself depends on wages and job opportunities. Migration can change the share of the total labour force in each sector. Migration into a sector (M_i) depends on the extent to which expected income in the sector exceeds that elsewhere; it also depends on the costs of belonging to the sector (e.g. the associated training cost or the climatic discomfort).[7] Thus the net immigration rate (M_i/L_i) is given by

$$\frac{M_i}{L_i} = h\left(W_i \frac{N_i}{L_i} \bigg/ (1+c_i)X \right) \quad (i = 1, \ldots, h-1) \tag{7.3}$$

where c_i reflects the differential costs of belonging to the sector.

Suppose initially that we define the long-run equilibrium as a condition of zero net migration. Then in equilibrium the *zero-migration condition* gives

$$W_i \frac{N_i}{L_i} = (1+c_i)\zeta X \quad (i = 1, \ldots, h-1) \tag{7.3'}$$

where $\zeta = h^{-1}(0)$

This is the long-run supply condition for the choice of sectors. The equalization of net advantage requires that if a sector has higher employment, it will have to have lower wages. This relationship reflects long-run migration behaviour, and could therefore be expected to show up in cross-sectional evidence. On the other hand, once workers are in a sector they will press for the setting of higher wages if employment is higher. This relationship repeated year after year could be expected to show up in time series evidence.

To understand why unemployment rates differ between sectors, we combine (3') and (2) to obtain

$$u_i = j^1\left(\frac{\beta_i}{1+c_i} \right)$$
$$W_i = j^2 (\beta_i, c_i, X)$$
$$\qquad +\ +\ +$$

This says that wage differentials between sectors must reflect cost differences, except that wages in a sector can be lower if its employment rate is unusually high. We note that relative unemployment rate and wage rates in the long run are determined by supply factors alone; demand conditions determine only the absolute magnitude of employment and of the labour force in each sector.

There are ($h-1$) zero-migration conditions. These, taken together with the wage-setting equations and the price equation (linking the set of feasible real wages), determine the real wages (W_i) and employment rates (N_i/L_i) in each group.

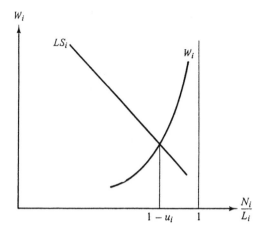

Figure 7.4 Employment and wages in a single sector: labour force endogenous, zero migration

The partial equilibrium for a sector is illustrated in Figure 7.4. As before, the wage-setting relation shows that wages rise as higher employment creates wage push. This reflects the way in which workers behave once they are in a sector. On the other hand, their migration decisions imply that higher wages must be associated with lower employment to equalise the net advantages of the different sectors. So long as the differential wage push in a sector is in proportion to its cost differential, it will have the same unemployment as elsewhere. But if the wage push is excessive, higher unemployment must result – otherwise the sector would continue to attract labour.

Consider, for example, the standard human capital model, where occupation 1 requires one more year of schooling than occupation 2. Under full unemployment

$$\frac{W_1}{W_2} = 1 + r = \text{(here)}\frac{1 + c_1}{1 + c_2}$$

Allowing for unemployment

$$\frac{W_1(N_1/L_1)}{W_2(N_2/L_2)} = \frac{1 + c_1}{1 + c_2}$$

as indicated by (7.3'). So long as $W_1/W_2 = 1 + r$ the unemployment rates will be equal. But suppose the differential is squeezed (because $\beta_1/\beta_2 < 1 + r$). Then the uptake of schooling will fall until the unskilled unemployment rate has risen sufficiently relative to the skilled rate.

A similar model was used by Harris and Todaro (1970) to explain urban unemployment in poor countries. If the urban wage gap (W_1/W_2) is excessive relative to any cost differences, people will pile into the towns until there is sufficient urban unemployment ($N_1/L_1 < 1$). Thinking along similar lines Hall (1970) showed that unemployment differences between US cities was positively correlated with their wage rates. A similar model was used earlier to explain the unemployment of educated people in India by excessive wages for the educated (Blaug, Layard and Woodhall, 1969).

So let us ask: how well does the notion that unemployment depends on $\beta_i(1 + c_i)$ explain the pattern of unemployment rates? There is strong evidence in Table 7.5 and 7.11 that those occupations and industries with high turnover rates (and thus high β_i have high unemployment rates. Wage pressure will also be higher the greater is union strength. Other things being equal, union power in an occupation or industry will thus increase its unemployment rate, as will factors increasing the firms' incentive to pay efficiency wages.

As regards training costs (c_i), occupations where these are high do tend to have low unemployment rates. This is partly because, for reasons of compensating differentials, their wages have to be high, with the result that they are kept well above the level of unemployment benefits.

Across regions, as we have seen, unemployment is also higher in those which have high turnover. But typically unemployment differences are greater than can be adequately explained on this basis. And in many countries, like Britain and Italy (but not the United States), the pattern of regional unemployment differences is highly persistent. The outmigration of labour from the high unemployment areas is only just sufficient to keep pace with the transfer of jobs. There is thus a *steady-state* migration of jobs *and* workers, with relative unemployment rates and relative wages very stable. Regions like the North of England or the South of Italy provide a steadily decreasing share of total employment, and this downward drift in employment share is matched by a downward drift in the share of the labour force. Matters are often made worse by the fact that the 'natural' growth rate of population (due to the difference between new entrants and retirements) is higher in the regions that are losing jobs. We also need to allow for this.

2.3 Labour force endogenous with steady-state migration

We can easily handle those long-run steady-state patterns with two small modifications of our earlier framework. First, employment is changing at a steady state rate $\hat{N}_i$ (which differs across sectors). This arises due to exogenous shifts in demand (e.g., due to changes in its industrial mix) – with relative wages unchanged. Since the employment rate (N_i/L_i) is constant, in this dynamic steady state it follows that

$$\hat{L}_i = \hat{N}_i = \text{(say)} \; \hat{\alpha}_i$$

In addition there is (as between regions) a differential 'natural' growth of working population (corresponding to the difference between new entries and exits from the population of working age).[8] If the total labour force is growing at $\hat{L}$, this is the average rate of 'natural' population growth. But a region has problems if its natural population growth Π_i exceeds that level.

To see this, we can now extend our (7.3) to show how the labour force changes due not only to net migration, $h(.)$, but to natural population growth (Π_i). This gives

$$\hat{L}_i = h\left(W_i \frac{N_i}{L_i} \Big/ (1 + c_i)\lambda X \right) + \Pi_i$$

Since the unemployment rates are constant in the steady state, with $\hat{L}_i = \hat{N}_i$, it follows that

$$h\left(\frac{W_i N_i}{L_i} - (1 + c_i)\lambda X \right) + \Pi_i - \hat{N}_i = 0$$

At given W_i a region will thus have a lower employment rate (N_i/L_i) if its rate of population growth exceeds its rate of job creation.

Turning to Figure 7.4, in such a region the long-run labour supply relation (LS_i) is shifted down – raising unemployment and lowering wages. This helps to explain persistent high unemployment, as in Southern Italy and Northern Ireland. People have constantly wondered why one-off injections of jobs into such areas have had no enduring effect on their unemployment rates; our story shows why. It also helps to explain low unemployment in skilled occupations; if skilled jobs are always increasing faster than unskilled, this will tend to lower steady-state unemployment in the skilled occupations.[9]

The analysis in this section is out of line with traditional analyses of structural unemployment, which emphasise the role of one-off demand shifts. However, as we showed in section 1, there are such striking persistent differences in unemployment rates that we feel these deserve the primary attention.

3 HOW MISMATCH IS RELATED TO THE NAIRU

The preceding analysis provides in principle a complete account of the unemployment rate for each separate group, and thus also of the aggregate unemployment rate. In principle our theory could thus stop at this point. However, many people are interested in explaining aggregate unemployment without going through the daunting task of explaining each of the individual rates. In particular, people ask: does increased structural imbalance help us to understand the recent high unemployment in Europe?

So is there some simple index by which one could assess how the structure of unemployment is related to its average level (both, of course, being endogeneous)? The answer is: yes. The basic idea goes back to Lipsey (1960). It is worth beginning with an analogous framework to his, before modifying it in the direction of greater rigour. Figure 7.5 sets out the wage function, assumed to be the same for each of two equal-sized groups. $\overline{W}$ is the feasible average wage. If both unemployment rates are equal, aggregate unemployment is at A. If the two unemployment rates differ but the average wage remains at W, the average unemployment will have to be at B. Overall unemployment is thus higher. The further apart the unemployment rates, the higher the average unemployment.

This result depends entirely on the convexity of the wage function, for which there is much evidence (see below). But the formulation is unrigorous. In particular, it relies on identical wage functions for each group, which on reasonable assumptions turn out to be unnecessary.

To see this, and to derive the relevant mismatch index, we begin with the feasible set of real wages, given by the price function. For simplicity we shall assume constant returns to scale in the different types of labour. If we also initially assume a Cobb–Douglas production function, the nominal price is given by

$$P = \Pi W_i^{\alpha_i} e^{-A} \quad (\textstyle\sum \alpha_i = 1)$$

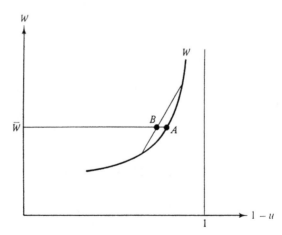

Figure 7.5 Introductory presentation of mismatch and the NAIRU

where A is a combined index of technical progress and of product market competition.

Setting the price level at unity and taking logs, the *price function* gives a feasible real wage frontier.

$$A = \Sigma\alpha_i \log W_i \tag{7.4}$$

In addition we shall assume double logarithmic wage functions (evidence for the United Kingdom follows, for other countries see, for example, Grubb, 1986). The *wage functions* are thus:

$$\log W_i = \beta_i - \gamma \log u_i \tag{7.5}$$

Substituting the wage functions into the price functions gives an *unemployment frontier*

$$A = \Sigma\alpha_i\beta_i - \gamma\Sigma\alpha_i \log u_i \tag{7.6}$$

This shows the locus of all combinations of sectoral unemployment rates which are consistent with the absence of inflationary pressure, given the behaviour of wage setters.

This frontier is illustrated in Figure 7.6 for the case of two sectors of equal size ($\alpha_1 = \alpha_2 = \frac{1}{2}$). Since the function is convex to the origin, the lowest possible *average* level of unemployment ($u_{\min}$) is where unemployment is the same in both sectors.[10] This occurs at point P in Figure 7.6. If, instead the unemployment rates differ, as at P', average unemployment is higher – in this scale it is u'. The further apart the different unemployment rates, the higher their average level.

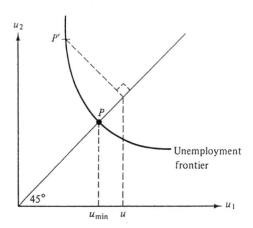

Figure 7.6 The unemployment frontier: wages responding to own-sector unemployment

We can readily derive an expression that shows how average unemployment is related to the dispersion of the unemployment rates across sectors. We start from (7.6) and add $\gamma \log u$ to both sides and divide both sides by γ. This gives

$$\log u = \text{const} - \Sigma\alpha_i \frac{\log u_i}{\log u}$$

Since $\Sigma\alpha_i = 1$, expanding $\log u_i/u$ around 1 gives[11]

$$\log u \simeq \text{const} - \sum\alpha_i(-\tfrac{1}{2})\left(\frac{u_i}{u} - 1\right)^2$$
$$= \text{const} + \tfrac{1}{2}\text{var}\frac{u_i}{u}$$

The minimum level of log unemployment is now given by the constant, $(\Sigma\alpha_i\beta_i - A)/\gamma$, and occurs when unemployment rates have been equalised. But, if unemployment rates are unequal, unemployment rises by the proportion $\tfrac{1}{2}\text{var}(u_i/u)$.

Given (7.7), the natural index of the structure of unemployment, viewed as a 'cause' of the average unemployment rate, is $\tfrac{1}{2}\text{var}(u_i/u)$; this measures the proportional excess of unemployment over its minimum. Since it is zero if labour demand and supply have the same structure, it is natural to give it the name 'mismatch' (*MM*).[12] Thus

$$MM = \tfrac{1}{2}\text{var}\frac{u_i}{u} = \log u - \log u_{\min}$$

As the data in section 1 showed, mismatch on this definition has not increased. In other words, we cannot use changes in the structure of unemployment as an explanation of the higher average level of unemployment rates.

At this point we need to deal with a misconception. We do *not* mean that the *number* of unemployed people who are 'mismatched' has failed to rise, for if unemployment rises for some *other* reason and the proportional mismatch is constant, the absolute numbers mismatched will rise. This corresponds well with the feeling of many Europeans that there are now more people who are structurally unemployed than used to be the case. The point is that it is possible *both* for this to be true *and* for structural factors as a *cause* of unemployment to have been constant.

Clearly this need not mean that mismatch is unimportant. In fact the figures we gave earlier for Britain show precisely how important it is. In 1985 the variances of relative unemployment rates were

'Across'	
7 occupations	0.22
322 travel-to-work areas	0.24
10 industries	0.14
10 age groups	0.22
2 race groups	0.03
2 sex groups	0.01
	0.86

Assuming these imbalances to be approximately orthogonal, we can add them together and conclude that the degree of mismatch equals approximately half their sum – i.e. 0.4. Mismatch thus would account for roughly one-third of total unemployment – a serious matter.

3.1 Qualifications

Clearly the measure of mismatch that we have developed is very model-specific. It depends on our assumptions about

1. the curvature of the price function
2. the curvature of the wage function, and
3. the assumption that wages depend on unemployment in the sector in question and not in some leading sector.

How much do things change if we vary these assumptions?

The first assumption is not that important. Suppose, for example, that the production function is CES with an elasticity of substitution σ between each type of labour. Then we show (in the Appendix) that the appropriate measure for mismatch is

$$MM = \tfrac{1}{2}(1 - \gamma(\sigma - 1))\operatorname{var}\frac{u_i}{u}$$

In general the elasticity of substitution between skill groups, age groups, sex groups and regional products exceeds unity (e.g. Hamermesh, 1986; Layard, 1982). But γ is quite small – of the order of 0.1 (see below). Thus $\gamma(\sigma - 1)$ will not be large. However, it is true, as one would expect, that for a given dispersion of u_i/u mismatch declines as types of labour become more substitutable. It is also true (given $\sigma > 1$) that mismatch declines as wage flexibility (γ) increases. Since $\sigma > 1$, mismatch may equal somewhat less than half $\operatorname{var}(u_i/u)$.

But many people object to the notion that mismatch should be measured by relative unemployment differentials. They feel that *absolute* differences are what matter – so that for constant $\operatorname{var}(u_i/u)$ mismatch will have arisen if average unemployment is higher; they are wrong; this is true whatever the curvature of the wage function.

To see this, we can assume quite generally that

$$\log W_i = \beta_i - \gamma \frac{u_i^\alpha - 1}{\alpha} \quad (-\infty < \alpha \le 1; \alpha \ne 0)$$

where the parameter α determines the curvature of the wage function.

With $\alpha = 1$, the function is linear and as α falls the curvature increases (with wages tending to $\beta_i - \gamma \log u$ as α tends to zero). The level of unemployment is now determined by[13]

$$\frac{u^\alpha - 1}{\alpha} = \frac{\Sigma \alpha_i \beta_i - A}{\gamma} + \frac{(1 - \alpha)u^\alpha}{2} \operatorname{var}\left(\frac{u_i}{u}\right)$$

As $\alpha \to 0$, this tends to

$$\log u = \frac{\Sigma \alpha_i \beta_i - A}{\gamma} + \tfrac{1}{2}\operatorname{var}\left(\frac{u_i}{u}\right)$$

but whatever α, u is increasing in $\operatorname{var}(u_i/u)$. Only relative unemployment matters, whatever the curvature of the wage function. Needless to say if there is no curvature ($\alpha = 1$) there is no problem of mismatch whatever the variance. However all the evidence supports the notion of curvature, and we shall in the next section provide evidence in support of the log formulation.

3.2 Leading sector issue

All the analysis so far is postulated on the basis that wages in a sector depend only on the unemployment rate in the same sector. This is not how many analysts of mismatch think. Suppose instead that wages depend only on unemployment in some leading sector (like the South of England or electrical engineering) whose unemployment rate is denoted u_L. Then

$$\log W_i = \beta_i - \delta \log u_L$$

and the unemployment function is

$$A = \Sigma \alpha_i \beta_i - \delta \log u_L$$

This tells us the minimum unemployment we can have in the leading sector before general overheating emerges in the economy. There is no point in having unemployment higher than u_L anywhere else since it would have no effect on wage pressure. On the other hand presumably unemployment elsewhere cannot be lower than in the leading sector (since the leading sector is likely to be the tightest market). Thus[14]

$$MM = \log u - \log u_L$$

This is much greater than mismatch as measured on the assumption that wages respond to unemployment in each sector (rather than in the leading sector only) for, with a given set of unemployment rates, the minimum level of unemployment is much higher in the 'own-sector' case than the unemployment rate in the 'leading-sector' case. In the own-sector case (7.6) shows that the same wage pressure is generated by $\Sigma \, \alpha_i \log u_i$ as by $\Sigma \, \alpha_i \log u_{min}$ (with all rates equal). Thus, since $\Sigma \alpha_i = 1$,

$$\log u_{min} = \Sigma \alpha_i \log u_i$$

In other words the minimum level of unemployment (u_{min}) is then the *geometric mean* of all the actual unemployment rates. But in the 'leading-sector' case, it is given by u_L which is the *lowest* of all the rates. The gap between u and u_{min} is thus greater in the leading-sector wage model than it is when wages respond to own-sector unemployment.

The point is illustrated in Figure 7.7. Assuming that the leading sector is the one with the lowest unemployment rate, the unemployment frontier becomes a right-angle. As we have drawn the actual pattern of unemployment at P', sector 1 is the leading sector and actual unemployment greatly exceeds u_{min}.

So have we grossly underestimated mismatch by ignoring the leading sector issue? This depends on whether the leading-sector theory of wages is right.

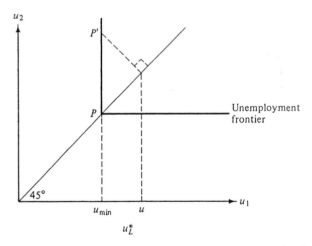

Figure 7.7 The unemployment frontier: wages responding to leading-sector unemployment

Before addressing this question, we should consider one further possibility: that wages in one group depend simply on the aggregate unemployment rate:

$$W_i = f^i(u)$$

In this case there is no mismatch, as we have defined it, since the NAIRU is independent of the distribution of unemployment and depends only on its average.

4 EVIDENCE ON SECTORAL WAGE BEHAVIOUR AND ON MOBILITY

4.1 Regional wage behaviour (Britain)

To check on our model, the first issue to study is the wage determination equation (7.2). We do this first in relation to regional wage behaviour, beginning with Britain. We investigate the following general time-series wage equation

$$w_i = a_i \log u_i + a_2 \log u_L + a_3 \log u + a_4 X + a_5 i t + a_6 w_{i,-1} + a_{0i} \qquad (7.8)$$

Here w_i is the log real hourly wage for male manual workers in region i (in units of GDP), and X is trend log output per worker (calculated by interpolating log output per worker between peaks).[15]

There is a regional fixed effect a_{0i} and regional time trend for each of the 10 regions of Britain. The equation was fitted to annual data for 1967 to 1987, and the results are shown in Table 7.14.

In row 1 we include as possible influences own-region unemployment (u_i), leading-region (South-East) unemployment (u_L), and national unemployment (u). We find that own-sector unemployment is insignificant and the national unemployment rate is significant but wrongly signed. Because of the collinearity between these measures we tried dropping first national unemployment (row 2) and then leading-sector unemployment (row 3). In both cases, own-sector unemployment remained significant and correctly signed, whereas leading-sector or national unemployment (respectively) too significant but wrongly signed coefficients.

This finding has parallels in other studies. The perverse sign on, say, national unemployment may arise from the fact that it stands as a proxy variable for unobserved aggregate supply shocks. An adverse supply shock will tend to raise unemployment in the nation as a whole and at the same time tend to raise wages at any given local unemployment rate in each region; hence it takes a positive sign in a regression equation. One may avoid this problem simply by

Table 7.14 Determinants of regional wage rates, Britain; dependent variables: w_i; other independent variables: x, t, allowing region-specific time trends

Regression	$\log u_i$	$\log u_L$	$\log u$	$\left(\frac{LTU}{U}\right)_i$	$\Delta \log u_i$	w_{i-1}	se	LM auto-correlation statistic
1	-0.074 (6.0)	-0.015 (1.1)	0.046 (2.7)	–	–	0.12 (2.2)	0.0123	5.7
2	-0.062 (5.2)	0.042 (3.9)	–	–	–	0.079 (1.5)	0.0125	13.3
3	-0.069 (6.0)	–	0.058 (4.7)	–	–	0.14 (2.7)	0.0123	3.8
4	-0.020 (3.9)	–	–	–	–	0.14 (2.7)	0.0130	7.6
5	-0.019 (3.6)	–	–	0.02 (0.9)	–	0.17 (2.7)	0.0131	9.5
6	-0.020 (3.2)	–	–	–	-0.0006 (0.1)	0.14 (2.3)	0.0131	11.4
7	-0.025 (3.5)	–	–	0.057 (1.5)	-0.013 (1.3)	0.16 (2.6)	0.0130	7.6

Notes:

Estimation by pooled time-series OLS for the 10 standard regions of Great Britain, 1967–87.

u is the national unemployment rate excluding regions i and L.

The small sample bias tends to bias the coefficients towards zero by a factor $\frac{1}{20}$ (Nickell, 1981). The constraints that the coefficients on u_i, w_{i-1} and R_i in 7.5 are the same in each region are jointly satisfied, with a test statistic of 1.7 against a critical 5% value of $F_{27,149),0.05} = 1.7$. The constraints on u_i and w_{i-1} in equation (7.4) are similarly accepted at the 5% level with a test statistic of 0.8 against a 5% critical value of $F_{(18,159),0.05} = 1.6$. The LM autocorrelation statistic is constructed by retrieving the residuals $\hat{u}$, from our estimated equation regressing $\hat{u}_i$ on X and $\hat{u}_{-1}$, then retrieving R^2 from this later equation. Under the (null hypothesis) H_0: serially independent disturbances the statistic TR^2 is $\sim \chi^2(1)$, $\chi^2(1)$, 0.05 = 3.8.

Our results are shown to be robust to possible endogeneity between u_i and w_i when we estimate by instrumental variables using lagged unemployment and lagged real national income as instruments. Our results are also unaffected by replacing regional trends and trend log output by year time dummies.
Source: Department of Employment Gazette; for details see Savouri (1989).

dropping the national unemployment term in the equation (as we do in rows 4–7) but the coefficient on own-sector unemployment is then biased towards zero (given that own-sector unemployment will also be correlated with supply shocks).

It is nonetheless interesting, using this formulation, to check the effect of the level of long-term unemployment in the region. In row 5 this comes in with the correct (positive) sign. Alternatively the change in unemployment, which is negatively correlated with long-term unemployment, comes in with a negative sign (row 6). As row 7 shows, when both variables are included, both are (marginally) significant and correctly signed. Given other evidence on the effects of long-term unemployment, our preference is for row 5. (When hysteresis variables are allowed for in the 'horse-race' of rows 1–3 the signs on the hysteresis terms are always wrong for leading-sector unemployment and aggregate unemployment, in the same way as reported in rows 1–3 for u_L and u.)

We may use the simplest of the own-sector unemployment wage equations (row 4) to test whether the unemployment coefficients are significantly different across regions. An F-test on constraining the coefficient values across regions to be the same is satisfied. This means that one can obtain more precise estimates of the regional wage equation by looking simply at relative wage movements. This procedure is not subject to biases coming from unobservable supply shocks. Thus we can take (7.8) and insert national average values and then subtract the averaged equation from (7.8). This gives[16]

$$w_i - w = a_1(\log u_i - \log u) + a_2(w_{i,-1} - w_{-1}) + (a_{0i} - a_0) + a_{3i}t$$

This procedure is more accurate since the estimates of the coefficients on local unemployment do not now depend at all on how the influences of any common national variables is modelled. The results of this analysis, comparable with rows 4 and 5 of Table 7.14, are

$$(w_i - w)_t = -0.049 (\log u_i - \log u)_t + 0.63 (w_i - w_t - 1) + (a_{0i} - a_0) + a_{3i}t$$
$$\qquad\qquad (5.8) \qquad\qquad\qquad\qquad (11.7)$$
$$(se = 0.0074 \quad LM = 5.1 \quad \chi^2(1), 0.05 = 3.8)$$

and

$$(w_i - w)_t = -0.045 (\log u_i - \log u)_t + 0.68 (w_i - w_t - 1)$$
$$\qquad\qquad (5.6) \qquad\qquad\qquad\qquad (12.9)$$
$$\qquad + 0.16 \left(\frac{LTU_i}{U_i} - \frac{LTU}{U}\right) + (a_{0i} - a_0) + a_{3i}t$$
$$\qquad\quad (4.2)$$
$$(se = 0.0070 \quad LM = 4.0 \quad \chi^2(1), 0.05 = 3.8)$$

On this basis we find that regional wages respond to local unemployment with a long-run elasticity of 0.13. This is greater than the value of 0.02 implied by row 4 of Table 7.14 and closer to elasticities of around 0.10 found at many other levels of disaggregation (Layard and Nickell, 1986; Nickell and Wadhwani, 1989; Oswald, 1986). But the key point is that we have confirmed the strong effect of the local labour market upon regional wages.

The next question is whether our use of the double-log-linear wage function is justified. Indeed is the wage function convex (downward) *at all* – or is it *more* convex than the double-log-linear formulation implies?

To investigate this in a reasonably general way we replace log u by a quadratic in the level of unemployment (the cubed term being found completely insignificant). The result is

$$(w_i - w)_t = 0.91 (u_i - u)_t + 0.84 (u_i^2 - u^2)_t + 0.59 (w_i - w)_{t-1}$$
$$(3.7) \qquad\qquad (1.02) \qquad\qquad (9.5)$$
$$+ a_{3i}t + (a_{0i} - a_0)$$
(se $= 0.0075$)

While a t-statistic of 1.02 suggests a degree of additional curvature, it is insufficiently well defined to justify abandoning the double logarithm form.

We should briefly contrast these estimates with the 'wage curves' estimated from cross-section data by Blanchflower and Oswald (1989). When estimated across British regions, these show $\partial w / \partial u$ becoming positive at high levels of unemployment. This is because the cross-sectional data capture a mixture of the wage equation and the long-run supply equation – the latter having the opposite slope to the former (see Figure 7.4).

4.2 Regional wage behaviour (United States)

Similar analyses have been made for wage determination at the level of US states, using annual data for 1975–88. Given the lack of stability in unemployment rankings across US states, there is no plausible leading sector. But it is interesting to compare the effects of state-level unemployment and national unemployment. This is done in Table 7.15. Again the powerful influence of local unemployment is apparent. This is even more so when we run the equation for relative wages:

$$w_i - w = -0.0280 (\log u_{i,-1} - \log u_{-1}) + 0.676 (W_{i,-1} - W_{-1})$$
$$(5.1) \qquad\qquad\qquad (23.0)$$
$$+ (a_{0i} - a_0)$$
(se $= 0.02599 \quad LM = 21.4$)

Table 7.15 Determinants of regional wage rates, United States; dependent variables: w_i; other independent variables: x, t

Regression	Independent variables			se	LM auto-correlation statistic
	$\log u_i$	$\log u$	w_{i-1}		
1	−0.023 (5.5)	0.032 (5.02)	0.82 (36.5)	0.0197	9.8
2	−0.010 (2.9)	−	0.83 (36.3)	0.0201	11.8
3	−	0.009 (1.8)	0.82 (35.8)	0.0202	15.5

Notes: Both the terms $\Delta \log u_i$ and $\Delta \log u$ were not significant.
Wages are hourly wages of production workers.
Sources:
Employment and Earnings.
Prices are GDP deflator.
Productivity is trend output per worker (peak to peak).

This gives an unemployment elasticity for wages of 0.09. We then tested for the constancy of this elasticity by running a quadratic in $u(u^3$ being again insignificant). The implied elasticities $(u \partial w / \partial u)$ were

u	$u \partial w / \partial u$
0.02	−0.019
0.04	−0.030
0.06	−0.032
0.08	−0.027
0.10	−0.013

This again lends reasonable support to the constant elasticity approach over the most relevant parts of the range.

4.3 Regional labour mobility

As regards the regional model, the next relationship to be investigated is the immigration function (7.3). The equation is

$$\frac{M_i}{L_i} = b_1 \log\left(\frac{N_i/L_i}{N/L}\right) + b_2 \log\left(\frac{W_i}{W}\right) + b_3 \log\left(\frac{P}{P_i}\right) + b_{4i}$$

or, for estimation purposes

$$\frac{M_i}{L_i} = b_1(u - u_i) + b_2(w_i - w) + b_3(p - p_i)$$

Here P refers to house prices, there being for Britain no more series on other cost of living differences between regions (which are in any case small).

The equation was fitted to annual data for 1968–86 (see Savouri, 1989), and the results were

$$\frac{M_i}{L_i} = \underset{(2.7)}{0.081}\,(u - u_i) + \underset{(3.9)}{0.058}\,(w_i - w) + \underset{(1.6)}{0.010}\,(p - p_i) + b_{4i}$$

(se $= 0.0031$)   ($LM = 37.3$)

Interestingly the equation is consistent with the idea that the real wages and the employment rates have the same proportional effect on migration. Pissarides and Wadsworth (1989) have argued that the absolute rate of migration falls when the general level of unemployment is high but we were unable to find such an effect.

For the United States we estimated the following equation for 1975–88:

$$\frac{\Delta L_i}{L_i} - \frac{\Delta L}{L} = \underset{(7.8)}{0.0546}\,(u - u_i) + \underset{(0.5)}{0.013}\,(w_i - w) + b_i$$

For the United States we do not (yet) have data on local price levels. This may be one reason why we find no significant effect of local wages, though this problem is common in US studies (Greenwood, 1985). But local unemployment has a much more powerful effect than in Britain.

4.4 Occupational wages and mobility

In due course we shall be able to report a similar analysis of the dynamics of the market for skills. At this stage we shall simply note that, in Britain at least, occupational unemployment has a strong effect on occupational wages, with an elasticity well above 0.1. In consequence the relative wages of manual workers have fallen sharply in the 1980s.

We have not been able to undertake any similar analysis for other European countries yet, due to lack of data on unemployment by occupation. But we are struck by the fact that in no other European country except Denmark have wage differentials increased during the 1980s as they have in Britain (see

Table 7.16   Non-manual wages relative to manual wages, 1970–86,
index 1980 = 100

	Belgium	Denmark	France	Germany	Holland	Italy	United Kingdom
1970	–	–	–	–	–	–	–
1971	–	–	–	–	–	–	–
1972	–	–	1.19	0.96	–	1.27	–
1973	–	–	1.15	0.97	–	1.23	0.95
1974	–	–	1.11	0.97	–	1.17	0.97
1975	1.03	1.10	1.09	0.97	0.99	1.12	0.96
1976	1.01	1.09	1.04	0.98	1.01	1.05	0.95
1977	1.01	1.08	1.02	0.99	0.99	1.01	0.96
1978	1.01	1.03	1.02	0.99	1.00	1.02	0.97
1979	1.01	1.02	1.01	1.00	1.00	1.04	0.98
1980	1.00	1.00	1.00	1.00	1.00	1.00	1.00
1981	0.99	1.00	0.98	1.00	1.01	0.98	1.01
1982	0.98	1.01	0.95	1.00	1.01	0.95	1.00
1983	0.97	1.03	0.93	1.01	1.02	0.95	1.06
1984	0.97	1.04	0.94	1.02	1.00	0.98	–
1985	0.97	1.06	0.94	1.02	0.98	1.01	1.04
1986	0.97	1.08	–	1.02	–	–	1.07

Source: *Eurostat Review* (1970–1980), (1977–1986).
Manual: Gross hourly earnings, all industries, nominal. Table 3.6.1.
Non-manual: Gross monthly earnings, all industries, nominal. Table 3.6.12.

Table 7.16). And in France and Belgium they have narrowed. Can this be a partial clue to high European unemployment?

Turning to skill formation, there is a strong effect of wages on the choice of skill. Thus if we interpret M_i as the excess of entrants to departures in a skill group, the number of entrants is highly sensitive to expected earnings. In the United States the earnings elasticity of entrants has been variously estimated in the range 1–4 (Freeman, 1986), while in the United Kingdom Pissarides (1981, 1982) gives figures of $\frac{1}{2} - 1\frac{1}{2}$. Relative unemployment effects on educational choice are less well determined.

Taking a unit elasticity and a working life of 50 years, we can thus infer that if wages in a skill group are higher by 1 per cent numbers in the skill group will rise by some 0.02 per cent per annum above what they would otherwise do. This is of the same order as the effect on a region's labour force if wages in the region are higher by 1 per cent (see above).

5 POLICY IMPLICATIONS

So are there any policies which can improve things when there is mismatch? Policies commonly advocated include:

1. shifting the jobs towards the workers (e.g. by cutting employers' taxes in those sectors where unemployment is high), and
2. shifting the workers towards the jobs (e.g. by subsidies to migration or training).

Frequently both are advocated (e.g. by Johnson and Layard, 1986). But is the analysis correct?

5.1 An illustrative case (W_2 totally rigid)

We shall begin with the highly simplified case of two skill groups, with the skilled wage (W_1) perfectly flexible and the unskilled wage (W_2) perfectly rigid. There is then full employment in the skilled labour market, and unemployment in the unskilled one. If unemployed leisure is of zero value (as we shall assume throughout), this outcome is clearly inefficient.

What is the appropriate policy response? We shall begin with the case where the labour forces (L_1 and L_2) are given. This is illustrated in Figure 7.8.

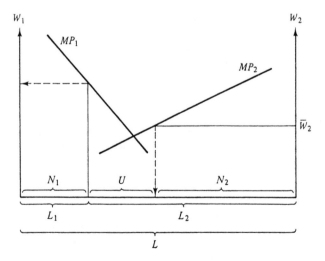

Figure 7.8 Skilled and unskilled labour markets: L_1, L_2 fixed (W_1 flexible, W_2 rigid)

In this situation two things are clear

1. An employment subsidy to employers hiring unskilled workers would increase unskilled employment. This would have to be financed. Since it is unrealistic to posit lump-sum taxation, we shall assume that any employment subsidies have to be financed by other employment taxes. In the present case this implies a tax on skilled labour; since wages of skilled labour are perfectly flexible and labour supply inelastic, this tax involves no efficiency costs. Skilled workers remain fully employed, and the increased employment of unskilled workers raised employment and thus output.
2. Equally if we could turn unskilled workers into skilled workers; this would increase (gross) output, for suppose we transfer one individual from group 2 to group 1: employment in the skilled sector will rise, since W_1 is flexible, and (to the first approximation) employment in the unskilled sector will be unaffected, since W_2 is fixed. To find the output effects we shall assume that $Y = F(e_1L_1, e_2L_2)$ where e_i is the employment rate. If we have one more skilled worker, output rises by approximately F_1. This is the net social return to training. By contrast, the net expected private return is $(F_1 - e_2F_2)$ which is much lower. This appears to suggest a case for subsidies to training and migration.

On the line of reasoning so far, we would then be willing to subsidise employment in group 2 *and* migration into group 1. These are the arguments commonly heard. But they will not really stand up. For subsidies to migration can be evaluated only within a general theory of migration behaviour. Once we do this, we realise that the employment *tax* on skilled workers (proposal 1) will reduce skilled wages and thus discourage migration. The migration subsidy (proposal 2), when amortised, would be equivalent to an employment *subsidy* to skilled workers, partially or wholly offsetting the initial tax. Is there any sense in such a combined operation? The answer is that employment taxes and migration subsidies cannot be thought of as distinct entities. The only question is: what should be the net taxes paid by each group of workers?

Let us pursue this issue in the context of our simple example, and ask: 'suppose there were initially no taxes on either group and W_2 is rigid; is there any subsidy to one group, paid for by a tax on the other, that would increase output?'

Net output is

$$Y = F(e_1L_1, e_2L_2) - c_1L_1$$

where c_1 is the amortised cost of training.

We want to maximise this subject to the constraints, including those coming from migration behaviour. In the steady state this implies the *zero-migration condition*, which for simplicity can be written in the additive form

$$W_1e_1 = W_2e_2 + c_1$$

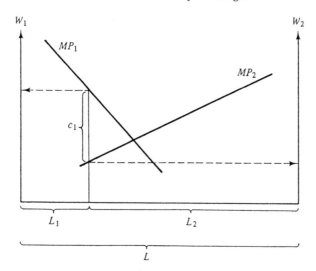

Figure 7.9 Skilled and unskilled labour markets: L_1, L_2 variable (W_1, W_2 flexible)

In other words, net expected income in sector 1 ($W_1 e_1 - c_1$) equals expected income in sector 2, the private and social costs of training (c_1) being for the present assumed to be the same.

If all wages were fully flexible, we should have full employment in both sectors ($e_1 = e_2 = 1$). This would maximise net output, as illustrated in Figure 7.9.

If, however, W_2 is rigid, output is reduced. The migration condition becomes (with $e_1 = 1$)

$$W_1 = \overline{W}_2 e_2 + c_1$$

The question is: if we start from zero taxes, is there any self-financing scheme of taxes and subsidies which would increase net output?

The answer is 'no', for given that $L_2 = L - L_1$, the change in net welfare when policy changes is

$$(F_1 - e_2 F_2 - c_1)dL_1 + F_1 L_2 de_2$$

But private choice has already set the first term to zero. So policy action can improve welfare only if it can alter the employment rate of the unskilled.

But this it cannot do (even though it *can* change L_1 and L_2); for, if $\overline{W}_2$ is fixed, so is W_1. Hence, by the zero-migration condition, e_2 is fixed.

To see why W_1 cannot change, note that (under perfect competition in product markets)

$$dW_1 = dF_1 - dt_1$$

The real wage frontier implies

$$dF_1 = -\frac{N_2}{N_1} dF_2$$

while the government budget constraint implies

$$-dt_1 = \frac{N_2}{N_1} dt_2 + s$$

But since W_2 is fixed, $dF_2 - dt_2$ is zero and hence $dF_1 - dt_1$ is also zero. There is no scope for improving things; the best taxes and subsidies are no taxes and subsidies. Though unemployment involves an externality, it is not an externality that can be offset by these kinds of taxes and subsidies.

There are two basic qualifications to this. First, if there is an external social cost or benefit, this must be corrected by taxation or subsidy. And second, if individuals differ in their costs, there may well be a case for taxing the costly sector. But to investigate these issues, let us proceed to the more general case where both wages are flexible, and taxes are non-zero, though differentially so.

We begin with the case where the labour forces are exogenous and observe the potent role of policy. Then we proceed to the case where the labour force are endogenous and policy analysis is more complex.

5.2 Labour force given

To find the ideal tax structure, we maximise net output subject to a revenue requirement and to the wage functions and labour demand functions. The problem is

$$\max_{t_i, W_i, e_i} Y = F(e_1 L_1, e_2 L_2)$$
$$+ \varphi(t_1 e_1 L_1 + t_2 e_2 L_2 - R)$$
$$+ \psi_1(W_1 - f^1(e_1)) + \psi_2(W_2 - f^2(e_2))$$
$$+ \theta_1(W_1 + t_1 - F_1) + \theta_2(W_2 + t_2 - F_2)$$

where R is a revenue requirement, W_i is take-home pay and t_i is a per-worker tax levied on employers. This requires

$$\frac{\partial Y}{\partial t_i} = \varphi e_i L_i + \theta_i = 0$$

$$\frac{\partial Y}{\partial W_i} = \psi_i + \theta_i = 0$$

which imply $\psi_i = \varphi e_i L_i = -\theta_i$, and in addition

$$\frac{\partial Y}{\partial e_i} = F_i L_i + \varphi t_i L_i + \psi_i \frac{\partial W_i}{\partial e_i} - \theta_i F_{ii} L_i$$

$$= L_i \left(W_i + t_i + \varphi t_i - \varphi e_i \frac{\partial W_i}{\partial e_i} + \varphi e_i L_i F_{ii} \right) = 0$$

Hence the standard Ramsey-like condition that[17]

$$\frac{t_i}{W_i} = \frac{\varphi}{1+\varphi} \left(\frac{1}{\eta_S} + \frac{1}{\eta_D} \right) - \frac{1}{1+\varphi} \tag{9}$$

where η_s is the wage elasticity of employment (in the wage function) and η_D is the wage elasticity of employment (in demand).

The tax rate should be higher the more flexible are wages and the less elastic demand. In general, unskilled labour markets are likely to have relatively inflexible wages and relatively elastic demand.

Concentrating on wage flexibility, if the wage function is double-log, then $\partial \log W_i / \partial \log u_i$ will be similar (e.g. $-\alpha$) in all groups and

$$\frac{\partial \log W_i}{\partial \log e_i} = \frac{\partial \log W_i}{\partial \log u_i} \frac{e_i}{u_i} = \alpha \frac{(1-u_i)}{u_i}$$

Hence wage flexibility will be inversely proportional to unemployment. Taxing flexible markets means taxing those with low unemployment; so long as t_1/W_1 is too low, output could be increased by raising t_1 and lowering t_2, thus stimulating employment where wages are inflexible and reducing it where they are flexible.

This argument has been used to justify subsidies to less skilled labour financed by taxes on skilled labour; it is a standard conclusion in much of the theory of manpower policy.

5.3 Labour force endogenous

But it is valid only if the labour force is exogenous (e.g. by age, race or sex). If the labour force is endogenous, everything changes. We shall show that, if there are no externalities, efficiency requires that the absolute level of the net tax (after netting out any subsidy) should be roughly equal for all groups. More precisely, the 'expected' net tax burden should be equal: that is, groups with lower employment rates should pay proportionately higher taxes.

The problem now is to maximise net output, $F(e_1L_1, e_2L_2) - c_1L_1$, subject to the budget constraint, the two wage functions, the two demand functions, and the *zero-migration condition*. The policy instruments are t_1 and t_2, but to examine the properties of the optimum we again choose the full set of variables $(L_1, t_1, t_2, W_2, e_1$ and $e_2)$ to maximise net output. Thus

$$\max_{t_i, W_i, e_i L_i} Y^* = F(e_1L_1, e_2L_2) - c_1L_1$$
$$+ \varphi(t_1e_1L_1 + t_2e_2L_2 - R)$$
$$+ \psi_1(W_1 - f^1(e_1)) + \varphi_2(W_2 - f^2(e_2))$$
$$+ \theta_1(W_1 + t_1 - F_1) + \theta_2(W_2 + t_2 - F_2)$$
$$+ \lambda(W_1e_1 - W_2e_2 - c_1)$$

where the last (and additional) constraint is the zero-migration constraint, enabling us to determine L_1.

Adding this zero-migration constraint changes everything. The focus of the analysis shifts to the first-order condition for L_1. This

$$\frac{\partial Y^*}{\partial L_1} = F_1e_1 - F_2e_2 - c_1 + \phi(t_1e_1 - t_2e_2)$$
$$= W_1e_1 - W_2e_2 - c_1 + t_1e_1 - t_2e_2 + \varphi(t_1e_1 - t_2e_2) = 0 \qquad (10)$$

The zero-migration condition ensures that the first three terms sum to zero, so that optimality requires that

$$t_1e_1 = t_2e_2$$

Expected taxes should be equal in each sector.[18] The Ramsey-type equation (9) is no longer valid since it fails to take into account the migration condition. Thus, even in the presence of wage rigidity and differential unemployment, the classic principles of public finance apply and there is no case for differential taxation unless there are externalities (other than simply unemployment itself).

However, there may well be externalities; the most obvious are the congestion externalities from regional migration. Suppose that net output is not $Y - c_1L_1$ but $Y - c_1L_1 - c_sL_1$, where the costs c_1 are privately borne but the remaining social costs c_s are not. Then the optimality condition becomes

$$t_1e_1 = t_2e_2 + \frac{c_s}{1 + \varphi}$$

The congested sector should pay higher taxes in the standard Pigovian manner in order to equate the private and social returns to migration. This argues for increased taxes in regions which are congested (typically low-unemployment regions) and subsidies to skill-formation, where there is an external benefit that is not privately appropriated.

There is, however, a more subtle form of externality. We have so far allowed only for one type of 'original' labour, which can then be allocated between two sectors. In fact there may be different types of original labour – say, of different ability or taste – for whom there are different costs (c_i) of entry to sector 1. The average cost (c_1) per sector 1 worker is thus an increasing function of L_1. If $C(L_1)$ is the total cost of L_1, the migration condition is thus

$$W_1 e_1 - W_2 e_2 - C' = 0 \qquad (C', C'' > 0)$$

Optimality now requires

$$\frac{\partial Y^*}{\partial L_1} = (W_1 + t_1)e_1 - (W_2 + t_2)e_2 - C' + \varphi(t_1 e_1 - t_2 e_2) - \lambda C'' = 0$$

where λ is the multiplier on the supply condition $e_1 + W_1 - e_2 + W_2 - C' = 0$. Hence

$$t_1 e_1 = t_2 e_2 + \frac{\lambda C''}{1 + \varphi} \tag{12}$$

The extent of the expected tax differential $(t_1 e_1 - t_2 e_2)$ is higher the less responsive migration is to changes in financial incentives. For λ and φ are positive,[20] and C'' is the inverse of the supply response dL_1/dW_1, suitably discounted.

As we have seen, both regional and occupational labour forces respond very slowly to wage differentials which could make the last term in (7.12) quite important (even after multiplication by the discount rate). (Even without standard externality arguments) there is thus certainly some efficiency case for lower absolute tax rates on occupations and regions with low-employment rates. But the standard externality arguments differ sharply between occupations and regions, favouring tax concessions for high-skilled groups and tax penalties for congested regions.

Of course, the whole discussion has as premise the assumption that unemployment of a group affects only the wage of that group. If there is a leading sector whose employment rate pushes up wages elsewhere, that sector generates external disbenefits which make it a candidate for extra taxation. The reader will find it easy to modify our framework to deal with that case.

What we have said in this section is not the last word on tax progressivity, for there are well-known equity arguments in its favour, which we have not considered. There is also the case for progressive taxes to discourage wage pressure (Layard *et al.*, 1991). In that context we recommend a linear tax structure $(tW - S)$ with quite high t and a high flat rate subsidy S. But the implication of the present study is that, if it is possible to have different subsidies, S_i, for different groups, the optimal tax structure (in the absence of externalities) involves $(tW_i - S_i)e_i$ being equated between groups.

6   MISMATCH AND THE UNEMPLOYMENT/VACANCY RELATIONSHIP

We have not so far referred to vacancies at all in discussing mismatch. This is because we believe that the main issue is the mismatch between the total labour force of each type (L_i) and the employment (N_i). Hence our index *MM*.

It is helpful to use the shift of the aggregate u/v curve to isolate changes over time in the effectiveness of the unemployed. One cannot do this without first isolating the effect of mismatch on the location of the u/v curve. Hence we need an index of mismatch between u and v, which we shall call *mm*.

6.1   Theory

We need to see how differences in the ratio u_i/v_i across different groups affect the location of the aggregate u/v curve. Suppose, first, that each group had the same u/v curve based on the hiring function

$$H_i = AV_i^\alpha U_i^{1-\alpha}$$

If the entry to unemployment in each sector is $S_i = sN_i$, where s is the entry rate (assumed common to all groups), then in the steady state (with $H_i = sN_i$) the u/v curve is

$$s = A\left(\frac{V_i}{N_i}\right)^\alpha \left(\frac{U_i}{N_i}\right)^{1-\alpha} \tag{13}$$

This is shown in Figure 7.10.

If U/N and V/N were always the same for each group, then the national aggregate u/v curve would be identical to that shown in Figure 7.10. But if group 1 was at P_1 and group 2 at P_2 (and the two groups were of equal size) the aggregate national observation would be at P. This follows from the convexity of the relationship, and implies that inequalities in U_i/V_i always increase U/N at given V/N.

The same is true even if the hiring functions differ, as they do (see below). To see the quantitative effect of variations in the U_i/V_i ratios, we can begin by modifying the hiring function, (7.13), for each group to obtain

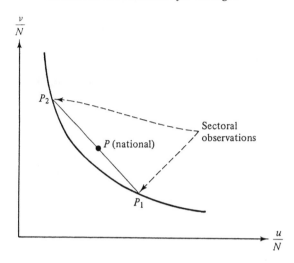

Figure 7.10 The u/v curve of a group

$$\frac{s_i}{A_i} = v_i^{\alpha} u_i^{1-\alpha}$$

where $u_i = U_i/N_i$ and $V_i = v_i/N_i$.

We then multiply and divide the right-hand side by $v^{\alpha}u^{1-\alpha}$ and take a weighted average of all the equations. This gives

$$\sum f_i \frac{s_i}{A_i} = \left[\sum f_i \left(\frac{v_i}{v}\right)^{\alpha} \left(\frac{u_i}{u}\right)^{1-\alpha}\right] v^{\alpha} u^{1-\alpha}$$

where $f_i = N_i/N$.

The term in brackets is a matching index, which has a maximum value of unity when the u_i/v_i ratio is the same in all groups.[21] At this point the aggregate unemployment rate is as low as it can be, for a given level of vacancies. But, as the u_i/v_i ratios diverge, the aggregate u/v curve shifts out.

It is natural to measure mismatch by the proportion to which unemployment is higher than it could be at given vacancies. u/v mismatch is thus measured by

$$mm = \log u - \log u_{min} = -\frac{1}{1-\alpha} \log\left[\sum f_i \left(\frac{v_i}{v}\right)^{\alpha} \left(\frac{u_i}{u}\right)^{1-\alpha}\right]$$

This is approximately[22]

$$mm \simeq \frac{1}{2}\alpha\left(\sigma_{v_i/v}^2 + \sigma_{u_i/u}^2 - 2\rho_{u_iv_i}\sigma_{u_i/u}\sigma_{v_i/v}\right)$$

where σ is the standard deviation and ρ the correlation coefficient (positive or negative).

6.2 Evidence

Let us examine the size of this mismatch index and its movements over time. Table 7.17 shows relative vacancy rates and relative unemployment rates by occupation, region and industry in Britain in 1982. To obtain the mismatch index we need a value of α, which can be taken as approximately $\frac{1}{2}$ (Pissarides, 1986; Jackman, Layard and Savouri, 1987; Blanchard and Diamond, 1989).[23] Using this value for α, Table 7.18 shows the movement of the mismatch index over time. The striking thing is the very small magnitude of the mismatch index, and the fact that it has not risen over time. In other words, any shift that has occurred in the aggregate u/v curve has also been a shift in the average u/v curve for each sector.

Jackman and Roper (1987) present similar evidence for France, Germany, the Netherlands, Austria, Finland, Norway and Sweden. Except in Sweden, there is no evidence of increased mismatch.

As regards the cyclical behaviour of mismatch, this was illustrated in Figure 7.1 using the index mm'. It shows a tendency for regional mismatch to fall in downturns and for industrial mismatch to rise.

Much has been made of the latter phenomenon by Lilien (1982). He has argued that fluctuations in unemployment are often *caused* by exogenous shifts in labour demand between industries, producing mismatch and hence changes in unemployment. But can we reasonably think of these cyclical shifts in mismatch as exogenous? If they were, we should expect the resulting mismatch to increase not only unemployment but vacancies. As Abraham and Katz (1986) show, this is not what happens when we see a short-run rise in the turbulence index. Instead unemployment rises and vacancies fall. Thus the notion that business downturns are typically initiated by structural demand shifts is implausible.

However over the longer term the degree of turbulence in industrial structure *is* clearly an important factor affecting unemployment. But for this purpose we need to take a moving average of the index. If we do this, as we have said, we find that industrial turbulence in the 1930s was double its postwar average in both Britain and the United States, and the same was true of Britain in the 1920s. Thus it is quite appropriate to blame a part of interwar unemployment on the 'problems of the declining industries'.

Table 7.17   Unemployment rates and registered vacancy rates by occupation, region and industry: Britain, 1982 (relative to national average)

	u_i/u	v_i/v
Occupation		
Managerial and professional	0.32	0.49
Clerical and related	0.80	1.05
Other non-manual	0.84	1.93
Skilled manual	0.87	0.84
Other manual	1.87	1.31
Region		
South-East	0.73	1.10
South West	0.89	1.30
East Midlands	0.92	0.92
West Midlands	1.24	0.67
Yorkshire and Humberside	1.11	0.74
North West	1.24	0.77
North	1.39	0.85
Wales	1.30	1.22
Scotland	1.17	1.24
Industry		
Agriculture	0.94	0.31
Mining and quarrying	0.88	0.12
Manufacturing	1.03	0.66
Construction	2.13	1.03
Gas, electricity and water	0.33	0.31
Transport	0.68	0.48
Distribution	0.86	1.31
Services	0.53	1.36
Public administration	0.68	1.31

Notes:
Unemployment data relate to previous occupation and industry of unemployed registered at Job Centres.
Vacancy rates relate to vacancies registered at Job Centres.
Source:
Occupation
Department of Employment Gazette (June 1982), Tables 2.11 and 3.4 (Employment figures from Labour Force Survey).
Region
Vacancies: *Department of Employment Gazette* (December 1985), Table 3.3.
Employment: *Regional Trends* (1985), Table 7.1.
Unemployment: *Department of Employment Gazette* (June 1982), Table 2.3 (made consistent with unpublished Department of Employment continuous series).
Industry
Department of Employment Gazette (June 1982), Table 3.3 and (July 1982), Table 2.9.

Explaining Unemployment

Table 7.18 u/v, mismatch: time series, Britain, 1963–88

	Mismatch index (%) $$2\left[1 - \sum \frac{N_i}{N}\left(\frac{u_i}{u}\frac{v_i}{v}\right)^{1/2}\right]$$		
Year	Regional (9 groups) (1)	Industrial (24 groups) (2)	Occupational (24/18 groups) (3)
1963	16	12	22
1964	20	10	22
1965	16	10	22
1966	12	10	24
1967	10	12	20
1968	14	12	20
1969	14	14	22
1970	10	12	22
1971	12	10	24
1972	14	8	22
1973	14	6	26
1974	12	10	26
1975	6	8	30
1976	4	6	24
1977	4	6	22
1978	8	4	22
1979	10	4	22
1980	8	8	24
1981	4	14	26
1982	4	12	24
1983	2	–	–
1984	4	–	–
1985	4	–	–
1986	4	–	–
1987	4	–	–
1988	5	–	–

Source: Author's calculations based on data published in successive issues of the *Department of Employment Gazette*.

6.3 Further evidence on occupations

Finally, we present some evidence on the duration of occupational vacancies in Britain. This is given in Table 7.19. The first point concerns the vacancy rates. These are based on a national survey which included all vacancies rather than adjusted data based on vacancies registered at Job Centres. It shows no clear tendency for higher vacancy rates in more skilled occupations, but the turnover rate is very much lower in the more skilled occupations; from this it follows that the duration of vacancies is very much longer in the skilled occupations. (The situation was very similar in 1977, the year of the only other national survey of vacancies: Jackman, Layard and Pissarides, 1984, p. 45.)

All of this raises obvious questions about which occupations are facing labour shortages. When employers in manufacturing were asked 'Do you expect your output to be limited by shortages of (a) skilled labour and (b) other labour', only 4 per cent replied Yes for 'other labour' compared with 20 per cent for 'skilled labour'. These replies coincide with the view that, from the employers' side, the proper pressure of demand variable is the *duration* of vacancies, rather than the vacancy rate. We must, however, note that from the point of view of workers the comparable duration (of unemployment) is similar in all groups, and it is the unemployment *rates* which differ. We have not yet found a satisfactory way of interpreting these fascinating data.

7 CONCLUSIONS

It may now be helpful to bring together in summary form some of the main arguments of this study.

1. There are huge differences in unemployment rates between occupations, regions, age groups and races. These differences are for the most part very persistent and do not reflect the legacy of structural shocks. They are however quite closely related to differences in turnover rates (i.e. in the rate of entry to unemployment), with differences in unemployment durations playing a minor role.

2 Unemployment rate differences between age groups are affected by demographic factors. But unemployment differences between occupations and regions can be explained only jointly with mobility between groups. In each case high unemployment is associated with low costs of entry and high levels of wage push. Where (as in Britain but not the United States) regional unemployment differences are highly persistent, these importantly reflect steady-state differences in job growth relative to the natural growth of population.

Table 7.19 Differences between occupations in vacancy flows and stocks: Britain, 1988

	Unemployment (1984)				Vacancies (1988)			% of firms reporting shortage of labour (January 1988) (7)
	Inflow rate (% per month) (1)	Average duration (months) (2)	Unemployment rate (%) (3)		Engagement rate (% per month) (4)	Duration of vacancies (months) (5)	Vacancy rate (%) (January) (6)	
Managerial and professional	0.50	11.2	5.3	Managerial and professional	1.0	2.2	2.2	
Clerical	0.88	10.1	8.0	Clerical	2.3	1.5	3.4	Skilled 20
Other non-manual	1.14	11.8	12.2	Skilled and semi-skilled manual	2.8	1.2	3.4	
				Retail and catering, personal services	5.8	0.9	5.1	
Skilled manual	1.02	14.2	12.6					
Semi- and unskilled manual	1.32	14.1	15.5	Unskilled manual	3.8	0.6	2.1	Other 4
All	0.94	12.8	10.8	All	2.8	1.0	2.9	

Sources:
Unemployment:
See Table 7.5.
Vacancies:
IFF Research Ltd, *Vacancies and Recruitment Study* (May 1988), 12 Argyll Street, London W1V 1AB.
Col. (4) = Engagements ÷ Employed (Table 4.3).
Col. (5) = Col. (6) ÷ Col. (4).
Col. (6) = Vacancies ÷ Employed (Appendix 9).
Labour Shortages: CBI Industrial Trends Survey.

3. One naturally asks whether the rise in European unemployment can be explained by increased mismatch. To investigate this we assume (and later check) that wage behaviour in a sector is primarily caused by unemployment in that sector, rather than by unemployment in some leading sector. Given this assumption, the relevant index of mismatch is a half the variance of the relative unemployment rates; on this basis mismatch has increased in no country we studied except Sweden, but the *level* of mismatch still in Britain explains at least one-third of all unemployment.

4. As regards policy, if the members in each group are exogenous (e.g., as in each age group), then it pays to subsidise employment where it is low and to tax employment where it is high. But where workers choose their sectors (as with occupations and regions) the matter is more complex. If there are no standard 'externalities' (other than unemployment), no leading sector in wage determination, and all workers are identical, there is no efficiency case for any tax/subsidy scheme to improve the structure of unemployment rates. Contrary to the standard notions of 'manpower policy', expected taxes should be equal for all groups.

   But tax/subsidy arrangements should be used to discourage bad externalities (e.g. congestion in low unemployment regions), to promote good externalities (e.g. skill training), and to discourage overheating in any leading sectors. In addition where workers vary (upward-sloping supply curves) it may be right to subsidise employment in high unemployment groups.

5. Finally we examine the mismatch between unemployment and vacancies. We show that this mismatch has not worsened either, and cannot be used to explain the outward shift of the u/v curve that has occurred in many countries.

Appendix: Mismatch and Substitution between Types of Labour

The curvature of the real wage frontier depends on the elasticity of substitution in demand between different types of labour.[24] Using a CES production function of the form

$$Y^\rho = \varphi \Sigma \alpha_i N_i^\rho \qquad (\Sigma \alpha_i = 1, \rho - 1 = -1/\sigma, \sigma \geq 0, \sigma \neq 1)$$

we obtain a price function[25]

$$P = \Sigma \alpha_i^\sigma W_i^{-(\sigma-1)}/A'$$

where A' is again a combined index of technical progress and product market competition.

Setting the price level at unity, the *price function* gives us a feasible real wage frontier

$$A' = \Sigma \alpha_i^\sigma W_i^{-(\sigma-1)}$$

If the *wage functions* are

$$W_i = \beta_i u_i^{-\gamma}$$

the *unemployment frontier* is now

$$A' = \Sigma \alpha_i^\sigma \beta_i^{-(\sigma-1)} u_i^{\gamma(\sigma-1)}$$

Using empirically relevant magnitudes such as γ 0.1 (see below), and $0 < \sigma < 10$, this is a concave function in the u_is.

To find the aggregate unemployment rate, we multiply by $u^{-\gamma(\sigma-1)}/A'$ to obtain

$$u^{-\gamma(\sigma-1)} = \frac{1}{A'} \Sigma \alpha_i \alpha_i^{\sigma-1} \beta_i^{-(\sigma-1)} \left(\frac{u_i}{u}\right)^{\gamma(\sigma-1)}$$

If α_i, β_i, u_i/u and L_i/L are approximately independent,[26] then

$$\log u \simeq \frac{1}{2}(1 - \gamma(\sigma - 1)) \text{ var } \frac{u_i}{u} + \text{constant}$$

Mismatch is now

$$MM = \frac{1}{2}(1 - \gamma(\sigma - 1)) \text{ var } \frac{u_i}{u}$$

Notes

1. Note that a temporary shock in favour of a high unemployment group will actually *reduce* the total imbalance.

2. Honourable exceptions are Lipsey (1960), Archibald (1967), Baily and Tobin (1977), Johnson and Blakemore (1979) and hopefully the chapters in this volume arising out of the CEPR/CLE/STEP conference, Venice (4–6 January 1990).

3. This is not because turbulence creates mismatch which creates aggregate unemployment (Lilien, 1982) – see Abraham and Katz (1986); it is because aggregate shocks are highly sectorally unbalanced – and thus create both aggregate unemployment *and* more turbulence and more mismatch. Such shocks particularly affect high unemployment sectors (e.g. construction).

4. Where the sectors considered are regions, we could introduce an equivalent CES utility function where σ reflected substitution elasticities between the products of different regions.

5. Neither bargaining theory nor efficiency wage theory have so far made much progress in explaining the wages of one group out of many groups employed. This is a key area for research. Honourable exceptions to this remark include Lazear (1989) who showed how envy could lead employers to prefer more egalitarian wage structures than otherwise. A related argument is developed in Akerlof and Yellen (1987).

6. X is not of course exogenous but can be solved for by substituting $N_i \ (= (1 - u_i)L_i)$ into the production function.

7. It is best to think of W_i as measuring the wage in terms of its power to purchase market bundles of goods.

8. This arises from differential age structures and differential change in participation rates.

9. The 'natural' population growth in *each* occupation (i.e. the growth in the absence of net migration) is $\dot{L}$.

10. This assumes $\alpha_i \quad L_i/L$, for the minimization of u requires

$$\min_{u_i} \Sigma \frac{L_i}{L} u_i - \varphi(\Sigma \alpha_i \log u_i - \text{const})$$

that is,

$$\frac{L_i}{L} - \varphi \frac{\alpha_i}{u_i} = 0$$

If $\alpha = L_i/L$, this requires $u_i = \varphi$ (all i).

11. This assumes that the weights α_i (which are shares of the wage bill) are either equal to L_i/L (which are shares of the labour force), or that $(\alpha_i - L_i/L)$ is independent of u_i/u.

12. Note that mismatch is the proportional excess of actual unemployment over the unemployment needed to yield the same inflationary pressure if all unemployment rates were equal. Readers familiar with the Atkinson (1970) index of inequality will note the close correspondence between his measure and our mismatch measure. Atkinson measured inequality as the proportion by which actual output exceeded the output needed to yield the same social welfare if individual incomes were equal.

13. Let

$$\gamma \frac{u_i^\alpha - 1}{\alpha} = f(u_i)$$

$$f(u_i) \qquad f(u) + f'(u)(u_i - u) + \tfrac{1}{2}f''(u)(u_i - u)^2$$

So

$$A = \Sigma \alpha_i \beta_i - \Sigma \alpha_i f(u_i)$$

$$= \Sigma \alpha_i \beta_i - \gamma \left[\frac{u^\alpha - 1}{\alpha} + 0 - \tfrac{1}{2}(1 - \alpha)u^{\alpha-2} \Sigma \alpha_i (u_i - u)^2 \right]$$

This gives

$$u^\alpha = \left(\frac{1 + \alpha(\Sigma \alpha_i \beta_i - A)/\gamma}{1 - \dfrac{\alpha(1 - \alpha)}{2} \operatorname{var} \dfrac{u_i}{u}} \right)$$

Since $0 < u < 1$, $\Sigma \alpha_i \beta_i - A < 0$ and u is increasing in $\operatorname{var}(u_i/u)$ for all values of α.

14. Of course wages could depend on both one-sector unemployment (u_i) and leading-sector unemployment (u_L):

$$\log u = \frac{\Sigma \alpha_i \beta_i - A}{\gamma + \delta} + \frac{\gamma}{\gamma + \delta}\tfrac{1}{2}\operatorname{var}\left(\frac{u_i}{u}\right) + \frac{\delta}{\gamma + \delta}\log\left(\frac{u}{u_L}\right)$$

15. We also did estimates in which X took the fitted values from regressing output per worker on a quintic in time. The coefficients in the corresponding wage equations were almost identical to those in Table 7.14.

16. No serious bias exists from letting W and u be the log of the averages, rather than the average of the logs.

17.

$$\frac{1}{\eta_S} = \frac{e_i}{W_i}\frac{\partial W_i}{\partial e_i} \quad \text{and} \quad \frac{1}{\eta_D} = \frac{e_i L_i}{W_i}\frac{\partial F_i}{\partial (e_i L_i)}$$

Strictly, the latter is $1/\eta_D$ only if t_i is small.

18. There are two further terms which sum to zero. These are

$$- \theta_1(F_{11}e_1 - F_{12}e_2) - \theta_2(F_{21}e_1 - F_{22}e_2)$$

$$= \varphi e_1(e_1 L_1 F_{11} + e_2 L_2 F_{21}) - \varphi e_2(e_1 L_1 F_{12} + e_2 L_2 F_{22})$$

$$= \varphi e_1(0) - \varphi e_2(0) \quad \text{(by Euler's Theorem)}$$

19. In the case of a migration subsidy of s paid to workers who get trained and employed in sector 1, we arrive at exactly the same conclusion. The tax condition is

$$(t_1 - s)e_1 L_1 + t_2 e_2(L - L_1) - R = 0$$

The migration condition is

$$e_1(W_1 + s) - e_2 W_2 - c_1 = 0$$

Hence $\dfrac{\partial Y^*}{\partial L_1} = 0$ implies

$$(t_1 - s)e_1 - t_2 e_2 = 0$$

20. The conclusion would be unaffected if costs were a proportion of $W_2 e_2$, φ is positive, because a reduction in R raises Y. As regards λ, if the zero-migration constraint did not hold and people could be physically allocated to sectors, the optimum allocation would be given by equation (10), with c_1 replaced by C'. We can assume that in this situation $t_1 e_1 - t_2 e_2 > 0$: in other words we should want to have a smallish number of unskilled people and then subsidise their employment to keep them in work. But we cannot do this since by equation (10) this would reduce incentives to migrate below the acceptable level. It follows that if there is a supply equilibrium constraint, an additional incentive to move would raise welfare. Hence $\partial Y^* / \partial$ net return $= \lambda > 0$.

21. We seek to

$$\max_{u_i, v_i} \sum \left(\frac{v_i}{v}\right)^\alpha \left(\frac{u_i}{u}\right)^{1-\alpha} + \lambda(\Sigma v_i - v) + \varphi(\Sigma u_i - u)$$

This requires

$$\alpha \left(\frac{v_i}{u_i}\right)^{\alpha-1} \left(\frac{1}{v}\right)^\alpha \left(\frac{1}{u}\right)^{1-\alpha} + \lambda = 0 \quad \text{(all } i\text{)}$$

If $v_i = \theta u_i$ (all i),

$$\sum \left(\frac{v_i}{v}\right)^\alpha \left(\frac{u_i}{u}\right)^{1-\alpha} = \sum \left(\frac{u_i}{u}\right)^\alpha \left(\frac{u_i}{u}\right)^{1-\alpha} = \frac{\Sigma u_i}{u} = 1$$

22. Expanding $\left(\frac{v_i}{v}\right)^\alpha \left(\frac{u_i}{u}\right)^{1-\alpha}$ around $\frac{v_i}{v} = \frac{u_i}{u} = 1$,

we have

$$\left(\frac{v_i}{v}\right)^\alpha \left(\frac{u_i}{u}\right)^{1-\alpha} \simeq 1 + \alpha\left(\frac{v_i}{v} - 1\right) + (1-\alpha)\left(\frac{u_i}{u} - 1\right)$$
$$+ \tfrac{1}{2}\alpha(\alpha-1)\left(\frac{v_i}{v} - 1\right)^2 + \tfrac{1}{2}(1-\alpha)(-\alpha)\left(\frac{u_i}{u} - 1\right)^2$$
$$+ (1-\alpha)\alpha\left(\frac{v_i}{v} - 1\right)\left(\frac{u_i}{u} - 1\right)$$

Hence

$$\sum \frac{N_i}{N} \left(\frac{v_i}{v}\right)^\alpha \left(\frac{u_i}{u}\right)^{1-\alpha} \simeq 1 - \tfrac{1}{2}\alpha(1-\alpha)\left[\sigma^2_{v_i/v} + \sigma^2_{u_i/u} - 2\mathrm{cov}_{v_i/v, u_i/u}\right]$$

Note also that this equals

$$1 - \tfrac{1}{2}\alpha(1-\alpha)\sum \frac{N_i}{N}\left[\left(\frac{v_i}{v} - 1\right) - \left(\frac{u_i}{u} - 1\right)\right]^2$$
$$= 1 - \tfrac{1}{2}\alpha(1-\alpha)\sum \frac{N_i}{N}\left(\frac{v_i}{v} - \frac{u_i}{u}\right)^2$$

Thus it is closely related to the index.

$$\sum \frac{N_i}{N}\left|\frac{v_i}{v}-\frac{u_i}{u}\right| = \sum\left|\frac{V_i}{V}-\frac{U_i}{U}\right|$$

used in Jackman and Roper (1987).

23. See Jackman *et al.* (1991, Chapter 5). The British studies find α about 0.3, while the US studies find a value nearly twice as high. For reasons given there the true value probably lies in between, and this is confirmed for British data in Jackman *et al.*, Chapter 5, Annex 2 which suggests a coefficient around $0.29/(0.46 + 0.29)$.

24. This reflects the elasticity of substitution in production or the elasticity of substitution in consumption between different products.

25. Under monopolistic competition with demand elasticity η,

$$W_i = \frac{\partial Y}{\partial N_i}(1 - 1/\eta) = A'\alpha_i\left(\frac{N_i}{Y}\right)^{-(1/\sigma)}(1 - 1/\eta)$$

By Euler's Theorem

$$1 = \sum_i \frac{\partial Y}{\partial N_i}\frac{N_i}{Y} = (1 - 1/\eta)^{-1+\sigma}A^\sigma \Sigma W_i\left(\frac{w_i}{\alpha_i}\right)^{-\sigma}$$

26. If $\Sigma\alpha_i = 1$ and α_i, x_i, y_i and z_i are independent, then $\Sigma\alpha_i x_i y_i z_i = \bar{x}\bar{y}\bar{z}$. Hence if α_i, β_i and u_i are independent, (7.5) implies

$$u^{-\gamma(\sigma-1)} = \frac{1}{A'}\sum \alpha_i\alpha_i^{\sigma-1}\sum \alpha_i\beta_i^{-(\sigma-1)}\sum \alpha_i\left(\frac{u_i}{u}\right)^{\gamma(\sigma-1)}$$

or

$$u^{-\gamma(\sigma-1)} = \sum \alpha_i\left(\frac{u_i}{u}\right)^{\gamma(\sigma-1)} x \text{ const}$$

Going on, if we assume $(\alpha_i - L_i/L)$ independent of u_i/u, we obtain

$$u^{-\gamma(\sigma-1)} = \sum \frac{L_i}{L}\left(\frac{u_i}{u}\right)^{\gamma(\sigma-1)} x \text{ const}$$

Since

$$\sum \frac{L_i}{L}\left(\frac{u_i}{u}\right)^{\gamma(\sigma-1)} \simeq 1 + \tfrac{1}{2}(\gamma(\sigma-1) - 1)\gamma(\sigma-1)\,\text{var}\,\frac{u_i}{u}$$

$$-\gamma(\sigma-1)\log u \simeq \tfrac{1}{2}(1 - \gamma(\sigma-1))\gamma(\sigma-1)\,\text{var}\,\frac{u_i}{u} + \text{const}$$

References

Abowd, J. and O. Ashenfelter (1981) 'Anticipated Unemployment, Temporary Layoffs and Compensating Differentials', in S. Rosen (ed.), *Studies in Labor Markets* (Chicago: University of Chicago Press).

Abraham, K. and L. Katz (1986) 'Cyclical Unemployment: Sectoral Shifts or Aggregate Disturbances?', *Journal of Political Economy*, 94, 507–22.

Akerlof, G.A. and J.L. Yellen (1987) 'The Fair Wage/Effort Hypothesis and Unemployment' (Berkeley: University of California), mimeo.

Archibald, G. (1967) 'Regional Multiplier Effects in the UK', *Oxford Economic Papers*, 19(1).

Archibald, G. (1969) 'The Phillips Curve and the Distribution of Unemployment', *American Economic Review*, LIX(2).

Atkinson, A. (1970) 'On the Measurement of Inequality', *Journal of Economic Theory*, 2, 244–63.

Baily, M. and J.M. Tobin (1977) 'Macroeconomic Effects of Selective Public Employment and Wage Subsidies', *Brookings Papers on Economic Activity*, 2, 511–41.

Blanchard, O. and P. Diamond (1989) 'Beveridge and Phillips Curve' (Cambridge, MA: MIT), mimeo.

Blanchflower, D. and A. Oswald (1989) 'The Wage Curve', London School of Economics, Centre for Labour Economics, *Discussion Paper*, 340.

Blaug, M., R. Layard and M. Woodhall (1969) *The Causes of Graduate Unemployment in India* (London: Allen Lane, The Penguin Press), see Chapter 11 in this volume.

Freeman, R. (1986) 'Demand for Education', in O. Ashenfelter and R. Layard (eds), *The Handbook of Labor Economics*, vol. 1 (Amsterdam: North-Holland), 357–86.

Freeman, R. and D. Bloom (1986) 'The Youth Labour Market Problem: Age or Generational Crowding', OECD *Employment Outlook* (September), 106–28.

Greenwood, M. (1985) 'Human Migration: Theory, Models and Empirical Studies', *Journal of Regional Sciences*, 25, 521–44.

Grubb, D. (1986) 'Topics in the OECD Phillips Curve', *The Economic Journal*, 96, 55–79.

Hall, R. (1970) 'Why is the Unemployment Rate so High at Full Employment?', *Brookings Papers on Economic Activity*, 3, 369–402.

Hamermesh, D. (1986) 'The Demand for Labor in the Long Run', in O. Ashenfelter and R. Layard (eds), *The Handbook of Labor Economics*, vol. 1 (Amsterdam: North-Holland), 429–71.

Harris, J. and M. Todaro (1970) 'Migration, Unemployment and Development: A Two-Sector Analysis', *American Economic Review*, 60, 126–42.

Jackman, R., R. Layard and C. Pissarides (1984) 'On Vacancies', Centre for Labour Economics, LSE, *Discussion Paper*, 165 (revised), Chapter 5 in this volume/OBES version.

Jackman, R. and S. Roper (1987) 'Structural Unemployment', *Oxford Bulletin of Economics and Statistics*, 49(1), 9–37.

Jackman, R., R. Layard and S. Savouri (1987) 'Labour Market Mismatch and the "Equilibrium" Level of Unemployment', London School of Economics, Centre for Labour Economics, working paper, 1009.

Johnson, G. and A. Blakemore (1979) 'The Potential Impact of Employment Policy for Reducing the Unemployment Rate Consistent with Non-Accelerating Inflation', *American Economic Review* (Papers and Proceedings), 69, 119–30.

Johnson, G. and R. Layard (1986) 'The Natural Rate of Unemployment: Explanation and Policy', O. Ashenfelter and R. Layard (eds), *The Handbook of Labor Economics*, vol. 2 (Amsterdam: North-Holland), 921–99.

Layard, R. (1982) 'Youth Unemployment in Britain and the United States Compared', in R.B. Freeman and D.A. Wise (eds), *The Youth Labor Market Problem: Its Nature, Causes and Consequence* (Chicago: University of Chicago Press).

Layard, R. and S. Nickell (1986) 'Unemployment in Britain', *Economica, Special Supplement on Unemployment*, 53, S121–S169.

Layard, R. and S. Nickell (1987) 'The Labour Market', in R. Dornbusch and R. Layard (eds), *The Performance of the British Economy* (Oxford: Oxford University Press) Chapter 4 in this volume.

Layard, R., S. Nickell and R. Jackman (1991) *Unemployment: Macroeconomic Performance and the Labour Market* (Oxford: Oxford University Press).

Lazear, E. (1989) 'Pay Equality and Industrial Policies', *Journal of Political Economy*, 97(3), 561–80.

Lilien, D. (1982) 'Sectoral Shifts and Cyclical Unemployment', *Journal of Political Economy*, 90, 777–93.

Lipsey, R. (1960) 'The Relation Between Unemployment and the Rate of Change of Money Wage Rates in the United Kingdom, 1862–1957: A Further Analysis', *Economica*, 27(1), 1–31.

Nickell, S. (1981) 'Biases in Dynamic Models with Fixed Effects', *Econometrica* 49(6), 1417–26.

Nickell, S. and S. Wadhwani (1989) 'Insider Forces and Wage Determination' Centre for Labour Economics, LSE, *Discussion Paper*, 334.

Oswald, A. (1986) 'Wage Determination and Recession: A Report on Recent Work', Centre for Labour Economics, LSE, *Discussion Paper*, 243.

Pissarides, C. (1981) 'Staying-on at School in England and Wales', *Economica* 48(192), 345–64.

Pissarides, C. (1982) 'From School to University: The Demand for Post-Compulsory Education in Britain', *Economic Journal*, 92(367), 654–67.

Pissarides, C. (1986) 'Unemployment and Vacancies in Britain', *Economic Policy*, 3, 489–560.

Pissarides, C. and J. Wadsworth (1989) 'Unemployment and the Inter-Regional Mobility of Labour', *Economic Journal*, 99, 739–55.

Savouri, S. (1989) 'Regional Data', Centre for Labour Economics, LSE, *Working Paper*, 1135.

8 European versus US Unemployment: Different Responses to Increased Demand for Skill? (1997)*

with R. Jackman, M. Manacorda and B. Petrongolo

In coffee-shop discussions of unemployment, skills mismatch is a usual suspect. Indeed authors like Krugman (1994) assert that European unemployment is rising because the demand for skills increases faster than the supply, and wages are not allowed to adjust.[1] Surprisingly, no one has so far checked the component parts of this assertion, nor analyzed them within a simple model which has a sensible definition of a neutral shift in demand and supply.

The aim of this paper is to develop a simple labour market model which explains the movement of wages and unemployment for each skill group – and then to apply it to what has been happening in Europe and the United States. The aim throughout is to tease out what part of the change in unemployment can be attributed to changes in skills mismatch, carefully defined.

There are two types of labour by skill (though it could be more). The demand for each is derived from a production function which is becoming steadily more skill-intensive. At the same time the pattern of supply (taken as exogenous) is also becoming steadily more skilled. By estimating the production function, we can assess the rate at which the demand for skill is shifting relative to supply. If demand is rising faster than supply, we call this an increase in 'ex ante mismatch' (M), meaning that if relative wages remained unchanged the employment rate of the skilled would rise relative to the employment rate of the unskilled.

What *actually* happens to unemployment depends, however, on how wages actually move. The wages of each group are determined by a wage-setting function which depends on the unemployment rate of that group.[2] Provided the balance of demand and supply remains unchanged (dM = 0), unemployment can only increase if the wage function for each group shifts up faster than its increase in productivity. We described a general 'unwarranted' increase in wages as an increase in aggregate wage pressure (AWP).

* We are grateful to the Economic and Social Research Council for financial support.

201

We can thus decompose historical changes in unemployment into three main sources – changes in the balance between demand and supply (M), changes in *relative* wage behaviour (which may or may not offset the effect of changes in M), and changes in *aggregate* wage pressure (AWP). The first component reflects 'ex ante mismatch', and the first two taken together 'ex post mismatch'.

We show why our definition of ex ante mismatch shocks (ΔM) is more meaningful than that used by previous writers such as Nickell and Bell (1995). And we also show how the aggregate measure of mismatch unemployment put forward in Layard *et al.* (1991), and now widely used, works out in terms of the detail of our structural model.

In Part 2 of the paper we assign numbers to each element in the model. In the key Tables 8.2A and 8.2B we decompose for Britain and the USA the reasons for the changes in unemployment of both skilled and unskilled workers. The key fact is that in Britain skilled unemployment rose, which cannot be explained by increased imbalance (M) and must be explained mainly by increased aggregate wage pressure (AWP). We also look at other European countries and show that in most of them the supply of skill grew more in line with increased demand than it did in Britain and the USA. This is an important reason why wage inequality increased less in continental Europe than it did in Britain and the USA. Thus Europe's especial difficulty arises not from a failure to adjust to increased skills imbalance but from a different set of problems. In this paper we group all these other problems under the heading of aggregate wage pressure, but we believe that this in turn stems largely from problems of the European welfare state (Jackman *et al.*, 1996; Nickell and Layard, forthcoming).

So, in what follows, Section 1 is the theory, and Section 2 the evidence. Section 3 concludes.

1   THE FRAMEWORK OF ANALYSIS

Skilled-specific unemployment

We begin by analyzing skill-specific unemployment. We concentrate on a binary division between two groups, skilled (group 1) and unskilled (group 2), though the approach can be generalized. The demand side comes from a Cobb–Douglas production function, which we show later is supported by the evidence. Thus

$$Y = AN_i^{\alpha} N_2^{1-\alpha}$$

where Y is output and N_i is employment.

We can see at once the dilemma motivating Krugman's argument. For in a competitive labour market, if W_i is the real wage,

$$\frac{W_1 N_1}{W_2 N_2} = \frac{\alpha}{1 - \alpha}$$

and thus

$$\frac{W_1}{W_2} \frac{N_1/L_1}{N_2/L_2} = \frac{\alpha}{1 - \alpha} \Big/ \frac{L_1}{L_2}$$

where L_i is labour supply. The right hand side represents the balance between relative demand and relative supply. If relative demand outruns relative supply, this leads (on the left hand side) either to widening wage inequality or widening employment differentials in favour of skilled labour.

This is the basis of Krugman's assertion that 'the European unemployment problem and the US inequality problem are two sides of the same coin'. In this argument it is *assumed* that in both regions relative demand has outrun supply, and the only issue is how this shows up – in higher wage inequality (the USA) or in higher dispersion of employment rates (Europe).

The argument is illustrated in Figure 8.1. The location of the isoquant depends on the level of $\frac{\alpha}{1-\alpha} / \frac{L_1}{L_2}$ which we call M – our measure of ex ante

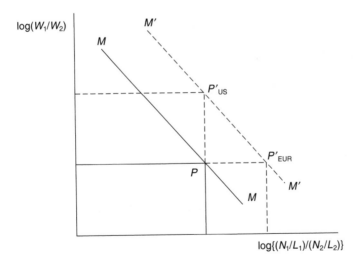

Figure 8.1 Responses to increases in *ex ante* mismatch: the 'Krugman' argument

mismatch. Originally we are at point P, but after M rises we can move to P'_{US} or P'_{EUR}, or anywhere else on the new M' isoquant.

However to make progress we need a framework in which we can look at absolute as well as relative employment rates. For this we need demand functions and wage functions for each type of skill. For skilled labour, demand is given by

$$\log W_1 = \log A + \log \alpha + (\alpha - 1)\log \frac{N_1}{N_2}$$

where W_1 is the real wage. Differentiating, and then adding and subtracting $(1 - \alpha)d\log(L_1/L_2)$, gives a *demand function*[3]

$$d\log W_1 = d\log A + \log \frac{N_1}{N_2}d\alpha - (1 - \alpha)d\log \frac{N_1/L_1}{N_2/L_2}$$
$$+ d\log \alpha - (1 - \alpha)d\log \frac{L_1}{L_2}$$

or

$$d\log W_1 = d\log A + \log \frac{N_1}{N_2}d\alpha + (1 - \alpha)d\log \frac{1 - u_2}{1 - u_1}$$
$$+ (1 - \alpha)d\log M \qquad (8.1)$$

At the same time skilled wages respond to skilled employment according to the double-log *wage function*[4]

$$\log W_1 = z_1 - \gamma \log u_1$$

or

$$d\log W_1 = dz_1 - \gamma d\log u_1 \qquad (8.2)$$

Unemployment outcomes

Combining (1) and (2) gives

$$du_1 = -\phi_1(1 - \alpha)d\log M + \phi_1\left(dz_1 - d\log A - \log \frac{N_1}{N_2}d\alpha\right)$$
$$+ \phi_1(1 - \alpha)(1 - u_2)^{-1}du_2 \qquad (8.3)$$

where $\phi_1 = u_1(1 - u_1)/(\gamma(1 - u_1) + (1 - \alpha)u_1)$. By analogy

$$du_2 = \phi_2\alpha d\log M + \phi_2\left(dz_2 - d\log A - \log \frac{N_1}{N_2}d\alpha\right)$$
$$+ \phi_2\alpha(1 - u_1)^{-1}du_1 \qquad (8.4)$$

where $\phi_2 = u_2(1 - u_2)/(\gamma(1 - u_2) + \alpha u_2)$. Thus unemployment rates are given by ex ante mismatch (M) and wage behaviour (given by

$$dz_i - d\log A - \log\frac{N_1}{N_2}d\alpha)$$

One key lesson emerges at once from (8.3) and (8.4) taken together. The unemployment rates of both groups will be constant ($du_1 = du_2 = 0$) if

(1) there is no change in M – the balance between relative demand and relative supply is unchanged, and
(2) the wage functions of each group move up by an amount equal to $d\log A + \log(N_1/N_2)d\alpha$

If however M changes, the unemployment rates will shift, unless the wage functions adjust appropriately so as to offset this effect. To see how they need to adjust, it is illuminating to divide the second (bracketed) term in each equation into two parts, one reflecting shifts in the average wage function and the other reflecting shifts in the relative wage function. If $d\bar{z} = \alpha dz_1 + (1 - \alpha)dz_2$, we can decompose the shift in a group's wage behaviour into the two parts – a shift in the relative wage functions and a shift in the aggregate wage function, as follows:[5]

$$dz_1 - d\log A - \log\frac{N_1}{N_2}d\alpha \equiv (dz_1 - d\bar{z}) + \left(d\bar{z} - d\log A - \log\frac{N_1}{N_2}d\alpha\right)$$

$$\equiv (1 - \alpha)(dz_1 - dz_2) + dAWP$$

and similarly for group 2. The overall shift in a group's wage behaviour comes from a shift in the relative wage function ($dz_1 - dz_2$) plus a shift in aggregate wage pressure defined as $dAWP = d\bar{z} - d\log A - \log\frac{N_1}{N_2}d\alpha$.

If we insert these changes into (8.3) and (8.4), we can get some real insight into what is going on. We have

$$du_1 = -\phi_1(1 - \alpha)d\log M + \phi_1(1 - \alpha)(dz_1 - dz_2) + \phi_1 dAWP$$
$$+ \phi_1(1 - \alpha)(1 - u_2)^{-1}du_2 \qquad (8.3')$$

$$du_2 = \phi_2\alpha d\log M - \phi_2\alpha(dz_1 - dz_2) + \phi_2 dAWP + \phi_2\alpha(1 - u_1)^{-1}du_1 \quad (8.4')$$

We can now see how the relative wage functions have to shift if M changes, in order to prevent unemployment changing, since sufficient conditions for constant unemployment rates ($du_1, du_2 = 0$) are

(1) $d\log M = dz_1 - dz_2$, and
(2) $dAWP = 0$

In other words, the wage functions must shift to offset the change in ex ante mismatch and there must be no change in aggregate wage pressure.

Aggregate unemployment

We can now look at the change in aggregate unemployment, du. To get this, we solve (8.3′) and (8.4′) to get the reduced form equations for du_1 and du_2 as shown in Appendix 1. To find the total change in unemployment we take a weighted average of du_1 and du_2 and allow also for any shift in the composition of the labour force. Thus the total change in unemployment is given by

$$
\begin{aligned}
du = {} & \theta_1 d\log M & & \text{(ex ante mismatch)} \\
& - \theta_1(dz_1 - dz_2) & & \text{(relative wave shock)} \\
& + \theta_2 dAWP & & \text{(aggregate wage shock)} \\
& + (u_1 - u_2)d(L_1/L) & & \text{(compositional effect)}
\end{aligned}
\tag{8.5}
$$

where the θ_is are defined in Appendix 1. In our empirical analysis we therefore show the breakdown of du_1, du_2 and du, for both Britain and the USA into the categories identified in (8.5).

This seems a reasonable breakdown. If unemployment rates change and there has been no altered balance between relative demand and supply, then in the most general sense the change in unemployment must result from inappropriate changes in wage behaviour at given unemployment.[6]

These changes in wage behaviour may result from all kinds of influences – changes in unemployment benefits, wage bargaining behaviour, taxes, import prices and so on. But if our focus is on the issue of skills imbalance, it is natural to group all the other issues together under the heading of wage pressure.

Justifying our definitions of neutrality

The question is precisely how one should define a neutral shift in relative demand and supply, and how one should define an appropriate change in aggregate wage behaviour. In our framework we are defining

(1)   a neutral shift in demand and supply ($dM = 0$) as one in which there is no change in

$$\frac{\alpha}{1-\alpha} \Big/ \frac{L_1}{L_2}, \text{ and}$$

(2)   a neutral change in aggregate wage behaviour ($dAWP = 0$) as one where $d\bar{z} = d\log A + \log(N_1/N_2)d\alpha$

The first point is that, if we redefined one of these criteria of neutrality, we should have to redefine the other, in order to ensure that there was no effect on unemployment if both changes were neutral. But how reasonable is each definition, taken on its own?

(1) *A neutral shift in demand and supply.* For neutrality we require

$$d \log \frac{\alpha}{1 - \alpha} - d \log \frac{L_1/L}{L_2/L} = 0$$

By contrast Nickell and Bell (1995 Box 2) and (Manning *et al.* 1996) implicitly assume that a neutral situation is characterized by

$$d \log \alpha - d \log L_1/L = 0 \quad \text{and} \quad d \log(1 - \alpha) - d \log L_2/L = 0$$

However, this condition can never be satisfied except when $\alpha = L_1/L$, which is never the case. Indeed in the historical statistics it is frequently the case that both $(d \log \alpha - d \log L_1/L)$ and $(d \log (1 - \alpha) - d \log L_2/L)$ have the same sign. Thus an analysis which is meant to imply that an increased relative demand for one type of labour accompanies a decreased relative demand for the other may in fact imply that both relative demands move in the same direction. Not surprisingly an illogical approach to imbalance goes hand in hand with an illogical approach to aggregate wage pressure.

(2) *A neutral shift in aggregate wage pressure.* For unemployment to be constant for each type of labour, wages at given unemployment must grow in line with the marginal product of that type of labour. From (8.1) and the comparable equation for unskilled labour, it is clear that if $d \log M = 0$, each unemployment rate will be constant if each wage changes by $d \log A + \log(N_1/N_2)d\alpha$. In other words we require $dz_i = d \log A + \log(N_1/N_2)d\alpha$. Any deviation from this causes trouble, which is why it is perfectly natural to define a neutral change in aggregate wage pressure (*AWP*) by $d\bar{z} = d \log A + \log(N_1/N_2)d\alpha$.

It is important to be clear what the aggregate wage pressure condition permits, in a context where N_1/N_2 is constantly rising. The condition does not allow for $d\bar{z}$ to be as large as the rise in *actual average* wages, since this latter includes the effect of changes in both of the marginal products *plus* a compositional effect as increasing N_1/N_2 increases the share of skilled workers in the workforce. The permitted $d\bar{z}$ is limited to a fixed-weight index of the changes in marginal products.[7]

Yet the procedure adopted by Manning *et al.* (1996) and others allows the wage function to rise by the actual rise in average wages, including the compositional effect. This naturally reduces the role of wage pressure in explaining rising unemployment, and increases the role of mismatch. Given these considerations, we are happy with our decomposition and believe that the results given in the first half of Section 2 give a good picture of what has been happening.

Ex post mismatch: a short-cut

However, for some purposes we can usefully use a simpler decomposition than that provided in equation (8.5). When people ask if higher unemployment is due to increased skills mismatch, they do not mean to include only the effect of $d \log M$. Suppose that wages have adjusted through an appropriate change in relative wage pressure – for example, an increase in M has been offset by an appropriate increase in $z_1 - z_2$. Then there is no reason why aggregate unemployment should rise. Indeed that is just what happened in the USA.

So when people discuss mismatch they mean to include the full effects of the 'ex ante mismatch shock' *and* the 'relative wage shock' which may have offset it. The combination of these then produces a change in 'ex post mismatch'. The remaining change in unemployment, as before, is due to aggregate wage pressure (or compositional effects which are small).

This suggests the following short-cut approach to the mismatch issue, in which we do not identify separately the 'ex ante mismatch shock' and the 'relative wage shock'. Instead we identify changes in 'aggregate wage pressure' and label everything else a change in mismatch.

To perform this decomposition, we first note that, from the demand functions[8]

$$\alpha d \log W_1 + (1 - \alpha)d \log W_2 = d \log A + \log \frac{N_1}{N_2} d\alpha$$

We then substitute for $d \log W_i$, by using the wage functions

$$d \log W_1 = dz_1 - \gamma d \log u_i$$

This gives

$$d\bar{z} - \gamma(\alpha d \log u_1 + (1 - \alpha)d \log u_2) = d \log A + \log \frac{N_1}{N_2} d\alpha$$

Dividing through by γ and then adding $d \log u$ to both sides gives

$$du = \frac{u}{\gamma}\left(d\bar{z} - d \log A - \log \frac{N_1}{N_2} d\alpha\right) + \left(-\alpha d \log \frac{u_1}{u} - (1 - \alpha)d \log \frac{u_2}{u}\right)u$$

$$= \text{Aggregate wage pressure effect} + \text{Ex post mismatch effect.} \quad (8.6)$$

The first term is the average excess rise in the wage function *times* u/γ (which reflects the degree of real wage resistance). This term is approximately equal to our previous measure of the effect of 'aggregate wage pressure' in (8.5).[9] The second term is therefore close to the sum of the other three terms in equation (8.5). It is a natural measure of mismatch and close to the measure advocated by Layard *et al.* (1991 p. 309)[10] and now widely used.

In the later part of Section 2 we show our new short-cut measure of the change in mismatch for all the main European countries and the USA. We also document how these changes reflect the changes in employment and in labour supply, for each skill group.

2 EVIDENCE ON EUROPE AND THE USA

To examine the evidence, we split the labour force into two groups, skilled and the rest, where 'skilled' includes everyone with the equivalent of at least English 'A' levels (obtained by academically-oriented school leavers). In Europe this is a fairly easy category to identify, while in the USA we take as the equivalent 'some college'.[11] In Appendix 2 we give the basic time series for L_1/L_2, N_1/N_2 and W_1/W_2 in each country.

Production function

The first step is to estimate the production function, pooling all the usable time-series data shown in Appendix 2 for all the nine countries. We assume the production function to be CES, which gives a demand function[12]

$$\log\left(\frac{N_1}{N_2}\right)_{it} = -\sigma \log\left(\frac{W_1}{W_2}\right)_{it} + \beta_i t + \lambda_i + v_{it}$$

where i indicates the ith country. The estimated value of σ was 1.024 (s.e. = 0.178).[13] This is support for the use of the Cobb–Douglas function.

Wage functions

The next step is to estimate the wage functions. This is done for Britain (1975–92) and the USA (1979–88) in Table 8.1. In each country the observations are average wages for each skill group in each region (10 regions in Britain, 9 in the USA). The estimated equation is

$$\log W_{srt} = a_1 D_1 t + a_2 D_2 t - \gamma \log u_{srt} + b Q_{srt} + \text{fixed effects for}$$

$$s + \text{fixed effect for } r$$

where W is the real gross wage (deflated by the GDP deflator), s is skill, r region, t time, D_1 and D_2 dummies for each skill group, and Q is a vector of quality variables including average experience, experience squared, and the proportions who are full-time, male, white, and in each 'industry'. Observations are weighted by the number of individuals in each cell.

The regression is done for average wages in each cell (rather than for each individual) partly because these cells are the units relevant to our theory and

Table 8.1 Wage equation
Dependent variable: log of average real region-skill-specific wage

	Britain		USA	
log u_{srt}	−0.0302	−4.4	−0.0363	−2.3
$D_1 t$	.0195	(13.3)	−.0054	(1.5)
$D_2 t$	.0191	(15.5)	−.0120	(4.4)
D_2(unskilled)	−0.4346	−10.5	−0.3048	−4.2
Average experience	0.0336	−3.1	0.0513	−2.5
(Average experience)^2	−0.0004	−1.9	−0.0014	−2.7
Proportion full-time	0.7148	−6.4	0.8846	−2.8
Proportion male	0.264	−2.1	0.0823	−0.4
Other variables	Race % in each industry (7) Regional dummies (9)		Race % in each industry (12) Regional dummies (8)	
N	357.976		162.98	
$\bar{R}^2$				
Dates	1975–92		1979–88	

Source of data:
UK: *General Household Survey*.
USA: CPS March outgoing rotation groups. 20 per cent random sample within each gender-education cell. 1987 data not included.

partly to avoid exaggerating the *t*-statistic on cell-specific unemployment. However the coefficient estimates obtained in regressions on individual data are very similar, provided cell-specific variables as well as individual variables are included as regressors in the regressions on the individual data.

As Table 8.1 shows, time series movements in unemployment affect real wages with a coefficient γ that is similar in the USA and Britain.[14] However in Britain the time trends in the real wage intercept are very similar for the two skill groups, while in the USA they are much lower for the unskilled.

There is one further point stemming from the wage function. The quality (Q_s) of each skill group is not static. If a group's quality improves, so does its labour input. As Appendix 3 explains, this requires a modification of equations (8.3) and (8.4) to adjust the labour supply for quality. But the coefficients α in the theory can continue to be measured exactly by the actual shares of the wage bill.[15] In Table 8.2 we make this adjustment for quality.

Changes in unemployment – Britain versus the USA

We can now proceed in Table 8.2 to explain the changes in unemployment over the sample period (UK 1975–92; US 1979–88). The theory we have developed relates essentially to the NAIRU and excludes nominal surprises. However, since within each country the beginning and end years we have chosen are at similar points in the business cycle, this is not a major problem.

As Table 8.2 shows, in *Britain* unemployment grew over the period by 5.9 percentage points. To implement the explanatory framework set out in Appendix (8A1–8A3) we evaluate the coefficients by taking mean values of the variables that appear in each coefficient, evaluated over the whole period. One could of course perform the explanation separately for each year and then add up, but our simpler approximation works adequately. The evaluation is done separately for each region-and-skill group, and only then added up.

Overall, our model predicts that British unemployment grew by 5.5 points (compared with 5.9 actual). The model also explains quite well the growth of skilled unemployment (by 3.5 points) and unskilled unemployment (by 7.5 points). The main explanatory factors are these.

(1) Imbalanced demand and supply shocks

In the labour market as a whole the relative demand for labour grew strongly, but relative supply of skill grew almost (but not quite) as fast. Thus over the period

$$\Delta \log \frac{\alpha}{1 - \alpha} - \Delta \log \frac{L_i}{L} = 12.4 \text{ per cent}$$

Table 8.2A Decomposing the change in unemployment rates (percentage points) Britain 1975–92

	Skilled	Unskilled	Total
Rise in $\alpha/(1 - \alpha)$	−33.56	40.19	22.40
Rise in L_1/L_2	32.51	−38.93	−21.69
Ex ante mismatch shock (M)	−1.05	1.26	0.71
Relative wage shocks $(z_1 - z_2)$	0.05	−0.35	−0.28
Aggregate wage shock (AWP)	4.85	6.07	5.98
Compositional change	0.05	−0.11	−0.97
Total explained	3.91	6.86	5.24
Actual	3.47	7.50	5.90

Table 8.2B   Decomposing the change in unemployment rates (percentage points) USA 1979–88

	Skilled	Unskilled	Total
Rise in $\alpha/(1 - \alpha)$	−5.34	14.36	5.66
Rise in L_1/L_2	4.75	−12.71	−5.00
Ex ante mismatch shock (M)	−0.60	1.65	0.66
Relative wage shocks $(z_1 - z_2)$	0.50	−1.36	−0.54
Aggregate wage shock (AWP)	−0.11	−0.15	−0.13
Compositional change	−0.05	−0.10	−0.33
Total explained	−0.27	0.04	−0.35
Actual	−0.07	0.27	−0.05

Note: The compositional change includes shifts in the composition of workers between regions as well as between skill groups. Table 8.2A and B use equations A.1–A.3 in Annex 1.

This had the predicted effect of reducing skilled unemployment and raising unskilled. The net effect was an extra 0.7 points on overall unemployment – not a very large amount.

(2) Relative wage shocks

A little of the preceding effect was offset by relative wage restraint among the unskilled. Thus, taking (1) and (2) together, increased skill mismatch offers little explanation of the rise in British unemployment.

(3) Aggregate wage pressure

By far the main explanation comes from increased wage pressure at a given unemployment rate – requiring unemployment to rise in order to offset it. This alone can explain the otherwise unexplained rise in unemployment among skilled workers.

Such wage pressure is of course a pure catch-all. For a proper understanding of why unemployment rose we have to look in detail at the impact of welfare systems, bargaining institutions, labour market regulations, tax systems and so on.[16] These issues have been discussed at length elsewhere (Layard *et al.* 1991). But, to isolate the impact of skills mismatch (as here), that is unnecessary.

Table 8.3 Decomposing the change in aggregate unemployment: simplified approach (percentage points)

	Britain (1975–92)	US (1979–88)
Expost mismatch shock	0.10	0.06
Aggregate wage shock	6.87	0.30
Total explained	7.87	0.36
Actual	5.90	0.36

Note: Both the first two rows are independently calculated, using (8.6).

(4) The compositional effect

This is in a downward direction, due to the shift of the labour force into skill groups with lower unemployment rates. But it is a small part of the story.

Turning to the USA, there is little story to tell. The evolution of demand and supply was as imbalanced as in Britain. But almost all of this imbalance was offset by relative wage restraint in the unskilled labour market. The big difference from Britain was the absence of aggregate wage pressure. So aggregate unemployment barely changed.

Finally, while comparing Britain and the USA, we can look at the simpler decomposition given by (8.6). This is shown in Table 8.3 and again attributes almost all the British increase in unemployment to increased aggregate wage pressure, rather than to Krugman's imbalanced supply and demand shocks and the response to them. The story is highly consistent with the more detailed analysis in Table 8.2, and thus provides us with some confidence in the short-cut approach.

Increased mismatch? Europe vs. the USA

It is therefore interesting to use this short-cut approach (which requires less data to compare the USA with a wider range of European countries and over a longer span of time. As Table 8.4 shows, unemployment has risen substantially in most European countries except the Netherlands. But in none of these countries has there been any significant increase in ex post mismatch.

Why has there been no increase in mismatch in Europe? It is due to the massive change in the supply of skilled people. Table 8.5 shows the annual

Table 8.4 Change in aggregate unemployment: simplified approach (percentage points)

Country	Period	Change due to ex post mismatch	Total change
US	1970–91	0.1	1.4
Britain	1975–92	0.1	5.9
France	1978–94	0.2	7.3
Germany	1976–89	0.4	2.9
Italy	1977–91	0.4	3.9
Netherlands	1979–93	0.1	1.3
Norway	1983–91	0.0	2.1
Sweden	1971–93	−0.3	5.8
Australia	1979–93	−0.6	5.0
Canada	1975–93	−0.8	4.3

Note: Change due to mismatch is calculated using (8.6).

Table 8.5 Annual change in relative demand and relative supply
All variables have been multiplied by 100

	Years	$d \log (\alpha/(1-\alpha))$ (1)	$d \log (L_1/L_2)$ (2)	$d \log M$ (3)	$d \log(W_1/W_2)$ (4)	$d \log(N_1/N_2)$ (5)	(5)–(2) (6)
US	1970–89	5.24	4.82	0.42	0.24	5.00	0.18
	1970–79	5.67	6.78	−1.11	−1.27	6.94	0.16
	1980–89	4.60	3.24	1.36	1.40	3.20	−0.04
Britain	1975–92	7.62	6.94	0.68	0.51	7.11	0.17
France	1984–91	6.47	6.11	0.36	0.16	6.31	0.20
Germany	1976–89	5.11	4.54	0.57	−0.18	5.29	0.75
Italy	1977–91	6.74	6.46	0.28	−0.13	6.86	0.40
Netherlands	1979–93	4.75	5.80	−1.05	−1.08	5.83	0.03
Norway	1983–91	6.38	6.50	−0.25	−0.50	6.88	0.38
Spain	1977–93		5.05			5.58	0.53
Sweden	1971–93	6.86	6.93	0.07	−0.08	6.94	0.01
Australia	1979–90	5.25	5.01	0.24	0.03	5.22	0.21
Canada	1979–83	5.85	5.49	0.36	0.39	5.46	−0.03

Note: Changes are calculated from regressing the data in Appendix 2 on time. Column (3) = Col (1)–Col (2).
The equation for Canada includes a dummy for the years after the break before 1989 and 1990.

change in relative demand and relative supply (unadjusted for 'quality').[17] The story is quite remarkable. Both demand and supply have shifted hugely. In most countries the relative demand for skill has slightly outrun supply. But considering the size of the two changes, the difference between them is remarkably small, as column (3) shows. The difference is particularly large in the USA in the 1980s, which is doubtless one of the reasons for the strong upwards pressure on skilled wages.

The relative wage adjustment can be seen in column (4). It was especially large in the USA in the 1980s. In most European countries it was much less – but less wage adjustment was also needed, due to a better process of skill development.

Thus the evidence suggests fairly powerfully that rigid relative wages cannot be the main source of the *rise* in European unemployment. If they were the main reason, mismatch would have increased substantially. It did not.

Comment

A natural reaction to this analysis is to say that we have not used a fine enough division of skill. However we also used a three-fold breakdown of the labour force and applied it to a generalized version of our model in which we continued to measure asymmetric shocks by differences between $d \log \alpha_i/\alpha_N$ and $d \log L_i/L_N$ where N was a numeraire group. The results were very similar to those in Table 8.2.

A further objection is more subtle. It rests on the undoubted fact that in the USA there has been an increase in wage dispersion *within* skills, reflecting a widening premium for other dimensions of productive characteristics. Suppose now that there is in Europe some rigidity that limits the minimum wage payable within each skill group. Though mismatch between educational groups may not have increased, unemployment may increase in each group if wages are not allowed to reflect the changing value put on other dimensions of skill. This could even cause unemployment to rise by the same proportion in each educational group.

The first comment on this is that it does not seem reasonable to assume such a high binding wage floor for the highly-educated group. But, second, in most European countries there have in fact been very small increases in within-group wage inequality.[18] This could in principle reflect total wage rigidity in the upwards as well as the downwards direction, but this would cause severe excess demand for good workers which we do not see in Europe. So we are cast back on the idea that wages are only sticky in a downwards direction, but this is inconsistent with stable wage inequality – if the relative demand for good workers has indeed increased. So it does look as though in Europe, unlike the US, the relative supply of skill has more or less kept pace with demand.

3 CONCLUSIONS

Thus we cast severe doubt on the widely-held view that unemployment rose in Europe, but not in America, due to less flexible skill differentials. The evidence in this paper says that the explanation lies elsewhere.

First we develop a framework which can decompose changes in skill-specific unemployment into changes due to (1) imbalanced demand and supply changes, (2) shocks to the relative wage behaviour and (3) changes in aggregate wage pressure. This shows that, both in the USA and Britain, imbalanced demand and supply changes raised unskilled unemployment and reduced skilled unemployment. But some of this effect was offset by appropriate shifts in relative wage behaviour. Thus, taking (1) and (2) together, changes in skill mismatch raised total unemployment in Britain since 1975 by under half a percentage point, and in the USA by even less. The real difference between Britain and the USA was the rise in aggregate wage pressure in Britain (arising largely from the dysfunctionalities of the British welfare state exposed by the oil and productivity shocks).[19] It is this alone which can explain the key fact about British and European unemployment – that skilled unemployment has risen as well as unskilled. It is the failure of the Krugman *et al.* hypothesis to explain this fact which renders it so implausible.

Thus if one constructs a simple measure of changes in mismatch, corresponding roughly to the sum of items (1) and (2) above, this has hardly risen in any country and in most of the European countries studied, it has fallen. In the 1980s wage differentials have increased much less in Europe than in the USA, but they needed to increase less because the rate of skill formation was so much higher in Europe.

While our analysis is quite limited, it surely calls in question the view that European unemployment rose because of increased relative demand for skill, interacting with rigid relative wages. There was simply not the fall in unemployment of skilled workers which the theory predicts.[20] Instead we have to look above all at explanations based on the European welfare state and its effect on all groups of labour.

Appendix 1: Deriving (8.5)

We first solve for du_1 and du_2, using equations (3') and (4'). This gives

$$du_1 = T\left\{-\frac{\gamma(1-\alpha)}{u_2}(d\log M - (dz_1 - dz_2)) + \frac{u_2 + \gamma(1-u_2)}{u_2(1-u_2)}dAWP\right\} \quad (8A.1)$$

where $T = \dfrac{u_1 u_2 (1-u_1)(1-u_2)}{\gamma(\gamma(1-u_1)(1-u_2) + \alpha u_2 + (1-\alpha)u_1 - u_1 u_2)} > 0$

Similarly,

$$du_2 = T\left\{\frac{\gamma\alpha}{u_1}(d\log M - (dz_1 - dz_2)) + \frac{u_1 + \gamma(1-u_1)}{u_1(1-u_1)}dAWP\right\} \quad (8A.2)$$

Aggregate unemployment is given by $u = u_1\dfrac{L_1}{L} + u_2\dfrac{L_2}{L}$. The change in unemployment is therefore

$$du = \ell du_1 + (1-\ell)du_2 + (u_1 - u_2)d\ell, \quad \text{where } \ell = \frac{L_1}{L}.$$

Hence

$$\begin{aligned}
du = &\ T\gamma\left\{(1-\ell)\frac{\alpha}{u_1} - \ell\frac{(1-\alpha)}{u_2}\right\}\{d\log M - (dz_1 - dz_2)\} \\
&+ T\left\{\ell\frac{u_2 + \gamma(1-u_2)}{u_2(1-u_2)} + (1-\ell)\frac{u_1 + \gamma(1-u_1)}{u_1(1-u_1)}\right\}dAWP \\
&+ (u_1 - u_2)d\ell
\end{aligned} \quad (8A.3)$$

Note that, in the case where $u_1 = u_2 = u$, the coefficient on $dAWP$ is

$$\begin{aligned}
&\frac{u^2(1-u)^2}{\gamma(\gamma(1-u)^2 + u - u^2)}\left(\ell\frac{u + \gamma(1-u)}{u(1-u)} + (1-\ell)\frac{u + \gamma(1-u)}{u(1-u)}\right) \\
&= \frac{u^2(1-u)^2}{\gamma(\gamma(1-u)^2 + u - u^2)}\frac{u + \gamma(1-u)}{u(1-u)} \\
&= \frac{u(1-u)(u + \gamma(1-u))}{\gamma(1-u)(u + \gamma(1-u))} = \frac{u}{\gamma}
\end{aligned}$$

Note also that a fall in wage pressure for one group reduces unemployment of both groups. For example,

$$du_1 = T\left\{-\frac{\gamma(1-\alpha)}{u_2} + \frac{u_2 + \gamma(1-u_2)}{u_2(1-u_2)}(1-\alpha)\right\}dz_2$$

$$= T\left\{\frac{1-\alpha}{1-u_2}\right\}dz_2$$

This is because the two groups are q-complements.

Appendix 2:   Basic Data

Australia

	L_1/L_2	N_1/N_2	W_1/W_2	u_1	u_2	u
1979	0.937	0.969	1.279	0.053	0.084	0.069
1980	0.952	0.989		0.047	0.082	0.065
1981	1.044	0.989		0.044	0.078	0.061
1982	1.113	1.082	1.248	0.052	0.087	0.068
1983	1.184	1.155		0.084	0.129	0.104
1984	1.261	1.245		0.079	0.129	0.101
1985	1.281	1.332		0.067	0.120	0.090
1986	1.329	1.359	1.281	0.065	0.113	0.085
1987	1.427	1.401		0.066	0.118	0.087
1988	1.487	1.510		0.062	0.103	0.078
1989	1.533	1.555		0.055	0.092	0.069
1990	1.613	1.678	1.270	0.053	0.090	0.067
1991	1.750	1.831		0.077	0.117	0.091
1992	1.886	1.986		0.096	0.142	0.112
1993	2.092	2.202		0.104	0.149	0.119

Canada

	L_1/L_2	N_1/N_2	W_1/W_2	u_1	u_2	u
1975	0.484	0.502		0.046	0.081	0.069
1976	0.460	0.475		0.050	0.081	0.071
1977	0.461	0.481		0.055	0.093	0.081
1978	0.454	0.473		0.058	0.096	0.084
1979	0.412	0.433	1.331	0.043	0.089	0.075
1980						
1981	0.465	0.485		0.048	0.088	0.075
1982	0.499	0.531		0.073	0.128	0.110
1983	0.541	0.575		0.083	0.137	0.118
1984	0.565	0.597		0.081	0.131	0.113
1985	0.590	0.626		0.072	0.125	0.105
1986	0.620	0.655		0.065	0.115	0.096
1987	0.646	0.680		0.059	0.108	0.089
1988	0.695	0.726		0.054	0.094	0.078
1989	0.715	0.747	1.384	0.052	0.092	0.075
1990	0.970	1.017		0.059	0.102	0.081
1991	1.009	10.71	1.363	0.076	0.130	0.103
1992	1.060	1.128		0.086	0.141	0.113
1993	1.142	1.213		0.087	0.141	0.112

Italy

	L_1/L_2	N_1/N_2	W_1/W_2	u_1	u_2	u
1977	0.221	0.206	1.334	0.121	0.059	0.071
1978	0.240	0.223	1.264	0.124	0.059	0.072
1979	0.256	0.241	1.237	0.122	0.064	0.076
1980	0.274	0.258	1.260	0.118	0.064	0.075
1981	0.291	0.275	1.198	0.124	0.071	0.083
1982	0.312	0.297	1.272	0.124	0.079	0.090
1983	0.334	0.138	1.266	0.131	0.088	0.099
1984	0.352	0.337	1.292	0.133	0.094	0.104
1985	0.379	0.364		0.128	0.092	0.101
1986	0.406	0.394	1.275	0.130	0.104	0.112
1987	0.435	0.425	1.287	0.134	0.114	0.120
1988	0.461	0.450		0.135	0.114	0.121
1989	0.489	0.478	1.242	0.134	0.114	0.121
1990	0.516	0.506		0.122	0.104	0.110
1991	0.544	0.532	1.237	0.123	0.103	0.110

France

	L_1/L_2	N_1/N_2	W_1/W_2	u_1	u_2	u
1978	0.731	0.734		0.057	0.061	0.059
1979	0.758	0.767		0.059	0.070	0.065
1980	0.816	0.826		0.063	0.075	0.070
1981	0.856	0.870		0.070	0.086	0.078
1982	0.810	0.834		0.063	0.090	0.078
1983	0.852	0.883		0.063	0.095	0.081
1984	0.888	0.926	1.343	0.075	0.113	0.095
1985	0.919	0.954	1.334	0.081	0.114	0.098
1986	0.979	1.032	1.286	0.078	0.126	0.102
1987	1.045	1.109	1.303	0.081	0.134	0.107
1988	1.100	1.168	1.308	0.076	0.130	0.102
1989	1.125	1.197	1.310	0.070	0.125	0.096
1990	1.248	1.325	1.325	0.077	0.131	0.101
1991	1.337	1.417	1.340	0.078	0.130	0.100
1992	1.417	1.508	1.352	0.088	0.143	0.111
1993	1.530	1.619	1.344	0.101	0.151	0.121
1994	1.603	1.712	1.342	0.111	0.167	0.133

Germany (West)

	L_1/L_2	N_1/N_2	W_1/W_2	u_1	u_2	u
1976	1.822	1.874	1.387	0.025	0.051	0.034
1977						
1978	2.322	2.413	1.386	0.021	0.058	0.032
1979						
1980	2.684	2.798	1.406	0.019	0.059	0.030
1981						
1982	2.558	2.774	1.391	0.043	0.117	0.064
1983						
1984						
1985	2.957	3.292	1.361	0.050	0.147	0.075
1986						
1987	3.255	3.673	1.368	0.047	0.155	0.072
1988						
1989	3.623	4.025	1.365	0.043	0.138	0.063

Netherlands

	L_1/L_2	N_1/N_2	W_1/W_2	u_1	u_2	u
1979	0.859	0.870	1.541	0.056	0.067	0.062
1980						
1981	1.038	1.084	1.463	0.058	0.098	0.078
1982						
1983	1.144	1.271	1.388	0.092	0.183	0.134
1984						
1985	1.274	1.411	1.328	0.090	0.178	0.128
1986						
1987						
1988						
1989						
1990	1.696	1.785	1.347	0.052	0.099	0.069
1991	1.788	1.88	1.323	0.048	0.095	0.065
1992	1.888	1.977	1.284	0.050	0.093	0.065
1993	2.015	2.130	1.288	0.058	0.109	0.075

Norway

	L_1/L_2	N_1/N_2	W_1/W_2	u_1	u_2	u
1972	0.532	0.537		0.012	0.022	0.019
1973	0.638	0.642		0.011	0.018	0.015
1974	0.640	0.643		0.012	0.017	0.015
1975	0.718	0.725		0.017	0.026	0.022
1976	1.858	1.868		0.016	0.021	0.017
1977	1.993	2.008		0.012	0.020	0.015
1978	2.114	2.129		0.017	0.024	0.019
1979	2.181	2.202		0.016	0.025	0.019
1980	2.327	2.353		0.013	0.024	0.017
1981	2.463	2.504		0.015	0.030	0.019
1982	2.608	2.641		0.022	0.035	0.026
1983	2.737	2.791	1.358	0.028	0.047	0.033
1984	2.864	2.915		0.026	0.043	0.030
1985	3.089	3.130		0.022	0.034	0.025
1986	3.339	3.376		0.016	0.027	0.019
1987	3.568	0.602	1.316	0.019	0.028	0.021
1988	3.834	3.913		0.027	0.047	0.031
1989	4.036	4.193		0.042	0.078	0.049
1990	4.217	4.401		0.044	0.084	0.051
1991	4.589	4.791	1.304	0.047	0.088	0.055
1992	4.848	5.040		0.053	0.089	0.059
1993	5.072	5.274		0.053	0.089	0.059

Sweden

	L_1/L_2	N_1/N_2	W_1/W_2	u_1	u_2	u
1971	0.431	0.435		0.018	0.027	0.024
1972	0.431	0.434		0.027	0.034	0.032
1973	0.460	0.465		0.026	0.035	0.032
1974	0.474	0.478	1.266	0.020	0.028	0.025
1975	0.505	0.508		0.014	0.020	0.018
1976	0.578	0.583		0.012	0.021	0.018
1977	0.612	0.618		0.012	0.022	0.018
1978	0.649	0.658		0.014	0.028	0.023
1979	0.706	0.716		0.015	0.028	0.023
1980	0.746	0.757		0.012	0.026	0.020
1981	0.789	0.802	1.151	0.016	0.032	0.025
1982	0.845	0.861		0.022	0.040	0.032
1983	0.983	0.954		0.028	0.045	0.036
1984						
1985	1.128	1.157		0.019	0.043	0.030
1986	1.177	1.194		0.021	0.035	0.028
1987	1.266	1.276	1.221	0.016	0.023	0.019
1988						
1989	1.416	1.423		0.011	0.016	0.013
1990	1.509	1.519		0.012	0.019	0.015
1991	1.598	1.613	1.233	0.023	0.032	0.027
1992	1.711	1.725		0.044	0.053	0.047
1993	1.780	1.806		0.078	0.091	0.083

Britain

	L_1/L_2	N_1/N_2	W_1/W_2	u_1	u_2	u
1975	0.179	0.181	1.622	0.028	0.041	0.039
1976	0.178	0.183	1.599	0.031	0.055	0.052
1977	0.203	0.211	1.732	0.018	0.056	0.049
1978	0.210	0.218	1.664	0.020	0.055	0.049
1979	0.210	0.217	1.674	0.020	0.053	0.047
1980	0.225	0.235	1.682	0.028	0.070	0.062
1981	0.229	0.246	1.777	0.044	0.111	0.099
1982	0.256	0.277	1.685	0.051	0.125	0.110
1983	0.304	0.329	1.676	0.062	0.134	0.117
1984	0.354	0.381	1.682	0.059	0.124	0.107
1985	0.380	0.416	1.675	0.042	0.124	0.102
1986	0.396	0.424	1.680	0.056	0.118	0.100
1987	0.424	0.448	1.738	0.057	0.108	0.092
1988	0.432	0.453	1.713	0.044	0.088	0.075
1989	0.456	0.478	1.752	0.033	0.079	0.064
1990	0.480	0.502	1.746	0.036	0.078	0.064
1991	0.480	0.509	1.817	0.056	0.109	0.092
1992	0.507	0.538	1.844	0.062	0.116	0.098

United States

	L_1/L_2	N_1/N_2	W_1/W_2	u_1	u_2	u
1970	0.349	0.355	1.580	0.020	0.037	0.033
1971	0.372	0.381	1.621	0.028	0.051	0.045
1972	0.387	0.396	1.568	0.027	0.048	0.042
1973	0.416	0.425	1.543	0.022	0.042	0.036
1974	0.453	0.462	1.516	0.024	0.042	0.037
1975	0.487	0.511	1.544	0.038	0.085	0.069
1976	0.529	0.549	1.470	0.036	0.071	0.059
1977	0.560	0.579	1.460	0.027	0.069	0.058
1978	0.590	0.608	1.445	0.030	0.056	0.045
1979	0.630	0.647	1.444	0.032	0.054	0.044
1980	0.656	0.678	1.448	0.045	0.062	0.049
1981	0.658	0.689	1.464	0.051	0.075	0.058
1982	0.678	0.718	1.517	0.038	0.098	0.076
1983	0.733	0.788	1.531	0.034	0.118	0.090
1984	0.757	0.797	1.567	0.034	0.086	0.066
1985	0.783	0.823	1.614	0.033	0.082	0.061
1986	0.795	0.837	1.642	0.026	0.082	0.061
1987	0.817	0.855	1.601	0.018	0.076	0.056
1988	0.832	0.866	1.646	0.019	0.065	0.047
1989	0.866	0.905	1.615	0.021	0.060	0.040
1990	0.898	0.935		0.019	0.058	0.039
1991	0.923	0.973		0.021	0.071	0.047

Spain

	L_1/L_2	N_1/N_2	W_1/W_2	u_1	u_2	u
1977	0.056	0.056		0.053	0.051	0.051
1978	0.064	0.064		0.065	0.070	0.069
1979	0.071	0.071		0.081	0.087	0.086
1980	0.075	0.076		0.102	0.115	0.114
1981	0.077	0.078		0.133	0.144	0.143
1982	0.082	0.084		0.148	0.165	0.163
1983	0.091	0.095		0.149	0.183	0.180
1984	0.093	0.099		0.149	0.204	0.199
1985	0.097	0.103		0.169	0.217	0.212
1986	0.102	0.109		0.158	0.213	0.208
1987	0.106	0.112		0.163	0.207	0.203
1988	0.109	0.114		0.159	0.197	0.193
1989	0.118	0.124		0.134	0.175	0.171
1990	0.122	0.129		0.119	0.165	0.160
1991	0.126	0.134		0.114	0.166	0.160
1992	0.128	0.139		0.120	0.188	0.180
1993	0.133	0.148		0.147	0.232	0.222

Sources: Note that wages exclude labour taxes on employers.

Employment, labour force and unemployment

Australia *Sample*: 1979–93. *Source*: Labour Force Status and Educational Attainment, Australia. Selection criteria: males and females, 15–64 years old. Skilled: attended highest level of secondary school available. Unskilled: other.

Britain *Sample*: 1975–92. *Source*: GHS individual record files. Selection criteria: males, 16–64 years old; females, 16–60 years old. Skilled: with 'A'-level (or equivalent), including senior vocational qualification. Unskilled: other.

Canada *Sample*: 1979–93. *Source*: The Labour Force Statistics, Canada. Selection criteria: males and females, 15 years old and over. Skilled: with some post-secondary education. Unskilled: other.

France *Sample*: 1978–94. *Source*: *La Population Active d'Après l'Enquête Emploi*, INSEE. Selection criteria: males and females, 15 years old and over. Skilled: with *baccalauréat general* or vocational qualification (CAP or BEP). Unskilled: other.

Germany (West) *Sample*: 1976, 1978, 1980, 1982, 1985, 1987, 1989. *Source*: *Mikrozensus*. Selection criteria: males and females, 15 years old and over. Skilled: with vocational qualifications (*Berufsbildung*) or higher education (*Fachhochschulqualifikation* or *Hochschule*). Unskilled: without vocational qualifications.

Italy *Sample*: 1977–91. Selection criteria: males and females, 14–70 years old. *Source*: *Annuario Statistico Italiano*. Skilled: with upper secondary qualification (*diploma di scuola media superiore*) including vocational qualification. Unskilled: other.

Netherlands *Sample*: 1975–93. Selection criteria: males and females, 15 years old and over. *Source*: 1975–85: *Arbeidskrachtetentelling*, 1990–93: *Enquete Beroepssbevolking*. Skilled: with senior secondary qualification, including senior vocational training. Unskilled: other.

Norway *Sample*: 1972–93. *Source*: *Arbeidmarkedstatistikk* (abs.), Norway. Selection criteria: males and females, 16–74 years old. Skilled: completed secondary school level II (*gymnasiva II*). Unskilled: other.

Spain *Sample*: 1977–93. *Source*: *Encuesta de Poblacion Activa*. INE. Selection criteria: males and females, 16 years old and over. Skilled: some college (*nivel anterior al superior*). Unskilled: without any college education.

Sweden *Sample*: 1971–93. *Source*: 1971–86, Labour Force Survey, February interviews; 1987–93, all months. Selection criteria: males and females, 16–64 years old. Skilled: with high school qualification (including secondary vocational qualifications). Unskilled: other.

United States *Sample*: 1970–91. *Source*: 1979–89: *Handbook of Labor Statistics, 1989*; 1990–1: *Statistical Abstract of the US, 1992*. Selection criteria: males and females, 25–64 years old. Skilled: with at least some college. Unskilled: other.

Wages

Same skill partition as above.

Australia *Sample*: 1979, 1982, 1986, 1990. Wage differentials computed as weighted averages of ratios reported in OECD *Jobs Study* (1994), males only. Earnings concept: annual earnings of full-year, full-time workers.

Britain *Sample: 1975–92. Source: GHS individual record files. Selection criteria: males 16–64 years old, females 16–60 years old. Earnings concept: weekly earnings.*

Canada *Sample*: 1979, 1989, 1991. Wage differentials computed as weighted averages of ratios reported in OECD *Jobs Study* (1994), males and females. Earnings concept: weekly earnings of full-time workers.

France *Sample*: 1984–94. *Source*: INSEE, *Enquête sur l'Emploi*. Selection criteria: males and females, 15 years old and over, employees only. Earnings concept: monthly wages.

Germany (West) *Sample*: 1976, 1978, 1980, 1982, 1985, 1987, 1989. *Source*: *Mikrozensus*. Selection criteria: males and females, 15 years old and over. Earnings concept: net monthly wages.

Italy *Sample*: 1977–84, 1986, 1987, 1989, 1991. *Source*: 'Indagine sui Bilanci delle Famiglie', Banca d'Italia, individual record files. Selection criteria: males and females, 16–65 years old, employees only. Earnings concept: net yearly earnings.

Netherlands *Sample*: 1985, 1990. Wage differentials computed as weighted averages of ratios reported on OECD *Jobs Study* (1994), males and females. Earnings concept: gross hourly wages.

Norway *Sample*: 1983, 1987, 1991. Wage differentials are top/bottom category ratios reported in OECD *Jobs Study* (1994), aggregated for males and females using total male and total female employed numbers. Earnings concept: hourly wages.

Sweden *Sample*: 1974, 1981, 1987, 1991. Wage differentials computed as unweighted averages of ratios reported on OECD *Jobs Study* (1994), women only. Earnings concept: gross hourly earnings.

United States *Sample*: 1970–89. *Source*: Annual demographic files, March Current Population Survey (Outgoing Rotation Group). Selection criteria: wage and salary earners, males and females, 16–69 years old, working at least 40 weeks and earning more than one half the minimum wage on a full time basis. Earnings concept: weekly wages (annual earnings divided by number of weeks worked). Our thanks to Steve Davis for providing the data.

Appendix 3: Adjustment for 'Quality'

To make a satisfactory analysis of the race between demand and supply, we have to control for the fact that workers vary in 'quality' not only according to skill but also experience, experience[2], full-time/part-time, sex and race. Call this vector Q, which affects the wage of skill groups according to

$$\log W_s = a_s t - \gamma \log u_s + b Q_s + \text{regional dummies}$$

where W_s is the average real wage per person.

We can for convenience designate bQ_s by the expression $\log X_s$. It follows that the wage equation for skill group 1 has to be re-written as

$$\log W_1 - \log X_1 = z_1(t) - \gamma \log u_1 \qquad (8B.1)$$

The demand function for persons in skill group 1 also has to be rewritten to allow for quality. Suppose the true production function is

$$Y = A(N_1 X_1)^\alpha (N_2 X_2)^{1-\alpha}$$

where $N_1 X_1$ is measured in efficiency units. The demand for an efficiency unit of skill group 1 is then

$$
\begin{aligned}
\log W_1 - \log X_1 &= \log A + \log \alpha - (1-\alpha) \log \frac{N_1 X_1}{N_2 X_2} \\
&= \log A + \log \alpha - (1-\alpha) \log \frac{N_1 X_1}{L_1 X_1} + (1-\alpha) \log \frac{L_2 X_2}{L_2 X_2} \\
&\quad - (1-\alpha) \log \frac{L_1 X_1}{L_2 X_2} \\
&= \log A + \log \alpha - (1-\alpha) \log(1 - u_1) \\
&\quad + (1-\alpha) \log(1 - u_2) - (1-\alpha) \log \frac{L_1 X_1}{L_2 X_2} \qquad (8B.2)
\end{aligned}
$$

Combining (8B.1) and (8B.2) gives a new version of (8.3) in which changes in labour supply have to be modified to allow for changes in quality – and the ratio N_1/N_2 must also be modified.

The new equation is

$$
\begin{aligned}
du_1 &= \phi_1 (1-\alpha) \left(d \log \frac{L_1 X_1}{L_2 X_2} - d \log \frac{\alpha}{1-\alpha} \right) \\
&\quad + \phi_1 \left(dz_1 - d \log A - \log \frac{N_1 X_1}{N_2 X_2} d\alpha \right) + \phi_1 (1-\alpha) \frac{du_2}{1 - u_2} \qquad (8B.3)
\end{aligned}
$$

228

We make these modifications to $d \log \frac{L_1}{L_2}$ and $\log \frac{N_1}{N_2}$ wherever we 'allow for quality'. Similarly for skill level 2.

Notes

1. For other discussions of US and European wage dispersion and its correlates see Freeman and Katz (1994) and the collection of papers in Freeman and Katz ed. (1995). See also Juhn *et al.* (1993).
2. This wage-setting function has in its elements of labour supply, of bargaining and of efficiency wages (see Layard *et al.*, 1991).
3. Note that $d \log \alpha = (1 - \alpha)\left(\frac{1}{\alpha} + \frac{1}{1 - \alpha}\right)d\alpha = (1 - \alpha)d \log \frac{\alpha}{1 - \alpha}$
4. This form is well-supported by much evidence, especially in Europe – see for example Layard *et al.* (1991) and Blanchflower and Oswald (1994).
5. Note that $dz_1 - d\bar{z} = dz_1 - \alpha dz_1 - (1 - \alpha)dz_2 = (1 - \alpha)(dz_1 - dz_2)$
6. This statement ignores the effect of changes in labour force composition.
7. The permitted level of $d\bar{z}$ is

$$
\begin{aligned}
d\bar{z} &= \frac{1}{W}\left(\frac{N_1}{N}dW_1 + \frac{N_2}{N}dW_2\right) \\
&= \alpha d \log W_1 + (1 - \alpha)d \log W_2 \\
&= \alpha d\left(\log A + \log \alpha - (1 - \alpha)\log\frac{N_1}{N_2}\right) \\
&\quad + (1 - \alpha)d\left(\log A + \log(1 - \alpha) + \alpha \log\frac{N_1}{N_2}\right) \\
&= d \log A + \log\frac{N_1}{N_2}d\alpha
\end{aligned}
$$

8. See note 7.
9. If $u_1 = u_2$ the two measures are identical (see Appendix 1). But when $u_1 < u_2$, the coefficient in equation (8.5) is less than u/γ because the aggregate wage shock leads to a fall in the dispersion of the relative unemployment rates (see also Nickell and Bell, 1995). The difference however is not large if say $u_1 = \frac{1}{2}u_2$.
10. The measure of the change in mismatch used in Layard *et al.* (1991, p. 309) is d $(-\alpha \log u_1/u - (1 - \alpha) \log u_2/u)$. The present measure is more logical. The previous measure equals the present measure plus $(\log u_2/u_1)d\alpha$. This may be positive or negative but in our sample of countries it is negative (with $d\alpha > 0$ and $u_2 > u_1$). There is no reason to include this extra term in $d\alpha$ in a measure of changing mismatch.
11. We do the same for Spain since the available classification provides no clearer breakpoint.
12. This corresponds to the production function $Y = A(a_1 N_1^\rho + a_2 N_2^\rho)^{\frac{1}{\rho}}$, with

$$
\left(\frac{a_1}{a_2}\right)^\sigma = e^{\beta t} \cdot \text{const}
$$

13. For Britain and the USA, it is possible to do separate regressions using lagged W_1/W_2 as an instrument. The estimates of σ were 1.13 (se = 0.19) and 1.74 (se = 0.64) respectively – very similar to the OLS estimates for those countries.
14. When lagged u is used as instrument, γ is -0.046 (3.8) for USA and -0.036 (5.5) for UK. For a discussion of identification of the wage equation see Layard, Nickell and Jackman (1991) p. 405.
15. $d \log A$ is calculated as $d \log A = d \log WN - D \, (\alpha_1 \log N_1 X_1) - d(\alpha_2 \log N_2 X_2)$, where X_i is defined in Appendix 3.
16. The best explanation of rising European unemployment is in terms of an economic system that worked alright if not shocked, but was fragile in the face of shocks – leading to the emergence of behaviour unfriendly to employment. Thus across countries we have Δu related to the *level* of institutional variables.
17. A similar table based on the same data also appears in Manacorda and Petrongolo (forthcoming).
18. See OECD, *Employment Outlook* (1993, p. 162).
19. In addition incomes policy which had helped to contain wage pressure from 1975–9 was abandoned in 1979.
20. This does not mean that the *level* of mismatch is not an important issue in both Europe and America, see Layard *et al.* (1991, Chapter 6, p. 310).

References

Blanchflower, D. and A. Oswald (1994) *The Wage Curve* (Cambridge, MA: MIT Press).
Freeman, R. and L. Katz (1994) 'Rising Wage Inequality: The United States vs Other advanced Countries', in Freeman, R. (ed.) *Working under Different Rules* (New York: Russell Sage Foundation).
Freeman, R. and L. Katz, ed. (1995) *Differences and Changes in Wage Structures* (Chicago: The University of Chicago Press).
Jackman, R., R. Layard and S. Nickell (1996) 'Combatting Unemployment: Is Flexibility Enough?', OECD: *Macroeconomic Policies and Structural Reform*.
Juhn, C., Murphy and Pierce, B. (1993) 'Wage Inequality and the Rise in the Returns to Skills', *Journal of Political Economy*, 101(3), 410–442.
Krugman, P. (1994) 'Past and Prospective Causes of High Unemployment', in *Reducing Unemployment: Current Issues and Policy Options*, Jackson Hole Conference, WY.
Layard, R., S. Nickell and R. Jackman (1991) *Unemployment: Macroeconomic Performance and the Labour Market* (Oxford: Oxford University Press).
Manning, A., J. Wadsworth and D. Wilkinson (1996) 'Making Your Mind Up: Skill Mismatch in the UK', LSE mimeo.
Manacorda, M. and B. Petrongolo (forthcoming) 'Skills Mismatch and Unemployment in OECD Countries', *Economica*.
Nickell, S. and B. Bell (1995) 'The Collapse in the Demand for Unskilled and Unemployment Across the OECD', *Oxford Review of Economic Policy*, 11(1), pp. 40–62.
Nickell, S. and R. Layard (forthcoming) 'Labour Market Institutions and Economic Performance', in O. Ashenfelter and D. Card ed. *Handbook of Labour Economics*, North-Holland Publishing Co.
OECD (1994) *Jobs Study*.

9 Why Does Unemployment Persist? (1989)*

with C. Bean

1 INTRODUCTION AND SUMMARY

Macroeconomics was invented to explain the persistence of unemployment. In thinking about this issue there are three key facts to be accounted for. Fact 1 is persistence itself: if unemployment becomes unusually high, it does not quickly revert to its earlier level, and the same is true if it becomes abnormally low. This is true in all countries and is illustrated for Britain in Figure 9.1. As the figure shows, the history of unemployment, consists of some minor wiggles plus occasional major changes of level. The main movements of unemployment do not correspond to business cycle fluctuations which correct themselves within a few years.[1]

However, Fact 2 is that unemployment is in the long run untrended. In other words there *is* a long-run 'natural' rate of unemployment to which the system tends eventually to return. To avoid the suggestion that this is beyond the power of man to affect we shall call this the long-run NAIRU (Non-Accelerating-Inflation Rate of Unemployment) – meaning the level of unemployment at which there is no upwards or downwards pressure on the inflation rate (or more precisely no 'price surprises'). The fact that the unemployment rate is untrended is quite remarkable, given the large changes in labour force which have occurred in most countries, mainly for demographic reasons. In the long run employment follows the labour force, and any meaningful model of the economy must reflect this tendency.

Fact 3 is that unemployment is often far from the long-run NAIRU without any upwards or downwards pressure on inflation. In the late 1980s European inflation has been very stable despite high unemployment, it was also stable in the 1950's and 1960's despite low unemployment. This means that in any year the prevailing (or short-run) NAIRU can be far away from the long-run NAIRU. In fact very little of the variation in unemployment is associated with changes in inflation (or 'price surprises'). It follows that most of the variation in

* *Scandinavian Journal of Economics*, 91(2) (1989), pp. 371–96.
The authors are grateful to the Economic and Social Research Council and the Esmée Fairbairn Charitable Trust for financial support, as well as to the discussants for helpful comments.

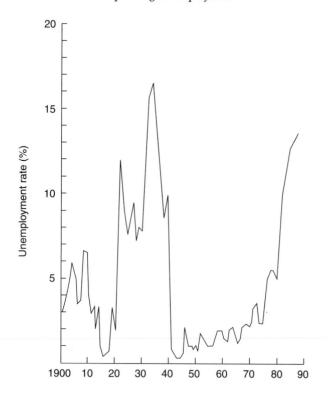

Figure 9.1 Unemployment in the United Kingdom, 1900–85
Source: Layard (1986, Figure 1).

unemployment reflects the evolution of the short-run NAIRU. Thus the short-run NAIRU has to become one of the central concepts in macroeconomics. The aim of this paper is to explain its evolution.

As we shall see, the initial impulse changing unemployment may come either from demand or supply shocks. But after such a shock, the continuing evolution of unemployment is most fruitfully thought of in terms of the evolution of the short-run NAIRU.[2]

This is a story of the supply side of the economy. One then asks: What causes such persistence in the economy's capacity to produce without increasing (or decreasing) inflation? One answer is in terms of the evolution of the physical capital stock; cf. Malinvaud (1982). As Modigliani *et al.* (1987) argue, this is not very plausible. The number of workers per machine, office or restaurant can be varied on any shift; the number of shifts can be varied; and new capacity can be quite quickly installed. The history of investment also suggests that capacity responds quickly to its rate of utilization. Thus, as Blanchard (1988) also argues, the main supply constraint originates in the labour market itself.

How the NAIRU is determined

To understand how this constraint operates, the first step is to develop the basic theory of the NAIRU. Unemployment is in equilibrium only when there is consistency between the intended mark-up of prices over wages and the intended mark-up of wages over prices; see Blanchard (1986). *The NAIRU brings peace in the battle of the mark-ups.*

Beginning with prices, firms set these on the basis of marginal cost. Thus in general

$$p - w^e = a_0 - a_1 u \tag{9.1}$$

where p is the logarithm of the price of output (value-added), w^e is the logarithm of the expected wage, u is the unemployment rate, and a_0 captures the effects of technical progress, the capital/labour-force ratio, and the degree of monopoly power in product markets. If the elasticity of product demand is constant, unemployment must reduce the price level for given wages if it raises the marginal product of labour. However a_1 could be zero (normal-cost pricing) if the marginal product was constant or if the elasticity of demand rose sufficiently in a boom.

Thus firms are setting prices as a mark-up on expected wages. By contrast wage-setters set wages as a mark-up on expected prices, the mark-up being lower the more unemployment there is. Thus

$$w - p^e = b_0 - b_1 u \tag{9.2}$$

To close the model we can assume an aggregate demand equation of the form

$$u = c_0 - c_1(m - p) \tag{9.3}$$

where m is the logarithm of the money stock. In the very short run (9.1)–(9.3) determine unemployment, wages and prices.

But if there are no nominal surprises ($p - p^e = w - w^e = 0$) then, by adding (9.1) and (9.2), unemployment is at the NAIRU given by

$$\text{NAIRU} = u^* = \frac{a_0 + b_0}{a_1 + b_1}$$

This is illustrated in Figure 9.2. Aggregate real demand is purely passive.

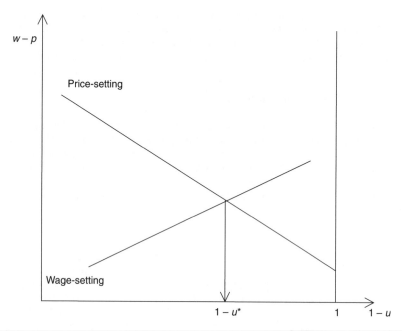

Figure 9.2   The NAIRU (with $p - p^e = w - w^e = 0$)

If however there *are* price surprises, then actual unemployment is

$$u = \frac{a_0 + b_0 - (p - p^e) - (w - w^e)}{a_1 + b_1} \tag{9.4}$$

Low unemployment is associated with positive price surprises and vice versa. However (9.4) is not a Lucas supply curve. It is a relationship obtained from price- and wage-setting behaviour – based in other words on the battle for distributive shares. If unemployment is too low, price-setters will be aiming at a profit mark-up incompatible with the real wage intended by wage-setters. The mechanism by which this inconsistency is resolved is the price and wage surprise (generally associated with changing inflation or changing prices, whichever variable is currently untrended).

If by contrast there are no wage and price surprises, then unemployment is at just the right level to bring peace in the struggle for shares. The leap-frogging of prices over wages and vice versa has been eliminated. We have also eliminated the leap-frogging of wages over wages (not modelled here) by ensuring that each group settles for the same wage as all equivalent groups, rather than trying to improve its relativity.

In this model pricing behaviour is relatively straightforward, and in equilibrium ensures that each group of labour is employed on the labour demand curve. But will each group also be employed on its labour supply curve? It could be so, in which case (9.2) can indeed be thought of as the labour supply curve. But job-queues exist widely and we shall therefore focus on those cases where more workers are willing to work at the prevailing wage than can find work.

This does not mean that we think all unemployment is involuntary. It may well be the case that everybody could get *some* job. In other words there is a 'secondary' labour market which is market-clearing. But there is also a larger 'primary' sector where job queues exist. Many of those who cannot get primary sector jobs are willing to take lower-paid and nastier jobs in the secondary sector. So unemployment results.[3] And in practice movements in unemployment are mainly the result of movements in primary sector employment. Since most of the action takes place in this sector we shall henceforth ignore the role of the secondary sector.

What stops the wage dropping and what causes persistence?

Two questions immediately arise: (i) What stops the wage dropping in the face of an excess supply of labour? (ii) What causes unemployment deviations to persist?

There are two main mechanisms which can cause wages to be above the supply price of labour. First, employers may voluntarily pay more – the case of efficiency wages. Second, they may be forced to pay more – the case of collective bargaining with unions.

But what causes persistence in each of these cases? Again there are two main mechanisms. First, there is the 'insider' mechanism. If the number of employed people falls due to some shock, the wage pressure at given unemployment will rise as there are fewer workers worried about their jobs. This effect most naturally operates when there are unions who can organize the insiders. Second, there is an 'outsider' mechanism. If the unemployed 'outsiders' are demoralized or stigmatized by, for example, long spells of unemployment, the wage pressure at given unemployment will also rise – because the effective excess supply of labour is reduced. This 'outsider' effect can operate whether wages are set by employers (efficiency wages) or by bargaining with unions.

In the rest of this overview we shall therefore review first the insider mechanism and then the outsider mechanism in a fairly schematic way. Then in the next section we shall explicitly derive the efficiency wage and the bargained wage, and show exactly how insider and outsider considerations operate within each.

Insider power

We begin with the role of insider power in generating persistence. This has been stressed both by Lindbeck and Snower (1988) and Blanchard and Summers (1986). It is convenient to begin with Blanchard and Summers' most extreme version of the story, which (unlike some of their later models) leads to total hysteresis – that is, employment follows a random walk with drift.

The idea is that insiders fix real wages to ensure their continued employment. If a shock reduces the number of insiders, next period's employment (with no further shocks) will be lower by the same amount. Thus the 'natural' level of employment this period (N^*) is simply equal to last period's actual employment (N_{-1}). Allowing for turnover at rate s, employment would be expected to drift down, unless there were positive shocks or sufficient risk aversion for workers to select N^* much higher than $(1 - s) N_{-1}$.

The model outlined above is one of 'pure hysteresis', with employment showing no tendency to converge on a given proportion of the labour force. Alternatively one could allow for an independent effect of outside unemployment, giving a model with 'partial hysteresis'. There would then be convergence to a long-run NAIRU but the short-run NAIRU would be much affected by recent levels of employment.

The most obvious source of insider power would come from trade union activity. This might help to explain the greater persistence of unemployment in recent years in Europe than in the USA (though in the 1930s, when unions everywhere were weak, the degree of persistence was the other way round).

Models of unemployment that focus on insider power leave much of the time-series variation of unemployment unexplained:[4]

(a)   The *extreme* version of pure hysteresis is inconsistent with our original Fact 2: in the long run the *labour force* clearly affects the level of employment. Furthermore in wage equations for 19 OECD countries over the period 1952–82 the negative effect of the labour force upon wages on average exactly offsets the positive effect of employment suggesting that it is only unemployment that matters; see Layard (1986). This explains *why* the labour force ultimately affects employment, one for one. Indeed Arrow (1974) has emphasized that a major triumph of economics as a social science is that it alone can explain this.

Thus the *extreme version* of insider power with pure hysteresis can be rejected. But does not the insider model still provide the main reason why the short-run NAIRU can diverge so long from the long-run NAIRU? Probably not. For there are two further facts which do not support the exclusive role of the insider mechanism in accounting for persistence.

(b)   In microeconomic *panel data studies of firms*, it is possible to examine the independent effect upon wages of (i) lagged employment *within* the firm and (ii) the unemployment rate in the *outside* labour market. The evidence is that outside unemployment has a powerful effect and inside employment (lagged) a weak effect, if any; cf. Nickell and Wadhwani (1988) and Nickell and Kong (1988). This illustrates a general point about the future of macro-economic research. There is little power in aggregate time series to discriminate between competing macroeconomic theories. There is, however, a wealth of disaggregated and microeconomic data which can also be brought to bear, both in distinguishing between models and in measuring the magnitude of parameters. Integration of this information should lead to a far better understanding of the mechanisms at work – so that the right policy conclusions can be drawn.

(c)   There is a third key fact which is inconsistent with the insider model. This is the *huge movement of the unemployment-vacancy (u/v) curve* in most countries where unemployment has risen sharply. If the insider model were correct, a large rise in unemployment should have no effect on the location of the *u/v* curve but should simply lead to a collapse in the vacancy rate. Yet in Britain there is now the same vacancy rate as in 1959 while unemployment is five times as high (see Figure 9.3). Britain is perhaps an extreme case, but in most high-unemployment countries the *u/v* curve has shifted out; see Johnson and Layard (1986).

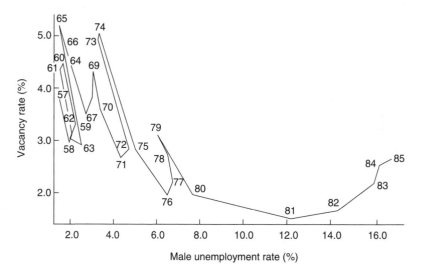

Figure 9.3   Unemployment and vacancies, Britain, 1957–85
Note: The definition of employment differs from Figure 9.1.
Source: Layard (1986, Figure 15).

Outsider ineffectiveness

To explain the shift of the u/v curve, one naturally turns to the characteristics of the unemployed. Have they become less well matched to the available vacancies (in terms of location, industry or skill)? There is no clear evidence that mismatch (except perhaps by skill) has worsened; cf. Jackman and Roper (1987). Perhaps they have become more choosy about which jobs they will accept? But there is little evidence that unemployment benefits have suddenly become more generous.

A key fact is that the unemployed have now been out of work for very much longer than in the past. There is also clear evidence that in all countries the rate at which unemployed people find work is at any instant much lower for long-term than for short-term unemployed. In Britain the rate is but one-tenth of its initial value for those who have been unemployed over 4 years. Psychological evidence indicates that this is largely due to the effect of prolonged unemployment, rather than heterogeneity among those who become unemployed (Warr and Jackson, 1985). The time-series evidence on the movement of exit rates at different durations also supports this thesis; see Jackman and Layard (1987).

If this is so, long-term unemployment reduces the 'effectiveness' of unemployed people as job-seekers – lowering their motivation, morale and skills and their quality as perceived by employers. Given this, it is easy to see how the u/v curve can shift out if the unemployed include a higher proportion of long-term unemployed. Econometric evidence supports the view that in many countries this has been an important mechanism shifting out the u/v curve; cf. Budd, Levine and Smith (1987) and Franz (1987). For the same reason unemployment exerts less downwards pressure on wages if a high proportion of the unemployed have been out of work for a long time; see Layard and Nickell (1987).

We have here a clear mechanism generating persistence. An adverse shock reduces employment. This reduces the outflow from unemployment. In consequence, a higher proportion of the unemployed have experienced long spells without work. This means that wage pressure at given unemployment is lower than it would otherwise be. Since the duration structure of unemployment is itself a function of current and past levels of unemployment, there *is* a long-run NAIRU. But in the short-term the NAIRU will exceed this, due to the high proportion of long-term unemployed.

Our original model therefore has to be modified as follows. We still have the same price equation (9.1) as before, but the wage equation is now

$$w - p^e = b_0 - b_1 \bar{c} u \tag{9.2'}$$

where $\bar{c}$ is an index of the average 'effectiveness' of the unemployed outsiders.

This effectiveness depends negatively on the average duration of unemployment, which in turn is positively related to past levels of unemployment. Allowing first for only one lag, we can approximate 'effective unemployment', $\bar{c}u$, by

$$\bar{c}u = c_0 + c_1 u - c_2 u_{-1} \qquad (c_2 < c_1) \tag{9.5}$$

We can now investigate how the short-run NAIRU evolves in this system, once unemployment has been displaced from the long-run NAIRU. To do this we proceed as usual by setting $w - w^e = p - p^e = 0$, and then add (9.1) and (9.2'), after first substituting in (9.2') for $\bar{c}u$. This gives an unemployment equation of the form

$$0 = d_0 - d_1 u + d_2 u_{-1} \qquad (d_1 > d_2)$$

where $d_0 = a_0 + b_0 - c_0 b_1, d_1 = a_1 + b_1 c_1$ and $d_2 = b_1 c_2$. This equation governs the evolution of the short-run NAIRU.

Clearly the long-run NAIRU is given by:

$$\text{Long-run NAIRU} = u^* = \frac{d_0}{d_1 - d_2}$$

But the short-run NAIRU is

$$\text{Short-run NAIRU} = \frac{d_0 + d_2 u_{-1}}{d_1} = \frac{(d_1 - d_2)u^* + d_2 u_{-1}}{d_1}$$

Thus in this model the short-run NAIRU always lies between the long-run NAIRU and last period's unemployment. It is a weighted average of the two, with weights depending on the ratio of d_2 to d_1. As d_2 tends to d_1, we tend to the special case of pure hysteresis, with the short-run NAIRU equal to last period's unemployment. But in general we have a system in which (given no further price surprises) unemployment converges monotonically on the long-run NAIRU. Each period the change in unemployment is

$$u - u_{-1} = \frac{d_1 - d_2}{d_1}(u^* - u_{-1})$$

so that a given fraction of the divergence is eliminated each period. This is the semi-comforting story that, if unemployment is high, it can always be reduced somewhat without inflationary pressure, but not by going directly to the long-run NAIRU.

However this story is rather too simple. For the evidence is that $\bar{c}$ depends on at least two lags of unemployment; see Layard and Nickell (1987) – a result which we rationalize formally in Section 3. Hence a more accurate representation of the NAIRU process is

$$0 = d_0 - d_1 u + d_2 u_{-1} + d_3 \Delta u_{-1} \qquad (d_1 > d_2) \tag{9.6}$$

where Δ denotes a first difference. This has the same long-run NAIRU. But after a one-off shock unemployment will now cycle before it converges on u^*. It can easily be the case that, if in one period unemployment is shocked upwards from the long-run NAIRU, the short-run NAIRU in the next period is *higher* than this period's unemployment.[5] This may well have been the case in many European countries after the two oil shocks, which helps to explain why it took so much unemployment to get inflation down.

We have talked so far as if the mechanism of persistence is only due to the ineffectiveness of the outsiders. We do not believe that. We also think the insider mechanism matters. Thus the dynamics in (9.6) in practice reflects both outsider *and* insider mechanisms.

Clearly the parameters of the persistence process in (9.6) depend on labour market institutions. For example the degree of persistence will be higher when unemployment benefits last indefinitely (thus raising c_2). Similarly reducing the role of insiders by limiting union power or alternatively ensuring that the interests of outsiders are respected in the wage-setting process as in the fully corporatist economies of the Nordic countries reduces persistence.[6]

Some concepts

Before going into greater detail we must clarify various matters of terminology. First, equilibrium. Our theory is one in which there is an equilibrium level of unemployment, the long-run NAIRU. This is not a market-clearing situation, nor indeed are most equilibria in natural or social sciences. It is a situation to which the system tends to return. There is also a short-run or temporary equilibrium, corresponding to the absence of price surprises.

Next, rationing. In product markets we shall assume monopolistic competition. Thus all firms are rationed, in the sense that they would like to sell more at the prevailing price. But *they* have fixed the price. By contrast workers without jobs are rationed because someone else has fixed the price (or rather the wage): at the prevailing wage no firm has an incentive to hire more workers. Whether we are in equilibrium or not, there is always rationing of this kind.

If we *are* in equilibrium, the level of employment is determined wholly by the supply side of the economy. Real aggregate demand has adjusted passively to the capacity of the economy to employ workers at constant inflation. Out of long-run equilibrium, there are two possible situations. In one, aggregate demand is extremely active, and forcing the economy to a level of unemployment different from the short-run NAIRU. In the other case aggregate demand is passive and merely lets the labour market evolve along the path of the short-run NAIRU.

We implicitly assume optimizing behaviour by individual agents at all times. But this does not lead to market-clearing, due to transactions costs and other externalities and imperfections.

Finally, there is the relation of unemployment to real wages. If the real wage implied in price-setting is higher when unemployment is higher (as is assumed in Figure 9.2), then one *could* say that unemployment was high because real wages were too high to sustain employment. This is the line taken by Bruno and Sachs (1985). But this focus can be quite misleading. For, if there were 'normal cost pricing', so that the price line were flat, the story would be quite wrong. Real wages could never be too high. By contrast if the price line had ever so small a slope, one could explain a huge amount of unemployment by a minute displacement of the real wage. The truth is that the whole approach gets us only a little way. For it does not tell us why wages are set as they are. For this we need to bring in the wage-setting line. It is the relationship between the two which *explains* unemployment.

In the rest of the paper we first develop in Section 2 two explicit models of wage-setting – in order to show *how* insider and outsider mechanisms arise. Then in Section 3 we integrate this into a fully dynamic model incorporating labour market flows. Finally Section 4 draws some policy conclusions from our analysis.

2   HELPFUL THEORIES OF UNEMPLOYMENT

Any fruitful theory of unemployment revolves around the battle of the mark-ups: of prices over wages and vice versa. Unemployment has to be high enough to prevent the wage–price spiral *and* the wage–wage spiral. This is so whether wages are set by firms or by union bargaining.

Efficiency wages

Let us begin with the case where firms set wages unilaterally. It has long been a commonplace of personnel management that wages should be set in a way that helps the firm to 'recruit, retain and motivate' staff. There is plenty of evidence that pay can have important effects on all these dimensions of performance. Wages have been shown to affect job queues, cf. Holzer, Katz and Krueger (1988); quits, cf. Pencavel (1972); absenteeism, cf. Krueger and Summers (1988); and output cf. Wadhwani and Wall (1991).

Efficiency wage models trace out the implications of these facts for the behaviour of rational firms, and thus for the equilibrium of the system.

Different models concentrate on different mechanisms. For example Shapiro and Stiglitz (1984) show how firms will pay workers more than their supply price in order to have a credible threat when they wish to discipline the worker. Jackman, Layard and Pissarides (1984) show how monopsonistic competition in hiring and retention of labour will also lead to a wage that prevents market-clearing. In all these stories the essential point is that firms have an incentive to bid up wages against each other (the wage-wage spiral). Only if unemployment is high enough does this incentive vanish, because the pay-off to paying above the going rate is eliminated.

The basic message of all these stories can be seen from the following simple model in which the relative wage affects the worker's effort (e). Hence

$$e = e\left(\frac{W}{\overline{W}}, \overline{c}u\right) \qquad (e_1, e_2 > 0; e_{12} < 0)$$

where $\overline{W}$ is the average outside wage, and $\overline{c}u$ measures the competition for jobs outside the firm.

For simplicity we shall assume that output is given by eN, where N is employment in the firm. Profits are

$$\pi = R(eN) - WN = R(eN) - (W/e)eN$$

which is to be maximized with respect to W and N. This can be done sequentially by first choosing W to minimize (W/e):

$$e - (W/\overline{W})e_1 = 0$$

In a symmetric general equilibrium $W = \overline{W}$. Hence the equilibrium unemployment rate is given by:

$$e_1(1, \overline{c}u) = e(1, \overline{c}u)$$

The lower is $\overline{c}$, the higher is u.

The source of unemployment in this model is that the wage performs two functions: it generates effort and it determines employment. Because firms use the wage to generate effort, it cannot also clear the market for employment. Thus critics of the theory ask why some other instrument could not be deployed to generate effort. Could not workers post bonds which they would lose if they are not efficient, or (if imperfect capital markets prevent that) could they not be underpaid while young and overpaid later, subject to good behaviour? The answer is that in general such schemes can never adequately achieve the efficiency objective; see Akerlof and Katz (1988).

But what positive evidence is there in support of these theories? Most businessmen recognize this account of their actions. If asked why they do not drop wages when people are queuing up for jobs, they give explanations of this kind; cf. Akerlof and Yellen (1986, 1987). We have already quoted evidence on the way in which firms can benefit from raising wages. There is also evidence that wages persistently differ between industries in ways that cannot be explained by worker quality or by union strength. The obvious explanation is that wages affect output differently in different industries and are therefore higher where effort matters more – for example where capital-intensity is high; see Krueger and Summers (1988).

In the model discussed in Section 1 persistence comes from the dependence of $\bar{c}$ on past levels of unemployment. But there may be another source of persistence in efficiency wage models; cf. Johnson and Layard (1986). We have so far assumed that effort depends on the wage relative to the *outside* wage. But workers may also compare their wage with what they think is *fair*, based on past experience. Suppose the fair wage (W_f), defined in real terms, adjusts adaptively to past experience:

$$\Delta W_f = \phi(W - W_f)_{-1}$$

And suppose individual output is given by

$$e = e\left(\frac{W}{W_f}, \bar{c}u\right)\lambda$$

Then, in the steady state, equilibrium unemployment will be independent of productivity λ. But now suppose λ falls, due for example to an oil price shock. The fair wage W_f will not instantly adjust downwards. Employers will therefore find it worthwhile paying a wage that is also out of line with productivity, and unemployment will rise. W will only converge on its long-run level as W_f converges on W at the new lower level.

Thus efficiency wage models can easily generate persistence if (i) outsider effectiveness depends on lagged unemployment, or (ii) the 'fair wage' that people expect adjusts slowly to supply shocks. Nevertheless it is noticeable that persistence has been stronger in economies where firms have to bargain with unions than where they do not. (The exception is some Nordic economies and Austria, where bargaining is highly centralized and the external diseconomies of bargaining can be overcome). This suggests that in most European countries a sensible story of the labour market also requires that we model collective bargaining and thus insider power.[7]

Union bargaining

If firms know that wages affect individual effort, they will take this into account in bargaining. However for simplicity we shall at this stage drop the efficiency wage issue and consider the following simple model of collective bargaining, based on Layard, Nickell and Jackman (1991). It is more consistent with reality than any other we have found, and does generate an insider effect provided certain key assumptions are satisfied.

Unions bargain over wages, knowing that employers will then determine employment on the basis of the bargained wage; see Oswald (1987).[8] Individual union members want to maximize their expected income (non-linear utility adds no further insight). Union policy is decided by the median voter's preferences.

Does this imply any persistence mechanism involving insider power? In other words, does last period's employment affect current wage demands? The answer is that this only happens if two assumptions hold: (i) It is uncertain how much employment there will be for a given wage, and (ii) It is uncertain which individual workers will be employed in a given total employment.

Suppose first that, once the wage is determined, the volume of employment is known. Under normal circumstances workers know that the outcome of the wage bargain will be similar to what it was last year (relative to productivity). So employment will be similar. Hence with say 30 per cent turnover, none of the existing workers is at risk. The *local* objective of the union will therefore be to maximize the wage.

Now suppose that the volume of employment is uncertain even after the wage is set, but workers know in what order they will be laid off. This order might most plausibly be in inverse order of seniority; see Oswald (1987). In this case the median voter will be far from the firing line. He will be quite happy if the union presses locally for the highest wage it can get – knowing that the countervailing power of the firm will prevent anything substantially different from last year's wage; cf. Layard (1990). Once again the union's local objective function is the wage, and the number of insiders plays no role.

However in reality the order in which workers will be laid off if wages rise is not certain. It is true that there is a general presumption in favour of last in – first out (LIFO), but this only operates within skill groups and (often) within individual plants or workshops. Firms will deliberately try to keep their workers uncertain about which shops or plants will be closed in the event of cut-backs – precisely in order to induce moderation in wage demands.[9] So we can assume for simplicity that, if employment turns out to be less than the number of insiders, lay-off is by random assignment.

In this case, the median voter's expected income is the same as everybody else's. So the union's objective function is this expected income, Ω^e, given by

$$\Omega^e = SW + (1 - S)A$$

where S is the probability of individual survival in the firm and A is expected outside income.

How is the survival probability determined? Each worker (which includes the median voter) knows that, if wages are raised, this reduces expected total employment. Hence there is a higher chance that there will be some layoffs and thus that any individual will be laid off. Thus the individual probability of surviving in employment depends inversely on the wage. But it also depends inversely on the number of existing employees (N_{-1}), since for given employment the more insiders there are the less likely any one insider is to be employed. Hence an individual's chance of survival is

$$S = S(W, N_{-1}) \qquad (S_1, S_2 < 0)$$

And how is A determined? It measures the expected value of the outside opportunities for someone laid off. These depend on outside wages $(\overline{W})$, benefits (B) and on the chances of getting a job if searching with given effectiveness. If discount rates are small relative to turnover rates, this expected value (in flow terms) is approximately[10]

$$A = (1 - \overline{c}u)\overline{W} + \overline{c}uB$$

We can now examine the outcome of the bargain. This is found by maximizing the Nash expression:

$$\max_W (\Omega^e - \overline{\Omega})^\beta (\pi^e - \overline{\pi}) = S^\beta (W - A)^\beta \pi^e(W)$$

where $\pi^e(W)$ is expected operating profit. We have assumed here that workers' fallback income during any dispute $(\overline{\Omega})$ equals A, that firms' fallback operating profit $(\overline{\pi})$ is zero, and that β is an index of the bargaining power of the union.[11] Differentiating logarithmically, the outcome of the wage bargain is given by

$$\frac{\beta S_1}{S} + \frac{\beta}{W - A} - \frac{N^e}{\pi^e} = 0$$

where N^e is expected employment. Multiplying by W and rearranging gives the partial equilibrium wage equation

$$\frac{W - A}{W} = \frac{1}{\left(\dfrac{WN^e}{\beta\pi^e}\right) + \varepsilon_{SW}} \tag{9.7}$$

where ε_{SW} is (the absolute value of) the elasticity of the survival probability with respect to the wage.

We turn now to general equilibrium. The economy consists of many sectors in each of which the representative bargain has proceeded as described. In equilibrium, unemployment must prevent a wage-wage spiral, so that $W = \overline{W}$.

Hence, substituting for A

$$\bar{c}u(1 - B/W) = \frac{1}{\left(\frac{WN^e}{\beta\pi^e}\right) + \varepsilon_{SW}}$$ (9.8)

In general ε_{SW} varies positively with N_{-1}/N^e.[12] For if the number of insiders is very low relative to expected employment, a change in expected employment has a small effect on the expected layoff rate. But, if there are many insiders, any change in expected employment will have a significant effect on layoffs. In fact using the simple Dixit–Stiglitz (1977) model of monopolistic competition with product demand elasticity η and constant marginal product of labour, ε_{SW} can be written as

$$\varepsilon_{SW} = \eta f[N_{-1}/N^e(W)] \qquad (f' > 0)$$

In addition $WN^e/\pi^e = \eta - 1$. Thus the wage equation is given by

$$\bar{c}u(1 - B/W) = \frac{1}{(\eta - 1)/(\beta + \eta f[N_{-1}/N^e(W)]}$$

The real wage is increasing in real benefits and decreasing in unemployment. It is also higher the higher the bargaining power of the union and the lower the elasticity of product demand – monopoly in the product market being a potent source of monopoly power in the labour market.

Since on reasonable assumptions $f(\cdot)$ is twice-differentiable, there is no asymmetry in wage behaviour: it is not true that a small fall in unemployment reduces the wage much less than a small rise in unemployment raises it. Asymmetries of this kind are usually based on models, such as Lindbeck and Snower (1988), without firm-level or individual uncertainty, and thus inconsistent with *any* insider effects (as explained above). Moreover there is no convincing empirical evidence for the existence of asymmetries; see, e.g., Nickell and Wadhwani (1988).

If we now take the replacement ratio as given, we can examine the evolution of unemployment. Ignoring turnover, the long-run NAIRU is given by

$$\bar{c}u(1 - B/W) = \frac{1}{(\eta - 1)/\beta + \eta f(1)}$$

But the short-run NAIRU is given by

$$\bar{c}u(1 - B/W) = \frac{1}{(n - 1)/\beta + \eta f\left(\dfrac{1 - u_{-1}}{1 - u}\right)}$$

assuming a constant labour force. This is an equation with persistence coming through insider power *and* outsider ineffectiveness (via $\bar{c}$). Linearizing and substituting for $\bar{c}u$ gives an equation of the form

$$0 = e_0 - e_1 u + e_2 u_{-1} + e_3 \Delta u_{-1} + e_4 B/W$$

as in Section 1.[13]

3 A FULLY DYNAMIC MODEL OF PERSISTENCE

We turn now to a more complete dynamic model. This goes beyond the model of Section 1 in two ways. First, it explicitly models the duration structure of unemployment. This requires us to develop a model of the flows into and out of unemployment, which in turn introduces the relationship between unemployment and vacancies. Second, the wage equation needs to be modified in the light of this.

Outflow from unemployment

We begin with the outflow from unemployment. This depends on the 'hiring function'. People are hired when a match is made between a vacancy and a job-seeker. Hirings will be increasing in both the number of vacancies, V, and the 'effective' unemployment level, $\bar{c}U$. Thus the number of hirings per year is given by the *hiring function*[14]

$$H = H(V, \bar{c}U) \qquad (H_1, H_2 > 0)$$

where V, U are the number of vacancies and unemployed, and stocks are measured at the beginning of the period.

For a large enough market the hiring function should exhibit constant returns to scale; see Hall (1977). Empirical evidence supports this; cf. Pissarides (1986) and Jackman, Layard and Savouri (1987). Thus the exit rate for a person seeking with unit effectiveness is

$$\frac{H}{\bar{c}U} = H\left(\frac{V}{\bar{c}U}, 1\right) = h(X) \quad (h' > 0)$$

where X (for excess demand) $\equiv V/\bar{c}U$. We can note in passing that the steady state (constant unemployment) relationship between U/N and V/N is obtained by setting H equal to the inflow to unemployment, sN. This makes it clear that the lower $\bar{c}$ is, the 'further out' is the curve relating U/N and V/N; cf. Jackman, Layard and Pissarides (1984).

For simplicity we shall think of the effectiveness of the unemployed as depending solely on how long they have been unemployed. We shall assume two categories of unemployed only: (i) the short-term unemployed (U^S) i.e. those who entered unemployment this period, having effectiveness normalized to unity; and (ii) the long-term unemployed (U^L) i.e. those who entered unemployment in earlier periods, having effectiveness c (< 1).

Clearly c will tend to be lower the longer benefits are payable and the less rapidly benefits decline with duration. It follows that

$$\bar{c}U \equiv U^S + cU^L = cU + (1 - c)U^S$$

Duration structure of unemployment

The next step is to discover how the distribution of the unemployed by duration moves and unemployment changes. Again for simplicity we shall take the inflow rate into unemployment (s) as constant, since it tends to vary much less than the exit rate from unemployment (at least in European countries). It follows that short-term unemployment equals this period's inflow:

$$U^S = sN_{-1} = s(L - U_{-1}) \tag{9.9}$$

where the labour force ($L \equiv N + U$) is assumed constant. Total unemployment is last period's unemployment plus inflows minus outflows, i.e.,

$$U = U_{-1} + sN_{-1} - (\bar{c}U)_{-1}h(X_{-1})$$
$$= [1 - s - ch(X_{-1})]U_{-1} - (1 - c)h(X_{-1})U^S_{-1} + sL \tag{9.10}$$

Wages and prices

Finally we need wage and price equations. The wage equation now has to be a modified version of our earlier equation. For a fully dynamic wage equation has wages depending not on $\bar{c}u$ as hitherto, but on the chances that a person seeking work with given (unit) effectiveness can expect to find work.[15] As we have seen, these chances depend on $V/\bar{c}U$ (or X as we now call it). Hence, allowing also for an insider effect (via N_{-1}), the *wage equation* is

$$\frac{W}{P} = Zg(X, N_{-1}) \qquad (g_1 > 0; g_2 < 0) \tag{9.11}$$

where Z is a shift factor that reflects *both* supply influences (like variations in benefit levels), *and* the effect of demand shocks (e.g. price 'surprises').[16]

Turning finally to the demand side of the labour market, we follow Dixit and Stiglitz (1977) by assuming that there are n firms producing n differentiated commodities with the aid of a constant returns to scale production technology,

$Y_i = N_i$, where Y_i is output of firm i, $i = 1, \ldots n$. The demand for the firm's product is the constant elasticity function $D(M/P)(P_i/P)^{-\eta}$, with $D' > 0$, and where M is the nominal money stock and P_i/P the firm's relative output price. Finally firm i's hirings are proportional to the share of its vacancies, V_i, in total vacancies: hence its new hires, H_i, are equal to

$$H_i = \frac{V_i}{V} H = \frac{V_i}{V} \bar{c} U h(X) = \frac{h(X)}{X} V_i$$

For simplicity we shall assume that opening a vacancy is costless. It is easy to generalize the analysis to incorporate costly vacancies, but at the cost of complicating the dynamics. Interested readers should consult Pissarides (1985) for a fully worked out model incorporating costly vacancies (but excluding insider and outsider dynamics); see also Mortensen (1989).

The firm's problem is:

$$\max_{(N_i, P_i, V_i)} (P_i - W)N_i$$

subject to:

$$N_i = (1 - s)N_{i-1} + V_i h(X)/X$$
$$N_i = D(P_i/P)^{-\eta}$$

which yields the familiar *price-setting* relationship

$$P_i/W = \eta/(\eta - 1)$$

In a symmetric equilibrium, however, we have $P_i = P$ (and $N_i = N/n$). In that case the price-setting rule above and the wage-setting rule (9.11) may be combined to give a *consistent-mark-ups-equation*

$$(\eta - 1)/\eta = Zg[X, (L - U_{-1}] \tag{9.12}$$

which provides an implicit relationship between labour market tension, unemployment, the labour force and the shift factor in the wage equation (Z). Together (9.9), (9.10) and (9.12) completely describe the dynamic evolution of the economy.

Before analyzing the dynamics in detail, however, it is instructive to examine the determination of steady-state equilibrium. (9.9) and (9.10) imply that in a stationary state the equilibrium unemployment level U^* is given by:

$$\frac{U^*}{L} = \frac{1 - (1 - c)h(X^*)}{1 - (1 - c - c/s)h(X^*)}$$
$$= j(X^*)$$

where $j' = -ch'/s[1 - (1 - c - c/s)h]^2 < 0$. Substituting into (9.12) yields the reduced-form equation for the long-run NAIRU:[17]

$$(\eta - 1)/\eta = Zg[j^{-1}(U^*/L), L - U^*]$$

Let us now examine the effect of a permanent supply shock, raising Z. Since $\partial U^*/\partial Z = g/(g_2 - g_1/j'L) Z$, it follows that, provided the insider effect (g_2) is not too large,[18] an increase in Z, due to say increased union pushfulness, raises equilibrium unemployment. Notice, however, that by virtue of the price-setting rule, real wages are unchanged in the long-run equilibrium (and indeed along the transition path as well). This is despite the fact that increased wage push by the workers in a single firm will lead to a rise in their real wages and a fall in the level of employment in that firm. A corollary is that a (policy-induced?) reduction in Z need not be associated with any decline in real wages, and will instead result in an increase in employment alone.

This emphasizes rather starkly the role of unemployment at a macro-economic level as an equilibrating device to reconcile potentially conflicting claims over the division of the output of the economy. Of course, in more general models with variable returns to scale and/or a price elasticity of product demand that varies with the level of activity, equilibrium real wages will as a rule be affected by changes in Z. Nevertheless the basic insight still holds that with imperfect competition in the product market an understanding of the co-movement of real wages and employment requires an understanding of both pricing and wage-setting behaviour.

Let us now return to the issue of dynamic adjustment. Linearizing (9.9), (9.10) and (9.12) and eliminating X yields the system:

$$\begin{bmatrix} 1 - (1 - s - ch)B - aB^2 & (1 - c)hB \\ sB & 1 \end{bmatrix}\begin{bmatrix} U \\ U^s \end{bmatrix} = \begin{bmatrix} bZ_{-1} \\ 0 \end{bmatrix} \quad (9.13)$$

where B is the backward lag operator, coefficients are evaluated at equilibrium, and all variables are now understood to be deviations from equilibrium values. The parameter a is defined as:

$$a \equiv -g_2\bar{c}Uh'/g_1 = \frac{H}{N}\frac{\varepsilon_{WN}\varepsilon_{hX}}{\varepsilon_{WX}} \quad (a \geq 0)$$

where ε_{WN} is the (absolute value of the) elasticity of the wage-setting function with respect to lagged employment (the insider effect), ε_{WX} is the elasticity of the same function with respect to labour market tension, and ε_{hX} is the elasticity of the hiring function. Thus, if insider considerations dominate in wage setting, a is large, while if external factors dominate a will be small. Similarly b is defined as:

$$b \equiv \bar{c}Uh'g/Zg_1 = \frac{H}{Z}\frac{\varepsilon_{hX}}{\varepsilon_{WX}}$$

Solving (9.13) gives the reduced form relationship for unemployment as:

$$U = \frac{bZ_{-1}}{\{1 - (1 - s - ch)B - [a + s(1 - c)h]B^2\}}$$

Hence unemployment is a second-order autoregressive process in the demand/wage push shocks. Note that if there are no insider effects ($a = 0$) and no outsider effects ($c = 1$) the dynamics become only first order. Thus the dynamics inherent in the matching process – it takes time for people to find jobs and for firms to locate potential workers – automatically introduces a degree of persistence into the behaviour of unemployment. Insider and outsider effects both extend this persistence.

To see this more formally the mean lag, μ, in the effect of Z on unemployment is given by:

$$\mu = \frac{[1 + a + s(1 - c)h]}{[s + ch - a - s(1 - c)h]} - 1$$

and hence $\partial\mu/\partial a > 0$ and $\partial\mu/\partial c < 0$.

It is also instructive to calculate the time series representation of 'effective' unemployment $\bar{c}U$ in terms of past values of unemployment and the forcing variables. This is easily shown to take the form:

$$\bar{c}U = [s(1 - c) + c(1 - s - ch)]U_{-1} + c[a + s(1 - c)h]U_{-2} + bZ_{-1}$$

This provides a justification for the expressions in Section 1.

4 POLICY CONCLUSIONS

There is good evidence (some of it cited earlier) to support the theory that persistent European unemployment is sustained mainly by the ineffectiveness of the unemployed outsiders. This points to two important policy conclusions. First, once long-term unemployment has emerged there is a high return to special measures to re-integrate the long-term unemployed into the effective labour force. Second, it is important not to allow large numbers of people to drift into long-term unemployment in the first place. Here it is striking that long-term unemployment is very much smaller in countries such as the USA, Sweden, Norway, Finland and Austria in which benefits are not available beyond 6–12 months, except for those on special work or training schemes.[19] Targeted training and job programmes for the unemployed, as in Sweden, also have a crucial role. This whole issue is in no sense marginal, since in the major European countries almost a half of all the unemployed have been out of work for over a year; see Jackman and Layard (1987).

Second, there is some (less powerful) evidence in support of the theory that unemployment tends to remain high because the number of insiders has been reduced. This suggests that steps to reduce trade union power at the workplace could not only reduce the NAIRU but also the persistence of departures from it. Corporatist behaviour by unions could also achieve the same results. In addition policies to reduce firing costs would help to reduce insider power; cf. Lindbeck and Snower (1988).

Third, if hysteresis is important (for whatever reason) an incomes policy could help greatly. The incomes policy would temporarily lower the short-run NAIRU, until it has been permanently reduced by the actual experience of lower unemployment. Thus even if the policy lasted for only as long as the period during which unemployment was being reduced, this could speed the return to the long-run NAIRU without increasing inflation.

Finally, there is a moral about stabilization policy. If higher unemployment raises next year's NAIRU, the returns to preventing higher unemployment in the first place must be that much greater. Countries like Sweden which have used a mixture of stabilization policy and incomes policy to offset adverse supply shocks have been proved far wiser than most economists would have thought 10 years ago.

But demand stabilization is unlikely to succeed without simultaneous efforts on the supply side. It is always best to be ambidextrous.

Notes

1. For formal tests of whether unemployment follows a random walk see Blanchard and Summers (1986). However the results of this type of test depend critically on the time period chosen, suggesting that it may not be helpful to view a hundred years of unemployment as simply the result of a given time-invariant stochastic process.
2. Thus there is no reason to assume (as real business cycle theorists are wont to do) that only technology shocks can have persistent real effects. Our view of the world provides an alternative explanation of high persistence which has the merit of explaining not only output but *also* unemployment.
3. See Bulow and Summers (1986) and Johnson and Layard (1986).
4. This is a *different* issue from whether insider power influences the NAIRU. Obviously trade union power affects the NAIRU – in *any* trade union model. Equally trade union behaviour explains why employers do not hire new workers at less than the insider wage – because the union believes this will ultimately undermine its bargaining strength; cf. Lindbeck and Snower (1988).

5. This requires $d_1 - d_2 - d_3 < 0$. In the Layard and Nickell results this condition does indeed hold when the sum of their equations (5.1') and (5.2') is expanded around a 12 per cent male unemployment rate, as prevailed in 1980–1.

6. Such reforms could also be expected to raise b_1, the effect of unemployment on wage setting behaviour, which would reduce the impact effect of a demand or supply shock (see (9.4)). Bean, Layard and Nickell (1986) provide empirical evidence on the link between corporatism and persistence as well as impact effects.

7. The number of insiders would have an effect in efficiency wage models if individual efficiency was reduced when the firm recruited more workers, e.g.,

$$e = e(W/\overline{W}, \bar{c}u, N/N_{-1}) \qquad (e_3 < 0)$$

    This seems improbable.

8. Bargaining over employment is extremely rare, bargaining over productivity extremely common. The latter does not radically alter the picture; cf. Layard, Nickell and Jackman (1991).

9. Moreover in the real world of voting behaviour there are many issues on which members vote, so that the wishes of the median number on one particular issue may not be decisive.

10. The present value to being unemployed (V_u) if a person searches with unit effectiveness is

$$V_u = \frac{1}{1+r}\left[B + \frac{\phi}{\bar{c}}V_e + \left(1 - \frac{\phi}{\bar{c}}\right)V_u\right]$$

    where r is the discount rate, ϕ the outflow rate from unemployment, $\bar{c}$ the effectiveness of those currently unemployed, V_e the present value of being employed elsewhere and wages and benefits are assumed to be paid at the end of the period. V_e in turn is:

$$V_e = \frac{1}{1+r}(\overline{W} + sV_u + (1-s)V_e)$$

    where s is the rate of separation into unemployment. Solving we find that

$$rV_u = (1-\lambda)\overline{W} + \lambda B$$

    where $\lambda = (r+s)/(r+s+\phi/\bar{c}) \approx s/(s+\phi/\bar{c})$ since $r \ll s$. Now in equilibrium $\phi u = s(1-u)$. Hence $\lambda \approx \bar{c}u/[1 - (1-\bar{c})u] \approx \bar{c}u$.

11. As regards workers, $\overline{\Omega}$ is unlikely to be exactly equal to A but it is certainly affected by both $\overline{W}$ and $\bar{c}u$. Note that the interior Nash solution only applies provided that both Ω^e and π^e exceed the outside option open to workers and firms respectively, assuming no agreement is reached. Unless there is full employment, Ω^e *will* exceed the workers' outside option, but a very high wage cannot be agreed on because the firm would rather sack the whole workforce and hire another one.

12. Some regularity conditions on the distribution function are also required; see Gottfries and Horn (1987).

13. In addition there is at least one other possible source of persistence in models with bargaining. Suppose that when unemployment rises, firms cease to be able

to bargain over productivity. Demanning ensues. In a 2-sector model the NAIRU is now higher, unless the rise in real wages leads to sufficient increase in secondary sector employment; see Layard, Nickell and Jackman (1991).

14. This ignores job-to-job movements. Allowing for this makes no significant difference – see Layard, Nickell and Jackman (1991, Chapter 7).

15. Suppose for example wages are set by bargaining, as in (9.7). With the Dixit–Stiglitz specification of the product market, and a proper intertemporal evaluation of expected income we get

$$\frac{W - rV_u}{W} = \frac{1}{(\eta - 1)/\beta + \eta f[N_{-1}/N^e(W)]}$$

From the third equation of n. 10 above

$$rV_u/W = (1 - \lambda + \lambda B/W)$$

where $\lambda = (r + s)/(r + s + \phi/\bar{c})$ Thus

$$W = W\left(\frac{\phi}{\bar{c}}, B, N_{-1}\right) \qquad (W_1, W_2 > 0; W_3 < 0)$$

By contrast, (9.2′) can be justified as follows. By definition $\phi = H/U$ and, in equilibrium, $H = sN$. Thus

$$\frac{\phi}{\bar{c}} \approx \frac{s}{\bar{c}u}$$

16. In this case one might wish to make wage settlements a function of X^e rather than X.

17. As written, this leaves the NAIRU, U^*/L, depending on the size of the labour force. This could be rectified by assuming the number of firms grows with the size of the economy so the wage equation becomes

$$\frac{W}{P} = Zg\left(X, \frac{N_{-1}}{L}\right)$$

18. The ambiguity arises because on the one hand higher equilibrium unemployment reduces the chances of finding a job and hence reduces wage pressure, but on the other hand is associated with a lower employment level for a given labour force, a smaller group of insiders and hence an increase in wage pressure. Thus an exogenous increase in wage pressure could require either an increase or a decrease in unemployment to equilibrate the reduced form NAIRU equation. However, for the system to be stable the 'outside' effect must dominate, i.e., $g_1 > g_2 j'L$ is a necessary condition for the stability of (9.13).

19. An important research project would attempt to correlate our parameter c with the benefit regime.

References

Akerlof, G. and L. Katz (1988) 'Workers' Trust Funds and the Logic of Wage Profiles', Berkeley, mimeo.

Akerlof, G. and J. Yellen (1987) 'The Fair Wage/Effort Hypothesis and Unemployment', Berkeley, mimeo.

Akerlof, G. and J. Yellen (eds) (1986) *Efficiency Wage Models of the Labor Market* (Cambridge: Cambridge University Press).

Arrow, K. (1974) 'General Economic Equilibrium: Purpose, Analytic Techniques, Collective Choice', *American Economic Review*, 64, 1–10.

Bean, C., R. Layard and S. Nickell (1986) 'The Rise in Unemployment: A Multi-country Study', *Economica Special Supplement on Unemployment*, 53, S1–S22.

Blanchard, O. (1986) 'The Wage–Price Spiral', *Quarterly Journal of Economics*, 101, 543–66.

Blanchard, O. (1988) 'Unemployment: Getting the Questions Right and Some of the Answers', MIT, mimeo.

Blanchard, O. and L. Summers (1986) 'Hysteresis and the European Unemployment Problem', *NBER Macroeconomics Annual*, 15–78.

Bruno, M. and J. Sachs (1985) *The Economics of Worldwide Stagflation* (Oxford: Oxford University Press).

Budd, A., P. Levine and P. Smith (1987) 'Long Term Unemployment and the Shifting U/V curve: A Multi-Country Study', *European Economic Review*, 31.

Bulow, J. and L. Summers (1986) 'A Theory of Dual Labor Markets with Application to Industrial Policy, Discrimination, and Keynesian Unemployment', *Journal of Labor Economics*, 3, 376–414.

Dixit, A. and J. Stiglitz (1977) 'Monopolistic Competition and Optimum Product Diversity', *American Economic Review*, 67, 297–308.

Franz, W. (1987) 'Hysteresis, Persistence and the NAIRU: An Empirical Analysis for the FRG', in R. Layard and L. Calmfors (eds), *The Fight against Unemployment* (Cambridge, MA: MIT Press).

Gottfries, N. and H. Horn (1987) 'Wage Formation and the Persistence of Unemployment', *Economic Journal*, 97, 887–4.

Hall, R. (1977) 'An Aspect of the Economic Role of Unemployment', in G.C. Harcourt (ed.), *Microeconomic Foundations of Macroeconomics*.

Holzer, H., L. Katz and A. Krueger (1988), 'Job Queues and Wages: New Evidence on the Minimum Wage and Inter-Industry Wage Structure', Princeton University, Industrial Relations Section, mimeo.

Jackman, R. and R. Layard (1988) 'Innovative Supply-Side Policies to Reduce Unemployment', in P. Minford (ed.), *Monetarism and Macroeconomics*, IEA Readings, 26.

Jackman, R. and R. Layard (1991) 'Does Long-Term Unemployment Reduce a Person's Chance of a Job? A Time-Series Test', *Economica* 58, 299, Chapter 6 in this volume.

Jackman, R., R. Layard and C. Pissarides (1984) 'On Vacancies', Discussion Paper 165 (revised), London School of Economics, Centre for Labour Economics, Chapter 5 in this volume.

Jackman, R., R. Layard and S. Savouri (1987) 'Labour Market Mismatch and the "Equilibrium" Level of Unemployment to Vacancies'. W.P. 1009, London School of Economics, Centre for Labour Economics.

Jackman, R. and S. Roper (1987) 'Structural Unemployment. Special Issue on Wage Determination and Labour Market Flexibility', *Oxford Bulletin of Economics and Statistics*, 49, 9–36.

Johnson, G. and R. Layard (1986) 'The Natural Rate of Unemployment: Explanation and Policy', in O. Ashenfelter and R. Layard (eds), *Handbook of Labor Economics* (North Holland: Amsterdam).

Krueger, A. and L. Summers (1988) 'Efficiency Wages and the Inter-Industry Wage Structure', *Econometrica*, 56, 259–94.

Layard, R. (1986) *How to Beat Unemployment* (Oxford: Oxford University Press).

Layard, R. (1990) 'Layoffs by Seniority and Equilibrium Employment', in *Economics Letters*, 32, North Holland.

Layard, R. and S. Nickell (1987) 'The Labour Market', in R. Dornbusch and R. Layard (eds), *The Performance of the British Economy* (Oxford: Oxford University Press), Chapter 4 in this volume.

Layard, R., S. Nickell and R. Jackman (1991) *Unemployment: Macroeconomic Performance and the Labour Market* (Oxford: Oxford University Press).

Lindbeck, A. and D. Snower (1988) 'Cooperation, Harassment, and Involuntary Unemployment: An Insider-Outsider Approach', *American Economic Review*, 78, 167–88.

Malinvaud, E. (1982) 'Wages and Unemployment', *Economic Journal*, 92, 365, 1–13.

Modigliani, F., M. Monti, J. Drèze, H. Giersch and R. Layard (1987) 'Reducing Unemployment in Europe: The Role of Capital Formation', in R. Layard and L. Calmfors (eds), *The Fight against Unemployment* (Cambridge, MA: MIT Press).

Mortensen, D.T. (1989) 'The Persistence and Indeterminacy of Unemployment in search Equilibrium' in *The Scandinavian Journal of Economics*, 91, 2.

Nickell, S.J. and P. Kong (1988) 'An Investigation into the Power of Insiders in Wage Determination', University of Oxford, Institute of Economics and Statistics, Applied Economics. Discussion Paper no. 49.

Nickell, S. and S. Wadhwani (1988) 'Insider Forces and Wage Determination', Mimeo, London School of Economics, Centre for Labour Economics.

Oswald, A. (1987) 'Efficient Contracts are on the Labour Demand Curve: Theory and Facts', Discussion Paper 284, London School of Economics, Centre for Labour Economics.

Pencavel, J. (1972) 'Wages, Specific Training, and Labor Turnover in U.S Manufacturing Industries', *International Economic Review*, 13.

Pissarides, C. (1985) 'Short-Run Equilibrium Dynamics of Unemployment, Vacancies and Real Wages', *American Economic Review*, 75.

Pissarides, C. (1986) 'Unemployment and Vacancies in Britain', *Economic Policy*, 499–560.

Shapiro, C. and J. Stiglitz (1984) 'Equilibrium Unemployment as a Worker Discipline Device', *American Economic Review*, 74.

Wadhwani, S. and M. Wall (1991) 'A Direct Test of the Efficiency Wage Model using U.K. Micro-Data', London School of Economics, Centre for Labour Economics, Working Paper no. 1022, revised.

Warr, P. and P. Jackson (1985) 'Factors Influencing the Psychological Impact of Prolonged Unemployment and of Re-employment', *Psychological Medicine*, 15, 795–807.

10 Combating Unemployment: Is Flexibility Enough? (1996)*

with R. Jackman and S. Nickell

What is the route to lower unemployment? Is it through greater labour market flexibility, involving deregulation and decentralization? Or are there areas where more collective action, rather than less, is required?

To examine this issue we have tried to see how differences of policy and institutions affect the unemployment levels in the different OECD countries. (We are concerned not with cyclical fluctuations but with the average levels of unemployment over a run of years.) The factors whose possible influence we examine are:

- how unemployed people are treated (benefit levels and active help with job-finding);
- how wages are determined;
- how skills are formed;
- how far jobs are protected by redundancy legislation;
- how heavily employment is taxed; and
- how far labour supply is reduced through reductions in hours of work and through early retirement.

Our conclusions are that the most important influences on unemployment come from the first three factors.

- The longer *unemployment benefits* are available the longer unemployment lasts. Similarly, higher levels of benefits generate higher unemployment, with an elasticity of around one half. On the other hand *active help* in finding work can reduce unemployment. So more 'flexibility' may need to be complemented by more intervention to provide active help.
- Union coverage and union power raise unemployment. But if *wage bargaining* is decentralised, wage bargainers have incentives to settle for

---

* *Macroeconomic Policies and Structural Reform* (Paris: OECD, 1996), pp. 19–49.

more than the 'going rate', and only higher unemployment can prevent them leapfrogging. Although decentralization makes it easier to vary *relative* wages, this advantage is more than offset by the extra upward pressure on the *general* level of wages. Thus, where union coverage is high, co-ordinated wage bargaining leads to lower unemployment.
– Conscious intervention to raise the *skill levels* of less able workers is an important component of any policy to combat unemployment. Pure wage flexibility may not be sufficient because it leads to growing inequality which in turn discourages labour supply from less able workers.

Thus in our first three areas it is clear what types of reform are needed. If well designed, such reforms might halve the level of unemployment in many countries.

But there are other proposed remedies some of which have been advocated either in the OECD Jobs Study or the Delors White Paper. These include: less employment protection, lower taxes on employment, and lower working hours. Our research does not suggest that lower employment taxes or lower hours would have any long term effects; while the effects of lower employment protection would be small.

– *Lower employment protection* has two effects. It increases hiring and thus reduces long-term unemployment. But it also increases firing and thus increases short-term unemployment. The first (good) effect is almost offset by the second (bad) one. The gains from flexibility are small.
– *Employment taxes* do not appear to have any long-term effect on unemployment and are borne entirely by labour. There may be some short-term effects, but it is not clear that there would be any fall in inflationary pressure if taxes on polluting products were raised at the same time as taxes on employment were lowered.
– *Hours of work* appear to have no long-term effect upon unemployment. Equally, if *early retirement* is used in order to reduce labour supply, it is necessary to reduce employment *pari passu* unless inflationary pressure is to increase. While flexible hours and participation can reduce the fluctuations in unemployment over the cycle, they cannot affect its average level.

We can now proceed to the evidence for these assertions. We begin by looking at the pattern of unemployment differences between countries and estimate an equation which explains it, using all the factors we find significant. We then discuss each factor in turn, drawing on other evidence where relevant. We end with policy conclusions.

COUNTRY DIFFERENCES

There are wide differences in unemployment rates across countries, but one feature of these differences has been little noticed: a large part of the variation is in long-term unemployment. This is shown in Table 10.1. It appears that countries can live with very different rates of long-term unemployment, whereas some short-term unemployment seems inevitable. The reason for this 'optional' nature of long-term unemployment appears to be that long-term unemployment has a much lower effect on wage pressure than does short-term unemployment (OECD, 1993, p. 94).

Table 10.1 Unemployment rates, total, long-term and short-term, per cent

	1983–8			1989–94		
	Total	Long-term	Short-term	Total	Long-term	Short-term
Belgium	11.3	8.0	3.3	8.1	5.1	2.9
Denmark	9.0	3.0	6.0	10.8	3.0	7.9
France	9.8	4.4	5.4	10.4	3.9	6.5
Germany	6.8	3.1	3.7	5.4	2.2	3.2
Ireland	16.1	9.2	6.9	14.8	9.4	5.4
Italy	6.9	3.8	3.1	8.2	5.3	2.9
Netherlands	10.5	5.5	5.0	7.0	3.5	3.5
Portugal	7.6	4.2	3.5	5.0	2.0	3.0
Spain	19.6	11.3	8.4	18.9	9.7	9.1
United Kingdom	10.9	5.1	5.8	8.9	3.4	5.5
Australia	8.4	2.4	5.9	9.0	2.7	6.2
New Zealand	4.9	0.6	4.3	8.9	2.3	6.6
Canada	9.9	0.9	9.0	9.8	0.9	8.9
United States	7.1	0.7	6.4	6.2	0.6	5.6
Japan	2.7	0.4	2.2	2.3	0.4	1.9
Austria	3.6	n.k.	n.k.	3.7	n.k.	n.k.
Finland	5.1	1.0	4.0	10.5	1.7	8.9
Norway	2.7	0.2	2.5	5.5	1.2	4.3
Sweden	2.6	0.3	2.3	4.4	0.4	4.0
Switzerland	0.8	0.1	0.7	2.3	0.5	1.8

Note: Long-term means over one year.
Source: Total OECD standardized rates except for Italy (which is the US BLS measure). Long-term: Total times share of long-term in total (as in *OECD Employment Outlook*, appendix).

To explain unemployment it is therefore useful to explain separately not only the total of unemployment but also its two different parts (short-term and long-term). We shall explain unemployment rates in 1983–8 and 1989–94, using the following main explanatory variables:

– Replacement rate (per cent).
– Benefit duration (years; indefinite = 4 years).
– Active labour market policy per unemployed person as per cent of output per worker (ALMP).
– Union coverage (1 under 25 per cent, 2 middle, 3 over 75 per cent).
– Co-ordination in wage bargaining (1 low, 2 middle, 3 high).
– Employment protection (ranking: 1 low, 20 high).
– Change in inflation (percentage points per annum).

The last variable is included because it is always possible to achieve a temporary fall in unemployment through allowing inflation to increase.[2] The values of the variables are in Table 10.2.

The explanatory regression was a pooled regression for the two sub-periods. (We checked that the two sets of coefficients in the two sub-periods were not as a set significantly different.) The results are in Table 10.3. In the equation for long-term unemployment we also include short-term unemployment as a regressor.

OECD countries do of course display quite severe persistence in unemployment, and our two six-year periods may not be long enough to eliminate these effects.[3] However, terms measuring lagged unemployment were either insignificant or incorrectly signed, and have therefore not been included. The pooled regression was however estimated by the random-effects method which to some extent discounts the effects of persistent country specific factors.

Turning to our results, we can first explain the cross-country variation of *long-term* unemployment. All the variables reflecting the treatment of unemployed people come in with the predicted sign. The system of wage bargaining is also important. Employment protection *raises* long-term unemployment.

However when we turn to *short-term* unemployment, things change. Not surprisingly, benefit duration and active labour market policy (ALMP) are unimportant. And, as expected, employment protection *reduces* short-term unemployment, by reducing the inflow to unemployment.

Turning to the effects on total unemployment, employment protection has an insignificant effect. But unemployment does respond to how unemployed people are treated and to how wages are determined.

Table 10.2 Explanatory variables[a]

	Replacement rate	Benefit duration	ALMP	Union coverage	Union coordination	Employer coordination	Employment protection	Employment	Change in inflation
Belgium	60	4	10.0 14.6	3	2	2	17	-0.76	-0.52
Denmark	90	2.5	10.6 10.3	3	3	3	5	-0.86	-0.46
France	57	3.75 3	7.2 8.8	3	2	2	14	-1.38	-0.30
Germany	63	4	12.9 25.7	3	2	3	15	-0.34	-0.04
Ireland	50 37	4	9.2 9.1	3	1	1	12	-1.52	-0.54
Italy	2 20	0.5	10.1 10.3	3	2	1 2	20	-1.68	-0.52
Netherlands	70 65	4	4.0 6.9	3	2	2	9	-0.14	0.14
Portugal	60 70	0.5 2	5.9 18.8	3	2	2	18	-2.74	-1.28
Spain	80	3.5 0.8	3.2 4.7	3 2	2	1	19	-1.24	-0.60
United Kingdom	36 38	4	7.8 6.4	3	1	1	7	0.16	-1.02
Australia	39 36	4	4.1 3.2	3	2	1	4	0.02	-1.24
New Zealand	38	4	15.4 6.8	2	2 1	1	2	0.36	-1.22
Canada	60 59	4 1	6.3 5.9	2	1	1	3	-0.08	-0.84
United States	50	0.5	3.9 3.0	1	1	1	1	-0.04	-0.48
Japan	60	0.5	5.4 4.3	3	2	2	8	-0.20	-0.36
Austria	60 50	4	8.7 8.3	3	3	3	16	-0.46	0.06
Finland	75 63	4 2	18.4 16.4	3	3 2	3	10	-0.26	-0.72
Norway	65	4	9.5 14.7	3	3	3	11	-0.34	-1.12
Sweden	80	1.5	59.5 59.3	3	3	3	13	-0.75	-1.02
Switzerland	70	1.2	23.0 8.2	2	1	3	6	-0.12	-0.50

Note:

[a] When variable changes between the two sub-periods, the first number is for 1983–88 and the second for 1989–94.

Source: Replacement rate and benefit duration: Mainly US Department of Health and Social Services. Social Security Programmes throughout the World (1985 and 1993). See Layard et al. (1991) Annex 1.3. ALMP: OECD Employment Outlook (1988 and 1995). For the first sub-period the data relate to 1987 and for the second to 1991. We include all active spending, except on the disabled. Union coverage – union co-ordination and employer co-ordination: See LNI Annex 1.4 and OECD Employment Outlook (1994) pp. 175–85. Employment protection: OECD Jobs Study (1994), Part II, Table 6.7, Col. 5, p. 74. Country ranking with 20 as the most strictly regulated. Inflation: OECD Economic Outlook.

Table 10.3 Regressions to explain long unemployment rate, 20 OECD countries, 1983–8 and 1989–94 per cent

	Total unemployment (1)		Long-term unemployment (2)		Short-term unemployment (3)	
Replacement rate (percentage)	0.011	(1.6)	0.004	(0.5)	0.009	(1.2)
Benefit duration (years)	0.09	(1.3)	0.16	(1.9)	0.04	(0.6)
ALMP (percentage)	–0.008	(0.7)	–0.03	(2.0)	–0.0008	(0.07)
Union coverage (1–3)	0.66	(2.7)	0.56	(1.7)	0.54	(2.2)
Co-ordination (1–3)	–0.68	(3.2)	–0.29	(0.9)	–0.57	(2.4)
Employment protection (1–20)	–0.005	(0.2)	0.09	(2.7)	–0.04	(1.6)
Change in inflation (percentage points per annum)	–0.17	(1.7)	–0.13	(1.1)	–0.15	(1.6)
Constant	–3.96	(7.3)	–3.28	(2.9)	–3.8	(7.0)
Dummy for 1989–94	0.16	(1.9)	0.1	(0.9)	0.16	(2.1)
Log (short-term unemployment)			0.94	(4.0)		
R^2	0.59		0.81		0.41	
se	0.51		0.59		0.52	
N	40		38		38	

Dependent variables:
(1)   Total unemployed as percentage of labour force.
(2)   Long-term unemployed (over one year) as percentage of labour force.
(3)   Short-term unemployed (under one year) as percentage of labour force.
t-statistics in brackets. These are based on the method of 'random effects'.
Notes:
ALMP is measured by current active labour market spending as percentage of GDP divided by current employment. To handle problems of endogeneity and measurement error this is instrumented by active labour market spending in 1987 as percentage of GDP divided by average unemployment rate 1977–9. The coefficients measure the proportional effect on unemployment of a unit change in an independent variable; where the unit is measured as in Table 10.2.

To understand why all these variables might affect unemployment, we need to see how they fit into an integrated framework. This is provided by the system of wage and price equations. Assuming no price surprises, we have

Wage equation

$$\log W = -\gamma \log(cu) + Z + \log(Y/L) \qquad (10.1)$$

Price equation (simplified)

$$\log W = \beta + \log(Y/L) \qquad (10.2)$$

where W is the real cost per worker, u the unemployment rate, c the 'effectiveness' of the unemployed, Z the impact of other wage pressure variables, and Y/L is output per head of labour force.

Thus the equilibrium unemployment rate is given by

$$\log(cu) = \frac{Z - \beta}{\gamma} \tag{10.3}$$

The key variables affecting unemployment are those which affect 'wage pressure' (namely c and the Zs) plus the effect of unemployment in offsetting wage pressure (γ). We can now examine each of the possible causes of unemployment for their effect on wage pressure.

POLICIES TO THE UNEMPLOYED

Benefits

Benefits work through two mechanisms. First, they reduce the fear of unemployment and thus directly increase wage pressure from the unions (a simple Z factor). But second, and more important, they reduce the 'effectiveness' of unemployed people (c) as fillers of vacancies. This encourages *employers* to raise wages. It also reduces the competition which newly unemployed workers will face in their search for jobs, which again encourages the *unions* to push for higher wages.

Since any reduction in effectiveness (c) leads to an equiproportional increase in unemployment, one can obtain an estimate of the effects of benefits (working through c) from micro cross-sectional studies which explain exit rates by benefits, holding vacancies constant. These estimates typically give an elasticity of exit rates with respect to the replacement ratio of around one half, with a wide range on either side (Narendranathan *et al.*, 1985; Atkinson and Micklewright, 1991).

A second key dimension of unemployment benefits is their potential duration. Long-term benefits increase long-term unemployment. There are two processes at work here. First benefits reduce exit rates in general. But the resulting long-term unemployment further reduces exit rates. For in those countries where long-term unemployment is common, the exit rates for the long-term unemployed are much lower than for the short-term unemployed – in other words they have lower c. At least in part this appears to reflect a state-dependence of exit rates on duration (Jackman and Layard, 1991). Thus the incidence of long-term unemployment shifts out the U/V curve in many European countries (Budd, Levine and Smith, 1988).

However when unemployment benefits run out quite quickly exit rates decline much less as duration lengthens. This is confirmed by Katz and Meyer (1991) and Carling *et al.* (1995) for the USA and Sweden, where benefits run out after 6 and 14 months respectively. By contrast in Britain and Australia, where benefits are long-lived, there is much more state dependence. (Jackman and Layard, 1991; Fahrer and Pease, 1993.)

Active labour market policies (ALMP)

If long-duration benefits have negative effects, one approach is simply to provide *no help* to unemployed people beyond some period. Given sufficient wage flexibility, this will increase employment. But the cost will be more unequal wages, and not all of long-term unemployment will be eliminated.

An alternative is to provide *some help* to all who do not get benefit, but to give it through activity rather than through benefits. This cuts off the flow of long-term unemployment at least for the period for which the active measures last, and gives all the unemployed at least a chance to prove themselves.

This latter alternative is the Swedish model: active labour market policy *replaces* benefits. It should be sharply distinguished from other systems of active labour market policy where the uptake of the help offered is voluntary, so that labour market activity is an *optional alternative* to benefits. While active labour market policies of the second kind do continue in many countries, there is an interesting shift towards the Swedish model in Switzerland, while Denmark which has always had a similar general approach to Sweden's has now shortened the 'passive' period of benefit duration to two years (Schwanse, 1995). In our regression equation, we find that dropping Sweden eliminates the effect of active labour market policy spending on long-term unemployment, consistent with the view that only Swedish-style ALMPs make a real difference.

The case for active labour market policy comes of course from social cost-benefit analysis. But it is also important to note that in terms of costs and benefits to the Ministry of Finance, *optional* ALMP is quite costly per unit reduction in unemployment, since those helped by the subsidy will include a disproportionate number of people who would have exited anyway (the problem of 'deadweight'). *Replacement* ALMP can more nearly break-even, since all of those still unemployed are helped; there is thus a known maximum for the proportion of those helped who would have exited otherwise (the problem of 'deadweight' is reduced, through avoiding creaming).

The other problem with active labour market policy is 'substitution and displacement' – if an employer employs someone who would not have exited otherwise, this may disemploy someone else who would otherwise have been employed. In normal discussions this problem is greatly exaggerated. For the aim of ALMP is to help people who would otherwise have had low exit probabilities. By positive discrimination in their favour, vacancies go to them rather than to others who had better exit probabilities (were more employable). The effect is to increase the total stock of employable workers who are still unemployed. So vacancies get filled faster and employment expands. By

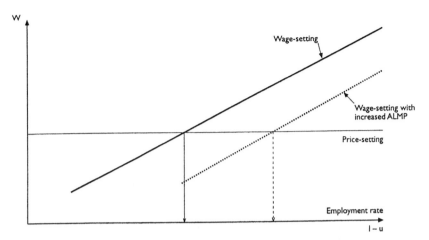

W

Wage-setting

Wage-setting with
increased ALMP

Price-setting

Employment rate

l − u

Figure 10.1 Effects of active labour market policies (ALMP)

helping the hard to place, the total stock of employable labour expands. In response the total stock of jobs expands.

We can easily see this in the context of our model – (10.1) and (10.2). There is a certain required level of cu. Through the active labour market policy the average effectiveness of the unemployed (c) is increased. This decreases wage pressure at each level of unemployment (see Figure 10.1). In consequence there is an increase in the equilibrium employment rate. Assuming that when prices are set the mark-up of prices over wages is constant, as in Figure 10.1, unemployment falls by the same proportion that average effectiveness (c) rises.

But what about substitution and displacement? If for example action is taken to help the long-term unemployed, does this increase short-term unemployment? The logic of our model says No.

Suppose the short-term unemployed have effectiveness c_s and the long-term unemployed have effectiveness c_L. Equilibrium requires a given level of $(c_s u_s + c_L u_L)$ in order to restrain wage pressure. We now through ALMP improve c_L, while c_s remains unchanged. What happens? u_L falls and u_s remains unchanged. Why?

The stock of short-term unemployed depends on the total inflow into unemployment (S) and on the exit rate from short-term unemployment. This latter is equal to c_s times the exit rate for a person with effectiveness equal to unity, i.e. it equals $c_s S/cu\,L$, where L is labour force. But cu is given. Thus if S/L and c_s remain unchanged, so does the exit rate from short-term unemployment and so does the stock of short-term unemployed.

The short-term unemployed get the same number of jobs per period because the long-term unemployed also get the same number of jobs per period. The only thing that has changed is that the *stock* of long-term unemployed has fallen since the exit rate from long-term unemployment has risen. Thus the long-term unemployed do not take jobs from the short-term unemployed.

There is no job-fund. Employment expands as the effective supply of labour expands. This should be obvious to anyone who contemplates the employment miracle which occurred when the Pilgrim Fathers landed at Cape Cod and found a sudden increase in the demand for labour on those inhospitable shores. But, as expressed so far, it is a medium term argument. In the short-run there may be some constraints on the demand side. For example, if nominal demand is fixed, an increase in the effective supply of labour will generate *some* new jobs, due to lower inflation, but the increase in jobs will be less than the increase in labour supply. If, however, the government has an inflation target, then even in the short-run employment will increase in line with the effective supply of labour.

This result provides important insights but may need modifying to suit the details of particular schemes. In any case it says nothing about the effectiveness of particular schemes. This depends on how well they do indeed improve the effectiveness of the individuals who are exposed to them.

Clearly schemes are more effective when they are not optional (see above) but then they are also more difficult to study – since there is no control group. Thus most studies of ALMP relate to optional schemes and compare people who were and were not exposed to such schemes. The microeconomic studies have been well summarised in OECD (1993) and Fay (1995). The general findings are (i) a good return to assistance with job-finding; (ii) a goodish return to subsidised self-employment; (iii) some return to targeted recruitment subsidies; (iv) a weaker return to public sector job creation and (v) an often weak return to the training of unemployed people. In most cases heavy deadweight is the main factor reducing the return.

Our conclusion is that major expansions of ALMP can only be justified where the aim is to achieve universal coverage of some group (e.g., the long-term unemployed). This will greatly reduce deadweight, since in any disadvantaged group the overall outflow rates are generally low. It is also the only way to make any large dent in unemployment.

Going further, what is needed is in fact a change of regime. When people enter unemployment they need to understand that there will be no possibility of indefinite life on benefits. Instead it should be made clear that, after a period of say one year, public support will be provided only through participation on a programme. But access to the programme is guaranteed. This will have the twin effect of (a) helping those who really need help and (b) driving off the public purse those who only want help in the form of cash.

This is the Swedish model, which played a central role in holding down Swedish unemployment to around 2 per cent until the end of the 1980s.[4] The model has of course come under heavy pressure recently due to bad macroeconomic management: over-expansionary policy in the late 1980s followed by over-contraction. The Swedes have been right to continue with ALMP, since institutional/cultural arrangements of this kind cannot easily be re-established once they have been abandoned (Layard, 1995). But the experience makes it clear that ALMP is not primarily a counter-cyclical device – it needs to be a permanent feature of the economic and social system.[5]

WAGE BARGAINING

The next key factor affecting equilibrium unemployment is the system of wage determination. In systems where wages are settled in a decentralised way (either by employers' fiat or by bargaining) there is always a problem of leapfrogging. Even in the absence of bargaining, some employers may have an incentive to pay an 'efficiency' wage above the supply price of labour, in order to motivate and retain staff. Indeed, unless unemployment is high enough, they will generally try to pay more than the going wage paid by other employers. Unions will also seek to raise their pay above that of other unions.

This problem of leapfrogging can be reduced when wages are centrally co-ordinated (namely by centralised positions adopted by the unions and the employers). A simple illustration will suffice, where unions can freely choose their pay so as to maximise the expected income of their members. If the choice is *decentralised*, the union chooses the firm-level wage (W_i) to maximise a function like $(W_i - A)N_i$ where N_i is firm-level employment, and A is expected income outside the firm. A is then given by $(1 - u)W^e + uB$, where W^e is the expected outside wage and B benefits. (The price level is taken as exogenous.) This leads to a wage given by

$$\frac{W_i - A}{W_i} = \left(\frac{\partial N_i}{\partial W_i}\frac{W_i}{N_i}\right)^{-1}$$

So, for equilibrium (W_i equal to W^e), unemployment is given by

$$u = \left(\frac{\partial N_i}{\partial W_i}\frac{W_i}{N_i}\right)^{-1}\left(1 - \frac{B}{W}\right)^{-1}$$

By contrast a *centralised* union would be setting the wage for everybody and would choose it to maximise NW, recognizing that workers disemployed by the wage settlement would have no alternative income opportunity (so that $A = 0$), unemployment benefits simply being a transfer from employed to unemployed union members. Unless an increase in employment required a more than proportionate fall in the real wage, the union would choose a wage consistent with full employment. A similar result can be obtained in a wage bargaining model. If by contrast employers set efficiency wages, there are also advantages from co-ordination to reduce leapfrogging, though employers would collectively choose non-zero unemployment as a worker-discipline device.

All this is on the assumption of homogeneous labour. If labour is heterogenous, the arguments for decentralization become more powerful. Under co-ordinated bargaining it is quite difficult to achieve the shifts in relative wages that may be required in response to differential shifts of relative demands and supplies. Thus co-ordinated bargaining reduces unemployment by cutting out leapfrogging, but increases it by worsening structural imbalances. The overall outcome is an empirical issue.

The issue appears to be quite clearly resolved in Table 10.2. Co-ordination has a powerful influence in reducing unemployment. An unco-ordinated economy will have, other things equal, an unemployment rate more than twice as high as an economy with highly co-ordinated wage-setting arrangements. Our results suggest, however, that a fully co-ordinated economy with a high degree of union coverage will have approximately the same unemployment rate as an economy with low union coverage and no co-ordination.

In this context we should perhaps refer to the view of Calmfors and Driffill (1988) that, while full centralization has advantages, co-ordination at the industry level gives the worst of all worlds (due to the low demand elasticity for labour in one industry). The implication is that if full centralization is too difficult, one should go for full decentralization. We believe this argument is misleading. On the empirical level the finding is not robust (Soskice, 1990). Moreover it ignores the obvious point that, when comparing countries, it is not only the degree of centralization which rises but the degree of union coverage. The United States does not have decentralised bargaining; it has hardly any unions. Other things equal, higher coverage is bad for employment but this effect can be offset by sufficient co-ordination. This is precisely what our equation shows.

With regard to the impact of relative wage flexibility, we tried introducing the degree of wage dispersion as a further independent variable in the Table 10.3 regressions. It turned out insignificant in relation to total unemployment ($t = 0.6$) and long-term unemployment ($t = -0.9$), but to have a significant positive effect ($t = 4.2$) in increasing short-term unemployment. These results suggest the complexity of the issues surrounding wage flexibility.

The truth is that co-ordination is a very subtle affair.[6] But the more there is, it appears, the better. Equally the task of achieving it appears to have become more difficult, possibly reflecting the greater exposure to international competition in both product and factor markets in recent years.

SKILLS IMBALANCE[7]

One possible reason why unemployment is higher than in the 1970s is the steady fall in the demand for unskilled workers. If this is not matched by an equal fall in supply, this can certainly cause an increase in unemployment.

To see this we can (for simplicity) divide the labour force into two categories, skilled and unskilled denoted 1 and 2 respectively. We shall assume that output is produced by a Cobb–Douglas production function

$$Y = AN_1^{\alpha_1} N_2^{\alpha_2} K^{\alpha_3} \qquad (\alpha_1 + \alpha_2 + \alpha_3 = 1)$$

Thus the demand for labour of type i is given by[8]

$$\log W_1 \quad \log \alpha_i + \log(Y/L) - \log l_i + u_i \tag{10.4}$$

where W is the cost per worker, L total labour force and $l_i = L_i/L$. It follows that, if the unemployment rate of a group is to remain constant when α_i rises or falls, wages must adjust in line. Equally, when the labour force composition changes, wages must also adjust.

The problem is that wages do not normally adjust as they 'should'. Usually it takes extra unemployment to get wages down. There is much evidence to support the following wage equation

$$\log W_1 = -\gamma \log u_i + z_i + \log(Y/L) \tag{10.5}$$

where z_i measures a return of wage pressure effects. From (10.1) and (10.2) we can see that the unemployment of a group is determined by

$$u_i + \gamma \log u_i = \log l_i - \log \alpha_i + z_i \tag{10.6}$$

If the relative demand for a group (α_i) falls faster than the relative supply of people in that group (l_i), then $(\log l_i - \log \alpha_i)$ falls, and the unemployment rate in that group rises. There is thus a ceaseless race between shifts in demand and shifts in supply.

The change in unemployment of group i is

$$du_i = \phi_i(d \log l_i - d \log \alpha_i)$$

where $\phi_i = u_i/(u_i + \gamma)$. We can interpret this in terms of Figure 10.2. The demand for type i labour (relative to its supply) shifts to the left by the same amount if the labour supply (l_i) increases by 1 per cent or the labour demand (α_i) falls by 1 per cent. Both of the shifts in supply and demand have the same effect. The effect on unemployment is greater the more rigid are wages. The lower is g the more rigid are wages and the greater the rise in unemployment. Moreover the absolute rise in unemployment is greater the higher the existing level of unemployment (u_i) – due to the curved nature of the wage function.

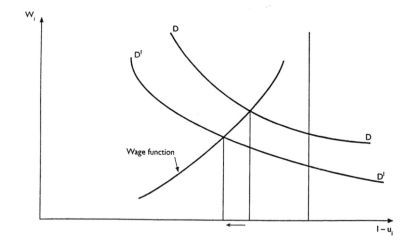

Figure 10.2 Effect of an upwards shift in the relative supply (l_i) and demand of labour (α_i)
Note: For definitions see text.

In modern societies a race is in progress between the increase in the demand for skilled labour (measured by α_l) and the supply of skilled labour (measured by l_l). If the supply of skill fails to increase as fast as the demand, total unemployment will rise. To see this, note that the total change in unemployment is

$$du = d(u_1 l_1 + u_2 l_2) = u_1 dl_1 - u_2 dl_1 + l_1 du_1 + (1 - l_1) du_2$$
$$= -(u_2 - u_1) dl_1 - (\phi_2 - \phi_1) dl_1 + (\theta_2 - \theta_1) d\alpha_1$$

where $\theta_i = \phi_i \, l_i / \alpha_i$.

The first of these terms is a pure composition effect – if the labour force becomes more concentrated in low-unemployment groups, unemployment will tend to fall. The second term reflects the problems which stem from wage rigidity. Since log wages depend on *log* unemployment, one extra point of unemployment reduces wages less for a group whose unemployment is high. Thus switching labour into the skilled group *reduces* overall unemployment – the downwards force on skilled wages outweighs the upwards force on unskilled wages $(\phi_2 - \phi_1 > 0)$. The third term shows the effect of technical progress raising the relative demand for skilled labour. Since $l_2/\alpha_2 > 1$ and

$l_1/\alpha_1 < 1$, a rise in the demand for skilled labour (α_1) *raises* overall unemployment, by raising the demand for labour where the wage pressure responds sharply to extra demand and reducing demand where wages are unresponsive to demand.

Empirical work

Empirical work using this kind of approach is still at a preliminary stage. However Nickell and Bell (1995a and b) give results using a similar model, with a more general CES production function. They tentatively estimated that on average one fifth of the rise in unemployment from the late 1970s to the late 1980s in Germany, Holland, Spain, the United Kingdom and Canada was due to structural shifts of demand relative to supply. Nickell (1995b) gives similar results.

EMPLOYMENT PROTECTION

It is widely believed that labour market flexibility is good for the macroeconomy and that employment protection legislation is an impediment to such flexibility. So it is argued that freedom of action for employers to dismiss workers on economic grounds is necessary for a smoothly functioning economy, though it is of course desirable to protect employees from arbitrary, unfair or discriminating dismissals. However, it may be tricky in practice to protect employees from arbitrary dismissal while simultaneously allowing freedom of action for employers to dismiss on economic grounds. Thus it may be felt necessary by benevolent legislators to circumscribe this freedom of action.[9] The macroeconomic consequences of this are, however, of major importance – both on the process of short-run adjustment and on the long-run equilibrium level of unemployment.

Theoretical background

Employment protection has a potential impact at a number of different points in the operation of the labour market. It obviously impedes employment adjustment by reducing both flows from employment, because of the legal hurdles, and flows into employment by making employers more cautious about hiring. It may also influence wage determination, for example by raising the power of insiders or by lengthening unemployment duration. Finally, because of the excessive caution of employers, it may impede the absorption of new entrants into the labour market thereby reducing participation rates and raising relative youth unemployment rates.

Consider the following model, where we ignore nominal inertia (wage/price stickiness), labour force growth and trend productivity effects. Wage setting is given by

$$\log W = -\gamma_1 u - \gamma_{11} \Delta u + z_w \tag{10.7}$$

where z_w are wage pressure shocks. The demand for labour is given by

$$n = \lambda n_{-1} - (1 - \lambda)\beta_1 \log W + (1 - \lambda)z_n \tag{10.8}$$

$n = \log$ employment, $z_n =$ labour demand shifts (e.g., productivity shocks) and β_l is the *long-run* labour demand elasticity. If we suppose the labour force to be fixed and normalised to unity, (10.8) can be written as

$$u = \lambda u_{-1} + (1 - \lambda)\beta_1 \log W - (1 - \lambda)z_n \tag{10.9}$$

Then, eliminating real wages from (10.7) and (10.9), we obtain

$$u = \alpha_{11} u_{-1} + (1 - \alpha_{11})u^* \tag{10.10}$$

where u^* is the equilibrium unemployment rate, given by

$$u^* = \frac{\beta_1 z_w - z_n}{1 + \beta_1 \gamma_1} \tag{10.11}$$

and the speed of adjustment, $1 - \alpha_{11}$, is given by

$$1 - \alpha_{11} = \frac{\beta_1 \gamma_1 + 1}{\beta_1 \gamma_1 + \beta_1 \gamma_{11} + (1 - \lambda)^{-1}} \tag{10.12}$$

From this analysis, we see that there are two important questions. First, how might employment protection influence the *speed of adjustment*, $1 - \alpha_{11}$? Second, how might employment protection affect the *equilibrium unemployment* rate, u^*? The first of these is straightforward. We would expect employment protection to raise employment adjustment costs and this would increase λ. Furthermore, employment protection may tend to increase long-term unemployment by reducing the rate of flow from unemployment to employment, as employers become more cautious about hiring. This will typically generate hysteresis effects in wage determination and thereby raise γ_{11}. Increases in both λ and γ_{11} will tend to reduce the overall speed of adjustment, $1 - \alpha_{11}$.

Turning to the second question, namely the impact on equilibrium unemployment, it is important to recognise that, just because employment protection may tend to lengthen the duration of unemployment spells, this does not mean that it will necessarily raise equilibrium unemployment, u^*. For offsetting the duration effect is the reduction in flows. The flow into unemployment is obviously reduced by regulations designed to restrict dismissals. Since the unemployment rate is the product of the inflow rate and the mean duration, the overall effect of employment protection on u^* is indeterminate.

Looking at the formula for u^* in (10.11), there are a number of possibilities. First, employment protection may influence wage pressure, z_w, directly, for example, by raising the power of insiders. Second, employment protection can raise the impact of unemployment on wages, γ_1, by making the threat of unemployment more unpleasant (longer duration, harder to find alternative employment). On the other hand, of course, since employees are protected against dismissal to some extent, the threat of unemployment is less germane and this will *reduce* γ_1. So the overall effect on u^* is ambiguous.

Finally, we have not modelled participation in this exercise but we should consider the implications of employment protection for employment rates as well as unemployment rates when we come to our empirical investigation.

Evidence on unemployment dynamics

Our purpose in this section is to explore the evidence on the relationship between employment protection, employment adjustment and both the dynamics of labour demand (λ) and the extent of hysteresis in wage determination (γ_{11}).[10]

We first investigate the relationship between some empirical measures of λ, a measure of the rate of turnover of employees within companies (the percentage of employees with job tenures less than two years, *PL2*) and the OECD composite ranking of the tightness of employment protection (*EP*). The data are reported in Table 10.4. The first point to note is the very strong correlation between *EP* and *PL2*, the correlation coefficient between the two variables being 0.9. So the variation in the rate of turnover (as captured by the proportion of employees with less than two years' tenure) is explained almost entirely by the strictness of the employment protection laws. The relationship between *PL2* and our various measures of λ is set out in Table 10.5. In two out of the three cases, we see that PL2 is significantly related to the aggregate measure of labour demand sluggishness (λ). Overall, therefore, there is some evidence in favour of the hypothesis that the speed of adjustment in labour demand is negatively related to the strictness of employment protection legislation.

Turning next to wage determination, we are concerned here with the relationship between the degrees of hysteresis (γ_{11}) and employment protection, operating via long-term unemployment. The impact of long-term unemployment on the extent of hysteresis is confirmed explicitly in Layard *et al.* (1991), Chapter 9, Table 9 and implicitly in OECD (1993, Chapter 3).[11] So we can simply focus on the impact of employment protection on long-term

Table 10.4 Further data used for analysing employment protection

	λ(LNJ)	λ(NS)	λ(BLN)	Percentage of employment with tenure < 2 years (PL2)	LTU 1985–93	LTU (standardized)	γ_1	Employment rate 1990	Employment protection
Belgium	0.64	0.92	0.76	18	67	35.9	4.06	55.0	17
Denmark	0.48	..	0.26	27	29.4	36.2	1.74	75.7	5
France	0.74	0.90	0.72	22.2	40.8	30.3	4.35	57.9	14
West Germany	0.86	0.88	0.36	21	44.1	21.2	1.01	62.9	15
Ireland	0.85	0.86	0.71	22	54.6	31.8	1.82	50.2	12
Italy	0.81	0.74	0.65	13	66.2	35.8	12.94	52.6	20
Netherlands	0.85	0.91	0.90	26.9	50.4	27.1	2.28	59.2	9
Portugal								67.2	18
Spain	0.66	..	..	13.6	55.4	27.5	1.21	47.4	19
United Kingdom	0.70	0.88	0.37	31	40.9	24.5	0.98	70.4	7
Australia	0.35	0.49	0.43	36.8	29.3	21.1	0.73	68.6	4
New Zealand	0.84	..	..	..	14.7	3.23	66.1	2
Canada	0.92	0.91	0.17	33.7	8.8	3.5	2.38	70.5	3
United States	0.38	0.10	0	39.7	8.2	4.2	0.94	71.6	1
Japan	0.85	0.83	0.65	20	15.1	18.8	14.50	71.7	8
Austria	0.85	0.84	0.56	..	..	13.3	3.11	65.0	16
Finland	0.45	0.91	0.32	26.3	17.4	12.0	1.55	73.5	10
Norway	0.88	0	0.07	17	14.5	10.8	10.59	73.6	11

Table 10.4 Continued

	$\lambda(LNJ)$	$\lambda(NS)$	$\lambda(BLN)$	Percentage of employment with tenure < 2 years (PL2)	LTU 1985–93	LTU (standardized)	γ_1	Employment rate 1990	Employment protection
Sweden	0.60	0.78	0.16	...	7.9	6.8	12.16	81.7	13
Switzerland	0.81	0.83	0.12	29.3	18.9	17.0	7.33	79.5	6

Notes:
λ = Coefficient on lagged dependent variable in an employment equation, *LNJ* = Layard, Nickell and Jackman (1991, Chapter 9, Table AI, p. 450), *NS* = Newell and Symons (1985), *BLN* = Bean, Layard and Nickell (1986) both as reported in Alogoskoufis and Manning (1988, Table 6), and in Layard, Nickell and Jackman (1991: Chapter 9, Table A3, pp. 454–66).

PL2 = Percentage of manufacturing employees with tenure less than 2 years. It is based on Metcalf (1986, Table 4), and on OECD (1993, Table 4.1). Where information for a given country appears in both places, the average is reported. The figure for Spain is derived as follows: In OECD (1993, Table 4.1). It is reported that 31.6 per cent of employees had tenure of less than 2 years. But much of this was a consequence of the introduction of fixed term employment contracts in the mid 1980s. Since our sample period is mostly prior to this date, we must try and remove the impact of these fixed term workers. In 1990, 23.8 per cent of employees held fixed term (53 year) contracts so, if we suppose that three quarters of these have a job tenure under 2 years, removing these leaves 13.6 per cent as reported in the table.

EP = γ a measure whereby countries are ranked by the strictness of their employment protection legislation (*i.e.* 1 = least strict etc.). These data are taken from OECD (1994), Table 6.7, col 5.

LTU 1985–93 = Percentage of unemployed with a duration of unemployment of more than 1 year using survey-based data and averaged over 1985 to 93. (OECD, *Employment Outlook*, various issues, statistical annex).

LTU (standardized) = Percentage of unemployed with a duration of unemployment of more than 1 year. Where possible, this is measured for each country when the aggregate unemployment rate is between 5 and 7 per cent (OECD, *Employment Outlook*, various issues. The data refer to various dates in the 1980s).

Employment rate = Employment as a proportion of the population of working age (OECD, *Jobs Study, Evidence and Explanations*, Table 6.8).

Explaining Unemployment

Table 10.5 Slope coefficients in a regression of λ on *PL2*

Dependent variable	λ(*LNJ*)	λ(*NS*)	λ(*BLN*)
PL2	–0.011 (2.1)	–0.0081 (0.6)	–0.010 (2.4)
N	16.00	14.00	15.00
R^2	0.23	0.04	0.23

unemployment, in particular on the proportion of the unemployed who have a duration of more than one year. As well as employment protection, we should also expect the long-term proportion to be influenced by the duration of benefit availability (*BD*) and by expenditure on active labour market policies (*ALMP*), many of which are designed to prevent the build-up of long-term unemployment. In Table 10.4 we provide two measures of long-term unemployment. The first is simply the 1985–93 average proportion of unemployed with durations exceeding one year. The second attempts to standardise this proportion, when possible, by measuring it for each country when unemployment lies between 5 and 7 per cent. The idea here is to focus on the extent of long-term unemployment at *given levels of aggregate unemployment*. Because the long-term proportion tends to be an increasing function of the overall unemployment rate in the long-run, anything which explains unemployment in general will tend to be correlated with the long-term proportion in a cross-section. The standardised measure will eliminate this problem.

The relevant regressions explaining the two measures of the long-term proportion are:

$$LTU(\text{standardised}) = 21.5 + 0.24BD - 0.51ALMP87 + 0.55EP + 13.8IT$$
$$(2.7) \qquad (3.2) \qquad (1.5) \qquad (2.8)$$
$$N = 19, \quad R^2 = 0.55$$

$$LTU85\text{-}93 = 37.4 + 0.55BD - 0.33ALMP91 + 1.77EP + 30.6IT$$
$$(3.4) \quad (3.9) \qquad (3.3) \qquad (3.6)$$
$$N = 17, \quad R^2 = 0.82$$

(*IT* is a dummy for Italy, which is included because although Italy has only a short benefit duration, the level of benefit is negligible, so its duration is irrelevant.) The overall picture is that there is some evidence that stricter employment protection legislation raises long-term unemployment and thus enhances hysteresis in wage-setting. When added to the results on labour demand, we feel that we have some fairly strong and coherent evidence that the strictness of employment protection legislation does influence labour market dynamics by raising unemployment persistence. Whether or not it influences the equilibrium level of unemployment is the issue we consider next.

Evidence on equilibrium unemployment

As we noted earlier, employment protection can influence equilibrium unemployment by directly influencing wage pressure and/or by affecting the impact of unemployment on wages (γ_1). This latter parameter is crucial in translating wage pressure into unemployment (see 10.11).

We begin by looking at the effect of employment protection on γ_1 and then move onto consider its overall impact on average unemployment. As we argue in Layard *et al.* (1991), there are a number of other possible factors which can influence γ_1. These include the structure of the benefit system (replacement rates and benefit duration), and the extent of union and employer co-ordination in wage bargaining. In Table 10.4, we present estimates of γ_1 from Layard *et al.* (Chapter 9, Table 7). The relevant regression to explain γ_1 is

$$\gamma_1 = 11.9 - 0.078\,RR - 2.12\,BD + 1.32\,(UNCD + EMCD) + 0.23\,EP$$
$$(0.9)(4.8)(2.3)(1.7)$$

$$N = 19, R^2 = 0.71$$

This indicates that if employment protection legislation is very strict, this tends to be associated with high values of γ_1. Of course, *EP* is not significant at conventional levels but it is most unlikely that there is, in reality, a strong effect in the opposite direction. So, from this channel the data indicate, if anything, employment protection reduces unemployment. But, since we know that employment protection can also increase wage pressure, we must also investigate its total impact on unemployment.

This was done in Table 10.3. As this showed, there is some weak evidence that employment protection tends overall to increase employment. But the *t*-statistics are never very significant. We ran a large number of further variations using alternative measures of union density and union coverage and also different measures of employment protection. In some eighteen regressions, we were able to obtain only two significant negative coefficients on *EP*. So there is no strong evidence that employment protection affects equilibrium unemployment. This is, of course, consistent with the fact that while we have good reason to expect employment protection legislation to reduce flows both into and out of unemployment, we have no strong reasons for believing either effect to dominate.

Conclusions

We would expect employment protection legislation to slow down the speed with which the labour market adjusts to shocks but to have only a minor impact on the long-run equilibrium. It may however affect the position of those entering or re-entering the labour market because of the effective restrictions on hiring. In practice, there is considerable evidence that employment protection reduces adjustment speeds in the labour market. But it is hard to find any significant effects on equilibrium unemployment rates.

TAXES ON EMPLOYMENT

Lowering payroll taxes is a perennial suggestion by those concerned to reduce unemployment. Thus the *OECD Jobs Study* (1994) recommends that we should 'Reduce non-wage labour costs, especially in Europe, by reducing taxes on labour' (p. 46). The European Commission's White Paper on Employment proposes a reduction in payroll taxes in conjunction with an increase in taxes on energy. Another straightforward policy would be to lower payroll taxes and make up the shortfall by raising consumption taxes. Phelps (1994) argues that 'such a substitution of tax instruments would achieve a major gain in employment and some gain in the general level of real wage rates as well' (p. 28). Presumably, such a switch would work equally as well in a non-European country, such as the United States, where the sum of payroll and income taxes is substantial.

The general argument for this switch goes as follows.[12] Payroll taxes apply only to labour income; consumption taxes apply to all income (which is spent). So a switch from the former to the latter raises the reward for working relative to not working and thereby reduces unemployment. More formally, we may write total real income in work net of taxes, Y, as

$$Y = \frac{W(1 - t_1)(1 - t_2)}{P(1 + t_3)} + \frac{Y_n(1 - t_2)}{P(1 + t_3)}$$

where W = labour costs, t_1 = payroll tax rate, t_2 = income tax rate, P = output price at factor cost, t_3 = consumption tax rate, Y_n = non-labour income. This may be rewritten as

$$Y = \frac{vW}{P}\left(1 + \frac{y_n}{(1 - t_1)}\right)$$

where $v = (1 - t_1)(1 - t_2)/(1 + t_3)$ $(1 - t_1 - t_2 - t_3)$, the tax wedge, $y_n = Y_n/W$, the ratio of non-labour income to labour costs. Consider now the real income when unemployed, Y^u. This may be written as

$$Y^u = \frac{B(1 - t_2)}{P(1 + t_3)} + \frac{Y_n(1 - t_2)}{P(1 + t_3)}$$
$$= \frac{vW}{P}\left(b + \frac{y_n}{1 - t_1}\right)$$

where $b = B/W(1 - t_1) =$ unemployment benefit/wage ratio. The definition of Y^u assumes that benefits are subject to income tax.

In most theories of wage determination, the wage cost which is set depends on Y/Y^u which is increasing in b, y_n and t_1. Increases in b, y_n and t_1 will, therefore, automatically raise equilibrium unemployment. So a reduction in t_1 and an equal increase in t_3 will leave the tax wedge, v, unchanged but will lower equilibrium unemployment so long as y_n is not zero.[13] How big is this effect? The crucial factor is the extent of non-labour income which is not subject to payroll tax. It is arguable that, for the typical person at risk of unemployment, this non-labour income is extremely small. For example, in 1987/88, only 7 per cent of unemployment entrants in Britain had savings of more than £3K, a sum which would produce an annual interest income of around 10 per cent of unemployment benefit.[14] So it may be that this tax switching effect is simply too small to have any noticeable effect.

A more fundamental question is whether any of the taxes (payroll, income or consumption) have an impact on labour costs in the long-run, or whether they are all eventually shifted onto labour. An obvious first approach to this issue is to see whether countries with high taxes have higher labour costs than those with low taxes. We must obviously correct for productivity which suggests that we correlate

$$\frac{W}{P}\bigg/\frac{Y}{N}$$

with tax rates across countries ($W =$ labour costs, $P =$ GDP deflator, $Y =$ GDP, $N =$ employment). But this procedure is open to objection. Real labour costs normalised on productivity is precisely equivalent to WN/PY, the share of labour. In a Cobb–Douglas world, for example, an increase in taxes might lead to a rise in W/P and a fall in N, with the share of labour unchanged. The proposed correlation will then understate the true impact of taxes because of the fall in N when labour costs rise. This suggests that we normalise real labour costs on Y/L where L is the labour force.

Taking average values over the period 1980–90 for 13 OECD countries[15] we obtain:

$$WL/PY = 7.06 + 0.017 t_1 + 0.033 t_2 - 0.12 t_3$$
$$(0.6) \qquad (0.5) \qquad (0.9)$$
$$(R^2 = 0.13, N = 13, t\text{-ratios in brackets})$$

where t_1 is the payroll tax rate, t_2 is the income tax rate, t_3 is the consumption tax rate. Basically there is no relationship between tax rates and labour costs, indicating complete shifting onto labour. A similar result due to James Symons and Donald Robertson and based on changes is reported in OECD (1990, Annex 6A). Using changes between 1974 and 1986 across 16 OECD countries,[16] they obtain

$$\Delta \log W/P = -0.05 + 0.09\Delta\,t_1 + 0.33\Delta\,t_2 + 0.68\Delta\,t_3 + 0.97\Delta\log PROD$$
$$\quad\quad\quad\quad\ (0.3)\quad\quad (0.6)\quad\quad (1.1)\quad\quad\ (5.3)$$

$(R^2 = 0.80, N = 16,$ t-ratios in brackets; $PROD$ is labour productivity)

Here again we see no significant effects of tax changes on real labour costs although the numbers suggest that consumption taxes have the biggest impact.

While these cross-section regressions are useful for looking at long-run tax shifting, only time-series analysis can shed light on the dynamics. First we report some further results in the same Annex due to Symons and Robertson, which are the average coefficients and t-ratios emerging from individual time-series regressions for 16 OECD countries. Thus we have:

$$\log(W/P)_t = \text{const.} + 0.84\log(W/P)_{t-1} + 0.12\log(K/L)_t$$
$$\quad\quad\quad\quad\quad\quad (9.6)\quad\quad\quad\quad\quad (1.4)$$

$$+\ 0.46\Delta\,(t_1 + t_2 + t_3) + 0.07\,t_1 - 0.07\,t_2 + 0.26\,t_3$$
$$\quad (2.3)\quad\quad\quad\quad\quad\ (0.3)\quad\ (0.1)\quad\ (0.2)$$

(average t-ratios in brackets)

These results suggest there is no systematic long-run impact of taxes on labour costs but that the short-run effects are substantial. A one percentage point increase in the tax wedge (from whatever source) leads to a short-run increase in labour costs of around 1/2 per cent which takes a long time to fade away. So even after four years, labour costs are still 1/4 per cent higher. Such effects will lead to significant and persistent temporary increases in unemployment, particularly in the light of the fact that tax wedges have risen by 10 to 20 percentage points in the last 30 years in most OECD countries. In the long run, however, these unemployment effects will disappear.

These significant and long-lasting temporary tax effects imply that, when looking at individual country data, it is very difficult to discriminate between the short- and long-run impacts of the individual taxes. There is simply not enough information. Consequently, the impression given by the collection of individual country time-series studies of wage determination is that the estimated tax effects are all over the place.

It is not worth repeating the summaries in Layard et al. (1991, p. 210) and OECD (1994, p. 247) but we may consider one recent example, namely the

Table 10.6 Labour cost responses to changes in tax rates

	Semi-elasticity of labour costs with respect to:		
	Employers' payroll taxes (t_1)	Income taxes and employees' social security contributions (t_2)	Value-added and excise taxes (t_3)
Australia	0.5	0.5	0.5
Canada	0.8	0.8	0.8
Finland	0.5	0.5	0.5
France	0.4	0.4	0.4
Germany	1.0	1.0	1.0
Italy	0.4	0.4	0.4
Japan	0.5	0.5	0.5
Sweden	0.0	0.0	1.0
United Kingdom	0.25	0.25	0.25
United States	0.0	1.0	0.0

Source: T. Tyrväinen, 'Real Wage Resistance and Unemployment: Multivariate Analysis of Cointegrating Relations in 10 OECD Economies', *The OECD Jobs Study: Working Paper Series*, 1994.

work of Tyrväinen reported in OECD (1994).[17] This work focuses on the long-run effects of taxes by using the Johansen method to estimate long-run cointegrating relationships between labour costs, taxes and other relevant variables. The long-run tax effects he obtains are given in Table 10.6. The first point that stands out is how big the tax effects are. Whereas our previous evidence indicated zero long-run tax effects, here we have a substantial long-run impact of taxes. Second, in all bar two of the countries, the tax effects are uniform across all taxes. Indeed, in no country is there any advantage in switching from payroll taxes to consumption taxes.[18]

We have investigated these matters further in the context of our pooled regression equation of Table 10.3. The payroll tax rate, as an additional explanatory variable turns out to be insignificant (with a *t*-statistic of 0.4) though the total tax burden as percentage of GDP comes in with a small significant positive coefficient (though no effect on long-term unemployment). These results require further investigation.

On balance, we may perhaps conclude that taxes may have an adverse effect on unemployment in the long run, but any such effect is smallish, and that it relates to the burden of taxation in total and not to payroll taxes in particular.[19]

WORK-SHARING AND EARLY RETIREMENT

Two final much-canvassed solutions to unemployment are reduced hours of work and early retirement. Advocates of these measures often seem to believe that there is some exogenous limit to the amount of work to be done. But history shows that, for a given institutional structure, the amount of work tends to adjust in line with the available supply of labour – leaving the equilibrium rate of unemployment unchanged. We can begin with some theoretical remarks, before supporting them with evidence.

Theoretical issues

We shall first examine the underlying theory in a long-term context, using for illustration a simple efficiency wage model. Efficiency per worker hour is e, which depends on hourly wages (W_i) relative to the expected wage ($\hat{W}$) and on the unemployment rate: $e_i = e(W_i/\hat{W}, u)$. Output is given by $f(eHN)$ where H is hours per worker, which can be varied exogenously. Then the profits of the representative firm are

$$\pi_i = f(e_iHN_i) - \frac{W_i}{e_i}e_iHN_i \qquad (f' > 0, f'' < 0)$$

The problem is recursive and the firm can first choose W_i to minimise W_i/e_i. The optimum wage is then given by

$$e_1\left(\frac{W_i}{\hat{W}}, u\right)\frac{W_i}{\hat{W}} = e\left(\frac{W_i}{\hat{W}}, u\right)$$

Hence in general equilibrium (with $W_i = \hat{W}$) unemployment is determined by

$$e_1(1, u) = e(1, u)$$

This holds irrespective of hours.

This result arises because the change in hours affects both those making the wage comparison and the reference group with which the comparison is being made. In the long run both groups must be paid the same. However in the short run things could be different, especially if people are comparing their wage with what they think they 'ought to' be paid – as in many models of real wage resistance. The problem here is that people's ideas of what they should be paid adjust only gradually to the reality of what they are paid. Thus

$$\Delta \log \hat{W} = \gamma(\log W_{-1} - \log \hat{W}_{-1})$$

Suppose there is now a downwards productivity shock. Sluggish adjustment of the reference wage will for a time prevent actual wages falling as much as is needed to preserve employment. In this case reduced hours can be an appropriate adjustment to temporary shocks. Indeed in general there can be no objection to allowing hours to act as shock-absorbers, as in Japan. But this is quite different from saying that lower hours will secure permanently higher employment. They will not, and they will also reduce the national output.

Similar arguments apply to the use of early retirement. Since labour market equilibrium requires a given unemployment rate, reductions in labour supply will simply reduce equilibrium employment. Employment will of course take a while to adjust down, and, until it does, there will be extra inflationary pressure in the economy – which eventually leads to the necessary fall in real aggregate demand (assuming nominal demand follows a steady path). However again a negative productivity shock together with real wage resistance will lead to less unemployment if the labour force is temporarily reduced.

Empirical analysis

It is fairly simple to check on these basic lines of reasoning. We ran the following wage equation for each of our usual 19 OECD countries for the years 1952 to 1990:

$$\dot{w} = a_1\dot{w}_{-1} + (1 - a_1)\dot{p}_{-1} + a_2(w - p)_{-1} + a_3\log L + a_4\log N$$
$$+ a_5\log H + a_6t + \text{const}$$

where w is log hourly earnings in manufacturing, p is log consumption deflator, L is labour force, N employment, H is average weekly hours in manufacturing and t is time. We then computed the average value of each coefficient (averaged across all countries) and its average t-statistic.

If our reasoning has been correct we would expect:

– $\log H$ to have no significant effect; and
– a_3 to be insignificantly different from $(-a_4)$, indicating that it is the unemployment rate which affects wage pressure and the size of the labour force exerts no independent influence.

Both expectations were born out. The equation looked as follows, with average coefficients and average t-statistics:

$$w = 0.37w_{-1} + 0.63p_{-1} - 0.12(w-p)_{-1} - 2.10\log L +$$
$$\quad (1.8) \qquad\qquad\qquad (0.7) \qquad\qquad (2.3)$$

$$1.82\log N - 0.16\log H + 0.008t + \text{const.}$$
$$(2.8) \qquad\quad (0.1) \qquad\quad (1.4)$$

Hours have no significant effect and a cut in the labour force raises wage pressure in a way that can only be offset by an equivalent cut in jobs.

We again examine these effects also in the context of our pooled cross-section regression of Table 10.3. Average hours worked, as additional explanatory variable, had a small but statistically insignificant ($t = 1.1$) negative effect on unemployment. A more rapid growth of the labour force was also associated with significantly ($t = 2.4$) lower unemployment, but this result is not very plausible, and may reflect largely the rapid growth of the labour force in the United States.

CONCLUSIONS

We have found clear evidence that unemployment is strongly affected by how unemployed people are treated and by how wages are determined. There are also indications that problems of skill mismatch have exacerbated European unemployment. As regards employment protection, there is no clear evidence of whether it decreases the outflow rate from unemployment by more or less than it decreases the inflow rate. And there appears to be no long-term effect on unemployment rates from employment taxes or from work-sharing/early retirement.

Thus it is unhelpful to focus the discussion of unemployment on the concept of flexibility. Clearly lower benefits and less employment protection are examples of more flexibility. But active labour market policy, co-ordinated wage bargaining, and skill training are not exactly forms of flexibility.

It seems better to focus on the proper role of government in affecting unemployment. Clearly lower benefits of shorter duration would reduce unemployment, but these policies should be accompanied by more (not less) active labour market policy. Similarly governments would be ill advised to encourage the dismantling of bargaining structures. And they ought certainly to ensure that most youngsters enter adult life with a basic level of competence.

Indeed if Europe's Social Chapter is to contribute to lower unemployment in Europe it needs to impose two further obligations on governments: (a) to prevent entry to long-term unemployment (by replacing long-term benefits by active labour market policy), and (b) to prevent young people ceasing their education (full-time or part-time) until they have acquired basic literacy, numeracy and vocational competence.

Notes

1. We are extremely grateful to Tim Hughes and Jan Eeckhout for help with Sections 1 and 7, to Marco Manacorda and Barbara Petrongolo for allowing us to draw on their work in Section 4, to W. Röger for helpful comments, and to Philomena McNicholas for typing the paper presented to the Conference.

2. We also used the less conventional measure of 'the change in inflation *relative* to its initial level' – to allow for the extra difficulty of reducing inflation when it is low. This was only marginally more significant than the conventional measure and barely affected the other coefficients. We also tried including the trade deficit since inflation can always be reduced by a real exchange rate appreciation; but it was insignificant and wrongly signed.

3. We are indebted to our discussant, W. Röger, for emphasizing this point.

4. The other main influence was co-ordinated wage-bargaining. We reject the view that high employment was based on money illusion and repeated devaluation.

5. Because of cyclical effects on the scale of ALMP it is difficult to study the effect of ALMP on wage pressure (and thus unemployment) from time series data, as has often been tried (Calmfors and Nymoen, 1990, Calmfors and Forslund, 1991). The best evidence must come from cross-sectional comparisons such as our international comparisons in Table 10.3 or (when available) more microeconomic comparisons of the effects of institutional differences.

6. For a full discussion of the degree of co-ordination in 12 countries see Soskice (1990).

7. This draws heavily on the work of our colleagues M. Manacorda and B. Petrongolo (1995).

8. Since $\ln W_i = \log \alpha_i + \log \left(\dfrac{YLL_i}{LL_i N_i} \right)$

9. There is also an important productivity argument. It is well known that a participatory environment is good for company productivity (see Nickell, 1995a, Chapter 5) and that, as part of this environment, some degree of job security is required. If the remainder of the economy is governed by very loose employment protection laws, any employer who wishes to introduce some degree of job security for the above reasons may be so beset by adverse selection problems that he is unable to operate a participatory system. This mechanism could easily operate to the detriment of national productivity growth.

10. When analyzing labour demand dynamics on the basis of aggregate data, it is necessary to face up to some criticism of this activity set out by Kramarz (1991), Caballero (1992) and Hamermesh (1992). Thus Hamermesh argues that 'one cannot use aggregate dynamics to examine or compare the structures or sizes of adjustment costs' (p. 8). Since we intend to do just this, we must examine the arguments closely. Hamermesh looks at three types of adjustment cost structures, namely fixed costs, linear costs and asymmetric quadratic costs. In each case he concludes that, *in aggregate*, the adjustment speed is related both to micro adjustments costs *and* to the cross-section variance of sectoral shocks. When looking across countries there is, therefore, the danger that any correlation between adjustment speeds and adjustment costs is corrupted by our inability to control for the variance of sectoral shocks. It is more or less

impossible to obtain comparable measures of the variance of sectoral shocks because of the difficulty of obtaining consistent sectoral breakdowns across a large number of countries. However, this corruption will only be serious if the cross-section variance of shocks is strongly correlated with adjustment costs across countries. While we have no evidence on this, there seem to be no strong *a priori* arguments in favour of such a correlation, in which case the omission of this variable is not a problem. Finally, it is worth remarking that estimated labour market dynamics look very similar at the aggregate and at the firm level. For example, the dynamics of a United Kingdom aggregate annual employ-ment equation have the form $n_t = 1.06n_{t-1} - 0.36n_{t-2} +$ etc., whereas a similar annual equation based on United Kingdom company data has dynamics $n_t = 0.83n_{t-1} - 0.14n_{t-2} +$ etc. (see Layard *et al.*, 1991, Chapter 9, Table 15, and Nickell and Wadhwani, 1991, Table III). Both exhibit a considerable degree of persistence, with shocks dying away at a very similar rate.

11. The results in OECD (1993, Table 3.5) indicate a strong positive relationship between wages and long-term unemployment at given unemployment rates. Since long-term unemployment is negatively related to unemployment changes in the short-run, this asserts a positive relationship between long-term unemployment and hysteresis effects (negative effects of unemployment changes on wages).

12. This is the non-labour income argument. Hoon and Phelps (1995) also provide a real interest rate argument, which we do not consider here.

13. The effect will be enhanced if B is exogenous, rather than $B/W(1-t)$. Typically, however, most countries (although not Britain) set the replacement ratio rather than the level of benefit.

14. See Layard *et al.* (1991, Table A6).

15. These are Australia, Belgium, Canada, Denmark, France, Germany, Italy, Japan, Netherlands, Spain, Sweden, United Kingdom, United States.

16. These are those recorded in n. 15 plus Austria, Finland, Ireland, Norway and Switzerland minus Denmark and Spain.

17. See OECD (1994, p. 246).

18. So long as the tax base for these is the same. If, of course, it happens that the consumption tax base is larger, then a lower consumption tax rate would raise the same revenue and have a lesser impact on labour costs.

19. There is a separate question about the effect of changing the progressivity of the employment tax. If skill formation responds very little to relative wages, there is a strong case for a fiscally neutral shift towards greater progressivity, raising the demand for unskilled labour and reducing it for skilled (Layard *et al.*, 1991, Sections 6.5 and 10.3).

References

Alogoskoufis, G. and A. Manning (1988) 'On the Persistence of Unemployment', *Economic Policy*, 7, 427–69.

Atkinson, A.B. and J. Micklewright (1991) 'Unemployment Compensation and Labour Market Transitions: A Critical Review', *Journal of Economic Literature*, 29 (4), 1679–1727.

Bean, C.R., R. Layard and S.J. Nickell (1986) 'The Rise in Unemployment: A Multi-Country Study', *Economica Special Study on Unemployment*, 53, S1–S22.

Budd, A., P. Levine and P. Smith (1988) 'Unemployment, Vacancies and the Long-Term Unemployed', *Economic Journal*, 28, 1071–1091.

Caballero, R.J. (1992) 'A Fallacy of Composition', *American Economic Review*, 82, 1279–92.

Calmfors, L. and J. Driffill (1988) 'Centralisation of Wage Bargaining and Macroeconomic Performance', *Economic Policy*, 6.

Calmfors, L. and A. Forslund (1991) 'Real Wage Adjustment and Labour Market Policies: The Swedish Experience', *Economic Journal*, 101.

Calmfors, L. and R. Nymoen (1990) 'Real Wage Adjustment and Employment Policies in the Nordic Countries', *Economic Policy*, 11.

Carling, K., P.A. Edin, A. Harkman and B. Helmlund (1995) 'Unemployment Duration, Unemployment Benefits and Labour Market Programmes in Sweden', *Journal of Public Economics*.

Fahrer, J. and A. Pease (1993) 'The Unemployment/Vacancy Relationship in Australia', Reserve Bank of Australia Economic Research Department, *Research Discussion Paper*, 9305.

Fay, R. (1995) 'Enhancing the Effectiveness of Active Labour Market Policies, the Role of – and Evidence from – Programme Evaluations in OECD Countries' (Paris: OECD), mimeo.

Hamermesh, D.S. (1992) 'Spatial and Temporal Aggregation in the Dynamics of Labour Demand', *NBER Working Paper*, 4055.

Hoon, H.T. and E.S. Phelps (1995) 'Taxes and Subsidies in a Labor-Turnover Model of the Natural Rate', Columbia University, mimeo.

Jackmann, R. and R. Layard (1991) 'Does Long-Term Unemployment Reduce a Person's Chance of a Job? A Time-Series Test', *Economica*, 58, 93–106, Chapter 6 in this volume.

Katz, L.F. and B.D. Meyer (1991) 'The Impact of the Potential Duration of Unemployment Benefits on the Duration of Unemployment', *Journal of Public Economics*, 41(1), 45–72.

Kramarz, F. (1991) 'Adjustment Costs and Adjustment "Speed"' (Paris: INSEE), mimeo.

Layard, R. (1995) 'Sweden's Road back to Full Employment', Rudolf Meidner Lecture, Centre for Economic Performance, LSE, mimeo.

Layard, R., S.J. Nickell and R. Jackman (1991) *Unemployment: Macroeconomic Performance and the Labour Market* (Oxford: Oxford University Press).

Manacorda, M. and B. Petrongolo (1995) 'The Race between the Supply and Demand of Skills: Some Evidence from OECD Countries', Centre for Economic Performance, LSE, mimeo.

Metcalf, D. (1986) 'Labour Market Flexibility and Jobs: A Survey of Evidence from OECD Countries with Special Reference to Great Britain and Europe', Centre for Labour Economics, LSE, *Working Paper*, 870.

Narendranathan, W., S. Nickell and J. Stern (1985) 'Unemployment Benefits Revisited', *Economic Journal*, 95, 307–329.

Newell, A. and J.S.V. Symons (1985) 'Wages and Unemployment in OECD Countries', Centre for Labour Economics, LSE, *Discussion Paper*, 219.

Nickell, S.J. (1995a) *The Performance of Companies* (Oxford: Blackwell).

Nickell, S.J. (1995b) 'The Distribution of Wages and Unemployment across Skill Groups' (Oxford: Institute of Statistics), mimeo.

Nickell, S.J. and B. Bell (1995a) 'The Collapse in Demand for the Unskilled and Unemployment across the OECD', *Oxford Review of Economic Policy*, 1, 40–62.

Nickell, S.J. and B. Bell (1995b) 'Changes in the Distribution of Wages and Unemployment in OECD Countries' (Oxford: Institute of Statistics), mimeo.

Nickell, S.J. and S. Wadhwani (1991) 'Employment Determination in British Industry: Investigations Using Micro-Data', *Review of Economic Studies*, 58, 955–69.

OECD (1990) *Employment Outlook* (Paris: OECD).

OECD (1993) *Employment Outlook* (Paris: OECD).

OECD (1994) *The OECD Jobs Study* (Paris: OECD).

Phelps, E.S. (1994) 'A Program of Low Wage Employment Tax Credits', *Russell Sage Foundation Working Paper*, 55 (New York: Russell Sage).

Schwanse, P. (1995) 'The Effectiveness of Active Labour Market Policies: Some Lessons from the Experience of OECD Countries', paper presented to OECD technical workshop (Vienna), (November).

Soskice, D. (1990) 'Wage Determination: the Changing Role of Institutions in Advanced Industrialized Countries', *Oxford Review of Economic Policy*, 6(4).

11 The Causes of Graduate Unemployment in India

(1969)*

with M. Blaug and M. Woodhall

The figures in Table 11.1 show that all levels of education in India are profitable investments for private individuals at 8 per cent; indeed, they remain profitable even at cut-off rates as high as 10 per cent; at higher rates, a first degree at least ceases to be *obviously* profitable. Apart from the first general degree, however, the results are insensitive to alternative rates as high as 12 per cent. Thus, despite the fact that educated unemployment has eroded some of the financial returns of additional education, and despite the fact that there is a relatively high incidence of unemployment even for the better educated, additional education right up to the degree level still remains a profitable investment for the average Indian parent.

It is a notable fact, however, that the private rate of return is much higher at the primary than at the matriculate and graduate level. This may seem contrary to the principle that rational private behaviour would be expected to lead to equality in the private rates of return. We must, however, consider the marginal parents at each level of education, whose behaviour determines the number of children that enter the level. At the primary stage, they come from small towns or villages where borrowing rates are much higher than in cities. They are also poorer and may have a higher rate of time preference, placing a high premium on present income and a high discount on future income. Again, they are almost certain to be less well-informed of the gains to be had from education than the parents of children already well up the educational ladder. These economic factors certainly help to explain the unequal private rates of return at different levels, though they are largely a matter of speculation. Some readers may prefer to argue that there are parents with and parents without a 'taste' for education. For example, educated parents may want to give their children more extra education than uneducated parents are willing to give. We cannot attempt to settle these issues here and we certainly do not want to claim

* Extract from Chapter 10 in R. Layard, M. Blaug and M. Woodhall, (1969) *The Causes of Graduate Unemployment in India* (London: Allen Lane, The Penguin Press), pp. 237–9.

Table 11.1 Social and private rates of return on education, urban India, 1960
(per cent)

	Social			Private		
	Crude rate	Fully adjusted		Crude rate	Fully adjusted	
		$\alpha = 0.65$	$\alpha = 0.5$		$\alpha = 0.65$	$\alpha = 0.5$
Primary over illiterate	20.2	15.2	13.7	24.7	18.7	16.5
Middle over primary	17.4	14.2	12.4	20.0	16.1	14.0
Matric. over middle	16.1	10.5	9.1	18.4	11.9	10.4
First degree over matric.	12.7	8.9	7.4	14.3	10.4	8.7
Engineering degree over matric.	16.6	12.5	10.8	21.2	15.5	13.5
Matric. over illiterate	18.1	13.9	12.2	21.4	16.5	14.7
First degree (BA, BSc, BCom) over illiterate	15.9	12.0	10.3	18.5	13.9	12.3
Engineering degree over illiterate	17.3	13.8	12.3	21.2	17.0	15.2

that rate of return analysis is adequate to explain the entire structure of the educational pyramid.

So far so good: Indian students are not deceived in pressing for matriculation and graduation. This explains why supply has continued for a long time to grow faster than demand. But why in the shorter run have wages not fallen faster so as to eliminate unemployment? The basic answer lies, we think, in the peculiar character of educated unemployment in India: it is not that some people are permanently employed and others are permanently unemployed, but rather that large numbers are made to wait a year or two or three before finding a first job. It is as if entry into the labour market were a slowly revolving turnstile that inevitably generates congestion and hence long queues. One moves to the head of the queue by having a first-class degree, or a matriculation with good pass marks, or by having scientific and technical qualifications rather than a BA or BCom. But because the longer a person looks, the more likely he is to find a satisfactory job, and because some preference is given to older applicants, everyone eventually finds a job.

But why a *slowly* revolving turnstile? What stops a graduate from taking the first job he finds and then looking around for a better one in his leisure hours? It is true that this is what some graduates have been doing: this is why the Live Register of the Employment Exchanges includes the names of educated people who already have jobs but who are looking for better ones. Nevertheless, this is not what the average matriculate or graduate does, the reason being that it is very difficult to canvass the possible vacancies in the labour market once one is employed. Despite the growth of labour exchanges and despite the increasing use of newspapers as sources of information about vacancies, Indians still rely to a surprising degree on personal contacts for information about employment, and it takes time to contact friends and relations. Furthermore, despite the considerable regional mobility that characterizes Indian employment, inter-occupational mobility seems to be much less frequent than in advanced countries. It is, 'once in a job, always in the same job'. In the public sector, it is often difficult to persuade one's superior to forward an application, but even in the private sector there appear to be strong taboos about moving elsewhere to enhance one's prospects.

All of these barriers to mobility induce matriculates and graduates to continue the search for employment until it leads to a 'satisfactory' job. In an advanced country, lack of family support would soon drive them into employment at almost any salary. In India, however, the institution of the joint family with its creed of pooling resources to help every member of the family, tends to underwrite the search for employment and, to that extent, to lengthen it. But the key to the length of search is the relatively inflexible reservation price of matriculates and graduates. Now, if it is difficult to move once a first job has been accepted, it may make perfectly good sense to wait a little longer rather than to accept a cut in starting salary which must affect the whole of one's life-time earning profile. The effect of this collective behaviour on the part of matriculates and graduates may also have helped to maintain the rate of return on these forms of education. For though a substantial proportion of educated people are unemployed (6.5 per cent), the proportion of their working life which is spent unemployed is much less, say 2.5 per cent. Thus, zero unemployment would reduce the wages of the employed by more than it would increase the proportion of his life for which a person worked, unless the elasticity of demand for educated people were quite high; it would thus reduce life-time earnings.[1]

From what we have said, it is immediately evident that mere vocational guidance, at least as it is traditionally understood, would do little to alleviate educated unemployment: the rational matriculate, presented with private rates of return on a first degree, suitably adjusted for the incidence of unemployment among graduates, would head straight for the nearest undergraduate college. But something must be done to improve the workings of the labour market. This is no mere academic point. A crude estimate of the social costs of educated unemployment in India in 1966–7 gives a figure of Rs 700 million, a sum roughly equal to one-ninth of national expenditure on education and a third of one per cent of national income.

What can be done about this? The essential remedy is much more flexible hiring policies on the part of employers' aimed at breaking the link between starting salaries and eventual salaries and at making it much easier for people to change their jobs. The public sector can exert tremendous leverage here, as it employs nearly two-thirds of the educated labour force. If salary scales were less rigidly applied and rules about applying for jobs through one's superior officer relaxed, much could be done to promote mobility and to break the close relation between starting and life-time salaries: more flexible age limits for recruitment and promotion would also help. And in the labour market as a whole, more use of employment exchanges and University Employment Information and Guidance Bureaux could greatly improve the matching of workers and jobs.

Notes

1. Suppose unemployment were eliminated. Annual wages would fall by $6.5/\eta$ per cent where η is the elasticity of demand. Life-time earnings would rise from 97.5 per cent of annual wages to 100 per cent. Thus, the absolute value of life-time earnings would rise only if $2.5 > 6.5/\eta$ that is, if the elasticity of demand were over 2.6.

2. The figure is derived by multiplying the starting salary of a nineteen-year-old matriculate in 1966 (about Rs 1,300) by the number of unemployed matriculates (440,000) and adding it to the salary of a twenty-three-year-old graduate in 1966 (about Rs 2,000) multiplied by the number of unemployed graduates (60,000).

12 Unemployment in Britain: Causes and Cures (1981)*

British unemployment is higher than in any other large European country, and it is still growing. However, as Chart 1 shows, it has been at over 5 per cent since 1976. In this essay, I want first to discuss why unemployment has been so high for so long, and then to suggest what should be done about it.

1 CAUSES

Let me begin with some of the things that are *not* causing the recession. Firstly, our abnormal unemployment since 1974 is not due to an abnormal burst of automation. Of course labour-saving investment is going on (robots in British Leyland, etc.) but the rate of this labour-saving investment is not abnormally high – rather the reverse. In fact one of the most striking features of our situation is the extraordinarily *high* level of employment, given the low level of output. There has of course been a long-run downward trend in the numbers of workers used to produce a given output. But, as Figure 12.2 (p. 296) shows, from 1973 to 1976 the trend was stopped in its tracks, and since then has been a lot slower than before 1973. It is possible that we shall in future be hit sideways by the chip, but the automation scare has continually recurred and been falsified. This is because inventions which reduce prices (for given wages) raise real purchasing power, which makes it possible to sell *more* output – not just the same amount of output produced by fewer workers. Interestingly the industries in which employment has risen most tend to be those with the most rapid productivity growth, like electronics. It could even be that, if our problem is excessive real wages relative to productivity, the extra productivity produced by the chip could lift us off the hook. Interestingly, I find that chips are far more discussed in Britain than in America, which has many more of them and no sign of chip-induced unemployment.

A second fallacy relates to employment protection legislation. This discourages both sackings and hirings, and the balance of these two contrary effects is not obvious *a priori*. However once again we get some evidence from

---

* *Work and Social Change*, 6, European Centre for Work and Society (Maastricht) (November), pp. 7–36.

the fact that employment is so high given the low level of output.[1] Of course output itself may have been reduced by the inefficiencies resulting from job protection, but it seems unlikely that this effect can have been very strong.

Thirdly, unemployment has not risen due to increasing structural mismatch of workers to jobs. Whether we analyse the labour force in terms of skills or geographical location, there is no evidence of a growing dispersion in the ratio of unemployment to vacancies.[2]

So what *is* the cause? There is of course little mystery about why unemployment has risen from around 6 per cent in 1978–9 to over 10 per cent. It results directly from the deflationary policies of the government, to which I shall return later. But what are the causes of the *6 per cent unemployment experienced in the later 1970s*? Some people argued that the recession then was more apparent than real. People, they said, were not willing to work, and the rise in unemployment was simply an increase in the numbers of the work-shy. But if this were true, employers ought to have been finding it as difficult to get workers as it ever was before. Yet, as Figure 12.1 shows, the proportion of firms experiencing shortages of skilled labour has been very low ever since 1974. Thus it is not true that, as the Chancellor of the Exchequer sometimes hints, Britain had a boom in 1978–9 but ran into major supply constraints. The level of employment has mainly reflected the demand for labour rather than the supply of willing workers.

The supply of labour and the effects of benefits

I shall shortly return to the factors affecting demand, but it is best to start by looking at supply. For even if supply is not the binding constraint on employment, supply plays an equal role with demand in affecting the degree of labour slack, and thus the evolution of wages and employment. Figure 12.1

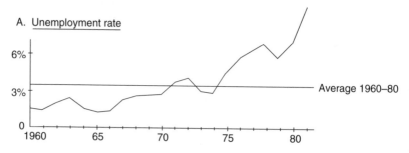

Figure 12.1   see page 295

points a clear lesson here. In 1979 the level of vacancies (Panel *B*) was roughly the same as the mid-point of previous cycles. Yet the level of unemployment (at 5.7 per cent) was much higher than at the mid-point of previous cycles – in 1961–2 it was below 2 per cent. If such a large increase in unemployment had not reduced the level of labour shortage, it follows that most of the extra unemployed in 1979 (over and above the number unemployed in 1961–2) were not effectively offering themselves for work.

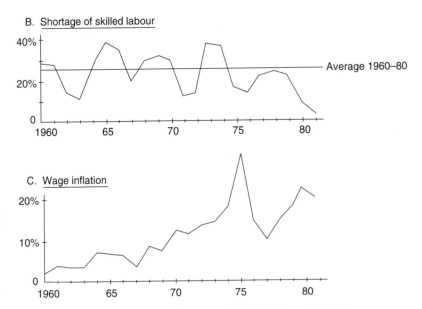

Figure 12.1 Firms experiencing shortages of skilled labour, 1960–80
Notes: Each observation is an annual average. 1981 observation is for January.
    A – Seasonally adjusted excluding school-leavers.
    B – Percentage of firms in manufacturing expecting their output over the next four months to be limited by shortages of skilled labour. (Percentage is weighted by number of employees.)
    Source: Confederation of British Industry, *Industrial Trends Survey.* This variable is more meaningful than the government's vacancy series, which is boosted progressively from 1974 onwards by the creation of the Job Centres. The fact that our series relates only to manufacturing may mean that it progressively under-estimates the level of shortage in the economy as a whole.
    C – Average weekly earnings. 12-monthly rate of increase.

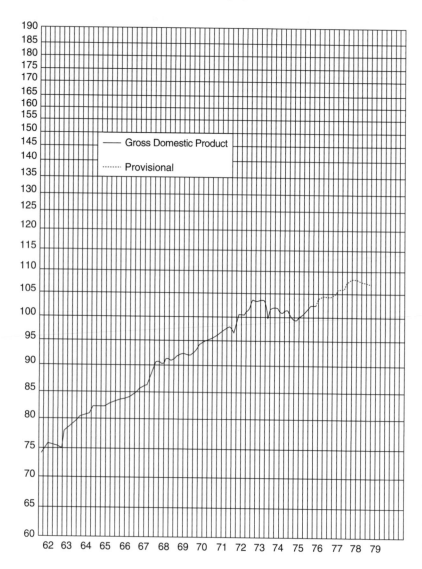

Figure 12.2 Gross domestic product per person employed
Source: Department of Employment Gazette (November 1979)

Table 12.1 Frequency with which unemployed are refused social security

| Year | Unemployed people refusing suitable employment or 'neglecting to avail' | | Number of unemployed people placed by Employment Service (000) |
	Number referred to Insurance Officer (1)	Percentage of (1) denied benefit (2)	(3)
1968	28,300	78	1,450
1969	25,500	78	1,440
1970	24,200	79	1,380
1971	19,600	79	1,250
1972	20,700	79	1,400
1973	18,900	83	1,490
1974	13,200	81	1,430
1975	6,900	75	1,220
1976	5,600	68	1,390
1977	8,400	69	1,480
1978	7,700	64	1,630

Source: Cols (1) and (2), Department of Health and Social Security; Col. (3), Manpower Services Commission, mainly from *Job Centres: An Evaluation*, p. 36.

There is no certain explanation of why this has happened, but one naturally thinks about the effect of social benefits, both in terms of the level of the benefit and its mode of administration. As regards the level of benefits, American work and that of my colleague Stephen Nickell suggests that a 1 per cent rise in benefit may induce something like a 1 per cent increase in unemployment. However social benefits have not risen relative to earnings in work since 1966. They did rise by about a third between the late 1950s and 1966 and this rise may have had a lagged effect. But it cannot explain much of the doubling of unemployment between the 1966 and 1973 boom.

Probably more important have been informal changes in the administration of social security, whereby throughout the 1960s and 1970s less and less pressure was put on the unemployed to find work. It is extremely difficult to get hard evidence on this. I have however assembled the time-series on the frequency with which unemployed people are refused social security (see Table 12.1). Such evidence can hardly be decisive, but it does at any rate add a dimension to the story.

Let us start with the denial of benefit. If a person on Unemployment Benefit refuses an offer of suitable employment or 'neglects to avail' of opportunities of work that exist, the employment service can refer his case to an Insurance Officer. If the Officer accepts the charge, then (subject to appeal) the person loses his Unemployment Benefit for up to 6 weeks. As the table shows, the numbers referred fell steadily up to 1973 after which they fell precipitously. In addition, from 1974 onwards there was a sharp fall in the proportion of all referred people who were eventually refused benefit.

However, a person who is disqualified from Unemployment Benefit can still get some Supplementary Benefit. Normally any individual whose income is below the national minimum gets Supplementary Benefit sufficient to raise him to the minimum. But if he has been disqualified for Unemployment Benefit he loses 40 per cent of the personal scale rate of Supplementary Benefit for up to 6 weeks (though his dependents' benefits and rent are paid in full). If the person continues to refuse work, he can be required to attend a Re-establishment Centre as a condition for getting Supplementary Benefit, and eventually he can be prosecuted for failing to maintain himself and his family. Prosecutions raise obvious difficulties and the number of prosecutions has fallen from around 100 a year in the sixties to under 10.

So what explains the trends shown in the table? They probably reflect, above all, profound changes in social attitudes towards people receiving public money. The most glaring example of this has been the altogether new phenomenon in the 1970s of large numbers of full time students on vacation receiving benefits designed for the 'unemployed'. But in addition there has been an interesting set of institutional changes in Britain since 1973 which may have further encouraged the tendencies at work.

In 1973 the employment service was completely restructured in three main ways. Until then it operated from labour exchanges in which the matching of workers and jobs was done at one desk, and benefit was paid out at another desk. From 1973 onwards the two functions were split into different buildings, often far apart. In this way the employment service hoped to escape the dole queue image and attract more jobs, by moving progressively into Job Centres on high street sites.

In addition the old process whereby an employment adviser matched person to job was supplemented by a new self-service system. All jobs are now advertised on open stands, and one half of all Job Centre placements are made as a result of the self-selection of a job by a job-seeker. An unemployed person need rarely visit the Job Centre unless he wants to. He signs on once a fortnight at the Benefit Office. And he goes to the Job Centre when he first becomes unemployed, and thereafter only if he wants to scan the boards or is summoned because he is to be submitted to a vacancy (which mainly occurs when vacancies are hard to fill).

Thirdly, the objectives of the service were changed. The idea now is to maximise the number of placements, with little separate concern for *who* is placed in the jobs. And the performance of offices is largely judged on their success in attracting and filling vacancies rather than on getting unemployed people off the register. The argument behind this change is that the labour market in general is imperfect and the public employment service should try to expand its activity at all levels of the market.

The effects of these changes can easily be guessed. Firstly, the splitting of the offices drastically reduced communication between the job-matchers and those responsible for paying benefit to the unemployed. Though the job-matchers had always been concerned to provide employers with suitable applicants, they had in the old days shared their colleagues' aims of getting people off the register. Now they increasingly saw themselves as providing a service to employers.

Secondly, the self-service system gave tremendous advantages to the newly unemployed and tended to divert jobs away from the longer-term unemployed. For, needless to say, the people who search the screens are mainly the most recently unemployed. Thus the proportion of the unemployed finding work who get their jobs through the employment service is much higher among those who find work within one month of becoming unemployed than it is among the longer-term unemployed. It seems strange that a public employment service should be providing so much of its support to those having the least difficulty. In fact in 1976 two thirds of all those who had been out of work for over one year had *never* been submitted for a job.

Finally there is the effect of the targets. These inevitably make employment advisers wary of submitting doubtful prospects, or people who are not so keen to work. There are obvious dilemmas here. Employment advisers argue that, even from the point of view of the long-term unemployed it is important to keep up the image of the service, otherwise employers will not use it. But this argument, if taken to extremes, leads to a *reductio ad absurdum* – the best way to help the long-term unemployed cannot always be to give priority to the short term.

Thus we have the picture of a service which has increasingly served the easy-to-place. Those who are work-shy are not offered jobs and because they are not offered jobs, no sanctions can be used against them: it is very difficult to force someone to help himself. I have described these institutional changes to the employment service at some length because they raise important practical issues. I do not think they explain more than a smallish fraction of the post-1973 rise in unemployment; and in so far as administrative influences have affected this rise, it is mainly through the direct application of a laxer work test.

The Thatcher government has naturally been worried about this alleged laxity in the payment of benefit, and the issue has recently been reviewed by an official 'Rayner committee' (1981). They concluded that it was best to accept that the Job Centres were going to play no role in putting pressure on the unemployed but that this should be done by increasing the number of Unemployment Review Officers, who are based at the Benefit Offices and look into individual cases of long-standing unemployment. They also propose administering a formal test of availability for work before beginning to pay benefit to anyone. They recommend more anti-fraud work, since they believe (on the basis of rather limited evidence) that at least 8 per cent of those on benefit have undisclosed work (often of course part-time), while 16 per cent are not seeking work. Finally they confirm the lax public attitude to benefit. A sample of the unemployed were asked whether 'a married woman who decided to stay at home with her children rather than work would be likely to get Unemployment Benefit'. One quarter said Yes, whereas the correct answer is naturally No. The Committee recommend better publicity about the rules!

The demand for labour and the mechanism of inflation

All this may help to explain why there are more people who are voluntarily unemployed. And a further important point may be that when society has experienced higher levels of unemployment for some time, the stigma of unemployment gets reduced and people who are out of work may feel less pressure (from within themselves and from society at large) to find work. This reduces the supply of labour available to firms at given levels of unemployment. However, having said all this, let me reiterate my basic point – though there may be more work-shy unemployed than there used to be, there have also in the late 1970s been more *work-hungry* unemployed than there used to be. And the total level of unemployment has been constrained by the shortage of jobs rather than of willing workers.

This raises the question of why there have been so few jobs. To answer this, one has only to look at panel *C* of Figure 12.1. Inflation has increased sharply. Most, though not all, economists believe that the level of unemployment affects whether inflation increases or decreases. So a key question is: If unemployment is reduced, at what level of unemployment will the inflation rate begin to increase? A glance at Panels *A* and *C* shows that, whereas in the early 1960s the inflation rate was fairly stable at around $2\frac{1}{2}$ per cent unemployment, in the later 1970s inflation increased even though unemployment was over 5 per cent. We have already seen one reason why the 'critical' level of unemployment (at which inflation is just stable) has risen: there have been more unemployed who are actively seeking work (as reflected in the relation of vacancies to unemployment). But on top of this one can see from the chart that the 'critical' level of vacancies at which inflation is just stable has fallen. For example up to 1968 an average labour shortage of 24 per cent was sufficient to stop inflation accelerating, whereas in the late 1970s inflation failed to decelerate, even though there was a much lower average level of tightness in the labour market. Thus something has happened which has made inflation accelerate when there is more slack in the labour market. The reasons for this are difficult to interpret. One possible explanation is that the real wage has been pushed up to a level where the number of workers that firms are willing to employ is less than before, relative to the number actively seeking work. The real wage affects labour demand through its effects on profitability and on competitiveness in world markets. If it is too high there will be fewer jobs, and attempts by normal methods to provide more jobs will only produce more inflation.

However this explanation, even if correct, does not explain why real wages have been pushed too high. The most likely reason for this is that workers have not fully adjusted their targets for real wages to the slower rate of growth of productivity that has prevailed since the early 1970s.[3] In most Western countries the rate of growth of real output per worker-hour has fallen by about 2 percentage points relative to what it was in the 1960s. Thus by now output per man-hour is some 15 per cent lower than it would have been if earlier trends had continued. In addition the rise in the real price of oil has twice reduced the sustainable income per head in OECD – by about 2 per cent in 1973 and the same again in 1979. If workers continue to aim at higher real wages than are consistent with full employment, two results may follow. Workers may in part achieve a higher real wage, but at the cost of less than full employment. Or they may not in fact achieve a higher real wage.

But even in the latter case we are in trouble. For suppose workers aim at a real wage increase of 4 per cent, but that productivity increases by only 2 per cent. If employers can maintain their profit margin by pushing up prices, workers will find that prices rise by 2 per cent more than they expected when they made their settlement. If they now try to offset this by further wage increases, inflation will tend to increase. If the monetary authorities accommodate this wage pressure, inflation will actually increase. But if they do not accommodate, unemployment will increase, which will thus offset the inflationary pressure. In general since 1974 European governments have been unwilling to accommodate inflationary pressure and have preferred to see unemployment increase. For a time after 1973 real wages did seem to rise relative to productivity, but then they fell. So it is not certain that actual real wages have been too high. But it seems very likely that *aspirations* for real wages would have been too high at normal levels of labour slack. Hence more slack in the labour market has been necessary to bring actual wage claims into line with reality.

There is one other obvious point. Western economies have been subjected to not only extra inflationary pressure from domestic sources but also to two external inflationary shocks (in 1973 and 1979). The problem with external price shocks is that they can easily lead to permanent increases in the levels of inflation which people expect. To offset this and to 'squeeze inflation back out of the system' governments naturally deflate.

Thus we have two reasons why governments may have been willing to see labour market slack emerge. Firstly, there were more domestic sources of inflationary pressure due to the slower rate of productivity growth. Secondly, there were external inflationary shocks. But in each case labour market slack has been deliberately allowed to develop as the stick to beat inflation.

2   CURES

So what can be done? The ideal solution would be to find some other instrument than labour slack for controlling the level of inflation. I believe there is such an instrument and I will reveal it at the end of this essay. However, it will take time to install and, even without it, there are avenues of hope.

To choose between policies we have to balance their effects, firstly, on the total net output of the economy, secondly, on the fairness with which it is divided, and thirdly on inflation. It is no good asserting that unemployment is costly (in lost output and peace of mind), and should therefore be reduced. We also need to allow for the possible *costs* of reduced unemployment, i.e. more inflation. Some schemes involve less inflationary cost than others, and less pressure on the exchange rate. With this in mind, we can now review the main possible approaches to the problem. If unemployment means an excess of supply over demand, it can in principle be cured either by reducing supply or increasing demand. Which is best?

Reducing supply

Supply reduction is in the air. The government subsidises early retirement (the Job Release Scheme), and the Trade Union Congress is campaigning for the shorter working week. But there is one strong objection to this approach. If people were willing to work the hours they did at the available wages, they must have valued the output they produced in the last few hours of work more than the leisure they gave up. In this case it is inefficient for the rest of society to bribe them to accept more leisure. It is better to increase demand. There might be arguments for removing one man's unemployment by increasing another man's leisure, if that were the only option. But since people would like to work more *it would be better to increase the amount of work*. However let us examine the effects of supply reduction, in order to see why the idea appeals to administrators and trade unionists.

From an administrative point of view the scheme has appeal, especially if it were possible (which it is not) to ensure that all the hours which the retired or the work-sharers give up are in fact allocated to unemployed workers. For in that case unemployment benefit is reduced by roughly the same amount as the cost of the subsidy to early retirement or work-sharing. Thus the public deficit is unaffected, but the number of registered unemployed has been cut. At the same time, since national output has not increased, we avoid the increase of imports caused by income growth.

The problem is that typically employers will find they can produce the same output with fewer man-hours. This could reverse our previous conclusions. It would be splendid for efficiency, but the savings in unemployment benefit would be far too little to offset the cost of the subsidy. Administrators might be disappointed.

Trade unionists like work-sharing partly because they see it helping a long-term move towards shorter hours on higher real hourly pay. But work-sharing can only reduce unemployment if real hourly labour cost keeps in line with productivity. This may mean short-run falls in weekly earnings. It is not clear how far those who would be involved in work-sharing are willing to accept this. It is therefore better to concentrate on expanding labour demand than to accommodate pessimistically to less work than people want.

Subsidizing extra jobs

Demand can be expanded either by special labour market measures or by general reflation; there is room for both. The argument for special measures is that they may be able to improve the trade-off between inflation and unemployment. One possible measure would be a subsidy to firms producing extra jobs. A firm would be paid a large sum per week for any increase in its work force over and above the number of workers it employed last year. The basic argument for such a subsidy is that it concentrates the give-away near to the margin at which firms make their decisions about whether to employ more workers or not. Thus whereas a *general* cut for example of 3 per cent in employers' social security contributions would only reduce the cost of an extra worker by 3 per cent, a subsidy costing the same to the government but concentrated on 1 in 20 of the work force would reduce the marginal cost by 60 per cent. This must be more effective. It would be particularly effective in manufacturing, where marginal costs may be particularly important in affecting the volume of exports and import-substitutes. But even in a closed economy it would be bound to work better than a general cut in taxes on labour. The subsidy would not be a subsidy to inefficiency – by only subsidizing expansions in employment the subsidy would be helping forward the firms with a future. The subsidy will often act simply as an inducement to bring forward in time an expansion that would otherwise happen later. This is much better than protecting firms that are in secular decline.

I first advocated such a scheme in 1976 (Layard, 1976)[4] and in 1977 a mini-version of it was introduced as the Small Firms Employment Subsidy. This gave £20 a week for 6 months for any increase in employment over its level in the previous year. It was originally limited to small firms in manufacturing in development areas but, owing to favourable evaluation of its effects, it was extended so that in 1979–80 it was expected to cover nearly one quarter of a million jobs (even though it was mistakenly limited to small firms). It has however been abolished by the present government.

A job subsidy of the kind proposed, especially if the subsidy is large, could substantially increase the number of jobs. But it matters not only how many jobs there are in the economy but who gets them. In Britain, unemployment, if you catch it, lasts much longer than in many other countries. It lasts twice as long as in the USA, which is why it is rightly considered a greater evil here than in the USA. At present those who are unemployed have been out of work *on average* for over half a year, and one quarter have been out for more than one year. This means that a given unemployment is concentrated on a smaller fraction of the population than it would be if durations were shorter. It would be fairer and more efficient to spread the unemployment around more, so that more people became unemployed but had shorter durations. To bring this about, one could have a recruitment subsidy for employers hiring people who have been unemployed for over six months. This could be paid at a given weekly rate for, say, a year, in order to ensure that the worker was not just hired and fired.

However the problem with a subsidy of this latter kind is to ensure that the subsidised workers do not, to a large extent, displace unsubsidised workers who would otherwise have been employed – with no net increase in jobs. If this happened, it would be an expensive way of securing greater fairness in the distribution of unemployment. For one of the main arguments for job subsidies is that to an important extent they can pay for themselves in budgetary terms, since extra jobs mean less social benefits being paid out and more taxes brought in. The public expenditure cost (in benefits and lost tax) of an extra unemployed man is put by the Treasury at about £70 a week. This makes one wonder whether we could not have a combination of the two proposals made so far. Firms could be offered a major subsidy (say £70 a week) for one year for anyone they employed who had been out of work for over six months, provided their total employment (net of subsidised workers) did not contract.

The right to work and selective public employment

This leads me to a more radical thought. Would it be possible for the government to guarantee some kind of work to anyone who had been unemployed for over 6 months? The British government has done something like this for school-leavers in that for the last few years it has promised to do 'something' for anyone of them who has not found work by the Easter after leaving school.[5] 'Something' means either being placed on 6 months' work experience with an employer (at no cost to the employer) or working on a publicly-funded project or taking a training course. This Youth Opportunities Scheme has worked quite well (though there are complaints from the trade unions that private employers are replacing regular workers by youngsters on work experience). And the present government remains firmly committed to trying to protect youth against the worst effects of the recession. But for adults they dismantled many of Labour's subsidies and public projects and are only now in a minor way developing a programme of projects.[6] It should surely be possible to do better than this. Though any kind of work guarantee would worsen the government's deficit, the effect might not be very great and the benefits considerable. Thus a policy one might consider would be two-pronged along the following lines. Firstly, employers would receive a £70 a week subsidy for hiring anyone who had been unemployed for over 6 months. The subsidy would last for one year but during that year the worker would be on a temporary contract with no rights under the Employment Protection legislation. He would however be paid the full rate for the job. Secondly, any worker unemployed for over 6 months would have the right to be employed on a publicly-supported project at a wage 10 per cent higher than his benefit entitlement.

The reason for proposing this combination is that I believe that work in regular workplaces (private or public) is much preferable to work on ad hoc publicly-supported projects. Firstly, the output is something which the market or the electoral system has shown to be demanded. Secondly, the individual worker is nearer to a regular job and a career. He is building up contacts with a regular employer. In YOPs the subsequent job history of those placed in work experience has been better than of those on ad hoc projects, and about one half have been hired by their existing employers on a permanent basis. Thus job subsidies should be the chief special measure for adults, but publicly-supported projects (generally on lower wages) are a necessary adjunct in order to deliver a right to work guarantee.

Where possible training should be part of employment programmes because this helps to reduce the supply of workers in over-supplied (unskilled) markets and increase the supply to under-supplied (skilled) markets. This reduces the long-run unemployment rate, and has much greater economic benefits than appear from comparing the histories of trained and untrained workers (as is done in most of the research). However, in the case of adults, it would be a mistake to *insist* on training, since this will reduce the number of jobs being available.

General stimulation of demand

We come now to the more contentious issues of general reflation. As I have already stressed, there is some limit to the level of employment consistent with non-accelerating inflation (though this level can be changed by some of the measures I discuss). But the problem facing the government today is that the British public is not willing to tolerate the *present* level of inflation even if it does not accelerate. It has therefore embarked on a road towards lower inflation that is leading to much higher unemployment, causing much misery and loss of output. Is it all worth it?

This is a matter of value judgement. My own view is that a low rate of inflation is much preferable even to 10 per cent inflation. Thus a policy that led to a permanent fall in inflation would yield valuable benefits. On the other hand such a policy would also have permanent costs (via a reduced stock of physical and human capital). In addition there are the major temporary costs, which must increase more than proportionately with each increase in the unemployment rate. This latter consideration suggests that the right way to reduce inflation is gradually rather than precipitously (unless there is some other non-linearity in the process by which inflationary expectations are formed, for which no evidence exists).

I would therefore think that the present British government is making a serious mistake in deflating the economy far more than any earlier British government or any current European one. In addition it is resolutely rejecting the other instrument by which inflation could be reduced – namely incomes policy.

Incomes policy[7]

There are, after all, two ways to attack inflation. One is the indirect method of controlling money spending. The other is by direct control of costs or prices, accompanied of course by controlled money spending. The difficulty with the indirect approach is that there is no way of ensuring that the reduced growth of money spending leads to reduced growth of prices, rather than to reduced output. If it goes into reduced output this will ultimately dampen inflation, but in the meantime there may have been horrendous costs in terms of increased unemployment and lost output. That is why an incomes policy is needed – to ensure that the reduced spending is linked to reduced costs rather than to reduced output.

But at this point a division of opinion arises. Some people believe that a temporary incomes policy would be sufficient; others think it would need to be permanent. There are two reasons for supporting a permanent incomes policy. Firstly, there is good empirical evidence that when inflation has been reduced by incomes policy (as in 1975–7), there has been a roughly equal increase in inflation in the years when the policy breaks down. In fact a temporary incomes policy almost inevitably ends in an episode when the government is still leaning on wages and is discredited by its failure to hold the line. Secondly, and more importantly, it seems that the level of long-run unemployment that is now necessary to keep inflation from increasing is unacceptably high.[8] According to this view, we must now look for some permanent instrument, other than unemployment, for keeping inflation in check. If one can find any instrument involving less real cost than unemployment one should adopt it, even if the costs are considerable.

This brings us to consider the different forms of possible incomes policies, and the costs associated with each. All recent incomes policies have been specified in terms of maximum permitted increases for groups of workers (and sometimes individuals). They have thus placed administrative limits on the outcomes of settlements. Whether the policy was compulsory or voluntary, the freedom of collective bargaining from administrative constraint has been suspended. One could perhaps have a more voluntary version of such policies, in which individual trade unions agreed on some carve-up of an agreed national cake. But in a country the size of Britain (rather than Sweden or Holland) such an arrangement would still involve strong elements of centralism and dirigisme, if it was to be a permanent feature of our system. This is why incomes policies which have limited the rights of collective bargainers have always been temporary, and would be likely to remain so. But we have already given arguments in favour of an incomes policy that can be permanent.

A second major problem with traditional incomes policies is their inability to handle the problem of differentials. These are left to administrative decisions. But it is notoriously difficult for people removed from the scene to be sensitive to the true degree of shortage or surplus in a particular sector. Sometimes of course one has to use an administrative tribunal to arbitrate a particular dispute and produce an acceptable solution taking into account equity, shortage/surplus and sheer market power. But arbitration in particular cases is quite different from a national system of administered wage structures.

In favour of such a system, some would argue that it is an important instrument of income redistribution. However, the evidence of the £6 a week policy suggests that it is very difficult to alter the distribution of gross incomes by administrative fiat. Moreover, a rise in gross pay for the lowest paid would not have much effect on the inequality of income per head in our society.[9] Redistribution has to be done by fiscal policy. And an incomes policy that tries to redistribute is likely to collapse: a major reason for the 1977–9 débâcle was that the 1975–7 policies had reduced a few key differentials in the engineering industry, leading to a quite disproportionate degree of aggro.

I conclude that we want a permanent incomes policy which will restrain the growth rate of all incomes in equal proportion. It need not become involved in trying to alter the pattern of wages, and must allow free collective bargaining. It should also not take money away from individuals but rather ensure that they never get it in the first place. This leads to the notion that the correct place to apply pressure is on employers. Is it possible, one asks, to devise a non-bureaucratic method of permanently reducing increases in employers' wage payments without interfering with free collective bargaining?

An employer-based tax on wage increases above a norm

The obvious method is to operate a tax on employers proportional to the excess of their increase in average hourly earnings above a national norm. This is a good idea because it bears directly on the actual payments that affect costs, rather than on settlements. (Between 1972 and 1977 hourly earnings generally rose about 3 per cent per annum faster than the maximum permitted level of settlements.) It is also better in a free society to affect settlements indirectly rather than directly. Since a £1 increase in payments would cost a firm more than £1 it would lead employers to be more resistant in wage negotiations and, after wage negotiations were over, it would lead to less upward drift in payments.

The tax is administratively feasible. The firm's liability could be checked from a duplicate copy of the firm's PAYE returns (showing its total wage bill) plus an extended version of the monthly returns on workers and hours currently made to the Department of Employment. (Non-manual workers would be deemed to work 35 hours a week unless there was evidence of paid overtime.) The tax would relate to the excess of a firm's average payments in each quarter over their level in the corresponding quarter a year earlier.

The more one wanted to reduce inflation in the current year, the higher the tax rate would have to be. This is no objection to the scheme. The public would not object to a stiff inflation tax in very inflationary conditions.[10] However, it might be easier to introduce the scheme in the wake of a cruder incomes policy that had reduced the inflation rate to an acceptable level. In such a situation there would be strong public pressure for a more flexible policy. To remove all controls would be a mistake and the kind of flexibility introduced by a tax-based policy might be very popular. I suggest that one should adopt a permanent tax-based incomes policy as the central policy, without ruling out an explicitly temporary policy as an initial short-term measure.

An incomes policy would have to control capital income as well as wages. The natural thing would be to have a similar scheme for dividends. There could be the same norm for dividend increases as for wage increases, and the same tax rate on increases above the norm. There would of course be complaints that reinvested profits were exempt from control. However these are only of distributional significance if there are corresponding capital gains accruing to households; and the share of real capital gains in household income is rather small these days. In any case capital gains can be handled by capital gains tax.

An important issue is what would happen to prices. The scheme would obviously only control domestic sources of inflation. With floating exchange rates, prices will, in the medium term, reflect normal domestic unit costs adjusted for changes in the terms of trade. There is no way in which a government can protect its population against fundamental changes in the terms of trade and this scheme would not attempt to do so. However, there is also the question as to how the norm should be adjusted in the face of speculative changes in the exchange rate, not reflecting current changes in purchasing power parity. I suggest that the norm should not be adjusted downwards if the exchange rate rises, nor upwards if it falls, since this would add to the instability in the inflation rate, and a major objective should be to stabilise inflation. But this procedure would mean that the real wage could oscillate somewhat (as it certainly does under traditional incomes policies).

There is one other point. The government should use the scheme to run the economy at a much higher level of activity than would otherwise be possible. The additional money spending could pull up prices relative to wages. But any small resulting fall in the real wage would be a small price to pay for a major reduction in unemployment.

If it was felt politically necessary, one could operate a prices policy as well as a wages policy. This could be of the traditional kind, aiming to maintain a reasonable level of mark-up over cost. There are however notorious difficulties in controlling for changes in the quality of products. And one thing is clear. A prices policy is almost certain to fail without a wages policy, whereas a wages policy can probably control inflation without a prices policy.

There are a number of possible objections to the wage scheme. Firstly, since it bears on average hourly earnings, it provides an incentive to firms to employ relatively more unskilled people, and by the same token penalises firms that wish to move towards a relatively more skilled work force. This may be a mild distortion, though some would regard it as a desirable subsidy to unskilled labour that could offset the inefficiency caused by too high wages for the unskilled.

Secondly, it taxes all increases in differentials. This will reduce the use of wage signals as instruments for attracting more labour. This again is a source of inefficiency, though one can plausibly argue that in inflationary conditions changes in differentials tend to be too frequent. Uncertainty about the underlying rate of inflation leads to a much greater dispersion in settlements than would 'normally' prevail – and most changes in differentials get unwound within a year or two.[11] In the meantime they cause great social discontent. So some dampening down of the rate of change of differentials might positively improve social welfare.

Thirdly, there is the problem of the public sector. It looks odd when the public sector taxes itself. However, this is only a wasteful book-keeping operation if the public sector is truly monolithic, which, thank God, it is not. In fact there is some decentralised decision-taking throughout the public sector – more in some places and less in others. Therefore the scheme should apply to the public sector like the private. At worst it might in some parts of the public sector have little effect.

Then there is the question of anomalies. Almost no incomes policy proposals have any plausible mechanism for remedying anomalies existing at the beginning of the scheme. Under our scheme anomalies *would* be gradually rectified, at some cost to employers. There should be no exceptions to the scheme.

Next, one might ask why the scheme is only operated in the form of a tax on super-normal increases in wages (i.e. a stick) rather than offering in addition a subsidy for sub-normal increases (i.e. a carrot). One could of course do this, but it is not politically appealing to pay firms for 'underpaying' their workers, while it may be all right to tax them for 'overpaying' them.

Finally, there is the question of the fiscal implications of the tax proceeds. These could not of course be easily forecast and thus the same would be true of the Public Sector Borrowing Requirement (PSBR). However, if this uncertainty arises from the action of an automatic stabiliser, it may not matter and may be a positive advantage. If one wants to get rid of it, one can plan in advance to redistribute the proceeds as a cut in Value Added Tax.

I conclude with the basic point that mass unemployment is unacceptable as a weapon against inflation. Any alternative involves some control on incomes, but we want to permit as much flexibility as possible, while controlling the average level of earnings. Any control automatically involves costs (including administrative costs). That does not rule it out. Unless one considers unemployment a less costly method of controlling inflation, we ought to have a tax-based incomes policy.

Income while unemployed

Finally a word on benefits for the unemployed. I believe these should be generous, linked to stringent administration to prevent abuse. At present unemployed people receive Unemployment Benefit for the first year of unemployment (often supplemented by Supplementary Benefit). After the first year Supplementary Benefit alone is available. This means a considerable income drop for some of the unemployed. Yet Nickell has shown that once a person has been unemployed for over 6 months, an increase in benefits will have no effect on his likelihood of leaving unemployment. Involuntary long-term unemployment is very unpleasant and its victims have generally exhausted any savings they might have had. Since the fraction of the long-term unemployed who are involuntary is going to rise sharply, those unemployed for over one year should be given the long-term rates of Supplementary Benefit, as paid to pensioners and single parents, rather than the short-term rate, which is all that is currently available. However if my right to work proposal was introduced, this proposal would lapse.

CONCLUSIONS

I have covered too much ground for an aerial photograph to be useful. Let me just remind you of a few main points.

1. Unemployment at a given level of vacancies has risen in a secular way mainly because of laxer administration of social benefits.
2. Inflationary pressure at a given level of vacancies has risen because of a failure of workers to adjust their real wage targets to lower productivity. Thus the Labour government allowed the labour market to remain slack in order to control inflation. In addition the inflation rate was jerked up twice by external shocks to energy prices. Since 1979 the government has increased labour slack by deflating the economy in order to reduce inflation.
3. Incomes policy rather than unemployment should be used to control inflation. But it should be a flexible policy, whereby the government declares a norm for the rate of growth of hourly earnings in each firm but firms can go above this if they are willing to pay a stiff tax.
4. There is a case for special measures, as well as general reflation, to offset excessive unemployment. Special measures should mainly aim to stimulate the demand for labour rather than to reduce the supply. There should be a two-pronged right to work guarantee for all workers who had been unemployed for over 6 months. Firstly, employers should receive a £70 subsidy for employing such people, provided their total employment (net of subsidised workers) is not reduced. Secondly, any such worker should have a right to be employed on a publicly supported project at pay 10 per cent above his social benefits while unemployed.

Notes

1. According to Nickell (1980), on balance the legislation has encouraged employment.
2. See Nickell (1980).
3. For further details on this argument see the work of the LSE Centre for Labour Economics project on OECD unemployment, undertaken jointly with D. Grubb and R. Jackman. *See* D. Grubb *et al.* (1982).
4. For a fuller analysis see Layard and Nickell (1980), Layard (1979, 1980a).

5. It is being considered whether this gap can be reduced to the Christmas after leaving.
6. Now called Community Enterprise and providing about 30,000 places, many of which will go to under 25s.
7. This section draws heavily on work done with R.A. Jackman.
8. See for example, Grubb, Jackman and Layard (1982).
9. For further discussion of these issues, see Layard (1980b).
10. Note that a current wage increase has a considerable value to an employer. It allows him to pay more in every subsequent year without any further tax. Thus the tax on a current increase may need to be quite high to discourage it. There is no reason why one should not consider taxes of the order of 100 per cent.
11. Layard (1980b).

References

Department of Employment and Department of Health and Social Security (1981) *Payment of Benefits to Unemployed People* (March).

Grubb, D., R. Jackman and R. Layard (1982) 'Causes of the Current Stagflation', *Review of Economic Studies*, XLIX 707–730.

Layard, R. (1976) 'Subsidizing Jobs without adding to Inflation', *The Times* (28 January).

Layard, R. (1979) 'The Costs and Benefits of Selective Employment Measures: The British Case', *British Journal of Industrial Relations*, 17 (July).

Layard, R. (1980a) 'Evidence to the House of Lords Select Committee on Unemployment' (12 March) (London: HMSO).

Layard, R. (1980b) 'Wages Policy and the Redistribution of Income', in D. Collard, R. Lecomber and M. Slater (eds), *Income Distribution: The Limits to Redistribution* (Bristol: Colston Society).

Layard, R. and S. Nickell (1980) 'The Case for Subsidising Extra Jobs', *Economic Journal* (March), Chapter 17 in this volume.

Nickell, S. (1980) 'The Determinants of Equilibrium Unemployment in Britain', Centre of Labour Economics, LSE, *Discussion Paper*, 78 (August).

Part II
Remedies for Unemployment

13 Introduction to Part II

What can be done to reduce unemployment? I have devoted many years of my life to this issue and written more articles than I care to count.

PREVENTING LONG-TERM UNEMPLOYMENT

I have always believed that the chief strategy is to prevent long-term unemployment through guaranteeing offers of work to everybody within a year of becoming unemployed. It seems absurd to pay billions to people for being in long-term unemployment rather than using the money to subsidise their re-employment. I also believe that it is a disaster to separate the payment of unemployment benefits from the organization of job placement, since it then becomes impossible to implement any job-search conditions for benefit recipients (see Chapter 12). In my mind the key idea has to be a pro-active employment service committed to helping people find work and preventing welfare dependency. In this sense I was perhaps a pioneer of what is now called Welfare to Work.

As early as 1979 the Labour Party election platform adopted the idea of a guarantee of employment for all people unemployed for over a year. I continued to push this idea and in 1985 it was the central proposal of the anti-unemployment campaign launched by the Employment Institute, which I founded.[1] In 1986 it was proposed by the all-party House of Commons Select Committee on Employment,[2] and it then featured in the Labour Party election platforms for 1992 and 1997. It is now being implemented. The key issue is how to analyse its effects.

The basic idea is that if people are paid indefinitely for not working, more people will be out of work. However, rather than simply cutting the duration of benefit, it seems better to use the benefit savings to take active measures to get them back into the world of normal work rather than starving them back into work at depressed wages. But, many people say, such a policy can only redistribute work from the unsubsidised to the subsidised, with little effect on the total.

Of course when employers are asked whether all the subsidised jobs are extra jobs they point out that some x per cent of the subsidised jobs would have existed anyway but filled with different people. In the literature this is called 'substitution' and it is generally assumed that those who were displaced in this way become permanently unemployed – or, more precisely, that the total expansion of jobs is $(1 - x)$ per cent of the jobs subsidised.

315

But what did happen to those displaced? Did they get absorbed elsewhere in the economy? To study this requires a model, such as that in Chapter 14. The basic idea is that the control of inflation requires a given number of effectiveness–units of unemployment. If we can reduce ineffective unemployment (such as long-term unemployment) we can live with lower total unemployment. Indeed on some assumptions, short-term unemployment need not increase at all.

These issues are very important to those who do cost-benefit analysis of the proposal. In 1997 I published a (rather crude) cost-benefit analysis of a policy that I proposed for a future British government (see Chapter 15). The social benefits (reduced unemployment) clearly exceed the social costs (of extra administration plus any new distortions). But the costs and benefits to the Treasury are more finely balanced. In the steady state once the new system is well established, it is likely to be roughly self-financing due to the savings on benefits and extra tax receipts. But in the start-up phase there is certainly a net cost to the Treasury.

The most powerful argument for this approach to unemployment is that it is targeted directly at those who reveal themselves to be at risk. The chances of success are greatest when there is a close link between the policy and its mechanism of working. For most other policies the link is more indirect.[3]

TAX-BREAKS FOR HIGH UNEMPLOYMENT GROUPS

One such policy is based on the idea that some groups, such as the unskilled, have higher unemployment rates than others. If wages are more rigid for the 'low-skilled' group than they are for the 'skilled', then total employment can be increased by reducing the employers' tax on the low-skilled and increasing it on the high-skilled. For the low-skilled unemployment can decline a lot without much increase in wages, while skilled unemployment need not increase much since skilled wages are so flexible.

This idea is developed in Chapter 16. In that paper, the different degrees of wage flexibility are attributed to differences in workers' supply elasticities in taking jobs. But the difference could equally well be derived from models where wages are determined not by supply and demand but by wage bargaining or by efficiency wages.[4] This line of thought has been pursued by many governments which have cut wage taxes for youth, or for high unemployment regions, or simply for low-paid workers (as in Britain in 1985).

It is certainly an efficient policy if people are trapped into their own particular group (be it age, region or skill). But, whereas people cannot choose their age, they can to some extent choose their region or skill. This then raises another issue. We would like people to move from the high-unemployment group into a lower-unemployment group, but if we reduce taxes on the higher-unemployment group we reduce the incentive to move. In the extreme case where everyone is as willing to change groups as everyone else (that is the case of infinitely elastic supply), there is no case as such for lighter taxation of high unemployment groups. The less elastic the supply of movers the stronger the case for light taxation of low unemployment groups (see Chapter 7).

Since most taxes are in the end borne by labour, it is not obviously logical to advocate simultaneously a subsidy to employers of high-unemployment groups and a subsidy to people to migrate out of the group. If a choice has to be made between subsidizing the employment of low-skilled people or subsidizing skill-formation, which should it be? The answer has to depend on the elasticities of supply of skilled people (as above) but also on the other externalities involved. In general these will favour subsidizing skill formation, which generates many positive externalities.[5] The analogous analysis will be less favourable to inter-regional migration, since this often induces negative externalities, like migration costs and costs of extra infrastructure.

MARGINAL EMPLOYMENT SUBSIDIES

Another form of tax relief (or subsidy) is one that is related to the growth in employment at the level of the firm. The idea here is to reduce the marginal cost of output (relative to wages), thus permitting a non-inflationary growth of output. The idea was simultaneously promoted by Layard and Nickell (see Chapter 17) and by Rehn.[6] The problem is that it can only work if firms are earning rents which can safely be eaten into. This is probably the reason why it has never been used on a large scale. But it was adopted for selected areas in Britain from 1977 to 1979 and proved rather successful.[7]

TAX-BASED INCOMES POLICY

In the most general sense the problem of unemployment arises from the problem of wage pressure. Most wages are set by some deliberate process of either wage bargaining or efficiency wages chosen by the employer – and not by the blind forces of supply and demand. There is therefore a huge problem of leap-frogging. Employers get positive net gains from increasing their relative wages (over a range), and decentralised unions take the outside wage as the reference point for their own bargaining position. There is therefore a problem of externality – each wage settlement imposes costs elsewhere.

To offset this, there is a strong theoretical case for a proportional (or other) tax on the level of hourly wages, which could be distributed back in the form of a fixed payment per worker hour. The tax could be levied either on the level of hourly wages or on the growth of hourly wages since the previous year. A tax on the growth of wages had been proposed by Wallich and Weintraub (1971), as well as by Lerner (1978), but not very satisfactorily analysed.

I was much attracted by this idea, as at the least an improvement on the administrative incomes policies of the 1970s. I made it the subject of my inaugural lecture as a Professor (see Chapter 18), and shortly afterwards it was adopted in the platform of the newly-founded Social Democratic Party. I later wrote a book and many more articles, including detailed proposals for implementation.[8]

The main problem was always the risk that the tax would reduce productivity through its negative effect on productivity bargaining or on employers' unilateral efforts to motivate effort by higher pay. This issue is investigated in Chapter 19, with relatively optimistic conclusions.

However tax-based incomes policy has, to my knowledge, never been implemented in OECD countries, though it has been common practice in Eastern Europe and the former Soviet Union, both before and after the end of Communism. This fact reflects a mixture of ignorance (the assumption that a massive bureaucracy is needed) and aversion to government intervention into business matters.

EMPLOYER SOLIDARITY

So nowadays the best hope of preventing leap-frogging is probably through employer solidarity. This has been shown clearly to be a major force against wage-pressure and thus against unemployment (see Chapter 10). Chapter 20 is a plea for more employer solidarity.

BARGAINING OVER EMPLOYMENT

The policies discussed so far are probably the main ones which can really affect unemployment. But there are many others that have been advocated. One, often urged by trade unions, is that employment issues should be covered by employer-union bargains. In the USA this is illegal; in Britain it is unusual – except for matters like severance payments.

What difference would it make if workers bargained over jobs as well as pay? A partial equilibrium approach would lead one to expect more jobs. But a general equilibrium approach shows that there would be no effect on aggregate unemployment (see Chapter 21).

Other widely advocated schemes also fail at the general equilibrium level. These include work-sharing; early retirement; and a general reduction in employers' taxes (see Chapter 10).

EUROPEAN MACROECONOMICS

Most of the preceding papers are relatively timeless – one of the merits of economists is that they stick with on-going problems rather than pretending that the main problems are new. However the last Chapter 22 is a report written for its time. It is one of the reports of the European Commission's Macroeconomic Policy Group, which I drafted in early 1984. The theme of our group both then and later was that European unemployment could be reduced by simultaneous supply-side improvement and demand expansion. Soon after writing it, I decided to launch the Employment Institute, which has campaigned against unemployment ever since. Now in other hands than mine, it continues to show that serious research-based ideas can be translated into practical actions which make life better.

Notes

1. See for example Charter for Jobs (1985). The job guarantee proposal is developed in more detail in Layard (1986).
2. House of Commons Employment Committee (1986); I was adviser to the Committee. For more detail see Layard and Philpott (1991). I was of course much influenced by the Swedish system.
3. For an early analysis of most candidate policies see Johnson and Layard (1986), written in 1983.
4. See for example Jackman and Layard (1986a).
5. Layard (1994).
6. Rehn (1975).
7. For a summary of the evaluations see Layard (1979).
8. See Layard (1982); Jackman and Layard (1982, 1986a and b); Layard and Nickell (1986).

References

Charter for Jobs (1985) *We Can Cut Unemployment* (London: Charter for Jobs).
House of Commons Employment Committee (1986) *Special Employment Measures and the Long Term Unemployed* (London: HMSO).
Jackman, R. and R. Layard (1986a) 'A Wage-Tax, Worker-Subsidy Policy for Reducing the 'Natural' Rate of Unemployment', in W. Beckerman (ed.), *Wage Rigidity and Unemployment* (London: Duckworth) (July).
Jackman, R. and R. Layard (1986b) 'The economic effects of tax-based incomes policy', in D. Colander (ed.), *Incentive-Based Incomes Policies* (New York: Ballinger).
Johnson, G. and R. Layard (1986) 'The natural rate of unemployment: explanation and policy', in O. Ashenfelter and R. Layard (eds), *Handbook of Labor Economics* (Amsterdam: North-Holland).

Layard, R. (1979) 'The costs and benefits of selective employment policies. The British case', *British Journal of Industrial Relations*, 17, (July).

Layard, R. (1982) *More Jobs, Less Inflation* (London: Grant McIntyre).

Layard, R. (1986) *How to Beat Unemployment* (Oxford: Oxford University Press).

Layard, R. (1994) 'The welfare economics of training', in R. Layard, K. Mayhew and G. Owen (eds), *Britain's Training Deficit* (Aldershot: Avebury).

Layard, R. and S. Nickell (1986) 'Unemployment in Britain', *Economica Special Supplement on Unemployment*, 53.

Layard, R. and J. Philpott (1991) *Stopping Unemployment*, The Employment Institute (September).

Lerner, A.P. (1978) 'A wage-increase permit plan to stop inflation', *Brookings Papers on Economic Activity*, 2.

Rehn, G. (1975) 'The fight against stagflation', University of Stockholm (August), mimeo.

Wallich, H.C. and S. Weintraub (1971) 'A tax-based incomes policy', *Journal of Economic Issues*, 5, 1–19.

14 Preventing Long-term Unemployment: An Economic Analysis (1997)*

1 INTRODUCTION AND REVIEW

The EU has set the target of halving unemployment by the year 2000 (CEU, 1993). How can this be done without increasing inflation? The strategy must be to reduce those kinds of unemployment which do little to restrain inflation. The most obvious such category is long-term unemployment.

1.1 Effects of long-term unemployment

Let us examine the evidence. In wage equations long-term unemployment is usually found to have a very small (or zero) effect in reducing wage pressure.[1] The reasons for this are obvious: long-term unemployed people are not good fillers of vacancies. This can be seen from data on exit rates from unemployment: exit rates decline sharply as duration increases. Equally, aggregate time series show that, for a given level of unemployment, vacancies increase the higher the proportion of unemployed who are long-term unemployed.

If long-term unemployment is an optional extra, depending on social institutions, it is not surprising that there are striking differences in its prevalence across countries. As Table 14.1 shows, in the 1980s the majority of countries had between 3 and 6 per cent of the labour force in short-term unemployment (of under a year). But there were huge differences in long-term unemployment. It was under 1 per cent in the USA, Japan, Canada and Sweden and over 8 per cent in Spain, Belgium and Ireland.

Clearly some short-term unemployment is necessary in any economy, to avoid the inflationary pressure which would develop in an over-tight labour market. But long-term unemployment is not needed for this purpose.

---

* Chapter 11 in D. Snower and G. de la Dehesa (eds), *Unemployment Policy: Government options for the Labour Market* (Cambridge: Cambridge University Press for the CEPR, 1997), pp. 333–49.

Table 14.1 Short- and long-term unemployment as a percentage of the labour force, 1980s average

	Long-term	Short-term	Total
Australia	1.9	5.5	7.4
Belgium	8.0	3.0	11.1
Canada	0.8	8.4	9.2
Denmark	2.4	5.6	8.0
Finland	0.7	4.1	4.8
France	3.9	5.0	9.0
Germany	3.0	3.6	6.7
Greece	2.9	3.6	6.6
Ireland	8.1	6.1	14.2
Italy	6.4	3.4	9.9
Japan	0.4	2.0	2.4
Netherlands	4.7	5.0	9.7
New Zealand	0.4	4.1	4.5
Norway	0.2	2.5	2.7
Portugal	2.5	4.7	7.3
Spain	10.1	7.4	17.5
Sweden	0.2	2.2	2.4
UK	4.2	5.2	9.5
USA	0.6	6.5	7.1

Sources: OECD, *Employment Outlook*; OECD, *Labour Force Survey*.

1.2 Causes of long-term unemployment

So how can it be prevented? To consider this we need to know under what conditions it occurs. Figure 14.1 provides a striking clue. It shows on the vertical axis the maximum duration of benefit in each country and on the horizontal axis the percentage of unemployed people in long-term unemployment (over a year). In countries like the USA, Japan, Canada and Sweden benefits run out within a year and so unemployment lasting more than a year is rare. By contrast in the main EU countries benefits have typically been available indefinitely or for a long period, and long-term unemployment is high.

The relationship shown in Figure 14.1 is of course a partial correlation. But if one allows for multiple causation, the effect of benefit duration upon the aggregate unemployment rate remains strong and clear.[2]

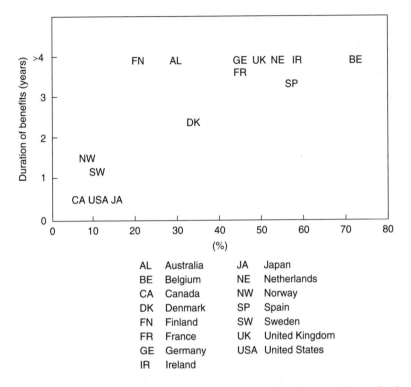

Figure 14.1 Percentage of unemployed people out of work over 12 months, by maximum duration of benefits, 1984

The effect of unemployment benefit availability upon unemployment is not surprising. Unemployment benefits are a subsidy to idleness, and it should not be surprising if they lead to an increase in idleness. In principle, of course, the benefits are meant to protect individuals against an exogenous misfortune and there is meant to be a test of willingness to work. But in practice it is impossible to operate a 'work test' without offering actual work. So after a period of disheartening job search, unemployed individuals often adjust to unemployment as a different life-style.

1.3 Preventing long-term unemployment

What should we do about the situation? One possibility would be to reduce the duration of benefits to, say, one year and put nothing else in its place. This would be the American-style solution. But we know this only works because people thrown onto the labour market accept an ever-widening inequality of wages. A much better approach would be to help people to become more employable so that they would justify a better wage. This leads to our central proposal. After 12 months the state should stop paying people for doing nothing. But at the same time it should accept a responsibility to find them temporary work for at least six months.[3]

In return, the individual would recognise that if he wishes to receive income, he must accept one of a few reasonable offers. These offers would be guaranteed through the state paying to any employer for six months the benefits to which the unemployed individual would have otherwise been entitled.

This would have huge advantages:

(i)   After the 12th month, it would relieve the public finances of any responsibility for people who are already in work. It is very difficult to prevent fraud without being able to offer full-time work.[4]

(ii)   Between months 12 and 18, people would be producing something rather than nothing.

(iii)   But the biggest effect would come after the 18th month. Provided the temporary work had been real work with regular employers, unemployed people would have re-acquired work habits plus the ability to prove their working capacity. They would have a regular employer who could provide a reference – or (even better) retain the individual on a permanent basis. The main justification for the proposal is not that it employs people on a subsidised basis but that, by doing so, it restores them to the universe of employable people. This is an investment in human capital.

That is the central objective of the exercise. Job creation schemes in the past have often failed because the jobs have been marginal and have failed to make the individual more employable thereafter. The job subsidy should therefore be available to any employer (private or public). There should also be the fewest possible restrictions on the kind of work that can be done. Clearly, no employer should be allowed to employ subsidised workers if he is at the same time dismissing regular workers. But there should be no condition (as there was in the UK's former Community Programme) that the work done should be work that would not otherwise be done for the next two years. Such a requirement is a formula for ineffectiveness.

The reason why job creation schemes have so often had these disastrous limiting conditions is the fear of substitution and displacement. This fear is understandable but misplaced.

1.4 Substitution and displacement

Most opposition to active labour market measures is based on fears of displacement and substitution. In their extreme form these derive from the 'lump-of-labour fallacy': there are only so many jobs so, if we enable X to get one of them, some other person goes without work. This is a complete fallacy.

However it is easy to see how it arises. In the most immediate sense, the proposition is true. If an employer has a vacancy and, due to a job subsidy, X gets it rather than Y, Y remains temporarily unemployed. But by definition Y is inherently employable. If he does not get this job, he will offer himself for others. Employers will find there are more employable people in the market and that they can more easily fill their vacancies. This increases downwards pressure on wages, making possible a higher level of employment at the same level of inflationary pressure.

On average over the cycle that level of unemployment is determined at the level needed to hold inflation stable. Active labour market policy increases the number of employable workers, and thus reduces the unemployment needed to control inflation. Equally, in the short run a government that has a given inflation target (or exchange rate target) will allow more economic expansion if it finds that inflationary pressures are less than would otherwise be expected.

Many people find it difficult to believe that (inflationary pressure equal) jobs automatically expand in relation to the employable labour force. So we devote the whole of section 2 of the chapter to that issue.

1.5 Benefits and costs

We can now proceed to sum up the effects of the scheme and its impact on human welfare. In a formal sense, it would abolish long-term unemployment. However this is to over-claim since someone who reverts to unemployment after 18 months (after his temporary job) is not really short-term unemployed, even though this would be his classification in the statistics. So let us consider the impacts on the flow of a cohort entering unemployment.

During the first 12 months, some people may, it is true, delay taking a job because their potential employer has an incentive to wait for the subsidy. But more people will take a job who would not otherwise have done so because they would not like to end up on the programme. The hope is that a completely new climate would develop in which neither individuals nor the Employment Service accept the idea that someone should reach the humiliating position of being confronted with temporary work as the only possible source of income. In Sweden in the 1980s typically about 3 per cent of the workforce reached the 14th month of unemployment (when benefit ran out): in Britain the figure was about five times larger.

Going on, between the 12th and 18th months all the cohort is now employed. After the 18th month the proportion employed should be very much higher than it would have been, due to the employability of those concerned.

Thus it is reasonable to suppose that unemployment would fall by roughly the same size as the stock of long-term unemployed, leading to a substantial increase in production. Suppose average European unemployment fell to 5 per cent compared with a counterfactual rate of, say, 9 per cent. Output would be at a minimum 2 per cent higher.

This is the *social gain* (not to mention an additional non-income-related gain in psychic well-being among those affected). What is the *social cost*? Very little. The Employment Service would need more administrative staff, but this is a tiny cost compared with the gain.[5] (The typical EU country spends only 0.1 per cent of GNP on its Employment Service.)

The balance is also favourable if we focus exclusively on the *benefits and costs to the public finances*:

(i)   After the 12th month the taxpayers stop supporting those who are already fraudulently in work.

(ii)   Between the 12th and 18th month, the taxpayers keep paying benefit but now it goes to employers not workers. However an employer who would anyway have hired somebody unemployed between 12 and 18 months will of course claim the subsidy, so that there would on this account be some deadweight – i.e. extra expenditure.

(iii)   After the 18th month, there will be major savings on benefits and extra taxes received. On any reasonable estimate the total of all these will be a positive saving to the government, and a saving higher than the extra cost of the Employment Service.

1.6   Carrot and stick

Why does this analysis seem so much more cost-effective than most existing active labour market policy? Because it is much more drastic. *Job subsidies without compulsion to accept an offer can easily be ineffective.*

Consider for example the proposal put forward by Snower (1997) which as inspired a recent British government initiative. The idea here is to make possible the conversion of a person's unemployment benefit into an employment subsidy, but not to make it mandatory. While the social net benefits should be positive, they may well be small. Major falls in unemployment are unlikely down this route. What is needed is a shift of regime.[6] No one would now design a system like the existing one. But it requires courage and commitment to change it. One thing, however, is sure. Unless it is changed, we shall be almost as far from the EU's target early next century as we are now.

In the rest of the chapter, we first discuss the issue of substitution and displacement (section 2). We then in section 3 review the effects of existing work-based policies in Sweden and the USA as a basis for evaluation of our own proposal.

2 SUBSTITUTION AND DISPLACEMENT

Programmes to help unemployed people have always been subject to two types of criticism. First, they may help people to do things they would have done anyway. Such expenditure is called 'deadweight' since it has no effect but involves a public outlay. The social cost of this public outlay is the excess burden of the tax that financed the outlay. While this can be an important issue, it is not the main criticism.

The second and more serious objection is that, if unemployed workers get jobs they would not otherwise have got, this may not increase total employment but simply deprive other workers of jobs. This can happen either if each firm employs the same number of people as before but just *substitutes* one lot of workers for another, or if some firms expand employment and output but *displace* employment in other firms.

2.1 No job fund

Such arguments taken to the limit are based on the idea that the total number of jobs is somehow fixed, presumably by the level of aggregate demand. But there is no reason to suppose that demand is ever the main constraint in an economy. The monetary and fiscal authorities can always generate more demand. The constraint is the inflation constraint.

This is illustrated by the Phillips curve. A_0A_0 in Figure 14.2. When the employment rate is about $(1 - u^*)$ inflation tends to rise, and vice versa. Most governments and electorates seem to have some kind of inflation objective. Given this objective, the level of employment depends on u^*. Only policies which alter u^* will change the actual level of unemployment. But, conversely, if a policy reduces u^*, it *will* reduce u. This is illustrated by the new inflation constraint A_1A_1. There is no fixed number of jobs to be done. Given the inflation target, the number of jobs is fixed entirely on the supply side of the economy.

2.2 Employability

The main thing that determines the number of jobs is the number of 'employable' people in the economy. Economists generally take for granted the idea that, *ceteris paribus*, the number of jobs rises in proportion to the labour

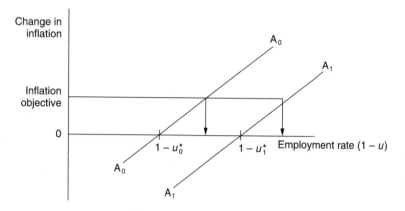

Figure 14.2 The inflation constraint

force, so we will for the moment take that as read. The more difficult issue is the notion of 'employability'. People clearly differ along a wide spectrum of employability. Near one end is A: a skilled worker who is willing to take any job and searches every day. Near the other is B: unskilled worker with an excessive reservation wage who only samples the job market once a month. If there are vacancies, A will probably be hired soon and B after a longer spell of unemployment.

More specifically, we can denote the 'employability' of an individual c_i, and the average employability of all unemployed people c. Then the total number of unemployed people hired in a given period (H) will depend on the number of vacancies (V) and on the number of unemployed people (U) weighted by their average employability (c).[7] Hence

$$H = f(V, cU) \qquad (f_1, f_2 > 0) \tag{14.1}$$

Thus our concept of 'employability' refers to the capacity to fill vacancies.

How, then, does the employability of the unemployed affect the number of jobs (for a given inflation path)? The path of inflation is given by the wage–price spiral, which we shall depict in the simplest possible form. Prices (p) are a mark-up on expected wages (w^e) so that, using small letters for logarithms:

$$p - w^e = \beta_0 \tag{14.2}$$

Wages (w) are a mark-up on expected prices (p^e), and this mark-up is affected by 'inflationary pressure', denoted by Φ and defined below. Thus

$$w - p^e = y_0 + \phi \tag{14.3}$$

Substituting expected prices from (14.2) we have

$$w - w^e = \beta_0 + y_0 + \phi$$

If price inflation is perceived as a random walk, then when $w = w^e$ inflation is stable; when $w > w^e$ inflation falls.

Thus the key determinant of the inflation path is Φ. Evidence suggests strongly that inflationary pressure increases with the chances of finding work for an unemployed person of given employability i.e. $\left(\dfrac{H}{cU}\right)$.[8] Thus

$$w - w^e = \beta_0 + y_0 + y_1 \frac{H}{cU}$$

If unemployment is constant, hires equal separations, i.e. employment (N) times the separation rate (s). So

$$w = w^e = \beta_0 + y_0 + y_1 \frac{s}{cU/N}$$

Hence for a given inflation path, unemployment is inversely proportional to average employability (c).[9]

The basic concept of this chapter is that cU is a constant. More generally, if U_i is the number of unemployed of type i, $\Sigma c_i U_i = $ constant. Going on, we could for simplicity assume that there are only two types of unemployment, short-term and long-term, and that long-term unemployment causes people to be less employable ($c_L < c_S$).[10] It follows that

$$c_s U_s + c_L U_L = \text{constant}$$

From this position we can immediately understand the effect of measures to increase the employability of the long-term unemployed (i.e. to raise c_i). It will be clearest if we simply compare the equilibrium positions before and after c_L is reduced. After c_L has fallen, this is what we observe:

(i)   The inflow into unemployment (sN) is unchanged (and so therefore is the outflow H).[11]

(ii) The exit rate from unemployment for a person with given employability is unchanged, since

$$\frac{H}{c_i U_i} = \frac{H}{cU}$$

Therefore the exit rate from short-term unemployment is unchanged.

(iii) Since (a) the entry to short-term unemployment is unchanged and (b) the exit rate is unchanged, the stock of short-term unemployment is unchanged. Therefore $c_s U_s$ is unchanged.

(iv) It follows that U_L is lower by the same proportion that c_L is higher. Since the outflow from long-term unemployment is given by

$$\frac{H_L}{c_L U_L} = \frac{H}{cU}$$

it follows that the long-term unemployed are filling exactly the same number of vacancies per period as before. *They do not prevent a single extra short-term unemployed person from being hired.* What happens is that there are fewer long-term unemployed but they are being hired at a faster rate. The position is illustrated in Figure 14.3.

Thus there is no substitution or displacement whatever in aggregate terms. Because long-term unemployed are more employable, their numbers fall. Total hirings of long-term unemployed have not increased.

In the transition from one equilibrium to another the hirings of long-term unemployed people do, of course, increase. But so, of course, do total hirings, which is the method by which employment increases and unemployment falls.

2.3 The proposed scheme

The preceding analysis does not of course reflect in detail our proposed scheme. In Figure 14.3, we assume that all who complete short-term unemployment enter long-term unemployment, but that people are helped to leave at double the previous rate. We can now depict our own scheme more exactly in Figure 14.4. In between short-term unemployment and long-term unemployment there is a six-month period of temporary work. This leads to two extra flows. Some people who complete short-term unemployment do not take temporary jobs (J). And some who take temporary jobs never re-enter unemployment at the 18th month. Total unemployment falls by the fall in U_L.

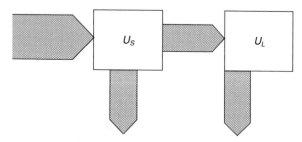

Figure 14.3   Stocks and flows

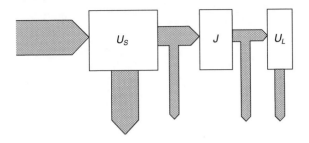

Figure 14.4   The Layard scheme

2.4   People cause jobs

Finally we revert to the question of whether in given institutional conditions the labour force determines the number of jobs (taking the cycle as a whole). Economists take this for granted, but rarely bother to document it. This is done in Figure 14.5. As the graph shows, there is nothing special about the USA or Japan as creators of jobs, as is constantly alleged. They just happen to be good creators of people.[12]

To ram home the point, Figure 14.6 shows that the same applies to 'jobs for men' and 'jobs for women'. These do not go their own merry way. They respond with remarkable precision to the ratios of men and women in the labour force. In almost every country the proportion of men aged 16–64 wanting to work has fallen and the proportion of women wanting to work has risen. This is the overwhelming source of the fall in the male–female ratio in employment, which has tended to occur within nearly all industries.

3   RELEVANT EXPERIENCE

What empirical evidence is there that could throw light on the feasibility of our proposal or its effects? We are aware of only two main types of evidence that really help.

First there is cross-sectional evidence of decadal unemployment rates across countries having different ways of treating unemployed people (see Figure 14.7). In Layard *et al.* (1994) we estimated such a regression, which showed that unemployment increases with the duration of unemployment benefit and falls with expenditure on active labour market policy (per unemployed person). Only with these variables is it possible to explain the extraordinarily low rate of unemployment in Sweden throughout the 1970s

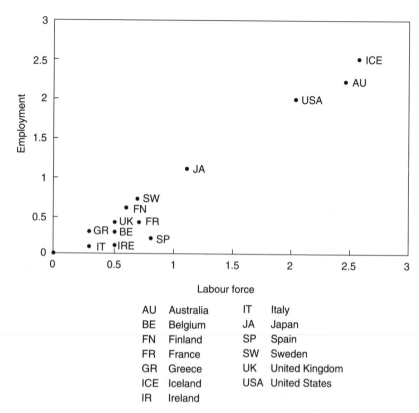

Figure 14.5   Percentage growth in the labour force and in employment, 1960–89, annual average percentage change
Source: OECD.

and 1980s (around 2 per cent on average). Sweden operated and still operates essentially the system we have been advocating.

Second, there are the randomised experiments with 'conditionality' for recipients of AFDC in the USA (Gueron, 1990). These show that AFDC recipients who are exposed to work requirements subsequently became more likely to be in work, and had higher earnings and lower AFDC receipts – adding up to higher total incomes.

Our proposal is, we believe, immune to the criticisms of many training programmes offered to unemployed people. These often show a poor rate of

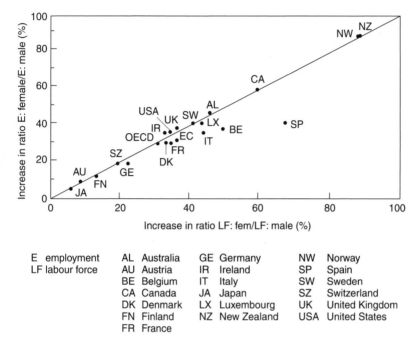

Figure 14.6 Change in relative labour force, and change in relative employment, by sex, 1970–90

return, especially when those retrained had little previous skill or where the quality of training was poor. For most people whose previous work experience was semi- or unskilled the best way to become employable is to work. We believe that only a regime change which makes this the normal course of affairs can make major inroads on European unemployment.

Notes

I am grateful to the ESRC and the Esmée Fairbairn Charitable Trust for financial support.

1. All remarks in this paragraph are based on Layard *et al.* (1991, Chapter 4). They apply only to countries which encourage long-term unemployment. The situation is different in the USA where there are no UI benefits for the long-term unemployed.

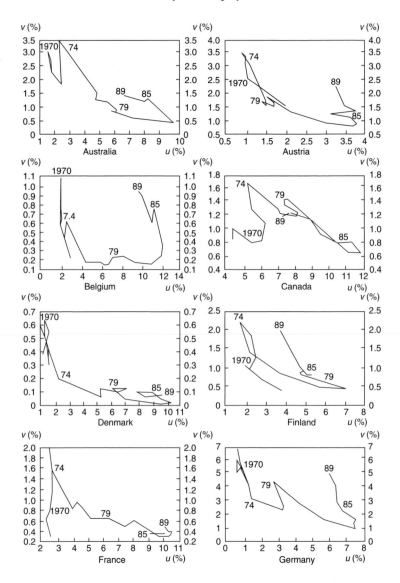

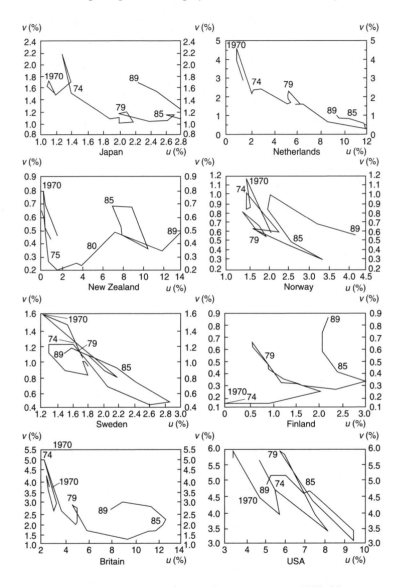

Figure 14.7   Vacancy rates, *v*, and unemployment rates, *u*, 1970–85

2.   Layard *et al.* (1994, p. 82). The other causal variables in the equation relate to the replacement ratio, active labour market policy, collective bargaining and the change in inflation.
3.   As in Sweden, anyone who failed to find regular work within that period would be entitled to go back onto benefits after six months; but re-entry onto benefits would be conditional on having worked at least 15 out of the last 52 weeks.
4.   In Sweden two-thirds of those entitled to temporary jobs because their benefits have come to an end do not exercise their right to subsidised work.
5.   We personally strongly favour more retraining of skilled workers with obsolete skills but in this chapter we focus on a virtually costless proposal.
6.   In passing, note that we have not suggested doing anything extra for the existing long-term unemployed. This is deliberate. Helping people who are already long-term unemployed is very difficult, and can easily fail. Therefore *prevent* long-term unemployment, and let the existing long-term unemployed find their own solutions within the existing programmes, as eventually they will.
7.   It is easy to allow for job competition from other employed people, but this makes no difference of substance.
8.   It may also increase with the duration of vacancies

$$\left(\frac{V}{H}\right).$$

But from (1) these two variables are positively related. Since (1) must exhibit constant returns to scale (in a large enough market),

$$\frac{H}{cU} = f\left(\frac{V}{cU}, 1\right)$$

and

$$1 = f\left(\frac{V}{H}, \frac{cU}{H}\right).$$

9.   In a more fully dynamic context we need to allow for changes in U. Since $\Delta U = sN - H$, $H/cU = (s - \Delta U)/N)/cU/N$.
10.   There are also of course selectivity reasons why the long-term unemployed have lower exit rates than short-term unemployed. But Layard *et al.* (1991) provides powerful evidence that long-term unemployment also *causes* lower employability.
11.   If s is constant, there is a second-order rise in sN and H, due to the rise in N.
12.   If the population of working age is used on the horizontal axis, the diagram still works well.

References

CEU (1993) *Growth, Competitiveness, Employment, The Challenges and Ways Forward into the 21st Century* (Brussels: Commission of the European Communities).
Gueron, J.M. (1990) 'Work and Welfare: Lessons on Employment Programs', *Journal of Economic Perspectives*, 4, 79–98.

Layard, R., S. Nickell and R. Jackman (1991) *Unemployment: Macroeconomic Performance and the Labour Market* (Oxford: Oxford University Press).

Layard, R., S. Nickell and R. Jackman (1994) *The Unemployment: Crisis* (Oxford: Oxford University Press).

Snower, D. (1997) 'The Simple Economics of Benefit Transfers', Chapter 6 in D. Snower and G. de la Dehesa (eds), *Unemployment Policy: Government Options for the Labour Market* (Cambridge: Cambridge University Press for the CEPR).

15 Preventing Long-term Unemployment: Strategy and Costings (1997)*

1 RATIONALE FOR PREVENTING LONG-TERM UNEMPLOYMENT

No free society has been able to contain inflation without having some unemployment. For wage inflation gets bid up unless employers face a reasonable supply of attractive applicants for their vacancies. But long-term unemployment does not provide such a supply of applicants. The longer people have been unemployed the less attractive they are to employers, as is illustrated dramatically in Figure 15.1. So long-term unemployment fails to control inflation, and at the same time is deeply damaging to the unemployed. It is therefore a total waste, economic and social. Although we now have the same level of vacancies as in 1972, we have eight times more long-term unemployed.

So the most dependable way open to us for reducing unemployment is to eliminate long-term unemployment. And the way to do this is to prevent people entering it. For, once people have entered, they become much more difficult to help in a cost-effective way. Thus *the key strategy is to have some positive solution for everybody by the time they reach the beginning of long-term unemployment*. This would normally mean within 6 months for the under 25s and within 12 months for the rest.

2 LESSONS FROM EXPERIENCE[1]

As the Swedish experience shows, it is very important to have something to offer to *everybody* in the group. For this ensures not only that all who need help get it, but also that those who do not need help (and therefore do not accept it) cease to be able to collect benefit. In Sweden benefit lasts 14 months and after that everyone is entitled to income support in the form of a guaranteed (temporary) job or training course. Only about a half of those entitled to such a job claim it, and the numbers of unemployed who find jobs on their own rises sharply as the end of benefits approaches. This 'sorting' effect is an important

---

* Employment Policy Institute, *Economic Report*, 11 (4) (March 1997), pp. 1–17.

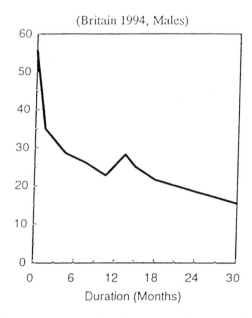

Figure 15.1 Percentage of unemployed people leaving unemployment in next 3 months, by duration of unemployment experienced so far
Source: These data relate to registered (claimant) unemployed and come from the *Employment Gazette* for 1994 and 1995.

reason why a policy of offering help to everyone can be quite cost-effective in public expenditure terms. It is also effective in real social terms. The evidence suggests that in Sweden the labour market policy reduces unemployment by at least 2 percentage points.

During the 1990s Denmark, Switzerland and Australia have moved towards the Swedish system. The Australian experience is particularly instructive. Their 1994 white paper called Working Nation promised a job to everyone unemployed for over 18 months.[2] But the Australians have failed to deliver their promise. The reason is that the Employment Services suddenly had to try to find something both for the 'flow' (everyone reaching 18 months) and for the 'backlog' (who were already unemployed for over 18 months). This was too great a challenge. It is probably better to begin with the manageable challenge of preventing *entry* to long-term unemployment and only a year later to guarantee something to the remaining backlog. (This suggestion has the support of many within the British Employment Service.)

The next question is, Which elements in the possible package of measures are the most cost-effective? There is a good deal of evidence on this, based either on controlled experiments (where some groups have been deliberately 'treated' and some not) or using statistical analysis of non-experimental situations. The view of OECD experts is that on average the cost-effectiveness of the different measures is in this order (starting with the most effective).[3]

(1) Job-search measures

These include counselling, job placement assistance, stricter tests of actively-seeking work, Job Clubs, etc. In Britain the Restart Programme appears to have reduced long-term unemployment by up to 10 per cent. More recently Project Work appears to be having an even stronger effect. The finding that job-search matters reinforces the view that it is crucial to be able to *offer* something to everyone. For no test of individual 'availability for work' can ever be fully effective unless work is made available.

(2) Recruitment subsidies

These have been a long-standing feature of the Swedish system (50 per cent of the wage can be paid for the first 6 months to a firm hiring a long-term unemployed person (LTU)). Recruitment subsidies have now become more central in Sweden, as belief in public sector job-creation has ebbed there, as in the rest of Europe. France has now made recruitment subsidies their key tool against unemployment and will subsidise 50 per cent of the wage for the first 2 years for anyone hiring an LTU (unemployed over a year). Their mistake is that they are not aiming at securing an offer for every LTU so that they will not have the advantage of the 'sorting' effect which results from a universal scheme.

In Britain we have two small-scale localised experiments to go on. The Workstart Programme is a recruitment subsidy of £60 per week for 6 months, followed by £30 per week for another 6 months, paid to employers hiring people unemployed for over 2 (or in one case 4) years. No attempt was made to find jobs for all such unemployed people in the locality, so that those recruited may have been of above average quality in their group. Employers were pleased with the quality of their recruits; 64 per cent said they were adequately skilled, and 83 per cent planned to keep them on after the subsidy ran out. Strikingly, one third of the vacancies had been hard to fill; employers were grateful that the Employment Service had sent along some candidates. This again illustrates the importance of effective job-placement in combatting unemployment.

One further finding is relevant. Employers were asked how they would have responded to a lower subsidy. Their replies showed that this would reduce the cost-effectiveness of the subsidy because a low subsidy would barely affect employers' behaviour.[4] This illustrates the ease of wasting money on labour market policy unless the policies are well designed.

Most of the jobs were provided by small firms, as occurs with wage subsidies in any country. Unfortunately there has been no follow-up of the subsequent history of people on Workstart, but the Institute of Employment Studies report on Workstart states the belief that even if people 'return to work at a relatively low rung on the job-ladder, it is nevertheless one from which they are better placed to progress than they were before'.

The government has now initiated a second experiment known as Project Work, which comes somewhat nearer what we have in mind. In certain areas all those unemployed for over 2 years get 13 weeks of intensive job-search help, including the offer of recruitment subsidies. Those who still have no work at the end of the 13 weeks get 13 weeks on a job-creation project.

(3) Job-creation projects (public or voluntary), such as the former Community Programme

This approach used to be favoured on the grounds that it would provide additional employment, while subsidised jobs provided by regular employers might simply displace other jobs. However job-creation programmes have three main difficulties. They cost more in terms of supervision, materials and possibly wages. They are inherently temporary and leave the client looking for work again at the end of the period. And they do not provide such a convincing work record as work with a regular employer. Indeed the British Community Programme was closed down in the late 1980s following the Normington Report which alleged that the pace of work was slow and the preparation given for 'real' work inadequate. For these reasons the emphasis in Europe is increasingly on getting the unemployed directly into employment with regular employers (even if there is sometimes a time limit on the contract).

This reflects in part a new view of the labour market which focuses more on labour market flows and outcomes than on the snapshot picture while people are on the programme. Policy is now judged more by its results in terms of future behaviour, and policies which involve mainly marking time have rightly fallen from favour. This new view of course partly reflects the perceptions of the unemployed themselves who have become increasingly sceptical of 'schemes' that lead nowhere.

(4) Adult training

It is surprising, but true, that training programmes for unemployed adults rarely show up in any country as very effective. Clearly some of them are, but the generality are not. They seem to be difficult to organise. Probably the most

successful are where a worker already has a skill which has become obsolete
and he now needs a new one. *Up* skilling after the age of 25 or so seems to be
very difficult.

For most adults the best thing is to find them an employer and leave it to the
employer to provide what training he thinks appropriate. But for under 25s we
should of course place a high priority on skill formation, with a strong
component of part-time or full-time off-the-job education. And for any worker
lacking basic skills of literacy and numeracy we should provide an intensive
course to equip them for the modern work environment. Where there is any
doubt unemployed people could be tested for literacy and numeracy to ensure
that this is not a barrier to their employment.

3   PROGRAMME STRUCTURE

Against this background, we can list some of the main decisions which need to
be taken in relation to:

(i)   those 18–25 unemployed for over 6 months,
(ii)   other long-term unemployed.

Recruitment rebates

1   How central a role should they play?

The evidence in section 2 suggests that recruitment rebates should be the
central tool, since it would be far better to get people back into contact with
regular employers than have them in some temporary situation on benefit plus,
outside the regular labour market. The latter is not the kind of experience that
employers value when they are looking for staff.

We should of course empower the individual to take the subsidy to any
employer and not confine the searching to the Employment Service. This could
be embedded in a clear promotion document made available to the
unemployed person.

The main argument against recruitment rebates is that the people hired as a
result of the subsidy may displace different people who would otherwise have
been hired: these people then become unemployed, so that total unemployment falls little if at all. The argument is fundamentally unsound. For the other
people who would have been hired are clearly attractive to employers. If they
are not hired 'here', they will soon be used by other employers to fill their
vacancies.

This is exactly the same process as occurs when a business ceases to hire
people. When hiring ceases there is of course a temporary rise in
unemployment, but soon those who would have been hired fill other vacancies

and the labour market adjusts. There is no permanent rise in unemployment (except perhaps in an isolated company town). Yet all traditional analyses of recruitment subsidies assume a permanent rise in unemployment in the rest of the economy. These analyses have no scientific foundation.[5]

In an isolated labour market the adjustment process can of course be difficult – and the problem of substitution is more serious. In such areas there will have to be major job-creation projects as well – and there will almost certainly have to be *some* job-creation projects in every area, in order to deliver the guarantee of job offers for everyone.

But the priority objective should be to get people into normal jobs at the regular workplace. If possible, people should be hired on indefinite contracts, but we could probably not get enough places if we refused to subsidise employers offering only temporary contracts: even when a person is hired on a temporary contract there is a chance he will be made permanent. But we should discourage 'churning' – where an employer sacks one person who is not subsidised and replaces him by someone else who is.

2   Should recruitment rebates apply in the public and voluntary sectors as well as the private sectors?

This seems the obvious approach.[6] It would be far better to get people taken on in these sectors as normal employees, working for a wage, than as temporary workers on a scheme for benefit plus. The local authorities and NHS should be able to play an important role as recruiters of the LTU. So should voluntary bodies. We should not find so many places in this way as we could if we allowed these sectors to employ people on benefit plus. But the places we got would be more worthwhile. We do not want to re-create the large 'unemployment industry' of the 1980s, with low quality supervisors supervising low quality activities. Only as a fall back should we have job-creation projects on benefit plus.

3   What level of rebate?

The basic idea of the rebate is that we *use the benefit money for a better purpose*. Thus the simple principle of benefit transfer is attractive. It is however less administratively simple than a flat rate 'rebate'. I suggest £60 for 18–24 and £75 for 25+. (This compares with average benefit rates of £37 for 18–24 and £70 for 25+).

4   What conditions?

People should be paid the rate for the job.[7] They should be employed for normal full-time working hours.[8] (The client group will include few people wanting part-time work.) Other normal conditions of work should apply.[9]

What about a training requirement? Such a requirement will undoubtedly make it more difficult to find the requisite number of jobs. Even if the off-the-job training is paid for out of public funds, day release disrupts the firm's schedule of work. If enforced on the individual, it also singles them out from other workers doing the same job in a way which the individual might resent. However it would be necessary to insist on day release for all youngsters on the programme who have not reached Intermediate level qualifications.

We turn now to the fall-back provision of direct job creation.

Job creation and the environmental task force

1 How would workers be paid?

Workers should be impatient to get into regular jobs. Thus it makes sense to have the fall-back activity paid at benefit plus £20 (similar to current practice in Sweden). In any case there are substantial other costs of supervision and materials, and we cannot afford to pay people more. Work should be full-time (to discourage fraud).

2 How would it be organised?

The best strategy would be for the money to go through the Employment Service – they have to find solutions for their clients and they should have the money to buy the solutions. They should invite bids from local authorities, voluntary organizations and others who want to organise these activities.

Full-time education

Full-time education may be the best route for some people. At present a person cannot continue to draw benefit if they study for over 16 hours a week. This should be changed and the LTU (as defined below) should be allowed one period of 6 months' study on benefit on a work-related sub-degree course leading to a national qualification. However no one should be put in a position where they *have* to do this – thus the guarantee should relate to an offer of work, but education could be chosen in lieu.

4 COVERAGE AND PHASING

The Labour Party is committed to guaranteeing opportunity for every person aged 18–25 unemployed over 6 months and all others unemployed over 2 years. There is a strong case for reconsidering the 2-year cut-off. Sweden has a one-year cut-off on the grounds that after one year people become increasingly difficult to help. Thus it is more cost-effective to help them after one year rather than later.

Moreover as we shall see later, even offering something to everyone after one year may not reduce unemployment in total by more than 450,000. To attempt anything less would be inadequate.

However we cannot attempt everything at once. It is *vital to succeed at each stage*, unlike the Australians. For this and many other reasons it is right to start with the under 25s, and it would be a mistake to simultaneously attempt the most difficult thing – to help all the existing people unemployed over 2 years.

I would suggest the following approach.

(i) Start with 18–24 years olds unemployed at 6 months plus in 1998, and include 25–34 year olds at 12 months plus in 1999, 35–44 year olds at 12 months plus in 2000, and so on.

(ii) The commitment to the backlog in each age group who are already LTU should permit a delay of up to a year. Thus with 18–24 year olds we should guarantee a solution to all who reach 6 months + by say beginning-1998, while the guarantee to those already over 6 months would come in by end-1998. This would substantially reduce the numbers in the backlog whom the Employment Service had to handle. In terms of public presentation the government could simply say that all 18–24 year olds reaching 6 months' unemployment are guaranteed a place by end-1998 but administratively instruct the Employment Service to handle the whole flow by beginning-1998.

Thus there could be a well-conceived and feasible programme which could be announced soon after the election. It could look like the scheme in Table 15.1.

The numbers that would have to be financed are shown in Appendix Table 15A.3. The commitment to the flow is of course on-going and represents the main commitment. Altogether it builds up to a commitment to place 700,000

Table 15.1 Guaranteed offers will be made by the following dates (January)

	1998	1999	2000	2001	2002
18–24 (6 months +)	Flow	Backlog			
25–34 (12 months +)		Flow	Backlog		
35–44 (12 months +)			Flow	Backlog	
45+ (12 months +)				Flow	Backlog

people a year. This sounds a lot until one realises that there are already this number of people flowing out of LTU each year – the problem is that they waste so long in LTU before flowing out. Our aim is to use the benefit money to make people flow out faster – not actually to place more people.

The only exception to the above is the additional commitment to do something for the backlog. This is a very difficult extra task, which is why the government should be cautious in how it expresses its commitment.

5 ADMINISTRATION: THE EMPLOYMENT SERVICE

None of this will work without a proper proactive Employment Service, with a clear method of handling each unemployed person.

(i) Every unemployed person should have an individual *caseworker*, whose job it is to find a solution within 6 months (if under 25) or 12 months (if over 25).

(ii) The *finance* for recruitment rebates and job-creation should go through the Employment Service, so that they can do their job. Education finance too should possibly go through the Employment Service rather than the TECs.

(iii) Unemployed people should be *interviewed* every month after the 3rd month (if under 25) or the 6th month (if over 25).[10] The Employment Service should also have resources to send anyone who needs it on an intensive Basic Skills course and to require half-time attendance at a Job Club in the 3 months before the job guarantee comes into force.

(iv) The *recruitment rebate* should be payable from the 22nd week (if under 25) and the 48th week (if over 25) so that by the deadline everybody had received at least two offers. In the worst case one or even both of these offers would be on job-creation schemes. People could not draw benefit after the deadline, if they had rejected two offers.

(v) After 13 weeks of employment all *employers should report* on the progress of those hired. If they do not plan to retain the worker, they should provide a profile and evaluation. The Employment Service should then make strenuous efforts to place the individual.

Staffing

The Employment Service now has 30,000 staff to handle around 2,000,000 people at any one time – roughly 1 to 70. They could probably find the number of places we are describing (with more intensive placement efforts) if they had

10 per cent more staff. One reason why no larger increase is required is of course that LTU would decrease, reducing the caseload at the same time that intensity per client was increased. The cost of such a 10 per cent increase is of the order of £50 million.

6 EFFECTS AND COSTS

Effects on unemployment

In thinking about the effects on unemployment, we make the following assumptions.

1. Only 80 per cent of those eligible to participate do so, as with Project Work.[11]
2. After the sixth month of supported work, 60 per cent of participants return to unemployment; their chances of leaving unemployment are then the same as at present for people with the same elapsed time since originally entering unemployment (counting the 6 months work experience as unemployment in this calculation).
3. The resulting fall in unemployment has some effect of displacing other workers, who are not then absorbed elsewhere, but swell the ranks of the unemployed. We assume that each initial fall in unemployment induces a 30 per cent increase in unemployment elsewhere through displacement.[12] This is a generous assumption, given the way in which the economy generally absorbs displaced workers.[13]

On this basis unemployment falls within 5 years by 440,000, as shown in Table 15.2. The figures are of course subject to considerable uncertainty.

Table 15.2 Fall in claimant unemployment (000s) (annual average)

	1997/8	1998/9	1999/2000	2000/1	2001/2	2002/3
Under 25s	10	70	120	120	120	120
Over 25s	0	0	100	190	300	320
Total	10	70	220	310	420	440

Cost

In estimating the cost, we assume the following

1. Participants are divided as follows (%)

	18–24	25
Recruitment subsidies	60	75
Full time education	15	–
Job-creation	25	25
	100	100

2. Of the 18–24 year olds not in full-time education, one half are on day release. Full-time education costs £1,500 p.a. and day release £500 p.a. People in full-time education are on benefit.
3. Job-creation costs £60 a week per place in supervision and materials. (The Community Programme cost £30 for half-time jobs and was very low quality.) People are on benefit plus £20. So this is the most expensive option.

   The gross cost to the government (excluding continuing payment of benefit) is shown in Table 15.3. The resulting savings which are subject to considerable uncertainty are shown in Table 15.4. Table 15.5 gives the net cost. By the end of a Parliament there is no net cost. But during the time when the programme is being brought in, there is substantial net cost because some of the savings come later than the outlays and there is the one-off cost of dealing with the backlog.

Table 15.3 Gross cost to government (£ million)

	1997/8	1998/9	1999/2000	2000/1	2001/2	2002/3
Under 25s	30	490	430	430	430	430
Over 25s	0	10	450	560	800	580
Job Clubs	0	60	80	90	110	110
Basic Skills	0	10	20	20	20	20
Employment Service	40	50	60	60	60	50
University for Industry	10	20	30	40	40	30
Total	80	640	1,070	1,200	1,460	1,220

Table 15.4 Savings by government (£ million)

	1997/8	1998/9	1999/2000	2000/1	2001/2	2002/3
Benefits						
Under 25s	0	30	130	130	130	130
Over 25s	0	10	280	580	910	1,010
NI and Housing Benefit	0	0	130	270	420	470
Total	0	40	540	980	1,460	1,610

Table 15.5 Total net cost to government (£ million)

	1997/8	1998/9	1999/2000	2000/1	2001/2	2002/3
Cost (from Table 15.3) Net Savings (from Table 15.4)	80	610	520	220	0	−390

Over the life of a 5-year Parliament the gross cost is £4.5 billion and the net cost is £1.5 billion, which, as the Labour Party has suggested, could be financed by a Windfall Tax on the excess profits of the privatised utilities.

7 CONCLUSION

It *is* possible to achieve a major permanent fall in unemployment if the right strategy is adopted. This is to prevent people entering long-term unemployment, through guaranteed offers of work. These should be introduced on a carefully phased basis, beginning with the under 25s. Now, during an economic recovery, is the ideal moment to introduce such a fundamental reform, which would prevent the waste of taxpayers' money and transform the lives of millions of our people.

Appendix: Background Tables

Table 15A.1 Numbers currently unemployed, October 1996 (000s)

Age	Under 6 months	6–12 months	12–18 months	18–24 months	24 months and over	Total
18–24	296	94	54	22	42	508
25–34	246	111	65	38	131	590
35–44	137	67	39	24	103	370
45+	175	93	48	31	146	492
Total	853	365	205	115	423	1,961

Table 15A.2 Flows per half-year, October 1996 (000s)

18–24 (past 6 months)	161
24–34 (past 12 months)	78
35–44 (past 12 months)	46
45+ (past 12 months)	61

Table 15A.3 Number of people being subsidized (person-years, 000s)

		1997/8	1998/9	1999/2000	2000/1	2001/2	2002/3
18–24 (6 months+)	Flow	8	121	129	129	129	129
	Backlog	0	26	0	0	0	0
25–34 (12 months+)	Flow	0	4	58	62	62	62
	Backlog	0	0	53	0	0	0
35–44 (12 months+)	Flow	0	0	2	34	36	36
	Backlog	0	0	0	41	0	0
45+ (12 months+)	Flow	0	0	0	3	46	49
	Backlog	0	0	0	0	58	0
Total		8	151	242	270	332	276

Source of Tables

Table 15.2: Fall in claimant unemployment (annual average)

In steady state:

(i)	Numbers unemployed in Table 15.A.1 for 6–12 months (under 25) and 12–18 months (over 25) × (0.2 + 0.8 (0.7))
+	
(ii)	Numbers unemployed 12–18 months (under 25) and 18–24 months (over 25) × (0.2 + 0.8 (0.4) (0.7))
+	
(iii)	Numbers unemployed over 18 months (under 25) and over 24 months (over 25) × (0.2 + 0.8 (0.4) (0.7))

In first year:

(i)	Above × 0.06

In second year:

(i)	Above × 0.94
+	
(ii)	Above × 0.25
+	
(iii)	Backlog

Table 15.3: Gross cost to government

Under 25s:

Recruitment rebate =	Table 15A.3 × 0.60 × 60 × 52
Job-creation =	Table 15A.3 × 0.25 × 80 × 52
Education =	Table 15A.3 × 0.15 × 30 × 52
Training =	Table 15A.3 × 0.42 × 10 × 52

Over 25s:

Recruitment rebate =	Table 15A.3 × 0.75 × 75 × 52
Job-creation =	Table 15A.3 × 0.25 × 80 × 52

Job clubs:
> Number now unemployed 3–6 months (under 25) and 9–12 months (over 25) – appropriately phased. Cost per person-year assumed to be £500.

Basic Skills:
> Same groups as job clubs. Assume one-fifth participate at cost of £500 per course.

Table 15.4: Savings by government

Under 25s:
> 37 × 52 × (Table 15.2–Table 15A.3 (× 0.40))

Over 25s:
> 70 × 52 × (Table 15.2–Table 15A.3 (× 0.25))

NI and Housing Benefit:

Under 25s:
> 2 × 52 × (Table 15.2–Table 15A.3 (× 0.40))

Over 25s:
32 × 52 × (Table 15.2–Table 15A.3 (× 0.25))

Table 15.5: Total net cost to government

Tables 15.3 and 15.4

Table 15A.1:   Numbers currently unemployed, October 1996

Employment Trends. (December 1996, Table 2.6).

Table 15A.2   Flows per half-year

Ditto

Table 15A.3   Number of people being subsidised (person-years)

'Flow' in steady state =	Table 15A.2 × 0.8
'Flow' in first year =	Table 15A.2 × 0.8 × 0.06
'Flow' in second year =	Table 15A.2 × 0.8 × 0.94
'Backlog' =	Number unemployed beyond 18 months (under 25) and beyond 24 months (over 25) × 0.8 × 0.5

Notes

1.   I am grateful to Tim Hughes and Fernando Goni for statistical help, and to Richard Jackman for constant advice.
2.   They also abolished unemployment benefit for people under 18, replacing it by a training guarantee.
3.   See Fay (1995).
4.   This is confirmed by recent experience of the NI rebate for hiring long-term unemployed. See also Stern *et al.* (1995, p. 28) showing that the proportion of deadweight increases as the level of subsidy falls.
5.   See for example Layard (1997, pp. 62–3).
6.   Most wage subsidy schemes abroad cover all sectors of employment.
7.   This would in effect ensure that everyone was employed on an income higher than benefits. For people with children, Family Credit would ensure this; and for childless people a Minimum Wage would have the same effect. Housing Benefit would of course also be payable in employment where appropriate.
8.   People on Income Support have to be available for full-time work. Those on UB have to have been in full-time work.
9.   We need to ensure that a worker who is helped but is not kept on by the first employer does not simply revert to unemployment. One possible step is to always offer help to the partner as well, where that partner is out of work (even if not a claimant).

10. This approach would build on existing experience with the programmes known as 1–2–1, Workwise and Jobplan.
11. For reference, note that, if all participated, the 'deadweight' would be approximately
18–24 (6–12 months) 45 per cent; 25–34 (12–18 months) 25 per cent; 35–44 (12–18 months) 30 per cent; 45+ (12–18 months) 30 per cent.
12. Some of these displaced workers may reach the point where they themselves qualify for entry to the subsidised programme. However, it is not possible to know how many there would be, and the number would not be large relative to the margins of error of the existing calculation.
13. See Layard *What Labour Can Do*, Warner Books, (1997 pp. 62–3).

References

Atkinson, J. and N. Meager (1994) 'Evaluation of Workstart Pilots', Institute for Employment Studies, *Report*, 279.
Carling, K. *et al.* (1994) 'Unemployment Duration, Unemployment Benefits, and Labour Market Programmes in Sweden', mimeo.
Fay, R. (1995) 'Enhancing the Effectiveness of Active Labour Market Policies. The Role of and Evidence from Programme Evaluations in OECD Countries' (Paris: OECD).
Layard, R., S. Nickell and R. Jackman (1991) *Unemployment: Macreconomic Performance and the Labour Market* (Oxford: Oxford University Press).
Jackman, R., R. Layard and S. Nickell (1996) 'Combatting Unemployment: Is Flexibility Enough?', in *Macroeconomic Policies and Structural Reform* (Paris: OECD), Chapter 10 in this volume.
Layard, R. (1997) *What Labour Can Do* (London: Warner Books).
Layard, R. and J. Philpott (1991) *Stopping Unemployment*, The Employment Institute (September).
OECD (1993) *Employment Outlook* (July).
Stern, J. *et al.* (1995) *OECD Wage Subsidy Evaluations: Lessons for Workstart* (NERA) (November).
(1994) *Working Nation. The White Paper on Employment and Growth* (Canberra: Australian Government Publishing Service).

16 The Efficiency Case for Long-run Labour Market Policies (1980)*

with R. Jackman

INTRODUCTION AND SUMMARY

Can long-run labour market policies do any good? Or, in other words, is there a role for labour market intervention, independent of the business cycle?[1] The test is, of course, whether it could raise the level of welfare consistent with non-accelerating inflation. One obvious case that calls for intervention is where real wages or relative wages are rigid. But there has been a tendency to suppose that, if wages were flexible, there could be no free lunch.[2] We therefore begin with the case of flexible wages, before considering the case of wage rigidity.

If wages were flexible, there would be no free lunch if there were no distortions in the labour market. However, the payment of unemployment benefit leads to such distortions. We assume that the solution of reducing benefit is ruled out on equity and insurance grounds. Given whatever benefit exists, there will be opportunities for reducing its efficiency cost by appropriate policies on wage subsidies, public employment or training. Provided that at the same time these policies do not dis-equalize the distribution of income, they ought to be followed. The policies we consider satisfy this equity condition, so we therefore concentrate on evaluating their efficiency effects in the standard fashion (see for example Harberger, 1971), though we do also measure the effects on output and employment, which have been the main criteria used by other writers.

The analysis is confined to the case of two types of labour (for example, skilled and unskilled). If unemployment benefit is being paid and wages are *flexible*, we show in Section 1 that efficiency can be increased if

(a) the supply of workers is more elastic in one market than the other; or
(b) the proportional distortion is greater in one market than the other.

* *Economica*, 47 (August 1980), pp. 331–49.
We are extremely grateful to George Johnson for invaluable help – our paper and his, though conceived independently, are concerned with closely related problems. We would also like to thank the Esmée Fairbairn Charitable Trust for financial support.

If demand-side policies are being used (wage subsidies and public employment), demand should be shifted towards the group with the higher supply elasticity or the higher proportional distortion. Since distortions are greatest in the low-wage market, the usual equity case for shifting demand towards unskilled workers is now reinforced by an efficiency argument. Our model thus provides an argument for greater progressivity, but only in so far as the existing structure fails to reflect the moral hazard implicit in the unemployment benefit system.

If wages are flexible, it makes no difference on which side of the market the subsidy and tax are levied. However, if unskilled wages are in some sense *rigid*, there is obviously no efficiency case for subsidizing the unskilled worker's pay packet. The subsidy must be paid to the employer, where it will lead to an efficiency gain by bringing the demand for unskilled workers up towards the supply. All this is well known, but it is less obvious how the tax on the skilled workers should be levied (see Section 4). This depends on the form of wage rigidity that is postulated. There is, however, evidence that suggests that the gross wages of the unskilled may be rigid *relative* to the skilled. In this situation, it is much better to levy any tax on skilled workers via the employer rather than the worker. For, if the tax is levied on the worker, it will tend to raise the gross wage of skilled workers. The gross wage of the unskilled will then have to rise in proportion, owing to the rigid differential, and this will reduce the demand for their services. Thus there seems to be a strong case for making employer taxes the main vehicle for progressivity in the tax system. This will reduce the labour cost of unskilled labour in two ways: first the tax on skilled workers will lead to a lower gross wage for the unskilled; and, second, the subsidy to unskilled workers will reduce the labour cost below the gross wage.

In what follows we begin in Section 1 with the case of flexible wages, and look at policies operating not only on the demand side (wage subsidies and public employment) but also on the supply side (training). In Section 2 we examine the same policies in the case of fixed relative wages (gross and net).

1 FLEXIBLE WAGES

We concern ourselves with a world in which there are only two types of labour – skilled (group 1) and unskilled (group 2). If a person works at all, he works for a fixed work week. The supply of workers in the *i*th group is an increasing function of their net wage;

$$S_i = h^i\{W_i(1 - t_i), B_i\} \cdot L_i \qquad (i = 1, 2)$$

where W_i is the gross weekly earnings, t_i the average personal tax rate, B_i the (untaxed) unemployment benefit and L_i the total population of group i.[3] In thinking about elasticities of supply it is convenient to focus on the way in which supply changes when the gross wage changes. Such an elasticity is defined only for a given tax schedule, since the gross wage elasticity is

$$e_i = \frac{\partial \log S_i}{\partial \log W_i} = \frac{\partial \log S_i}{\partial \log\{W_i(1 - t_i)\}} \frac{\partial \log\{W_i(1 - t_i)\}}{\partial \log W_i}$$

On the demand side, production is described by a constant returns-to-scale function $X(D_1, D_2)$, where D_1, D_2 are the numbers of workers. Government and private firms have the same production function. To avoid problems of valuing public output, we assume that the government has a fixed output and minimizes the cost of producing it. Private firms are competitive profit-maximizers, equating labour cost to marginal product for each type of worker. Unemployment benefit rates are given, and personal tax rates are set so as to raise the tax revenue needed to pay for the benefits and for government production. The equality of supply and demand in each market closes the system $(D_1 = S_1; D_2 = S_2)$

Wage subsidy

Suppose now that a proportional subsidy is paid to employers of unskilled labour at a rate s and a proportional tax imposed on employers of skilled workers at a rate q which exactly pays for the subsidy. This procedure raises the gross wage of unskilled workers (W_2) and lowers that of skilled workers (W_1), leading to an increased supply of unskilled workers and a reduced supply of skilled workers.

How big are these changes? From our supply relation (and given that $S_1 = D_1$ and $S_2 = D_2$)

$$dS_2 = D_2 e_2 d \log W_2$$

and

$$dS_1 = D_1 e_1 d \log W_1 = D_1 e_1 \frac{d \log W_1}{d \log W_2} d \log W_2$$

where the term $d \log W_1/d \log W_2$ reflects the pattern of changes that are possible on the demand side. As Appendix 1 shows, given constant returns and a self-financing subsidy, $d \log W_1/d \log W_2 = -W_2 D_2/W_1 D_1$. Hence

$$dS_1 = -D_2 \frac{W_2}{W_1} e_1 d \log W_2$$

We are now in a position to evaluate the change in the efficiency of the economy. The appropriate efficiency measure V (unweighted for distribution) is the value of output minus the cost of leisure forgone by workers:

$$V = X(S_1, S_2) - C_1(S_1) - C_2(S_2)$$

where $C_i(.)$ is the cost of leisure forgone in the ith group. Thus the efficiency change is

$$dV = \left(\frac{\partial X}{\partial S_1} - \frac{\partial C_1}{\partial S_1}\right)dS_1 + \left(\frac{\partial X}{\partial S_2} - \frac{\partial C_2}{\partial S_2}\right)dS_2$$

$$= (t_1 W_1 + B_1)dS_1 + (t_2 W_2 + B_2)dS_2$$

This follows since workers are paid their marginal product, and the marginal worker equates his supply price ($\partial C_i / \partial S_i$) to the net return to work ($W_i(1 - t_i) - B_i$). Thus the change in efficiency is the change in labour supply times the distortion in each market, summed over both markets. And there is a gain if the benefit from having the extra unskilled workers exceeds the loss from having fewer skilled workers.

Substituting in,

$$dV = \left(-\frac{t_1 W_1 + B_1}{W_1}e_1 + \frac{t_2 W_2 + B_2}{W_2}e_2\right)W_2 D_2 d\log W_2$$

Each ratio term is the sum of the average tax rate and the gross replacement ratio. This proportional distortion we shall call m_i. Hence,

$$dV = (-e_1 m_1 + e_2 m_2)W_2 D_2 d\log W_2$$

Thus there is an efficiency gain from shifting demand to unskilled workers if

$$e_2 > e_1 \frac{m_1}{m_2} \tag{16.1}$$

It would of course be most unlikely that (16.1) would hold as an equality, so that, if the government had sufficient knowledge, it should be able to help by subsidizing one or other of the groups.

However, the preceding analysis ignores the fact that altered labour supply will alter the budget balance. This would invalidate our conclusion if it turned out that, when (16.1) was just satisfied, it was necessary to alter personal tax rates in order to make the budget balance. Fortunately this is not the case, for the following reason. The budget surplus is

$$\Pi = S_1 t_1 W_1 - (L_1 - S_1)B_1 + S_2 t_2 W_2 - (L_2 - S_2)B_2 - Q$$

where L_1, L_2 are again the total numbers of each type of person and Q is the cost of government production. So if r is the marginal tax rate, assumed to be the same for both groups,

$$d\Pi = dS_1(t_1 W_1 + B_1) + dS_2(t_2 W_2 + B_2) + r(S_1 dW_1 + S_2 dW_2) - dQ$$

But, as we show in Appendix 1, $S_1 dW_1 + S_2 dW_2 = 0$, and in addition $dQ = 0$.[4] Hence

$$d\Pi = dS_1(t_1 W_1 + B_1) + dS_2(t_2 W_2 + B_2)$$

This is exactly the same as the change in efficiency. Such a finding is not surprising, since the change in efficiency *is* the sum of the changes in the welfare of type 1 workers, type 2 workers and taxpayers. If the marginal tax rate is constant, the welfare gains of type 2 workers exactly equal the welfare losses of type 1 workers, and the gains of the taxpayers exactly equal the change in efficiency.[5]

It follows that if condition (16.1) is just satisfied there is no need to alter personal tax rates, and condition (16.1) does indeed give the break-even conditions for the efficiency change. For if condition (16.1) is more than satisfied, a demand shift to type 2 workers would increase efficiency if income taxes were held constant. But in fact income taxes can be cut, which will lead to further increases in labour supply and more efficiency. Likewise, if condition (16.1) is not satisfied, income taxes will have to be raised, which will further reduce labour supply and efficiency.

Some writers have focused more strongly on employment and output as objectives than on efficiency (see for example Baily and Tobin, 1977). There seems no obvious justification for this, except that this is what many politicians think they care about. However, it is easy to see how employment and output change in our model. The condition for *employment* to increase is that $dS_1 + dS_2 > 0$, or in other words (without allowing for personal tax rate changes) that

$$e_2 > e_1 \frac{W_2}{W_1} \tag{16.2}$$

This is clearly less demanding than (16.1), since $t_1 W_1 + B_1 > t_2 W_2 + B_2$. But if (16.1) is not satisfied tax rates will have to be raised. So (16.2) understates the requirement for an increase in employment, though (16.1) of course overstates it.

By contrast, the requirement for *output* to increase is that $dS_1 W_1 + dS_2 W_2 > 0$, or in other words (again not allowing for personal tax rate changes) that

$$e_2 > e_1$$

However, since tax rates can be cut, this is an over-demanding condition for an output increase, though (16.1) is not sufficiently demanding.

Reverting to our efficiency criterion, if (16.1) holds, the government should subsidize unskilled workers. But is (16.1) likely to hold, and how substantial are the gains that are available?

The size of the distortions and elasticities

There is every reason to suppose that in Britain both $e_2 > e_1$ and $m_2 > m_1$. Starting with the elasticities, we would expect the main impact of benefits on labour supply to arise through their effects on the duration of spells. Following Nickell (1979) and Ehrenberg and Oaxaca (1976), the elasticity of unemployment duration with respect to the replacement ratio lies between 1 and 0.5. Allowing for the possibility that benefits may also affect the incidence of spells, our preferred estimate will be the former. In Britain, unemployed men receive a benefit that is roughly independent of their previous earnings,[6] so that the elasticity with respect to the net wage is equal to that with respect to the replacement ratio. The elasticity of labour supply is the elasticity of unemployment multiplied by $u/(1 - u)$, where u is the unemployment rate. If the elasticity with respect to the replacement rate is the same at all wage levels – and we have no evidence to the contrary – the supply elasticities will be roughly proportional to the unemployment rates of the two groups. Suppose we take group 2 as the bottom 10 per cent of men and group 1 as the top 90 per cent (both groups married with no children, in 1977–8). Taking the unemployment rates of the two groups as 16 and 4 per cent respectively, our preferred assumption about the duration elasticity suggests supply elasticities with respect to the net wage of 0.19 and 0.04 respectively.[7]

If we take the gross wages of the two groups as £50 and £100 and assume a tax structure of the form $t_i W_i = -b + r W_i$, and assume b (the lump-sum grant implicit in the tax system) is £10 and r, the marginal tax rate, is 39 per cent (to allow for national insurance contributions, etc.), then the gross wage supply elasticities are:

$$e_1 = 0.03 \quad e_2 = 0.14$$

Turning to the distortions,[8]

$$m_i = \frac{t_i W_i + B}{W_i}$$

Hence, if B is constant, our tax schedule implies

$$m_i = r + \frac{B - b}{W_i}$$

This is a decreasing function of W, provided $B > b$, as is the case in Britain, where we calculate, for B of £30, and allowing for employers' national insurance contributions and indirect taxes,

$$m_1 = 0.76 \quad m_2 = 0.97$$

Needless to say, the values of e_i and m_i that we have given will be used more to provoke thought than to settle matters. But they do seem to establish that there would be gains from intervention.

How big are the likely gains? A natural statistic to examine is the change in efficiency per pound sterling of gross expenditure on subsidies. As we show in Appendix 1, the exact formula for welfare change is

$$dV = (-e_1 m_1 + e_2 m_2)\frac{\sigma}{A} W_2 D_2 . ds$$

where ds is the proportional subsidy, σ is the elasticity of substitution in production, and A is $\sigma + e_1 a_2 + e_2 a_1$, given $a_i = D_i W_i / (D_1 W_1 + D_2 W_2)$. This result is presented in Table 16.1, together with all our other main results.

If $\sigma = 1$[9] and our other numbers hold, the increase in welfare per pound sterling of subsidy is

$$\frac{dV}{W_2 D_2 ds} = (-e_1 m_1 + e_2 m_2)\frac{\sigma}{A} = 0.11$$

This is a non-negligible number compared with the usual calculations of the marginal welfare gain from tax reductions.[10] We therefore conclude that, in the case of flexible wages, a wage subsidy can provide a free lunch, even if a somewhat frugal one.

Public sector employment

An alternative way of altering the pattern of demand is for the public sector deliberately to employ more unskilled workers than it would if it were minimizing the money cost of a given output. Let us consider this from first principles before reverting to the question of magnitudes. As before, we assume that public output is to be held constant:

$$g^0 = g(G_1, G_2)$$

where G_1, G_2 are government employees of the two types. If E_1, E_2 refer to private employment, equilibrium now requires that

$$E_1 + G_1 = S_1 \qquad E_2 + G_2 = S_2$$

Initially the government minimizes the money cost of producing g^0 – so rates of substitution are the same in the public and private sectors. Now the government employs a few more people of type 2 and a few less of type 1, holding g constant. This will create a relative shortage of type 2 people in the private sector. Once again, W_2 (measured in units of private output) will rise and W_1 will fall. This again induces changes in labour supplies, which are the only source of changes in welfare.

Table 16.1 Effects of different policies

	$d \log W_1$	$d \log W_2$	$d \log D_1$	$d \log D_2$	dV
I: Flexible wages					
Subsidy	$-\frac{\sigma a_2}{Aa_1}ds$	$\frac{\sigma}{A}ds$	$-\frac{e_1\sigma a_2}{Aa_1}ds$	$\frac{e_2\sigma}{A}ds$	$(-e_1m_1+e_2m_2)\frac{\sigma W_2 D_2}{A}ds$
Public sector employment	$-\frac{a_2}{AS_2a_1}dG_2$	$\frac{1}{AS_2}dG_2$	$-\frac{e_1a_2}{Aa_1}dG_2$	$\frac{e_2}{AS_2}dG_2$	$(-e_1m_1+e_2m_2)\frac{W_2}{A}dG_2$
Training	$-\frac{La_2}{AL_1L_2}dL_1$	$\frac{La_1}{AL_1L_2}dL_1$	$\left(\frac{1}{L_1}-\frac{e_1La_2}{AL_1L_2}\right)dL_1$	$\left(\frac{e_2La_1}{AL_1L_2}-\frac{1}{L_2}\right)dL_1$	$(-e_1m_1+e_2m_2)\frac{a_1SW_2}{AS_1}dL_1$
II: Fixed relative wages					
Subsidy					
Gross relative wages fixed					
Employer tax	0	0	0	$\frac{\sigma}{a_1}ds$	$>\frac{\sigma m_2}{a_1}W_2S_2ds$
Worker tax	a_2ds	a_2ds	$-\frac{e_1a_2^2}{a_1}ds$	$\left(\sigma-\frac{e_1a_2^2}{a_1}\right)ds$	$>\left\{\sigma m_2 - \frac{e_1a_2}{a_1}(a_1m_1+a_2m_2)\right\}$ W_2S_2ds
Net relative wages fixed					
Employer tax	0	0	0	$\frac{\sigma}{a_1}ds$	$>\frac{\sigma m_2}{a_1}W_2S_2ds$
Worker tax	$\frac{a_2}{a_1}ds$	0	0	$\frac{\sigma}{a_1}ds$	$>\frac{\sigma m_2}{a_1}W_2S_2ds$
Public Sector employment	0	0	0	$\frac{1}{a_1S_2}dG_2$	$>\frac{m_2}{a_1}W_2dG_2$
Training	0	0	$\frac{1}{S_1}dL_1$	$\frac{1}{S_1}dL_1$	$>m_2\frac{SW_2}{S_1}dL_1$

Notes:
1. $S = S_1 + S_2$
2. $A = \sigma\lambda + e_1a_2 + e_2a_1$, where $\lambda = 1$ in the subsidy and training cases and is equal to the propotion of the workforce in the private sector (E_1/S_1) in the public sector employment case, which we have set equal to 0.75 in the numerical examples.

The conditions for an efficiency gain (or an employment or output gain) are the same as for a wage subsidy. The reason for this is that, as before, $d \log W_1/d \log W_2 = -W_2 D_2/W_1 D_1$, so the relation between one wage change and the other is the same as before. Thus the procedure for deriving condition (16.1) is exactly the same as that used above (p. 357). Likewise, the change in the budget surplus is equal to the efficiency change, since the total cost of government labour is unchanged.

The exact expressions for the changes in wages, employment and efficiency are derived in Appendix 2 and are set out in Table 16.1. As one would expect, cost-effectiveness (measured by efficiency change per pound of gross expenditure) is higher for public employment relative to wage subsidies the lower the elasticity of substitution (see Table 16.1).[11] If the elasticity is low, the effect of price on demand is so small as to make the wage subsidy less effective than a direct boost to employment in the public sector. In fact, if the elasticity of substitution is less than unity, public employment is always more effective, whatever the size of the public sector. And, interestingly, the cost-effectiveness case for using public employment is stronger, the more public employees there already are.

Training

We turn now to training. This also raises the relative wage of the unskilled, not by raising their relative demand but by reducing their relative supply. It is thus an instrument for the elimination of distortions just as much as wage subsidies and public employment are. Hence, even if the capital market were perfect and private choices were not inefficient on that account, they would still be inefficient in the context of labour markets distorted by unemployment benefit.

To see this, we assume that somehow the government causes one worker to shift himself from type 2 to type 1. This reduces the relative supply of type 2 workers, which raises W_2 and lowers W_1, subject to the usual demand relation that $d \log W_1/d \log W_2 = -D_2 W_2/D_1 W_1$. The policy must therefore be beneficial, subject to exactly the same conditions as the other policies.

To get an idea of the possible magnitude of the gains from training, one can compare the welfare gain per period with the wage cost of a trainee per period. (If there were no direct costs this ratio would equal the supranormal rate of return per x years where x was the duration of the training.) As Table 16.1 shows, this ratio is approximately

$$\frac{dV}{W_2 dL_1} = (-e_1 m_1 + e_2 m_2)\frac{a_1}{A}\frac{S}{S_1} = 0.12 \text{ (for } \sigma = 1)$$

$$= 0.22 \text{ (for } \sigma = 0.5)$$

2 FIXED RELATIVE WAGES

Though there is some evidence that in the United States many wage relativities are fairly flexible (Johnson and Blakemore, 1979), some are not; and the problem of wage rigidity may be more serious in some European countries than in the United States, owing to greater union strength. So it is interesting to see how our policies fare in a rigid wage context. We could assume either that the absolute wage of group 2 was fixed or that its wage was fixed relative to group 1. History provides no obvious evidence that the real wages of the unskilled are rigid: they certainly change a lot.[12] But there may well be rigidities in the structure of *relative* wages. There are two sorts of evidence here. First, there is the well-known stability of the degree of wage dispersion.[13] This is somewhat of a mystery, given that inter-occupational differentials have varied over time. It thus provides only limited support for any notion of rigidity. Stronger evidence comes from the fact that, not only are unemployment rates always higher for the unskilled than the skilled, but vacancy rates are much lower. Whereas the difference in unemployment could be explained from the supply side (as in Section 1), the simultaneous differences in vacancy rates suggests that rigidities may be present. It could of course be either relative *gross* pay or relative *net* pay that is fixed, but we shall focus on the case where gross pay is fixed, leaving the question of net pay to Appendix 1.

The model is as before, with one difference. Though the skilled workers are always assumed to be on their supply curves, the unskilled are now assumed to be in excess supply. Thus their supply equation is dropped from the system and replaced by the equation that fixes relative wages. The details are given in Appendixes 1 and 2 and Table 16.1, and we can simply summarize the conclusions.

For wage subsidies (financed by an employer tax) the gain is always greater than it would have been with flexible wages. This is because the absolute gross wages of both groups of workers remain unchanged, and so therefore do their net wages. Thus the supply of type 1 workers does not fall when the demand for type 2 workers rises. Hence there is no offsetting loss to be set against the gain from extra employment of the unskilled. The reason why the absolute gross wages remain unchanged can be loosely expressed as follows. If there are constant returns to scale and marginal product is equated to labour cost, then if the costs of the different types of labour change, the total labour cost evaluated at the original quantities of labour must be constant. (This is related to the notion of product exhaustion.) It follows that, if we have a tax/subsidy scheme that is self-financing, unskilled wages and skilled wages will have to move in opposite directions, if they move at all.[14] But their ratio is fixed; so they will not move.

Although we can compute how many unskilled jobs are generated, we cannot derive an exact measure of the resulting efficiency change, since we do

Table 16.2

	With fixed wages	With flexible wages
Wages subsidies	> 1.02	0.11
Public employment	> 1.02	0.14
Training	> 1.08	0.12

not know the supply price of the additional workers employed. But we can set a lower bound to the change in welfare, which indicates that

$$dV \geq dS_2 W_2 m_2 (= d\Pi)$$

Table 16.1 gives the relevant expressions, which are unambiguously higher for rigid wages than for flexible wages, not only for wage subsidies financed by an employer tax, but also in the case of public employment and training (see Appendix 1).

Using our previous numbers, the gains in welfare per gross pound expended are as in Table 16.2.

However, the same advantages could not be expected if a wage subsidy were financed by an increased *income* tax on type 1 workers. For, although in a flexible wage model it makes no difference which side of the market pays the taxman, in a model with a fixed relative gross wage it makes a lot of difference. Suppose, for example, that, with relative wages (W_1/W_2) fixed, we shift a tax on group 1 from the employer to the worker. The gross wage W_1 rises. This raises W_2 (given fixed relative wages) and hence reduces the demand for type 2 workers. In fact it is even possible that, starting with no tax or subsidy, a move to a subsidy linked to a worker tax will lower the employment of type 2 workers. This suggests that, if a tax is to be levied on the higher paid, it is better to levy it on the employers than on the workers.

By contrast, if it is relative net wages that are fixed, it makes no difference which side of the market pays the taxman, and the real consequences are in fact the same as in the case of fixed gross wages with an employer-based tax.

3 CONCLUDING REMARKS

We have discussed three possible policies – wage subsidies, public employment, and training – and shown that they can improve the efficiency of the economy. If relative wages are flexible, this is achieved by increasing W_2 and lowering W_1. The resulting increased supply of type 2 workers is of greater value than the loss through the discouraged type 1 workers. If relative wages are fixed, there is no change in net wages (except with an undesirable employee tax) and the gain comes entirely from increased demand for type 2 workers, who are in excess supply.

But this leaves unresolved at least three important issues: what policy mix is best? can other policies do the job? and how far should our policies be taken?

We can start with an obvious point. If wage subsidies were to be confined to the private sector, any non-marginal scheme would lead to a difference in the rates of substitution of type 1 for type 2 labour as between the public and private sectors. This would be inefficient. A similar difference (though of opposite sign) would result from large-scale expansion in the public employment of type 2 workers in place of type 1, unaccompanied by wage subsidies in the private sector. Thus, the public sector should either be faced with the same wage subsidy and tax as the private sector, or be instructed to behave as if it were. It is a pity that wage subsidies are so often not extended to public sector agencies – as if micro-efficiency is not a problem in decentralized public sector decision-making.

We have so far taken the levels of benefit as given. This seems reasonable in relation to B_2, which might correspond to some socially acceptable minimum level of living. Casual thought might suggest that it would be a good thing to raise B_1 in order to reduce the difference between the distortions in the two markets. However, more careful reflection will refute this notion; for a higher level of B_1 will reduce the supply of the skilled, which will reduce the demand for the unskilled. It is therefore inefficient.[15]

But how far should our policies be taken? If relative wages are fixed the answer is: until the excess supply of type 2 workers has been eliminated. If wages are flexible, our analysis provides a further argument in favour of redistribution. As we have already said, there are obvious limits to redistribution, which arise from the distorting effect of taxes on other dimensions of labour supply. However, we believe that distortions in the supply of hours could be greatly reduced by making hourly earnings rather than weekly earnings the tax base for the social security tax (at any rate in respect of employees).[16]

Thus our basic conclusions are as follows:

(a) If wages are flexible, the existence of unemployment benefit provides an efficiency argument for progressivity in the tax system.
(b) If relative wages are rigid, the arguments of subsidizing the unskilled are even stronger; and if it is *gross* relative wages that are rigid, there is a strong case for levying any progressive tax on employers rather than workers.

Appendix 1: Derivation of Results for 'One-Sector Model'

The 'one-sector model' in fact incorporates both a private sector and a government sector, but because the production function is the same in the two sectors, and both minimize costs, the system behaves as a one-sector model.

We begin with the demand side, where there are two conditions. The first derives from the assumption of constant returns to scale. In the private sector we have

$$X = X(E_1, E_2) = E_2 f(k)$$

where X is private output, E_1 and E_2 are private employment of type 1 and type 2 workers, and $k = E_1/E_2$. If c_i is the unit labour cost of the ith type of worker, profit maximization requires

$$c_1 = f'(k) \qquad c_2 = f(k) - kf'(k)$$

so

$$\frac{dc_1}{dc_2} = \frac{f''dk}{(f' - f' - kf'')dk} = -\frac{E_2}{E_1}$$

Because both sectors face the same production function and the same relative factor prices, and both minimize costs, it follows that $E_2/E_1 = G_2/G_1 = D_2/D_1$ (where G_i is the employment of type i workers in the government sector).

If there are no taxes or subsidies on employers,

$$\frac{dc_1}{dc_2} = \frac{dW_1}{dW_2} = -\frac{D_2}{D_1}$$

so

$$D_1 dW_1 = D_2 dW_2$$

or

$$D_1 W_1 d\log W_1 = -D_2 W_2 d\log W_2$$

or

$$a_1 d\log W_1 = -a_2 d\log W_2 \tag{16A.1}$$

where

$$a_i = D_i W_i / (D_1 W_1 + D_2 W_2)$$

(16.1) also holds if a self-financing tax subsidy scheme is introduced. If a proportional tax on employers (at rate q) is levied on the wage bill of type 1 workers, and a proportional subsidy (at rate s) is paid on type 2 workers, we have

$$\frac{dc_1}{dc_2} = \frac{dW_1 + W_1 dq}{dW_2 - W_2 ds} = -\frac{D_2}{D_1}$$

If the subsidy is self-financing, $D_1 W_1 dq = D_2 W_2 ds$. Hence $D_1 W_1 = -D_2 W_2$ in this case, and (16A.1) follows.

The second relation is the definition of the elasticity of substitution

$$-\sigma = \frac{d \log D_1 - d \log D_2}{d \log W_1 - d \log W_2 + ds + dq} \tag{16A.2}$$

Then, on the supply side we have (assuming market clearing and no change in employee tax rates)

$$d \log D_1 = e_1 d \log W_1 + d \log L_1 \tag{16A.3}$$
$$d \log D_2 = e_2 d \log W_2 + d \log L_2 \tag{16A.4}$$

Flexible wages: wage subsidies

The system is equations (16A.1)–(16A.4), together with the condition that

$$d \log L_1 = d \log L_2 = 0$$

By substituting (16A.3) and (16A.4) into (16A.2) we have to equations in $d \log W_1$ and $d \log W_2$. The solutions are

$$d \log W_1 = -\frac{a_2 \sigma}{a_1 A} ds \quad \text{and} \quad d \log W_2 = \frac{\sigma}{A} ds$$

where $A = \sigma + a_2 e_1 + a_1 e_2$. Hence we can solve for $d \log D_1$, $d \log D_2$ and dV, and the resulting expressions are given in Table 16.1.

Flexible wages: training

We assume that the man who gets trained is the marginal person who nearly became trained in the absence of the government programme. If capital markets are perfect there is then no social benefit from his being trained except that which results from the effect of induced wage changes in eliminating distortions.

But how *do* wages change? To determine this we need to know the supply characteristics of the marginal man. Clearly, he will not get trained unless he intends to work if he becomes skilled. Equally, the returns to training are greater for those unskilled workers who would choose to work (if unskilled) than for those who would choose not to work, because the net unskilled wage was less than their supply price. Hence if one man is trained, he will both work in occupation 1 and would have worked in occupation 2. It follows that, if this policy is pursued in respect of one trainee,

$$\frac{dS_1}{S_1} = \frac{1 + S_1 e_1 d \log W_1}{S_1}$$

and

$$\frac{dS_2}{S_2} = \frac{-1 + S_2 e_2 d \log W_2}{S_2}$$

where e_1 refers to the supply function of workers initially in occupation 1 and e_2 refers to the supply function of workers initially in occupation 2. These equations together with (16A.1) and (16A.2) give

$$d \log W_1 = -\frac{a_2}{A} \frac{S}{S_1 S_2}$$

where $S = S_1 + S_2$, and

$$d \log W_2 = \frac{a_2}{A} \frac{S}{S_1 S_2}$$

To evaluate the efficiency change, we only take into account the changes in S_1 and S_2 that are induced by the wage changes. Hence

$$dV = (dS_1 - 1)(t_1 W_1 + B_1) + (dS_2 + 1)(t_2 W_2 + B_2)$$
$$= (-e_1 m_1 + e_2 m_2)\frac{SW_1 W_2}{AX}$$

These results are reported in Table 16.1 for the general case where dL_1 takes any value (and not unity, as above).

Fixed relative wages: wage subsidies

If relative wages are fixed we assume this leads to market clearing for type 1 labour and excess supply for type 2. Therefore we drop (16A.4) and replace it by the relevant assumption about the fixity of wages.

We also have to specify the type of tax to pay for the subsidy and the exact fixity assumption. As is well known, if there are flexible wages the real effect of a tax on type 1 labour is the same whether the tax is paid by employer or worker. But if there are *fixed* relative wages the effect may differ according to who pays it. It turns out that there is a difference if it is the *gross* relative wage that is fixed, but not if it is the *net* relative wage.

(i) Gross relative wage fixed: employer tax

The system is (16A.1)–(16A.3), together with

$$d \log W_1 = d \log W_2 \tag{16A.5}$$

Hence, from (16A.1), it follows immediately that

$$d \log W_1 = d \log W_2 = 0$$

There is no change in the supply of type 1 workers ($d \log D_1 = 0$ from (16A.3)). The employment of type 2 workers is determined by the demand for them (16A.2).

The efficiency gain resulting from the reduced distortion is

$$(t_2 W_2 + B_2)dD_2 = m_2 \frac{\sigma}{a_1} W_2 D_2 ds$$

This will be greater than the efficiency gain in the flexible wage case if

$$\frac{m_2}{a_1} > (-e_1 m_1 + e_2 m_2)\frac{1}{A}$$

$$\sigma m_2 + m_2(a_2 e_1 + a_1 e_2) > (-a_1 e_1 m_1 + a_1 e_2 m_2)$$

$$\sigma m_2 + e_1(a_2 m_2 + a_1 m_1) > 0$$

which will always hold.

(ii) *Gross relative wage fixed: worker tax*

With a subsidy but no employer tax, (16A.1) and (16A.2) must be revised to allow for $dq = 0$. This gives

$$a_1 d \log W_1 = -a_2(d \log W_2 - ds) \tag{16A.1$'$}$$

and

$$-\sigma = \frac{d \log D_1 - d \log D_2}{d \log W_1 - d \log W_2 + ds} \tag{16A.2$'$}$$

If z is the rate of the worker tax levied as a proportion of the gross wage, the effect on the supply of type 1 workers is given by[17]

$$d \log D_1 = e_1\left(d \log W_1 - \frac{dz}{1-r}\right)d \log L_1 \tag{16A.3$'$}$$

To compare the worker tax with the employer tax, it must be set at a rate that generates the same total tax revenue as did the employer tax. In that case gross wages, and hence income tax receipts, were unaffected. With the worker tax gross wages change. We therefore require

$$W_1 D_1 dz + W_1 D_1 r d \log W_1 + W_2 D_2 r d \log W_2 = W_2 D_2 ds$$

Substituting from (16A.1$'$) gives

$$a_1 dz = a_2(1-r)ds \tag{16A.6}$$

The system is therefore (16A.1$'$), (16A.2$'$), (16A.3$'$), (16A.5) and (16A.6). From (16A.1) and (16A.5) we solve for wages, then from (16A.3$'$) and (16A.6) for $d \log D_1$ and from (16A.2$'$) for $d \log D_2$. The result is that gross wages rise since money has been put into the production system, but the net wages of type 1 people fall since they bear all the tax that pays for that money. Hence their supply falls. This would of itself (at given factor proportions) tend to reduce the demand for type 2 workers, while the subsidy will increase the demand for them. The direction of the effect can not therefore be determined *a priori*.

(iii) Relative net wage fixed: employer tax

The system is as in **(i)** above, provided average personal tax rates are not changed.

(iv) Relative net wage fixed: worker tax

The system is as in **(ii)** above, except that (16A.5) is replaced by

$$d \log W_1 - \frac{dz}{1 - t_1} = d \log W_2 \tag{16A.5'}$$

(16A.1'), (16A.5') and (16A.6) solve for $d \log W_1$ and $d \log W_2$ and this gives $d \log D_1$ from (16A.3') and (16A.6) and $d \log D_2$ from (16A.2'). If relative net wages are fixed and no net resources are injected into the system, absolute net wages cannot change, and hence supplies of type 1 workers do not change. The gross wages of type 1 rise by enough to pay for the subsidy. If the tax on type 1 workers were proportional $(r = t_1)$ the solution would be the same as for the employer tax, and these are the results set out in Table 16.1.

Fixed relative wages: training

In the case of training we assume the tax system given, and therefore it makes no difference (to a first approximation) whether we focus on fixed relative gross or net wages. We therefore assume the former. The system is equations (16A.1), (16A.2) and (16A.5) and

$$dq = ds = 0$$

As before, gross wages do not change. Again we assume that only people who would choose to work if trained actually get trained. So the labour supply of type 1 workers increases by dL_1. This raises the demand for type 2 workers by the same proportion, that is by dL_1/S_1. The efficiency gain resulting from the elimination of the distortion is the reduction in the unemployment of type 2 workers, multiplied by their distortion. (The actual gain is of course greater since many of those brought into employment were not previously at the margin of indifference between work and unemployment.)

The efficiency gain from the reduced distortion is given by $(Sm_2/S_1)W_2dL_1$. This is greater than the corresponding measure in the flexible wage case if

$$m_2 > (-e_1m_1 + e_2m_2)\frac{a_1}{A}$$
$$\sigma m_2 + e_1a_2m_2 + e_2a_1m_2 > -e_1a_1m_1 + e_2a_1m_2$$
$$\sigma m_2 + e_1(a_1m_1 + a_2m_2) > 0$$

which will always hold.

Appendix 2: Derivation of Results for Two-sector Model

Flexible wages

We use E_1, E_2 to refer to private sector employment and S_1, S_2 to refer to total employment. The demand side in the private sector is described by (16A.1) and (16A.2) of Appendix 1; that is

$$a_1 d \log W_1 = -a_2 d \log W_2 \tag{16A.1}$$

and

$$-\sigma = \frac{d \log E_1 - d \log E_2}{d \log W_1 - d \log W_2} \tag{16A.2}$$

Hence

$$d \log W_1 = -\frac{a_2}{\sigma}(d \log E_1 - d \log E_2) \tag{16A.7}$$

and

$$d \log W_2 = \frac{a_1}{\sigma}(d \log E_1 - d \log E_2) \tag{16A.8}$$

The supply side is given by

$$G_1 + E_1 = S_1(W_1(1 - t_1), B_1)L_1$$
$$G_2 + D_2 = S_2(W_2(1 - t_2), B_2)L_2$$

or, with t_i, B_i, L_i given,

$$dG_1 + dE_1 = dS_1 = e_1 \frac{S_1}{W_1} dW_1 \tag{16A.9}$$

$$dG_2 + dE_2 = dS_2 = e_2 \frac{S_2}{W_2} dW_2 \tag{16A.10}$$

If initially the government were minimizing costs, it follows that

$$W_1 dG_1 + W_2 dG_2 = 0 \tag{16A.11}$$

371

from (16A.9), (16A.10) and (16A.11);

$$-\frac{W_2}{W_1}dG_2 + dE_1 = e_1\frac{S_1}{W_1}dW_1$$

$$dG_2 + dE_2 = e_2\frac{S_2}{W_2}dW_2$$

or, in logarithmic form,

$$-\frac{W_2}{W_1}dG_2 + E_1 d\log E_1 = e_1 S_1 d\log W_1$$

$$dG_2 + E_2 d\log E_2 = e_2 S_2 d\log W_2$$

Substituting from (16A.7) and (16A.8),

$$\left(E_1 + e_1 S_1\frac{a_2}{\sigma}\right)d\log E_1 - e_1 S_1\frac{a_2}{\sigma}d\log E_2 = \frac{W_2}{W_1}dG_2$$

$$-e_2 S_2\frac{a_1}{\sigma}d\log E_1 + \left(E_2 + e_2 S_2\frac{a_1}{\sigma}\right)d\log E_2 = -dG_2$$

This gives $d\log E_1$ and $d\log E_2$ as functions of dG_2:

$$d\log E_1 = \frac{1}{\Delta}\begin{vmatrix}\frac{W_2}{W_1}dG_2 & -e_1 S_1\frac{a_2}{\sigma} \\ -dG_2 & E_2 + e_2 S_2\frac{a_1}{\sigma}\end{vmatrix}$$

$$= \frac{1}{\Delta}\left\{\frac{W_2}{W_1}\left(E_2 + e_2 S_2\frac{a_1}{\sigma}\right) - e_1 S_1\frac{a_2}{\sigma}\right\}dG_2$$

$$d\log E_2 = \frac{1}{\Delta}\begin{vmatrix}E_1 + e_1 S_1\frac{a_2}{\sigma} & \frac{W_2}{W_1}dG_2 \\ -e_2 S_2\frac{a_1}{\sigma} & -dG_2\end{vmatrix}$$

$$= \frac{1}{\Delta}\left\{-\left(E_1 + e_1 S_1\frac{a_2}{\sigma}\right) + \frac{W_2}{W_1}e_2 S_2\frac{a_1}{\sigma}\right\}dG_2$$

where

$$\Delta = \left(E_1 + e_1 S_1\frac{a_2}{\sigma}\right)\left(E_2 + e_2 S_2\frac{a_1}{\sigma}\right) - e_1 S_1\frac{a_2}{\sigma}e_2 S_2\frac{a_1}{\sigma}$$

$$= E_1 E_2 + e_1 S_1 E_2\frac{a_2}{\sigma} + e_2 S_2 E_1\frac{a_1}{\sigma}$$

So

$$d\log S_1 = \frac{E_1}{S_1}d\log E_1 + \frac{1}{S_1}dG_2$$

$$= \frac{E_1}{S_1\Delta}\left\{\frac{W_2}{W_1}\left(E_2 + e_2 S_2\frac{a_1}{\sigma}\right) - e_1 S_1\frac{a_2}{\sigma} - \frac{\Delta}{E_1}\frac{W_2}{W_1}\right\}dG_2$$

$$= -\frac{e_1 E_2 W_2}{\sigma\Delta W_1}dG_2$$

In the case of equal factor intensities, we may write $E_1/S_1 = E_2/S_2 = \lambda$ and

$$A = \frac{\sigma\lambda\Delta}{E_1E_2} = \sigma\lambda + e_1a_2 + e_2a_1$$

Then

$$d\log S_1 = -\frac{e_1W_2}{AS_1W_1}dG_2$$

and

$$d\log S_2 = \frac{E_2}{S_2}d\log E_2 + \frac{1}{S_2}dG_2$$

$$= \frac{E_2}{S_2\Delta}\left\{-\left(E_1 + e_1S_1\frac{a_2}{\sigma}\right) + \frac{W_2}{W_1}e_2S_2\frac{a_1}{\sigma} + \frac{\Delta}{E_2}\right\}$$

$$= \frac{e_2E_1}{\Delta\sigma}dG_2$$

or, with equal factor intensities,

$$= \frac{e_2}{AS_2}dG_2$$

The change in efficiency, for the case of equal factor intensities, is given by

$$dV = dS_1W_1m_1 + dS_2W_2m_2$$

$$= \left(-\frac{e_1W_2}{A}m_1 + \frac{e_2W_2}{A}m_2\right)dG_2$$

$$= (-e_1m_1 + e_2m_2)\frac{W_2dG_2}{A}$$

Fixed relative wages

The model is as above, except that equation (16A.10) is replaced by

$$d\log W_1 = d\log W_2 \qquad\qquad (16A.12)$$

(16A.1) and (16A.2) imply that wages do not change. Hence

$$d\log S_1 = 0$$

(from (16A.9)) and

$$d\log E_1 = d\log E_2$$

(from (16A.2)). Hence

$$d\log E_1 = \frac{S_1}{E_1}d\log S_1 - \frac{1}{E_1}dG_1$$

$$= \frac{W_2}{W_1E_1}dG_2$$

(from (16A.1)); so

$$d \log E_2 = \frac{W_2}{W_1 E_1} dG_2$$

and

$$d \log S_2 = \frac{E_2}{S_2} d \log E_2 + \frac{1}{S_2} dG_2$$

$$= \frac{1}{a_1 S_2} dG_2$$

Inspection of Table 16.1 shows that the condition for the efficiency gain to be greater with fixed than with flexible wages is the same as that for the tax-subsidy policy (see Appendix 1).

Notes

1. For a rather crude attempt to apply welfare economics to the analysis of contra-cyclical labour market policies, see Layard (1979).
2. There are of course many honourable exceptions (e.g. Baily and Tobin, 1977). Our model has some features in common with their model and is in one sense an attempt to derive similar results without assuming from the start that the rate of inflation in each market is affected not only by unemployment in that market but also by relative wages. Where they begin with a reduced form of this kind, we use standard demand and supply functions to obtain our results.
3. Wages and benefits are measured in units of private sector output.
4. If G_1, G_2 are government employees of type 1 and type 2 respectively,

    $$dQ = d\{W_1 G_1 (1+q) + W_2 G_2 (1-s)\}$$

    Thus, if q and s are small,

    $$dQ = (W_1 dG_1 + W_2 dG_2) + (G_2 dW_1 + G_2 dW_2) + (W_1 G_1 q - W_2 G_2 s)$$
    $$= \text{term } 1 + \text{term } 2 + \text{term } 3.$$

    Term 1 is zero since, if we start from a cost-minimizing point, $dG_2/dG = W_1/W_2$. Term 2 is zero, since $S_1 dW_1 + S_2 dW_2 = 0$, and, by equal factor intensities, $G_1/S_1 = G_2/S_2$. Term 3 is zero owing to the self-financing tax/subsidy and equal factor proportions.
5. If we give one line each to the welfare change for type 1 workers, type 2 workers and taxpayers,

    $$dV = S_1 dW_1 (1-r)$$
    $$+ S_2 dW_2 (1-r)$$
    $$+ S_1 r dW_1 + S_2 r dW_2 + dS_1 (t_1 W_1 + B_1) + dS_2 (t_2 W_2 + B_2) - dQ$$
    $$= dS_1 (t_1 W_1 + B_1) + dS_2 (t_2 W_2 + B_2)$$

6. Only about 20 per cent of the unemployed get earnings-related supplement, and for those people the increase in weekly benefit per pound of previous weekly earnings is never more than a third.

7. If we were to attribute these differences in unemployment rates wholly to differences in the replacement ratio, the implied elasticity of unemployment with respect to the replacement ratio would be 2.3 rather than 1 as calculated by Nickell. We think Nickell's figure gives a better indication of the likely supply side behavioural response to changes in the wage-benefit ratio, and we therefore adopted it in gauging the empirical effects of the policies we consider. The estimates we use are thus based on evidence rather than prior assumptions.

8. This may be an overestimate in so far as efficiency calls for an insurance system which subsidizes productive search.

9. On our assumptions $a_1 = 0.95$ and hence A is approximately equal to σ for values of σ within a reasonable range (say between 0.25 and 2). For evidence on σ see for example Fallon and Layard (1975) and Hamermesh and Grant (1979) and the references therein. The welfare gain is thus not sensitive to the value chosen for σ (provided it is not zero). On the other hand, it is approximately proportional to the value of the supply elasticities, and if we had assumed a duration elasticity with respect to the replacement ratio of 0.5 the welfare gain per pound of subsidy would have been 0.056. On the other hand, if the duration elasticity with respect to the replacement ratio were 1 for the unskilled and zero for the skilled, the welfare gain per pound of subsidy would be 0.14.

10. If the income tax is reduced, the welfare gain per unit loss of tax revenue is $t\varepsilon/(1 - t - t\varepsilon)$ where t is the marginal tax rate and ε is the compensated elasticity of labour supply. If $t = 0.3$ and $\varepsilon = 0.1$, this is approximately 0.04. If such an exercise is to be self-financing it has to be assumed that public goods are sacrificed and have the same value as private goods that cost the same.

11. Thus if $\sigma = 1$, $dV/\text{subsidy} = 0.14$; if $\sigma = \frac{1}{2}$, $dV/\text{subsidy} = 0.28$.

12. If any group's real wage is rigid and too high, efficiency is improved by subsidizing that type of labour.

13. See for example Thatcher (1968) and Ashenfelter and Layard (1983). These provide evidence of the long-run stability of the percentile ratios in the wage distribution. For a discussion of other possible reasons for this phenomenon see Layard, Piachaud and Stewart (1978).

14.
$$(dW_1 + qW_1)D_1 + (dW_2 - sW_2)D_2 = 0$$
$$qW_1D_1 - sW_2D_2 = 0$$
$$\therefore dW_1D_1 + dW_2D_2 = 0$$

15. In the flexible wage model one can check that $dV < 0$ by an appropriate use of Appendix 1's equations (16A.1), (16A.2), (16A.4) and (16A.6), together with (16A.3) modified as follows:

$$d\log S_1 = e_1 d\log W_1 - e_1' d\log B_1$$

The result is even more obvious in the fixed model.

16. Non-manual workers do not always have well defined hours. No worker whose hours were not well defined would be allowed to claim more than 40 hours, but

there could be a ceiling on hourly earnings above which tax liability ceased to increase. To avoid discouraging part-time workers, they could also be taxed as though they worked 40 hours.

17. dz is 'grossed up' by $1/(1-r)$ because e_1 is the gross wage elasticity. If we denote the net wage elasticity, which is behaviourally determined independently of taxes, as η_1, then

$$d \log D_1 = \eta_1 \left(\frac{1-r}{1-t_1} d \log W_1 - \frac{1}{1-t_1} dz \right)$$

and

$$e_1 = \eta_1 \frac{1-r}{1-t_1}$$

References

Ashenfelter, O. and R. Layard (1983) 'Incomes Policy and Wage Differentials', *Economica* 50, No 198.

Baily, M.N. and J. Tobin (1977) 'Macroeconomic Effects of Selective Public Employment and Wage Subsidies', *Brookings Papers on Economic Activity*, 2, 511–41.

Ehrenberg, R.G. and R.L. Oaxaca (1976) 'Unemployment insurance, duration of unemployment and subsequent wage gain', *American Economic Review*, 66, 754–766.

Fallon, P. and R. Layard (1975) 'Capital-skill complementarity, income distribution and output accounting', *Journal of Political Economy*, 83, 279–301, Chapter 10 in R. Layard, *Tackling Inequality* (London: Macmillan, 1999).

Hamermesh, D.S. and J. Grant (1979) 'Econometric studies of labor-labor substitution and their implications for policy', *Journal of Human Resources*, 14, 518–542.

Harberger, A.C. (1971) 'Three basic postulates for applied welfare economics', *Journal of Economic Literature*, 9, 785–797.

Johnson, G. and A. Blakemore (1979) 'Estimating the potential for reducing the unemployment rate consistent with non-accelerating inflation', *American Economic Review*, 69, 119–130.

Layard, R. (1979) 'The costs and benefits of selective employment measures: the British case', *British Journal of Industrial Relations*, 17 (July), 187–204.

Layard, R., D. Piachaud, and M. Stewart (1978), *The Causes of Poverty*, Background Paper 5, Royal Commission on the Distribution of Income and Wealth (London: HMSO).

Nickell, S. (1979) 'The effect of unemployment and related benefits on the duration of unemployment', *Economic Journal*, 89, 34–49.

Thatcher, R. (1968) The distribution of earnings of employees in Great Britain, *Journal of the Royal Statistical Society* (Series A), 131, 133–170.

17 The Case for Subsidizing Extra Jobs (1980)*

with S. Nickell

Unemployment is expected to remain high for some time. Given the well known problems of general reflation, it is worth exploring other possible anti-unemployment measures. The one we shall consider in this paper is the marginal employment subsidy. Under such a scheme, any firm which expands its employment will be paid a subsidy of, say, £20 a week for each additional job it provides above its average level of employment during some base period.

Such a scheme was first proposed in Britain in Layard (1976) and Layard and Nickell (1976). A similar scheme was put forward in the TUC Economic Reviews for 1976 and 1977, and a mini version was introduced in the 1977 Budget. By January 1979 it had been extended to all firms with under 200 workers except for service industries outside the development areas.[1] The actual scheme differed from ours both in its limited coverage and because the subsidy is only paid for six months after the expansion occurs. The scheme which is analyzed here visualises a take-up period of about two years, with the additional jobs being subsidised for a considerably longer period during which there is a gradual phasing out of the payments. We present the general arguments for the scheme in Section 1, followed by a discussion of the analytical model in Section 2. Section 3 assesses the likely impact of the scheme and compares it with a number of other possible policies; we conclude with more general remarks.

1 SOME GENERAL ARGUMENTS

A country with large-scale unemployment is in a familiar dilemma, which can be crudely depicted thus. General reflation, by tax cuts or expenditure increases, will have bad effects on the balance of payments, and on the budget deficit and prices. The balance of payments might be remedied by a

* *Economic Journal*, 90 (March 1980), pp. 51–73.
The authors are grateful to David Allen, Lucien Foldes, Richard Jackman, Lord Kaldor and Gosta Rehn for helpful discussions, and to John Flemming, John Black and the referee for useful comments.

devaluation – but this only helps if it is possible to reduce the real wage. For devaluation involves price increases. Without real wage resistance these price increases could be once-for-all; but if real wage resistance makes it impossible to reduce real wages, the price increases will only call forth wage increases which will obliterate the improvement in the balance of payments.[2] Moreover, however wages are determined, reflation is bound to worsen the budget deficit, which is bad for prices, investment or both.

These harmful effects would stem equally from ordinary tax cuts or from, say, a general employment subsidy. However, a subsidy to *marginal* employment or output offers a different range of opportunities. Since a marginal value-added subsidy is difficult to administer in a period of inflation, we shall confine ourselves to a marginal employment subsidy.[3] The ideal arrangement would be to *confine the subsidy to extra jobs provided as a result of the subsidy*. Such a 'marginal' job subsidy has enormous advantages over a general one. A given expenditure, if concentrated on marginal workers, will generate many more jobs than the same expenditure spread over all workers. We discuss the reasons more fully in the next section. But the basic idea is this. Any subsidy can have only a limited effect on domestic demand. For, taking wages as given, it has its effect mainly by reducing prices, and prices cannot fall below the average cost of the marginal firm. So, since the price elasticity of aggregate domestic demand is low, the effect of *any* subsidy upon domestic demand is limited. But with exports and import-substitutes matters are quite different, and a marginal subsidy can have a much bigger effect than an average subsidy costing the same amount. For many firms are price-takers in markets for internationally traded goods. Thus a large fall in the marginal cost of producing them will have a profound effect on the quantity sold, even if there is only a small fall in their average costs. Since exports and import-substitutes will rise, the balance of payments is likely to improve. And since the same expenditure generates more jobs this way than if it were spent on general reflation, the budget deficit is much less adversely affected. In fact, an ideal marginal job subsidy would pay for itself. For where an extra man was employed, the saving on unemployment relief plus additional taxes paid would exceed the subsidy, unless the subsidy were very large.

The advantage of a counter-cyclical marginal subsidy would be further strengthened if it were only paid out for additional jobs provided *within two years*. Such a device would encourage firms to bring forward their expansion plans so as to qualify for the subsidy, and quite substantial employment effects might be secured by relatively small expenditures of public money. Further dynamic gains might be secured if initially output grew faster than demand, inducing downward pressure on prices (Rehn, 1975). In addition, if the subsidy were at a flat rate for each extra worker, it would encourage firms to produce extra output by employing extra men, rather than by lengthening the hours of those already employed. So there would be fewer people unemployed at any given level of capacity utilization, and thus, one hopes, less inflationary pressure at any particular level of unemployment.

We seem to have found the philosopher's stone. But is an ideal marginal wage subsidy administratively possible? Unfortunately not. For it requires that the government can get firms to report truthfully what their employment would have been in the absence of the subsidy. In principle this is what they are meant to do to obtain the UK Temporary Employment Subsidy.[4] To get this a firm has to 'prove' that it would have made redundant 10 or more workers in the absence of the subsidy. Having proved this, it qualifies for £20 per week for a year for each job preserved. But proving these claims has become an increasingly slippery business. It would be even more difficult to require expanding firms to prove that they would not have expanded their labour force but for the subsidy. And yet it is at least as important to induce expanding firms to expand more, as it is to induce contracting firms to contract less. The main reason why unemployment has risen in Britain is not that more people have become unemployed, but that those who are unemployed have remained unemployed longer. So what can be done?

We propose a perfectly general subsidy to *all* new jobs created, whether due to the subsidy or not. If introduced in year t, the scheme could be guaranteed to last in this form until the end of year $t + 2$ and to go on being paid thereafter in relation to the average number of jobs in year $t + 2$ or the then current level, whichever is the less. However, the subsidy per worker would fall progressively to zero over, say, four years. The reason for a six-year guarantee is that this will induce employers to act more strongly in taking on workers before year $t + 3$, while the gradual reduction in the subsidy should discourage them from any precipitate layoffs as the subsidy is dismantled. If, of course, the gloomier forecasts of unemployment prove right, then the subsidy could be extended later.

The subsidy would have to relate to changes in employment at the level of the firm, not of the establishment. For, if it related to the latter, this would encourage firms to transfer jobs from one establishment to another and so obtain the subsidy without providing extra jobs. If two firms merged, the original calculated level of those employed in year t should include workers in both the constituent firms.[5] The subsidy would be paid at, say, £20 a week for full-time workers, and £10 for part-timers. The flat rate nature of the subsidy means, of course, that it raises the relative demand for unskilled workers. But its supreme virtue is its administrative simplicity. The firm would supply an easily checked record of its employment and be paid the relevant sum.[6]

Clearly it would be nice to analyze the effects of such a scheme in a fully dynamic model. However, economic science does not seem to be at the stage where such an analysis is possible. We therefore confine our analysis to the medium-term impact of the scheme as indicated by a relatively simple static macro model.

2   A MACRO MODEL

We start by presenting a Keynesian model and then consider a monetarist variant. Both of these models are simple-minded but we feel that they capture most of the crucial points. They are based on a fixed money wage and a fixed exchange rate, for reasons which we shall explain at the beginning of the next section.

Starting with the less controversial aspects of our model we first have the *ex ante* equilibrium condition

$$y = e\left[y^d, \frac{\Pi(1-t_2)}{p}\right] + g + \frac{x}{p} - \frac{p_m m(p, y, p_m)}{p} \tag{17.1}$$

y is real domestic value added and e is private expenditure which comprises both consumption and investment and is a function of personal real disposable wage income, y^d, and real after-tax profits, $\Pi(1-t_2)/p$, where t_2 is the rate of profits tax and p is the domestic price level. g is real government expenditure, x is the value of exports, m is real imports, all of which are assumed to be inputs, and p_m is the price of imports in pounds. p_m is assumed to be normalised so that it is initially equal to p. It is worth commenting on the aggregation of private consumption and investment in the light of the fact that we are proposing a wage subsidy which will presumably have an adverse relative price effect on investment in the long run. Since the subsidy is only temporary, however, and applies to but a small proportion of the work force, it will only have a tiny relative price impact on total investment demand, which may safely be ignored.[7]

Disposable wage income, y^d, comprises real after-tax wages and unemployment benefits. We treat earnings as subject to a proportional tax, t_1, since, in the medium term with given wages, aggregate earnings vary mainly due to changes in the numbers employed. Real unemployment benefit is paid only to some fraction of the difference between full employment n^*, and the number currently employed, n. Thus when we say that the total of real unemployment benefits is $u(n^* - n)$, the coefficient u has to allow for cyclical variations in labour force participation as well as the fact that not all the unemployed receive benefits. Thus we have

$$y^d = \frac{wn(1-t_1)}{p} + u(n^* - n) \tag{17.2}$$

where w is the exogenous money wage. Profits Π equal domestic value added less labour costs. The subsidy is, of course, a (negative) part of labour costs. If we assume that n_0 is base period employment, $\bar{n}$ is the number of workers who receive the subsidy minus the expansion of aggregate employment and s is the proportional subsidy, then the total government handout is $sw(n - n_0 + \bar{n})$.

Profits are then given by

$$\Pi = \frac{py}{1+t_3} - wn + (n - n_0 + \bar{n})ws \tag{17.3}$$

where t_3 is the rate of indirect taxes. An important point to notice about the subsidy is that some firms which would have contracted in the absence of the subsidy will in fact expand in order to obtain it. This has two consequences. First, it implies that $\bar{n}$ is not equal to the total of gross expansions that would have occurred in the absence of the subsidy with aggregate employment unchanged. Second, it has the consequence that $\bar{n}$ is a function of the size of the subsidy. We shall henceforward assume that this effect is small (being mainly confined to firms in the export sector) and may therefore be ignored. (Its importance is in any case proportional to the level of subsidy s and therefore affects only the scale of the optimum subsidy.)

On the production side we assume the simple relationship

$$y = f(n) \tag{17.4}$$

where f' is assumed to be positive but we make no assumptions concerning f''. In order to close the model it remains for us to specify an export function and a relationship between prices, wages and employment. This latter function is of vital importance and, if we are to use this model to determine the order of magnitude of the impact of a marginal wage subsidy, we must choose a function which bears some relationship to known facts.

In textbook macroeconomic models of this type the function most commonly used is the equality between the marginal product of labour and the (marginal) real wage which is a necessary condition for profit maximization by a price-taking firm.[8] So we have

$$f'(n) = w/p \tag{17.5}$$

which determines aggregate employment as a simple function of the marginal real wage. Unfortunately there are two extremely strong objections to the use of such an equation in an aggregate model. First, it implies that the level of employment is inversely related to the real wage whereas we know that real wages (net of trend) do not move contra-cyclically during business cycles. Second, we are not aware of any satisfactory estimated aggregate labour demand function which is specified in terms of (17.5), or a dynamised version of it, without including output.[9] Since we are concerned to use our model to make rough predictions of the impact of policy changes, to use a relationship such as (17.5), which is completely at variance with observed facts, is clearly out of the question.

The rejection of (17.5) seems to neutralise what is, at first sight, one of the major arguments in favour of a *marginal* wage subsidy. A naive microeconomic analysis might conclude that since a profit-maximizing firm is solely concerned with the *marginal* wage in determining its output and employment levels, a large subsidy on the wages of marginal employees would have a dramatic effect on the firm's level of employment at very little cost. This argument is, however, grossly misleading at a more aggregate level at least in a closed economy. Suppose *all* the firms in a competitive industry in equilibrium are offered a marginal wage subsidy and there is a consequent dramatic expansion in industry output. This will immediately lead to an equally dramatic fall in price in this industry and since average costs will have fallen but a little, the firms will be making losses. The industry will then contract, and in the new equilibrium the price of output will be equal to average cost in the marginal firm. Aggregate employment in the industry will have risen only to the extent that average cost has fallen as a result of the marginal subsidy; that is, not very much. This is of course a long-run argument, and since the subsidy is but a short-term phenomenon it is difficult to say precisely what will happen in a short period. If all firms in the industry were of identical efficiency, we might argue that in the short run they would implicitly collude to avoid making losses, in which case the short-run expansion would be determined again on the basis of average cost pricing as in the long run. This is the *worst possible result* as far as the marginal policy is concerned. If the firms differ in efficiency, those which are most efficient would be able to expand output to maximise their profits without fear of making a loss due to the fall in price when all their competitors do the same. Temporary losses will, however, be inflicted on the marginal firm which might be borne in the short term. In this case industry output would be determined to some extent by marginal cost and the expansion would be greater than if output and price were determined exclusively on an average-cost basis. Nevertheless, we feel it is better to err somewhat on the side of caution and suppose that prices, at least in the home market, are determined by the average cost of the representative firm. We shall, therefore, assume an aggregate 'normal' cost pricing relationship which has some empirical support from Godley and Nordhaus (1972) and Sargan (1977). Prices are determined as a fixed mark-up on the 'normal' average cost of production where 'normal' means that inputs and outputs are taken to be on their trend paths. The resulting equation for the home price level is then given by

$$p = (1 + \pi)[w\hat{n} + p_m\hat{m} - (n + \bar{n} - n_0)ws\alpha]/(\hat{y} + \hat{m}) \tag{17.6}$$

The 'hats' indicate trend levels, π is the mark-up including the indirect tax rate, t_3,[10] and α is the proportion of the subsidy which is 'passed on' in price reductions.[11] The denominator is equal to gross output, the sum of domestic value added, $\hat{y}$, and imports, $\hat{m}$, all of which are assumed to be inputs into some firm.[12]

It is worth noting, in the context of the marginal employment subsidy scheme, that in (17.6) we have made no distinction between expanding firms in receipt of the subsidy and contracting firms which receive nothing. Instead we have averaged over the two sets of firms to produce the aggregate price index p. Within this index there will be some changes in relative prices which will lead to so-called displacement effects; that is, falling prices and expanding employment in some firms will directly contribute to contractions in others. This is another aspect of the dependence of $\bar{n}$ on s which we gave reasons above for ignoring. The displacement effects will be automatically netted out when we consider any expansions in demand due to falls in the aggregate price level p, and consequently they need trouble us no further.

The final equation we must specify in our model is the one which determines the value of exports, x. Pricing in export markets must be sharply distinguished from the policies employed by firms in the home market, particularly in so far as they relate to marginal costs. First, a firm which is a price-taker in export markets will export up to the point where marginal cost is equal to the price received, but with the difference that a subsidy on marginal units will lead to expansion of output *without* any corresponding fall in price, since foreign firms competing in the same markets will not be expanding their output simultaneously. Furthermore, a marginal subsidy may also enable a firm to enter a new export market where the price was originally too low to cover marginal costs.[13] Second, a monopolistic firm in an export market will use marginal costs to determine its optimal price, and any marginal subsidies are likely to have more of an expansionary effect than in the home market because elasticities of demand are generally likely to be higher.

Evidence that marginal considerations are deemed important by exporters is provided by the results of surveys described in Gribbin (1971) (particularly pp. 19–20) and in Rosendale (1973, pp. 47–8). Rosendale notes that about one-third of the firms in her sample of 29 large engineering companies sell abroad at prices which do not fully cover overhead costs, and Gribbin records that 68 per cent of firms in his sample distinguish marginal costs in their accounting systems, with those firms making this distinction selling abroad at prices considerably lower relative to the home price than those that do not. Rosendale also reveals that over half of the products sold abroad by the firms in her sample are, in fact, sold in price-taking markets (Table 2, p. 47).

This analysis thus leads us to consider in our model three types of exports. Type (1): those sold by firms who simply charge a mark-up on average normal cost, which yields for them a total export revenue $px_1(p)$. Type (2): those sold by firms which equate marginal revenue to marginal cost in export markets, yielding a total revenue $p_2x_2(p_2)$, where p_2 is the export price index for such firms. Type (3): those sold by firms which are price takers in export markets, giving a revenue $p_3x_3(c)$, where p_3 is the world price level in export markets and c is the marginal cost of production. p_2, p_3 are both measured in pounds and hence the total value of exports is given by

$$x = px_1(p) + p_2x_2(p_2) + p_3x_3(c) \tag{17.7}$$

Our Keynesian macro model is now completely determined by (17.1), (17.2), (17.3), (17.4), (17.6) and (17.7). In the next section it will also be convenient to have a monetarist model to hand, and here we go to the opposite extreme and simply add a quantity theory equation, based on domestic absorption, to (17.4), (17.6) and (17.7). Thus we have

$$M = pk\left(y + \frac{p_m m(y, p, p_m)}{p} - \frac{x}{p}\right) \tag{17.8}$$

M being aggregate nominal money balances.

3   THE IMPACT OF THE MARGINAL EMPLOYMENT SUBSIDY AND OTHER POLICIES

We are now ready to look at the effects of the marginal employment subsidy. Our main aim is to compare these with the effects of other policies generating the same number of extra jobs, in order to see which policy or mix of policies is the most desirable. For this purpose we need only look at the initial effect of each policy on the level of employment, the balance of payments,[14] the budget deficit and the short-run price level. The policies we consider are non-marginal employment subsidies, government expenditure changes, indirect tax changes and exchange rate changes (all other policy effects being computed for fixed exchange rates). The resulting effects (which we shall eventually show in Table 17.3, p. 392) can be used to answer the following types of question.

(i)   If the exchange rate is taken as fixed, are there policy mixes which dominate others in terms of their effects on the balance of payments, the budget deficit and the short-run price level?

(ii)   If the exchange rate is flexible, so that the sum of balance of payments effects has to be zero, are there policy mixes which dominate others in terms of their effects on the budget deficit and the short-run price level?[15]

Notice that we do not need to trace through the longer-run effects of changes in the budget deficit and the short-run price level since these will be the same, independent of the policy mix that brought them about. All the formulae used are derived in the Appendix. We shall only consider impact effects since the multipliers in all these policies turn out to be approximately unity, as we also demonstrate in the Appendix.

The effect of the marginal employment subsidy on employment comes about via a number of distinct channels. Taking the Keynesian model first, it is clear that it will have a direct impact on expenditure via the changes in prices and profits consequent on the subsidy being paid for intra-marginal workers, who are $\bar{n}$ in number. This leads to the following proportional employment effects $(\Delta n/n)$.

Proportional effect via price reductions increasing real personal incomes

$$= \frac{ae_1(1-t_1)}{e(1+\pi)(1+b)} \frac{\bar{n}s}{n} \tag{17.9}$$

Proportional effect via profits

$$= \frac{[1-\alpha/(1+b)]e_2(1-t_2)}{e(1+\pi)} \frac{\bar{n}s}{n} \tag{17.10}$$

Proportional effect via price reductions leading to import substitution

$$= \frac{\alpha\tilde{m}e_{mp}}{e(1+\tilde{m})} \frac{\bar{n}s}{n} \tag{17.11}$$

Proportional effect via price reductions leading to increased

$$\text{type (1) exports} = \frac{-\alpha\tilde{x}_1(1+e^1)}{e(1+\tilde{m})} \frac{\bar{n}s}{n} \tag{17.12}$$

In these formulae, e_1 is the marginal propensity to consume out of personal disposable income, e_2 is the same out of profits, $\tilde{m}, \tilde{x}_1$ are the ratios of imports and type (1) exports to domestic value added and e_{mp} and e_1 are the elasticities of imports and type (1) exports with respect to the home price level. Finally b is the import bill divided by labour costs and $e = nf'(n)(1+b)/y(1+\tilde{m})$, where $nf'(n)/y$ is the elasticity of value added with respect to the labour input.[16]

There are a number of things worth noting about these results. First, these expansionary effects bear no relation to the marginality of the employment subsidy but arise solely from the lump sum subsidy, $\bar{n}s$, received by firms. This aspect of the marginal employment subsidy is thus identical to any other policy which transfers funds directly to firms. Its effectiveness depends crucially on how much of the subsidy is 'passed on' in price reductions for, if it accrues entirely as profits, we have $\alpha = 0$ and effects (17.9), (17.11) and (17.12) are all zero because there are no price reductions. The only impact is via expenditure out of profits, which in the short term is generally considered to be rather low at the margin.

The impact on employment which is associated particularly with the marginal aspect of the policy, is that due to increases in exports, especially in markets where firms operate as price takers. Here we have the following.

Proportional effect via type (2) and type (3) exports

$$= \frac{s(1+b)}{e(1+\tilde{m})} \left[\tilde{x}_2(1+e^2)\frac{\partial \log p_2}{\partial s} + \tilde{x}_3 e^3 \frac{\partial \log c}{\partial s} \right] \tag{17.13}$$

$\tilde{x}_2, \tilde{x}_3$ are the ratios of type (2) and (3) exports to domestic value added and e^2, e^3 are the elasticities with respect to selling price p_2 and marginal cost c, respectively. The point to notice about this effect is that it operates completely at the margin, both p_2 and c being crucially affected by marginal changes. In this particular aspect, the policy is similar to an export subsidy, albeit of a rather special kind. In determining the size of the subsidy's impact on the selling price p_2 and marginal cost c, it is not necessarily the case that all exporting firms will be in receipt of the subsidy. If the exporting firm happens to be simultaneously contracting in the home market, it will only take up the subsidy if its export sales are a large enough proportion of its total output, so that its induced expansion in exports outweighs the home market contraction and leads to a take-up of the subsidy. This we shall assume to be the typical case. The whole difficulty could, however, be avoided altogether if we took the baseline employment level beyond which the subsidy is paid as being, say, 90 per cent of the current employment level. In such circumstances nearly all firms would receive the subsidy, and this would have the additional advantage of discouraging contractions as well as encouraging expansions. It would, however, be more costly, as we shall see.

The fact that a particular policy is expansionary is, of course, of no particular interest unless it can also be demonstrated that it is particularly unsusceptible to the usual drawbacks of such policies. As we have already indicated, these drawbacks may be conveniently classified under the headings of balance of payments effects, budget deficit effects and price level effects, and we shall consider each in turn. Because one of the major expansionary effects of the policy comes via exports, it is to be expected that the balance of payments effect will be favourable. The change in the balance of payments, B, which is defined by

$$B = x - p_m m(y, p, pm) \tag{17.14}$$

is given by

$$\frac{\Delta B}{py} = \frac{\alpha[\tilde{m}e_{mp} - \tilde{x}_1(1 + e^1)]}{1 + b}\left(\frac{\bar{n}}{n} + \frac{\Delta n}{n}\right)s$$
$$+ \left[\tilde{x}_2(1 + e^2)\frac{\partial \log p_2}{\partial s} + \tilde{x}_3 e^3\frac{\partial \log c}{\partial s}\right]s - \frac{\tilde{m}e_{my}e(1 + \tilde{m})}{1 + b}\frac{\Delta n}{n} \tag{17.15}$$

$\Delta n/n$ being the proportional employment effect of the policy. The first term is the favourable effect of import substitution and type (1) export expansion brought about by the falling price level, and the second is the direct export expansion brought about by the fall in the marginal costs. The last is the only negative effect, which is the rise in imports due to the expansion of domestic expenditure. As we shall see, this should generally be offset by the export terms.

Turning now to the budget deficit, D, this may be written as

$$\frac{D}{p} = g + \frac{sw}{p}(n - n_0 + \bar{n}) + u(n^* - n) - t_1 \frac{wn}{p} - \frac{t_2 \Pi}{p} - \frac{t_3 y}{1 + t_3} \qquad (17.16)$$

where constant elements are omitted for convenience. In order to see the impact of the subsidy clearly, we make the not unreasonable assumption that falls in the price level affect the tax and expenditure elements of the government balance sheet in an identical manner. The one exception to this is that we shall include the loss in corporation tax due to the fall in profits following the fall in prices. The change in the budget deficit resulting from the policy is then given by

$$\frac{\Delta D}{py} = \left[\frac{(1 + b)(1 + \pi)}{(1 + \tilde{m})}\right]^{-1} \left(\left\{1 - t_2\left[1 - \frac{\alpha(1 + \pi)}{(1 + \tilde{m})(1 + t_3)}\right]\right\}\frac{\bar{n}s}{n}\right.$$

$$\left. - \left[\frac{u}{w/p} + t_1 - s + t_2 k + \frac{t_3 e(1 + \pi)}{1 + t_3}\right]\frac{\Delta n}{n}\right) \qquad (17.17)$$

where $\quad k = e\dfrac{(1 + \pi)}{1 + t_3} - (1 - s)$

The important point to notice here is that the impact of the policy depends crucially on the money paid out to firms which would have expanded without any increase in aggregate employment, $\bar{n}s$, compared with the expansion induced by the policy, Δn.

Finally, the impact effect of the policy on prices can be nothing other than favourable and is given by

$$\frac{\Delta p}{p} = -\frac{\alpha s}{(1 + b)}\left(\frac{\bar{n}}{n} + \frac{\Delta n}{n}\right) \qquad (17.18)$$

Here, of course, the extent to which the subsidy is 'passed on' in price reductions, as measured by α, is the vital factor.

Before considering the order of magnitude of these effects it is worth noting the employment changes which would ensue if the monetarist model was correct. The impact effect is given by

$$\frac{\Delta n}{n} = \frac{\alpha \bar{n}s}{en} + \frac{\alpha}{e}\left[\tilde{m}e_{mp} - \tilde{x}_1(1 + e^1)\right]\frac{\bar{n}}{n}s$$

$$+ \frac{s(1 + b)}{e(1 + \tilde{m})}\left[\tilde{x}_2(1 + e^2)\frac{\partial \log p_2}{\partial s} + \tilde{x}_3 e^3 \frac{\partial \log c}{\partial s}\right] \qquad (17.19)$$

The similarities with the Keynesian model are most striking, with the first term corresponding to the domestic expenditure effects (17.9) and (17.10), the second to the import substitution and type (1) export effects (17.11) and (17.12), and the last being identical to the export effects of (17.13). The differences are in fact minimal and, unlike some other policies, such as changing government expenditure, it matters little whether one takes a Keynesian or a monetarist view of the world; the efficacy of the policy is unaltered. We shall hereinafter use the Keynesian model to analyse all policies.

In order to discuss the likely size of these policy impacts it is necessary to attach numbers to the parameters which appear in the formulae. Our plan here is to fix the relatively non-contentious ones and then consider variations in the less certain parameters, grouping them under pessimistic, reasonable and optimistic headings. The parameters considered as non-contentious are allotted values as follows.

$$b = \frac{\text{import bill}}{\text{labour cost}} = 0.35; \quad \tilde{m} = \frac{\text{import bill}}{\text{domestic value added}} = 0.30$$

$$\tilde{x}_i = \frac{\text{type } i \text{ exports}}{\text{domestic value added}}; \quad \tilde{x}_1 = 0.15; \quad \tilde{x}_2 = \tilde{x}_3 = 0.075$$

e_{my} = elasticity of imports with respect to income = 2

t_1 = tax rate on personal incomes = 0.15

t_2 = *marginal* tax rate on profits = 0.5

π = mark-up = 0.25 of which 0.15 is indirect taxes (t_3)

$$\frac{u}{w/p} = \frac{\text{marginal reduction in benefit payment}}{\text{wage}} = 0.3$$

$$\frac{f'(n)n}{y} = \text{elasticity of value added with respect to labour input} = 1.5$$

e_1 = marginal propensity to spend out of personal disposable income = 0.8

$$\frac{\partial \log p_2}{\partial s} = \frac{\text{proportional change in type (2) export prices}}{\text{subsidy}}$$

$$= \frac{\text{proportional change in marginal cost}}{\text{subsidy}} \quad \text{(assuming constant demand elasticity)}$$

$$= -\frac{\text{wage costs}}{\text{total costs}} \text{ in export industries}$$

$$= -0.3$$

It is worth noting that we have assumed half the exports to be priced at normal cost p, which is somewhat higher than the evidence suggests is correct. This may be thought of as adjusting for the fact that some price-taking exporters will

Table 17.1 Alternative assumptions on contentious parameters

	Pessimistic	Reasonable	Optimistic
α = proportion of the subsidy passed on in price reductions	0	0.5	1
e_2 = marginal propensity to spend out of profits	0	0.5	0.5
e_{mp} = elasticity of imports with respect to the home price level	0	0.5	1
$e^1 = e^2$ = price elasticity of demand for type (1) and (2) exports	–1	–1	–2
e^3 = marginal cost elasticity of supply of type (3) exports	–0.5	–1	–1

not be in receipt of the subsidy because of home market contractions, by effectively lumping them in with the normal-cost pricing group. For the contentious parameters we have three sets of values and the details are set out in Table 17.1.

Given these parameters, we present in Table 17.2 the impact effect of the marginal employment policy on employment, the balance of payments, the budget deficit and the price level. In order to incorporate as much information as possible into the table, we show at the bottom the general formula containing $\bar{n}/n$, the proportion of the labour force in receipt of the subsidy when aggregate employment remains fixed, and at the top the actual numbers resulting if $\bar{n}/n$ is set at 3 per cent, 6 per cent and 10 per cent. The derivation of the first two figures is discussed in the Appendix. The 10 per cent figure would arise if the baseline was taken as 90 per cent of the current employment level, assuming that no firms were going to contract naturally by more than 10 per cent. It should be borne in mind that the export effects for this latter policy will be larger than those we have predicted.

Under the reasonable assumptions, a marginal employment subsidy equal to one-third of average weekly earnings would yield an increase in employment of between 0.7 and 1.0 per cent, improve the balance of payments by between 0.2 and 0.3 per cent of GNP, worsen the budget deficit by between 0.2 and 0.5 per cent of GNP and lower prices by between 0.5 and 0.9 per cent. The budget deficit cost per job is between £1,100 and £2,500 per annum, this figure being obtained by setting py/n in the last column at £5,000.[17] One of the drawbacks of the policy is its minuscule effect under pessimistic assumptions, with all the subsidy disappearing into profits never to emerge again. This could lead to a

Table 17.2 Effect of a marginal employment subsidy at rate s

	Employment $\Delta n/n$	Balance of payments surplus $\Delta B/py$	Budget deficit $\Delta D/py$	Price level $\Delta p/p$	Budget deficit cost per job $\Delta D/\Delta n$
		If $\bar{n}/n = 0.03$			
Pessimistic	$0.0075s$	$0.006s$	$0.008s$	0	$1.6py/n$
Reasonable	$0.022s$	$0.0084s$	$0.004s$	$-0.014s$	$0.18py/n$
Optimistic	$0.046s$	$0.017s$	$-0.003s$	$-0.033s$	$-0.06py/n$
		If $\bar{n}/n = 0.06$			
Pessimistic	$0.0075s$	$0.006s$	$0.019s$	0	$3.8py/n$
Reasonable	$0.030s$	$0.005s$	$0.012s$	$-0.026s$	$0.40py/n$
Optimistic	$0.062s$	$0.01s$	$0.006s$	$-0.06s$	$0.1py/n$
		If $\bar{n}/n = 0.10$			
Pessimistic	$0.0075s$	$0.006s$	$0.034s$	0	$0.7py/n$
Reasonable	$0.040s$	0	$0.026s$	$-0.042s$	$0.64py/n$
Optimistic	$0.085s$	0	$0.020s$	$-0.096s$	$0.24py/n$
		General formula			
Pessimistic	$0.0075s$	$0.006s$	$(0.37n/\bar{n} - 0.0033)s$	0	
Reasonable	$(0.015 + 0.25\bar{n}/n)s$	$(0.012 - 0.11\bar{n}/n)s$	$(0.36\bar{n}/n - 0.01)s$	$-(0.4\bar{n}/n + 0.002)s$	
Optimistic	$(0.03 + 0.54\bar{n}/n)s$	$(0.024 - 0.24\bar{n}/n)s$	$(0.36\bar{n}/n - 0.016)s$	$-(0.9\bar{n}/n + 0.006)s$	

budget deficit cost per job as high as £19,000 per annum (with $\bar{n}/n = 6$ per cent) although under these circumstances the government would have no trouble in borrowing the money back again to finance the deficit, with little impact either on the money supply of interest rates. It is worth noting how susceptible the change in the budget deficit is to assumptions about $\bar{n}/n$, and this implies that there is a high degree of uncertainty attached to estimates of the budget deficit cost per job. On the other hand, if a baseline of 90 per cent of current employment were used, the value of $\bar{n}/n$ is almost certain to be around 0.1, with results illustrated in the third row of Table 17.2. The employment effects are generally larger but the budget deficit cost per job rises to around £3,750 per annum.

We next consider some other possible policies for comparative purposes, and the ones we have chosen are a proportional labour subsidy, s', on all jobs, an increase in government expenditure, Δg, a change in the exchange rate, $\Delta \eta$, where η is the price of pounds in terms of foreign currency and a change in indirect taxes, Δt_3. In order to compute the impact of a devaluation we assume that the elasticity of import prices with respect to the exchange rate is $-\frac{2}{3}$ and that of type (2) export prices (in pounds) is $-\frac{1}{2}$. The impact effects of all these policies, given the same parameter values, are shown in Table 17.3.

Comparing the marginal employment subsidy with an across the board employment subsidy (such as a cut in employers' National Insurance contributions) we can see that a proportional marginal wage subsidy of one-third is equivalent in its employment effect to a non-marginal subsidy of about 3 per cent. But this latter would lead to a worsening of the balance of payments and a larger budget deficit cost per job. It is, therefore, an inferior policy. Similar remarks apply to a cut in indirect taxes.

The obvious advantage of a government expenditure increase is the comparative certainty about its effects, for, as can be seen from the table, these are insensitive to those parameter values which are crucial in determining the effects of the other policies. It should be remembered, however, that if the world is as monetarists view it, marginal employment subsidies remain highly effective whereas *ceteris paribus* government expenditure increases make no impact whatever. Furthermore, the balance of payments effects of government expenditure increases are adverse and the budget deficit cost per job is about £3,250 per year, higher than all but the most pessimistic calculations for marginal employment subsidies.[18]

Turning to the effects of a devaluation, we can see that the balance of payments effect of a marginal subsidy of one-third of average earnings is equivalent to a devaluation of about $1\frac{1}{2}$ per cent. Devaluation, as an instrument of employment expansion, appears to be rather effective but it does, of course, have an adverse impact on the price level. It is an overt 'beggar my neighbour' policy which invites retaliation, whereas the marginal employment subsidy whose action is, in part, that of an export subsidy, is more of a covert 'beggar my neighbour' policy and only partly one at that. Of course, the fact that one is doing down the rest of the world by subtle rather than obvious means is not necessarily something to be pleased about, but then if the economically stronger countries of the world had not pursued such contractionary policies in the recent past, papers such as this might well not have been worth writing.

So far we have compared the marginal employment subsidy with each alternative in turn. The question remains as to whether there does not exist some combination of policies which is superior to the marginal subsidy. The obvious candidate is devaluation linked to a non-marginal employment subsidy or a cut in indirect taxes to offset the adverse price effects. A non-marginal employment subsidy of 2.6 per cent plus a devaluation of 2.9 per cent will have

Table 17.3 Effects of various possible reflationary policies ($\bar{n}/n = 0.03$)

	Employment $\Delta n/n$	Balance of payments surplus $\Delta B/py$	Budget deficit $\Delta D/py$	Price level $\Delta p/p$	Budget deficit cost per job $\Delta D/\Delta n$
Pessimistic					
MES*	$0.0075s$	$0.006s$	$0.008s$	0	$1.6py/n$
NMES	$0.005s'$	$-0.003s'$	$0.32s'$	0	$0.42py/n$
Govt expenditure	$0.66\Delta g/y$	$-0.60\Delta g/y$	$0.43\Delta g/y$	0	$0.65py/n$
Devaluation	0	$0.13(-\Delta\eta/n)$	0	$0.18(\Delta\eta/n)$	–
Cut in indirect taxes	$0.34(-\Delta t_3)$	$-0.3(-\Delta t_3)$	$0.45(-\Delta t_3)$	$-0.8(-\Delta t_3)$	$1.3py/n$
Reasonable					
MES	$0.022s$	$0.0084s$	$0.004s$	$-0.014s$	$0.18py/n$
NMES	$0.24s'$	$-0.07s'$	$0.29s'$	$-0.38s'$	$1.40py/n$
Govt expenditure	$0.66\Delta g/y$	$-0.60\Delta g/y$	$0.43\Delta g/y$	0	$0.65py/n$
Devaluation	$0.10(-\Delta\eta/n)$	$0.16(-\Delta\eta/n)$	$-0.06(-\Delta\eta/n)$	$0.18(-\Delta\eta/n)$	$-0.60py/n$
Cut in indirect taxes	$0.42(-\Delta t_3)$	$-0.18(-\Delta t_3)$	$0.38(-\Delta t_3)$	$-0.8(-\Delta t_3)$	$0.90py/n$
Optimistic					
MES	$0.046s$	$0.017s$	$-0.003s$	$-0.033s$	$-0.06py/n$
NMES	$0.58s'$	$-0.02s'$	$0.21s'$	$-0.75s'$	$0.41py/n$
Govt expenditure	$0.66\Delta g/y$	$-0.60\Delta g/y$	$0.43\Delta g/y$	0	$0.65py/n$
Devaluation	$0.22(-\Delta\eta/n)$	$0.26(-\Delta\eta/n)$	$-0.10(-\Delta\eta/n)$	$0.18(-\Delta\eta/n)$	$-0.48py/n$
Cut in indirect taxes	$0.54(-\Delta t_3)$	0	$0.3(-\Delta t_3)$	$-0.8(-\Delta t_3)$	$-0.55py/n$

*MES = marginal employment subsidy, NMES = non marginal employment subsidy.

precisely the same balance of payments and price level effects as a one-third marginal employment subsidy and will generate about 20 per cent more employment, but at over four times the budget deficit cost or over three times the budget deficit cost per job. Similarly, a 1.3 per centage point cut in indirect taxes plus a 3.2 per cent devaluation will again have the same balance of payments and price level impact as the marginal subsidy generating 17 per cent more employment at about three times the budget deficit cost per job.

One of the possible problems with our analysis of these policies, in particular with the marginal subsidy, is our assumption of a fixed exchange rate. If the subsidy generates an improvement in the balance of payments there is always of course, the temptation to allow the exchange rate to move up, thereby reducing its employment effect and improving its effect on the home price level. This can clearly be avoided by combining the marginal subsidy with, say, tax cuts which can be such a size as to nullify the balance of payments effect. Thus, for example, a one-third marginal employment subsidy combined with an indirect tax cut of some 1.6 percentage points will have a zero balance of payments effect and generate an increase in employment of 1.4 per cent, although increasing the budget deficit by some 0.7 per cent of GNP. The combination of devaluation and indirect tax cuts, which achieves the same employment and balance of payment effects, has a budget deficit effect which is about 20 per cent worse and a fall in the price level which is some 15 per cent smaller.

Finally, there are a number of further general points to be made about the marginal employment subsidy. First, as has been made clear, the deadweight cost incurred through the payment of the subsidy to workers in firms which expand even at constant aggregate employment is crucial in determining the budget deficit cost per job. This deadweight cost is extremely difficult to estimate, and although our analysis in the Appendix comes up with a rather low figure of 3 per cent of the labour force, this estimate has a very high variance and it could be a great deal higher.[19]

Another problem which we have not mentioned is the possibility that the expanding firms in a particular industry will obtain such a cost advantage over the remainder in the home market that they will drive them out of business. This is a particular danger given that their cost advantage will grow as their market share increases. The upshot would be to raise the deadweight burden to an enormous size while driving a large number of firms out of business. Given the limited time horizon of the proposed subsidy, however, this seems a somewhat unlikely scenario given that the typical firm would have to expand fairly dramatically in order to gain an appreciable cost advantage.[20]

The scheme has also been criticised as being a charter for over-manning. But it is difficult to see why firms should create jobs where nothing is produced if it costs them £50 a week to do so. Overmanning may be a problem in many existing jobs, but it is hardly encouraged by steps to bring forward the creation of new jobs.

4 CONCLUDING REMARKS

So we conclude that there is much to be said for a scheme whereby firms are paid a subsidy proportional to their increase in employment over its level in some initial period. Compared to a general employment subsidy costing the same amount of money, this is bound to generate more jobs (mainly in the export sector) and thus a healthier balance of payments and a smaller budget deficit. Concentration of the subsidy at the margin gives it that much more leverage. Compared to an increase in government expenditure, the performance of the marginal employment subsidy depends on the size of the deadweight subsidy to additional jobs that would have been provided anyway. However, provided this is not too large, the budget deficit cost per additional job is less for the marginal employment subsidy, and the balance of payments effects are always more favourable. So are the price level effects. Devaluation is of course an attractive alternative on all counts other than its price level effects. If there were real wage resistance, so that price increases led to equivalent wage increases, devaluation could not work. But the marginal employment subsidy works even if there is a real wage resistance, since real wages improve slightly.

The analysis leading to these conclusions uses a 'normal' cost theory of pricing over the cycle. Thus the model involves an essentially recursive approach to the cyclical behaviour of the economy: wages determine prices, real demand determines output, and output determines employment. But similar conclusions to ours have been reached by economists using a longer term approach to the labour market in which employment is always a unique negative function of the real wage.[21] According to this approach, recent unemployment has been due to an excessive real wage, and a marginal wage subsidy would be a good antidote. It is not always the case that opposed theories lead to the same conclusion, and the fact that they do here gives us added confidence in putting forward our proposal.

Appendix

The Keynesian model

The basic model consists of the following equations.

$$y = e\left[y^d, \frac{\Pi(1-t_2)}{p}\right] + g + \frac{x}{p} - \frac{p_m m(p, y, p_m)}{p} \tag{17A.1}$$

$$y^d = \frac{wn(1-t_1)}{p} + u(n^* - n) \tag{17A.2}$$

$$\Pi = \frac{py}{1+t_3} - wn + (n - n_0 + \bar{n})ws \tag{17A.3}$$

$$y = f(n) \tag{17A.4}$$

$$p = (1+\pi)[w\hat{n} + p_m\hat{m} - (n + \bar{n} - n_0)ws\alpha]/(\hat{y} + \hat{m}) \tag{17A.5}$$

$$x = px_1(p) + p_2x_2(p_2) + p_3x_3(c) \tag{17A.6}$$

In order to compute the employment effects of any particular policy, it is necessary to differentiate these equations with respect to the appropriate policy variable and solve for the derivative of n. In the case of changes in government expenditure the model is as above except that $s = 0$. For an across-the-board wage subsidy we assume, for simplicity, that (17A.3) and (17A.5) are replaced by

$$\Pi = \frac{py}{1+t_3} - w(1-s')n \tag{17A.3a}$$

$$p = (1+\pi)[w(1-\alpha s')\hat{n} + p_m\hat{m}]/\hat{y} + \hat{m}) \tag{17A.5a}$$

When the exchange rate, η, is changed, it must be remembered that p_m, p_2 and p_3 are all functions of η and that $\dfrac{\eta}{p_3}\dfrac{\partial p_3}{\partial \eta} = -1$, by definition.

In order to obtain the formulae below, the partial derivatives are evaluated at the point where $n = n_0, y = \hat{y}, m = \hat{m}$ and the balance of payments deficit is zero. It is further assumed that $n_0 = \hat{n}$.

First we state the *multipliers* for all the policies. For the marginal employment subsidy it is given by K^{-1}, where

$$K = 1 + \tilde{m}e_{my} - \frac{e_1}{e(1+\pi)}\left[(1-t_1)\left(1 - \frac{\alpha s}{1+b}\right) - \frac{u}{w/p}\right]$$
$$+ \frac{e_2(1-t_2)}{e(1+\pi)}\left[\frac{e(1+\pi)}{1+t_3} - (1-s) - \alpha s\right] + \frac{\alpha s}{e(1+\hat{m})}\left[\tilde{m}e_{mp} - \tilde{x}_1(1-e^1)\right]$$

For the other three policies it is given by K_1^{-1}, where $K_1 = K$ when $s = 0$. It is easy to check that for the parameter configurations used in the paper, $K_1 \simeq K \simeq 1$ and so the impact effects are the primary concern.

The *impact effects on employment* are as follows.

Marginal employment subsidy:

$$\frac{\partial n/n}{\partial s} = \frac{\alpha e_1(1-t_1)}{e(1+\pi)(1+b)}\frac{\bar{n}}{n} + \frac{[1-\alpha/(1+b)]e_2(1-t_2)\bar{n}}{e(1+\pi)}\frac{}{n}$$
$$+ \frac{\alpha}{e(1+\tilde{m})}[\tilde{m}e_{mp} - \tilde{x}(1+e^1)]\frac{\bar{n}}{n}$$
$$+ \frac{(1+b)}{e(1+\tilde{m})}\left[\tilde{x}_2(1+e^2)\frac{\partial \log p_2}{\partial s} + \tilde{x}_3 e^3 \frac{\partial \log c}{\partial s}\right]$$

Change in government expenditure:

$$\frac{\partial n/n}{\partial g/y} = \frac{(1+b)}{e(1+\tilde{m})}$$

Employment subsidy:

$$\frac{\partial n/n}{\partial s'} = \frac{\alpha e_1(1-t_1)}{e(1+\pi)(1+b)} + \frac{[1-\alpha/(1+b)]e_2(1-t_2)}{e(1+\pi)} +$$
$$\frac{\alpha}{e(1+\tilde{m})}[\tilde{m}e_{mp} - \tilde{x}_1(1+e^1)] + \frac{(1+b)}{e(1+\tilde{m})}\left[\tilde{x}_2(1+e^2)\frac{\partial \log p_2}{\partial s'} + \tilde{x}_3 e^3 \frac{\partial \log c}{\partial s'}\right]$$

Devaluation:

$$\frac{\partial n/n}{\partial \eta/\eta} = \frac{1+b}{e(1+\tilde{m})}\left\{(1+\pi)\tilde{m}e_{p_m\eta}\left[\frac{\tilde{x}_1(1+e^1)}{(1+\tilde{m})} - \frac{e_1(1-t_1)}{(1+\pi)(1+b)}\right.\right.$$
$$\left. + \frac{e_2(1-t_2)}{(1+\pi)(1+b)} - \frac{\tilde{m}e_{mp}}{(1+\tilde{m})}\right] - \tilde{m}(1-e_{mp})e_{p_m\eta} + \tilde{x}_1 e^1$$
$$\left. + \tilde{x}_2[(1+e_{p_2\eta})(1+e^2) - 1] - \tilde{x}_3(1-e^3)\right\}$$

Cut in indirect taxes:

$$\frac{\partial n/n}{\partial t_3} = -\frac{1+b}{e(1+\tilde{m})(1+\pi)}\left\{\frac{e_1(1-t_1)(1+\tilde{m})}{(1+\pi)(1+b)}\right.$$
$$\left. + e_2(1-t_2)\left[(1+\pi) - \frac{(1+\tilde{m})}{(1+\pi)(1+b)}\right] + \tilde{m}e_{mp} - \tilde{x}_1(1+e^1)\right\}$$

Next we present the *balance of payments effects* of the policies where the balance of payments is defined as

$$B = x - p_m m(y, p, p_m)$$

Marginal employment subsidy:

$$\frac{\partial B/py}{\partial s} = \frac{\alpha[\tilde{m}e_{mp} - \tilde{x}_1(1+e^1)]}{(1+b)}\left(\frac{\bar{n}}{n} + \frac{\partial n/n}{\partial s/s}\right) + \tilde{x}_2(1+e^2)\frac{\partial \log p_2}{\partial s}$$

$$+ \tilde{x}_3 e^3 \frac{\partial \log c}{\partial s} - \frac{\tilde{m}e(1+\tilde{m})e_{my}}{(1+b)}\frac{\partial n/n}{\partial s}$$

Change in government expenditure:

$$\frac{\partial B/py}{\partial g/y} = -\frac{\tilde{m}e_{my}e(1+\tilde{m})}{(1+b)}\frac{\partial n/n}{\partial g/y}$$

Employment subsidy:

$$\frac{\partial B/py}{\partial s'} = \frac{\alpha[\tilde{m}e_{mp} - \tilde{x}_1(1+e^1)]}{(1+b)} + \tilde{x}_2(1+e^2)\frac{\partial \log p_2}{\partial s'} + \tilde{x}_3 e^3 \frac{\partial \log c}{\partial s'}$$

$$- \frac{\tilde{m}e(1+\tilde{m})e_{my}}{(1+b)}\frac{\partial n/n}{\partial s'}$$

Devaluation:

$$\frac{\partial B/py}{\partial \eta/\eta} = \tilde{x}_1\left[e^1 + (1+e^1)\frac{(1+\pi)}{(1+\tilde{m})}\tilde{m}e_{p_m\eta}\right] + \tilde{x}_2[(1+e_{p_2\eta})(1+e^2) - 1]$$

$$- \tilde{x}_3(1-e^3) - \tilde{m}\left[(1-e_{mp}) + \tilde{m}\frac{(1+\pi)}{(1+\tilde{m})}e_{mp}\right]e_{p_m\eta} - \frac{\tilde{m}e(1+\tilde{m})e_{my}}{(1+b)}\frac{\partial n/n}{\partial \eta/\eta}$$

Cut in indirect taxes:

$$\frac{\partial B/py}{\partial t_3} = \frac{1}{1+\pi}[\tilde{x}(1+e^1) - \tilde{m}e_{mp}] - \frac{\tilde{m}e_{my}e(1+\tilde{m})}{(1+b)}\frac{\partial n/n}{\partial t_3}$$

The following are the *budget deficit effects*, where we assume that pure price level effects net out. The budget deficit is defined as

$$\frac{D}{p} = g + \frac{sw}{p}(n - n_0 + \bar{n}) + u(n^* - n) - t_1\frac{wn}{p} - t_2\frac{\Pi}{p} - t_3\frac{y}{1+t_3}$$

In the formulae, $k = e(1+\pi)/(1+t_3) - (1-s)$, where $s = 0$ in the second and fourth policies.

Marginal employment subsidy:

$$\frac{\partial D/py}{\partial s} = \frac{(1+\tilde{m})}{(1+b)(1+\pi)}\left(\left\{1 - t_2\left[1 - \frac{\alpha(1+\pi)}{(1+\tilde{m})(1+t_3)}\right]\right\}\frac{\bar{n}}{n}\right.$$

$$\left. - \left[\frac{u}{w/p} + t_1 - s + t_2 k + \frac{t_3 e(1+\pi)}{1+t_3}\right]\frac{\partial n/n}{\partial s}\right)$$

Change in government expenditure:

$$\frac{\partial D/py}{\partial g/y} = 1 - \frac{(1+\tilde{m})}{(1+b)(1+\pi)}\left[\frac{u}{w/p} + t_1 + t_2 k + \frac{t_3 e(1+\pi)}{1+t_3}\right]\frac{\partial n/n}{\partial g/y}$$

Employment subsidy:

$$\frac{\partial D/py}{\partial s'} = \frac{(1+\tilde{m})}{(1+b)(1+\pi)}\left(\left\{1 - t_2\left[1 - \frac{\alpha(1+\pi)}{(1+\tilde{m})(1+t_3)}\right]\right\}\right.$$
$$\left. - \left[\frac{u}{w/p} + t_1 - s' + t_2 k + \frac{t_3 e(1+\pi)}{1+t_3}\right]\frac{\partial n/n}{\partial s'}\right)$$

Devaluation:

$$\frac{\partial D/py}{\partial \eta/\eta} = -\frac{(1+\tilde{m})}{(1+b)(1+\pi)}\left[\frac{u}{w/p} + t_1 + t_2 k + \frac{t_3 e(1+\pi)}{1+t_3}\right]\frac{\partial n/n}{\partial \eta/\eta}$$
$$- \frac{t_2(1+\pi)\tilde{m}e_{p_m \eta}}{(1+\tilde{m})(1+t_3)}$$

Cut in indirect taxes:

$$\frac{\partial D/py}{\partial t_3} = -\frac{1}{1+t_3} + t_2\left[1 - \frac{1}{(1+t_3)(1+\pi)}\right]$$
$$- \frac{(1+\tilde{m})}{(1+\pi)(1+b)}\left[\frac{u}{w/p} + t_1 + t_2 k + \frac{t_3 e(1+\pi)}{1+t_3}\right]\frac{\partial n/n}{\partial t_3}$$

The *price level effects* are as follows.
  Marginal employment subsidy:

$$\frac{\partial p/p}{\partial s} = -\frac{\alpha}{(1+b)}\left(s\frac{\partial n/n}{\partial s} + \frac{\tilde{n}}{n}\right)$$

Change in government expenditure:

$$\frac{\partial p/p}{\partial g/y} = 0$$

Employment subsidy:

$$\frac{\partial p/p}{\partial s'} = -\frac{\alpha}{(1+b)}$$

Devaluation:

$$\frac{\partial p/p}{\partial \eta/\eta} = \frac{(1+\pi)}{(1+\tilde{m})}\tilde{m}e_{p_m \eta}$$

Cut in indirect taxes:

$$\frac{\partial p/p}{\partial t_3} = \frac{1}{1+\pi}$$

Finally, in this section of the Appendix we consider the impact of the marginal employment subsidy in the context of a monetarist model. Such a model would consist of (17A.4), (17A.5) and (17A.6) plus

$$M = pk\left[y + \frac{p_m m(y, p, p_m)}{p} - \frac{x}{p}\right]$$

The employment effect of the marginal employment policy is given by

$$\frac{\partial n/n}{\partial s} = \left\{\frac{\alpha}{e}[1 + \tilde{m}e_{mp} - \tilde{x}_1(1 + e^1)]\frac{\bar{n}}{n} + \frac{1+b}{e(1+\tilde{m})}\left[\tilde{x}_2(1 + e^2)\frac{\partial \log p_2}{\partial c}\right.\right.$$
$$\left.\left. + \tilde{x}_3 e^3 \frac{\partial \log c}{\partial s}\right]\right\}\left\{1 + \tilde{m}e_{my} - \frac{\alpha s}{e}[1 + \tilde{m}e_{mp} - \tilde{x}(1 + e^1)]\right\}^{-1}$$

This analysis has been rather cryptic. A full derivation is available from the authors on request.

Spontaneous labour force growth

The marginal employment subsidy is paid to all firms which experience labour force growth. As we noted in the main body of the paper, the amount of subsidy paid out, even when aggregate employment is fixed, is a crucial parameter in predicting the effects of the policy. Here we present a derivation of the likely size of this parameter.

There is evidence that in manufacturing industry, over a two-year period the sum of gross increases at the *establishment* level would be 6 per cent of a constant labour force. But we are interested in increases at the *firm* level. There are two extreme cases. First, the percentage growth in all establishments within any given firm is the same. In this case the sum of gross increases at the firm level is 6 per cent. At the other extreme there is perfect negative correlation between the growth of establishments in the same firm – one establishment grows by the transfer of workers from another establishment in the same firm. In that case the sum of increases at the firm level is roughly zero. An intermediate assumption is that there is no correlation between the growth of establishments in the same firm. Let us explore this case.

First, suppose each firm has n establishments. G_{ij} is the growth in ith establishment of the jth firm. Then the growth of the firm, assuming it has n establishments, is $(G_{1j} + G_{2j} \cdots + G_{nj})$. Call it Q_j. If all firms have n establishments and G_{ij} is a random normal variable, then

$$\text{var}(Q_j) = \text{var}(G_{1j} + G_2 j + \ldots + G_{nj}) = n \, \text{var}(G_{ij})$$
$$\text{and} \quad SD(Q_j) = SD(G_{1j} + G_{2j} + \ldots + G_{nj}) = \sqrt{n} SD(G_{ij})$$

so $\quad \dfrac{\sum(Q_j|Q_j > 0)}{J.SD(Q_j)} = \dfrac{\sum(G_{ij}|G_{ij} > 0)}{nJ.SD(G_{ij})}$

where J is the number of firms. Thus

$$\frac{\sum(Q_j|Q_j > 0)}{\sum(G_{ij}|G_{ij} > 0)} = \frac{1}{\sqrt{n}}$$

However, not all firms have the same number of establishments. The Census of Production gives grouped data on firms according to their number of establishments and their total workforce. Suppose there are K groups. In kth group each firm has n_k establishments. Now let us assume that the (known) ratio of gross employment increases at the establishment level to total employment is the same (0.06) in each group of firms. Then in size group k the sum of gross increases at the establishment level is $0.06\,E_k$, where E_k is total employment in the group. The sum of gross increases at the firm level, following the argument just developed, is $0.06\,E_k/\sqrt{n_k}$. So the ratio of the sum of gross increases at the firm level to the total labour force is

$$0.06 \sum_k \left(\frac{1}{\sqrt{n_k}} \frac{E_k}{\sum E_k} \right)$$

Using data on manufacturing industries from the *Census of Production* (1968), volume 158, table 42, pp. 158–60, this equals 0.06/2.5 (or 0.06/3.2 if only establishments with more than 100 workers are included). Thus on the assumptions given, the spontaneous sum of increases at the firm level in a static labour force would be about 2 per cent. To this must be added 1 per cent to allow for the natural rate of increase of the labour force. However, the resulting estimate of 3 per cent may be too low and we therefore also use the extreme estimate of 6 per cent.

Notes

1. The US Employment Tax Credit is another version of the same basic idea. See Ashenfelter (1977).
2. This has been used as an argument for import controls, but these involve other familiar problems.
3. If the word subsidy is unattractive, the same scheme could be conceived as a rebate to employers' National Insurance contributions.
4. This is now being phased out.
5. The definition of 'firm' would be the same as for Corporation Tax.
6. The idea is not new. It dates back to at least April 1932 when it was an important part of the German recovery measures announced by the then Chancellor Von Papen (Rustow, 1932). By the 'Papen Plan' employers were paid a large subsidy per week for each additional job created after the plan was announced, and the Chancellor said that he expected this to reduce unemployment by 1 3/4 million. Unfortunately, it is difficult to isolate the actual effects of the measure, partly because it was accompanied by a very large cut in business taxes. However, the

actual course of German unemployment is striking. The number of unemployed (seasonally adjusted) was climbing steadily until it reached 5 3/4 million in August 1932. It then turned down quite sharply, falling by a quarter of a million within four months, over a million within a year, and nearly three million within two years. Meanwhile, of course, Hitler had come to power in January 1933, but his expansion of public expenditure can have had little impact within the first year of the Papen Plan. More important perhaps, the world recovery also began in 1933, but since German exports continued to decline, the German recovery must have occurred to some extent independently of trends elsewhere. Perhaps on the strength of this experience, the West Germans again operated a job-expansion subsidy in 1975. The fraction of the wage subsidised was over a half. But the payment lasted only six months, the period during which the extra jobs had to be created was short, the extra jobs had to be occupied by men already unemployed for over three months, and the scheme was confined to areas of high unemployment (about a third of the country). Given this, it is perhaps not surprising that the subsidy was only claimed for about 90,000 workers.

7. We have computed that a 30 per cent wage subsidy lasting for four years would affect private investment to the tune of less than 1/2 per cent. This computation was performed assuming a putty-clay world and an ex-ante elasticity of substitution of 0.77, an estimate taken from Hausman (1974).

8. See for example, Dernberg and McDougall (1960, chapter 11).

9. Killingsworth (1970) discusses a very large selection. See also Hamermesh (1976).

10. Note that the total indirect tax revenue is given by $pt_3y/(1 + t_3)$, where $p/(1 + t_3)$ is the price before taxes are added. We implicitly assume that $(1 + n) = (1 + \pi')(1 + t_3) \simeq (1 + \pi' + t_3)$, where π' is the non-tax mark-up.

11. It is worth emphasizing again that even if all the subsidy is 'passed on', this is still somewhat pessimistic and ignores the fact that some firms in the home market will determine output on the basis of marginal cost. In this case, we have $p = w(1 - s)/f'(n)$ and the subsidy has a dramatic effect compared with (17.6), even when $\alpha = 1$.

12. Remember that p_m has been normalised to be equal to the initial value of p and is, therefore, approximately equal to p throughout.

13. Such entry will, however, be restricted by the knowledge that the subsidy is only temporary, particularly if the fixed costs of entry are considerable.

14. We assume no change in the capital account.

15. If we wished to proceed formally we could find the optimal mix of three policies by finding for each combination of three policies what level each policy would need to be set at in order to achieve a given Δn and zero ΔB and ΔD. We would then choose that policy mix which gave the lowest Δp.

16. If the reader becomes confused by the number of symbols, their definitions are repeated in a compact form on pp. 388 together with Table 17.1.

17. The cost per job would be greatly reduced if the subsidy were confined to manufacturing. For the effect on exports would be more or less the same but the deadweight loss much reduced. The effects of the subsidy would then be very approximately as indicated in the bottom section of Table 17.2, but with $\bar{n}/n$ replaced by $\frac{1}{2}\bar{n}/n$, where $\bar{n}$ refers to the value it would take in the case of an economy-wide subsidy.

18. The preceding argument does not allow for possible forms of government expenditure that are either markedly less import-intensive than general expenditure on goods and services, or that employ low wage labour, e.g. the Job Creation Scheme. On the effects of special labour market measures other than employment subsidies, see Layard (1979).
19. If the subsidised employment growth had an upper limit, this would exclude the deadweight cost of some very large expansions that would happen anyway.
20. The scheme *has* to be contracyclically operated. For imagine a permanent scheme with the base period being moved forward by one period each period. Knowing this, a firm evaluating the undiscounted present value of the stream of subsidy associated with alternative employment streams would find them all the same. So the incentive to expand earlier rather than later would be fairly weak. Notice also that the scheme has to be introduced in an unexpected way otherwise firms will rig their level of employment in the base period (unless this is made very long).
21. Flemming (1976). General employment subsidies were advocated by Kaldor (1936), using the same model. Our model could also lead to the conclusion that too high a real wage would lead to unemployment, but by a different mechanism: the excessive real wage would make impossible the devaluation needed to maintain balance of payments equilibrium at full employment.

References

Ashenfelter, O. (1977) 'Evaluating the Effects of the Employment Tax Credit', Princeton University (November), mimeo.

Dernberg, T.E. and D.M. McDougall (1960) *Macro-Economics* (New York: McGraw-Hill).

Flemming, J. (1976) 'The British Economy in 1977', *Financial Times* (New Year).

Godley, W. and W. Nordhaus (1972) 'Pricing in the Trade Cycle', *Economic Journal* (September), 853–82.

Gribbin, J.D. (1971) 'The Profitability of UK Exports' Government Economic Service, *Occasional Papers*, No. 1.

Hamermesh, D.S. (1976) 'Econometric Studies of Labour Demand and Their Application to Policy Analysis', *Journal of Human Resources*, 11(4).

Hausman, J.A. (1974) 'A Theoretical and Empirical Investigation of an Aggregate Putty-Clay Technology for Great Britain, 1946–1970', MIT, mimeo.

Kaldor, N. (1936) 'Wage Subsidies as a Remedy for Unemployment', *Journal of Political Economy* (December).

Killingsworth, M.R. (1970) 'A Critical Survey of Neoclassical Models of Labour', *Bulletin of the Oxford Institute of Economics and Statistics* (May), 133–66.

Layard, R. (1976) 'Subsidizing Jobs Without Adding to Inflation', *The Times* (28 January).

Layard, R. (1979) 'The Costs and Benefits of Selective Employment Measures: The British Case', *British Journal of Industrial Relations*, 17 (July), pp. 187–204.

Layard, R. and S.J. Nickell (1976) 'Using Subsidies as a Means of Cracking the Unemployment Nut', *The Guardian* (2 April).

Rehn, G. (1975) 'The Fight Against Stagflation', University of Stockholm (August), mimeo.

Rosendale, P.B. (1973) 'The Short-run Pricing Policies of Some British Engineering Exporters', *National Institute Economic Review* (August), pp. 44–51.

Rustow, H.J. (1932) 'Stimulating the Economy. The Reich Government's Economic Programme', *Reich and Staat* (September).

Sargan, J.D. (1977) 'The Consumer Price Equation in the Post War British Economy. An Exercise in Equation Specification Testing', Econometrics Programme, SSRC, LSE, *Discussion Paper*, A.11.

Trades Union Congress (1976), *Economic Review*, Congress House, London (March).

Trades Union Congress (1977), *Economic Review*, Congress House, London (February).

18 Is Incomes Policy the Answer to Unemployment? (1982)*

In Western Europe unemployment has remained obstinately high ever since 1975. What has prevented governments from reducing it? The answer is simple. If unemployment were reduced by normal methods, inflation would rise. It follows that the only way to cut the long-run level of unemployment is to find some other way of controlling inflation. No such device will be costless. But if we could find any method that was less costly than unemployment, we ought to adopt it. Maurice Chevalier was asked in later life what he thought of old age. 'It's not so bad', he replied, 'when you consider the alternative'. That was a true economist talking, and it is also the spirit in which I shall approach the unhappy choices open to us.

My argument will proceed roughly as follows. First, imagine that a costless incomes policy is available. Then most people would probably agree that, if inflation was too high, a temporary incomes policy would be a good idea – in order to get inflation down. But what then, when it was down? We would still be left with far too high an unemployment rate. Only a permanent incomes policy can substantially reduce the non-inflationary level of unemployment. However, against these benefits have to be set the costs of an incomes policy. A conventional incomes policy, which permanently suspended collective bargaining, would be out of the question in a free society. So we have to have an incomes policy that works by incentive rather than by regulation. The best thing would be a tax on wage increases, levied on employers and proportional to wage increases above a prescribed norm. I shall spend some time discussing this tax using various different models of wage-setting to explain how it would have its effect. And finally, I shall try producing a first draft of the Operator's Manual.

* *Economica*, 49 (August 1982), pp. 219–39.

The Appendix to the paper is not reprinted here.

This is a revised version of an inaugural lecture presented at the London School of Economics (7 October 1981). I should like to thank the following for many helpful discussions and comments: O. Ashenfelter, J. Bray, D. Grubb, O. Hart, C. Huhne, R. Jackman, J. Kay, J. King, J.E. Meade, S. Nickell, D. Piachaud, C. Pissarides, C. Smallwood, A. Zabalza and A.P. Lerner, whose paper (Lerner, 1978) first aroused my interest in this subject.

1 THE CASE FOR A PERMANENT INCOMES POLICY

So let me start with the case for an incomes policy, assuming that it is costless. One must at once distinguish between the case for a policy designed to *reduce* inflation (which could be a temporary policy) and one designed to hold inflation *steady* (which would presumably be permanent). The case for a temporary policy is pretty obvious. The government wants to reduce inflation and can do this indirectly, by reducing the growth of total money spending, and possibly in addition by exerting direct control over wages or prices. We have only to look around us to see the problems of the indirect method. For if you control only money spending (which equals price times the quantity of output), there is in the short run no way of ensuring that what gets held down is price rather than quantity. In fact, comparing 1980 with 1979, about two-thirds of the reduced growth of money GNP went into a reduced growth of output rather than a reduced growth of prices.[1] By contrast if we use the direct method of control, we try to hold down unit costs as such, and leave quantity to be determined by the relation between money spending and unit costs. In this way, having two instruments instead of one, we can achieve two targets – a satisfactory inflation rate and a satisfactory level of employment.

We can formalize this argument using the standard inflation relation:

$$\dot{p} = \dot{p}^e - \gamma(U - U^*) \tag{18.1}$$

where $\dot{p}$ is price inflation, $\dot{p}^e$ expected price inflation and U is unemployment. This says that inflation will be less than expected only if unemployment is higher than some level U^*. If inflationary expectations depend on past experience of inflation, the inflation rate will fall only if unemployment exceeds U^*.

Now this relation holds in the absence of an incomes policy. Without an incomes policy any government that wants to reduce inflation has to raise unemployment, unless it can somehow reduce inflationary expectations by announcing monetary targets or other such tricks. By contrast, a government with an incomes policy can affect costs directly and may also in the process find that the inflationary pressure is itself reduced as expectations change.[2] Once inflation has been held down to a steady rate for long enough, inflationary expectations will come to equal inflation, and the level of unemployment will settle down at U^*.

That is how an incomes policy could ease the transition to a lower inflation rate. But could we then put incomes policy to bed? The answer to this question depends mainly on whether we are satisfied with the level of unemployment that would prevail with no incomes policy (which is U^*) – in the sense that it is the best that is open to us over a run of years.[3] Among what might be called *laissez-faire* economists, the usual line is that long-run unemployment can be reduced by microeconomic measures such as reducing benefits, but not by anything as macroeconomic-looking as an incomes policy. One line of reasoning is this. Long-run unemployment reflects an equilibrium where, apart from frictions, demand is in balance with effective supply. Those who want work at prevailing wages can get it. It follows that no form of wage control can increase the quantity of labour that is bought and sold, since, if wages are held down, fewer people will be willing to work.

This analysis can be challenged on theoretical and empirical grounds. First, a wage-inflation tax (though not a traditional incomes policy) could lower long-run unemployment even in a virtually competitive labour market, once one allows for the simultaneous existence of vacancies and unemployment. But second, and much more important, the labour market in Western Europe is not competitive. If all the main labour markets are affected by union monopoly, then any incomes policy can increase employment.[4]

I shall come back to these theoretical issues when I have developed my proposal. But first I have to establish the empirical evidence for the view that the competitive model is irrelevant in explaining Western European stagflation. To see this one has only to look at the data on labour shortage, which can be taken to reflect the tightness of the labour market. According to the competitive model, this tightness should not vary from one cycle to another, unless there is a major acceleration or deceleration of inflation. Yet in most Western European countries the labour market has been much more slack since 1975 than in any previous period since at least 1960. This is illustrated for Britain in Figure 18.1(a), which shows that since 1975 the shortage of skilled labour was in every year below its 1960–80 average. The official vacancy series for Germany, Belgium and the Netherlands tell an almost equally melancholy tale.[5] Yet if we compare early 1981 with 1976 there has been no net fall in the 12-monthly rate of wage inflation in the EEC, and very little even in Britain.[6] So evidently the labour market has to be much slacker nowadays in order to contain inflation than it did in earlier times.

2 THE CAUSES OF STAGFLATION

Some economists will say this cannot be. So let me help with a brief digression to explain how this wretched turn in our affairs has come about. This means we must investigate what determines the constant-inflation rate of unemployment U^* in (18.1). Contrary to what is often taught, this depends not only on the wage equation but also on the price equation. The wage equation is

$$\dot{w} = \dot{p}^e - \gamma(U - U_0) + \dot{x}^* \tag{18.2}$$

where $\dot{w}$ is wage inflation and $\dot{x}^*$ is the target real-wage growth that would be embodied in settlements when unemployment was at U_0. This is pretty

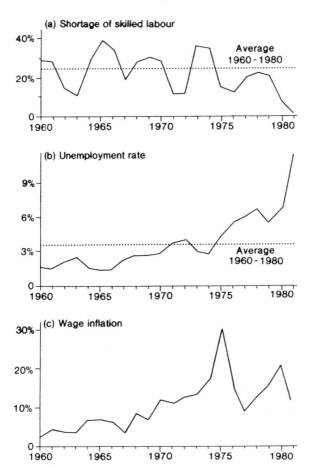

Figure 18.1 Labour shortages, unemployment rates and wage inflation, 1960–81. Each observation is an annual average; 1981 observation is for June–July.
(a) Shortage of skilled labour: percentage of firms in manufacturing expecting their output over the next four months to be limited by shortages of skilled labour (percentage is weighted by number of employees).
Source: Confederation of British Industries, *Industrial Trends Survey*.
(b) Unemployment rate, seasonally adjusted, excluding school-leavers. (c) Wage inflation: average weekly earnings, 12-monthly rate of increase.

familiar. The price equation is, say,

$$\dot{p} = \dot{w} - \dot{x} \tag{18.3}$$

where $\dot{x}$ is the feasible rate of real wage growth when unemployment is constant.[7] This also is pretty familiar. Yet substituting (18.2) into (18.3) we get something not so familiar:

$$\dot{p} = \dot{p}^e - \gamma \left\{ U - \left(U_0 + \frac{x^* - \dot{x}}{\gamma} \right) \right\} \tag{18.1'}$$

This says that the long-run unemployment rate will rise if the feasible rate of growth of real wages falls, assuming that this fall is not matched by a fall in the level of real wage settlements that would occur at a given unemployment rate.

Well, there has certainly been a fall in the rate of feasible real wage growth since 1973. Let me take Britain as an example and give some purely illustrative calculations. Comparing the period since 1973 with the 15 years before that, the long-run annual rate of growth of labour productivity has fallen by $1\frac{1}{2}$ percentage points. In addition, relative import prices, which improved by $1\frac{1}{2}$ per cent a year up to 1972, have worsened on average by $2\frac{1}{2}$ per cent a year since then. This, after allowing for the share of imports in GDP, implies a further fall in feasible real wage growth of nearly 1 percentage point a year. Thus, the feasible annual growth rate of real wages $\dot{x}$ has fallen by nearly $2\frac{1}{2}$ percentage points altogether, implying a rise in the long-run unemployment rate of $2\frac{1}{2}$ points divided by γ. To find γ I have here estimated a highly simplified Phillips Curve, in which expected inflation is proxied by lagged inflation.[8] This indicates that γ is around 1.6. Thus the long-run unemployment rate rose by $1\frac{1}{2}$ percentage points, which helps to explain the increase in unemployment between the early 1970s and the late 1970s.

David Grubb, Richard Jackman and I have developed a somewhat more sophisticated version of this model and applied it to each of 19 OECD countries. We have found that it explains quite well the change in the relation between labour slack and inflation on a country-by-country basis.[9] Interestingly enough, most of these countries have pretty well defined Phillips Curves. Of course, many of them, like Britain, have also experienced substantial increases in unemployment, owing not to increased slackness in the labour market, but rather to supply-side forces. For Britain this effect can be seen by comparing Figures 18.1(a) and 18.1(b), which show how, from the mid-1960s onwards, the unemployment rate at a given level of labour shortage has risen. It can also be seen from the time trend in the wage equation.[10] Since there is no evidence of growing mismatch between workers and jobs (Nickell, 1982, Table 3), this increase in the degree of labour shortage at a given level of unemployment must mean that unemployed workers became, over the 1960s and 1970s, more choosy about what work they would accept – perhaps owing in part to a less stringent application of work test (Layard, 1981, Table 1).

But the key point for today is that the rise in unemployment in the 1970s was due not only to supply side forces of this kind; it was also due to a failure of the wage-setting process, which has required more labour slack than ever before in order to contain inflation.

One would of course expect that in due course the target real-wage growth in the wage equation would change to reflect whatever changes had happened to the feasible rate of growth of real wages. But there is no reason why adjustment should be quick. Employers and workers may feel they have implicit long-term contracts guaranteeing significant real wage growth (see e.g. Okun, 1981). Or alternatively, if we think of the unions as the prime movers in real-wage determination, union members may misperceive the general rate of real wage growth in the economy. The model of union wage-setting that I shall develop later gives one a Phillips Curve just like (18.1′), with $\dot{x}^*$ corresponding to individual unionists' perception of what is happening elsewhere in the economy.

Thus my basic argument so far is this. Unemployment has to be high enough to prevent inflation from increasing. The required level of unemployment does not correspond to a competitive equilibrium. Long-run unemployment is higher the lower the real-wage increase that people have to be forced to accept (given their target). But unemployment could be permanently reduced if some other force in addition to unemployment could be brought to bear, which would help induce people to accept the rate of growth of real wages that is feasible. Incomes policy is the obvious candidate, and I would therefore without question support a permanent incomes policy, if it were costless.

3 REQUIREMENTS OF AN INCOMES POLICY

But, alas, no incomes policies are costless. So let me set our four required characteristics of an incomes policy and see how each can be achieved at least cost. As I have already argued, the first requisite is permanence. This immediately rules out traditional incomes policies. For the essence of these is that they prohibit the free bargaining of wages between employers and workers. This may be tolerable for short periods, but is intolerable on a permanent basis. It is not just that regulatory agencies or procedures are unlikely to produce an efficient pattern of wages. A more important cost is the politicization of an area of life that is best left to decentralized decision-making. Regulation in this area breeds frustration and discontent. The main cost of a permanent incomes policy is the loss of liberty that it involves. Any attempt to impose a permanent incomes policy of a traditional type would almost certainly, as in the late 1970s, lead to unrest and probably to the humiliation of the government. That is why both Tory and Labour Parties are now so leery of incomes policies. However, the answer to their fears lies in a policy that works by incentive rather than by regulation. The virtue of tax-based incomes policies is that individual agents have all the decision-making powers they had before. They just face an additional tax constraint, which forces them to take into account the interest that the public has in full employment.

The second requisite of a policy is that it should not take away from workers any part of their gross pay. A scheme that did this would face impossible political opposition and would soon be dropped. So the tax must be levied on employers, and not on workers.[11] But there are also technical reasons. Employees could not be taxed on the basis of their own personal increases in earnings, since this would make it impossible to operate incremental scales and would discourage job mobility and promotion effort. So an employee tax should have to be levied on the basis of increases in group earnings, which would lead to endless arguments about what group an individual belonged to.

Third, the tax should be based on the money that employers actually pay out and not on the notional value of settlements. It is hourly earnings that determine the cost of labour, and these should be the tax base. If instead we used earnings per *worker*, we should penalize an employer who increased overtime and provide an incentive for employers to dilute their tax base by hiring lots of very part-time workers – perhaps ones who did practically no work at all.

Fourth, there is the issue of income distribution. Most incomes policies in the past have had some bias in favour of the low-paid – the clearest case being the £6 a week flat rate policy introduced by Denis Healey. Though I believe income distribution matters desperately, it should be dealt with through taxes and transfers and not through pay policy. There are three reasons for this (see Layard, 1980). First, there is the employment effect on the low-paid, for which there is some good evidence (see, for example, Hamermesh, 1981). Second, the relation between low pay and low income per family member is very weak, suggesting that fiscal policy should be the main instrument of redistribution. And, third, it is in any case very difficult by administrative fiat to alter the distribution of gross earnings when other forces are pulling in defence of the status quo: between April 1975 and April 1976, while the lowest decile got the prescribed £6 a week, the upper decile got £17.

So an incomes policy should be proportional in design. It should permit as much as possible of the medium-run adjustment of differentials that is dictated by market forces. But it would be no bad thing if it suppressed some of the random year-to-year variations in differentials, which are one of the most costly results of inflation, demoralizing the temporary losers more than they satisfy the temporary gainers. Perhaps as much as 80 per cent of the year-to-year changes in relativities that occurred in the 1970s were disfunctional. I arrive at this figure as follows. First take the annual wage increase in each bargaining group in each year and look at the dispersion of this across groups. Now, taking the earnings increase in each group over the ten years 1970–80 expressed as an annual average, and look at the dispersion of this across groups. The first figure is on average five times as large as the second (Ashenfelter and Layard, 1983, Table 4). In other words, most short-run changes in relativities get reversed soon after – and have no useful effect on the allocation of labour. Needless to say, the higher the level of inflation, the higher the dispersion of year-to-year pay increases. Low inflation, especially when linked to an incomes policy, tends to reduce the amount of pointless change in relativities.

4 A WAGE-INFLATION TAX AND HOW IT HAS ITS EFFECT

So if you accept my four requirements, there is just about only one way of doing things, which is this. Each year the government would declare a norm for the rate of growth of hourly earnings. If an employer increased his average hourly earnings by more than this, all his excess payments would be subject to a tax; likewise, he could be rewarded for payment below the norm. The tax would have nothing to do with the pay of any individual – only with the average hourly earnings at the level of the firm.

The idea of an employer-based wage-inflation tax is not new.[12] The challenge is to find an appropriate design for the tax, and a satisfactory way of analyzing its effects in the whole-economy context.[13] Let me first suggest an important additional feature of the design. We do not want the tax to increase the net tax burden on companies, for three reasons. First, we do not want to treat firms unfairly as compared with workers. Second, we do not want any net passing-on of the tax into prices. Third, we want a revenue-neutral scheme: we do not want a scheme that (like monetarism) automatically increases unemployment if wages go up faster than is expected. So I suggest that in each period the rate of social security contributions should be reduced (or 'rebated') by an amount that would in aggregate just offset the tax proceeds from the wage-inflation tax. This 'rebate' would be proportional to the firm's total wage-bill, while the tax was proportional to its excess wage bill.[14]

So what would be the effect of the scheme? Would it really reduce inflationary pressure at given unemployment and thus permit a lower long-run unemployment rate? My claim is that the tax in effect modifies the Phillips Curve by adding an extra term ($-\beta t$ where t is the tax rate):

$$\dot{w} = \dot{p}^e - \gamma(U - U_0) + \dot{x}^* - \beta t$$

In this way, in the short run it permits *either* the same inflation path and lower unemployment *or* the same unemployment and a lower inflation path. This effect is, of course, strengthened if the tax also affects price expectations. In the long run, the inflation rate has to be determined by the rate of growth of money income (adjusted for potential output). So the inflation tax becomes exclusively a mechanism for raising the level of employment.

To establish my claim, let me first give some rather intuitive arguments before becoming more formal. Under the tax any firm that gives a £1 wage increase will lose not only the pound, but also £1 times the tax rate. If the tax rate were 100 per cent, it would lose £2; if the tax rate were infinite, it would lose everything. This affects inflationary pressure by modifying the behaviour of both employers and workers. It provides employers with a stronger incentive to resist wage claims. This is so even though the employer with an average wage increase receives roughly as much rebate as he pays tax (see n. 14). For the rebate is unaffected by his current wage increase, while the tax depends crucially upon it. If the firm can now save £2 by paying £1 less, it will be more likely than before to pay £1 less. Of course, if all firms conspired to give the same increase, then there would be no way in which they could affect their net tax liability by paying less. But British industry is fortunately not monolithic, and British firms will respond to a wage-inflation tax just as British drivers respond to a tax on speeding – even though British drivers, if they colluded, would notice that higher fines would be offset by lower taxes.

The tax will also discourage workers from pushing wage claims so far. For the tax reduces the employer's demand for labour at high wages (when he pays a net tax per worker) and increases the employer's demand for labour at low wages (when he receives a net subsidy per worker). The union realizes this and concludes that an additional wage claim will now have more of an effect on unemployment than it would without the tax. It therefore chooses a lower wage claim.

To examine both these effects more rigorously, we have to specify some formal model of the economy and then work it through. I shall concentrate on the long-run level of employment. There are essentially three possible models of this, each of which has elements of truth in it, and in each of which we shall find that the inflation tax does reduce unemployment.

The first model is one in which workers are organized into unions but employers are fragmented. The unions are thus the prime-movers in wage determination and do the best they can for their members, after taking into account the employment effects of their actions. Let me briefly discuss a model of this kind that Richard Jackman and I have developed.

Each representative union faces a competitive demand curve for labour in its sector, illustrated as *DD* in Figure 18.2. Subject to this constraint, it maximizes the wage bill in its industry *plus* the income that members who cannot get work in this industry can expect to get elsewhere. This latter, of course, depends on the general national level of unemployment, which is why in this model unemployment has such a dampening effect on wage settlements. Point A

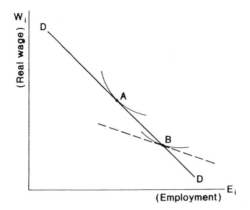

Figure 18.2 The labour market in the *i*th industry

shows the union's choice of wage and employment in the absence of an inflation tax. If we assume that *ex post* workers have to get paid the same wages as they think prevail elsewhere, then unemployment equals $\theta/(\eta - 1 + \theta)$, where η is the elasticity of demand and θ the fraction of workers in an industry hired from outside. Thus the unemployment rate is higher, the lower the elasticity of demand and the greater the consequent monopoly power of the unions.[15]

So how can one reduce the level of unemployment? Obviously, by making the effective demand curve faced by unions more elastic. This is exactly what the inflation tax does. If a firm gives more than the average wage increase, the firm is subject to a net tax per worker, while if it gives less than the average wage increase it is subject to a net subsidy. This reduces the demand for labour at high wages and raises it at low wages. Thus, tax-based incomes policy (TIP) works, appropriately enough, by tipping the demand curve – to the dotted line shown in Figure 18.2. Unemployment is now given by $\theta/\{\eta(1 + \delta t) - 1 + \theta\}$ where t is the rate of inflation tax and δ is the union's real rate of discount. So unemployment has fallen and employment risen. This is illustrated in point B.

This model seems to me quite powerful. Unlike many models of union-determined wages, it gives rise to a standard Phillips Curve wage equation. And this equation predicts that unemployment rises if unions have exaggerated impressions of real-wage growth elsewhere in the economy – a possible explanation of our (18.1′). But the basic point of this model is that an inflation tax works by confronting the unions with worse consequences if they raise wages. It thus reduces their monopoly power, but does this by a tax rather than by the thorny route of labour legislation.

A second model is one in which both employers and workers are actively involved in wage determination through a process of bargaining at industry level or below. Unfortunately, there is no very satisfactory model of bargaining outcomes, but a rather crude line of argument goes like this (see Seidmann, 1978). Wages are determined where the downwards push from the employers equals the upwards push from the workers. A unique wage bill will be determined, because, the higher the wage being considered, the more employers push down and the less hard workers push up. Now suppose a wage inflation tax is introduced. Even if employers expect it to have no effect on wages and prices in the rest of the economy, they will push harder for lower wages in their industry, because by paying lower wages they now save more money than they would have without the tax. Hence, even if the push from workers remains the same, a lower wage will be settled for. This analysis, of course, assumes that the general level of unemployment (which affects the bargaining power of the two sides) is the same in both cases. Thus, in a climate of given price expectations, the tax produces less wage inflation for a given unemployment. Hence, in a steady-state inflation, where price expectations are fulfilled, we must have less unemployment than we would if we had no tax.

This line of reasoning is rather casual and better models of bargaining outcomes are needed. Stephen Nickell and Christopher Pissarides have been working on the bargaining case and have found that the conclusions of the first model hold in a world of bargaining between firms and workers (Nickell, 1981; Pissarides, 1981 and 1982).

Finally there is a third model, where neither workers nor firms are organized, but where firms have complete control over wage determination. Christopher Pissarides (1981) has developed a useful model of this kind. The firms believe they can get more workers only by raising wages, but this monopsony power is only temporary, and does not lead to any permanent profit. This model is thus the nearest we can get to describing a competitive equilibrium, while assigning an explicit wage-setting role to firms. However, unlike normal competitive models, where employment is determined by supply or demand, whichever is the less, this model allows for the obvious fact that vacancies and unemployment co-exist. How, then, would unemployment change if a tax were introduced? Each firm now has an additional incentive to lower real wages, because it saves more money by doing so. This leads to a fall in real wages and an increase in vacancies. With more vacancies unemployed workers can find jobs more easily, so equilibrium unemployment falls. Thus, even in a purely competitive model, a wage inflation tax can work. Obviously, some labour markets in the economy are more like one of our three models and some are more like another. But the reassuring point is that the tax works whatever the model.

It is more difficult to analyze its effects in the short run than in the long run because the effects on expectations are not easy to model. However, there is every reason to suppose that the mechanisms I have described for the long run would also work in the short run, plus some added gain through effects on expectations.

I have not so far mentioned the public sector. Here one must distinguish between central government, local government and the nationalized industries. Only the last two would pay the tax. But all sectors would benefit from the tax, in two ways. First, if comparability is used as an argument in pay settlements, any scheme that helps in the private sector must contribute to the problem of public sector pay. I regard that as crucial. there is a strong tendency to suppose that it is one or two settlements in the public sector (especially the miners) that somehow determine the national inflation rate. That is absolutely wrong, as one can see from what is going on now. Broadly, private sector pay is determined by the economic forces at work in the private sector, and public sector pay follows the private sector inflation rate with some lurches in the name of catch-up.

Moreover, a sensible general norm could help to provide a frame of reference in public pay negotiations. In central government there could be a presumption that workers get the norm plus a catch-up equal to the difference between last year's norm and last year's actual wage increase in the private sector. This formula would be modified to allow extra increases for central government employees whose occupation was in shortage or whose comparator group has grown faster than the private sector average. Any extra payments of this type would of course be deducted when calculating the catch-up. In this way average pay in central government and the private sector would grow in line,[16] although individual occupations in the public sector would rise or fall relative to the national average, according to their shortage position or the movements in the comparator groups.

So much for public services. In the nationalized industries the tax would have an additional effect through the incentive that it provided to employers to resist wage increases (just as in the private sector). This incentive would obviously not hold if it was known that the cash limit would be reduced to pay the tax, and doubtless this would sometimes occur. Thus, it may be that the tax would have little effect on miner's pay. But if it affected the pay of the other 99 per cent of us, it would be well worth having.

5 INCIDENCE

Let me now turn to the incidence of the tax. Clearly, anything that increases employment benefits the genuinely unemployed. But would an inflation tax also benefit those who already have work? A common left-wing argument against incomes policy is that it will lower real wages. This is partly true and partly not. In the very short run, if wage inflation starts falling before price inflation does, real wages can fall quite sharply at the beginning of an incomes policy. But equally, under mark-up pricing, price inflation would go on falling after wage inflation had stopped falling, so real wages would at that stage be restored.

However, there is some evidence that mark-up pricing is not the whole story, and that in the medium term prices have to rise relative to wages if employment is to rise (Symons, 1981).[17] This is what I have been assuming in my earlier analysis. But, if it is true, then a successful inflation tax must lower real wages for a given capital stock. However, we must then allow for the fact that if employment is higher the tax rates needed to finance a given government expenditure will be lower, not to mention the reduced financing of unemployment benefit. Moreover, with higher activity there will be more investment. The capital stock will become larger and this will tend to raise the real wage. So workers have little to fear from incomes policy in the medium and long run. But union leaders inevitably have a short time-horizon, and may find it difficult to agree to a policy.[18] That is why it is so essential to have a policy that can, if necessary, be implemented without union agreement, although it is sincerely to be hoped that union leaders would prefer to have the necessary restraint imposed by a tax, rather than by unemployment which is the only alternative.

6   DESIGN

Let me now turn to some more nuts-and-bolts issues of tax design. Should one provide for a negative range of tax? Let me first put the argument in favour of providing for this. The reason is this. If firms that pay below the norm in any quarter get no credit for it in the form of a negative tax, then the tax penalizes those firms where wages grow in jumps relative to those with the same long-run wage growth but having a steadier growth path. If this is unacceptable, we have to have a negative range of tax, within which slow wage growth is rewarded. For the same reason, the rebate cannot be confined to firms paying below the norm or some other cut-off.

This leaves us with a positive and negative range of tax, and a rebate payable to all. Thus, taking the tax and rebate together, we have a net tax schedule in which firms paying above the average pay positive net tax and those paying below the average pay negative net tax. In such a set-up, what is the function of the norm? In terms of formal economic theory it has no role,[19] in which case we might just as well have a zero norm and tax all earnings growth.

This line of thought has its attractions. But against it one must allow for the psychological value of a realistic norm. The norm could have an important effect of its own if it could be chosen so that the *ex post* inflation rate was usually fairly near it. One must also allow for the massive political difficulties of rewarding firms by paying below the norm. So it would probably be best to have no negative range of tax and to aim at a realistic norm.

Turning to the tax rate, this would obviously have to be quite high. For when a firm raises its wage it pays a once-for-all tax. The true annual cost to the firm of raising its wage by £1 is (in pounds sterling) only the tax rate times the discount rate.[20] For this reason, the tax rate will need to be at least 50 per cent and probably 100 per cent.

As regards the definition of hourly earnings, earnings could probably be defined as for PAYE. Hours pose more problems. For the 90 per cent or so of workers whose pay varies according to their hours, there is no problem. We want to know the actual hours they worked (since these determine output). If we confine the tax-cum-rebate scheme to firms with over 100 workers (which is desirable on many grounds), we shall find that nearly all the firms have an automatic record of the hours worked by workers whose pay is related to hours worked. Problems arise with other workers, since firms will not normally know the hours that they actually worked. For workers who have contractual hours firms could be asked to enter in each quarter their annual contractual hours divided by 4. For workers like academics and some salesmen, who have no contractual hours, employers would be asked to enter a nominal figure. If in one year a firm recorded an increase in the average hours of workers not paid by time, it would have to supply detailed evidence to the Inland Revenue.

Next, the start-up problem. In the year after the announcement of the tax, firms may not have adequate records of earnings and hours for the previous year. But if the tax were announced in advance there would be a danger of firms conceding big wage increases before the tax came in, so as to reduce their tax liability in the following year. This suggests that the government might have to announce simultaneously the introduction of a one-year incomes policy of the old style, plus the fact that it would be followed in the second year and thereafter by a tax. Thus, when the tax eventually came in every firm would have a data base for the previous year.

As regards the problem of anomalies existing at the beginning of the scheme, the scheme should make no explicit allowance for them. They will of course be gradually rectified, at some cost to employers, but there is little more that can be done about them. No other incomes policy has found any successful method of handling this problem. There is also a problem connected with the timing of the wage round. To ensure that a firm's inflation tax liabilities do not vary widely from quarter to quarter, the tax should relate to the excess of a firm's average payments in each quarter over their level in the corresponding quarter a year earlier.

7   COSTS OF THE TAX

These are the outlines of the scheme. I have already praised it for its benefits. What costs should be set against them? The main cost is the fact that the tax discourages adjustment in the labour market. It will discourage expanding firms from raising wages in order to attract more labour,[21] and thus slow down the redeployment of the workforce. The tax will also discourage productivity agreements, though less than might at first sight appear, since over a run of years pay rises no faster in industries of high productivity growth than in those of low productivity growth. These costs are important, but are worth bearing for the sake of substantially higher employment.

Next, since the tax bears on average hourly earnings irrespective of the skill composition of the workforce, it provides an incentive to firms to employ relatively more unskilled people, and by the same token penalizes firms that wish to move towards a relatively more skilled workforce. This is a more mild distortion, and some would regard it as a desirable boost to the demand for unskilled labour that could offset the inefficiency caused by too high wages for the unskilled. The tax also discourages overtime, which some would count as a virtue.

Third, there is the administrative cost. This would not be horrific. The tax would be paid quarterly to the Inland Revenue, and self-assessed by the company (like PAYE and National Insurance). The company would send a tax cheque quarterly to the relevant computer centre, and receive its 'rebate' as a quarterly cheque from the same computer centre. The company would be subject to a spot audit at one week's notice (as with PAYE and national insurance). At present the audit of the whole of PAYE and national insurance at the firm's end requires under 500 inspectors, so there is no reason why the audit of the inflation tax should require more than another 100 or so.[22]

8   DIVIDENDS AND PRICES

An incomes policy would of course have to control capital income as well as wages. The natural thing would be to have a similar scheme for dividends as for wages. There could be the same norm, and the same tax rate on increases above the norm. There would also of course have to be a share-out of the tax proceeds.

There would of course be complaints that reinvested profits were exempt from control. However, these are of distributional significance only if there are corresponding capital gains accruing to households; and the share of real capital gains in household income is rather small these days. In any case, capital gains can be handled by capital gains tax.

If it were felt politically necessary, one could operate a prices policy as well as a wages policy. This could be of the traditional kind, aiming to maintain a reasonable level of mark-up over cost. There are however notorious difficulties in controlling for changes in the quality of products, as well as efficiency costs even if you do. One thing is clear: a prices policy is certain to fail without a wages policy, whereas a wages policy can work without a prices policy.

9 CONCLUSION

Before summing up I should like to thank most warmly my colleagues at the Centre for Labour Economics, and especially Richard Jackman, for the uncountable hours we have spent discussing these issues. The questions are enormously important, but also, alas, enormously difficult, involving as they do the whole question of how the labour market works. No one understands this very well, and if it were not for the magnitude of the issue I would hesitate to suggest another change in our social arrangements.

But suppose that such a tax enabled us permanently to reduce unemployment by 2 percentage points, as well as avoiding the horrors of the temporary unemployment required to change the inflation rate. What magnitude of costs should be set against these benefits? Some microeconomic inefficiency, without a doubt. But the whole cost of monopoly and tariffs is often estimated at less than 2 per cent of GNP (see for example Harberger, 1954, and Johnson, 1960). Surely the costs of an inflation tax will be trivial compared with the cost of monopoly and tariffs, and therefore far less than the benefits of lower unemployment. The more we actually experience of the real costs of unemployment, the more compelling becomes the case for fighting inflation some other way.

Notes

1. If Y is log-nominal GDP, y log-real GDP and p the log GDP deflator, then $\Delta^2 Y \equiv \Delta^2 y + \Delta^2 p$. If Δ^2 is $\{1981(\text{I}) - 1980(\text{I})\} - \{1980(\text{I}) - 1979(\text{I})\}$, $\Delta^2 y = \frac{2}{3}\Delta^2 Y$.
2. The legal effect of incomes policy would tend to supersede equation (18.1), but the effect of it on $\dot{p}^e$ would also help to reduce incentives to break the law. The evidence on effects on $\dot{p}^e$ is ambiguous. There is evidence of price expectations from the Gallup Poll, FT and CBI surveys and of wage expectations from FT and CBI surveys. Only the Gallup Poll price series and the FT wage series show any sharp drop in late 1975.
3. There is also the catch-up argument that, in the period *after* the temporary incomes policy, inflation will go back to its former level, partly because price expectations have never really altered and partly, perhaps, because of troubles

over real wages. However, the econometric evidence on this in relation to past policies is not conclusive either way. Wadhwani (1985) suggests that the inflationary leap in 1978–79 was not a straightforward catch-up. The main causes were the earlier price increases (owing to depreciation) and the increase in vacancies.

4. Minford (1981) has a union sector *and* a competitive sector, and would therefore deny the potential effectiveness of incomes policy. However, his estimates imply a rise in the union mark-up from 10 per cent in 1963 to 74 per cent in 1979, which is not consistent with the evidence of the New Earnings Survey (Ashenfelter and Layard, 1983) or with other results (Layard, Metcalf and Nickell, 1978). The findings would imply massive falls in real wages in the competitive sector.

5. In 1981 vacancies were down more in Britain than anywhere else.

6. *Department of Employment Gazette*, July 1981, Table 5.9.

7. (18.3) should be $\dot{p} = \dot{w} - \dot{x} - \delta U$, but has been simplified for expositional purposes.

8. Using annual data for 1960–80 inclusive, I find

$$\dot{w} = \dot{p}_{-1} - 1.61\,U + 0.0054\,T - 0.10D + 0.098$$
$$\quad\quad\quad (1.9)\quad\ \ (2.5)\quad\quad (4.6)$$

where T is years since 1970 and D is an incomes policy dummy for 1976 and 1977. (*t*-statistics in brackets); $D - W = 2.02$; se $= 0.027$. Chow-test compared with 1960–74 is $F(5, 12) = 1.66$. An incomes policy catch-up dummy for 1978 and 1979 was insignificant.

9. Grubb, Jackman and Layard (1982).

10. The wage equation implies that unemployment has been growing for supply-side reasons by 0.34 percentage points a year. If one regresses the percentage rate of unemployment on the pressure of demand and on time, we get, for 1960–80,

$$U = 3.63 - 0.045\,S + 0.217\,T + 0.013\,T^2 \quad D - W = 1.22$$
$$\quad\quad\ \ (5.0)\quad\ \ (16.1)\quad\ \ (5.5)$$

and

$$U = 4.15 - 0.0084\,V + 0.229\,T + 0.016\,T^2 \quad D - W = 1.41$$
$$\quad\quad\ \ (8.0)\quad\quad\ \ (24.6)\quad\quad (9.1)$$

where S is percentage of firms experiencing shortage of skilled labour, V is vacancies at employment exchange ('000), and T is years since 1970. These regressions imply a rather slower average increase in supply-side unemployment over the period (0.22 points a year). We explain the difference in a moment.

We can compute the level of unemployment in 1980 that would correspond to the average level of labour market tightness in the period 1960–80. Using either of the equations in this note, this comes out at about $6\frac{1}{4}$ per cent. We can now compare this with the constant-inflation rate of unemployment implied by the wage equation at the average rate of growth of real wages over the period 1960–80 of 2.6 per cent. This gives a figure of $7\frac{1}{2}$ per cent. The reason for the difference is that, at the average level of labour market tightness, inflation increased by about

15 per cent over the period plus an additional 20 per cent which was 'suppressed' by incomes policy. To eliminate this $1\frac{3}{4}$ per cent per annum acceleration of inflation would require an additional $1\frac{1}{8}$ per cent of unemployment.

As regards the constant-inflation rate of unemployment at the *current* rate of real wage growth of, say, $1\frac{1}{2}$ per cent (assuming no further rises in relative import prices), this would on the above reckoning be $8\frac{1}{4}$ per cent.

11.   For a useful discussion of various schemes see Blackaby (1980).

12.   A tax of this type was originally suggested by Wallich and Weintraub (1971). In their version, the firm's corporation tax rate was varied in relation to the rate of its excess wage increase. A whole issue of the *Brookings Papers* (1978, No. 2) was devoted to discussing the proposal. In Britain the tax was independently suggested by Wiles and Roberts (1971) and became Liberal Party policy in the early 1970s.

13.   For other analyses of the Wallich-Weintraub tax see Seidmann (1978), Meade (1982) and Kotowitz and Portes (1974). Seidmann's bargaining model and his monopsony model have no general equilibrium context, and his general equilibrium treatment makes the inflation tax work via reduced profits, in which case why not just have a profits tax? Meade offers a monopsony model in a general equilibrium context, but relies on a somewhat *ad hoc* effect of the tax in the wage equation (resulting in a reduced mark-up of prices over wages). Unemployment does not appear in his wage equation. An analysis that is explicitly partial equilibrium is that by Kotowitz and Portes, who look at one market with unions setting wages. The unions' 'utility' depends on the rate of growth of money wages and the rate of growth of employment. If there is a tax, a union facing a demand curve rising at a given rate will choose a lower rate of growth of wages and a higher rate of growth of employment.

14.   Thus, the tax liability of a firm would be

$$t\left(\frac{g-\pi}{1+g}\right)(EW)$$

and its rebate would be $s(EW)_{-1}$, where t is the tax rate, g the growth rate of hourly earnings, π the norm growth rate, and EW the wage-bill. The self-balancing character of the scheme ensures that

$$s = t\frac{\bar{g}-\pi}{1+\bar{g}}$$

where $\bar{g}$ refers to the national average.

15.   Identical results would follow if the tax were levied on workers. It is natural to ask how inflation enters into our tax since it is essentially a marginal tax on wages. Given this, could not the same results be achieved by an ordinary proportional tax on labour, linked to an equal-yield flat-rate subsidy – such as we have in the present income tax? There are two insuperable difficulties. First, our proposal is for a tax on hourly earnings, whereas an income tax or social security tax is levied on weekly earnings and thus has a much greater efficiency cost in terms of labour supply. It *could not* be levied on individual hourly earnings because there are enough *individuals* for whom these could be defined only in an arbitrary way. Second, one would like to levy our tax at quite high marginal rates

(e.g. 50–100 per cent on wages net of the tax). Such rates are politically unthinkable if levied on the base of *all* earnings, even though the later (linked to an equal yield subsidy) is analytically equivalent to the same tax rate levied on all hourly earnings above a norm (linked to a much smaller subsidy).

16. This is so only if inflation is stable. Rising inflation would hurt public sector workers and vice versa. Note that in the long run public and private sector pay do in any case grow at the same rate (*Department of the Employment Gazette*, December 1977, pp. 1338–1339).

17. For the debate on this issue see the references in Symons (1981).

18. As Isard (1973) pointed out, it is possible but not certain that the policy would lead to more strikes. But a few more strikes are surely more acceptable than mass unemployment. To investigate this question one might start from the model of Ashenfelter and Johnson (1969). If the tax left the workers' reaction function unchanged, it would lead employers to choose lower wages and more strikes. But in the transition phase the tax could well lower the reaction function of workers. However, this whole model is based on wage-setting by employers rather than by workers, and the latter seems on the whole more relevant (see my first model above).

19. A glance at Figure 18.2 shows that the level of W and E is determined only by the level of the marginal tax rate.

20. For a similar argument using the union's discount rate see the appendix.

21. For evidence that changes in relative wages are an important mechanism for redeploying labour, see Pissarides (1978).

22. For further discussion of administration issues see Jackman and Layard (1982).

References

Ashenfelter, O. and G. Johnson (1969) 'Bargaining Theory, Trade Unions, and Industrial Strike Activity', *American Economic Review*, 59, 35–49.

Ashenfelter, O. and R. Layard (1983) 'Incomes Policy and Wage Differentials', *Economica*, vol. 50, No. 198.

Blackaby, F. (1980) 'An Array of Proposals', in *The Future of Pay Bargaining* (F. Blackaby, ed.), (London: Heinemann).

Grubb, D., R. Jackman and R. Layard (1982) 'Causes of the Current Stagflation', *Review of Economic Studies*, 707–730.

Hamermesh, D. (1981) 'Minimum Wages and Demand for Labour', National Bureau of Economic Research, Working Paper no. 656.

Harberger, A.C. (1954) 'Monopoly and Resource Allocation', *American Economic Review*, 64, 77–87.

Isard, P. (1973) 'The Effectiveness of Using the Tax System to Curb Inflationary Collective Bargains: An Analysis of the Wallich-Weintraub Plan', *Journal of Political Economy*, 81, 729–740.

Jackman, R. and R. Layard (1982) 'An Inflation Tax', *Fiscal Studies*, 3, 47–59.

Johnson, H.G. (1960) 'The Cost of Protection and the Scientific Tariff', *Journal of Political Economy*, 68, 327–345.

Kotowitz, Y. and R. Portes (1974) 'The "Tax on Wage Increases"', *Journal of Public Economics*, 3, 113–132.

Layard, R. (1980) 'Wages Policy and the Redistribution of Income', *Income Distribution: The Limits to Redistribution* (D. Collard, R. Lecomber and M. Slater, eds) Colston Society, (Bristol: Bristol University Press).

Layard, R. (1981) 'Unemployment in Britain: Causes and Cures', *Work and Social Change*, 6, European Centre for Work and Society (Maastricht) (November) pp. 7–36. Chapter 12 of the present book.

Layard, R. (1982) *Jobs without Inflation. The case for a counter-inflation tax* (London: Grant McIntyre).

Layard, R., D. Metcalf and S. Nickell (1978) 'The Effects of Collective Bargaining on Relative Wages', *The Economics of Income Distribution* (A. Shorrocks and W. Krelle, eds) and *British Journal of Industrial Relations*, 16, 287–302.

Lerner, A.P. (1978) 'A Wage-Increase Permit Plan to Stop Inflation', *Brookings Papers on Economic Activity*, no. 2.

Meade, J.E. (1982) *Stagflation*. Volume 1: *Wage-Fixing* (London: Allen and Unwin), Chapter X and Appendix C.

Minford, P. (1981) 'Labour Market Equilibrium in an Open Economy', paper presented at the Cambridge Conference on Unemployment, University of Liverpool, mimeo.

Nickell, S. (1982) 'The Determinants of Equilibrium Unemployment in Britain', *Economic Journal*.

Nickell, S. (1981) 'Some Notes on a Bargaining Model of the Phillips Curve', Centre for Labour Economics, LSE, *Working Paper*, no. 338.

Okun, A.M. (1981) *Prices and Quantities* (Oxford: Basil Blackwell).

Pissarides, C. (1978) 'The Role of Relative Wages and Excess Demand in the Sectoral Flow of Labour', *Review of Economic Studies*, 45, 453–467.

Pissarides, C. (1981) 'The Effects of a Wage Tax on Equilibrium Unemployment', Centre for Labour Economics, LSE, *Discussion Paper*, no. 118.

Pissarides, C. (1982) 'Trade Unions and the Number of Jobs in a Model of the Natural Rate of Unemployment', Centre for Labour Economics, LSE, *Discussion Paper*, no. 124.

Seidmann, L.S. (1978) 'Tax-Based Incomes Policies', *Brookings Papers on Economic Activity*, no. 2.

Symons, J. (1981) 'The Demand for Labour in British Manufacturing', Centre for Labour Economics, LSE, *Discussion Paper*, no. 91.

Wadhwani, S. (1985) 'Wage Inflation in the UK', *Economica*, May 1985.

Wallich, H.C. and S. Weintraub (1971) 'A Tax-Based Incomes Policy', *Journal of Economic Issues*, 5, 1–19.

Wiles, P.J. and B.C. Roberts (1971) *Evening Standard*, 8 March, 1971.

19 The Real Effects of Tax-based Incomes Policies (1990)*

with R. Jackman

1 INTRODUCTION AND SUMMARY

In most countries the citizens desire lower unemployment. They also understand that this raises a problem of inflation and are consequently sympathetic to incomes policy. However, most actual incomes policies have collapsed – often after a period of success.

There are three main reasons why mandatory attempts to impose wage norms fail. First, of necessity they involve interferences with (or even suspension of) free collective bargaining between individual employers and their workers. Neither individual firms nor local union leaders like this. Second, they rigidify the wage structure, which can lead to labour shortages that are undesirable and generate huge pressures on wages. Third, the policies are typically too crude to contain earnings drift, through regrading of staff, bonuses and other evasive tactics.

In order to deal with these problems, some economists, beginning with Wallich and Weintraub (1971), have suggested replacing the law (or social sanction) as the mechanism of enforcement by a financial inducement.[1] This would (i) permit free wage bargaining, (ii) permit changes in the relative pay and (iii) apply to actual earnings per worker (or worker-hour) rather than to notional wage scales.

In Britain, such a policy was in the election platforms of the Alliance parties in both the last two elections. The idea was also implemented in France in 1975, but not for long enough to permit an analysis of its effects. It is currently being debated in many countries.

In this paper we analyze the economic effects of such a scheme. We concern ourselves with the situation where the inflation rate is fairly steady, as it has

* *Scandinavian Journal of Economics*, 92(2) (1990), pp. 309–24.
The authors are grateful to the Economic and Social Research Council and the Esmée Fairbairn Charitable Trust for financial support.

been in most advanced countries for some years. The problem is to reduce unemployment without an increase in inflation.

Thus this is a long-run analysis in which inflation is determined by the growth of nominal demand, and the aim of the scheme is simply and solely to lower the NAIRU.[2] For simplicity we use a one-sector model of identical firms, in which the labour market fails to clear.[3] This failure may arise from one of two sources, which we model in turn. The first is efficiency wages set by employers, and the second is collective bargaining.

In the proposed scheme there is a norm (n) for the proportional growth of money earnings per worker (or worker-hour). If a firm pays more than the norm, it pays a tax equal to t times the excess wage-bill (and this tax can be negative). As a result, a 1 per cent increase in the earnings (W) received by the worker involves a $(1 + t)$ per cent increase in the firm's labour cost per worker (C). This reduces the firm's willingness to pay high wages in order to satisfy its workers.

As we shall see, the key requirement is not simply a wedge between labour cost and earnings but a wedge that increases faster than either. Thus a progressive tax on the *level* rather than the *growth* of wages will also bring about the desired effect. Since a tax on the wage level is simpler to explain, we begin (in Section 2) with this case, using the efficiency wage model. We show that on the (slender) available evidence, the tax will have a significant effect on unemployment. We then show the equivalence of TIP, using the same model.

We next (in Section 3) turn to the case where wages are set by collective bargaining. Again we find significant reductions in unemployment. However the evaluation of these effects becomes more complicated once we allow for possible adjustments in effort. When we analyze this case, we find that TIP will lead to lower effort, but using reasonable parameter estimates social welfare will improve.

In Section 4 we expand the model to include a secondary market-clearing sector of the labour market. The effects of TIP upon unemployment now vary labour supply, the unemployment effect of TIP is greater than in a one-sector model. With completely inelastic labour supply it is less.

Many people, while conceding the economic case for TIP, have dismissed the idea on the grounds that it would be an administrative nightmare; c.f. Dornbush and Fischer (1987, p. 530). But as we have shown elsewhere, in Colander (1986, Ch. 9), it can in fact be relatively simple to administer. It should be judged on the economic case.

The tax should be based on average *hourly* wages at the level of the firm and would thus be free of one of the most serious objections to the taxation of weekly earnings. There would of course be *some* distortions, which we discuss in the Colander volume, but the main one is discussed in Section 3 below. Taking everything into account, our judgement is that the benefits outweigh the costs.

2 TIP UNDER EFFICIENCY WAGES

Suppose each firm pays a net real tax per worker of $tW - S$, where W is real earnings per worker, t the tax rate and S a positive per worker subsidy. Hence labour cost is

$$C = W(1+t) - S$$

and

$$\frac{dC}{dW} \cdot \frac{W}{C} = (1+t)\frac{W}{C} > 1$$

We assume that the scheme is self-financing, so that the *ex post* general equilibrium $tW = S$ or $C = W$. Thus at general equilibrium values of W and C

$$\frac{dC}{dW} \cdot \frac{W}{C} = 1+t$$

To see how this affects equilibrium unemployment, we begin with the case where wages are set by firms, as efficiency wages. Efficiency (e) is increased by higher relative take-home pay ($W/\overline{W}$) and by unemployment (u):

$$e = e\left(\frac{W}{\overline{W}}, u\right) \qquad e_1, e_2 > 0$$

This is a convenient general formulation which captures the implications of most efficiency wage models based on gift exchange, shirking, adverse selection, turnover, etc.; cf. Jackman *et al.* (1988).

The firm chooses W and N to maximize its profit:

$$\pi = R(eN) - CN$$

$$= R(eN) - \frac{C}{e}eN$$

where the revenue function $R(\ )$ includes the labour input as one variable and N is employment. The problem can be solved sequentially for W and N. W is chosen to minimize C/e – or maximize e/C. This requires

$$\frac{Ce_1}{\overline{W}} - e\frac{dC}{dW} = 0$$

or

$$e_1 = e\frac{dC}{dW} \cdot \frac{\overline{W}}{C}$$

Hence in general equilibrium (with $W/\overline{W} = 1$)

$$e_1(1, u) = e(1, u)(1 + t)$$

While each firm sets wages taking the unemployment rate and wages in other firms as given, the equilibrium unemployment rate must be such that all firms choose to set the same wage. The equilibrium unemployment rate then determines employment in equilibrium (the labour force being taken as given) and employment together with labour productivity and product market competition determines the *ex post* equilibrium real wage.

Returning to the effects of the tax, as t is increased, unemployment changes according to

$$\frac{du}{dt} = \frac{e}{e_{12} - e_2(1 + t)}$$

This expression is negative if the efficiency wage function is in terms of expected incomes:

$$e = e\left(\frac{W}{\overline{W}(1 - u)}\right) \qquad e'' < 0$$

Or some readers may prefer a function in which it is assumed that $e_{12} < 0$ due to the reduced relevance of relative wages $(W/\overline{W})$ in the presence of high unemployment. Either way the tax reduces unemployment.

In fact, empirical estimates by Wadhwani and Wall (1988), which assume that wages are based on efficiency wage considerations, give

$$\frac{e_{12}}{e} = -\frac{0.08}{u}; \frac{e_2}{e} = \frac{0.26}{u}$$

This implies approximately (with t $1/2$)

$$-\frac{du}{dt} = 2u$$

Clearly the effect of the tax is the same whether it is levied on firms or workers, as can be seen by using instead the expression $W = C(1 - t) + S$. All that matters is the degree of progressivity.

However, wage level taxes of this kind may raise political problems, in a world of heterogeneous labour, and they may also distort work effort. Since the objective is to attack the leap-frogging of wages, it may be more politically acceptable to have a tax on wage-growth rather than on the level of wages. It may even be more effective, since human responses are affected in part by perceptions and not simply by what economic calculus would dictate, given fully accurate perceptions.

Tax-based incomes policy

This leads to the proposal for a tax-based incomes policy. The original proposal, by Wallich and Weintraub (1971), envisaged a variable rate of profits tax depending on whether a firm was sticking to the wage norm or not. However, in many countries, many firms avoid profits tax. Wallich and Weintraub's purpose in using the profits tax was to stop firms passing on the tax in prices. But the latter can easily be prevented at the aggregate level through a wage tax whose proceeds are distributed as a uniform per worker subsidy. This is the scheme we propose.

Thus the real tax per worker is $T(W - W_{-1}(1 + n)) - S$, where T is the tax rate, and n is the norm for the growth rate of real earnings. The tax is of course expressed in nominal terms, but from the firm's point of view the general rate of inflation is exogenous. Thus the real norm (n) is the nominal norm minus expected price inflation. (One obvious possibility is to fix the nominal norm equal to expected price inflation, in which case $n = 0$.)

Let us analyze such a system. If differs from the simple tax on the wage level in that if a firm raises it wages now (and expects the tax to continue), its wage growth next year will, other things equal, be *lower*. Hence it will save on future taxes, even though it pays more taxes now. In fact the tax will only work because of discounting, and we shall discover that, if the tax rate on wage growth is T,

$$\frac{\mathrm{d}u}{\mathrm{d}T} = \frac{\mathrm{d}u}{\mathrm{d}t}(r - n)$$

where r is the real discount rate, n the real norm and $\mathrm{d}u/\mathrm{d}t$ is the effect of a wage *level* tax.

The firm wishes to maximize its present value. If $R(\ )$ is real revenue, the present value of real profit is

$$PV = \sum_j (1 - r)^j \left\{ R_j \left[e \left(\frac{W_j}{\overline{W}_j}, u_j \right) N_j \right] - N_j[W_j(1 + T) - TW_{j-1}(1 + n) - S] \right\}$$

which is maximized with respect to W_j and N_j. Hence

$$\frac{\partial PV}{\partial W_j} = (1 - r)^j \left(R_j' \frac{e_1}{\overline{W}_j} N_j - N_j(1 + T) \right) + (1 - r)^{j+1} N_{j+1} T(1 + n) = 0$$

$$\frac{\partial PV}{\partial N_j} = (1 - r)^j [R_j' e - W_j(1 + T) + TW_{j-1}(1 + n) + S] = 0$$

Thus a steady-state employment we have (in general equilibrium with $(W/\overline{W} = 1)$ a wage equation

$$R'e_1(1,u) = W(1+(r-n)T)$$

and a price/employment equation

$$R'e(1,u) = W$$

(since $T(W_j - W_{j-1}(1+n)) = S$). Combining the wage and price equations gives

$$e_1(1,u) = e(1,u)(1+(r-n)T)$$

Hence a wage growth tax at rate T has an effect $(r-n)$ times the effect of a wage level tax at the same rate. This makes it clear that a tax on wage growth must be very high (e.g. 100 per cent) and the nominal norm must be set at or below the rate of price inflation (thus making $n \le 0$). Needless to say a given tax on wage growth would be much more effective if it were not expected to last. But it is not desirable to design such taxes on a temporary basis – it is precisely the on/off nature of previous incomes policies that we are trying to get away from.

3 TIP UNDER WAGE BARGAINING

We now assume that wages are set by a bargain between the employer and a union representing all those currently employed in each firm. For simplicity we assume that each union is specific to a firm, that there are no employers' federations and that each firm is sufficiently small to be treated atomistically (i.e. it ignores the impact of its decisions on the rest of the economy). Throughout we assume the union is concerned about wages (and effort where this is endogenous). We ignore any concern the union may have over employment. There are many reasons why under certainty a union would not at the bargaining margin care about employment: natural wastage provides existing workers with wide safety margins, and seniority rules further protect the median voter; see Layard *et al.* (1991) and Oswald (1987).

The unions do not bargain over employment, c.f. Oswald (1987), which is determined by firms. Initially we assume the bargain is only over wages, with workers' productivity exogenous. Later we modify this. We confine ourselves to the case of a tax on the wage level, which again can be shown to be equivalent to a tax on wage growth.

The outcome of the bargain is the wage which maximizes the Nash expression

$$\Omega = (W - \overline{Z})^{\beta\pi}$$

where β measures the relative discount rate of firm and union, π measures *operating* profits (so that the firm's fall-back is zero) and $\overline{Z}$ is the union fallback.

We assume that $\overline{Z}$ is a weighted average of wages paid in other jobs $(\overline{W})$ and unemployment benefits payable to strikers (B), the weights depending on unemployment:

$$\overline{Z} = (1 - \varphi(u))\overline{W} + \varphi(u)B. \qquad (\varphi' > 0)$$

The optimal wage is given by

$$\frac{d \log \Omega}{dW} = \frac{\beta}{W - \overline{Z}} + \frac{1}{\pi} \cdot \frac{d\pi}{dC} \cdot \frac{dC}{dW}$$

$$= \frac{\beta}{W - \overline{Z}} - \frac{NC}{\pi}\left(\frac{dC}{dW} \cdot \frac{W}{C}\right)\frac{1}{W} = 0$$

Hence in general equilibrium (with $W = \overline{W}$)

$$\frac{W - \overline{Z}}{W} = \frac{\beta\gamma}{1 + t}$$

where $\gamma = \pi/NC$, which is constant in a Cobb–Douglas world with monopolistic competition and constant demand elasticities. Thus

$$\varphi(u) = \frac{\beta\gamma}{(1 + t)(1 - \rho)}$$

where $\rho = B/W$, taken as exogenous. Again the system solves for the equilibrium unemployment rate, which then determines employment and real wages in equilibrium. And, once again, the tax reduces equilibrium unemployment.[4]

To get an idea of magnitudes, note that if $\varphi(u)$ is a proportional function

$$-\frac{du}{dt} = \frac{u}{1 + t}$$

Effort endogenous

However, many commentators have criticized TIP on the grounds that it might discourage productivity bargains. This in turn has led to the view that productivity bargains would have to be exempt – and, since that is administratively impossible, that TIP is a non-starter. To find how TIP affects productivity bargaining, we now assume that effort (e) is observable (e.g. it varies inversely with manning ratios) and is bargained over.[5] Individual workers dislike effort and their utility is given by

$$Z = Wg(e) \qquad g' < 0$$

(This gives a vertical labour supply curve, which is realistic). Hence the Nash maximand is

$$\Omega = (Wg(e) - \overline{Z})^{\beta\pi}$$

where

$$\overline{Z} = (1 - \varphi(u))\overline{W}g(\overline{e}) + \varphi(u)B$$

where B denotes the utility of unemployment. Since both wages (W) and effort (e) are bargained over, Ω has to be maximized with respect to each, subject to the firm's demand for labour. The optimal wage is given by

$$\frac{\partial \log \Omega}{\partial W} = \frac{\beta g(e)}{Wg(e) - \overline{Z}} + \frac{1}{\pi}\frac{d\pi}{dC} \cdot \frac{dC}{dW} = 0$$

Hence, after performing the usual manipulations, we get the usual answer:

$$\varphi(u) = \frac{\beta\gamma}{(1 + t)(1 - \rho)} \tag{19.1}$$

where ρ is now the replacement ratio in utility terms. Thus, as before, TIP reduces unemployment.

But what dreadful things does it do to effort? The optimal effort is given by

$$\frac{\partial \log \Omega}{\partial e} = \frac{\beta W g'}{Wg(e) - \overline{Z}} + \frac{1}{\pi}\frac{\partial\pi}{\partial e} = 0$$

But[6] $\partial\pi/\partial e = CN/e$, so that

$$\frac{Wg(e) - \overline{Z}}{Wg(e)} = -\beta\gamma\frac{g'e}{g}$$

Thus

$$\varphi(u)(1 - \rho) = -\beta\gamma\frac{g'e}{g} \tag{19.2}$$

and hence, using (19.1)

$$-\frac{g'e}{g} = \frac{1}{1 + t}$$

This conclusion would also follow if effort were set unilaterally by the employer.[7] It implies that the tax reduces effort.

Going on, it is helpful to set

$$-\frac{g'(e)e}{g(e)} = h(e) = \frac{1}{1+t} \qquad h' > 0$$

so that

$$\frac{de}{dt}\frac{1}{e} = -\frac{1}{(1+t)^2 h'(e)e}$$

We know of no estimates of the value which workers place on effort but an indication may be provided by the value which they place on leisure. We might, for example, assume that workers dislike a 10 per cent increase in effort about as much as they dislike a 10 per cent increase in hours. If e were hours, the compensated labour supply elasticity would be $1/h'(e)e$.[8] The most relevant estimates of this relate to male workers, since for female workers the whole choice of participation is involved and the spread of hours much wider. Typical estimates of the male compensated elasticity are around 0.1; see Pencavel (1986). Then

$$\frac{de}{dt}\frac{1}{e} = -\frac{0.1}{(1+t)^2}$$

We can now look, first, at the effects of the tax upon national output and then upon welfare. For simplicity we assume output (Y) proportional to labour input eN. Then

$$\frac{d \log Y}{dt} = \frac{d \log e}{dt} - \frac{du}{dt}$$

$$= \frac{-0.1}{(1+t)^2} + \frac{u}{1+t}$$

On this basis the tax would increase GDP provided initial unemployment was higher than say 7 per cent.

But on top of this we should allow for the fact that workers dislike effort and are glad to be making less of it.[9] The proportional change in welfare due to this source is

$$\frac{g'e}{g}\frac{de}{dt}\frac{1}{e}S_L = \frac{0.1S_L}{(1+t)^3}$$

where S_L is the share of labour. Thus the overall change in welfare is

$$\frac{1}{1+t}\left[u - \frac{0.1(1+t-S_L)}{(1+t)^2}\right]$$

For a 50 per cent tax rate and $S_L = 0.75$ this is positive for any unemployment above around 3 per cent.[10]

4 ADDING A MARKET-CLEARING SECTOR

All the estimates arrived at so far relate to a world in which there is a single non-market-clearing sector. We now ask whether, in the more realistic case where there is also a secondary market-clearing sector, TIP has a larger or smaller proportional effect upon unemployment.

We shall show that the proportional effect of the tax on unemployment may be higher or lower than we have so far suggested. If the supply to the secondary sector is infinitely elastic, the cut in unemployment is higher, and if supply is completely inelastic the cut in unemployment is lower.

To understand why this is so consider the case of highly elastic supply. The tax cuts the primary sector wage. This increases employment in the primary sector and reduces the pool of workers available for the secondary sector. This tends to raise the wage in the secondary sector and increases the proportion of people outside the primary sector who are willing to work in the non-union sector. Thus employment falls proportionately more than the fall in the number of people outside the primary sector. If by contrast the supply is inelastic, this bonus is lacking. To sharpen the argument we shall concentrate on the two extreme cases.

Infinitely elastic supply

First, we assume that the supply to the secondary sector is infinitely elastic at a wage B. The unemployed are all those who have no primary jobs *minus* demand in the secondary sector (see Figure 19.1).

Union bargaining or efficiency wages determine the mark-up of the primary wage over B. From now on we talk of the union wage and use the union as the model of the primary sector. But the analysis could apply equally well for the efficiency wage case in the primary sector.[11]

We continue to assume that the tax is self-financing and that it is self-financing *within* each sector (as it would be if it were in the form of a tax on wage growth). Hence, using t to mean the effective tax rate, $(r - n)T$, the union wage $(W_u = C_u)$ is given by

$$\frac{W_u - \overline{Z}}{W_u} = \frac{\beta\gamma}{1+t}$$

In the present case, normalizing on a labour force of unity,

$$\overline{Z} = (1 - \varphi(1 - N_u))W_u + \varphi(1 - N_u)B$$

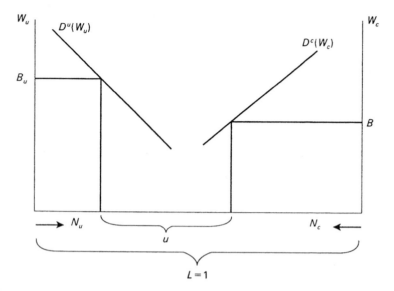

Figure 19.1 A primary sector (subscript u) and a secondary sector (subscript c)

Hence

$$\varphi(1 - N_u)(1 - B/W_u) = \frac{\beta\gamma}{1+t}$$

Thus if B/W_u is independent of t (as we shall show) then the change in union employment when t rises is

$$\frac{dN_u}{dt} = \frac{1 - N_u}{1 + t}$$

The change in total employment (fall in total unemployment) is

$$-\frac{du}{dt} = \frac{dN_u}{dt} + \frac{dN_c}{dt}$$

where N_c is employment in the competitive sector. If the proportional change in employment is the same in both sectors (as we shall show), then

$$-\frac{du}{dt} = \frac{dN_u}{dt} + \frac{dN_c}{dt} = \frac{1 - N_u}{1 + t}\left(\frac{N_u + N_c}{N_u}\right) > \frac{u}{1 + t}$$

This greatly exceeds the findings of the one-sector model.

It can now be shown why, if B is constant for given productivity, B/W_u and N_u/N_c are invariant when t changes – using some rather specific assumptions. We assume monopolistic competition *à la* Dixit-Stiglitz, with each worker producing one unit of output. All firms are identical and face demand curves with elasticity η. It follows that in each firm i the relative price will be proportional to the real wage W_i:

$$P_i = W_i(1 - 1/\eta)^{-1}$$

Hence the firm's demand for labour is given by

$$N_i = W_i^{-\eta} \overline{Y} (1 - 1/\eta)^{-\eta}$$

where $\overline{Y}$ is aggregate demand per firm. Hence the demand for labour in union firms (N_u) relative to competitive firms (N_c) is

$$\frac{N_u}{N_c} = \left(\frac{W_u}{W_c}\right)^{-\eta} \frac{n_u}{n_c} \tag{19.1}$$

where n_u, n_c are the relevant number of firms in the two sectors.

In addition pricing behaviour is such that

$$\overline{P} = 1 = \left(\frac{N_u}{N_u + N_c} W_u + \frac{N_c}{N_u + N_c} W_c\right)(1 - 1/\eta)^{-1} \tag{19.2}$$

or

$$1 - 1/\eta = \frac{N_u}{N_u + N_c} W_u + \frac{N_c}{N_u + N_c} W_c$$

For given $W_c = B$, (19.1) and (19.2) determine W_u and N_u/N_c

Thus, when the tax is imposed, real wages in each sector are unchanged. But wage pressure in the union sector is reduced so that unemployment can be reduced. This happens through an equiproportional rise in union and non-union employment.

Infinitely inelastic supply

We now consider the case of inelastic labour supply to the competitive sector. In this case there is a fixed proportion (S) of non-union personnel who are willing to work in the non-union sector.

The union mark-up is given by

$$\frac{W_u - \overline{Z}}{W_u} = \frac{\beta \gamma}{1 + t}$$

where $\bar{Z}$ now is

$$\bar{Z} = [1 - \varphi(1 - N_u)]W_u + \varphi(1 - N_u)[SW_c + (1 - S)B]$$

Hence

$$\varphi(1 - N_u)\left(1 - S\frac{W_c}{W_u} - (1 - S)\frac{B}{W_u}\right) = \frac{\beta\gamma}{1 + t}$$

When t rises W_c/W_u now rises, as does B/W_u (taking B as invariant, like W). Hence the fall in $(1 - N_u)$ is partially offset and

$$-\frac{d(1 - N_u)}{dt}\frac{1}{1 - N_u} < \frac{1}{1 + t}$$

In addition since $u = 1 - N_u - N_c = (1 - N_u)(1 - S)$

$$-\frac{du}{dt}\frac{1}{u} = -\frac{d(1 - N_u)}{dt}\frac{1}{1 - N_u}$$

Hence

$$-\frac{du}{dt} = -\frac{-d(1 - N_u)}{dt}\frac{u}{1 - N_u} < \frac{u}{1 + t}$$

This is less than the findings of the one-sector model. For some supply elasticity between zero and infinity, the one-sector and two-sector models would show the same effect of a TIP.

Notes

1. For more recent discussions, including by ourselves, see Colander (1986).
2. In cases where the aim is to alter the inflation rate, additional issues arise about the effect of TIP on the length of the lags in wage and price dynamics.
3. In Section 4 we add on a second market-clearing sector and show that our results still hold.
4. If we consider a tax on annual wage growth we choose W_0 to maximize

$$\Omega_0 = (W_0 - \bar{Z}_0)^\beta \pi_0$$

where subscripts reflect time-periods and we include in $d\pi_0/dW_0$ the discounted effect of W_0 on profits in period 1. Thus

$$\frac{d \log \Omega}{dW_0} = \frac{\beta}{W_0 - \bar{Z}_0} + \frac{1}{\pi_0}\left[-N_0\frac{dC_0}{dW_0} - \left(N_1\frac{dC_1}{dW_0}\right)(1 - r)(1 + n)\right]$$

$$= \frac{\beta}{W_0 - \bar{Z}_0} + \frac{1}{\pi_0}[-N_0(1 + T) + (1 - r)N_1 T(1 + n)] = 0$$

Hence in a steady state

$$\frac{W_0 - \overline{Z}_0}{W_0} = \beta \frac{\pi}{N_0 W_0} \frac{1}{1 + (r - n)T}$$

5. Efficiency wage theory is, of course, concerned with those dimensions of effort which are unobservable.

6. $\pi = R(eN) - CN$, so

$$\frac{\partial \pi}{\partial e} = R'N + (R'e - C)\frac{\partial N}{\partial e} = R'N = \frac{CN}{e}$$

7. The employer will choose effort knowing that this will affect the wage outcome in the bargain. Hence the employer chooses effort to maximize

$$\pi = R(eN) - (W(1 + t) - S)N$$

subject to

$$\frac{\partial \log \Omega}{\partial W} = \frac{\beta g(e)}{Wg(e) - \overline{Z}} + \frac{1}{\pi}\frac{d\pi}{dC} \cdot \frac{dC}{dW} = 0$$

that is

$$W = \frac{\overline{Z}(1 + t)}{(1 + t - \beta\gamma)g(e)}$$

Thus

$$\frac{\partial \pi}{\partial e} = N\left[R' + \frac{(1 + t)g'(e)}{g(e)} \cdot W\right] = 0$$

and, since when N is optimal $R' = C/e$

$$-\frac{eg'(e)}{g(e)} = \frac{1}{1 + t}$$

8. If w is the net reward per unit of effort, the individual maximizes

$$(we + Y)g(e)$$

where Y is non-employment income. This gives a supply curve

$$\frac{w}{we + Y} + \frac{g'(e)}{g} = 0$$

or

$$-\frac{g'(e)e}{g} = \frac{1}{1 + Y/we} = h(e)$$

We now vary w and Y simultaneously, with $dY = -edw$. Since we assume Y approximately zero, it follows that

$$-\frac{dY}{we} = \frac{dw}{w} = h'(e)de$$

and

$$-\frac{1}{h'(e)e} = -\frac{de}{e} \bigg/ \frac{dw}{w}$$

9. We are assuming that when an unemployed worker becomes employed, social welfare rises by his output.

10. The cost of lower effort and lower wages could be much less if we allowed for jealousy over wages in the utility function; cf. Boskin and Sheshinski (1978) and Layard (1980). The fall in the wages of others would then raise individual utility.

11. Under efficiency wages we can obtain a neat formula for the mark-up if one assumes, with Summers (1987), that

$$e = (w - A)^\alpha$$

where A is the expected outside income. In this case a firm maximising e/C with respect to W sets

$$\frac{\alpha}{W - A} - \frac{1}{C}\frac{dC}{dW} = 0$$

so that in general equilibrium with $C = W$

$$\frac{W - A}{W} = \frac{\alpha}{1 + t}$$

References

Boskin, M.J. and E. Sheshinski (1978) 'Optimal Redistributive Taxation when Individual Welfare Depends Upon Relative Income', *Quarterly Journal of Economics*, 92(4) (November).

Colander, D. (ed.) (1986) *Incentive-based Income Policies* (Cambridge, MA: Ballinger).

Dornbush, R. and S. Fischer (1987) *Macroeconomics*, 4th edn (New York: McGraw-Hill)

Layard, R. (1980) 'Human Satisfaction and Public Policy', *Economic Journal*, 90, 737–50 (December), chapter 14 in R. Layard, *Tackling Inequality* (London: Macmillan, 1999).

Layard, R., S. Nickell and R. Jackman (1991) *Unemployment: Macroeconomic Performance and the Labour Market* (Oxford: Oxford University Press).

Oswald, A. (1987) 'Efficient Contracts are on the Labour Demand Curve, Theory and Facts', Centre for Labour Economics, LSE, *Discussion Paper*, 284.

Pencavel, J. (1986) 'Labor Supply of men: A Survey', in O. Ashenfelter and R. Layard, 'Handbook of Labor Economics', vol. 1 (Amsterdam: North-Holland).

Summers, L. (1987) 'Relative Wages, Efficiency Wages and Keynesian Unemployment', mimeo.

Wadhwani, S. and Wall, M. (1988) 'A Direct Test of the Efficiency Wage Model using UK Micro-data', Centre for Labour Economics, LSE, *Discussion Paper*, 313.

Wallich, H. and Weintraub, S. (1971) 'A Tax-based Incomes Policy', *Journal of Economic Issues*, 5 (June) 1–19.

20 How to End Pay Leapfrogging (1990)*

1 WHY COORDINATION IS BETTER[1]

It is easy to see why uncoordinated bargaining has such bad effects. We can begin by looking at what it does to wages *claims*. In a decentralised bargain workers in one sector can, if successful, raise their wages relative to other wages and thus to the general price level. This will in the process also raise the relative price of what they produce, but the workers concerned will not mind this (provided the employment effects are not too severe).

In *aggregate*, however, it is impossible for all workers to raise their relative wages, except temporarily as inflation escalates. To prevent such leapfrogging requires a sufficient level of unemployment. If unemployment is not high enough, inflation will rise, as each group of workers leapfrogs its predecessor in the pay round. In the end nobody improves his real wage, but all suffer from higher inflation.

Thus, in the words of Harold Wilson, the problem with decentralised bargaining is essentially that '*one* man's wage increase is *another* man's price increase'. By contrast, when bargaining is centralised, all workers know that, if their wages go up, so will the prices *they themselves* pay. In consequence less unemployment is required to ensure that inflation is kept in check.

There is a further element involved. This arises from the fact that each year many workers leave their firm voluntarily for another job (some 10–15 per cent in most countries). This means that, if a wage claim reduces employment in a firm, the existing workers may well retain their jobs – the contraction being accommodated by the 'natural wastage' of workers moving to other jobs. Since few workers fear job loss, there is little pressure here to restrain wage claims.

By contrast, at the level of the whole economy, a fall in employment *must* mean that some workers become unemployed. Thus centralised bargainers will be more cautious in seeking higher wages than are firm-level bargainers, due to the more serious effect of wages upon job security. Thus wage pressure will be less under centralised bargaining, and so will equilibrium unemployment.

Turning to employers' wage *offers*, centralised bargains stiffen the backbone of the employers. For, when each employer strikes his own bargain, he may feel that higher wages involve not only costs but also benefits – in terms of his ability

---

* Economic Institute, *Economic Report*, 5(5) (July 1990), pp. 1–18.

to recruit, retain and motivate workers. But, if all employers agree to raise wages equally, these benefits are smaller or non-existent.

One would expect that coordination among employers would be more important in resisting wage pressure than coordination among unions. For employers generally have a stronger interest in wage restraint than unions. If a national employers' federation stood firm on the wages front, wage pressure could not easily get out of hand.

2 HOW OTHER COUNTRIES DO IT

So let us see whether the experience of different countries supports these predictions. Figure 20.1 provides some *prima facie* evidence. On the horizontal axis we measure the average level of coordination in each country and on the vertical axis its average unemployment rate for 1983–8 (when inflation was fairly stable in most countries). There is a noticeable association.

Our first job is to explain how we measure coordination, by describing the bargaining systems in the different countries. Then we can examine more precisely how bargaining affects wage pressure, by allowing also for other relevant factors pushing up wages.

Nearly all OECD countries other than Canada and the USA have a more coordinated system of wage bargaining than Britain. The most centralised systems are in *Scandinavia and Austria*, where there are *national framework agreements* about the broad level of settlements.

In most *EEC countries* except the UK there are *industry-level bargains* in each industry, whose results apply with the force of law or custom in most firms, unionised and non-unionised. These industry-level bargains can then (except in Portugal) be supplemented by firm-level deals, but countries differ in the importance of these.

In *Germany*, the formal industry-level bargains occur at the level of the 'Land', but the national (industry-level) union has to authorise any strike. Though there may also be firm-level negotiations, strikes at the firm level are illegal, as in Scandinavia.

Thus even in a formal sense the German system is quite centralised. Informally there are national consultations within the union federation and the employers' federation, and between the two federations. The national industry-level unions and federations then adopt their positions. This leads to a pattern settlement, generally in the metal industry, which is then broadly followed elsewhere.

In Belgium and the Netherlands there are also consultations at the national level but there are three federations in each country (Catholic, Protestant and non-denominational), making for less coordination. In France firm-level wage determination is more important, often at the employer's discretion. But the

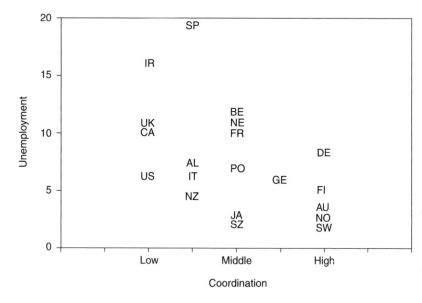

Figure 20.1 Average unemployment rate (1983–8) by level of coordination in wage bargaining
Note: Coordination equals average level of employer and union coordination.

AL: Australia; AU: Austria; BE: Belgium;
CA: Canada; DE: Denmark; FI: Finland;
FR: France; GE: Germany; IR: Ireland;
IT: Italy; JA: Japan; NE: Netherlands;
NO: Norway; NZ: New Zealand; PO: Portugal;
SP: Spain; SW: Sweden; SZ: Switzerland;
UK: United Kingdom; US: United States.

employers' federation is not without influence. In Italy and Spain by contrast private employers are ill-coordinated even at industry level.

In *Switzerland*, bargaining is exclusively at firm level, but employers' federations are quite strong. Negotiations are often conducted subject to 'peace agreements', ruling out strikes.

The *Japanese* system is not unlike the Swiss. Before the Spring bargaining season, there are intensive consultations among employers about the appropriate going rate, and likewise among unions. These objectives are then sought in uniform pattern bargains in one industry (often steel) and the settlement here is then broadly followed elsewhere. Strikes occur but are normally short.

The *Australian and New Zealand* systems are *sui generis*, since the national and industry basic wage increases are normally determined by a court after hearing evidence from both sides and from the government. These 'awards' can then be supplemented by 'over-award' payments negotiated at firm level. Employer coordination is weak, so that only union coordination offers much guarantee that the central award will hold. Since 1983 however the Australian system has been fundamentally over-ridden by the Accord between government and unions.

Thus in all countries other than Canada and the US there is more coordination than there is in Britain (or Ireland). But *we* get the worst of all worlds, because we also have a very high union density.

In order to investigate the effects of coordination, we start by explaining how it is measured. There are basically three levels at which bargaining can occur. In Table 20.1 we award a mark of 3 to national-level coordination, 2 to industry-level and 1 to firm-level.

In Figure 20.1 we measured the level of coordination by the average score for employer coordination and union coordination. But we can do better than this. In Appendix 1 we separate out employer coordination and union coordination and estimate the following relationship:

Unemployment 1983–8 (adjusted for changes in inflation) is explained by

- employer coordination,
- union coordination,
- proportion of workers covered by collective agreements,
- benefits relative to income in work,
- maximum number of years for which benefits can be paid, and
- expenditure on adult training, placement and job creation per unemployed person.

Remarkably, this equation explains over 90 per cent of the huge cross-country variation of unemployment levels across 20 countries in the 1980s. And, as we would expect, employer coordination plays an even more important role than union coordination.

3   COORDINATION AND THE NEEDS OF DIFFERENT FIRMS

So how could Britain do better? Though decentralised pay settlements cause problems, there is clearly also a problem about over-centralised pay – that it fails to take into account each firm's circumstances. Individual employers do need an element of discretion over pay, if they are to use pay to help them recruit, retain and motivate staff. In recruiting and retaining staff, employers need to take into account the local labour market for the relevant skills, and also whether they are themselves trying to expand or contract their workforces. And, in motivating their staff, they need to use pay as a bribe for better working practices.

Table 20.1 Unemployment rates and collective bargaining structures in
20 OECD countries

	Unemployment rate 1983–88 (1)	Union coordination (2)	Employer coordination (3)
Belgium	11.3	2	2
Denmark	9.0	3	3
France	9.9	2	2
Germany	6.7	2	3
Ireland	16.4	1	1
Italy	7.0	2	1
Netherlands	10.6	2	2
Portugal	7.7	2	2
Spain	19.8	2	1
UK	10.7	1	1
Australia	8.4	2	1
New Zealand	4.6	2	1
Canada	9.9	1	1
USA	7.1	1	1
Japan	2.7	2	2
Austria	3.6	3	3
Finland	5.1	3	3
Norway	2.7	3	3
Sweden	2.2	3	3
Switzerland	2.4	1	3

Sources: Col. (1) OECD standardized rates where available and otherwise
unstandardized, except for Italy (where we use the US Bureau of Labor Statistics
figure) and Switzerland (where we adjust registered unemployment by a
multiple of 3, this being the ratio in the 1980 Census).
Cols (2) and (3) see Layard (1991).

All this is plain. But if coordination is not overdone, it can all be handled
within a system that has a going rate that applies in the absence of exceptional
circumstances.

But unfortunately it has recently become fashionable in government and
CBI circles to argue that every circumstance is different and that the going rate
is therefore a hindrance rather than a help. One argument above all has been

used to press the view that every circumstance is different. This is the argument that pay should be related to performance. What performance means varies from one person to another. Some definitions (e.g. better working practices) make sense. But the definition most commonly used is productivity growth.

The argument here is wrong. It goes like this: 'If a firm's pay rises only as fast as the firm's productivity, then the firm's unit labour costs will be constant and so will its prices. So productivity-based pay will eliminate inflation.'

Unfortunately this argument is like the voice of the siren: it sounds sweet reason and it leads to disaster. For there are huge differences in productivity growth between sectors, which are mainly due to technological factors and not to the efforts of the workers. Thus some sectors have inherently greater productivity growth than others. For example in 1979–86 productivity growth in manufacturing varied hugely between industries – doubling in man-made fibres while it was constant in brewing. If pay had been based on productivity, wages in man-made fibres would have doubled relative to those in brewing.

Would this have been reasonable? Of course not. And in fact, the wage increase was identical in both industries (70 per cent). *For competition for labour will always produce a going rate*. But this rate will be unreasonably high if high-productivity growth enterprises are encouraged to pay large pay increases, while other industries end up paying the same in order to retain labour.

Since there is so much confusion on this point, let us pursue it a little further. If one compares the 54 main branches of manufacturing between 1979 and 1986 there is no correlation between the rate of productivity growth and the rate of wage increase. (The correlation coefficient is a negligible 5 per cent).

So what has been happening? Two things. First, the huge differences in productivity growth between industries have been mainly due to technological differences and nothing whatever to do with differential work effort. For this reason they have not been reflected in wage-setting, nor should they have been. Second, employers have of course rewarded workers for improved manning practices, as they should. But improvements here have been scattered across industries in a way that was unrelated to overall productivity growth.

So does this mean that all is well? Unfortunately not, for inflationary pressure has been excessive. And talk of productivity-related pay may well have increased this pressure.

Consider for example the argument referred to earlier that it is all right for pay to double in an industry where productivity doubles because this will cause no increase in unit labour costs. The argument is unbelievably dangerous. For, as the evidence shows, competition for labour will tend to ensure that wages rise at the same rate in the low-productivity-growth industries as well. Thus in these latter industries unit labour costs will inevitably rise. Hence average unit labour costs in the economy will rise. And so will average prices.

If, instead, we want average prices to be stable, some prices must fall while others rise. In fact roughly half of all prices must fall. So it is not good enough for high productivity growth enterprises to contain their unit labour costs. They must reduce them.

It is tragic that this simple piece of arithmetic is not more widely understood, but hopefully it is becoming better known. Competition in the labour market will always generate a going rate. But what is essential is the *going rate be determined by some process that makes it reflect the national concern for price stability*. Employers will then deviate from that rate when they feel they have truly exceptional circumstances: recruitment needs or better manning practices. But different levels of technological progress are *not* an appropriate reason.

So what institutions will help to produce the right kind of going rate?

4   WHAT WE SHOULD DO

1   Change of attitude

To begin with, there has to be a change of attitude, especially among employers. Everyone believes that inflation is bad. Thus *a stable average level of prices is a public good, like clean air*. When a firm increases its workers' wages by more than the average national productivity growth, it is contributing to a rise in the average price level.[2] *Such wage increases are a form of pollution*, and need to be seen as such. If other firms are giving wage increases, it is in any one firm's interest to do the same. So we cannot stop this pollution by moral suasion. The only way to stop it is by some kind of pact whereby each firm stops doing it on condition that others stop doing it also.

This is what coordination is about. But it need not be heavy-handed. All that is required is that everyone act on the basis of a sensible going rate.

How can this be determined? We need two major types of institutional reform. First, we need an authoritative demonstration of the implications of different levels of going rate for the whole economy, and then we need a bargaining structure that can deliver a sensible outcome.

2   A council of economic advisers

The source of analysis must be independent. In Germany there are two sources of analysis. There is the annual report of the Council of Economic Advisers each November, preceding the first national pay deal around February. And there is the twice-yearly economic forecast agreed by the 5 economic institutes. Both the Council and the institutes publish analyses of the implications of different going rates – contributing to a consensus view of what is reasonable.

In the British context the urgent need is to establish a Council of Economic Advisers which can initiate a rational debate about what going rate is needed to lower British inflation to the European level.

3   A lead from the CBI and TUC

In Germany the other major input into a rational consensus about the going rate is talks among employers within their federation (the BDI) and among unions within their federation (the DGB) and (informal) talks between the two federations. We desperately need this in Britain. The CBI is the key, since as we have seen, it is more important that employers coordinate than unions. Eventually the CBI will have to say to its members: we think the going rate should be x per cent and you should only depart from this for demonstrable cause.

4   The role of government

What is the role of government in all this? In the ideal case it happens without the government doing anything. But in Britain we are so far from these arrangements that the government will have to do something. First, it will have to set up the Council, but the Council should have no government officials as members. Second, the government will have to cajole the CBI members to talk to each other and to the TUC about pay (the TUC currently appears more willing). Quite possibly there is only one thing which will ultimately mobilise the CBI to do this – the threat that, if self-regulation does not work, there will be government regulation (i.e. incomes policy).[3]

But one hopes that the challenge of ERM entry will at least encourage some re-think in the CBI. For under a fixed exchange rate it is much more apparent that a firm which raises the going rate raises other firms' costs and thus lowers their ability to compete.

5   Public information on relative pay

There is one final issue: the problem of relative pay. Leapfrogging occurs because groups want to improve their relative pay. Yet in the long run the pay structure is remarkably stable. If one takes for each group its average ranking in the pay structure over the previous 20 years, this fluctuates remarkably little over time. Groups that get pushed down eventually bounce back, and vice versa. The reason is simply the need to recruit. In the long-run there is a pattern of differentials which is required to sustain any employment in an occupation (and this ranking is relatively independent of the occupation's size). Thus discussion about pay relativities should begin by comparing existing pay rankings with the 20-year average. It should never begin by comparisons with the previous peak – a formula for a rapid move to hyper-inflation.

The Council of Economic Advisers could therefore perform an extremely useful function in relation to the structure of pay structure as well as its general level. It should provide an authoritative set of data, publicly available in intelligible form, about movements in relative pay. This would help to dispel much of the misinformation which leads to conflict, and encourage a more orderly evolution of relativities as well as absolute pay. Just as no-one gains from wage rises which only produce price rises, so no occupation gains from getting 10 per cent more than its competitor occupation for 2 years followed by 10 per cent less for the following 2 years.

CONCLUSION

To conclude, Britain is not the USA. In Britain, like the rest of Europe, we set most wages by collective bargaining. But in Britain we do it in a less orderly way than most European nations.

For Britain ERM entry will remove the option of high inflation. But low inflation will not follow automatically. There are two ways we can have it:
- by high unemployment, or
- by reforming our wage bargaining.

Now is the time to choose.

Appendix: Explaining Inflation–Unemployment Trade-offs in the 20 OECD Countries

The following equation was estimated by ordinary least squares (*t*-statistics in brackets):

Average unemployment rate 1983–88 (%) =		(*t*-statistic)
−0.35	change in inflation 1982–8 (%) (points)	(2.8)
−4.28	Employer coordination	(7.0)
−1.42	Union coordination	(2.0)
+2.45	Coverage of collective bargaining	(2.4)
+0.17	Replacement ratio	(7.1)
+0.92	Maximum duration of benefits	(2.9)
−0.13	Active labour market spending	(2.3)

$\overline{R}^2 = 0.91;$ se = 1.41

Note: Coverage: Greater than 75% = 3; 25–75% = 2; Under 25% = 1.
Maximum duration of benefits: Over 4 years is set at 4.
Active labour market spending. Expenditure per unemployed person relative to output per worker.
Source: See Layard (1991).

Notes

1. Sections 1 and 2 draw heavily on Layard (1991).
2. There is no reason why low-productivity-growth industries should not raise their relative prices, and thus raise their money prices while average prices are unchanged. What is generally inflationary is for a firm to raise wages above national average productivity growth, since this leads to a rise in the average price level.
3. The least damaging form of incomes policy would be one which imposed a tax on excess wage increases, rather than simply forbidding them. See Layard and Nickell (1986).

449

References

Layard, R. (1991) 'Wage Bargaining, Incomes Policy and Inflation', in Simon Commander (ed.), *Managing Inflation In Socialist Economies in Transition* (New York: The World Bank).

Layard, R. and S. Nickell (1986) 'An Incomes Policy to Help the Unemployed', Employment Institute; reprinted in J. Shields (ed.), *Making the Economy Work* (London: Macmillan, 1989).

21 Is Unemployment Lower if Unions Bargain over Employment? (1990)*

with S. Nickell

1 OVERVIEW

Would there be more employment if unions bargained over employment, and not only over wages? Most economists seem to answer Yes.[1]

Proposition 1 If unions bargain over employment *and* wages, employment will be higher than if they bargain only over wages.

Many economists also believe the following.

Proposition 2 If unions bargain over employment and wages and are utilitarian and risk averse, then 'equilibrium employment is higher than in the equivalent competitive labour market' (Oswald, 1985).

So, in the eyes of many, bargaining over employment is a good thing.

In this paper we show that the first proposition is only true on limited assumptions, while the second is simply false. The propositions are obtained from a *partial*-equilibrium analysis, in which the environment outside the representative firm is assumed to be the same whatever bargaining scheme is in operation. Once a general equilibrium framework is adopted, the propositions collapse, and the view that featherbedding can maintain jobs is called into question.

We assume an economy in which all firms are unionized and bargain with their own union, although our results can be interpreted in a two-sector framework as we shall see. We then find Proposition 1'.

Proposition 1' If unions bargain over employment as well as wages, unemployment will be the same as if they bargain over wages only, provided

* *Quarterly Journal of Economics* (August 1990), pp. 774–87. © 1990 by the President and Fellows of Harvard College and the Massachusetts Institute of Technology. The authors are grateful for comments to participants in the Pinhas Sapir Conference on Unemployment in Tel Aviv (June 1987), especially to S. Stern, L. Summers and Y. Weiss. We are also grateful to the two referees for helpful comments on an earlier draft.

451

that the production function is Cobb–Douglas. It will be lower if the elasticity of substitution between labor and capital is smaller than unity.

We also find Proposition 2'.

Proposition 2' If we start from a fully competitive labor market and then move to one of efficient bargaining (over wages and employment), unemployment rises. This is so even if the marginal utility of income is constant, so that bargaining is 'strongly efficient'.

The partial-equilibrium story

To understand the source of the original confusion, we can start with the explicitly partial-equilibrium diagram used by McDonald and Solow (1981); see Figure 21.1. Workers are assumed to have real outside opportunities worth $\overline{W}$. The marginal revenue product function is shown as DD. In a competitive labor market, it is said, employment will therefore be at P_c.

Now consider possible outcomes of bargaining. If bargaining is over wages only, with the firm then choosing employment, the outcome will be a point on the demand curve at a wage higher than $\overline{W}$, say at P_W. At any point on the

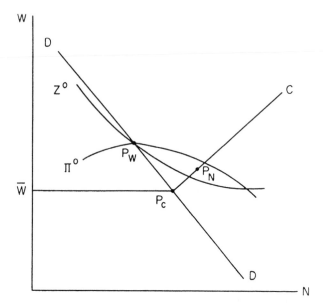

Figure 21.1 Partial equilibrium analysis of the representative firm

demand curve, the firm's real isoprofit contour ($\Pi^0 = R(N) - WN$) is horizontal. (Here $R(N)$ is the firm's revenue function, N being employment. $R(N)$ and W are measured in units of GNP.) But the union's objective $Z(W,N)$ is increasing in both W and N, so the iso-Z contour slopes down. Hence P_W is not an efficient point from the point of view of the bargainers. If bargaining covered employment as well as wages, both firm and union could be better off. The contract curve is a line rising from P_c and lying to the right of the demand curve. It contains the bargaining outcome P_N, which will be to the right of P_W.[2] This is Proposition 1.

To throw further light on the contract curve, we could assume in addition that the union is utilitarian, with objective function $Z = NU(W) + (M - N)) U(\overline{W})$, where $U()$ is utility and M is membership. If the marginal utility of income is constant, the contract curve is vertical; and the bargain is 'strongly efficient', since the marginal revenue product of labor equals the value of its outside opportunity. If there is diminishing marginal utility of income ($U'' < 0$), the contract curve slopes to the right, as drawn. In this case the bargaining point P_N lies to the right of the competitive level of employment – hence Proposition 2.

The general equilibrium story

The weakness of this whole analysis is that it assumes that the external opportunities are the same regardless of the system of wage determination in each representative firm. Let us begin with the competitive labor market. If the market is competitive, then everybody who wants a job gets one. If total labor supply (L) is inelastic, then total employment is L. It follows that employment with bargaining over wages and employment *cannot* exceed the level shown at P_c. Proposition 2 is simply false.

So what has gone wrong in the interpretation of Figure 21.1? The answer is that in a competitive labor market anyone can get a job at the prevailing wage. $\overline{W}$.[3] But in a bargaining situation the outside environment is different.

It is characterized as follows. There is an aggregate employment rate $\overline{N}/L$, say. Anyone who is not employed in the representative firm has opportunities that *depend* on $\overline{N}/L$. The analytical task is to determine the equilibrium level of $\overline{N}/L$.

This is done in Section 3 of the paper. To show the drift of the argument, we shall straightaway discuss the results in simplified form. These are based on monopolistic competition in the product market, with a fixed number of firms and constant elasticity product demand curves for each firm's output. Capital is fixed. Unions are assumed to be utilitarian. There is Nash bargaining.

We can first compare the results of the efficient bargaining with the outcome of a perfectly competitive labor market. Figure 21.2 depicts the perfectly competitive labor market. Employment in each firm is L/n, where there are n firms: and the

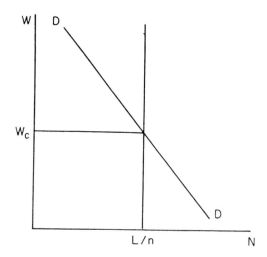

Figure 21.2   The competitive labor market

wage is W_c. Now introduce efficient bargaining, and for illustration suppose that it were strongly efficient (with $U'' = 0$). Then if there were no unemployed and the outside wage were W_c, the bargained level of employment would be L/n – full employment. But there will in fact be unemployment. For the bargained wage (W) will be above the union's fallback, and unless there is some unemployment, the union fallback will be the outside wage $\overline{W}$, which in equilibrium must equal W. Thus, there *must* be some unemployment. So the union fallback will exceed W_c, and the actual wage will be even higher.

This argument establishes Proposition 2′. The new equilibrium is illustrated in the upper part of Figure 21.3. Employment is N^*. The inside and outside wage is W_N, and the union's indifference curves are asymptotic to a level somewhat below W_N (due to the existence of unemployment).

Now compare efficient bargaining with bargaining over wages only. In Figure 21.3 we illustrate the case where equilibrium employment is the same in both cases, this being true when production functions are Cobb–Douglas (as we demonstrate below). The wage is now lower,[4] because unions are more worried about the employment implications of high wages. The union's indifference curves are therefore asymptotic to a lower asymptote than before (due to a lower outside wage). There is thus no reason why P_W should not be directly below P_N, with the new contract curve $C_W C_W$ lower than the earlier curve ($C_N C_N$)

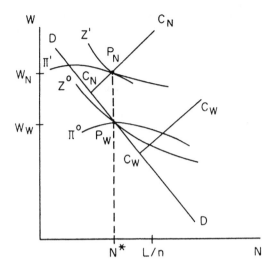

Figure 21.3 General equilibrium analysis of the representative firm

If the elasticity of substitution in production exceeds unity, efficient bargaining will actually raise unemployment. This is because a highly elastic demand for labor leads unions to be relatively cautious when bargaining is only over wages, and relatively more pushy when bargaining is also over employment.

This is Proposition 1'. To some it may appear counterintuitive that bargaining over employment could be bad for employment, even though unions like employment. The reason is that, if unions can bargain over employment (and not only over wages), *this gives them more power*. They may thus secure higher wages. And the effects of extra power may outweigh the employment gains from giving more expression to the unions' concerns over employment.

The argument that we have employed until now assumes that all firms in the economy are unionized. However, the model can also be interpreted within a two-sector framework where, in addition to the union sector, there is a competitive sector with an infinitely elastic supply of labor at a wage equal to the benefit level. In this case unemployment is essentially benefit-induced, and both the unemployed *and* those working in the secondary sector have utility equal to the utility of benefits. Employment in the secondary sector depends only on benefits (given that capital is fixed), and hence unemployment is determined by benefits and the size of the union sector. So, as the latter falls, unemployment rises. Our results now relate not to the aggregate rate of employment but to the rate of employment in the union sector (or, to be more precise, our results for unemployment now refer to the level of non-employment in the union sector). There is one other general point. As is now well known (Pohjola, 1986), bargaining over employment and wages is equivalent to bargaining over profit sharing, with the employer fixing employment. For the base wage that is chosen in profit sharing determines employment, and the profit share then determines total remuneration. Thus, our findings about the ineffectiveness (or otherwise) of efficient bargaining imply the same ineffectiveness (or otherwise) for profit sharing.

This completes our overview, and we can now derive our results systematically.

2 THE BARGAINING SETUP

The first step is to be clear about the bargaining setup. We shall use the Nash bargaining approach, because this is well suited to the analysis of union-employer bargains. This was first noted by Bishop (1964), and his analysis implies all the main features of modern bargaining theory most relevant to union-employer bargains (see Binmore, Rubinstein, and Wolinsky, 1986).

The nature of the agreement will correspond to the result of maximizing the Nash formula $(Z - \overline{Z})(\Pi - \overline{\Pi})^\beta$, where Z is the value of the union's objective and Π of the firm's objective if a bargain is struck, and $\overline{Z}, \overline{\Pi}$ are the corresponding values if agreement is not reached.

At this point we need to define these terms more closely. We assume that the union is utilitarian and cares about the welfare of M 'members' associated with the firm. It may seem artificial to assume that the population of concern is constant, but the alternative approach leads to all the well-known problems associated with membership dynamics and disappearing unions.[5] So we suppose that the union objective, Z is given by

$$Z = NV + (M - N)\overline{V} \tag{21.1}$$

where N is employment, M is membership, V is the individual welfare associated with a job within the firm, and $\overline{V}$ is the individual welfare associated with entering unemployment. $\overline{Z}$ is the value of the union objective if a bargain is not struck, and this we take simply as $M\overline{V}$ asserting thereby that members achieve the same utility as entry into unemployment.[6] As a consequence, the union contribution to the Nash bargain is given by

$$Z - \overline{Z} = N(V - \overline{V}) \tag{21.2}$$

and it now remains to specify how $V, \overline{V}$ relate to wages within the firm and opportunities outside.

As we noted in the introduction, one of our aims is to capture the notion that individuals who do not gain employment in the particular firm under consideration have potential employment opportunities elsewhere. We are also concerned to look only at steady states in an economy with n identical firm–union pairs. Consequently, we must introduce an exogenous source of turnover into the model, otherwise individuals who find themselves unemployed will remain so indefinitely, thereby defeating one of our objects and eliminating a key feature of the real world from our model. So we simply assume that a proportion δ of employees leave employment and enter unemployment voluntarily in each period for exogenous non-pecuniary reasons.[7] If we now define a as the per period exit probability from unemployment, then in steady state the unemployment rate, u, is given by

$$u = \delta/(a + \delta) \tag{21.3}$$

Next we define individual welfare at time t as

$$\sum_{s=0}^{\infty} \frac{U(I_{t+s})}{(1 + r)^{s+1}}$$

where I is income and r is the discount rate. Suppose that W is the wage within the firm under consideration, $\overline{W}$ is the outside wage, and B is the level of unemployment benefit. Then, in steady state (u constant) we must have

$$V_t = (1/(1 + r))(U(W) + \delta \overline{V}_{t+1} + (1 - \delta)V_{t+1}) \tag{21.4}$$

$$\overline{V}_t = (1/(1 + r))(U(B) + aV_{1t+1} + (1 - a)\overline{V}_{t+1}) \tag{21.5}$$

$$V_{1t} = (1/(1 + r))(U(\overline{W}) + \delta \overline{V}_{t+1} + (1 - \delta)V_{1t+1}) \tag{21.6}$$

where $V, \overline{V}, V_1$ refer to welfare associated, respectively, with a job within the firm, unemployment, and a job elsewhere.

We next consider two possibilities, a bargain that lasts forever and a bargain that lasts for one period.

Infinite bargain

In the infinite bargain case it is clear in the steady state context that $V_t = V, \overline{V}_t = \overline{V}, V_{1t} = V_1$ for all t. Solving out (21.4), (21.5), and (21.6), using (21.3), then gives

$$V - \overline{V} = (1/(r + \delta))[U(W) - \{(1 - \hat{\omega}(u))U(\overline{W}) + \hat{\omega}(u)U(B)\}] \tag{21.7}$$

$$\hat{\omega}(u) = ((r + \delta)u)/(ru + \delta) \qquad \hat{\omega}'(u) > 0 \tag{21.8}$$

In this case the 'outside opportunity' for the individual is a convex combination of employment at wage $\overline{W}$ and unemployment with benefit B. The weights $\hat{\omega}, 1 - \hat{\omega}$, simply reflect the expected proportion of time an unemployed entrant will be unemployed and employed, respectively. Note that as $\delta \to 0, \hat{\omega}(u) \to 1$, and the only alternative is unemployment. The model then collapses to the partial-equilibrium framework.

One-period bargain

If the wage bargain lasts for one period,[8] then not only are the outside opportunities $(\overline{W}, B, u)$ taken as exogenous but so are all events beyond this initial period, since these events are unaffected by current choices. So wage bargainers know that, in future periods, wages will be the same in all firms, including their own, and that there will be a stationary state. Thus, in (21.4), (21.5), and (21.6) we have $V_{t+1} = V_{1t+1} = V$ and $\overline{V}_{t+1} = \overline{V}$. From (21.4) and (21.5) we thus have

$$V_t - \overline{V}_t = (1/(1+r))[U(W) - U(B) + (1 - \delta)(V_{t+1} - \overline{V}_{t+1}) - a(V_{1t+1} - \overline{V}_{t+1})]$$

$$= (1/(1+r))[U(W) - U(B) + (1 - \delta - a)(V - \overline{V})]$$

Using (21.7) and (21.3) then gives

$$V_t - \overline{V}_t = (1/(1+r))[U(W) - \{(1 - \overline{\omega}(u))U(\overline{W}) + \overline{\omega}(u)U(B)\}] \qquad (21.9)$$

$$\overline{\omega}(u) = ((1+r)u)/(ru + \delta) \qquad \overline{\omega}(u) > \hat{\omega}(u) \qquad \overline{\omega}(u) > 0 \qquad (21.10)$$

So in the one-period bargain, given the steady state context, the 'outside opportunity' attaches more weight to the unemployed state and less to the employed state, essentially because there is less chance of becoming employed before the end of the bargaining period. Only if $\delta = 1$ and all labor turns over at the end of each period do the two models become equivalent.

In general, therefore, we can use (21.2), (21.7), and (21.9) to specify the union contribution to the Nash bargain as

$$N(U(W) - \overline{U}) \qquad (21.11)$$

$$\overline{U} = (1 - \omega(u))U(\overline{W}) + \omega(u)U(B) \qquad \omega'(u) > 0 \qquad (21.12)$$

which covers both infinite and one-period bargain cases. Note that the multiplicative constants which appear in (21.7) and (21.9), namely $1/(r + \delta)$ or $1/(1 + r)$, are irrelevant to the Nash solution and are simply omitted.

Turning now to the firm's contribution to the Nash bargain, we define Π as the profit per period given by

$$\Pi = R(N) - WN - F$$

where R is the revenue function and F reflects capital and other fixed costs. If we then suppose $\overline{\Pi}$ to be $-F$, the firm's contribution is given by

$$\Pi - \overline{\Pi} = R(N) - WN$$

and so the outcome of a bargain is obtained by maximizing

$$\Omega = N(U(W) - \overline{U})[R(N) - WN]^{\beta} \tag{21.13}$$

subject to whatever constraints are imposed by the rules of bargaining.

3 THE GENERAL EQUILIBRIUM

We are concerned here with determining the equilibrium unemployment rate in a stationary state in an economy with n identical firm-union pairs[9] engaged in Nash bargaining with the objective defined by (21.13). The decision variables for each bargain are employment, N, and wages within the firm, W. Each firm and union bargains taking outside wages $\overline{W}$ and benefits B, as *given*. However, once each firm-union bargaining outcome is determined, we investigate the general equilibrium by setting $W = \overline{W}$, since all bargaining units are identical. Total labor supply in the economy is taken as exogenously fixed at L so we also have the relation.

$$u = (L - nN)/L \tag{21.14}$$

Bargaining over wages only

We begin with the model where unions and firms bargain over *wages only* and where employment is set unilaterally by the firms. The outcome of each firm's bargain will be a level of employment N and a wage W which solve

$$\max_{N,W} N(U(W) - \overline{U})[R(N) - WN]^{\beta}$$

subject to

$$R_N - W = 0$$

where recall that $\overline{U}$, defined in (21.12), is taken as parametric. Notice that the constraint, which traces out the labor demand curve, follows as a result of the firm choosing employment to maximize profits at the given wage. The first-order conditions for this problem are

$$(U - \overline{U})(R - WN)\beta + \gamma R_{NN} = 0 \tag{21.15a}$$

$$NU'(R - WN)^\beta - \beta N^2(U - \overline{U})(R - WN)^{\beta-1} - \gamma = 0 \tag{21.15b}$$

$$R_N - W = 0 \tag{21.15c}$$

where γ is the Lagrange multiplier associated with the constraint. These equations provide the solutions to each individual bargain for given $\overline{W}$ and B. In order to derive the general equilibrium unemployment rate, we make use of the following. First, assume that U has a constant elasticity form, so that

$$U' = \alpha U/W \qquad (\alpha \le 1) \tag{21.16}$$

Second, note that the labor demand elasticity η is given by

$$\eta = R_N/NR_{NN} \tag{21.17}$$

since the demand curve (21.15c) implies that $R_{NN}\partial N/\partial W = 1$. Third, note that in static general equilibrium, wages are the same in all firms. This implies that $W = \overline{W}$. So from (21.12) and (21.16) we have

$$U - \overline{U} = \omega(u)(U(W) - U(B)) = \omega(u)(1 - b^\alpha)U(W) \tag{21.8}$$

where $b = B/W$, the replacement ratio. Defining $\eta_R = NR_N/R$, we can use (21.15c), (21.16), (21.17), and (21.18) to rewrite (21.15a) and (21.15b) as

$$\omega(u)(1 - b^\alpha) = \gamma R_N/(UN|\eta|(R - WN)^\beta) \tag{21.19a}$$

$$\alpha - (\beta\eta_R/(1 - \eta_R))[\omega(u)(1 - b^\alpha)] = \gamma R_N/(UN(R - WN)^\beta) \tag{21.19b}$$

If we now divide (21.19a) by (21.19b) to eliminate γ, we can solve out for the general equilibrium unemployment rate, u_w, as[10]

$$\omega(u_w) = \frac{\alpha(1 - \eta_R)}{(1 - b^\alpha)[|\eta|(1 - \eta_R) + \beta\eta_R]} \tag{21.20}$$

Before going on to the efficient bargain model, it is worth noting that, in general, both η_R and η are variable, and so they will depend on employment. (21.14) gives

$$N = (1 - u_w)L/n$$

and hence

$$\eta = \eta((1 - u_w)L/n) \qquad \eta_R = \eta_R((1 - u_w)L/n) \tag{21.21}$$

So, unless η and η_R are constant (e.g. the Cobb–Douglas case), (21.20) is only an implicit equations for u_w

Efficient bargaining

Turning now to the *efficient bargain model*, the outcome of the bargain for each firm will solve

$$\max_{W,N} N(U(W) - \overline{U})[R(N) - WN]^{\beta}$$

The first-order conditions with common factors removed are

$$(U - \overline{U}) + \beta[N(U - \overline{U})][R_N - W)/(R - WN)] = 0 \tag{21.22}$$

$$U' - \beta[N(U - \overline{U})]/(R - WN) = 0 \tag{21.23}$$

If we divide, we obtain the standard contract curve equation,

$$R_N = W - (U - \overline{U})/U' \tag{21.24}$$

As in the previous case, we compute the general equilibrium level of unemployment, u_N by setting $W = \overline{W}$. So using (21.16) and (21.18), we find that (21.22) becomes

$$\omega(u)(1 - b^{\alpha})U + \beta U[\omega(u)(1 - b^{\alpha})] \times [(NR_N - WN)/(R - WN)] = 0 \tag{21.25}$$

and (21.24) is

$$R_N = W[1 - (\omega(u)(1 - b^{\alpha}))/\alpha] \tag{21.26}$$

If we now use (21.26) to eliminate W from (21.25) we have, after some manipulation,

$$\omega(u_N) = [\alpha(1 - \eta_R)]/[(1 - b^{\alpha})(1 + \beta\eta_R)] \tag{21.27}$$

Precisely the same caveats apply as before: in particular, this is only an implicit equation for u_N since, in general, $\eta_R = \eta_R((1 - u_N) L/n)$

Comparison

When comparing the unemployment rates across the two steady states with different bargaining structures, a key question is what should be held constant. It is natural to keep technology, utility functions, demand elasticities, and the exogenous turnover rate fixed, and in our analysis we shall also keep the replacement ratio $b = B/W$ fixed. Thus, if the wage is different in the two steady states, we suppose that real benefits are also different. We are thus arguing that in comparing unemployment rates in two different economies, it makes more sense to interpret *ceteris paribus* as meaning equality of replacement ratios rather than equality of real benefits if for no other reason that, in the long run, it is the former rather than the latter which tend to be stable.[11]

In the light of this, we may simply compare u_N and u_w using the formulae in (21.27) and (21.20), and these reveal immediately that $u_N = u_w$ when $|\eta|\,(1-\eta_R)=1$. In order to interpret this condition, we must go behind each firm's real revenue function, $R(N)$. Since there is no reason to assume that the product market is perfectly competitive, we suppose that each firm faces a constant elasticity demand curve:

$$Y = P^{-e}\overline{Y}, \qquad e > 1 \tag{21.28}$$

where P is the firm's real output price, Y is output and $\overline{Y}$ is an index of aggregate real demand. Furthermore, each firm has a constant returns production function:

$$Y = F(N, K) \tag{21.29}$$

So real revenue R is given by

$$R = PY = (F, (N, K))^{1-1/e}\overline{Y}^{1/e} \tag{21.30}$$

From (21.30) we find that

$$\eta_R = NR_N/R = (1 - 1/e)_{s_N} \tag{21.31}$$

where $s_N = NF_N/F$. Further differentiation then yields

$$\begin{aligned}
|\eta| &= -R_N/NR_{NN} \\
&= (s_N/e + (1-s_N)/\sigma)^{-1}
\end{aligned} \tag{21.32}$$

where α is the elasticity of substitution, $F_N F_K/FF_{NK}$.

As a consequence of (21.31) and (21.32) we find that

$$|\eta|(1 - \eta_R) = \sigma/(1 + a)$$

where $a = (\sigma - 1)s_N/(s_N + e(1 - s_N))$. It is immediately clear that $|\eta|(1 - \eta_R) = 1$ when $\alpha = 1$. So, given a Cobb–Douglas technology and our other assumption (constant elasticity product demand and utility functions, and Nash bargaining), the aggregate unemployment rate is exactly the same, irrespective of whether firms and unions bargain over employment as well as wages. In addition, it is obvious by comparing (21.24) with (21.15c) that when employment is the same, wages must be higher when bargaining takes place over employment as well as wages.

We can go a little further along these lines by noting that, if we write the unemployment rates as functions of the elasticity of substitution $u_w(\sigma)$ and

$u_N(\sigma)$, then it is easy to demonstrate that

$$\frac{\partial u_w(1)}{\partial \sigma} < \frac{\partial u_N(1)}{\partial \sigma}$$

Thus, if we are close to $\sigma = 1$, $u_w > u_N$ if σ is below unity, and $u_w < u_N$ if σ is above unity.

Having derived our main results, it is worth looking a little more closely at the expressions for u_w and u_N. The comparative statistics are the same in both cases, and it is easy to show that under weak conditions, the unemployment rate is increasing in b, α, and δ, and decreasing in β. Furthermore, in all cases the wage rate will move in the same direction as the unemployment rate (see (21.15c) and (21.26)). All these results make good sense. In particular, it is worth noting that as α rises toward unity, the unemployment rate rises despite the fact that, under efficient bargaining, the level of employment in each firm approaches the 'strongly efficient' level which is achieved when employees are risk neutral.

Conclusions

We have demonstrated that in a fully unionized economy, the aggregate unemployment rate when firms and unions bargain over wages and employment can be either higher or lower than that arising when bargaining takes place over wages alone with firms setting employment unilaterally. In particular, if the technology is Cobb–Douglas, firms face constant elasticity demand curves for their product and workers have constant elasticity utility functions, then the unemployment rate is the same in both cases as long as the benefit replacement ratio is kept constant. These results contrast with the well-known partial-equilibrium result that employment is higher under efficient bargaining than when bargaining is only over wages.

Notes

1. An honorable exception is Pissarides (1986, Appendix 7A), who points out that in one special case, discussed below, the answer is neither more nor less. By contrast, according to Brown and Ashenfelter (1986), 'public policies that weaken trade unions will have different effects on employment according to whether employment contracts are struck as efficient bargains'.
2. This is obvious if the contract curve slopes to the right. If it slopes backwards, it is easy to show that under Nash bargaining the bargaining outcome (P_N) must lie to the right of (P_W).
3. Throughout this paper we ignore frictional unemployment.

4. Pissarides (1986, Appendix) erroneously says the opposite in words, but comparison of his equations (7.4) and (7.A3) shows the true situation.
5. Here we are simply concerned with the consequences of the standard utilitarian union model, since this is well situated to the point of issue. Thus, we also assume that membership always exceeds employment ($M \geq N$) in order to avoid the discontinuity in the objective when N rises above M.
6. It is obvious that we could make more sophisticated assumptions – for example, that strike pay was such as to provide a higher value. This issue is not, however, germane to our main line of argument, so we keep the model as simple as possible.
7. In reality, of course, turnover is also generated by exogenous demand shocks of various kinds. This is ignored here, since we do not wish to introduce such explicit stochastic elements into the model. However, we feel that our model will mimic closely the consequences of a stochastic steady state model.
8. This model is discussed in Manning (1988).
9. For an analysis of the monopoly union with an endogenous number of firms see Jackman and Layard (1986).
10. Note that $\alpha/(1 - b^\alpha) > 0$ for all $\alpha \leq 1$ if $b < 1$.
11. This is consistent with standard cross-country analyses of unemployment differences, for example, where a key variable in such comparisons is the replacement ratio.

References

Binmore, K., A. Rubinstein and A. Wolinsky (1986) 'The Nash Bargaining Solution in Economic Modelling', *Rand Journal of Economics*, 17, 176–88.

Bishop, R., (1964) 'A Zeuthen-Hicks Theory of Bargaining', *Econometrica*, 32, 410–17.

Brown, J. and O. Ashenfelter (1986) 'Testing the Efficiency of Employment Contracts', *Journal of Political Economy*, 94, 540–87.

Jackman, R. and R. Layard (1986) 'A Wage-Tax, Worker-Subsidy Policy for Reducing the "Natural" Rate of Unemployment', in W. Beckerman, ed., *Wage Rigidity and Unemployment* (London: Duckworth).

Manning, A. (1988) 'Unemployment Is Probably Lower If Unions Bargain Over Employment', Birkbeck College (August), unpublished mimeo.

McDonald, I. and R. Solow (1981) 'Wage Bargaining and Employment', *American Economic Review*, 71, no. 5, 896–908.

Oswald, A. (1985) 'The Economic Theory of Trade Unions: An Introductory Survey', *Scandinavian Journal of Economics*, 87, 160–93.

Pissarides, C. (1986) 'Equilibrium Effects of Tax-Based Incomes Policies', in D. Colander, ed., *Incentive-Based Incomes Policies* (Cambridge, MA: Ballinger).

Pohjola, M. (1986) 'Profit-Sharing, Collective Bargaining and Employment', Labour Institute for Economic Research, Helsinki, *Discussion Paper*, 52.

22 Europe in 1984: The Case for Unsustainable Growth

(1984)*

with G. Basevi, O. Blanchard, W. Buiter and R. Dornbusch

SUMMARY

The European economy remains in the doldrums. Though output is rising, the general opinion, reflected in the EC Commission's projections, is that unemployment will remain at around 10 per cent for some years. Thus when Europeans speak of recovery these days, they mean that output will soon be growing at its trend rate of growth. This will not increase employment, for output per worker will grow as fast as output. With the labour force constant, there will thus remain the same margin of unemployed labour as at present.

This depressing prospect is illustrated in Figure 22.1. By 1983 output was more than 8 per cent below its former trend and the Commission's central projection implies no narrowing of the gap at all by 1987.[1] In fact unemployment is expected to be higher this year than last.

There is only one way to reduce this gap. *The economy must for some years grow faster than its sustainable long-run growth rate*. Only thus can we reduce the margin of unused resources. This is a simple point of logic. But is it feasible?

Many analysts believe it would be dangerous to try to do better than the Commission's forecast. The argument is that the old ways did no good, so we should therefore give the new restrictive policies a chance. The worrying aspect of this approach is that it tends to accept the new situation as the best that can be achieved. As the situation becomes worse, the level of aspiration is further reduced.

By contrast, in the USA analysts have expected a recovery of employment and it has come about. The most obvious reason for the difference between continents is that fiscal policy in the USA became increasingly expansionary from 1982 onwards, while in the EC the full-employment deficit was progressively reduced from that year onwards.[2] From now on European fiscal

* *Centre for European Policy Studies Paper*, 8/9 (May 1984), pp. 4–50.

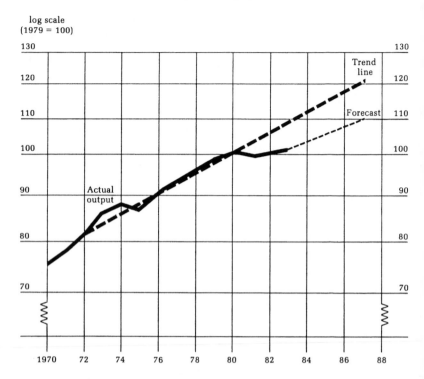

Figure 22.1   GDP at 1975 market prices: EC
Note: The log-linear trend line is the authors' and goes through the average
for 1970–4 (plotted at 1972) and the average for 1975–9 (plotted at 1977).
The implied growth rate is 2.3 per cent p.a., compared with the forecast of 2.0
per cent between 1983 and 1987. We attach no special importance to this trend
line; any other that excluded the last three years would make much the same point.
Source: Actual and forecast: Commission of the EC, *European Economy*,
18 (November 1983, pp. 64, 67).

policy is expected to become even more contractionary and US fiscal policy
more expansionary. (By contrast, European monetary policy has been roughly
as contractionary as in the USA, with European real interest rates having
followed US rates upwards.

We believe that instead of maintaining their deflationary stance, European
governments (especially the Federal Republic of Germany and the United
Kingdom) should undertake a temporary fiscal expansion, with monetary

policy accommodating to prevent a rise in interest rates and exchange rates. If the policy were temporary, there need be no fear that when employment had been restored the public deficit would crowd out private investment. Thus an excellent form of stimulus would be increased public infrastructure investment, with temporary investment subsidies in the private sector and a temporary marginal employment subsidy.[3]

The three constraints

Many people will say this cannot be done: that Europe has special problems which make recovery possible in America but not in Europe.[4] There are three possible constraints which might impede reflation: real resource constraints, financial constraints, and constraints arising from lack of coordination between countries. The first three parts of our report review these constraints as they apply in the European context.

1 The real resource constraint

The real resource constraint manifests itself in the fact that if unemployment is reduced below a certain level, inflation tends to increase. This 'non-accelerating inflationary rate of unemployment' (called the NAIRU) thus imposes a limit on the sustainable level of economic activity. The actual employment rate in the Community is now more than 10 per cent. However we estimate that the weighted average value of the NAIRU in the EC is no more than $7\frac{1}{2}$ per cent. Vacancies are now at an unprecedentedly low level and the utilization of physical capacity is also very low. In addition there is no good evidence that the European economy is suffering from abnormally high mismatch between the pattern of labour demanded and that supplied.

Thus there is certainly room for a Keynesian expansion and no reason to suppose that a modest reflation would run into major obstacles on the inflation front. However if governments really fear inflation, they would do better to implement some form of incomes policy than to resign themselves to 10 per cent unemployment for years to come. We outline a scheme for tax-based incomes policy which could be practicable in a number of countries.

2. The financing constraint

The second objection to reflation is that it will lead to higher budget deficits. These, it is said, must lead either to higher inflation (if financed by money creation) or to higher real interest rates (if financed by borrowing). But this does not follow. Suppose that, as we favour, the deficit increases temporarily and money is allowed to expand at a rate which holds real interest rates constant.[5] Then output will grow and the monetary expansion will not go into prices rather than output.

If expansion were pursued too far, inflationary pressure would of course develop in the labour market, but that is a general point that would apply whether expansion occurred through a higher budget deficit or a surge in exports. Few people, surprisingly, oppose a recovery based on exports, but many resist the notion that the public deficit can be the propellant. Their fears are only justified in a long-run context. In the long-run (at the NAIRU), a higher public sector deficit will lead to higher real interest rates, reducing private investment and thus the economy's potential for growth.[6] That is why the fiscal reflation we propose is temporary in form. Given this, there should be no fears about a modest reflation, since, as we show, there is nothing unsustainable about the current stance of fiscal policy in most European countries.

3. The coordination constraint

The constraints we have discussed so far affect the US as much as Europe: the NAIRUs may differ, but the logic of the problem is the same. However there is one outstanding difference between Europe and the United States: Europe is not a country. This poses a problem of coordination.

If a small open economy reflates on its own, it has two main practical alternatives. Either it allows its exchange rate to depreciate, in which case it can achieve a satisfactory expansion but at the cost of increasing inflation. Or if it is unwilling to accept this inflation, it has to maintain its exchange rate by increased interest rates. The higher interest rates distort the pattern of expansion away from investment. But, more seriously, much of the extra employment created by the increased deficit is overseas. A country wondering whether to expand will not take this extra foreign demand into account when performing its own cost-benefit calculus. It may be unwilling to incur the extra deficit (and future tax liabilities implied) for largely foreign jobs. But if all countries expanded at the same time, each country would obtain more extra jobs for a given increase in its budget deficit than if it expanded on its own. The country would therefore be more willing to expand.

1984 is not 1978

Some will say that these policies were tried after the Bonn Summit of July 1978, and failed. It is crucial therefore to note the differences between 1984 and 1978. The fundamental difference is in the margin of slack (in Figure 22.1 this is measured as the gap between the trend line and actual output). This gap is far greater now than in 1978. Thus it would be perfectly logical to believe that the 1978 reflation was misconceived (even if the Shah had not fallen) and to believe that concerted reflation now is essential.

What problems could arise? First, take oil and commodity prices. Oil prices are unlikely to surge.[8] Commodity prices have risen somewhat, but this may be essentially a restoration of their long-run relative price. Next, consider wages: a wage-led increase in inflation is unlikely.[9] Thus in all respects 1984 is different from 1978.

The danger of not reflating

Of course one would be less keen on reflation if one thought that a future *reduction* of inflation should be a top priority. Whether it should be is largely a matter of value judgment. It has been argued that a permanently high rate of inflation imposes a permanent annual cost whose present value is very high and may even be infinite. By contrast the cost of unemployment is reckoned as small, since it lasts only as long as the unemployment lasts.[10] However this last point is by no means obvious. In a period of prolonged unemployment net investment in machines and in workers is lower than normal, and this leads to a capital stock that is permanently lower than it would have been. Investment has been low in recent years and is unlikely to recover substantially unless there is a boost to aggregate demand. Moreover there is no evidence of the hoped-for productivity breakthrough occurring as the weaker firms (or parts of firms) go to the wall. On top of this unemployment undermines work habits and leads to the rusting of skills in a way that may permanently reduce the sustainable rate of employment. (This, however, is speculation rather than established fact.) For all these reasons our own judgment is that in most countries attempts to reduce inflation still further should be abandoned and a concerted (though controlled) reflation put in hand.

Why work-sharing is wrong

The form of reflation that we favour is explicitly temporary – to get the economies moving again. However there is also the longer term question of measures to reduce the sustainable level of unemployment, which we discuss in Section 4.

Some people advocate a reduction of working time. This is based on a fundamental misunderstanding of the nature of the unemployment problem. Work-sharing could be justified if there were some limit to the demand for person-hours because human wants had been satiated or because of insufficient capital to employ the workforce. But this is not why we have unemployment, either now or in the long-term. We have unemployment because otherwise we should have more inflationary pressure.

If unemployment is reduced, inflationary pressure will be higher, whether unemployment is reduced by cutting hours per worker (with output constant) or by expanding output (with hours per worker constant). If we are willing to increase inflationary pressure, it would clearly be better to get more output in return. So we consider the present vogue in favour of work-sharing to be one of the more dangerous and depressing features of the current European loss of confidence. It is basically a counsel of despair and distracts attention from the positive steps which could be taken.

The restructuring of employment taxes

There are a number of constructive measures that can be taken to reduce the long-run level of unemployment. The long-run problem is that, whether wages are set by firms, or by bargaining between the two, wage-setters have an incentive to set real wages above the level that is sufficient to employ all those who want work. The natural solution to the problem is to offer employers a credit for each worker employed, financed by a proportional tax on the wage bill. The credit will stimulate employment while the wage-bill tax will tend to reduce wages. The overall effect will be a fall in the real cost of labour.

This change can be introduced with no net increase in employers' taxes on labour and no new administration. Existing employment taxes can simply be restructured by raising the percentage element in the taxation of earnings and introducing a per worker 'credit'. The rates of tax and credit should be chosen so that at the whole economy level the net tax take is unchanged. Apart from the general advantages we have already described, the scheme will also reduce the net tax on unskilled workers, whose unemployment rates are typically four times the average rate. This element of discrimination in favour of the employment prospects of less skilled groups is an additional plus for the scheme.

Tax-based incomes policy

The same objectives can also be pursued by a tax-based incomes policy. In this case, the tax will be on the *growth rate* of wages rather than the level. Employers will pay a tax on that part of their wage bill that exceeds the norm for the growth of average hourly earnings. Linked to this there will be a small per worker subsidy. The advantage of this incomes policy approach is that it is explicitly linked to inflation. The disadvantage is the political difficulty of security consensus over the norm. But unless countries are willing to contemplate new social institutions, we are going to be saddled with high unemployment for the indefinite future.

Conclusion

However, the immediate problem is that unemployment is unnecessarily far above the NAIRU. There are no constraints limiting a return to the NAIRU. The financial problems could be overcome by a temporary fiscal stimulus with monetary accommodation, were it not for the problem of exchange rate effects. Thus there is a crucial need for concerted action. Individual countries

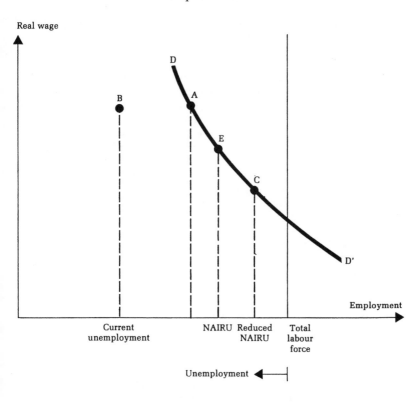

Figure 22.2 Different levels of unemployment

cannot be expected to go it alone. But if they concerted their actions, all would be better off. 1984 is not 1978.

1 THE REAL RESOURCE CONSTRAINT

Let us begin with some basic concepts about the level of unemployment. For this purpose, Figure 22.2 is helpful. *DD'* is the long-run demand curve for labour, which depends on the real wage. With existing labour market institutions, the lowest unemployment we can have without increasing inflation is that shown as the NAIRU. To achieve employment at that level, the real wage would have to be that shown at point *E*. If the real wage were higher, for example at point *A*, unemployment would have to be at least as high as at *A*. But at the same wage level, unemployment might be even higher than that, as at point *B*, with employment inside the long-run demand curve.

The crucial issues are whether our current unemployment is above the NAIRU – and by how much. If actual unemployment is well above the NAIRU (as at point *B*) there will be strong downwards pressure on the rate of growth of real wages and the level of real wages will be falling relative to trend productivity. In this situation a judicious reflation will not run into bottlenecks, especially if there is an element of 'Keynesian unemployment' (as at point *B*).

We therefore begin by examining the existing margin of slack, the subject of Section 1 of our report. We then consider what problems might arise in trying to take up the slack: the financing constraint (Section 2) and the problem of coordination (Section 3). Our proposals come in Section 4. We first give our suggestions for the reflation of demand, which we consider our most urgent message, and then deal with the important question of what can be done on the side of 'supply' to reduce the NAIRU. This would involve moving to a point such as *C*. We end by suggesting how to do this.

The margin of slack

The first point is to establish the margin of slack. Figure 22.3 shows the extraordinary rise in unemployment that has occurred in Europe in the last three years. It is important to remember that only four years ago EC unemployment was below 6 per cent, compared with just over 10 per cent today. Yet the Commission forecast that unemployment will continue at around 10 per cent for the next four years – with employment and labour force virtually constant and both output and labour productivity both growing at about 2 per cent a year. The forecast may well be somewhat too gloomy, but is striking fact that such a recent change is widely accepted as semi-permanent.

By contrast, the USA is recovering and is expected to recover further. The OECD forecast an 8 per cent US unemployment rate in 1984, and this may well prove too high. Even more striking perhaps is the trans-Atlantic comparison of employment growth. The US generated 13 million new jobs between 1973 and 1979, while employment in the EC was virtually constant (see Figure 22.4). In 1983 US employment was back to its 1979 level and was expected to grow by around 3 per cent in the following year, while European employment is now 4 million down on 1979 (with a static labour force) and expected to remain constant for the next few years.

What explains these differences? Clearly the time trend is mainly related to different movements of the labour force. But US employment fluctuates around its trend much more. This is probably due to the US system of employment at will. If the costs of firing and hiring are lower, it is rational for employers to vary their output more through fluctuations in men and less

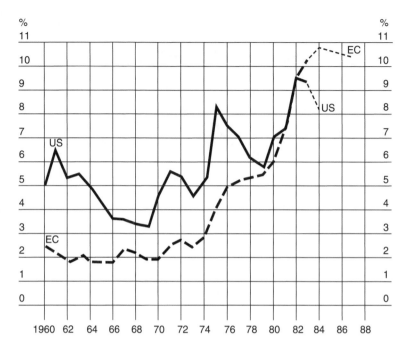

Figure 22.3 Unemployment rates as % of civilian labour force: EC and USA
Sources: EC: *European Economy*, No. 18, Table 3 and pp. 64, 67 for forecast to 1987.
USA: *Economic Report to the President*, Table B29; OECD forecast for 1983 and 1984, *Economic Outlook*, p. 45.

through fluctuations in hours per man.[11] This must be a partial explanation of the current strength of the US employment recovery. But more than this is needed to explain why the European economy is expected to stay down for so long. The most plausible explanation is the difference in budgetary stance, which we shall discuss in the next section.

For the present our main aim is to document how much slack exists in the European economy over and above that needed to contain inflation. If the unemployment rate goes up, the fact does not by itself indicate that the slack has increased. Four possible bottlenecks could be causing the high level of unemployment; if any of them were binding, an attempt at reflation would be pointless.

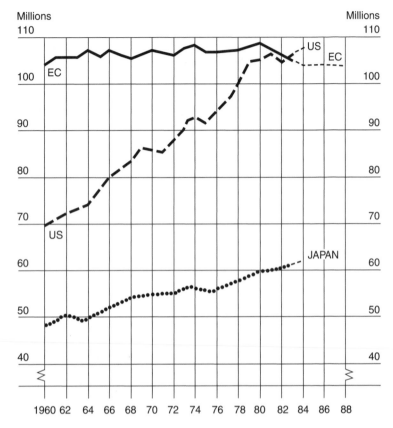

Figure 22.4 Employment: EC, USA and Japan
Source: Commission of the EC (forecast as in Figure 22.3).

- First, there could have been a reduction of the capital stock, so that, even though workers are available, there is no capital for them to work with.
- Second, the unemployed could be work-shy and not available for work.
- Third, there could be a structural mis-match in the labour market, so that although the unemployed are available for work, a resurgence of demand will not re-employ them because they have the wrong skills or are in the wrong place.

• Fourth, there could have been an increase in the degree of slack needed to contain inflation.

Let us examine each of these possibilities.

The hypothesis of capital shortage can be ruled out straight away. Figure 22.5 shows employers' reports of capacity utilization. This shows that in 1983 capacity utilization was way below its normal level and almost as low as in 1975. This is sufficient to rule out the story of technological unemployment, which alleges that capital now requires so few workers that even when all capital is used it cannot employ the willing hands. However, let us add another nail to that particular coffin. If capital has suddenly become so much more labour-saving, we should see a striking increase in the rate of growth of output per worker. As Figure 22.6 shows, we see nothing of the kind.

So let us turn to the second and third possibilities: that the unemployed are not willing to work or are in the wrong skills or locations. If this were a bottleneck, one would expect the number of job vacancies would be at least as high as normal. But it is at an all-time low, as Figure 22.7 shows. So the problem looks like one of 'not enough jobs' rather than 'not enough willing and

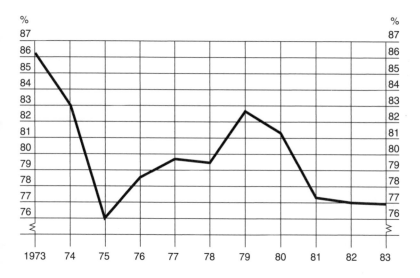

Figure 22.5 Capacity utilization in manufacturing industry: EC
Source: *European Economy*, Supplement B, No. 6 (June 1983, p. 5).
Notes: Weights by volume of industrial production. UK data are adjusted from data on percentage of firms working below capacity.

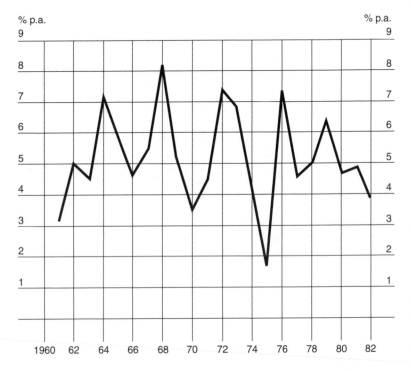

Figure 22.6 Rate of growth of output per person-hour in manufacturing: EC
Source: Commission of the EC: based on US Bureau of Labor Statistics,
press release (26 May 1983)

suitable workers'. In fact the striking thing is that in Europe vacancies have
been well below their historic average ever since 1975. This contrasts sharply
with the USA, where the 1979 boom looks as bullish as any before it.[12]

The NAIRU

We have therefore ruled out shortages of capital or willing workers, as well as
mis-match of skills or location as binding physical constraints on reflation. But
what about the inflation constraint? Suppose that there have been shifts in
wage-setting behaviour so that high levels of unemployment (and low levels of
vacancies) are now necessary to contain inflation. To investigate this we have

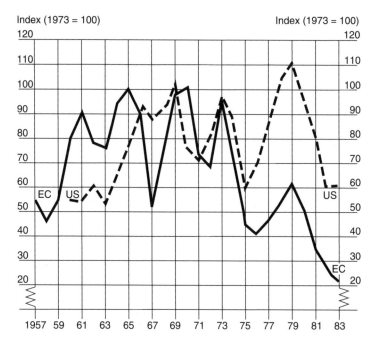

Figure 22.7 Vacancy rates
Source: See Figure 22.8
US index: Help-Wanted Index.
European index: Based on registered vacancies. The index is

$$100 \ e^{\Sigma a_i \log v_{i,t}} / e^{\Sigma a_i \log v_{i,1973}}$$

where a_i is the employment share of the ith country in 1975.

to look at the relationship between the level of unemployment and inflation. Wage (and price) inflation have been falling sharply recently (see Figure 22.8), which suggests that we are well above the level of unemployment at which inflation would start to rise.

However we must do our best to estimate the critical 'non-accelerating inflation rate of unemployment'. Unemployment is higher than the NAIRU if the rate of wage inflation is falling or if the rate of real wage growth is below its long-run trend. To find the NAIRU one therefore takes the actual rate of unemployment and adjusts it downwards for the fall in the rate of wage

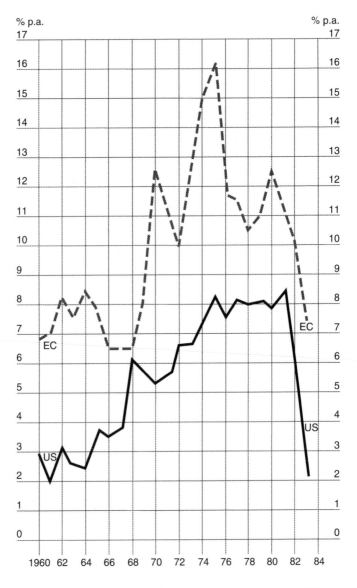

Figure 22.8 Rate of growth of hourly earnings in manufacturing: EC and USA
Source: OECD, *Main Economic Indicators*. 1983 figures relate 1983 (Q2) to 1982 (Q2).

Table 22.1

	Actual unemployment (%) 1981–3	Estimated NAIRU 1981–3	Estimated actual unemployment (%) 1984
France	7.3	6.9	9.0
FRG	6.7	5.3	7.8
Italy	9.4	7.7	11.9
UK	10.8	9.5	11.4
EC	8.8	7.3	10.4

inflation and for the excess of trend real wage growth over actual real wage growth. (Of course if wage inflation is increasing or if real wage growth is too high, one adjusts unemployment *upwards* to get the NAIRU). The estimates we get for the NAIRU are shown below. They are very approximate since they depend on the estimated parameters of the wage equation which are subject to wide margins of error.

We show first the average unemployment rates for 1981–3 and then the corresponding NAIRU obtained by applying the relevant adjustments (Table 22.1).[13]

These estimates give a NAIRU for the EC of about $7\frac{1}{2}$ per cent, compared with a 1984 forecast 3 points higher than that. We should also explain that the estimates do not allow for any effect which an incomes policy, such as that now operating in France, might have on the NAIRU.

Some people may feel that estimates of the NAIRU should be based on a longer run of years than just the last three, and on a less atypical period. If so, they may prefer to look back at the period 1976–80, when the estimated NAIRU averaged $5\frac{1}{2}$ per cent, and the country estimates shown in Table 22.2.[14]

However realism may require that we give more weight to recent than to earlier experience. In fact our estimates suggest that the NAIRU has risen fairly steadily in the EC (Table 22.3).

Although the causes of the higher NAIRU do not affect our estimates of whether slack exists, it is worth saying what we can about why the NAIRU has risen. The rise has two components. First, the fall in the rate of sustainable productivity growth since the early 1970s means that more unemployment is needed to make workers willing to accept the feasible rate of real wage growth. This appears explicitly in our calculation and accounts for an increase in roughly 2 per cent points of the NAIRU.[15]

Table 22.2

	Actual unemployment (%) 1976–80	Estimated NAIRU 1976–80
France	5.3	5.3
FRG	3.7	3.7
Italy	7.1	8.9
UK	5.5	4.6
EC	5.4	5.3

Table 22.3

	Actual EC unemployment (%)	Estimated EC NAIRU
1966–70	2.4	2.6
1971–5	3.2	5.3
1976–80	5.4	5.3
1981–3	8.8	7.6

But there is a residual unexplained element in the rise in the NAIRU. This could reflect (a) changes in the match between the pattern of labour demanded and labour supplied, (b) changes in willingness to work, (c) changes in employment protection legislation, or (d) changes in trade union power.

No growth in structural mis-match

Let us consider first the question of *mis-match*. The evidence suggests that this has not increased. We begin with Britain (Table 22.4). A reasonable index of structural mis-match is achieved by comparing the share of unemployment and the share of vacancies in each sector. If there were no structural mis-match, one might expect these shares to be the same in each sector. So an index of mis-match is provided by $\frac{1}{2}\sum_i |U_i - V_i|$, where u_i is the proportion of the unemployed in the sector, v_i the proportion of the vacancies, and $|\ |$ indicates absolute value. The index shows what proportion of the unemployed would have to move sector in order to bring about perfect balance. This index is

Table 22.4 The mis-match of unemployment and vacancies in the UK[a], 1962–82

	By occupation (6)[b]	By region (11)	By region and occupation (66)	By industry (27)
1962				0.25
1963				0.25
1964				0.25
1965				0.25
1966				0.25
1967		0.27		0.27
1968		0.27		0.29
1969		0.26		0.25
1970		0.23		0.24
1971		0.26		0.22
1972		0.30		0.22
1973		0.29		0.23
1974		0.28		0.23
1975	0.39	0.16		0.20
1976	0.35	0.13		0.19
1977	0.35	0.17	0.35	0.18
1978	0.37	0.21	0.37	0.17
1979	0.37	0.24	0.37	0.23
1980	0.31	0.23	0.37	0.31
1981	0.29	0.18	0.35	
1982[c]	0.26	0.18	0.33	

Notes:
[a] The mis-match index is $1/2\Sigma_i(u_i - v_i)$, where u_i is the proportion of the unemployed in each sector and v_i is the proportion of vacancies in each sector.
[b] Numbers in brackets indicate number of sectors.
[c] 1982 is based on 3 quarters only.
Source: Department of Employment Gazette and *Monthly Digest of Statistics* (second column only).

shown in the four columns of the Table 22.4 for different classifications of jobs. Remarkably, the index tends to have a downward trend.

Another approach is to look at possible sources of mis-match. These would be more likely to come from shifts in demand than from shifts in supply. Unfortunately there is no easy way to measure shifts in demand between sectors. But assuming that the flexibility of the supply responses is unaltered, the actual shifts in employment should be a reasonable proxy for the shifts in demand. Thus in Table 22.5 we compute an index of the shift in the pattern of employment across industries for the main EC countries. This starts from the annual net change in the structure of employment, which is a highly cyclical variable. To smooth the series we show its five-year moving average. In France, the FRG, Netherlands, and UK the index tends to rise up to the early 1970s, but to remain constant or fall thereafter. In Italy the series tends to fall fairly steadily over the whole period, and in Belgium to rise over the whole period. Thus, except in Belgium, there is absolutely no evidence of unusual disturbance in the mid to late 1970s.[16] Evidently demand shifts caused by the energy shock were not particularly strong compared to earlier demand shifts. So there is no reason to suppose that Europe is suffering from an 'increased pace of change' or from 'increased structural imbalance'.

Willingness to work and employment protection

We turn now to the *effects of any change in the willingness to work and employment protection*. If the unemployed have become more choosey about jobs, one would expect to see an increase in the numbers of unemployed at any given level of job availability (as measured by vacancies).[17] Similarly, if it were made more difficult for employers to fire workers, they would become more choosey about workers and the number of unemployed would again rise relative to the number of vacancies. It turns out that unemployment has risen sharply relative to vacancies in both Belgium and Britain, but the reverse has happened in the Federal Republic. In the Netherlands there is little shift either way.[18]

If the unemployed have become more choosey about jobs, there could be many reasons: a rise in the ratio of unemployment benefits to net income in work, a slacker administration of unemployment benefits, or a more general decline in the work ethic. In Britain there has been no rise in the ratio of benefits to net income in work since 1966, though there was a substantial rise in the ten years before. However there is evidence of slacker administration of benefits and of changes in attitudes to living off the state.[19] Thus in some countries there is evidence of a decline in the intensity of job search by the unemployed and perhaps of problems arising from employment protection legislation. But it is not clear that this applies to all countries.

In any event this is not the whole story, even in countries where it applies in part. For in addition to the rise in unemployment at given vacancies (in some countries), there has been a big decline in the non-inflationary level of vacancies in Britain, the Federal Republic, and the Netherlands.[20] In both the UK and FRG the fall has been more than is explained by the fall in productivity growth. This must be due to unfavourable change in *wage-setting behaviour* of

Table 22.5 Annual change in the structure of employment, 1953–81
(5-year moving average)

| | 8 industrial sectors | | | | | | 24 industrial sectors |
	Belgium	France	FRG	Italy	Neth	UK	UK
1953	1.8				1.5	1.1	1.9
1954	1.7				1.6	1.0	1.9
1955	1.4				1.3	1.0	1.6
1956	1.7				1.3	0.9	1.6
1957	1.8	1.5		4.3	1.3	1.0	1.6
1958	1.9	1.6		4.2	1.3	1.1	1.6
1959	2.0	1.6		3.8	1.4	1.2	1.7
1960	2.1	1.4	2.5	3.4	1.4	1.4	1.8
1961	1.9	1.5	2.7	3.1	1.4	1.5	1.9
1962	1.7	1.6	2.5	3.2	1.5	1.4	2.1
1963	1.6	1.7	2.3	2.9	1.6	1.4	1.9
1964	1.7	1.7	2.2	2.7	1.6	1.5	1.9
1965	1.9	1.7	2.2	2.4	1.9	1.6	2.0
1966	1.9	1.8	1.8	2.7	2.0	1.5	2.0
1967	1.9	1.6	2.0	2.5	2.0	1.6	2.0
1968	1.8	2.5	2.1	3.0	2.0	1.6	2.2
1969	1.8	2.2	2.9	2.6	2.0	1.8	2.4
1970	1.7	2.1	2.8	2.8	2.1	1.9	2.5
1971	1.7	2.0	2.7	2.5	1.9	2.1	2.7
1972	1.7	1.6	2.6	2.4	1.9	2.0	2.6
1973	2.1	1.7	2.8	2.1	1.9	2.4	2.6
1974	2.2	1.7	2.1	2.3	2.1	2.3	2.6
1975	2.3	1.5	2.0	2.1	2.0	1.9	2.2
1976	2.5	1.6	2.0	2.0	1.9	1.6	1.8
1977	2.7	1.6	1.8	2.0	1.9	1.6	2.0
1978	2.5	1.3	1.4	1.7	1.9	1.4	1.9
1979	2.6	1.3	1.4	2.0	2.0	1.8	2.3
1980							2.5
1981							2.8

Notes: The index is a centred 5-year average of $\sum |e_{i,t} - e_{i,t-1}|$ where e_i is the percentage share of the ith sector in total employment. The sectors are the usual ISIC sectors, except that sectors 8 and 9 have been aggregated. Each index covers the whole labour force.
Sources: *OECD Labour Force Statistics, Department of Employment Gazette* (for the last column).

various kinds. One cannot pin down the causes of this, but clearly the unions have had a role to play.

All of these influences are implicitly allowed for in our estimate of the current NAIRU. These estimates are sufficiently below actual levels (especially in Britain and the Federal Republic) for a judicious reflation not to run into bottlenecks. There is of course one bottleneck we did not mention in our earlier list. This is the real wage constraint. The reason is two-fold. First there is the likelihood, discussed above, that Europe is now off its neo-classical labour demand curve. The second is that, even if real wages are now binding, they may be temporarily out of line, and a reflation will tend to raise prices relative to wages. So the path of reflation is clear of physical obstacles.

The real costs of not reflating

Before coming to the financial obstacles, we wish to stress the physical costs of not reflating. The most obvious of these is the permanent effect on the capital stock of years of low investment. Recent experience is shown in Figure 22.9. A part of this dismal performance is due to the fall in the realized rate of return on capital (see Table 22.6), and high nominal and real interest rates (see Figure 22.10). But investment functions suggest that the dominant influence on investment is the future prospective level of demand, which affects the anticipated rate of return. Unless this improves, investment is not likely to pick up much, whatever happens to interest rates and to current realized profits.

2   THE FINANCING CONSTRAINT

Many people will say that a fiscal reflation through deficit spending is either not feasible, unnecessary, or perverse in its effect. In this school of thought there are thus three main lines of argument.

The first is that further fiscal expansion is simply not feasible. Current deficits are already so high that further increases would almost surely be unsustainable. They would lead later to monetization and inflation, or to repudiation of debt. Such a path is too uncertain and too dangerous. Fiscal restraint is therefore essential.

The second is that European fiscal policy is not in fact contractionary, but neutral. It points to the continuing high level of government borrowing in both 1983 and 1984. It argues that, given the large US fiscal deficits, further fiscal expansion in Europe is probably not necessary.

The last and related line of argument is that, even when feasible, fiscal policy does not work as well as its proponents suggest. Borrowing from the US debate, this line argues that further deficits may simply raise real interest rates,

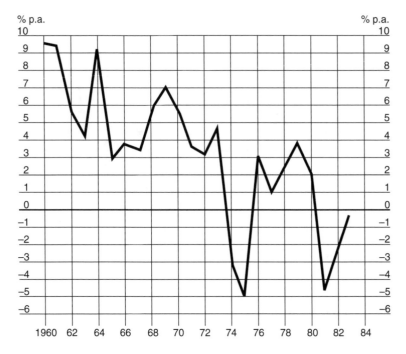

Figure 22.9 Growth rate of gross fixed investment at 1975 prices: EC
Source: European Economy, No. 18 (November 1983, Table 15).

having little effect on aggregate demand, but decreasing investment and
prospects for growth and a steady recovery.

We shall now review facts and arguments. But before we do so, we first focus
on two issues of measurement.

Issues of measurement

Two corrections are often made to the raw deficit numbers: the inflation
correction and the cyclical adjustment correction. Corrected and raw numbers
give different signals. Which ones should we look at?

We start with the inflation correction. The simplest inflation correction
deducts from the government deficit the capital gain which the government
experiences when inflation erodes the real value of its debt. Thus the inflation
adjustment counts as government revenue the size of the debt times the rate of

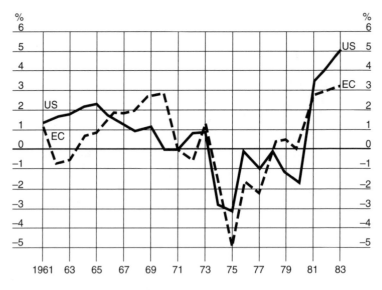

Figure 22.10 Short-run realized real interest rate: EC and USA
Source: Commission of the EC.
Note: Nominal interest rates minus growth rate of CPI. For country figures
see Table 22A.9 in the Statistical Appendix.

Table 22.6 Net rate of return on fixed capital (enterprises excluding construction)[a], 1960–81

	Belgium	FRG	France	Italy	Nether-lands	UK	EC-6	USA	Japan
1960–73	11.0	11.6	14.2	7.5	10.1	8.0	10.6	9.9	14.3
1974–80	6.8	8.3	7.7	1.9	8.4	2.8	5.9	7.9	3.4
1978	6.2	9.1	7.1	0.8	10.1	4.5	6.2	8.5	3.3
1979	6.0	9.6	6.8	2.9	9.0	2.5	6.1	7.8	2.7
1980	3.6	8.6	4.8	3.6	7.7	0.7	4.9	6.9	2.3
1981	2.8	7.6	5.1	0.7	6.8	0.2	4.0	6.7	2.1

Note: [a] Net operating surplus as percentage of the capital stock calculated at replacement cost.
Source: Estimates of the German Bundeswirtschafts Ministerium.

inflation. The resulting adjusted deficit simply measures the real increase in the government debt.[21] If the adjustment is not made, one gets quite the wrong impression about the increase in the burden of the debt. This adjustment should therefore be uncontroversial.

So why would anybody look at the raw deficit numbers? There are two possible reasons. The first is that monetary authorities may, as a rule, finance part of the raw deficit by monetization. The second is that households, as holders of government bonds, suffer from money illusion and perceive nominal interest payments as real interest. There is substantial evidence against the first,[22] and no evidence in favour of the second. Thus we should only look at the deficit numbers after inflation correction. Raw and corrected numbers are given in Table 22.7, columns (1) and (2). While the raw numbers show consistently large deficits, corrected numbers show small but decreasing deficits after 1980.

We can now look at a second approach to the inflation correction. This is concerned not with measuring the current year's change in the real government debt but with the long-run sustainability of the government's fiscal stance. To investigate this we need to measure the real interest burden of the debt by multiplying the (non-money) debt by the long-run real rate of interest. This magnitude fluctuates less from year to year than the real interest burden implied by our previous approach.[23] It is difficult to measure the real long-term interest rate, since we have no measure of long-term inflationary expectations, except where there are indexed bonds (as in the UK since 1981). Clearly the long-term real rate is not constant, but for simplicity we assume it is $2\frac{1}{2}$ per cent in every year (as in the UK in 1981). This gives us the second inflation-corrected series in Table 22.7, column (4). This is a smoother series than column (2), and rather too smooth. The proper figure for our present concept lies somewhere between the two columns.

We turn now to the cyclical correction. This adjusts the deficit downwards to what it would be on existing tax/transfer schedules if the economy were at 'full employment'. When this adjustment is added to the actual deficit, we have a series which shows the effect of discretionary policy changes. Columns (3) and (5) show this series plus the adjustments for inflation. Concentrating on column (5) one can see a pronounced tightening of policy stance from 1982 onwards.

This column gives the best evidence we can provide on the sustainability of present policies. We therefore now turn to the first of the three financial arguments against reflation that we raised at the beginning of this part.

Are the current deficits unsustainable?

This argument is that Europe cannot afford larger, even temporary, deficits without governments running the risk of bankruptcy or large money creation.

Table 22.7 General government deficit as a percentage of GDP:EC, 1973–87

	Actual deficit (1)	Deficit corrected for inflation (I) (2)	Deficit corrected for inflation (I) and cycle (3)	Deficit corrected for inflation (II) (4)	Deficit corrected for inflation (II) and cycle (5)
1973	0.8	–0.3	0.1	0.3	0.7
1974	1.9	0.3	0.0	0.9	1.2
1975	5.5	4.1	2.4	4.4	2.7
1976	3.7	3.1	3.0	2.4	2.3
1977	3.3	1.8	1.8	1.8	1.8
1978	4.0	2.7	3.3	2.1	2.7
1979	3.6	1.3	2.5	1.6	2.8
1980	3.5	0.9	1.5	1.3	1.9
1981	5.4	2.8	1.9	3.0	2.1
1982	5.4	3.3	1.4	2.7	0.8
1983	5.7	3.7	0.9	2.7	–0.1
1984	5.2	3.7	0.4	1.8	–1.5
1987	2.7				

Note: Individual country figures are shown in Table 22A.7 and figures for the USA in Table 22A.8 in the Statistical Appendix.

Source: Calculations kindly provided by B. Connolly.

Inflation adjustment I: Minus December to December change in CPI multiplied by the mid-year estimate of net general government debt excluding the monetary base.

Inflation adjustment II: Minus nominal interest plus $2\frac{1}{2}\%$ of net interest-bearing general government debt.

Cyclical adjustment: (Actual output – trend output) $\times$ (marginal tax rate + benefit withdrawal rate). The marginal tax rate is assumed equal to the average trend tax rate (the trend being by interpolation between 1973 and 1979). Adjustment is also made for unemployment benefits. Trend output is obtained from a regression of actual output on time for 1960–79 with a spline for 1973 on. Years of near to trend output (and trend growth rates since 1973) are as follows: Belgium 1979 (2.48%); Denmark 1976 (1.84%); France 1976 (2.87%); FRG 1977 (2.23%); Ireland 1975 (3.85%); Italy 1979 (2.41%); Netherlands 1973 (2.08%); UK 1974 (1.43%); USA 1977 (2.46%).

The large current deficits are already leading to increases in debt, increases in interest payments, and, thus, increases in future deficits. Stabilization of this debt explosion requires decreases, not increases in the deficit.

To get a feel for the urgency of the problem, we can start with a simple exercise. Let's assume that the economy was at full employment and growing on trend, and that money growth and inflation were at desired levels. We can then ask what real deficit/GNP ratio would be consistent with a constant debt/GDP ratio. In other words, what kind of numbers would be acceptable in Table 22.7, column 5?

Simple manipulations give:[24]

$$d = gb + (g + \pi)m$$

where d is the real deficit/GDP ratio, b the debt/GDP ratio, g the trend rate of growth of real GNP, π the rate of inflation, and m the ratio of high powered money to GNP. The first term captures the effect of trend real growth, which permits some deficit finance even with a constant debt/income ratio. The second term captures the effect of inflation finance. If target inflation is positive, some of the deficit can be safely financed by money creation. Using, for example, 2 per cent for g, 5 per cent for target inflation and actual Community values of b and m, one obtains a value of d of around $1\frac{1}{4}$ per cent, divided equally between the two components.

This computation suggests that corrected *deficits* of $1\frac{1}{4}$ per cent of GDP are perfectly sustainable. Let us turn now to Table 22.7 column (5) and Table 22A.7. These suggest that most countries are now running surpluses rather than deficits, Denmark and Italy being exceptions. So present policy is easily sustainable. However, the table also shows that in the late 1970s the position was different, and some countries, such as Ireland, were well outside the sustainable range. Since then there has been a major retrenchment in most countries. Clearly some was necessary, but it has unfortunately been overdone.

It may be argued of course that we are over-optimistic to compute deficits as they could be if output returned to its former trend. If instead there were no recovery of employment, we should compare our number for d to the actual deficit, not to the full-employment deficit. But even this comparison does not suggest serious problems of sustainability, once allowance has been made for inflation. (See the 1984 entry in column (4).)

We are in fact being over-cautious in our approach. For even if deficits exceeded their sustainable levels it would obviously not imply bankruptcy – only that fiscal policy would have to change at some time in the future. The relevant set of issues would then be about the rates at which taxes could be increased, or, expenditures decreased. In this respect, a large ratio of debt to GNP – and thus a high level of debt service – considerably reduces the degree of flexibility of fiscal policy. This raises the question of the optimal debt/income ratio. In what range can a country easily afford further real debt growth and in what range do serious issues of financial instability arise?

There is very little systematic evidence available on this point. It is clear that in Europe, debt/income ratios show a wide range across countries, but no systematic study has been done to show whether these debt ratios play an important role in public finance or in generating inflation. Of course in principle we would expect that debt/income ratios are closely linked to questions of supply side economics. If taxation is used to service the debt, the presumption of an increasing marginal social cost of taxation may imply that issues of efficiency could come long before those of financial instability.

A complicating point emerges from the experience of many less developed countries that borrowed extensively in the period of the oil shocks, when real interest rates were negative. (For the history of short-run real interest rates see Figure 22.10.) They are finding today, with positive real interest rates, that they have suffered an extreme, adverse, real income shock. The debt service burden has risen from nothing to a significant share of GDP and proves to be the source of domestic financial and economic instability. The example points to the fact that debt/income ratios are only meaningful indicators of fiscal policy if real interest rates move little and if the determinants of tax receipts are unlikely to shift much. Unanticipated changes in real interest rates or in the tax base can imply that comfortable debt/income ratios suddenly become unsustainable.

Overall, the sustainability argument does not seem well founded. Europe as a whole can well afford larger deficits for a few years without governments running into bankruptcy or excessive money finance.

What is the current EC fiscal impact?

It is wrong to assess the effect of fiscal policy on aggregate demand by looking only at actual or full employment deficits. One has to look at both the level of public spending and the level of the debt, as well as the deficit, to get an accurate assessment of the effects of fiscal policy.

It is useful to distinguish between the spending and finance components of fiscal policy. Suppose, for example, that the government always ran a balanced budget. Any permanent level of expenditures would then be associated with an equivalent level of taxes. Even if the effect of taxes on consumption were to offset the direct effect of permanent changes in government spending, leaving aggregate demand unchanged, short-run changes in government spending would still affect total demand. For example, temporary decreases in government expenditures, even accompanied by lower taxes are unlikely to be fully matched by a corresponding increase in private spending. Table 22.8(a) looks at the deviations of government expenditures from trend for the EC, the US, Japan and Canada. Deviations are positive for the EC during the whole

Table 22.8 Aspects of fiscal policy, 1977–84 (% of trend GDP)

(a) Deviations of government non-transfer expenditures from trend

	EC	(Expenditures as % of trend GDP in brackets) USA	Japan	Canada
1977	0 (20.2)	0 (19.8)	0 (16.7)	1.3 (23.6)
1978	0 (20.3)	0 (19.8)	1.0 (18.3)	1.1 (23.4)
1979	0.2 (20.6)	−0.2 (19.6)	1.5 (19.4)	0 (22.3)
1980	1.7 (22.2)	0.7 (20.5)	1.6 (20.1)	1.0 (22.0)
1981	1.5 (22.1)	0.5 (20.3)	1.8 (20.9)	1.2 (22.2)
1982	1.0 (21.6)	0.2 (20.0)	1.3 (21.0)	1.2 (22.2)
1983	0.8 (21.3)	0.2 (20.0)	0.3 (20.6)	0.7 (21.7)
1984	0.6 (21.1)	0.3 (20.1)	−0.3 (20.0)	0.6 (21.6)

(b) General government debt

	EC	US	Japan	Canada
1977	17.5	29.0	4.9	17.0
1978	19.9	27.6	5.0	20.7
1979	20.3	24.6	10.6	26.7
1980	20.7	20.0	12.5	30.1
1981	21.9	18.3	16.8	34.3
1982	24.5	18.5	21.5	36.1
1983	27.4	20.2	25.2	47.4
1984	30.6	21.8	28.5	59.2

(c) Actual deficit, excluding interest payments

	EC	US	Japan	Canada
1977	1.4	−0.3	3.2	0.4
1978	1.9	−1.3	5.2	0.7
1979	1.3	−1.8	3.4	−0.7
1980	1.0	−0.1	3.2	−0.3
1981	2.3	−0.8	2.7	−2.0
1982	2.0	1.8	2.6	1.2
1983	1.8	1.6	1.4	1.9
1984	1.0	1.1	−0.1	0.5

Table 22.8 continued

(d) Full-employment deficit, excluding interest payments

	EC	US	Japan	Canada
1977	1.4	–0.3	3.0	0.0
1978	2.4	–0.5	5.7	0.5
1979	2.4	–1.0	4.5	–0.8
1980	1.6	-0.4	4.1	–1.6
1981	1.5	–1.1	3.5	–3.4
1982	0.2	–0.4	3.0	–4.2
1983	–0.9	–0.1	1.4	–3.2
1984	–2.1	0.4	–0.3	–4.0

Note: Calculations kindly provided by B. Connolly.

period.[25] They have however steadily decreased since 1980. Thus the effect of the spending component of EC fiscal policy has been contractionary since 1980.

There is however a second component to fiscal policy: the finance component. Governments run deficits and issue debt, and this has additional effects on aggregate demand. Debt is net wealth to its holders and positively affects consumption demand. Likewise (given government spending) large current or anticipated deficits, which imply a deferral of taxes, increase private spending. Table 22.8(b) gives the movement of debt to GDP ratios over time.[26] The figures for the EC show a steady increase in the debt to GDP ratios during the whole period. Table 22.8(c) and 22.8(d) give actual and full employment deficit measures. (These are net of interest payments, since we have already looked at debt in Table 22.8(b), and leaving interest payments in the deficit measure would be double counting.) It is reasonable to assume that anticipations of future deficits lie between actual and full-employment deficits and thus both are reported. The EC is experiencing positive but decreasing actual deficits; this corresponds to growing full-employment surpluses (again, not including interest payments).

How do all these elements combine to affect aggregate demand? This is a matter of theory, not of statistics. Extreme Ricardians would for example argue that only the spending component of fiscal policy matters, and that deficits and debt are irrelevant. However we derive an index based on a less extreme view of the world and allow for a role of the finance component. The values of this index are given in Table 22.9. The index gives substantial weight to the

Table 22.9 Index of fiscal stance, 1977–84 (% of trend GDP)

	EC	USA	Japan	Canada
1977	2.8	2.2	3.5	2.5
1978	3.9	1.5	6.8	3.1
1979	4.0	0.6	6.3	1.4
1980	4.0	1.8	6.2	1.8
1981	4.6	0.8	6.1	0.5
1982	3.3	1.6	5.6	0.8
1983	2.4	1.7	3.6	2.3
1984	1.5	2.2	1.9	2.1

full-employment deficit; as a result, it shows a positive but sharply decreasing contribution of fiscal policy to aggregate demand. If, for example, we assume a multiplier of 2,[27] the fiscal contraction from 1982 to 1983 may be responsible for 2 to 3 per cent less growth. The index is based on many assumptions which can all be questioned. But the message is quite clear: current fiscal policy is a drag on the recovery.

Can fiscal expansion impede recovery?

Can fiscal expansion be perverse – that is, can it slow down the recovery? The answer is that it can, but only under very special circumstances. These might have been there in the USA in 1982, but they are easy to avoid in Europe in 1984.

The perverse effect might arise as follows. Ignore for the moment the fact that Europe is a very open economy, and consider a move of fiscal policy towards larger deficits. If these deficits are expected to be there even after the economy has returned to full employment, then real interest rates will be expected to be high in the future. These high expected real interest rates lead to current high long real rates. There is little that monetary policy can do to lower these long real rates: fiscal expansion at full employment must be associated with higher real rates, irrespective of monetary policy. These high long rates may in turn depress economic activity more than current deficit spending directly stimulates it. Fiscal expansion would then be perverse. In an open economy such as Europe, the effect on long rates will clearly be much smaller, but a similar perverse effect might arise through exchange rate appreciation.[28]

This analysis makes it clear that perverse effects are avoided if the fiscal expansion is explicitly temporary and planned to be phased out when the economy returns to full employment. Thus we recommend a temporary fiscal expansion, with an emphasis on investment. Investment responds more strongly to temporary fiscal stimulus than consumption and is currently affected adversely by high world real rates and the deep recession.

To the extent that such a fiscal expansion is successful, it will increase interest rates through increased activity and tend to make the ECU appreciate. Monetary policy could then be used to maintain the real effective value of the ECU.

3 THE COORDINATION CONSTRAINT AND THE ROLE OF THE EC

The previous parts of this paper have established the need and feasibility, in principle, of an expansion. But there remains a highly controversial issue regarding the means. One camp claims that coordination is the *sine qua non* of expansion, while another camp asserts it is unnecessary.

The Kieler Schule maintains that the pursuit of national self-interest will ensure an optimal national policy without the need for coordination. Useful international interaction is limited to the exchange of information. This point has been most uncompromisingly stated by Roland Vaubel:[29]

> International differences in stabilization policies lead to temporary real exchange-rate changes only if stabilization policies are volatile and unanticipated. Thus, all countries have an incentive to avoid unanticipated stabilization policies: monetary expansion, public expenditure, and public debt 'management' should all be preannounced. By preannouncing their policies, or the rules by which they are formed, governments would ensure an optimal supply of the only (international and national) public good that is at stake in regard to stabilization policy as such: the public good of knowledge about government behaviour. But there is no welfare-theoretic argument to the effect that such knowledge should be supplied on the basis of joint international decision-making.

The view that pre-announcement of policies is the cure-all in macroeconomics is both naive and extreme. As an objection to coordinated international policies, it is inappropriate in two respects. First, by *assuming* that there is no macroeconomic problem (other than alleged policy instability) it dismisses the case for stabilization policy before the issue of coordination even arises. Second, among the range of pre-announced policies or policy rules is certainly the possibility of vigorous anti-cyclical policy. An activist rule might go as follows: whenever EC unemployment exceeds x per cent, and is identified in good part as Keynesian, every member country will create investment incentives and marginal employment credits on a scale y. Policies of this kind are indeed necessary, over and above the existing automatic stabilizers. Having failed to follow these policies in time, the recession now makes it imperative to catch up with the task.

Another adverse reaction to coordination is based on the poor experience of 1978. At that time coordinated expansion was given little chance to prove itself because of the second oil shock. Hence even some of those who, in principle, accept the desirability of coordinated expansion have a lingering fear that everybody expanding together might just lead to another bad experience.

This is a peculiar line of argument in the current deep recession. Few, if any, of its proponents would feel that export-led growth is hazardous. Indeed, they would all express a preference for (miraculous) export growth over home-made expansion. But that is an important part of what a coordinated expansion provides.

The argument for coordination

So let us examine the general argument for coordination. If a country reflates, it can either maintain its exchange rate by keeping a high enough interest rate, or it can allow its exchange rate to depreciate.[30] Consider these cases in turn. At a faxed exchange rate, a reflating country captures only part of the employment benefits of the extra money spent or the money not collected in tax. Thus debt is issued, in part, to finance an employment programme in the rest of the world.[31] To service the extra debt (much of it owed to foreigners), future taxes have to be raised. Since much of this pays for employment creation abroad (the counterpart of the deterioration in the current balance), this limits the country's enthusiasm to spend its way to prosperity.

The alternative is to let the currency depreciate in order to stimulate employment while maintaining external balance. But most countries will not wish to do this since depreciation is inflationary. A country is therefore caught in a position where it will choose the path of maintaining the exchange rate through increasingly tight money and high interest rates. If the expansion eventually raises inflation relative to inflation rates abroad, devaluation will ultimately become inevitable unless the expanding country quickly contracts again.

There are significant differences between hard- and soft-currency countries in the cost-benefit ratio for home-made, isolated expansion. (The key difference between a hard- and a soft-currency country is that in the former a temporary monetary or fiscal expansion is not so likely to be interpreted as a permanent expansion.) For soft-currency countries expansion implies an exchange rate problem relatively soon. At that point a country faces one of three options: it can raise interest rates to defend the exchange rate, implying the need to accept the unfavourable effects of a lop-sided expansion; or it can accept an exchange depreciation that closes the current account, but at the expense of sharply increased inflation; or it can forego the expansion altogether. If expansion is in fact pursued, that policy will be effective in creating employment – the more so if there is an exchange rate depreciation, giving additional help through improved net exports – but it will also increase inflation.

In a hard-currency country the exchange rate is not a problem and therefore fiscal policy is less effective. More of the extra deficit spills into increased jobs abroad, and therefore the cost-benefit ratio is adverse to expansion. Even though it is not costly in terms of inflation, it buys relatively less in terms of jobs.

The coordinated expansion solves everyone's cost-benefit problem. The hard-currency country does not 'lose' so much of its fiscal expansion abroad and the soft-currency country, in exchange, enjoys a better inflation performance. In a coordinated expansion both types of country face more favourable cost-benefit ratios and will therefore be willing to pursue more nearly optimal policies. In principle there should be a 'market' for these policies, but the transactions costs require the operation of an intermediary. It is a major rationale for the institutions of the EC to perform this function.

We developed the argument in our last report,[32] but let us repeat a few basic points. If one country expands on its own at a constant exchange rate, it boosts demand in other countries. In making its own selfish plans it does not place much weight on this. But if it could persuade others to do the same, it would benefit from the other's expansionary policies. Coordination is thus in the selfish interest of each country. But it is difficult to achieve. This is a classic case of externality, which can only be overcome by the development of institutions which reduce the transactions costs and truly promote the common good.

In the process each country will experience a given expansion of output at a lower net budgetary cost and a lower balance-of-payments cost than if it had acted on its own. The potential gains are thus large. We cannot however expect all countries to contribute the same. We therefore repeat our previous suggestion for a package which would leave the weak currency countries with an unchanged budget deficit or an unchanged current account.

When we first suggested this, unemployment in the Community was 9.6 per cent. It is now 10.4 per cent and is not expected to fall below this before 1988. Our proposals therefore seem even more pressing than when we last made them. And, we repeat, 1984 is not 1978. *If there was ever a time when the case for reflation was compelling, this is it.*

There is one further direction in which coordination should be pursued. There is world-wide agreement, it seems, that the prospective US long-run deficits are harmful to the world economy. It is also the case, less generally agreed, that European recovery is too slow and too precarious. The natural conclusion is some inter-temporal trade: more rapid European recovery through fiscal stimulus traded off for reduced long-run US deficits.

4 POLICY ACTION

We come now to our proposals. First, the most urgent, are those relating to the reflation of demand – proposals 1 to 3. These are implicit in what we have already said, but we spell them out again here. Second, we turn to the problem of reducing the NAIRU: the most important problem facing the EC in the long run. We make three proposals (4 to 6) which we consider crucial in this context.

1 Fiscal reflation

There should be an aggregate fiscal expansion, linked to an accommodating monetary policy designed to maintain the effective exchange rate of the ECU.

2 Coordination with an emphasis on the Federal Republic of Germany and Britain

The fiscal expansion should be coordinated by the EC and be greater in countries with currently tight fiscal policies (especially the FRG and UK). Countries with weak fiscal positions or weak external current accounts should not be expected to expand beyond the point where their deficits become worse. If possible, the European fiscal expansion should be coordinated with a reduction of the US fiscal deficit.

3 Temporary investment boost and marginal employment subsidies

The fiscal expansion should be temporary. There should be a temporary boost to public investment plus an extra subsidy to private investment paid only on investment undertaken by a certain date.

In addition there should be a temporary employment credit linked to employment growth. For example each firm could be given a credit of sECUs for each worker they employed over and above 90 per cent of their previous year's employment. The financial cost (in a period of steady employment) would be approximately s $(0.1N)$ ECUs, where N is employment. If, instead, this same amount of money had been used to subsidize all workers, the credit per worker would have been only $1.0s$, that is only 10 per cent of the amount under the marginal employment credit. Thus, in so far as it is the marginal cost of labour which determines employment, the marginal credit would be ten times as effective as the average credit. It should therefore impart a substantial boost to employment.

But the subsidy should be temporary, for two reasons. First, we envisage it as being financed by an increase in the budget deficit. We have always argued that such increases should be temporary. Second, a marginal subsidy will be much more effective if it is explicity temporary, so that firms can only collect the subsidy if they expand within the stated period rather than later.[33] We believe that a major marginal subsidy of this kind is an ideal component of an expansionary package.[34]

4   Incomes policy using tax incentives

We turn now to measures to reduce the NAIRU. Some possible steps follow from our earlier analysis of the determinants of the NAIRU. Better training arrangements and better housing policies can reduce the mis-match between workers and jobs in terms of skill and location. Stricter administration of unemployment benefits can reduce abuse, though we would strongly oppose reduced levels of benefit. Modifications of employment protection legislation can encourage firms to hire more workers. Restrictions of union monopoly powers can also help. But more than this will be needed. We concentrate on two major proposals.

To prevent the resurgence of inflation, countries will have to be willing to experiment with various forms of incomes policy. The distortions involved will almost certainly be less than the costs of high unemployment.

One approach is direct central control of the rate of growth of wage rates, or better still average hourly earnings. This could be either by statute or by voluntary agreement between the social partners. There are however two main difficulties with this type of approach. First, it impedes the adjustment of relativities which is necessary for economic efficiency. Second, it eliminates any meaningful collective bargaining (except possibly at the highest level where the incomes policy itself is bargained). This often generates massive political unrest which leads to the breakdown of the policy.

There is therefore a strong case for promoting wage moderation by fiscal incentives rather than by regulation from above. Tax-based incomes policy has been discussed but never implemented in a form that had any hope of success.[35] Success requires simplicity. We therefore suggest for consideration a tax where there is a norm for the growth of average hourly earnings at the level of the firm. If the firm exceeds the norm, it pays a tax on that part of the wage bill corresponding to the excess wage growth. Smaller firms could be exempt from the tax (and if necessary given less favourable tax treatment in some other way to offset this advantage).[36] To ensure that at the aggregate level the tax is not passed on in prices, the tax proceeds should be used to finance a per capital employment subsidy. Thus since the tax will lower wages it will also lower average labour costs.

It may or may not be the ideal scheme. But it would be a tragedy if countries did not search out for themselves new methods of controlling inflation, rather than relying indefinitely on high unemployment to do the job for them.

5 The reform of employment taxes

We also have to find some permanent method of pricing more people into jobs. In other words we have to find a way of reducing the long-run real labour cost (relative to productivity). The obvious way is to subsidize employment. This normally raises heckles because it is assumed that the costs of raising the necessary money would be at least as great as the benefits from the subsidy. However if we have a per worker subsidy financed by a wage-bill tax, this will do the trick in a whole variety of possible types of labour market.

If the economy is one where wages are basically set by unions, the switch of tax structure will make the effective demand curve faced by unions much more elastic. Thus if they demand an extra ECU in wages, they will suffer a greater loss of employment. They will thus settle for lower real wages, and employment will rise. If the economy is one where wages are basically set by firms, the wage tax will lead to a fall in wages equal to the tax (thus leaving labour cost unaffected), while the subsidy will reduce labour cost and thus boost employment.

The argument we have developed so far is in terms of homogeneous labour. It is even more powerful when one takes into account the differences between markets. The unemployment rates of unskilled workers are, in many countries, as much as four times the national average. This almost certainly means that there is more slack to be taken up in these markets than in others. Thus a shift in demand into those markets would enable us to raise the aggregate employment rate and aggregate welfare. This could be achieved by reducing net taxes in the unskilled market, financing this by some increase in net taxes in the skilled market. This is exactly what would come about with the restructuring we have been discussing, since a given per worker credit is a higher fraction of a low wage than a high wage. If it is financed by a tax proportional to wages, the net tax burden on low wage workers will fall and the net tax burden on high wage workers will rise.

We therefore suggest for urgent consideration a restructuring of employment taxes to include a lump-sum credit linked to a higher rate of proportional taxation on the wage bill. There should be no net increase in tax burden.

6 No to work-sharing

We have listed many things that should be done, but we wish to end by saying what not to do. Many Europeans have become very pessimistic and have begun to think there is no way to create more work. They therefore advocate spreading the available work over more people by reducing the hours worked by each person. But the question is whether the amount of work to be done would stay constant if there were a reduction in hours per worker. The obvious danger is that if hours per worker were reduced, there would be a rise in real hourly wages, which would then reduce the total demand for person-hours. One might of course argue that an employment subsidy could be used to offset this, but in that case why not use the employment subsidy to promote an expansion of person-hours rather than to avert a contraction.

In order to think about the effect of a reduction of hours one must specify how wages are set. Suppose they are set by unions, with decentralized unions setting wages in each sector. The level of unemployment in the long term will be such that each union is willing to settle for what they expect each other union to get. For if not, there would be accelerating inflation as one group tried to outdo the other. So this is the *function* of unemployment: to make unions settle for the prevailing wage. It is easy to see that a change in hours is not going to change the level of unemployment at which the necessary discipline on wages is exerted. It follows that if hours per worker are reduced, *unemployment will not fall*, but person-hours will and so will output. If by contrast we think of wages as set by firms, the same conclusion follows. Again it takes a certain amount of unemployment to stop firms trying to outbid each other for labour and thus set in motion an inflationary spiral.

We can thus summarize the dangers of artificial reductions in hours of work. As unemployment falls, inflationary pressure develops. The government is not willing to accept this inflationary pressure and the economy becomes deflated. So total output is not constant (as the advocates of work-sharing assume), but falls. The community thus becomes poorer and there is a smaller tax base from which to finance the social services.

Exactly the same analysis applies to early retirement. It appears to provide work for younger people. But by tightening up the labour market, it adds to inflationary pressure and thus encourages governments to cut back on the level of demand.

Having given our views in this forthright manner, we should add some points of qualification. First, we are of course in favour of the long-run trend to shorter hours of work and shorter working lives. As people become richer, they naturally choose to take more leisure. But this should be a matter of choice. An artificial limitation on hours, even if 'voluntarily' negotiated by a trade union, is not necessarily what the individual would choose. It is this which should count.

Similarly we favour more flexibility in work arrangements. It may make sense to provide part-time unemployment benefits for people unemployed for part of the week, if this helps to reduce the number of people wholly unemployed.

Finally, there may be certain circumstances in which it makes sense to treat the total level of output as given in the short-run. If this is the case and there is excess labour around, it is more humane to share the work than to concentrate it on fewer workers. Thus as an emergency measure, temporary work-sharing schemes can make sense. But this assumes that real hourly wage costs are held constant. This may be easier to achieve in schemes where a new job is split between two new recruits than in schemes where existing workers are expected to take cuts in their real weekly earnings.

Given these qualifications, the advocates of work-sharing are probably hoping for more than it can deliver, even in the short run. As we have said, we do believe there are other ways of reducing unemployment – both in the short term and longer term. In the short term, a westward look could do no harm.

Statistical Appendix

Table 224.1 Growth rate of domestic product, 1958–83 at 1975 market prices (per cent year on year)

Year	Belgium	Denmark	France	FRG	Greece	Ireland	Italy	Lux	Neth	UK	EC	USA	Japan
1958	-0.7	2.6	3.0	3.4	3.4	-2.1	4.9		-1.0	0.4	2.2		
1959	2.3	6.4	2.6	6.6	3.7	4.5	6.1	3.8	3.9	3.8	4.7		
1960	5.8	6.6	7.2	10.5	3.8	5.8	6.7	5.6	9.9	5.0	7.6		
1961	5.0	6.4	5.5	5.2	11.1	5.0	8.2	4.4	2.9	3.3	5.2	2.5	4.6
1962	5.2	5.7	6.7	4.5	1.5	3.2	6.2	1.4	4.3	1.0	4.3	5.5	7.1
1963	4.3	0.6	5.3	3.2	10.1	4.8	5.6	2.6	3.3	3.9	4.3	4.1	0.5
1964	6.9	9.3	6.5	6.7	8.3	3.8	2.8	7.5	8.6	5.2	5.8	5.3	3.2
1965	3.6	4.6	4.8	5.5	9.4	1.9	3.3	1.7	5.3	2.3	4.1	6.1	5.1
1966	3.2	6.4	5.2	2.7	6.1	0.9	6.0	1.7	2.7	2.0	3.7	5.8	0.6
1967	3.9	3.7	4.7	0.0	5.5	5.8	7.2	1.6	5.3	2.6	3.4	2.8	0.8
1968	4.2	3.8	4.3	5.7	6.7	8.2	6.5	4.2	6.4	4.1	5.2	4.0	2.8
1969	5.9	6.5	7.0	7.4	9.9	5.9	6.1	8.9	6.4	1.5	5.6	2.9	2.3
1970	6.2	2.3	5.7	5.2	8.0	2.7	5.3	2.2	6.7	2.2	4.8	-0.3	9.8
1971	3.9	2.4	5.4	3.3	7.1	3.5	1.6	4.3	4.3	2.7	3.4	3.1	4.6
1972	5.3	5.4	5.9	4.2	8.9	6.5	3.2	6.2	3.4	2.2	4.1	5.3	8.8
1973	6.2	3.8	5.4	4.5	7.3	4.7	7.0	10.8	5.7	7.5	5.9	5.5	8.8
1974	4.4	-0.7	3.2	0.7	-3.6	4.3	4.1	3.6	3.5	-1.0	1.7	-0.7	9.0
1975	-1.9	-1.0	0.2	-1.6	6.0	2.0	-3.6	-6.1	-1.0	-0.7	-1.2	-0.8	2.3
1976	5.7	6.9	4.9	5.4	6.4	1.9	5.9	1.9	5.3	3.6	5.0	4.9	5.3
1977	0.7	2.0	3.1	3.1	3.4	6.8	1.9	0.6	2.4	1.3	2.4	5.2	5.3
1978	3.0	1.8	3.3	3.1	6.7	5.9	2.7	4.5	2.7	3.7	3.2	4.6	5.0
1979	2.4	3.7	3.2	4.1	3.7	2.5	4.9	4.0	2.1	1.6	3.3	2.4	5.1
1980	3.0	-1.1	1.3	1.9	1.6	2.8	3.9	1.7	0.9	-2.0	1.3	-0.3	4.4
1981	-1.8	0.1	0.2	0.2	-0.7	1.1	-0.2	-1.8	-1.2	-2.0	-0.4	2.3	3.1
1982	1.0	3.4	1.8	-1.0	-0.0	1.2	-0.3	-1.1	-1.6	1.5	0.4	-1.7	2.9
1983	–	2.0	0.3	1.0	0.3	0.5	-1.4	-2.4	1.0	3.2	0.8	3.4	3.3

Source: See Figure 22.1.

Table 22A.2 Unemployment as % of civilian labour force, 1958–83

Year	Belgium	Denmark	France	FRG	Ireland	Italy	Lux	Neth	UK	EC	USA	Japan
1958	3.1	3.2	0.5	2.9	5.7	8.1	0.1	1.8	1.9	3.3	6.8	2.1
1959	3.5	2.2	0.7	2.1	5.4	7.7	0.1	1.2	1.8	3.0	5.5	2.2
1960	3.1	1.5	0.7	1.0	4.7	7.2	0.1	0.7	1.6	2.5	5.5	1.7
1961	2.5	1.2	0.6	0.7	4.2	6.6	0.1	0.5	1.4	2.2	6.7	1.4
1962	2.0	1.1	0.7	0.6	4.2	5.5	0.1	0.5	1.9	2.0	5.5	1.3
1963	1.5	1.5	0.7	0.7	4.5	5.2	0.2	0.6	2.3	2.1	5.7	1.3
1964	1.5	0.9	0.6	0.6	4.3	5.2	0.0	0.5	1.6	1.9	5.2	1.1
1965	1.8	0.7	0.7	0.6	4.5	5.7	0.0	0.6	1.4	1.9	4.5	1.2
1966	2.0	0.8	0.7	0.6	4.3	5.5	0.0	0.8	1.4	1.9	3.8	1.3
1967	2.6	1.0	1.0	1.8	4.5	5.0	0.1	1.7	2.2	2.4	3.8	1.3
1968	3.1	1.7	1.3	1.3	4.8	4.7	0.1	1.5	2.3	2.3	3.6	1.2
1969	2.3	1.4	1.1	0.7	4.6	4.4	0.0	1.1	2.3	2.0	3.5	1.1
1970	2.2	1.0	1.3	0.6	5.3	4.4	0.0	1.0	2.5	2.0	4.9	1.1
1971	2.2	1.2	1.6	0.7	5.2	5.1	0.0	1.3	3.0	2.5	5.9	1.2
1972	2.8	1.2	1.8	0.9	6.0	5.2	0.0	2.3	3.4	2.7	5.6	1.4
1973	2.9	0.7	1.8	1.0	5.6	4.9	0.0	2.3	2.4	2.4	4.9	1.3
1974	3.2	2.0	2.3	2.2	6.0	4.8	0.0	2.8	2.4	2.9	5.6	1.4
1975	5.3	4.6	3.9	4.1	8.5	5.3	0.2	4.0	3.7	4.3	8.5	1.9
1976	6.8	4.7	4.3	4.1	9.5	5.6	0.3	4.3	5.1	4.9	7.7	2.0
1977	7.8	5.8	4.8	4.0	9.2	6.4	0.5	4.1	5.4	5.3	7.1	2.0
1978	8.4	6.5	5.2	3.8	8.4	7.1	0.7	4.1	5.3	5.4	6.1	2.2
1979	8.7	5.3	6.0	3.3	7.4	7.5	0.7	4.1	4.9	5.5	5.8	2.1
1980	9.4	6.1	6.4	3.3	8.3	8.0	0.7	4.7	6.3	6.1	7.1	2.0
1981	11.6	8.3	7.8	4.7	10.2	8.8	1.0	7.2	9.6	7.9	7.6	2.2
1982	13.2	8.9	8.7	6.8	11.7	9.1	1.3	12.7	11.0	9.5	9.7	2.4
1983	14.4	10.5	8.9	8.4	14.6	10.7	1.6	15.4	11.7	10.6	9.5	2.6

Source: See Figure 22.3.

Table 22A.3 Employment, 1960–83 (million)

Year	Belgium	Denmark	France	FRG	Greece	Ireland	Italy	Neth	UK	EC	USA	Japan
1960	3.48	2.05	19.6	26.1	3.39	1.05	20.5	4.20	24.3	104.8	71.0	48.3
1961	3.51	2.08	19.6	26.4	3.42	1.05	20.5	4.26	24.6	105.6	71.1	49.9
1962	3.57	2.12	19.6	26.5	3.39	1.06	20.3	4.35	24.8	105.8	72.5	50.5
1963	3.59	2.14	19.8	26.6	3.37	1.07	20.0	4.41	24.8	105.9	73.3	49.8
1964	3.64	2.19	20.0	26.6	3.34	1.07	20.0	4.48	25.1	106.5	74.8	50.4
1965	3.65	2.23	20.1	26.8	3.31	1.07	20.0	4.52	25.3	106.7	77.1	51.2
1966	3.66	2.24	20.3	26.7	3.28	1.07	19.2	4.56	25.5	106.6	80.6	52.2
1967	3.65	2.22	20.3	25.8	3.25	1.06	19.5	4.54	25.1	105.6	82.5	53.1
1968	3.65	2.25	20.3	25.8	3.22	1.06	19.4	4.59	24.9	105.4	84.5	53.9
1969	3.71	2.27	20.3	26.2	3.20	1.07	19.5	4.66	25.0	106.4	86.9	54.3
1970	3.69	2.28	20.6	26.6	3.17	1.05	19.7	4.72	24.8	107.1	86.7	54.4
1971	3.73	2.30	20.8	26.6	3.14	1.05	19.7	4.74	24.5	106.9	86.5	54.7
1972	3.72	2.35	20.9	26.7	3.16	1.05	19.5	4.70	24.5	106.8	88.5	54.8
1973	3.77	2.38	21.0	26.8	3.17	1.06	19.7	4.71	25.0	108.1	91.9	56.2
1974	3.83	2.37	21.3	26.5	3.17	1.07	19.9	4.71	25.1	108.3	93.5	56.1
1975	3.78	2.34	21.5	25.7	3.19	1.07	20.0	4.68	25.0	107.2	91.8	55.9
1976	3.75	2.38	21.2	25.5	3.23	1.06	20.1	4.67	24.8	107.1	94.1	57.0
1977	3.75	2.40	21.4	25.5	3.20	1.08	20.3	4.68	24.9	107.5	97.3	57.7
1978	3.75	2.42	21.6	25.6	3.25	1.11	20.4	4.71	24.9	108.0	101.9	58.5
1979	3.79	2.45	21.6	26.0	3.30	1.14	20.6	4.77	25.1	109.0	105.2	59.2
1980	3.79	2.44	21.6	26.2	3.36	1.16	20.8	4.80	24.7	109.1	105.8	59.8
1981	3.71	2.39	21.5	26.0	3.36	1.14	20.9	4.74	23.4	107.3	106.9	60.3
1982	3.65	2.40	21.3	25.5	3.32	1.13	20.8	4.62	23.0	106.0	104.8	60.9
1983	3.58	2.39	21.1	25.0	3.28	1.10	20.9	4.52	22.9	105.0	105.1	61.8

Source: See Figure 22.4.

Table 22A.4 Capacity utilization in manufacturing industry, 1974–83 (per cent)

Year	Belgium	France	FRG	Ireland	Italy	Neth	UK	EC
1974	83.4	85.8	82.5		78.2	84.3	82.5	82.9
1975	71.8	78.4	76.0		70.7	77.1	77.7	76.2
1976	75.1	83.0	80.2		71.9	77.7	76.1	78.6
1977	72.6	83.4	80.8		73.8	79.3	79.2	79.8
1978	71.9	83.7	80.8		72.0	79.7	79.2	79.5
1979	76.1	84.7	84.2		75.6	81.2	84.4	82.7
1980	77.6	85.0	84.1	65.0	75.7	81.3	76.4	81.2
1981	74.0	82.1	78.9	60.9	72.8	78.4	72.5	77.4
1982	75.7	81.9	77.3	59.1	71.9	76.8	74.3	77.0
1983	75.7	81.5	76.8	57.8	69.9	79.4	76.4	77.0

Note: The series for the United Kingdom are estimated using the national (Confederation of British Industry) data on the percentage of firms reporting below-capacity working. EC total is country data weighted by the volume of industrial production in 1975.
Source: European Community business surveys, quoted in *European Economy, Supplement* B, *No. 6* (June 1983) and 12 (December 1983).

Table 22A.5   Productivity growth in manufacturing, 1961–82
(output per person-hour)

Year	Belgium	Denmark	France	FRG	Italy	Neth	UK	EC
1961	1.5	6.1	4.5	5.1	7.6	5.3	0.9	3.3
1962	6.8	4.9	4.7	6.2	10.1	3.2	2.5	5.0
1963	3.1	3.2	5.2	4.6	3.0	3.4	4.9	4.4
1964	5.9	8.0	5.3	7.4	5.6	8.6	7.0	7.3
1965	3.9	4.7	5.7	6.3	10.5	6.0	3.2	6.0
1966	6.8	5.0	6.8	3.5	6.4	6.3	3.5	4.2
1967	6.1	8.5	5.3	6.4	5.7	6.4	4.7	5.6
1968	8.3	8.5	10.8	6.7	7.8	11.8	6.9	8.3
1969	8.4	4.1	3.5	5.7	7.3	8.7	2.3	5.2
1970	9.4	8.2	5.0	1.6	4.5	8.9	0.8	3.4
1971	6.1	5.9	5.3	4.0	2.8	6.5	3.8	4.5
1972	10.7	7.9	5.8	6.1	7.9	7.6	7.6	7.4
1973	10.2	9.9	4.8	5.8	11.4	9.7	6.0	6.9
1974	5.7	3.3	3.2	5.4	4.7	8.2	1.0	4.1
1975	4.2	9.9	3.1	5.2	−4.5	−2.0	−2.0	1.6
1976	9.9	3.7	7.9	6.8	8.2	12.1	3.9	7.6
1977	6.3	2.0	5.0	4.8	1.1	4.0	1.6	3.5
1978	4.9	2.4	5.5	3.3	3.0	6.4	3.3	4.0
1979	6.4	5.6	4.7	4.7	6.9	5.9	3.3	5.3
1980	3.0	1.4	1.7	1.5	5.5	1.9	1.1	3.5
1981	5.4	5.5	1.6	2.6	3.5	2.7	5.7	3.9
1982		3.0	6.6	1.8	1.3		3.3	2.9

Note: The 1982 EC figure is based on forecasts for Belgium and Netherlands.
Source: See Figure 22.6. The base-year is 1970, which helps to explain differences
between the UK data and those in the *Department of Employment Gazette*.

Table 22A.6 Vacancy rates, 1957–83 (per cent of labour force)

Year	Belgium	FRG	Neth	UK	USA (index)	Japan
1957	0.38	0.91	2.15	3.95		0.69
1958	0.17	0.90	1.08	2.95		0.69
1959	0.16	1.14	1.51	3.38		0.80
1960	0.23	1.79	2.20	4.46	0.10	0.90
1961	0.36	2.10	2.80	4.41	0.10	0.97
1962	0.44	2.17	2.82	3.06	0.11	0.69
1963	0.48	2.09	2.78	2.95	0.10	0.78
1964	0.36	2.29	2.93	4.46	0.12	0.84
1965	0.23	2.42	2.86	5.30	0.14	0.65
1966	0.20	2.01	2.53	5.61	0.17	0.75
1967	0.12	1.16	1.50	3.52	0.16	0.89
1968	0.13	1.88	1.68	3.85	0.17	0.89
1969	0.31	2.83	2.28	4.31	0.19	0.98
1970	0.63	2.98	2.70	3.62	0.14	1.02
1971	0.35	2.42	2.26	2.65	0.13	0.88
1972	0.22	2.05	1.34	2.83	0.15	1.20
1973	0.37	2.14	1.43	5.00	0.18	1.31
1974	0.35	1.20	1.47	5.00	0.16	0.91
1975	0.11	0.93	1.01	2.67	0.11	0.65
1976	0.11	0.94	1.01	1.90	0.13	0.66
1977	0.09	0.92	1.18	2.20	0.16	0.59
1978	0.11	0.97	1.34	2.79	0.19	0.61
1979	0.15	1.19	1.43	3.10	0.20	0.70
1980	0.15	1.19	1.14	1.93	0.16	0.70
1981	0.12	0.81	0.45	1.49	0.15	0.67
1982	0.11	0.42	0.25	1.71	0.11	0.62
1983	0.16	0.31	0.20	2.07	0.11	0.61

Notes: European and Japanese data relate to vacancies registered at employment exchanges, except that in Britain these have been adjusted upwards to allow for the share of employment exchanges in the total labour market flows. Data for USA relate to Help Wanted Index.
Source: OECD, *Main Economic Indicators*, various issues.

Table 22A.7 General government deficit: actual, corrected for inflation (II)[a], and corrected for inflation (II) and cycle: EC, 1973–84 (per cent of GDP)

Year	Belgium Actual	Belgium Corr. for infl.	Belgium Corr. for infl. and cycle	Denmark Actual	Denmark Corr. for infl.	Denmark Corr. for infl. and cycle	France Actual	France Corr. for infl.	France Corr. for infl. and cycle	FRG Actual	FRG Corr. for infl.	FRG Corr. for infl. and cycle	Ireland Actual	Ireland Corr. for infl.	Ireland Corr. for infl. and cycle
1973	2.7	1.4	-1.9	-5.9			-0.9	-1.0	-0.7	-1.2	-1.7	-1.1	4.1		
1974	1.8	0.1	1.6	-1.8			-0.6	-1.0	-0.6	1.4	0.8	0.5	7.5	6.4	7.3
1975	4.1	2.5	1.7	2.0			2.2	1.5	0.4	5.8	5.0	2.9	11.6	10.1	10.1
1976	6.1	4.3	5.1	0.8	0.5	0.5	0.5	0.0	0.0	3.5	2.5	1.7	7.5	5.5	4.6
1977	6.4	4.1	4.0	1.7	1.0	1.2	0.8	0.2	0.2	2.4	1.3	1.0	6.9	4.9	5.3
1978	6.8	4.1	4.2	2.2	1.2	1.7	1.9	0.2	0.5	2.5	1.4	1.7	8.8	6.5	7.8
1979	7.6	4.4	4.5	3.1	1.7	3.6	0.7	-0.2	0.3	2.8	1.6	2.9	10.8	8.2	8.8
1980	9.9	5.4	5.4	6.1	4.5	4.5	-0.3	-1.3	-1.7	3.1	1.7	2.8	11.8	9.2	9.3
1981	12.6	7.1	4.6	7.1	5.5	4.3	1.8	0.4	-1.4	3.9	2.4	2.4	15.8	9.7	8.4
1982	11.6	4.8	1.5	9.2	7.1	6.9	2.6	1.3	-1.1	3.5	1.6	-0.3	16.2	8.9	6.3
1983	11.6	4.4	-0.3	8.2	3.9	3.9	3.4	1.7	-2.1	3.0	0.7	-1.8	13.4	5.6	1.1
1984	10.9	2.8	-2.5	6.9	2.3	2.6	3.5	1.3	-3.6	1.8	-0.6	-2.7	12.3	4.5	-0.9

Table 22.7 continued

Year	Italy			Netherlands			UK			EC		
	Actual	Corr. for infl.	Corr. for infl. and cycle	Actual	Corr. for infl.	Corr. for infl. and cycle	Actual	Corr. for infl.	Corr. for infl. and cycle	Actual	Corr. for infl.	Corr. for infl. and cycle
1973	5.8	4.6	4.6	-1.1	-1.7	-2.0	3.4	2.5	3.7	0.8	0.1	0.7
1974	5.4	3.6	4.3	0.1	-0.4	0.2	4.1	2.8	2.7	1.9	0.9	1.2
1975	13.3	10.5	8.5	2.7	2.1	0.7	5.0	4.0	2.7	5.5	4.4	2.7
1976	9.0	5.8	5.2	2.4	1.8	2.4	4.9	3.4	3.3	3.7	2.4	2.3
1977	8.0	4.5	3.7	1.8	1.0	1.9	3.4	1.8	1.7	3.3	1.8	1.8
1978	9.7	5.4	4.7	2.7	1.9	3.2	4.3	2.6	3.5	4.0	2.1	2.7
1979	9.5	5.4	5.8	3.7	2.8	4.2	3.2	1.1	2.3	3.6	1.6	2.8
1980	8.4	3.9	5.1	4.0	2.7	3.2	3.4	0.8	0.1	3.5	1.3	1.9
1981	11.7	6.2	6.1	5.2	3.8	2.2	2.7	0.0	-2.7	5.4	3.0	2.1
1982	11.9	5.2	3.6	7.2	5.8	3.4	2.0	-0.5	-3.1	5.4	2.7	0.8
1983	11.9	4.6	1.0	6.6	4.5	-0.3	3.5	1.1	-0.5	5.7	2.7	-0.1
1984	12.1	-4.6	0.8	6.8	4.4	-0.7	2.5	0.2	-0.8	5.2	1.8	-1.5

Note: [a] Inflation adjustment II: minus nominal interest plus $2^{1}/_{2}$ per cent of net interest-bearing general government debt.
Sources and notes: See Table 22.4.

Table 22A.8 General government deficit: actual, corrected for inflation (II)[a], and corrected for inflation (II) and cycle: USA, 1974–84 (per cent of trend GDP)

Year	Actual (1)	Corrected for inflation (II) (2)	Corrected for inflation (II) and cycle (3)
1977	0.9	0.4	0.4
1978	0.0	−0.6	0.2
1979	−0.6	−1.2	−0.4
1980	1.2	0.4	0.1
1981	0.9	−0.3	−0.6
1982	3.8	2.2	0.0
1983	3.9	2.0	0.3
1984	3.7	1.5	0.8

Note: [a] Inflation adjustment II: minus nominal interest plus 2 1/2 per cent of net interest-bearing general government debt.
Source: See Table 22.4.

Table 22.4.9 Short-run realized real interest rates[a], 1961–83 (per cent per annum)

Year	Belgium	Denmark	France	FRG	Neth	Ireland	Italy	UK	EC	USA
1961	3.6	2.0	1.1	1.0	-0.2		1.4	1.7	1.3	1.2
1962	1.9	-0.8	-1.4	-0.4	-0.5		-2.2	0.0	-0.7	1.5
1963	1.0	-0.2	-1.9	0.9	-1.1		-3.6	1.6	-0.5	1.9
1964	0.6	3.1	1.4	1.7	-2.2		-2.3	1.5	0.6	2.2
1965	0.9	0.2	1.4	1.8	-0.6		-1.0	1.9	1.0	2.3
1966	1.3	-0.8	2.1	2.9	-0.8		1.2	2.9	2.0	1.8
1967	2.5	-1.2	1.9	2.5	1.1		-0.2	3.7	1.9	1.4
1968	1.6	-1.3	1.6	2.1	0.8		2.2	3.0	2.0	1.1
1969	4.2	4.4	2.5	3.8	-1.5		1.0	3.5	2.6	1.2
1970	3.3	2.4	2.9	5.7	1.6		0.2	1.6	2.7	0.3
1971	0.4	1.6	0.6	1.7	-2.8	-2.1	0.7	-3.0	-0.0	0.0
1972	-1.4	-0.3	-0.7	0.1	-4.9	-1.4	-0.4	-0.2	-0.6	0.8
1973	0.4	-1.0	1.7	4.8	-0.5	0.7	-3.4	2.3	1.4	0.9
1974	-1.7	-1.6	-0.5	2.6	0.5	-2.0	-3.4	-2.1	-0.6	-2.8
1975	-5.1	-2.9	-3.6	-0.9	-4.1	-8.2	-5.7	-10.8	-4.9	-3.0
1976	0.8	1.1	-0.8	-0.0	-1.4	-5.2	-0.5	-4.3	-1.2	-0.7
1977	0.2	3.0	-0.3	0.6	-1.8	-4.7	-3.8	-6.7	-2.1	-1.0
1978	2.6	4.8	-1.3	0.9	2.5	1.9	-0.5	1.0	0.4	-0.2
1979	6.2	2.7	-0.8	2.6	4.8	2.5	-2.4	0.5	0.7	-1.0
1980	7.1	4.0	-1.3	3.8	3.3	-1.7	-3.5	-1.0	0.2	-1.6
1981	7.3	2.7	1.7	6.0	4.6	-2.9	-0.1	2.0	2.7	3.2
1982	4.9	5.6	2.2	3.3	2.1	0.1	2.9	3.2	2.9	4.1
1983	2.3	4.6	2.7	2.5	2.7	3.5	2.6	5.5	3.1	5.2

Note: [a] Nominal interest rates minus growth rate of CPI from December to December.
Source: Commission of the EC.

Notes and references

1. For the Commission's projection see *European Economy*, 18, (November 1983, Table 2.6). The trend line is ours. For most of the graphs in this report there is a corresponding table in the Statistical Annex showing data for each country.
2. For the EC see Table 22A.7 (p. 508). For the USA see Table 22A.8.
3. If a country thought it was probably going to experience a boom anyway, it would still be wise to promise now to pay a conditional subsidy for investment undertaken in 1984, the payment being made only if a boom had not occurred. Firms investing would thus be guaranteed a return whichever outcome occurred.
4. *European Economy* (November 1983, p.11).
5. In that sense we are not recommending what some people see as the current US error: fiscal expansion linked to a degree of monetary restraint likely to inhibit the long-run growth potential of the economy.
6. This assumes that the extra public spending is not primarily for productive investment.
7. See for example M. Emerson, *Western Europe's Capacity for Sustained Growth*, Centre for European Policy Studies, *CEPS Papers*, 2 (Brussels) (November 1983). For a discussion of the case for coordination in the light of historical evidence see C.R. Bean, 'The case for coordination: theory and history', CEPS mimeo. We are grateful to C.R. Bean and R.A. Jackman for helpful discussions on these issues.
8. If the Straits of Hormuz were closed there would be a temporary rise, but spare capacity outside the Gulf is sufficient to prevent a major permanent rise.
9. For some econometric estimates of the likely effects of a concerted reflation see F. Bergsten and L. Klein, 'The need for a global strategy', *The Economist* (23 April 1983).
10. M.S. Feldstein, 'The welfare cost of permanent inflation and short-run economic policy', *Journal of Political Economy* (August 1979).
11. See for example R.J. Gorden, 'Why US wage and employment behaviour differs from that in Britain and Japan', *Economic Journal* (March 1982).
12. There are of course difficulties in interpreting figures on vacancies. The European figures are based on numbers registered at public employment exchanges. For Britain we have adjusted these for changes in the coverage of the exchanges (see R. Jackman, R. Layard, and C. Pissarides, 'On Vacancies', *Oxford Bulletin of Economies and Statistics*, 51.4 pp. 377–94, 1989, Chapter 5 of this volume). The US figures are based on the Help-Wanted Index of newspaper advertisements. There is evidence from Wisconsin and Minnesota that this tracks total vacancies well (see K. Abraham, 'What Does the Help-Wanted Index Measure?', MIT mimeo).
13. The figures are based on those given in the country data section of OECD *Main Economic Indicators* and relate to unemployed as a percentage of total labour force (including self-employed). The actual for 1983 is based on Q2. The forecasts are based on EC estimates of the growth of unemployment.
14. The low estimated NAIRU in the UK in 1976–80 reflects the success of the 1975–7 incomes policy in holding down inflationary pressures at that time. The estimates of NAIRU thus vary with the institutions prevailing at the time.

15. See for example, D. Grubb, R. Jackman and R. Layard, 'Wage Rigidity and Unemployment in OECD Countries', *European Economic Review*, 21 (1983), Chapter 3 in this volume.
16. If the table is recalculated excluding the agricultural sector, this conclusion is not altered.
17. See R. Jackman, R. Layard and C. Pissarides (1989).
18. There are no consistent vacancy series for France or Italy.
19. R. Layard, *More Jobs, Less Inflation* (London: Grant McIntyre, 1982), p. 43.
20. See Appendix I in the accompanying CEPS working document.
21. See A. Cukierman and J. Mortensen, Commission of the EC, *Economic Paper*, 15 (May 1983).
22. See G. Demopoulos, G. Katsimbris and S. Miller, Commission of the EC, *Economic Paper*, 19 (September 1983).
23. In the previous approach the implied real interest burden was the debt times [(interest payments/debt) – inflation], a short-run concept.
24. If D is the deficit, B the debt, M high-powered money, and Y income (all in nominal terms), then

$$D = \dot{B} + \dot{M} \text{ and } \frac{D}{Y} = \frac{\dot{B}}{B}\frac{B}{Y} + \frac{\dot{M}}{M}\frac{M}{Y}$$

If nominal bonds, money, and income grow at the same rate $(\pi + g)$, this implies that

$$\frac{D - \pi B}{Y} = g\frac{B}{Y} + (\pi + g)\frac{M}{Y}$$

25. We assume that up to 1981 people assumed that 'permanent' exhaustive spending was as in 1977 augmented by trend. After 1981 they assumed permanent exhaustive spending to equal the full employment tax-take at 1981 average tax rates (less transfer payments at full-employment).
26. Debt figures for the EC are based on Commission work on sectoral balance sheet data. The figures therefore differ from those reported in Table 5.5 of the EC Annual Review. Extrapolations to the most recent years have been shown on the basis of general government financial deficits, which do not include changes in the market value of the debt.
27. This reflects the influence of short-run liquidity or disposable-income constraints on private consumption and investment. The 'balanced-budget multiplier' is therefore not zero but positive.
28. See O. Blanchard and R. Dornbusch, 'US deficits, the Dollar and Europe', Centre for European Policy Studies, *CEPS Papers* 6 (Brussels) (April 1984).
29. R. Vaubel, 'International Coordination or Competition of National Stabilisation Policies? A Welfare-Economic Approach', Institute of World Economics, Kiel (March 1983, p. 20).
30. We omit the possibility of appreciation, since this is harmful to the internationally-exposed sector and would raise interest rates more than most countries would wish.
31. If reflation can be achieved by a balanced budget expansion, then there is no 'cost' of reflation stemming from a higher public debt but there is still (i) the

problem of the current account deficit increasing, and (ii) the problem that the financing of this worsening of current account, at the existing exchange rate, may require a rise in real interest rates.

32 R. Dornbusch, G. Basevi, O. Blanchard, W. Buiter and R. Layard, 'Macroeconomic Prospects and Policies for the European Community', *Centre for European Policy Studies Papers* 1 (April 1983). See also O. Blanchard and R. Dornbush (1984).

33. A permanent credit for increases in employment over the previous year will only induce increases in employment this year rather than next in so far as the firm values a credit more this year than next. Thus if the scheme were expected to last forever, the effective rate of subsidy is δs where δ is the discount rate and s the subsidy.

34. On marginal employment subsidies see OECD, *Marginal Employment Subsidies* (1982) and R. Layard and S. Nickell, 'The Case for Subsiding Extra Jobs', *Economic Journal* (March 1980), Chapter 17 in this volume. The British Small Firms Employment Subsidy of 1977–9 is a prototype of what we are advocating.

35. The French *prélèvement conjoncturel* which lasted for 8 months in 1975 was an employer levy on the excess growth of value added per unit of factor input above a norm. There are obvious difficulties in the calculation of factor input, and obvious planning problems for the firm since real value added per unit of input is so sensitive to unpredictable demand factors.

36. For a fuller discussion, including administrative issues, see R. Layard, 'Is incomes policy the answer to unemployment?', *Economica*, 49 (August 1982) or more briefly D. Grubb, R. Layard and J. Symons, 'Wages, unemployment and incomes policy', in M. Emerson (ed.), *Europe's Stagflation* (Oxford: Oxford University Press, 1984), or R. Jackman and R. Layard, 'An inflation tax', *Fiscal Studies*, 3(1) (1982), pp. 47–59. For an earlier discussion see the special issue of the *Brookings Papers on Economic Activity*, 2 (1978) devoted to this proposal.

Appendix: Richard Layard's Publications

1 EDUCATION AND INEQUALITY

Books

(1963) *Appendix Volumes One–Three of Higher Education. Report of the Robbins Committee* (London: HMSO) Cmnd 2154, I, II, II–I, III (One: The Demand for Places in Higher Education: Two (A and B): Students and their Education: Three: Teachers in Higher Education) (co-author), see Chapter 18 in R. Layard, *Tackling Inequality* (London: Macmillan, 1999).

(1968) *Manpower and Education Development in India, 1961–86* (London: Oliver and Boyd) (with T. Burgess and P. Pant).

(1969) *The Impact of Robbins: Expansion in Higher Education* (Harmondsworth: Penguin) (with J. King and C. Moser).

(1971) *Qualified Manpower and Economic Performance: An Inter-plant Study in the Electrical Engineering Industry* (London: Allen Lane, The Penguin Press) (with J. Sargan, M. Ager and D. Jones).

(1978) *The Causes of Poverty, Background Paper, 5.* Royal Commission on the Distribution of Income and Wealth (London: HMSO) (with D. Piachaud and M. Stewart).

(1979) *Human Capital and Income Distribution*, Special issue of *Journal of Political Economy*, October 1979 (edited).

(1985) *Trends in Women's Work, Education, and Family Building*, Special issue of *Journal of Labor Economics*, January (edited with J. Mincer).

(1994) *Britain's Training Deficit* (Aldershot: Avebury) (edited with K. Mayhew and G. Owen).

Articles

(1964) 'Planning the scale of higher education in Great Britain', *Journal of the Royal Statistical Society* (with C. Moser).

(1966a) 'Manpower needs and the planning of higher education', in B.C. Roberts and J.H. Smith (eds), *Manpower Policy and Employment Trends* (London: G. Bell).

(1966b) 'Educational and occupational characteristics of manpower: an international comparison', *British Journal of Industrial Relations* (with J. Saigal).

(1970a) 'How profitable is engineering education?', *Higher Education Review* (Spring) (with L. Maglen).

(1970b) 'The LSE as a graduate school', *Universities Quarterly* (Autumn) (with J. King).

515

(1971) 'The scale of expansion to come' and 'Meeting the cost restraint', in G. Brosan, C. Carter, R. Layard, P. Venables and G. Williams (eds), *Patterns and Policies in Higher Education* (Harmondsworth: Penguin) (with G. Williams).

(1972) 'Economic theories of educational planning', in M. Peston and B. Corry (eds), *Essays in Honour of Lord Robbins* (London: Weidenfeld and Nicolson), Chapter 15 in R. Layard, *Tackling Inequality* (London: Macmillan, 1999).

(1973a) 'Denison and the contribution of education to national income growth: a comment', *Journal of Political Economy* (July–August).

(1973b) 'University efficiency and university finance', in M. Parkin (ed.), *Essays in Modern Economics* (London: Longman) (with R. Jackman), Chapter 16 in R. Layard, *Tackling Inequality* (London: Macmillan, 1999).

(1974a) 'The screening hypothesis and the returns to education', *Journal of Political Economy*, 82(5) (with G. Psacharopoulos), Chapter 9 in R. Layard, *Tackling Inequality* (London: Macmillan, 1999).

(1974b) 'The cost-effectiveness of the new media in higher education', in K. Lumsden (ed.), *Efficiency in Universities. The La Paz Papers* (New York: Elsevier); reprinted in *Minerva* and the *British Journal of Educational Technology*, Chapter 17 in R. Layard, *Tackling Inequality* (London: Macmillan, 1999). (with M. Oatey)

(1974c) 'Traditional versus Open University teaching methods: a cost comparison', *Higher Education* (August) (with B. Laidlaw).

(1975a) 'Cost functions for university teaching and research', *Economic Journal* (March) (with D. Verry).

(1975b) 'Capital–skill complementarity, income distribution and output accounting', *Journal of Political Economy*, 83(2) (with P. Fallon), Chapter 10 in R. Layard, *Tackling Inequality* (London: Macmillan, 1999).

(1977) 'On measuring the redistribution of lifetime income', in M.S. Feldstein and R.P. Inman (eds), *The Economics of Public Services* (London: Macmillan), Chapter 3 in R. Layard, *Tackling Inequality* (London: Macmillan, 1999).

(1978) 'The effect of collective bargaining on relative and absolute wages', in A. Shorrocks and W. Krelle (eds), *The Economics of Income Distribution* (Amsterdam: North-Holland) and *British Journal of Industrial Relations* (March) (with D. Metcalf and S. Nickell), Chapter 7 in R. Layard, *Tackling Inequality* (London: Macmillan, 1999).

(1979a) 'Family income distribution: explanation and policy evaluation', *Journal of Political Economy* 87(5), pt 2 (with A. Zabalza), Chapter 4 in R. Layard, *Tackling Inequality* (London: Macmillan, 1999).

(1979b) 'The causes of poverty', *National Westminster Bank Review* (February) (with D. Piachaud and M. Stewart), Chapter 6 in R. Layard, *Tackling Inequality* (London: Macmillan, 1999).

(1979c) 'Human capital and earnings: British evidence and a critique', *Review of Economic Studies* (July) (with G. Psacharopoulos), Chapter 8 in R. Layard, *Tackling Inequality* (London: Macmillan, 1999).

(1979d) 'Education versus cash redistribution: the lifetime context', *Journal of Public Economics*, 12(3) Chapter 5 in R. Layard, *Tackling Inequality* (London: Macmillan, 1999).

(1980a) 'Wages policy and the redistribution of income', The Colston Research Society Annual Lecture, in D. Collard, R. Lecomber and M. Slater (eds), *The Limits to Redistribution* (Bristol: Colston Society).

(1980b) 'Married women's participation and hours', *Economica* (February) (with
M. Barton and A. Zabalza), Chapter 11 in R. Layard, *Tackling Inequality* (London:
Macmillan, 1999).

(1980c) 'One the use of distributional weights in social cost-benefit analysis: comment',
Journal of Political Economy, 88(5), Chapter 13 in R. Layard, *Tackling Inequality*
(London: Macmillan, 1999).

(1980d) 'Human satisfactions and public policy', *Economic Journal* 90 (December),
Chapter 14 in R. Layard, *Tackling Inequality* (London: Macmillan, 1999).

(1982) 'Trends in civil service pay relative to the private sector', in *Report of the Inquiry
into Civil Service Pay* (Chairman Sir John Megaw), vol. 2, Cmnd. 8590–1(London:
HMSO) (July) (with A. Marin and A. Zabalza).

(1983) 'Incomes policy and wage differentials', *Economica* (May) (with O. Ashenfelter).

(1985a) 'Why are more women working in Britain?', *Journal of Labor Economics*, 3 (1)
(with H. Joshi and S. Owen), Chapter 12 in R. Layard, *Tackling Inequality* (London:
Macmillan, 1999).

(1985b) 'Overseas students' fees and the demand for education', *Applied Economics*,
17 (with E. Petoussis).

(1985c) 'Public sector pay: the British perspective', in D. Conklin *et al.* (eds), *Public
Sector Compensation*, Ontario Economic Council, Special Research Report.

(1993) 'The Training Reform Act of 1994', *International Journal of Manpower*, 14 (5)
(with K. Mayhew and G. Owen).

(1994) 'The welfare economics of training', in R. Layard, K. Mayhew and G. Owen
(eds), *Britain's Training Deficit* (Aldershot: Avebury).

2 UNEMPLOYMENT

Books

(1969) *The Causes of Graduate Unemployment in India* (London: Allen Lane, The
Penguin Press) (with M. Blaug and M. Woodhall), Chapter 11 in this volume.

(1982) *More Jobs, Less Inflation* (London: Grant McIntyre).

(1984) *The Causes of Unemployment* (Oxford: Oxford University Press) (edited by
C. Greenhalgh and A. Oswald).

(1986a) *Restoring Europe's Prosperity* (Cambridge, MA: MIT Press) (with O. Blanchard
and R. Dornbusch).

(1986b) *How to Beat Unemployment* (Oxford: Oxford University Press). Translated
into Swedish.

(1987a) *The Rise in Unemployment* (Oxford: Basil Blackwell) (edited with C. Bean and
S. Nickell), reprint of *Economica*, Unemployment Supplement (1986).

(1987b) *The Fight against Unemployment* (Cambridge, MA: MIT Press) (edited with
Lars Calmfors).

(1991a) *Unemployment: Macroeconomic Performance and the Labour Market* (Oxford:
Oxford University Press) (with S. Nickell and R. Jackman). Translated into Spanish.

(1991b) *Stopping Unemployment*, The Employment Institute (September) (with
J. Philpott).

(1992) *Helping the Unemployed: Active Labour Market Policies in Britain and Germany*, The Anglo-German Foundation (March) (with Richard Disney, Lutz Bellmann, Alan Carruth, Wolfgang Franz, Richard Jackman, Hartmut Lehmann, John Philpott).

(1993) *UK Unemployment*, Studies in the UK Economy (London: Heinemann Educational), 2nd edition 1993, 3rd edition 1997 (with A. Clark).

(1994) *The Unemployment Crisis* (Oxford: Oxford University Press) (with S. Nickell and R. Jackman). Translated into Spanish, 1996.

Articles

(1979) 'The costs and benefits of selective employment policies. The British case', *British Journal of Industrial Relations*, 17 (July), also in the National Commission for Manpower Policy, *European Labor Market Policies* (September 1978).

(1980a) 'The case for subsidising extra jobs', *Economic Journal*, 90 (March) (with S. Nickell), Chapter 17 in this volume.

(1980b) 'The efficiency case for long-run labour market policies', *Economica*, 47 (August) (with R. Jackman), Chapter 16 in this volume.

(1980c) 'Evidence to the House of Lords Select Committee on Unemployment', *Minutes of Evidence* (London: HMSO).

(1981a) 'Measuring the duration of unemployment: a note', *Scottish Journal of Political Economy* (November).

(1981b) 'Unemployment in Britain: causes and cures', *Work and Social Change*, 6, European Centre for Work and Society (Maastricht), (November), Chapter 13 in this volume.

(1982a) 'Efficient public employment with labour market distortions', in R. Haveman (ed.), *Public Finance and Public Employment*: Wayne State University Press (with G. Johnson).

(1982b) 'Youth unemployment in Britain and the US compared', in R. Freeman and D. Wise (eds), *The Youth Labor Market Problem: Its Nature, Causes and Consequences* (Chicago: The University of Chicago Press).

(1982c) 'An inflation tax', *Fiscal Studies* (March) (with R. Jackman).

(1982d) 'Is incomes policy the answer to unemployment?', *Economica* 49 (August), with Appendix 'Trade Unions, the NAIRU and a Wage-Inflation Tax' (with R.A. Jackman), Chapter 18 in this volume, excluding Appendix.

(1982e) 'Causes of the current stagflation', *Review of Economic Studies* (October) (with D. Grubb and R. Jackman).

(1982f) 'Incomes policy, employment measures and economic performance', in 'Could Do Better', *IEA Occasional Paper Special* 62.

(1983a) 'Agenda for Liberal Conservatism. A comment', *Journal of Economic Affairs* (January).

(1983b) 'Wage rigidity and unemployment in OECD countries', *European Economic Review*, 21 (with D. Grubb and R. Jackman), Chapter 3 in this volume.

(1983c) 'Macroeconomic prospects and policies for the European Community', *Centre for European Policy Studies Paper*, 1 (April) (with R. Dornbusch, G. Basevi, O. Blanchard and W. Buiter).

(1984a) 'Europe: the case for unsustainable growth', *Centre for European Policy Studies Paper* 8/9 (May) (with G. Basevi, O. Blanchard, W. Buiter and R. Dornbusch), Chapter 22 in this volume.

(1984b) 'Wages, unemployment and incomes policy', in M. Emerson (ed.), *Causes of Europe's Stagflation* (Oxford: Oxford University Press) (with D. Grubb and J. Symons).

(1984c) 'Neo-classical demand for labour functions for six major economies', *Economic Journal* (December) (with J. Symons).

(1985a) 'The causes of British unemployment', *National Institute Economic Review* (February) (with S. Nickell).

(1985b) 'Cutting unemployment using both blades of the scissors', *Catalyst* (Spring).

(1985c) 'Employment and growth in Europe: a two-handed approach', *Centre for European Policy Studies Paper*, 21 (May) (with O. Blanchard, R. Dornbush, J. Drèze, H. Giersch and M. Monti).

(1985d) 'European unemployment is Keynesian and classical but not structural', Centre for European Policy Studies, *Working Document*, 13 (June) (with R. Jackman and S. Nickell).

(1985e) 'On tackling unemployment', *Economic Affairs* (July–September).

(1985f) 'Unemployment, real wages and aggregate demand in Europe, Japan and the US', in K. Brunner and A. Meltzer (eds), *Carnegie-Rochester Conference Series on Public Policy*, 23 (Autumn) (with S. Nickell).

(1986a) 'Policies for reducing the natural rate of unemployment', in J.L. Butkiewicz, K.J. Koford and J.B. Miller (eds), *Keynes' Economic Legacy* (New York: Praeger) (with R. Jackman and C. Pissarides).

(1986b) 'The economic effects of tax-based incomes policy', in D. Colander (ed.), *Incentive-Based Incomes Policies* (New York: Ballinger) (with R. Jackman).

(1986c) 'A wage-tax, worker-subsidy policy for reducing the "natural" rate of unemployment', in W. Beckerman (ed.), *Wage Rigidity and Unemployment* (London: Duckworth) (July) (with R. Jackman).

(1986d) 'A new deal for the long-term unemployed', in P.E. Hart (ed.), *Unemployment and Labour Market Policies* (London: Gower) (with D. Metcalf and R. O'Brien).

(1986e) 'Unemployment in Britain', *Economica Special Supplement on Unemployment*, 53 (with S. Nickell).

(1986f) 'The rise in unemployment: a multi-country study', *Economica Special Supplement on Unemployment*, 53 (with C. Bean and S. Nickell).

(1986g) 'Employment – the way forward', Stockton Lecture, *London Business School Journal*, 11 (Winter).

(1986h) 'Reducing unemployment in Europe: the role of capital formation', *Centre for European Policy Studies* (with F. Modigliani, M. Monti, J. Drèze and H. Giersch).

(1986i) 'An incomes policy to help the unemployed', Employment Institute; reprinted in J. Shields (ed.), *Making the Economy Work* (London: Macmillan, 1989) and in abbreviated form in *Economic Review*, 5 (November 1987) (with S. Nickell).

(1986j) 'The natural rate of unemployment: explanation and policy', in O. Ashenfelter and R. Layard (eds), *Handbook of Labor Economics* (Amsterdam: North-Holland) (with G. Johnson).

(1987) 'The labour market', in R. Dornbusch and R. Layard (eds), *The Performance of the British Economy* (Oxford: Clarendon Press) (with S. Nickell), Chapter 4 in this volume.

(1988) 'Innovative supply-side policies to reduce unemployment', in P. Minford (ed.), *Monetarism and Macroeconomics*, IEA Readings, 26 (with R. Jackman).

(1989a) 'On vacancies', *Oxford Bulletin of Economics and Statistics*, 51(4) (with R. Jackman and C. Pissarides), Chapter 5 in this volume.

(1989b) 'Why does unemployment persist?', *Scandinavian Journal of Economics*, 91(2) and in S. Honkapohja (ed.), *The State of Macroeconomics* (Oxford: Blackwell, 1990) (with C. Bean), Chapter 9 in this volume.

(1989c) 'Lessons for another country', in E. Wadensjo, A. Dahlberg and B. Holmlund, (eds), *Vigarnas Tryggnet*, Essays in Honour of Gösta Rehn.

(1990a) 'Lay-offs by seniority and equilibrium employment', *Economics Letters*, 32 (Harvard University).

(1990b) 'The real effects of tax-based incomes policies', *Scandinavian Journal of Economics*, 92(2) (with R. Jackman), Chapter 19 in this volume.

(1990c) 'Is unemployment lower if unions bargain over employment?', *Quarterly Journal of Economics* (August) and in Y. Weiss and G. Fishelson, (eds), *Advances in the Theory and Measurement of Unemployment* (London: Macmillan) (Spring) (with S. Nickell), Chapter 21 in this volume.

(1990d) 'European unemployment: cause and cure', *Revista de Economia*, 4, also in J. Velarde *et al.* (eds), *La Industria Espanola* (Colegio de Economistas de Madrid, 1990).

(1990e) 'Wage bargaining and EMU', in R. Dornbush, C. Goodhart, and R. Layard (eds), *Britain & EMU* (London: Centre for Economic Performance and Financial Markets Group).

(1990f) 'How to end pay leapfrogging', Employment Institute, *Economic Report*, 5(5) (July), Chapter 20 in this volume.

(1991a) 'Does long-term unemployment reduce a person's chance of a job? A time-series test', *Economica*, 58 (22) (with R. Jackman), Chapter 6 in this volume.

(1991b) 'Unemployment and inequality in Europe: what to do', in A. Atkinson and R. Brunetta (eds), *Economics for the New Europe*, IEA Conference Volume 104.

(1991c) 'Mismatch: a framework for thought', in F. Padoa Schioppa (ed.), *Mismatch and Labour Mobility* (Cambridge: Cambridge University Press) (with R. Jackman and S. Savouri), Chapter 7 in this volume.

(1993) 'The squeeze on jobs: getting people back to work', *Worldlink* (May–June).

(1994a) 'Unemployment in the OECD countries', in T. Tachibanaki (ed.), *Labour Market and Economic Performance: Europe, Japan and the USA* (London: Macmillan) (with S. Nickell).

(1994b) 'Preventing long-term unemployment in Europe', in P.-O. Bergeron and M.-A. Gaiffe (eds), *Croissance, compétitivité, emploi: à la Recherche d'un Modèle pour l'Europe* (Collége d'Europe), reprinted in various forms in House of Commons Employment Committee, *The Right to work/workfare: minutes of evidence* (Tuesday 22 November) (London: HMSO), and in *Work in future. The future of work*, Alfred Herrhausen Society For International Dialogue (Stuttgart: Schäffer-Poeschel Verlag) and as *Preventing long-term unemployment*, Employment Policy Institute (October) and as 'Preventing long-term unemployment', in H. Sasson and D. Diamond (eds), *LSE on Social Science* (London: LSE Books, 1996) and as 'How to cut unemployment', in *Policy Options*, Institute for Research on Public Policy, Montreal, 17(6) (July–August 1996) and as 'Preventing long-term unemployment', in J. Philpott (ed.), *Working for Full Employment* (London: Routledge, 1997).

(1994c) 'Subsidising employment rather than unemployment', *Rivista di Politica Economica*, Fascicolo XI, Anno LXXXIV (November).

(1995) 'Reforming national labour markets', in W.D. Eberle, E.G. Corrigan and W. Moller (eds), *The Future of the World Economy* (Washington DC: The Aspen Institute).

(1996a) 'Preventing long-term unemployment: an economic analysis', in J. Gual (ed.), *The Social Challenge of Job Creation* (Aldershot: Edward Elgar) and in D. Snower and G. de la Dehesa (eds), *Unemployment Policy: Government Options for the Labour Market* (Cambridge: Cambridge University Press, 1997), Chapter 14 in this volume.

(1996b) 'Vägen Tillbaka Till Full Sysselsättning' (The 1995 Rudolf Meidner Lecture), *Arbetsmarknad & Arbetsliv*, 2(1); reprinted as 'Sweden's Road Back to Full Employment', *Economic and Industrial Democracy* (London: Sage, 1997), 99–116.

(1996c) 'Combatting unemployment: is flexibility enough?', in *Macroeconomic Policies and Structural Reform* (with R. Jackman and S. Nickell) (Paris: OECD), Chapter 10 in this volume.

(1997) 'Preventing long-term unemployment strategy and costings', Employment Policy Institute, *Economic Report*, 11(4) (March), Chapter 15 in this volume.

3 TRANSITION

Books

(1991) *Reform in Eastern Europe* (Cambridge, MA: MIT Press) (with O. Blanchard, R. Dornbusch, P. Krugman and L. Summers).

(1992a) *East–West Migration: The Alternatives* (Cambridge, MA: MIT Press) (with O. Blanchard, R. Dornbusch and P. Krugman). Translated into Italian.

(1992b) *Russian Economic Trends*, 4 quarterly issues and 12 'monthly updates' (London: Whurr) (editor and co-author 1992–7).

(1993a) *Changing the Economic System in Russia* (London: Pinter Publishers) (edited with Anders Åslund).

(1993b) *Postwar Economic Reconstruction and Lessons for the East Today* (Cambridge, MA: MIT Press) (edited with R. Dornbusch and W. Nölling).

(1993c) *Post-Communist Reform: Pain and Progress* (Cambridge, MA: MIT Press) (with O. Blanchard *et al.*).

(1994) *Macroeconomics. A Text for Russia* (Moscow: Wiley) (in Russian).

(1996) *The Coming Russian Boom* (New York: The Free Press) (with J. Parker).

Articles

(1990) 'Economic change in Poland', in J. Beksiak *et al. The Polish Transformation: Programme and Progress*, Centre for Research into Communist Economies (London) (July) (with O. Blanchard).

(1991a) 'Wage bargaining, incomes policy, and inflation', in S. Commander (ed.), *Managing Inflation in Socialist Economies in Transition* (Washington, DC: Economic Development Institute of The World Bank) (June).

(1991b) 'How to privatise', in H. Siebert (ed.), *The Transformation of Socialist Economies: Symposium 1991* (University of Kiel) (with O. Blanchard), Chapter 22 in R. Layard, *Tackling Inequality* (London: Macmillan, 1999).

(1992) 'Post-stabilization inflation in Poland', in F. Coricelli and A. Revenga (eds), *Wage Policy during the Transition to a Market Economy, Poland 1990–1991*, World Bank Paper, 158 (Washington, DC: World Bank) (with O. Blanchard), Chapter 23 in R. Layard, *Tackling Inequality* (London: Macmillan, 1999).

(1993a) 'Prices, incomes and hardship', in A. Åslund and R. Layard (eds), *Changing the Economic system in Russia* (London: Pinter Publishers) (with M. Ellam).

(1993b) 'Eldorados in Russia', in A. Raphael (ed.), *Debrett's Euro-Industry 1993* (London: Debrett's Peerage Limited).

(1993c) 'Why so much pain, and how to reduce it', *Voprosy Ekonomiki* (Questions of Economics), 2.

(1993d) 'The future of Russian reform', *The Economics of Transition*, 1(3).

(1993e) 'Stabilization versus reform? Russia's first year', in O. Blanchard *et al.* (eds), *Post Communist Reform* (Cambridge, MA: MIT Press).

(1994a) 'Who gains and who loses from credit expansion?', *Communist Economies & Economic Transformation*, 6(4) (with A. Richter), Chapter 24 in R. Layard, *Tackling Inequality* (London: Macmillan, 1999).

(1994b) 'The conditions of life', in A. Åslund (ed.), *Economic Transformation in Russia* (London: Pinter Publishers) (with A. Illarionov and P. Orszag).

(1994c) 'Can Russia control inflation?', in J. Onno de Beaufort Wijnholds, S.C.W. Eijffinger and L.H. Hoogduin (eds), *A Framework for Monetary Stability* (Boston: Kluwer Academic Publishers), Chapter 25, in R. Layard, *Tackling Inequality* (London: Macmillan, 1999).

(1994d) 'The current state and future of economic reform', in *European Expertise Service 1992–1994; 1st Review Exercise*, TACIS European Commission (Brussels) (21–22 September).

(1995a) 'Labour market adjustment in Russia', in A. Åslund (ed.), *Russian Economic Reform at Risk* (London: Pinter Publishers) (with A. Richter).

(1995b) 'How much unemployment is needed for restructuring the Russian experience', *Economics of Transition*, 3(1) (March) (with A. Richter), Chapter 26 in R. Layard, *Tackling Inequality* (London: Macmillan, 1999).

(1996) 'The coming Russian boom', *The American Enterprise*, 7(4) (July–August) (with J. Parker).

(1998) 'Why so much pain?', Chapter 1 in P. Brone, S. Gomulka and R. Layard (eds), *Emerging from Communism: Lessons from Russia, China and Eastern Europe*, (The MIT Press), Chapter 27 in R. Layard, *Tackling Inequality* (London: Macmillan, 1999).

4 GENERAL

Books

(1971) *Cost-benefit Analysis* (Harmondsworth: Penguin) with long introduction; 2nd edition (Cambridge: Cambridge University Press, 1994) (edited with S. Glaister).

(1978) *Microeconomic Theory* (New York: McGraw-Hill) (with A.A. Walters), reissued as International Student Edition (1987). Translated into Japanese.

(1987a) *Handbook of Labor Economics* (Amsterdam: North-Holland) (edited with O. Ashenfelter). Translated into Spanish.

(1987b) *The Performance of the British Economy* (Oxford: Oxford University Press) (edited with R. Dornbush).

(1989) *World imbalances*, Report of the WIDER (World Institute for Development Economics Research) World Economy Group (with O. Blanchard, R. Dornbusch, M. King, P. Krugman, Y. Chul Park, and L. Summers).

(1990) *Britain & EMU*, Centre for Economic Performance and Financial Markets Group (edited with R. Dornbusch and C. Goodhart).

(1997a) (Signatory) *Promoting Prosperity*, Report of the Commission on Public Policy and British Business (London: Vintage).

(1997b) *What Labour Can Do* (London: Warner Books).

Articles

(1972) 'The determinants of UK imports', *Government Economic Service Paper*, 3 (with R.D. Rees).

(1976) 'The date of discounting in cost-benefit analysis', *Journal of Transport Economics and Policy* (July) (with A.A. Walters).

(1977) 'The income distributional effects of congestion taxes', *Economica* (August).

(1989) 'The Thatcher miracle?', *American Economic Review, Papers and Proceedings*, 79(2) (May); also *Economic Affairs* (December 1989–90); also *Wirtschaft und Gesellschaft*, 4 (1989) (with S. Nickell), Chapter 19 in R. Layard, *Tackling Inequality* (London: Macmillan, 1999).

(1993) 'Varför Överge den Svenska Modellen?', in V. Bergström (ed.), *Varför Överge den Svenska Modellen?* (Helsingborg: Nationalekonomiska Föreningen och Tidens Förlag).

Over 100 newspaper articles.

Index

Note: page numbers in **bold** type refer to illustrative figures or tables.